DATE DUE

MAR 0 9 09		

#47-0108 Peel Off Pr

Dream of Life

MICHAEL PHILLIPS

T 26463

TYNDALE HOUSE PUBLISHERS, INC.
CAROL STREAM, ILLINOIS

Visit Tyndale's exciting Web site at www.tyndale.com

TYNDALE and Tyndale's quill logo are registered trademarks of Tyndale House Publishers, Inc.

Dream of Life

Designed by Beth Sparkman

Scripture quotations are taken from the *Holy Bible*, King James Version.

This novel is a work of fiction. Names, characters, places, and incidents either are the product of the author's imagination or are used fictitiously. Any resemblance to actual events, locales, organizations, or persons, living or dead, is entirely coincidental and beyond the intent of either the author or publisher.

Library of Congress Cataloging-in-Publication Data

Phillips, Michael R., date.
  Dream of life / Michael Phillips.
    p. cm. — (American dreams ; v. 2)
  ISBN-13: 978-1-4143-0177-8
  ISBN-10: 1-4143-0177-4
  ISBN-13: 978-0-8423-7778-2 (pbk.)
  ISBN-10: 0-8423-7778-6 (pbk.)
  1. Cherokee Indians—Fiction.   2. South Carolina—Fiction.   I. Title.
  PS3566.H492D743 2006
  813'.54—dc22   2006000185

Printed in the United States of America

11   10   09   08   07   06
7   6   5   4   3   2   1

Dedication

To the Cherokee People and their noble ancestry,
to my "one-fourth" Cherokee mother-in-law, Cherokee,
to my "one-eighth" Cherokee wife, Judy,
and to our three "one-sixteenth" Cherokee sons Patrick,
Robin, and Gregory.

Seven Americans in the Royal Court

1730

*I*n the year 1729, the Scottish trader Ludovick Grant, enlisted by London adventurer Sir Alexander Cuming, a Scotsman by birth, ventured with Cuming through the rugged wooded region and along the trail over Ooneekawy Mountain into the heart of Cherokee land in the new world called America.

The idea for a voyage to the colonies to meet with native tribes had actually come to Cuming's wife in a dream back at their home in England. A daring man by nature, Cuming had endorsed the prospect with enthusiasm. It would be an adventure, as well as a chance to help solidify relations with the Indians for the English over the French. Most of all it would increase his standing in the eyes of the English court.

Grant had been into Cherokee territory many times. He had traded with the Cherokee and knew both the settlement of Telliquo as well as that of Tannassy, named for the river, some sixteen miles away. Reaching some lasting agreement with the Cherokee was imperative. Their mission was all the more critical in light of evidence that the Indians were showing more favor toward the French. If another war broke out, the French could take control of all Carolina. Cuming hoped to prevent that by allying the Cherokee with England once and for all.

He had not exactly been sent by King George. But he was loyal to the Crown, and if he could win the Indians over, the English colonies would benefit enormously from the alliance. If it earned him the king's favor, what Englishman would turn away kindness from the king's eye?

When asked by Cuming to take him to the chief of the Cherokee, Grant had replied that the Cherokee had many chiefs.

"How many?" asked Cuming.

"Several for each village, and they have more than forty towns— there may be over a hundred chiefs, several hundred. I don't know."

"Then take me to the most important of them," replied Cuming.

"I will take you to Moytoy," replied Grant in thick Scottish brogue. "He is called the headman of Great Telliquo. But there are other powerful chiefs as well."

Cuming was amazed at what he saw as they entered what was a village of remarkable size, with dozens of lodges of wood, bark, and mud, a variety of growing crops, and beasts of many kinds, the whole surrounded by a palisade perimeter of vertical logs bound side by side to a height of eight feet or more. He had heard that the Cherokees of DeSoto's time had lived in sizeable cities. But he had envisioned something far more primitive than this. These people were obviously living a structured, semicivilized, community form of life.

Grant exchanged greetings in the native tongue. He was quickly speaking English again with a young man in his late teens or early twenties, anxious to try out his own broken English. Grant introduced him to Cuming as Ukwaneequa, nephew to the chief, a slight but engaging and personable young man of scarcely more than five feet in height but of keen intellect. His English was sufficient to quickly communicate Sir Alexander's mission to his fellow villagers.

"And here is the chief's son, my cousin Oconostota."

Again Cuming offered his hand in friendship. The young warrior just introduced, however, neither took it nor betrayed any hint of welcoming expression. A momentary shudder went through Cuming's frame as he glanced at the sheathed knife at his side. He would not want to meet *this* fellow alone in the forest on a dark night!

He turned again to the short and friendly Ukwaneequa, who now spoke to his cousin in the Cherokee tongue. Oconostota nodded, answered him a few words, then turned and left the group.

"My cousin says his mother is not well," said the personable youth. "But I will tell my uncle that you are here, and that you come with greetings from the English king. In the meantime, be welcome in our village."[1]

He turned and spoke to some of the others gathered around in his native tongue. While he went in search of his uncle, the rest of the villagers eagerly crowded about their visitors and made them to understand where they would stay. As they made their way through the village to the accompaniment of a growing throng of curious natives, Cuming could not help noticing the scalps of dead enemies hanging from poles in front of warrior houses. The Cherokee may have been one of the advanced tribes in this land, but he shuddered at this visual display of one of their customs.

When at last Moytoy made his appearance, warmly greeting Grant and speaking to Cuming through his nephew, he gave the British a tour of the palisaded town. After being introduced to the powerful priest Jacob the Conjurer, as the English called him, the village priest led them to several nearby caves of stunning beauty, where crystals of unmatched color and clarity grew out of the ground amid hundreds of stalactites and stalagmites. Neither Cuming nor any of his party had seen the like before.

"This is why they are sometimes called the cave people," said Grant to Cuming. "This region is full of caves, and they make full use of them."

By many signs and with the help of the chief's nephew, the priest asked which color of crystal they fancied.

"The light purple," replied Cuming. "It is the color of royalty."

"He says for me to tell you," said Ukwaneequa, "that it will be

---

[1] The Cherokee often adopted orphans and captives from other tribes, and raised them as true sons. The genealogy of both these young men is in some doubt. Ukwaneequa is listed in some sources as the son of Moytoy's sister Nanye'hi (*not* Nanye'hi Ward), but other sources indicate that he was an ophan *adopted* by Nanye'hi. Oconostota, too, may have been adopted by Moytoy's family, for his exact genealogy is likewise unclear. Moytoy the younger, likewise, *may* have been the nephew not son of Amatoya Moytoy—genealogies of early Cherokee chiefs conflict in various sources, and nearly all had multiple names.

done, that he will find one the spirit of the cave will allow him to give as a gift to your king."

Cuming nodded to the priest in gratitude.

"And there, at the far end of the great room of the cave is the great Uktena crystal. The blood of small animals must be fed it twice a week, and the blood of a deer twice a year."

"Why?" asked Cuming.

"The crystal protects the tribe, as do the caves," answered the chief's nephew. "In times of war we hide our treasures, as well as our women and young, in the caves."

"What kind of treasures?" asked Cuming.

"The yellow stones that come from the earth," replied Ukwaneequa, "our paint and skins and royal feathers, and of course the crystals from the caves."

Cuming and Grant exchanged glances but said nothing. Had they just heard what they thought they heard—yellow stones! Had DeSoto's fabled quest for Cherokee gold actually been based on fact!

Back in the village, after a meal of roasted rabbit and venison, Cuming and his two servants were invited to the headman's lodge. At last Cuming got down to the business for which he had come so far into the wilds, to gain favor with the Cherokee over the French.

"We come in peace, Great Chief," he began, "in the name of our king across the water. You are a mighty people whose fame travels far. It is our desire to make alliance between you—your chief and all your people—and my king and his people."

Ukwaneequa turned to his uncle Okoukaula, Moytoy the younger, and, with occasional help from Grant, gave his uncle to understand Cuming's words.

"We have many chiefs," said Moytoy.

"I have heard of this—red chiefs and white chiefs."

Moytoy nodded. "We have chiefs for war and for peace, and others as well."

"But it is said that *you* are chief among your chiefs."

"Perhaps, but only because I am the great Moytoy's son. I am still only one among many."

"You have no emperor, no headman among headmen?"

"I do not know this word. What is an emperor?"

"The ruler of all people."

"I do not rule all our people. The council rules, not a single chief."

Cuming thought a moment. "Perhaps you, great headman called Moytoy, shall *become* king of the chiefs. I shall appoint you *emperor*."

Again it was silent. Now it was the Cherokee's turn to revolve much in his mind.

"The War Chief of Tannassy, the other chiefs of the great council," said Moytoy. "It may not be that all would agree."

"But if I could persuade them to give their allegiance to you?" suggested Cuming.

"How would you do such a thing?"

"Give your allegiance to *my* king," said Cuming, "and I will see that many gifts come to your people. You will be wealthy among the tribes, with blankets and beads and knives, perhaps even guns. For this would not the rest of the Cherokee give you their allegiance?"

As the explanation—translated between Grant and his nephew— came to Moytoy, it seemed a small price to pay to receive so much from the Englishman. They had traded for many goods from the French and English. The women of the tribe coveted the fine cloth and soft blankets and many variety of beads. And if they could obtain more guns . . . the French had never made them such an offer.

Slowly Moytoy nodded. "So it shall be," he said. "I will give my oath of allegiance to your king in exchange for the title and the goods you promise."

During the entire exchange, the chief's son Oconostota had not spoken a word.

Two days later, Grant led Cuming and his small band along a sixteen-mile trail to the village of Tannassy where they would find the greatest challenge to their scheme. There dwelt the most powerful war chief among the Cherokee. Carolina trader Eleazer Wiggan, who lived with the Cherokee in Tannassy and whom the Cherokee called the Old Rabbit, met the party of Englishmen and acted as interpreter. With yet more offers of gifts as well as assistance in times of war,

Cuming's smooth tongue resulted in another pledge of loyalty to King George II, as well as an agreement by the Warrior of Tannassy to accept Moytoy as Emperor of the Cherokee. The new word meant as little to the war chief as it had to Moytoy. But his agreement had been secured by the promise of weapons. The Warrior of Tannassy removed his crown of dyed opossum hair and handed it to Cuming in pledge of his word.

As Cuming took the strange crown, obviously of great value in the warrior's eyes, yet so primitive and from such an ugly and despised animal, the contrast struck him anew between this people and the splendor of the English court.

Suddenly his brain filled with the most extraordinary idea!

"Great Warrior," he said as Wiggan translated his words. "You shall *yourself* present your crown to my king, and tell him in your own tongue of your pledge of loyalty."

A confused expression met Wiggan's attempted translation.

"You shall accompany me back to England!" added Cuming.

Again Wiggan translated. Slowly the warrior chief shook his head. He had no interest in travel. He only wanted the Englishman's guns.

"Then perhaps some of your other chiefs shall go with me," suggested Cuming.

But Wiggan's words of translation roused no more enthusiasm from any of the other chiefs. Cuming returned to Great Telliquo with the news of the war chief's agreement to a pledge of loyalty to Moytoy. But now he had on his mind the exciting idea of a visit by native chiefs to England. The party that left Great Telliquo several days later, including Moytoy himself, Jacob the Conjurer, and many of the chief's attendants, was bound again over the mountain, this time to the valley towns on the other side, where the agreement of a pledge between the Cherokee "emperor" Moytoy and the king of England would be placed before the Cherokee national council at Nequassee. By now the word had spread from village to village, and their coming was greeted with much fanfare and anticipation. With feasting and dancing and much ceremony, and with the continued smooth negotiation of Sir Alexander Cuming, the national council recognized Moytoy as Emperor of all the Cherokee, and gave its allegiance to King George II of England.

Under the agreement, the Cherokee would not trade with the French. The English would favor the Cherokee among other native tribes with the best of its goods. The Cherokee would be rewarded for the capture and return of fugitive slaves from the Carolina colonies. And should war break out against them, either from the French or other tribes, the Cherokee would receive military assistance from the colonial militia. Immediate arrangements were also made for the shipment to the Cherokee villages numerous guns with ammunition, as well as the coveted red paint produced in the colonies.

The Cherokees had their half of the bargain, and Cuming had his so-called Emperor. It was the first of many such agreements between the English and the Cherokee.

Only one other arrangement needed to be concluded to make Cuming's coup with the Cherokee nation complete. But from none of the villages could he interest a single chief in a voyage to England. All asked how long it would take, and, being told three months, quickly declined.

Cuming pled with Moytoy one last time.

"Great Emperor of the Cherokee, I earnestly entreat you to accompany me to my homeland across the sea, to meet my king to whom you have pledged your loyalty."

"The distance is too great," replied Moytoy shaking his head. "You say it is a full moon each way."

"That is true. But you would see dazzling sights none of your people have ever beheld. Your name would be great for all time."

"My wife is unwell. I cannot be away from our people so long."

Cuming thought of the short, young, enthusiastic Ukwaneequa to whom he had already grown attached. It would be better, he thought, to take a youth than to return empty-handed. He suggested the boy to the chief. Moytoy nodded in consent.

Others of the young men in the towns and villages of the Cherokee soon heard that young Ukwaneequa was planning to go with Cuming. Interest in the voyage across the water began to spread.

When Sir Alexander Cuming at last returned over the mountains to the settlement in eastern Carolina, seven Cherokee men, one of them Chief Oukah-Ulah, accompanied him, bound for the adventure of their lives.

Diamonds and precious stones glittered from white necks and wrists, mingled with subdued laughter from the ladies of the court. An air of cultured gaiety, the fluttering of fans, rustling of silk dresses, and a murmured undercurrent of hushed voices filled the great hall. The clusters of ladies and gentlemen numbering several hundred before the closed doors of the throne room represented the aristocratic elite of Europe. None had spared the least effort to adorn themselves for the upcoming audience with His Majesty, King George II of England.

The occasion was the king's installation of his Knights of the Garter. Though but a few would be honored, many of those present hoped for a momentary word with the king or perhaps some mark of recognition during the day's ceremony and following banquet.

Into the middle of the assembly walked a tall man, lean, for he had not recently been feasting on the soft foods of refinement, but hale and hearty from spending so much of his time out of doors. In contrast with the setting, his eyes shone with a keen look of adventure. His approach turned several heads, and exclamations followed.

"Cuming!" called a gentleman nearby. "A great pleasure to see you again! We heard a rumor that your recent voyage to the colonies left you in poor health. I am glad to see otherwise. You are thin, I must say, but I have never seen you looking better."

"The colonies are not nearly so bad as the crossing!" laughed Cuming. "Primitive of course, but in most ways tolerable."

"Do tell us what the colonies are like, Sir Alexander!" gushed a young lady. "Did you encounter any of those frightful savages one hears about?"

"Encounter them!" laughed Cuming. "I ate with them, slept with them, sojourned in the wilds with them, and am privileged to call many from the Cherokee tribe my friends."

Expressions of astonishment went round the slowly expanding circle. The adventurer's name had become well-known throughout London due in large measure to the exaggerated reports of his wife.

"Are they as backward and savage as the reports say?" asked another.

"Perhaps in some ways so they might appear," replied Cuming. "The sight of enemy scalps hanging from war poles to adorn the homes of their warriors is shocking at first, I admit—"

Gasps sounded from the women. Several faces turned faint at the hideous thought.

"Some of their customs take getting used to. They have sent several scalps as a gift to the king. But believe it or not, our own English colonists also collect the black-haired scalps of Indians."

"Disgusting!" exclaimed one of the men.

"I am not sure whether to believe you, Sir Alexander. No *Englishman* would do such a thing."

"It is true. There is cruelty and barbarism on both sides across the sea, let me assure you."

He paused briefly, allowing some of the hubbub over scalps to die down.

"Furthermore," Sir Alexander added, "seven of their men have accompanied me here to England."

The expressions of surprise now rose yet higher and spread throughout the great hall. Soon every eye rested upon Cuming. He turned and gestured widely, obviously enjoying this moment he had anticipated for more than a month.

Through the door at which he had entered a minute earlier emerged seven men. The one chief among them was dressed in English garb suitable for the occasion. The smooth tan skin of the other six was painted with spots of red, blue, and green. Feathers of many colors adorned their long black hair. The only clothing upon their brown, muscular bodies was the leather apron around each waist extending to the knees. Their feet were wrapped in leather moccasins.

"Indians!" sounded several exclamations of astonishment, for the discussion of scalps had not yet been forgotten. Murmured questions flew through the room. But even with hundreds of eyes staring at them, the seven Cherokee men remained calm, stoic, and dignified. Whether they were terrified or awestruck by the assembly, no hint of expression crossed their faces. Lean though muscular, all were of above average height, except for the nephew of Chief Moytoy, whose head barely reached the shoulder of the others.

In the midst of the commotion, a sudden double rap of the royal staff on the floor announced the arrival of the king.

"His Majesty, King George the Second!" called the court herald in a loud solemn voice.

The great double doors swung open. The crowd parted as the king advanced behind his guards.

Ladies and gentlemen bowed low. The king walked through the aisle of adoring subjects, smiling and nodding graciously. Pacing the length of the room he directed his steps straight towards Cuming, then paused and spoke.

"Sir Alexander," he said, "we had heard of your return, and of the natives who accompanied you," he added with a glance behind Cuming. "You are the talk of London. And it would appear with good reason!"

Cuming bowed low. "Your Majesty," he said, "these seven men from the Cherokee tribe in the New World have come to pay homage to Your Majesty—in recognition of a treaty between ourselves and the Cherokee nation and their newly proclaimed Emperor, Chief Okoukaula Moytoy."

"Is the chief one of these?" asked the king, nodding toward the seven silent Americans.

"He is not, Your Majesty," replied Cuming. "His nephew has come in his stead. I have also brought one of their chiefs called Oukah-Ulah."

"I see," replied the king. "Take me to meet them."

Cuming led the way toward the seven silent men who stood erect and unembarrassed to one side of the assembly. To the king's surprise Cuming stopped in front of the shortest of the delegation and addressed him. The king had entertained princes and kings over the years and visited every court of Europe. George II was one familiar with power and dignity. Though the men before him were dressed as primitives, their carriage spoke more clearly than words that they understood the language of greatness.

A red-faced baronet began to chuckle as he watched the display, mistaking the king's silence for condescension.

"They will at least provide the king's court some much needed entertainment," he began to one beside him. "I daresay, I have never seen such savagery—"

Suddenly the king spun around, his face flushed with anger.

"Are we to understand, my lord, that you find humor in these men!" he snapped. "How dare you mock or belittle them? These men are no mere savages. They are princes. Can you not see it in their eyes?"

Humiliated, the baronet shrunk back under the king's glare and said no more

The king turned again toward his guests.

"Your Majesty," said Cuming, "may I present Ukwaneequa, nephew of Emperor Moytoy. If the name is too difficult, we call him the Little Carpenter. He is familiar with our tongue. Beside him stands Chief Oukah-Ulah, the headman of their town of Tassetchee."

The king shook the hands of both men. "I bring you greetings from my uncle, and from our people," said Ukwaneequa, the youngest of the group. At the sound of his voice, speaking in their own language, again murmurs spread throughout the hall. The young man's voice seemed to ring with the same dignity as their strange but compelling demeanor.

The king now offered his hand to each of the other five in turn as Cuming recited their unusual names—Kettagusta, Tathtiowie, Clogittah, Collanah, and Ounakannowie.

At last the king turned to his attendants. "I would have them dine with us today," he said. "There is much we would learn of their people and their land. They may stand behind my table."

When the ceremony and installation were complete an hour later, the assembly filed into the great dining hall where the feast had been prepared. The king's attendants conducted Cuming's seven guests to a place behind the king's table.

During the meal the king asked many questions about the New World and declared himself astonished at the intelligence and nobility of his guests. He asked about their "emperor" as Cuming called Chief Moytoy and about the habits of their people in times of war and peace. Although the official spokesman for the group was Oukah-ulay, who presented the king with the crown of dyed opossum hair, the king directed most of his questions to Ukwaneequa. His quick and courteous answers won him the favor of all present.

Over the course of the next days and weeks, the king bestowed many gifts upon his visitors. Besides the opossum crown, they had also brought the king a vest of soft deerskin, a flint-tipped arrow, a wampum necklace of precious shells, the crystal from Jacob the Conjurer . . . and the Creek scalps.

Chief among the king's gifts to the seven were signet rings he himself placed on the hand of each young Indian. The rings were a mark of honor and respect for those whom he called Cherokee princes, made of pure gold, a metal with which the Cherokee were well familiar, and containing the king's signet. With the exchange of gifts the king declared that peace and friendship should exist forever between the kings of the Old World and the New.

Before the seven stepped upon their own lands they determined that the seven rings the king had given would be worn in times of peace, but kept in the tribal council lodge in times of war lest they fall into the hands of the war council and become a tool for death and destruction for a war chief of the red feather.

⟜⟝

Soon after his return from England, Ukwaneequa began to rise in the leadership of the Cherokee. His name was changed to Attacullaculla and he became chief of the white feather. For the rest of his life, Attacullaculla remained steadfast in his loyalty to the British crown and was the leading Cherokee spokesman for peace. As the white settlers took more and more of the Cherokee land, however, there were many other Cherokee chiefs who did not share his sentiments.

Toward the end of his life, Attacullaculla knew he must somehow preserve the legacy of the seven sacred rings. He looked to his niece Nanye'hi Ward, she who had been most greatly honored among all Cherokee women with the title Ghigua, or "Beloved Woman," as one whom he could entrust with the sacred charge.

When Nanye'hi, herself by now a woman of advancing years, glanced up to see the aging chief approaching in his chieftain's garments, she sensed something momentous at hand. An hour later, uncle and niece, the most respected chief and the most revered woman among all the Cherokee, were on their way up the sacred mountain together.

The charge given to Nanye'hi that day was one she herself passed on years later to Attacullaculla's great-grandson Long Canoe, whose faithfulness to their people she had been watching since the day of his birth. The rings must be hidden and their legacy kept safe.

As Attacullaculla had passed that solemn responsibility on to her, she now passed it on to the young man whose destiny would fade from the view of his fellow Cherokee. But the heritage he carried, though shrouded over for a season like the mists covering the mountains his people had long called home, would like those same Smokey Mountains, reappear in time to give new life to the legacy of a proud and ancient people.

From the Old Books continues at the end of this volume.

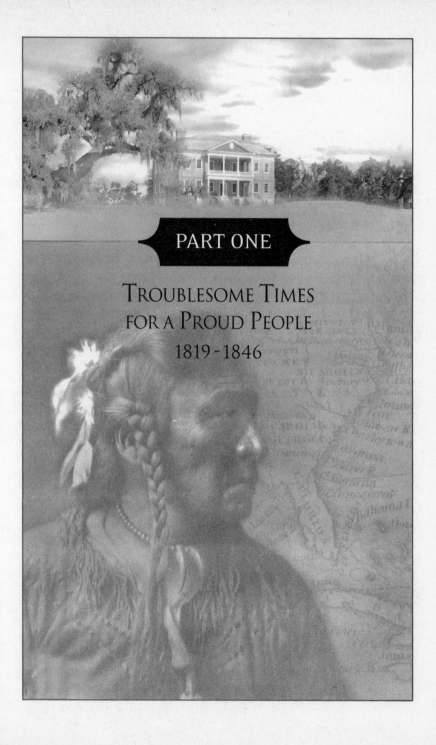

PART ONE

TROUBLESOME TIMES
FOR A PROUD PEOPLE
1819 - 1846

One

*W*hile darkness still covered the land, a man and boy, both more pale of skin than would have seemed likely from their heritage, made their way on horseback away from the land their people had possessed for more generations than any of their wisest men now remembered.

Long Canoe led the way up the mountain in the darkness. His nephew was still in a tragic stupor from the events of earlier in the evening. They paused briefly beside the sound of a waterfall, made more thunderous in the still of night. Behind it the man must tend to one final errand.

By daybreak they were well away through the valley and the deer-skin pouch of she known as the Ghigua was several times heavier than before. It not only bore five sacred rings but enough gold to cover the expenses of a long journey and much else besides. His intuition told him that his nephew's life depended on the speed and secrecy of their flight. They must travel far beyond the borders of the Cherokee and keep their identity hidden. Surely the assassins would not soon forget either the son or the brother of Swift Water.[1]

When would it be safe here? With a sudden twinge of melancholy Long Canoe wondered if he and his nephew would ever return to the

---

[1]The story of the sacred Cherokee rings, the history of that ancient people, and the reason for the secret midnight flight of this man and this boy to whom had been entrusted their legacy, is recounted in the legends From the Old Books.

once quiet mountain valley where they had both been born. This was indeed a sad moment. But he knew that for now, they must disappear without a trace.

Theirs was a legacy already being overrun by the rush of two new races—one white, one black—across this continent that the brown tribes of a diverse but related people had for millennia had to themselves. There would be no turning back of history's relentless march. Henceforth it would be a shared land, and the white man would write its new history, not the brown or the black. It would depend on a few like him to preserve the ancient legacy of his people. Both man and boy were of Attacullaculla's seed. The man's reasons for leaving were to preserve the past, not abandon it.

In the north he hoped to protect that heritage, even if to do so meant hiding it for a time.

By the time Long Canoe was missed, the rest of his kinsmen assumed that he too had died that night, or perhaps had fled west. His close friends shook their heads in bewilderment. Long Canoe had never expressed a desire to go west. His distant cousin Major Ridge thought he might have hidden himself in the mountains. But as the months passed and Long Canoe never returned to his seat on the Cherokee council, gradually the others assumed he was either dead or had joined the Old Settlers in the west.

What had happened to the boy likewise remained a question no one could answer.

After they were found to be missing and never returned, no one ever knew that aging Nanye'hi had, with the help of her daughter Katy Harlan, braved one more arduous journey to the top of the sacred mountain. What was her mission she never even told Katy. But when she emerged from the cave behind the waterfall, leaning on her trusted walking stick, a knowing smile spread across her lips which said more than she ever told another soul.

She could die in peace. The legacy would go on. Where destiny would take the rings, even her prophetic vision could not tell. But she was at peace. Long Canoe had been faithful to his charge. The Great Spirit would watch over them now.

Long Canoe was never heard from again. The suddenness with which he had vanished was forever after shrouded in mystery. The few who in later years came to know of his whereabouts, and even visited him from time to time, never divulged his secret. Most assumed that he had followed the Old Settlers west. In after years, however, when contact between eastern and western Cherokees was reestablished, there was no trace of his arrival among the western Cherokee.

Thus the mystery of his disappearance grew into legend.

In a small brick boarding school in New England the headmaster was concluding his final arrangements for a new pupil.

The boy said little as his uncle spoke with the man. He sensed that his past lay behind him and that his future was here. But at twelve, even the stoicism of his race could not prevent his being intimidated at sight of his future home.

The headmaster rang a bell. His assistant appeared and took the lad to his classroom to introduce him to his teacher and fellow students. When the two men were alone, the discussion continued.

"How long will the boy be with us?" asked the headmaster.

"I will leave you enough to cover two years' expenses," said the traveler from the south. "At that point I will assess his progress."

"How will I contact you?"

"You will not be able to for a while. I will be in touch with you. I will be relocating myself. It is best for the boy to remain ignorant of my whereabouts for a time. He must learn to make a place for himself here."

"As you wish, sir," said the headmaster, a little skeptically. "But if the boy's tuition is not paid I will have no choice but to turn him out—"

"Do not worry, my friend. The boy's expenses will be paid in full.

Money does not happen to be one of our problems. But the boy is in no little danger, as am I—"

The expression of concern on the headmaster's face registered clearly enough that he wondered if he had made a mistake by admitting the new student.

"Have no worries," said his strange visitor. "The danger I speak of is far away. Much farther than you can imagine. Not a trace of it will follow him here. We have traveled a great distance. Our movements are untraceable. But if his true identity were to become known to the wrong people, or my whereabouts discovered, there could be consequences. The boy must not know where I am. For the present he must be cut off from his roots. There is much danger. That is why I have brought him to you. It is for his own safety. I do not know what the future holds for me. Eventually he may contact me through you. I am sorry to be secretive, but it is for the boy's best. I ask you to trust me. I will reveal more in time."

The headmaster nodded, apparently satisfied.

"One more thing I would ask," added the boy's uncle. "Please watch him closely for a time. He has suffered a terrible shock with the loss of his parents. His need of love will be great. He is alone in the world. Even I as his closest relation cannot be near without endangering him."

"My wife and I will do all we can for him."

"He is a good boy, intelligent, quick to learn. He will adapt."

"I will be sure he receives all he needs."

"I am more grateful than I can say for your kindness. I will contact you when I can. Now . . . will you take me to him? I would have a few final words alone before I depart."

The man who now changed his name for a second time in his life, taking again to himself his father's English surname, left the wintry skies of New England where he had studied at Dartmouth years earlier, and traveled south again. He used a portion of his gold to purchase a fertile track of land suitable for many purposes, and settled in the heart of Virginia. The tract was only some sixty acres, whose rocky ground and thin topsoil had never attracted a buyer. But its location, several small but choice fields, and two or three extensive caves beneath the northern ridge, would suit his purposes perfectly.

Within a few short years, the ground had become profitable, verdant, and was the envy of every plantation owner for miles around.

Young Swift Horse, nephew of Long Canoe, grew into manhood. Gradually the events of his early life faded into the mists of memory along with his Cherokee name. None of his fellows ever suspected the true origins of his bloodline, nor did he himself pay much heed to events occurring within the nation of his heritage. Old chiefs were dying and with them an ancient way of life slowly passed into history. He was one of the new breed who thoroughly integrated into the modern life of New England America.

Two

The westering sun sank slowly behind a tree-lined ridge. In a remote region of the North Carolina mountains known as Winding Creek the hot afternoon seemed endless. Four women counted out the slow hours in a little log cabin where they were gathered to help in the birth of the newest child of the Cherokee Wolf Clan. The oldest woman was herself a matriarch of the clan. Her once dark hair gleamed with the silver of many winters that had come and gone since she was first laid in *her* mother Nanye'hi's arms. The birth she was attending now was for the child of her own daughter Ailcey.

It had been a difficult birth. The young mother had been laboring since dawn but the child seemed little closer to entering the world than when she began. Some of the women spoke in concerned whispers. But Katy Harlan, as she was called, knew that the child would survive. She had seen a white doe on the ridge the previous night. She knew that it signified the arrival of peace and prosperity to the clan.

Cata'quin placed a cool cloth on the young mother's forehead and squeezed her sweaty hand.

"Courage, Ailcey. The child is almost here."

The mother opened her mouth but a pang seized her. The words became instead a cry of pain.

Two women hurried with rags and hot water from the kettle. The taller of them, a young black woman in her early twenties, crushed some herbs into the steaming water to freshen the air. She understood the anguish in the eyes of the young mother. She had given birth to a child of her own a few months before. She and her husband were black slaves on the Harlan farm. She had grown up with Ailcey like a sister. She leaned over the bed.

"Miz Ailcey, you's 'most dere," she said softly. "I ken see a little head now."

As she spoke the young mother made a final desperate effort. Eight or ten minutes later the thin wail of a newborn greeted her ears as she dropped back in complete exhaustion.

Grandmother Katy Harlan took the baby in her arms and presented it to its mother.

"You have a daughter!" Katy announced proudly. "This one is a special child, Ailcey." Her eyes took on a faraway look as she gazed down on the tiny red face of her granddaughter. "She will have a long and eventful life. She will travel far from her home if my eyes do not deceive me and she will make peace between many people before the end. Perhaps she will even wear the ring of my mother the Ghigua."

Katy touched the gold ring on her right hand and then smiled as she saw how large it looked next to the tiny curled fists of the newborn.

"What you gwine call her, Miz Ailcey?" asked her black friend.

With the sound of her legendary ancestor still faintly in her ears, she replied.

"Chigua," whispered the mother, then closed her eyes.

When Chigua's birth was announced in the village there was great rejoicing. But the happiness of the clan was brief. The toll of the birth had been too great for the mother and young Ailcey's strength was too far gone. She could not recover and steadily weakened. Within a week she was gone. Little Chigua had lost her mother.

The family held council and came to a quick decision. The newborn would need a mother's milk for many months. The obvious choice for a wet nurse was the young black slave Sudina Magodan who had attended the birth. Her own child was but three months of age.

Thus little Chigua, descendant of the legendary Cherokee chief
Moytoy, suckled and then grew up with Sudina's children,
descendants of the youngest son of an ancient forgotten African chief
called Tungal whose son Magoda, known as Moses, had lived during
the time of Moytoy the elder.

Young Chigua, great-granddaughter of the Nanye'hi Ward the
legendary Ghigua, was three when she first remembered hearing
Sudina telling one of her older children of the five rivers of her native
land.

"Look at dat han' er yers, chil," whispered Sudina softly, unaware
that Chigua was listening as intently as her own five-year-old daughter. "Dem's da lines ob doze five ol' ribers dat da ol' king from da ol'
country tol' his chilluns 'bout. Doze be da five ribers er freedom dat
our people once knew, an' dat dey's gwine know agin one day. Dey
say da blood er kings is inside us, chil', an' dat we'll gib birth ter kings
one day agin. So don' you neber fergit ter look at dat han' er yers an'
doze lines ob da five ribers, cuz dey'll tell you who you is, an' where
you cums from."

Though her own race would in time ingrain into her consciousness
its own legends from the old books of *her* ancient past, this slice of
history from the black race with which she shared her youngest years
also became so deeply part of her from constant repetition in her hearing that all her life Chigua could not look at her hand without silently
wondering if she too might somehow be distantly connected not only
to Moytoy but also to the ancient chieftain of the blacks whose name
time had forgotten.

Three

*A*n adventurous aristocratic Frenchman decided to seek for himself a new life in the New World where land was cheap and opportunity unlimited. Twenty-four-year-old Jacques LeFleure sailed in 1798 to the island of Jamaica, where he used a portion of a sizeable inheritance to purchase a sugar plantation. Behind him in France he left a wife, also of high breeding and aristocratic blood, and baby daughter. It took LeFleure about a year to get the plantation and home in order and suitable for the style of living to which they were accustomed. Then he sent for his family. Accompanying Madame LeFleure as lady's maid and governess to the child was a young statuesque French Negro girl of sixteen. Like her mistress, Calantha Billaud was well-educated and spoke three languages and also commanded a reading knowledge of Latin. She possessed enough of an adventuresome spirit to find the prospect of travel to the New World exciting and full of challenge.

Over the next several years the plantation prospered. LeFleure and Madame LeFleure had two sons and another daughter. Though black, Miss Billaud was treated as an equal member of the family. LeFleure, already wealthy before arriving in Jamaica, refused to own another human being. He did not operate his plantation with the use of slaves, but employed freedmen, white and native, and paid them a fair wage. He grew to become a respected member of the Jamaican community.

When the two LeFleure sons reached seventeen and eighteen, they were sent to the mainland of the United States to study at the University of Georgia. While they were away, Madame LeFleure took ill with a fever and died. The sons came home briefly for the funeral, then returned to their studies on the mainland. There they learned the agricultural methods of the great southern plantations, with an eye to introducing cotton to their father's enterprise. They also became intrigued with the dependency of the South's cotton economy on slavery. By the end of their schooling they had thoroughly adapted themselves to the peculiar institution of slavery their father despised. This change in outlook, however, they thought it best not to divulge to him.

In the next two years following his wife's death, while his sons were still away, Jacques LeFleure came to realize how attached he had become to his wife's maid and friend, Miss Billaud. The grieving Frenchman, wealthy but now lonely, one daughter grown and married, his two sons away, began to haunt the classroom where Miss Billaud continued to tutor his youngest daughter, now in her teen years, watching and listening to every word that fell from the enchanting black lips. He began inviting the governess, now a majestic and stately black woman of regal beauty and thirty-nine years, to walk with him in his expansive gardens when the days' lessons were done. Their conversations grew gradually more relaxed. Intimidated somewhat at first, in time Miss Billaud grew comfortable with the man's gentleness, kindness, and humor. Laughter gradually accompanied their time together and slowly the sun returned to the countenance and heart of Jacques LeFleure.

Though LeFleure was nine years senior to his governess, before long they were nearly inseparable. The two were married in 1824. A son was born to them in 1825 whom they called Sydney.

Upon completion of their studies, the two sons, now in their twenties, returned to help their father on the plantation and to institute some of the changes they had planned. Now older and having grown accustomed to the feelings toward the Negro in the American South, whatever fondness they might once have felt for their childhood governess had disappeared. In their minds they had forgotten how very *black* she was. The sight of her on their father's arm, speaking in cultured French as if she was his equal, was enough to turn their stomachs. In many ways, though they still treated him with the respect of his station, they had become thorough sons of the American South, and despised their father for what he had done.

As for the half-black child of their father's unbelievable marriage, he was nothing but a bastard in their eyes, certainly not the half brother to which the blood in his veins testified. They hated him and lost no opportunity to treat the poor youngster with cruelty and contempt behind their father's back.

Calantha did her best, however, in the occasionally unpleasant circumstances, to bring up her son in the culture and refinement of a Jamaican plantation atmosphere. She taught him the classics, stories from the Bible, and to read and write, in addition to French and Latin, Spanish and English. The boy's aging father Jacques doted on his tan-skinned young son and gave him every advantage that his wealth afforded him. His older grown sons resented the boy all the more bitterly, seeing him lavished with privileges they had forgotten that they too had enjoyed.

Four

*O*n a fateful night of 1833, two young Virginians—in their mid-twenties, both unmarried, both presumed inheritors of wealth and consequently in little haste to grow into responsible manhood—stumbled on a plot that would change their lives forever.

They had been drinking heavily and would have been an embarrassment to their respective fathers in such condition. Their drunkenness may have heightened their sense of drama at what they saw, though it also made recalling the strange nighttime images difficult in the days that followed.

Four men, strangers to the region, rode with stealthy step, as if they had shod their horses in the silent moccasins of their forebears, through the moonless night toward the only dwelling for miles, a small farmhouse that sat roughly between the homes of the two drunken watchers. That they had nearly passed out beside the road, accounted for the riders coming so close that they nearly stumbled over them, yet never saw them.

"Who are *they*?" said one of the youths with slurred speech as he sat up.

"Keep your voice down!" replied the other in a loud whisper. "I don't know who they are. But I intend to find out."

"What are you going to do?"

"Follow them. Come on," he said, climbing with some difficulty to his feet. "They're heading toward the ridge. We can get there on foot."

"Wait for me," said the first, stumbling with difficulty after his friend.

"You're drunk!"

"And you're not?"

"At least I can keep my feet beneath me."

It was the younger of the two by a year who now led the way through the night across a cultivated field, reducing by about half the distance to the house. By the time they reached them, the dogs were occupied on the other side of the home greeting the four riders and their horses.

"Look at them!" said one of the youths as the light from a welcoming lantern fell upon the riders. "They're—"

"Keep your voice down, I tell you!" interrupted his friend. "I can see well enough what they are."

The two crept toward the house, where they collapsed under an open window and waited.

The peculiarities of the farmer who led his guests inside were well-known. Everyone suspected that his real name was so long and impossible to pronounce that he had changed it upon his arrival here. Rumors abounded concerning his ethnic origins. But he had earned the respect of most of his neighbors. Had the man suspected that the words of the four who had come all this way with worrisome tales from the south were being overheard, he would have urged greater discretion in their speech, or would have spoken to them in their native tongue. But he did not know it. Therefore much was revealed that the four riders had come so far to keep secret. Each of the four was well-known. How they had all managed to slip away unnoticed was little short of a miracle. Though he had been gone fourteen years, and the three younger of his visitors had been but boys at the time, he recognized them all instantly. They were Kahnungdatlageh, his son Skahtlelohskee, Degodoga, and his brother Kilakeena—all now known as Major Ridge, John Ridge, Stand Watie, and Elias Boudinot.

"The time is short," said the elder Ridge after they had gone inside and had spoken for some time. "If President Jackson continues on his present course, our people are doomed. The land will be taken from us as well as everything we possess. That is why we four have decided that perhaps the Old Settlers were right."

"You!" exclaimed their host in astonishment. "*You* are thinking of going west, when you have fought it so long?"

"I now believe that we have no choice. We four are about to announce the formation of a new party. We will call it the New Treaty Party. Our purpose will be to convince the rest of Cherokee leaders to join us in a final negotiated settlement with Washington."

"Is there a chance the leadership will go along?"

"It may be difficult," now said the younger Ridge. "But we must take steps to preserve what we can. Better to get something for our land than nothing."

"That is what my brother urged so many years ago. And he was killed for such a view. Will you risk a similar fate?"

"We have no choice, my friend," replied Ridge. "We walk a path with danger on all sides. If we refuse to leave the white men will eventually kill us all or drive us off the land. Already they are dividing up our land and selling it to white settlers. If we leave, our brothers call us traitors and seek our blood. If we stay, our people will be left with nothing. What path would you have us choose?"

"I am no counselor," replied the man. "I have lived out of sight of our people for many years. If you came wishing me to speak on your behalf I fear you were mistaken. I no longer have a voice in the nation."

"Perhaps you will again," suggested Ridge. "Times are changing. New leaders are speaking out, like these three young men with me."

"I fear the time of our generation, or at least my own part in it, has passed."

"We have not come for that reason," said the younger Ridge. "We come to you with a different request. You are a descendant of our great father Attacullaculla. You have carved a place for yourself outside the Cherokee nation. With you the treasures of our people will be safe until such time as they are needed. If we must leave, we must attempt to preserve what we can, to build up a safe treasure for the future of our people."

"In other words . . . the gold?"

One by one, the four looked at one another, then nodded.

"That, and other artifacts, records, and tribal treasures. They must be kept safe."

Their host thought to himself that even these four did not know of the greatest treasure of all that he had brought here years before.

"What does Ross say about all this?" he asked.

"He does not yet know of our plan. He will be furious when he learns of it."

"He is convinced he can still work out a compromise with Jackson to keep our people in the east," added Boudinot.

"He has refused to let us speak publicly," said the younger of the Watie brothers. "He has taken away Elias' editorship of the *Cherokee Phoenix* for that very reason. If he knew of our errand tonight, our lives would be in grave danger. He tells our people that Jackson will honor the old agreements. But it is a fool's hope. The Removal Act of three years ago is the only agreement Jackson intends to carry out."

"And I know Jackson," Ridge added. "I fought side by side with him. I know how he thinks. Stand is right. Nothing but complete removal of our people will satisfy him. That is why we must take the initiative and get something in return before it is too late. We think we can negotiate for five million dollars."

"What will you do?"

"We will conclude a treaty with Washington, with or without Ross's support."

"A dangerous policy," said the man. "There are those who have been assassinated for less." He did not think it prudent to bring up the Doublehead murder, nor the conviction he had held all these years that the Major may also have been involved in his own brother's death.

"If Ross has his way, it will be the end of the Cherokee nation," said Boudinot. "It is not right. We all hate it. But it is the reality. We want to keep our lands, but we must be practical. Yes, it is a great risk, but it is the only way. We *will* be forced to leave. So we want to negotiate while there is still time to get enough from Washington to build homes for our people and rebuild our nation."

"Do you really think Washington will pay? They have never honored such treaties in the past."

"That is a risk we take. But we see no other alternatives."

The conversation continued in lower tones.

"Did you hear what they were talking about?" said the older of the two drunken eavesdroppers outside the house. "Gold!"

"Shut up, you fool!" barked his companion softly. "Let me listen."

"But if the danger is as great as you say, will the gold and tribal treasures be safe here?" asked the man.

"You are more likely to escape the tears to come, my brother. They do not know you."

"The moment gold was discovered we knew we must find a way to smuggle away what we could," said Boudinot. "Nothing is safe on our land. They no longer honor our boundaries. The Georgia government is in the process of parceling out Cherokee land to sell in a state lottery. Catastrophe looms and Ross is blind to it. They will eventually find all our secret places."

"Take it west with you," suggested their host.

"The journey is long and dangerous. With gold to tempt thieves, how many would reach the Arkansas River alive? We need a place where the gold can rest undisturbed."

The man sighed. "I will help however I am able."

The four travelers exchanged looks of relief.

"Our people do not know we are here," now said Stand Watie. "Your whereabouts remain safely concealed."

"But we would not deceive you," said the younger Ridge. "If you help us, your life will be in danger too."

"It is no more than what I feared. For this very reason I left the land of our fathers and came north many years ago. Still, I had hoped it would not come to this."

"It has come to it, our brother."

"What about our cousin?" asked Boudinot.

"He is safe. But I am concerned he is forgetting his Cherokee roots.

I may have been mistaken to leave him as I did. Being in the North changed him. When we left his life was in danger. I may have emphasized the danger too greatly. He was at an impressionable age."

"Back then his life probably was in danger . . . I am sorry to say it . . . even from me," said Ridge sadly. "But we must all change with the times. There is no doubt you saved his life by doing what you did. We can only hope he will once again honor his heritage."

As they continued to talk, their speech became so low that the befogged minds of the two eavesdroppers could not make out what was said. Their heavy eyes drooped and they almost fell asleep before a louder tone jolted them into momentary wakefulness.

The voice was their neighbor's. "If the time comes when I must leave there is a man I would trust with our secrets—a man I would trust with my very life."

"Is he one of us?"

"He is a white man. But he can be trusted completely. Even should I be unable to, he will insure that our secret is secure until our people are safe once again."

Their voices grew yet softer in the night. The alcohol-soaked brains of the two listeners became muddled and confused. Before many more minutes had passed, they were both asleep again.

They awoke groggily with the first light of dawn. No sign remained of the four strange midnight visitors. With heads splitting, the two youths slunk away toward their homes wondering if they had imagined the whole thing.

Five

After the midnight visit in 1833, dark forebodings filled the heart of the man who as an infant had been plunged into the chilly Tannassy in the ancient rite of his mother's people. He knew that his kinsmen had spoken the truth when they predicted the end of Cherokee life in the east. Public opinion across the country had gradually turned against the Cherokee. With President Jackson's Indian Removal Act it was only a matter of time before they would be forced to vacate their homes.

More visitors from the South came to visit, always at night, and, like the first four, always with horses heavily laden with that which they hoped would one day secure, if not Cherokee freedom, at least the power to buy back some of the land that had been so cruelly taken from them over the years. Then suddenly the visits ceased. Their friend in the North feared for the worst, though he hoped that perhaps those few who knew of his whereabouts had made it safely to the west.

He hoped his own land was secure. The people nearby might gossip about his peculiarities but none other than his neighbor to the west knew his true heritage. Furthermore his farm was miles north of Cherokee borders. Yet he could not banish a growing sense of impending danger. He sometimes feared that one night the knock on the door would bring an assassin instead of a messenger laden with Cherokee wealth. In case of his own death he must leave record of where he had hidden what had been entrusted to him.

Who could he trust with such a secret?

His nephew was now a grown man. Whether he even remembered his Indian name, the man did not know, so effectively had he adapted to the white man's ways. He still felt that his nephew was destined to play some role in the legacy of their people. But it was a destiny he would have to discover for himself, in his own way, and in his own time.

He must leave the secret in the hands of his neighbor. His neighbor was an honorable man. But as he considered the implications more thoroughly, the more troubled he became. His neighbor's health was not good and if he should die then everything would go to his eldest son, a young man of weak character and scheming mind. He must devise a way to hide the secrets of his people so that ignorant eyes would not be able to interpret the signs.

He went out the next day, and the next after that, to walk his land, knife and hammer in hand, searching for suitable locations for the markers. Late the following night, alone at his table, he sat down in the flickering light from his lantern and began to draw.

After the strange images they had seen and cryptic words they thought they heard, the two drunken youths racked their brains trying to remember the exact words. Had there *really* been talk of gold? Had they heard the words "a place where it will be safe?" Over the following weeks and months, they became obsessed with finding whatever the four strange men had brought that night.

They began using their every available minute to spy on their neighbor and snoop about his land, but discovered nothing. The wily Cherokee knew well enough that he was being watched, and more than half suspected the reason.

When the summons came to Grantham Davidson, he knew immediately by his friend's demeanor and expression that something momentous was at hand. He went out to Brown's home late the following afternoon. His son watched him go with more curiosity than was good for him. He would have followed if he thought he could get away with it. As it was, he had to content himself to await his father's return to see what he might learn.

Grantham Davidson arrived at Brown's house. The two men sat down. Brown's expression was solemn. Two papers lay on the table in front of him.

"I have asked you here," Brown began, "because you are my friend, and I know I can trust you."

"Of course," nodded Davidson. "How may I help you?"

"You know I am Cherokee."

"You have made no secret of it to me."

"I assume you have been following the development of events in Georgia, how President Jackson is systematically taking what remains of our native lands."

"Yes. I am sorry. What is being done is wrong. I hope you know that I do not condone it in any way."

"Certainly. I came north fourteen years ago to do what I could to protect—"

He paused, considering how much to divulge even to a trusted friend.

"There were others involved," he went on, "others to protect. My brother was murdered. Dreadful things were afoot then, just as there is much danger again now."

"Surely *you* are not—" began Davidson.

"We are all in danger," said Brown. "Anyone of Cherokee blood is at risk, some more than others. There is danger even from within our own tribe. My brother was murdered by our own tribesmen. Even now, I am being watched. But more than that, these are seriously troublesome times for our tribe as a whole. Our lands and possessions are being stripped from us. If my identity were to become known to the wrong people, even here, this very land, this very home where we sit, could be confiscated and taken from me."

"But you hold legal title to the land."

"As do our people in the South. Legalities matter nothing to Jackson and those who do his bidding and those of the state governments

who would seize what is ours. They are bent on the complete destruction of all native tribes. My people have legal title to lands that are
being stolen from them with the full sanction of the government. We
have legal title to Dahlonega where gold was discovered. But it has all
been taken away. The Cherokee have no rights in the eyes of the
American government."

Davidson shook his head sadly. He knew it was true. "I am so sorry,
my friend," he said. "But surely here, nothing so drastic will happen to
you. I was witness when you purchased this parcel. I will attest to the
legality of your ownership."

"Don't you see—none of that matters," said Brown. "Where
Negroes and Indians are concerned, there *are* no legalities, no rights,
no freedoms. In the current climate, I would not want to take my
claim to this land, even with a legal deed in my hand, into any court
in this country. I could lose everything. It is a terrible time. The chiefs
in the South have taken their case all the way to the Supreme Court to
fight the Indian Removal Act and the court upheld them. Yet Jackson
has openly vowed that he will not abide by the decision and will rid
the states of the Cherokee one way or another. That is why I say that
legalities matter nothing. It is why I have decided on another course of
action . . . one that involves you."

"What can I do to help?" asked Davidson.

Brown picked up the document on the table in front of him.

"This is the deed to this tract of land that borders your own," he
said. "I have signed it over to you."

At the words, immediately Davidson opened his mouth to object.
Brown's uplifted hand silenced him.

"Please, hear me out," he said. "Then you will understand. This is
my way of protecting the land and insuring that it cannot be taken or
confiscated. I have noted a purchase price of one dollar, so there can
be no questioning that it is a legal transaction."

"I understand," said Davidson, now nodding. "If no Cherokee
name is associated with the legal title, the land will not be in jeopardy.
But it will always be yours . . . you know that—in spite of the deed."

"You are an honorable man," said Brown. "Perhaps a time will come when such troubles as these will no longer follow my people. For now, this is the best way. If something should happen to me, I must know that the land, and what it contains, is safe."

"What it . . . *contains*?"

"There are secrets . . . secrets that belong to my people. There are others, in addition to yourself, to whom I will entrust knowledge how to find them should I myself not be able to return or should harm befall me."

"You make it sound as if you are going away."

"I must leave tomorrow to see one of those of whom I speak. It is a journey that has perhaps waited too long, but one which I must no longer delay making. You will know the others I speak of by their possession of a portion of that which I am about to give you. If I should be detained or killed, all three of you together will be capable of finding what will secure our legacy."

Brown now took the second paper from the table, a single sheet, and tore off about a third of it and handed it to Davidson. "Guard this, if not with your life, with your most valued possessions, my friend. The future of my people may depend on it."

Davidson nodded in solemn agreement.

The two men continued to talk of many things late into the night.

When Grantham Davidson returned to his home, he little suspected that his son had been waiting for him, watching from the shadows, nor with what interest the youth noted the papers in his father's hand which went straight into the safe in his office.

True to his word, Brown released all his animals and was himself gone before the next day's sun had risen above the horizon into the Virginia sky.

It took Clifford Davidson a month of constant sleuthing to come upon his father's office unoccupied and the safe open. He hurried to it, rummaged through his father's papers until his eyes fell on a torn portion of paper attached to the deed to the Brown land. For an instant he stood staring. His pulse drummed in his ears. Then he snatched it from the deed, crammed it down his shirt, and ran from the office, glancing hastily over his shoulder to make sure he had not been seen.

Seconds later he was out of the house. He hurriedly saddled a horse and galloped away.

Brown returned to Virginia several weeks after his departure, his errand in the north completed, the ring of the ancients no longer on his finger. His return was brief, and no one saw him. Circumstances had changed again. His next mission to the south demanded secrecy and haste.

But though Brown was not seen, he saw that which would change the lives and fortunes of many when he arrived early one evening as dusk was falling. Riding toward his house, he overheard voices on a high ridge of his land raised in heated argument.

He was tired and hungry and was looking forward to one more restful night before setting off for the South. Sensing evil afoot, he dismounted and crept silently toward the voices.

"Let's just kill him when he gets back," said one. "He's only an Indian. We'll beat the truth out of him."

"You're crazy," replied the other. "I'm no murderer."

"Then we'll burn him out, burn his house down."

It was obvious the two had been drinking. This time, however, instead of producing sleep, the alcohol had produced anger.

"What good would that do? We don't even know where the gold is."

"We'll find it!" shouted the other, raving recklessly. "Now give me that paper!"

"I'm not going to let you do anything stupid. I should never have even shown it to you. We can't make any sense of it anyway."

"Give it to me, I tell you!"

"This whole thing was a mistake. I'm going home. We'll talk about it when you're not so drunk."

Brown heard the sound of horse hooves over the rocky ground. But they did not go far before the voices erupted in violent argument again.

"You're not going anywhere until you give it to me! It's ours . . . that gold is ours. If you don't want your half, then I'll take it. You're not going to ruin this for me!"

A sound followed . . . a fall from a horse . . . a thud and grunt, followed by shouts and threats . . . scuffling, high words, fists, more shouts. Then another fall . . . a cry . . . at last silence.

Brown listened intently, trying to make out what had happened. With the stealth of his ancestors, he crept closer, then peered over the ledge just in time to witness the final wickedness of treachery. He stole back out of sight.

After a minute or two he heard footsteps scuffling over rocks. A few seconds later a horse galloped away. The moment he was alone Brown scrambled down the incline to see what could be done. But he was too late to help. He knew the look of death well enough.

Most of the night he lay sleepless in his house, which he had found ransacked, no fire in the hearth to betray that he was here, debating with himself what to do. But this was not his fight. He could not prevent what had happened. He could only hope the truth would come out without him. A higher calling rested with him and he could not delay. After a lengthy silence, his own destiny beckoned.

When Clifford Davidson's blood-spattered body was found on Harper's Peak it seemed likely that a fall off his horse was responsible for the vicious wound on the side of his head.

The smoke which had risen from Brown's chimney for fourteen successive winters was seen in the Virginia sky no more. Though speculation about his absence hovered in the area for some time, gradually it too, like the smoke that was no more, drifted away on the currents of the wind and was heard little more of as the years turned the strange man who had occupied the hilly region into little more than a vague memory.

In his grief it was not for two or three years when Grantham Davidson's mind happened to recall it, and then realized he had not seen the small mysterious paper of Brown's in all that time. He went

through his safe where he knew he had put it, but found nothing. He
searched high and low through his entire office but still did not
uncover it, and never knew what became of it.

In time it became known that Brown had sold his land, for an
undisclosed sum, to Grantham Davidson. Some in the neighborhood
hinted at irregularities. But Davidson possessed the deed, and the
courts saw no evidence to force him to relinquish it.

Six

$\mathcal{B}$y 1838 all Cherokee who remained on their traditional lands in Georgia and the Carolinas were to be removed to the Oklahoma Territory. Those who had not complied with the government's order voluntarily would be rounded up by force and sent to camps where they would await their time to be herded west.

Young Chigua Eaglefeather and her aging grandfather, along with her sister, were among the many who formed the long train of wagons, carts, and walkers who set out from Fort Campbell on the long journey to the Oklahoma Territory which would come to be known as the Trail of Tears.

"Grandfather, why do some of the soldiers look so sad?" she asked as they went. "It is *our* people who are being driven from our home-lands."

"Everyone knows that what is happening is wrong," he answered. "Everyone except their chiefs in Washington who have ordered us away from the land of our fathers."

Many traveled with the Cherokee as they headed out over the mountains. There were French trappers, Scottish scouts, English adventurers, suppliers, whites married to Cherokees who refused to leave their families, and a few doctors who had been ordered along by the army.

After traveling for several weeks, nine-year-old Chigua and her

older sister had become good friends with the army private named
Burnett who was kind to the Indian families. They spoke to him in
Cherokee, which he could speak nearly as well as they. To pass the
time Burnett taught them some French words he had learned from a
Frenchman when trapping in the wilds of the South as a young man.
Young Chigua was intrigued with the strange-sounding language that
Private Burnett called French. She liked the feel of the words on her
tongue. She learned quickly, and with the help of one of the French-
men who was along, soon she and Burnett were carrying on brief
conversations in French as they walked along.

"Why are you not like the others who speak to us like animals?"
Chigua asked, speaking in her own tongue.

"Because I believe all people are God's children," replied Burnett,
also in Cherokee. "Just because God wanted to make his children
different colors, why should we treat anyone differently because of it."

One day as the train paused for its midday stop, one of the soldiers
sent Chigua and her sister and several other girls into the woods to
gather firewood. They knew that to disobey would invite the whip,
and so, though exhausted, they did as he said.

Unknown either to the Cherokee or their army captors, almost
from the beginning of the long drive west, the weary steps of the
displaced Cherokee and the plodding hooves of three thousand horses
had been silently and invisibly dogged by a renigade band of Seminoles. The fate of the other southeast tribes had been sealed long
before this last dying gasp of native culture now being ground beneath
the wagon wheels of a cruel trail of Cherokee tears. Many other tribes
had been rooted and stomped out before this. Those that remained in
small groups and clans and war parties survived however they could.
In these years of discontent, they had seen the rise and profitability of
the slave trade throughout the South and had learned to exploit it.
Though the white man was their enemy, they were not above taking
his money. Runaway blacks were their preferred stock-in-trade. But
they would capture and sell their own kind, too, when it suited them.
Tribes had always enslaved their enemies. Now they realized that
white plantation owners would pay cash money for muscular men,

and for any women who could make babies who would grow into muscular men.

So like the beasts of prey who dog a herd of elk to isolate one or two that lag behind or stray too far from the rest, the band of Seminoles who had been following the wagons for three days now saw the five girls leave the camp in the direction of the woods. They waited patiently until the girls were inside the cover of the trees and out of sight. Then with marvelous stealth, they snatched, bound, and gagged them without the escape of a peep of noise. Within minutes the raiding party and its captives was two miles away.

When his two granddaughters and the other girls did not return, the old man called Eaglefeather wandered from the camp in the direction of the woods. His shouts in the direction he had last seen them brought no answer. They did, however, succeed in arousing the notice of one of the guards, a certain Lieutenant Benjamin McDonal. He turned his horse in the direction of the sound and galloped toward Chigua's grandfather.

"Hey, old man, where do you think you're going?" he shouted as he rode up.

"Our daughters went for wood, sir," he answered. "My own and three other girls. They have not come back."

"What's that to me? Get back to the wagons!"

"I must find them."

"I gave you an order, old man. We're ready to pull out."

"I cannot leave them out there," persisted the grandfather, taking another step or two toward the woods. "We have to find them."

Angered by now, McDonal pulled his horse whip with its tiny wire tip from his saddle and let fly a vicious lash that ripped half an inch of skin off the bare back of the Indian.

The man screamed out in pain and fell to his knees as McDonal jumped off his horse. The poor man could not hide from a second lash, then a third.

The sound of galloping hooves interrupted the torment. As McDonal raised his whip for a fourth blow, he suddenly felt it wrested from his hand from behind.

In a white fury, he spun around to see a blue-clad member of his own detail staring down from his saddle, holding the whip he had grabbed from his commander's hand. The man threw down the whip at McDonal's feet.

"You fool, Burnett!" he shouted. "What do you think you're doing?"

"Stopping you from killing this poor man, Lieutenant," replied Burnett.

"You're just a private, I could have you court commissionered for what you've done."

"Perhaps, sir. But I won't let you kill a defenseless old man."

"The savage defied my order."

"His name is Eaglefeather. He is honored among his people."

"What kind of ridiculous name is that! It means nothing. I told him we were pulling out and to return to his wagon."

Burnett dismounted, walked forward, and stooped down beside Chigua's grandfather.

"The daughters, sir," the man said feebly, wincing in pain. "You know them for you have been kind to them."

"Yes, I know them—young Chigua and Betsy. What about them?"

"They were sent with three others for wood, sir. They have not returned."

Burnett turned to McDonal.

"It's true, Lieutenant," he said. "I heard Ensign Bullock send them off an hour ago."

"What's that to me, Private!" spat McDonal, stooping to retrieve his whip. "We are about to leave and can't hold up the entire train for a few girls who wandered off. Now stand aside, Private! And you get up, old man, and get back to the wagon!"

Another sudden crack of his whip found the Cherokee's shoulder. The private jumped to his feet and stood to face his superior officer. The next sting of the whip caught Burnett in the face and drew blood from a gash across his cheek. The normally even-tempered young man was at last fully aroused. He leapt to one side to avoid the next blow, even as his hand grabbed the small tomahawk he had worn on his belt for years. A minute later McDonal lay senseless on his back, his head bleeding from two deft whacks from the blunt end of the small hatchet. In truth, he was lucky to be alive. Any Indian wielding the same instrument would have cleft his skull in two.

The shouting brought half a dozen others to the scene, including Captain McClellan on his mount. Already the wagons had started to move behind them. Whatever this was about it had to be wrapped up quickly.

McClellan looked about hurriedly, saw one of his lieutenants laying on the ground with a private standing over him with what looked like an Indian tomahawk.

"Put this man under arrest," he said to the men who had accompanied him to the scene. "Then get this Indian who is doubtless responsible for the whole thing back to his wagon. I'll get to the bottom of it later."

As he galloped off, Burnett's hands were bound behind him and he was led away. The last he saw as he glanced back was the poor old Cherokee man, tears streaming down his brown wrinkled face, wailing and calling for the Cherokee daughters in the direction of the wood, while two of McClellan's men dragged him back toward the wagons.

No one saw any of the five missing girls again. Neither did any doubt their fate. For girls so young to survive in the wilds would be impossible.

Two hours later, the train had moved on, and the site was quiet and desolate. All that remained were a few dried splotches in the dust where an old man's tears had fallen to the ground as he lamented the loss of the two girls he loved with all his heart.

Seven

Jacques LeFleure died suddenly in 1842 at the age of 68. His two older sons immediately seized control of his Jamaican estate. Though LeFleure's will left control of his affairs in the hands of his wife, now 59, for her lifetime, and equal shares beyond that to all *five* of his children, his white sons vowed that neither their black stepmother nor her bastard son, Sydney, now 17, would see one cent of their father's fortune.

Secretly they made their plans.

On Sydney's eighteenth birthday his stepbrothers marched into the parlor where Sydney and Calantha were sharing a quiet celebration together. Following close behind were four surly looking men, recently hired by the LeFleure sons. The expressions that met Sydney and his mother said clearly enough that evil was afoot.

"David . . . Pierre . . . what are you doing?" said the young men's stepmother.

"Insuring what is ours," replied David, the eldest.

"What do you mean?"

"We are taking control of the plantation."

"But your father left the plantation to all of us!"

"Yes, and we are taking it. Get them out of here!"

First to the astonishment, then the protestations, and finally the horror of Sydney and his mother, the strangers proceeded to bind them with rope, drag them from the house, and heave them into a waiting cart as if they had been two sacks of grain, while Sydney's stepbrothers looked on with cool approval.

The cart rumbled away. All the rights, privileges, wealth, culture, breeding, and legal status of Calantha and Sydney LeFleure vanished as dust beneath its wheels. From the only home Sydney had ever known, and what had been Calantha's for more than forty years, mother and son were borne away into the slavery that had already become hell's curse upon this New World across the sea from the France from which their lineage had come.

Some four hours later the cart stopped at a nearby port town. One of the men walked around to the back, reached in and dragged Calantha out and onto her feet. Her hands were still bound.

"Sydney!" she screamed as he yanked at her and pulled her away.

Sydney scrambled out of the cart to follow. But a terrible whack from the fist of one of the men laid him flat on the dirt beside it. He struggled to his feet, lips and nose streaming blood.

"Mother!" he cried, stumbling forward.

"Sydney," she said again, though her voice was now failing, overwhelmed in sobs she could not control. She twisted from the man's grasp and cast a final forlorn look back at her son. "Sydney . . . Sydney!" she wailed softly through her tears, "Je t'aime . . . God be with you . . . *Je t'aime.*"

A rude hand grabbed her and twisted her away, ripping the corner of her elegant dress off at the shoulder, then shoved her stumbling along the walkway as she wept uncontrollably.

Once more Sydney made a vain attempt to follow. But another great blow fell on the side of his head, and he knew no more.

Sydney LeFleure awoke in the black fetid hold of a French slave ship bound for the coast of Florida, where the French had been doing a vigorous slave trade for years. The next weeks passed as the blur of a dark nightmare.

As Joseph of old was sold into Egypt's slavery by his own flesh and kin, there to be purified and tested for the destiny that awaited him, so was the young Jamaican Sydney LeFleure handed over to the taskmaster of a new and cruel Egypt of the American South, to see what the refiner's fire could likewise make of him.

By the time he had been sold to a Florida plantation owner, the blistering welts across his back and shoulders testified to lessons cruelly learned, that it would do him no good to protest, to try to explain that it was all a mistake, that he was educated and free, that he was the son of a white landowner and aristocrat, that he was even himself legal owner of a portion of a Jamaican sugar plantation. Every protest earned him fresh welts atop those still oozing from previous attempts to reason with his captors. Slowly he learned the invaluable first lesson of slavery—silent compliance.

Sydney learned, too, that to speak with intelligence angered his white overseers. He modified his speech to mimic the Negro dialect of the slaves around him, and in other ways used his intelligence to make the hideous captivity more tolerable. But in his heart of hearts, he never forgot who he was or where he had come from. He had come of French and Negro stock. He was a native Jamaican. But now, for better or worse, he was an "American." He vowed one day to be free again, no matter how long it took to realize that dream. One day he would be a *free* American.

Unfortunately, long years of slavery yet lay in his future, though of more varied kinds than he could have anticipated.

A roving band of Seminoles raided the plantation where Sydney LeFleure had just begun to learn what was expected of him sufficiently for his wounds to heal. At sight of the bare-chested Indians, the two white overseers scrambled for their rifles. But they lay dead in the field seconds later, and the eight blacks that had been their charge were bound and spirited away to be sold yet again, either to some native tribe or to another plantation owner.

Several nights later, after much travel, Sydney found himself alone in a Seminole encampment. Selling the other blacks, his Indian captors were fascinated by Sydney's moderate features, mannerisms, and unusual inflection of voice. What they would do with him, Sydney didn't know, but they seemed considering some means to increase his value at the slave auction. Or perhaps they merely intended to make him their own slave.

Months went by. Sydney found himself worked hard but in general treated well enough. He was not the only slave being held in the Florida wilderness by the Seminole band that had captured him, though all the rest were Indians from other tribes and spoke in tongues he could not understand. He did as he was told, said little, and waited and watched to see what he could learn.

A young lanky but stately Indian girl of fifteen or sixteen came to him one morning with his bowl of corn mush.

"Merci," said Sydney absently in French.

"Bien sur. Pas de quoi," she replied pleasantly. Sydney glanced up in surprise.

"You speak French very well," he said, smiling. "Are you Seminole?" he asked, now in English

"No, I am Cherokee," she answered in English. "I am a captive like you."

"How do you come to speak French and English?"

"I was from a Cherokee family of some means. We were well educated. Many Cherokee attend white schools. The French I learned from a trapper. I know only a few phrases."

"I am from Jamaica—I know nothing about your ways."

"Jamaica—where is that?" asked the girl.

"Across the sea, in the Carribbean."

"Is it near the place where the great king lives that my ancestors visited, far, far across the water?"

"I think you mean England," said Sydney. "No, Jamaica is nowhere near England, though now I am not certain exactly which direction it lies, or even where we are now. Do you know?"

"Not exactly. I think in Florida."

"Ah yes, I have heard of Florida also. Many Spanish are said to live there. But how do Cherokees come to attend white schools?"

"Cherokees are different than many other Indian tribes, though the white man has no eyes to see it and treats us with equal cruelty."

"Different . . . how?" asked Sydney.

"We have a great heritage of chiefs and laws. We are educated and many of our people own land and slaves and wealth—at least we once did. Many of our great men have been educated in the white man's schools and colleges and are very intelligent."

"How do you come to be here?"

"I was captured, like you."

The memory seemed unpleasant and the girl glanced away.

"You appear troubled," said Sydney. "You are afraid?"

Tears filled the girl's eyes as she nodded. "I have been with them many years since I was a girl. At first they mostly ignored me and made me do things that were not severe. But now they are looking for a man for me, or will sell me. They do not know that I understand when they talk about me. I am frightened. What if they sell me to an evil white man who does horrible things to me?"

"Have no fear, I will protect you."

"How can you? You are a slave, and a black man."

"I cannot say, but I will try. I will stand beside you and will not let them hurt you."

In the following days and weeks, the quiet Cherokee captive, reassured by his gentle kindness, spent more and more time, whenever she could, near the black Jamaican slave. Gradually their Seminole captors took notice of the poise and dignity of the two as they stood side by side. They made a striking couple together, as how could they not. Sydney was unable to disguise the carriage that revealed his aristocratic blood. The girl called Chigua would never be able to hide that she was descended from the greatest chiefs of Cherokee legend. The blood of dignity from both their races ran in their veins, and their regal carriage seemed heightened when they were together.

The Seminoles soon came to realize that they could make a small fortune by selling them as a couple.

A year later, at twenty-one and seventeen, they were on their way, under Seminole guard, to the slave auction at the ancient city of St. Augustine.

The night before the sale, as they slept on the ground beside one another, Sydney was awakened by a soft voice.

"Sydney . . . Sydney," Chigua whispered. "I have something to give you . . . to keep safe for me."

He turned to face her, doing his best not to draw the notice of the dozing Seminole guard.

She held her hand out to him in the darkness. In it she clutched a gold ring, whose reflection he could see clearly in the moonlight.

A brief gasp of astonishment escaped his lips.

"Where did you—"

"It is mine," she said, "from my grandmother and her mother before her. I have managed to hide it all this time from the Seminoles. But tomorrow . . . the white men do terrible things . . . they will look at me and—"

She stopped. The thought of it obviously terrified her.

"—they will want to see . . . everything . . . where I will not—"

"I understand," whispered Sydney.

"Please . . . you take it," she said. "I give it in pledge of my love for you. If you will protect me, I will never leave you."

Sydney took it in his grasp. "I will do what I can to keep it for you. There are certain places where no white man will look on the body of a black man, even to protect his investment."

She crept close to him. Sydney stretched his arm around her and pulled her close in reassurance that, whatever the morrow held, he would be her protector.

"Je t'aime," he said softly.

"Wadan," she answered in the ancient tongue of her people.

The two were sold for a handsome price to a Georgia cotton plantation owner, as man and wife. Though the passage of the ring between them that night would not have been recognized by the state of Florida, it was enough to seal between them a love that had grown slowly and that continued to grow stronger with every passing year.

Chigua bore four children. Sydney never forgot his vow to be free. He knew for the present that the safest way to protect his family and not be sold away from them was to cause no trouble. He continued to watch and listen and wait.

When he began to hear of the Underground Railroad, he began to think that perhaps their time was nearly at hand.

PART TWO

The Harvest Brings Life
SUMMER, 1859

Eight

A man of tan skin lay awake in the darkness. That his skin was lighter than most of his fellow slaves whose heavy breathing sounded about him in the open field where they slept made him no less an *owned* man. They were human oxen . . . beasts of labor and burden. Their only purpose in life was to serve their master in humble, ingratiating, dumb, unquestioning subservience. That he was only half black, that he possessed more refinement and education than his master, indeed, that the blood of ancient aristocracy flowed in his veins, mattered nothing. He had been a slave for sixteen years. And he would always be a slave.

Unless . . .

Unless perhaps the words he had heard that day were true.

Could it be . . . that escape was truly possible! The day just past had been long and grueling—fourteen hours of brutal toil. The next would be equally long and hard. He needed to sleep. His body would require all its strength to endure it. To slacken from fatigue, even for a moment, would invite the overseer's whip.

But he was too keyed up to sleep. He drew in a deep breath and tried to relax.

The stench of two dozen men's bodies in the still, heavy air was nearly as persuasive a preventative to sleep as the snoring of two or three of the larger men. They had spent the past two days digging and dredging out the stinking, fetid mud from a canal grown sluggish from years of inattention. Several plantation owners from the south-western corner of Georgia's Mitchell County, whose plantations depended on the water to irrigate their crops, had joined to clear it with the combined efforts of their stronger man slaves.

The water was mosquito infested, the mud foul, and stank with evidence that sewage flowed into it as well as excess from the Flint River that fed it. None of the blacks had bathed in a week and the dried mud and smell of honest labor was enough to make a grown man swoon. To say they became accustomed to it would be untrue, but they learned to endure it, as slaves throughout the South did a thousand other unpleasantnesses, along with outright cruelties.

The waking man's thoughts, however, were not occupied with his own plight nor with that of his fellow slaves. He was thinking instead of the runaway that the dogs and overseers from two of the plantations had hauled out of the canal off a makeshift raft. The incident had occurred within sight and earshot from where the rest had been work-ing. He had heard every word of the man's ranting, wild cries.

"I's git back . . . I's git to dat house er freedom . . . I's fin' hit!"

The words lodged in the would-be sleeper's brain. *"Dat house er freedom . . . I's fin' hit . . . I's git to dat house er freedom."*

He had heard rumors of such houses . . . places where runaways might find refuge. But this was the first he had heard of someone who might actually know where one was located.

When and how to attempt his own escape to freedom was a quan-dary he had wrestled with since the day his first daughter was born twelve years before. To make the attempt and fail could mean separa-tion, even death. He had always known the danger. He would likely have but one chance. He knew he had to be ready when it came.

But he had not expected it on this day.

As he lay, tingling with growing excitement mingled with terror, he sensed an increasing certainty that his moment had come to seize free-dom and the dream of new life.

Another hour he lay. His anticipation mounted. He had run the daring plan through his brain a dozen times, searching for every possible unforeseen danger.

He thought it could work. It *had* to work! Once he left the canal there would be no turning back. He would be a runaway. The lives of his family would be at stake.

He had to succeed . . . or die in the attempt.

When and how the final decision was made, he could not say for certain. But before another hour had passed, he had crossed the threshold in his mind that would mark out the steps of his future.

He would do it!

Tonight was the night! Before dawn came, he would flee this place never to return.

When the night was at its blackest, slowly the waking slave turned over on the ground where he lay, drew in a lungful of air for courage, then began to rise to his feet.

Suddenly a hand gripped his forearm and held it in the grip of a vise.

"I knows wha'chu's doin'," whispered a barely audible voice in the night beside him. "I been watchin' an' listenin' . . . I knows you's leavin'. Take me wiff you."

Still reeling that his plot had been discovered before it had even begun, he bent low to keep from waking anyone else.

"I can't," he said softly to the teenage boy whose voice had so startled him. "I gots my family ter git out."

The night was silent a moment. They were words that would haunt him for more than a year. Slowly he felt the hand on his arm relax.

"Den da good Lor' go wiff you, man," said the boy. "I's pray dat you'll make it ter a better life."

He climbed the rest of the way to his feet, then stole stealthily away from the other sleepers in the humid night.

There was no moon.

He only hoped the myriad smells from the disturbed waters of the

foul canal and piles of dredged mud beside it would keep the dogs'
noses from detecting anything amiss. If he chanced to step on a twig
or otherwise disturb their sleep, he could claim the need of nature's
beckoning. But once he reached the runaway, his danger would
increase a hundredfold.

Not knowing immediately where he had come from, they had tied
the runaway to the posts and boards of a nearby fence, and whipped
him till he passed out. He was now sound asleep on the hard ground.
The plantation owners had all returned to their houses for the night.
Only two overseers remained to guard the herd of slaves. But they had
been drinking heavily hours ago and now were dead to the world,
shotguns laying over their laps where they slept.

Across the ground he crept with care. As his eyes accustomed themselves to the blackness, he spotted the runaway on the ground ahead.
He reached him and knelt down noiselessly, then clamped his hand
hard on his mouth.

"Don't move, boy," he whispered in his most polished speech.
"Don't utter a peep and you won't be hurt."

The young man, who appeared to be in his early twenties, squirmed
and tried to free himself, terrified at being awakened so suddenly and
finding himself restrained. But his efforts availed nothing.

"Lie quiet, I tell you. I'm a friend."

Gradually the boy stilled. His eyes glistened wide with terror.

"I am going to take my hand off your mouth, do you understand?
If you make a sound, I'll whack your ear. But if you keep quiet, I'll tell
you how you just might escape from here and not be sent back where
you came from."

Slowly he released his hand.

"What's your name, boy?" he whispered. "And be quiet or those
dogs'll be on us."

"Silas, suh?" answered the runaway.

"Shush—whisper, boy! What's your last name?"

"Don' know, suh. Don' got one, I reckon. Dey jes' call me boy, er
Silas . . . er nigger."

"Where you come from?"

"Don't know, suh . . . yonder sumplace."

"Listen to me, Silas, I ain't no sir, I'm a slave just like you."

"You don't soun' like no confound nigger I eber heard! Why you talkin' like a w'ite man effen you's a nigger?"

"To show you that you'd better do what I say if you want to get out of here. And also so that if you do anything stupid and I have to leave you to the dogs, you won't recognize my voice later and they won't believe a word you say about me."

"Ah bleve you, suh . . . ah bleve anythin' you tells me effen you's git me outta here. I can't let dem sen' me back. Massa'll string me up effen he gits his hands on me."

"I won't let them send you back. All I want to know is if what you said earlier today is true, that you know a house where runaways are safe?"

"Dat I do, suh! I heard 'bout hit an' I wuz jes' nearly dere w'en dey got me wiff dem vicshus dogs. Hit's on dat railroad, suh, dat nigger railroad."

"Could you find it?"

"Sho nuff, suh! I reckon I cud do dat, sho nuff! Dey gib me direckshuns. I learned 'em jes' like dey tol' me. I wuz on my way down da riber w'en I got inter dis fool canal."

"It's down the river then?"

"Deed, dat's da truf. But who *is* you, suh?"

"I'm a slave, just like you, Silas—a slave who's ready to make a run for freedom."

"What I call you, suh?"

"You can call me—"

He paused, then added, "—call me Paul. And if you'll help me find that house, then Paul and Silas are going to break out of this prison."

An hour and a half later, Paul, so-called, and the runaway Silas had made good the first short leg of their escape and were well out of reach of the canal laborers and their sleeping guards. They were approaching the slave quarters of the plantation now, with most of the men at the canal, only about half occupied. The leader stopped and turned to his companion.

"I have to leave you here for a while, Silas," he said. "You will be safe. You are half a mile from any house or dog. But you must stay here until I return, do you understand?"

"Yes, suh. Where's you goin'."

"To get my family. Then we will all make for the river."

"What effen you gits caught, Paul, suh?"

"I won't. Don't worry. They won't expect me, and no one will miss me from the canal until morning. With so many slaves from three plantations, those two guards may not miss me at all."

"Dey'll know dat I ain't dere, dat's fo sho!"

"They won't trace you here. Don't worry, Silas, by morning we will be miles away. But listen to me, there are swamps all around. You must wait for me or you will never escape. I will be back, and we will get to the river together. You must wait for me right here."

"Yes, suh."

Moments later Silas was alone in the night. He crouched down, terrified and still bewildered by the strange tongue and confident manner of his savior, but not too bewildered to keep from falling fast asleep.

Twenty minutes later, a slave mother of fair skin found herself likewise awakened with a hand over her mouth and whispered words in her ear.

"What are you doing here!" she exclaimed in a low voice as her husband released his hand. "I thought—"

"We're leaving," he interrupted in an urgent whisper, speaking now in his normal voice. "We're leaving tonight."

"Leaving!" she repeated, suddenly wide-awake.

"We've got to get the children up and out without a sound."

"But how—"

"I'll explain later. Just listen," he whispered. "Get enough clothes to keep them warm if the weather turns. But we mustn't take more than we can carry. Get up, we must hurry. We have to be miles away before morning."

As his brave wife roused the older children and headed toward the woods, her husband fumbled in the darkness for a loose floorboard. Beneath it he had stashed a small bag full of items he had managed to steal over the years, including two knives, flints and a broken piece of glass for making fire, several candles, a compass, a well-worn map of Georgia, the Carolinas, and Virginia, and two books.

Ten minutes later, carrying his sleepy seven-year-old daughter, the daring slave father rejoined his wife near the edge of the wood where she waited, trembling though the night was warm, with the three older children.

He set the girl on the ground, then gathered them all close about him and gazed earnestly into their eyes. Nothing was visible but the whites of six sets of eyes suddenly bound together by a more immediate bond even that they were of one family. They were now fleeing for their lives.

"Listen to me, all of you," he said. "We are going to run away. We are going to escape to the North where slavery does not exist. There is a runaway waiting for us in the woods who has directions to a safe house. But we are in great danger. We mustn't make a sound and we have to move fast. If we are caught, we will all be whipped and then separated."

"But, Papa—," began one of the girls.

"Not a sound. Now come with me."

He led the way through the night. In another ten minutes they heard a voice in the night.

"Dat you . . . dat you, massa Paul?"

"Who's Paul, Papa?"

"That's me, son," replied the boy's father. "Yes, it's me, Silas, we're all here now."

"Why he call you dat, Papa?" asked the eleven-year-old.

"Because I didn't want him to know who I was in case we were caught. But there's no turning back now. I'll explain everything as we go. Silas, this is my family. Come, all of you . . . we must hurry!"

"Where are we going, Papa?" asked the youngest, a girl of seven.

"To the river."

Forty minutes later, now and then casting an anxious glance toward
the east to see whether night was beginning to wane on the horizon,
the leader of the small band of runaways led his troop to the river
landing. A barge, connected by ropes and pulleys to the opposite
bank, joined the roads of the two sides of the river and made access
possible to what limited commerce was required across it. The landing
was not heavily used and was unguarded.

"Come, Silas," he said. "You and I will cut the barge from the
ropes. Leave the overhead rope and pulley secure—just cut those
attached to the platform."

He produced two knives from the bag he was carrying, handed the
bag to his wife, then slid into the cool water. At last sensing his own
freedom within grasp, Silas leaped onto the barge and set vigorously to
work. In the darkness it was difficult work, especially where the ropes
were submerged. But one strand at a time gave way until at last they
felt the platform float free.

"That's it . . . good work, Silas!" cried his savior from the water.
"Children, jump on board."

The baying of a hound sounded somewhere in the distance.

"Dey's comin' after me!" cried Silas.

"That dog's miles away, Silas, don't worry!"

Even as he said it, however, the daring slave suddenly realized that a
thin glow had become visible on the horizon. "Sit down, everyone, in
the middle of the barge," he said, remaining in the water to steady it.
When all were in place, he began gently shoving the platform toward
the middle until the shoreline sank below his feet and he had to swim.

"Pull, Silas," he said, "pull on the upper rope."

Silas did so. Gradually the barge eased farther from the shore.

"Papa . . . get on!" cried one of the children.

"I will, don't worry, just as soon as we're in the middle of the river."

He pushed as he swam from behind, while Silas pulled the rope
attached by pulley to the opposite shore. Slowly the barge continued
toward the center of the river.

"All right, Silas—that's good! We'll give ourselves to the current
now. Help me up!"

He struggled aboard and sat down dripping beside his family. Already he felt their little craft picking up momentum. The waters of the Flint were not swift but steady. Slowly the landing receded from sight in the dim light of dawn.

"We should be six or eight miles away before we are missed, and well out of reach of the hounds' noses."

"What will we do then, Papa?" asked the man's twelve-year-old daughter, the oldest of the four children.

"We will find a place to go ashore and hide out for the day, Azura. After that, Silas will be our guide."

"But won't they find the barge?" asked his wife.

"They will find it all right. But it will be miles downriver by then. Once we land, I'll haul it back out to midstream and send it on its way without us. Then we'll keep under cover through the day, and after that, hope the directions Silas was given to the safe house are reliable."

"What's a safe house, Papa?" asked the man's nine-year-old son.

"It's a place where folk like us can find help," he replied.

Forty or more hours later, not daring approach until the cover of darkness had well settled over the Georgia countryside and the lights in the place were mostly out for the night, a black man stole from his hiding place where he had been keeping his eye on the front porch of a two-story blue farmhouse for several hours.

The directions that had been passed to the young man called Silas had proved accurate thus far—leave the river at sharp right bend where rapids give way to wide slow water, head straight east approximately two miles from the river, look for hill covered in scrub oak in center of four cultivated fields, climb to top, look north where several farms and one large plantation house will be visible. The safe house is a farmhouse facing east, painted blue, with three chimneys on roof of main house. Do not approach, the directions had concluded, until after nightfall.

"You sure that's all they told you, Silas?" the man asked one last time.

"Dat's all, massa Paul—dat be it."

"All right. But if anything happens to me, if you see danger, you get my family away from here."

"You kin depend on Silas, massa Paul."

The runaway slave kissed his wife, then left the security of the trees and walked toward the house in the darkness. Slowly he crossed the yard, then climbed the steps and knocked on the door.

From somewhere inside he heard footsteps. A moment later the door opened.

A white man stood expressionless, holding a lantern and looking him over carefully.

"I understand a man can book railroad passage here," he said.

"What kind of passage?" asked the man.

"Second class, though coloreds can't be too particular."

"You alone, son?"

"No, sir. There's seven of us—my family and a single man."

"You from nearby?"

"The Addison place, six or seven miles upriver close as I can figure."

The man nodded. "Yeah, I know the place. How long you been gone?"

"Two days."

The man was silent a minute, thinking to himself. Then he called back over his shoulder.

"Marjory," he said, "better stoke the fire and warm up the stew. We got travelers—and hungry ones by the sound of it."

He turned again to the open door.

"Bring the rest of them in, son," he said. "We'll get some food inside you, then find you a place to sleep in the barn."

Nine

*W*hen Scully Riggs heard the rumors of Veronica Beaumont's engagement to Seth Davidson, he went mad with suppressed rage. Whereas he had once vowed to make Veronica his own, now he vowed that she would *never* become the wife of Seth Davidson.

Seth accepted the news stoically, doing his best to don the chivalrous pride of a Southern gentleman who would never let humiliation or embarrassment fall upon a woman. He still wasn't quite sure how it had come about. Perhaps it wouldn't be so bad, he tried to tell himself. Veronica *was* pretty. He had always enjoyed being with her as they grew up. And it could not be denied that it felt good to have her depend on him. It made him feel like a man. He had always figured to marry her anyway.

In his quieter moments, pangs of disappointment went through him to realize that he would never enjoy a marriage like the one he had been part of every day of his life—that of his parents, where friendship, sharing, laughter, communication, and common objectives and spiritual values lay at the heart of it. Did he really want to spend the next forty years of his life in a marriage like Lady Daphne's and Denton Beaumont's rather than one like that of his own father and mother?

But, he said to himself, the gentlemanly thing was to press on without complaint. He had somehow let himself get into it, and he would either find a way gracefully to get out of it or see it through like a man.

Every time Seth saw Veronica now, she was more forward. Every day that passed made it more and more difficult to talk to her about some of his concerns. Veronica was one of those kinds of people who deflected serious conversation rather than encouraged it. Every time he tried to bring the conversation around to spiritual things, she flitted off into trivialities, usually having something to do with herself. Did she ever *think* seriously about anything? Seth wondered. Was her whole life nothing but dresses and hairdos and fashions and perfume and, up till now, what every boy in the neighborhood thought about her?

Seth's parents, meanwhile, also hearing the rumors of Seth's engagement, assumed from his silence that he had made his decision and that this was the outcome of it. They could hardly be happy about it. But if this was what Seth wanted, they must do their best to show support. For the present, therefore, they kept whatever thoughts they had on the matter between themselves, and waited for him to tell them whatever he chose to of it.

As the summer passed, Seth and his parents remained oblivious to how far the discussions, goings-on, and wedding preparations were progressing just a few short miles over the ridge to the east. Seth squirmed from silent embarrassment at not coming altogether clean with his parents and about his subsequent misgivings, while trying to resolve what was the gentlemanly thing to do. Richmond and Carolyn prayed and discussed privately what ought to be their position with regard to Seth's dilemma, as they perceived it. At Oakbriar, meanwhile, the mood concerning the future of the two young people could not have been more upbeat.

Veronica and her mother had already been to the city to gather fabric samples for the dresses. They were looking at several patterns and had ordered several more from Paris. And they were settling on names for the guest list, for which Lady Daphne's prior efforts in regard to their failed Washington plans proved enormously helpful. She could not, however, prevent pangs of disappointment at sight of it. Veronica was also making her own list for bridesmaids. Sally and Marta were obvious choices. And she simply had to include Julia along with the other two. Poor Brigitte would be disappointed to tears to be left out. But she was younger than her other friends. She would get over it.

In the end Veronica settled on three bridesmaids and three attendants—six in all to stand with her. The more lavish her adoring train the better! She doubted that Seth even had six friends—but his brother and her two brothers made three . . . surely he could scrape together three decent-looking boys to stand with him.

A wicked smile crossed Veronica's lips.

Perhaps she could suggest that Scully Riggs be one of them, as a favor to an old friend of her father's. He wasn't at all good-looking. But the thought of it was absolutely too delicious—it would drive Scully insane with jealousy!

None of these plans and machinations did Veronica mention to Seth. She continued to visit and invited him often to Oakbriar. Now that his sling was off and he was mostly back to normal, he went around most often on horseback like before. That made rides by buggy together more difficult. Nor had she failed to notice that he seldom came to Oakbriar on his own as would seem to be the customary tradition for an engaged young man. He seemed distracted and distant. It was obvious he was not completely comfortable in the role she had thrust upon him. He would get used to it, she told herself confidently. And she would help him do so.

Out of necessity, therefore, Veronica's visits to Greenwood became even more frequent than the other way around. Thus, whenever they were seen together, which it served her purposes to be often, it was in her father's most expensive carriage. And such sightings confirmed yet the more in the minds of the residents of Dove's Landing what the observant townspeople had heard.

As to an actual date, Veronica and her mother had been looking at the social calendar for the remainder of the year. The Christmas season looked to be a logical choice. A lavish wedding ball could be substituted for the annual Christmas ball. Their discussions took place beyond the ken of Veronica's father. No sense stirring up old wounds until the plans were so thoroughly set in motion that it was too late for him to do anything about them. He would go along. Men always did. Left to themselves, they bungled everything anyway. How badly were affairs managed without the delicate influence of a woman to guide them!

At last Veronica thought it time to tell her three friends so they could begin helping her with plans for hair and dress, and with the music and the dance cards and all the rest.

"But you mustn't tell a soul," she said. "Not yet. Seth, bless his dear heart, is still getting used to the idea of being married, you know. I don't want him to have to agonize over such details. No word of any of this must reach him until I am ready. And poor Brigitte will be hurt, but it cannot be helped."

"But Veronica," said Julia, "now that it is so close, aren't you . . . having any second thoughts? You know how they all get once they're married—all fat and boring and pregnant . . . ugh!"

"Remember Jessica Whitman," nodded Sally. "She was one of us too. But the minute she was married, she changed. I never see her anymore."

"They live near us in town," added Marta. "Whenever I see her, she is chasing those two brats of hers around. She looks like she's thirty. It's dreadful!"

"That won't happen to me!" laughed Veronica. "I do not intend to get fat, and I intend to maintain just as full a social life as I do now."

"But what about . . . babies?" said Sally.

"There are ways to avoid such inconveniences," smiled Veronica cunningly. "There will be certain times when Seth will just have to cool his heels and sleep in another room."

"Oh, you are a sly one!" said Marta as the other two tittered in embarrassment. "But how do you know all about it—did your mother tell you!"

"No, silly. My mother doesn't know the first thing about such things as *that*. I have a book."

Gasps of wonder escaped the other three almost in unison.

"Can . . . we see it?" asked Julia.

"It's hidden away," answered Veronica. "And it's private. So you see, being married won't change a thing. I intend for no children to complicate my life. And besides," she added, "Seth will be twenty a month after the wedding, and I will turn twenty next summer. If a girl isn't married by the time she's twenty, people start thinking she's an old maid! It's *time* for me to be married . . . it's expected."

She glanced at Marta and realized her words had stung.

"Oh, Marta, I'm sorry! I forgot that you just turned twenty. I didn't mean—"

"It's all right," laughed Marta. "I've nearly got Walter's mind made up for him too. I may not be far behind you!"

Meanwhile, at Greenwood, an unexpected but enthusiastically received letter had just arrived by mail. It was addressed,

> *Richmond Davidson*
> *Greenwood Acres*
> *Dove's Landing, Virginia*

"Dear Richmond," Richmond read aloud at the breakfast table the morning after it had been received,

> *"It has been some time since we saw one another. I now find myself in the awkward, yet I hope not too unseemly, position of writing to ask of you a favor, which is simply to say that the time has come when I would like to presume upon your kindness and take you up on the kind offer to visit which you have now twice extended me, and which your lovely wife reiterated so warmly. The fact is, my work has been suffering of late and I have found it necessary to take a brief leave of absence from the paper. I hope that the peaceful*

*surroundings of your village of Dove's Landing might restore not
only my vigor, but my desire to write again with something of the
force that I flatter myself I once possessed when I took pen in hand.*

 *"I realize the presumption in thus "inviting myself" as it were, yet
I trust between friends, as I hope to some degree we are, that such
forthrightness is not outside the bounds of decency.*

 "I am,

*Sincerely yours,
James Waters*

*Number 42, the Larches
Constitution Common, Boston."*

"Who is this guy anyway, Dad?" asked Thomas.

"You remember," answered Richmond. "He's the man I met in
Boston several years ago who put me up for two nights. He and his
daughter came for a brief visit three years ago."

"Oh, yeah."

"What are you going to tell him, Dad?" asked Seth.

"Why, that he is welcome, of course, and that we are delighted!
This great house of ours has so many rooms we don't know what to
do with them all. We can give him the entire south wing. He can
recuperate to his heart's content—why he can stay at Greenwood and
write a whole book if he wants to!"

"He makes no mention of his daughter," commented Carolyn.
"You must tell him to bring her along."

"I shall write back this very day."

A return letter from Boston arrived at Greenwood, in response to
Richmond's, fourteen days later.

 Dear Richmond, it read,

 *You are so kind with your words of invitation and welcome—thank
you very much. Please greet and thank your wife also. Having guests*

underfoot, I realize, falls more to a woman than a man. The invitations of a man are cheap—it is the woman whose hospitality must back them up!

Your inclusion of my daughter is generous indeed. She, of course, has begged to accompany me. She has not forgotten your horses! I considered sending her to one of her sisters, but of course we are happy and grateful to accept your invitation and the warm offer of your hospitality to us both.

You asked about my health. In short, it has not been of the best. My doctor, who is constantly fussing, an occupational hazard for his profession, insists that I need to get away from the city to regain my strength. He agreed that the Virginia countryside might suit such a need admirably. As long, he says, as I have nothing to do but relax and sleep and walk about in the country air and absorb its sunlight, he will be happy. It sounds rather tedious to me, but in the pastoral countryside of Greenwood, with cows and horses and growing crops about me, perhaps I shall be able to endure it.

I am, again,

Warmly and appreciatively yours,
James Waters

PS—My daughter adds her greetings.

"Well," said Carolyn, smiling broadly, "Maribel and I had better air out those rooms and set out fresh linen. This is exciting—it will be nice to have a girl in the house again! I can hardly wait!"

"Where will you put them?" asked Richmond, turning again to his wife.

"I am thinking that the two center rooms of the second floor would suit their needs perfectly, with its double windows looking south onto the fields in the distance. It will be bright and cheery and spacious and has the smaller adjoining room where James can sleep. It should be a roomy and comfortable little apartment away from home."

"And the girl?"

"Next to his, the corner room with the window looking east upon the great oak. They can use the room between as a common sitting room."

"It sounds like it should be ideal."

"Maribel and I will get started with preparations today. With Lucindy and her young ones gone, it has seemed too quiet. It will be nice to have guests again!"

With the coming of August arrived a warm and fragrant season in the cycle of life in Virginia, when the harvest gets under way and the humidity at times seems to rise straight out of the fertile ground, bringing with it odors of grass and honeysuckle and pine needles, and, after a rain shower and return of the sun, the warmth of the earth itself. It was a good time to be alive, and to feel the life of the world all around. It was a different life than nature exuded in springtime, when all is bursting anew and the streams and rivers rush cold and full. Now the streams ran low and the rivers warm and lazy. Now the earth, rather than breaking out with buds and leaves of new growth, yielded instead its bounty, having turned the hopefulness of spring into the wheat and corn that fed, the cotton that clothed, and the tobacco that gave men pleasure. All around *life* was being gathered into barns, as slaves and free blacks poured out their sweating energies for their masters, who gathered the profits of their labors into the storehouses called banks.

It was just this latter phenomenon that was the subject under consideration between one Stuart McCloud and his cousin Harland Davidson where they sat in private counsel in the latter's office in the state capital of Richmond.

"It would seem," McCloud had just commented a little peevishly, "that your plan has had anything but the desired results."

He handed back the papers he had been perusing, which amounted to a current review of the finances of Greenwood Acres, the disputed estate of their mutual cousin Richmond Davidson.

"We all agreed to it, Stuart," replied his cousin testily, pausing to drain the contents of his glass of scotch and pour himself another from the bottle that sat on the desk between them. "As I recall, you were just as enthusiastic as I was, singing the praises of it to Peggy and Pam. How could any of us foresee that the fool would actually make a go of it with a parcel of freedmen to care for. The thing is beyond me . . . but these numbers don't lie."

"By the way, how did you come by these figures?" asked Stuart, pouring himself out another liberal libation from the bottle. "They seem remarkably detailed and up-to-date."

"The banker in Dove's Landing, a man by the name of Perkins—he and I have, shall we say, a discreet arrangement. I assist him with his occasional legal affairs for the most nominal of fees. In exchange, from time to time he does certain favors for me."

"I see," smiled McCloud. Whatever their differences, he couldn't help liking this one of his Davidson cousins. They thought alike. "But the point is," he went on, "our gambit failed. We did not press the suit at the time and now more time has gone by. It was three years ago that we decided to sit on it . . . and look at his bank account. I say we act. It is time to press the suit forward and formally contest the estate."

"You're sure a suit is the course you want to follow?" asked Harland. "I am afraid the passage of time weakens what would probably already have been a weak case. In that light, I have been mulling over another option, one that is not dependent on the courts, but on Richmond's own ridiculous sense of ethics."

"What do you suggest, then?"

"What if, rather than press the suit, we put a settlement before him as an out-of-court arrangement?"

"Such as?"

"We agree to drop the contestation of the will in exchange for four promissory notes, one to each of us."

Stuart nodded his head, turning the thing over in his mind.

"What would induce him to agree?" he said after a moment.

"The fact that he is a fool," rejoined Harland.

"Do you think he might really do it?"

"I don't know. Who can predict the response of such religious types. I admit, it is a gamble. But I do not think the lawsuit would stand up after all this time. So what do we have to lose?"

"How much do you suggest we make the notes for?"

"Ten thousand each . . . or five. What do you think?"

"Ten thousand apiece . . . that is a great deal of money," said Stuart. "I would rather ask for ten and get it, than to aim too high and get nothing. If he refuses, we are left holding blue sky."

"I think you are right," rejoined Harland. "And I will slip in a clause, in fine print of course, guaranteeing each of the notes by a one-fourth interest in the land and assets of Greenwood. It is perfectly standard in such cases. Perhaps he will sign without noticing and then we'll have him."

"I do like the way you think, Harland. Well done!"

"We won't file a formal lien and call his attention to it. If he fails to comply with the terms of the notes, we will file a suit of nonperformance and foreclosure against him and take it to the courts. With his signature on the notes, I think we would win hands down."

"Just make sure the notes you draw up are ironclad and that there is no way he can weasel out of them later."

"My dear Stuart," smiled Harland, "I am an attorney. We earn our weekly envelope making sure people don't weasel out of things!"

The two men raised their glasses to one another. At last their plans seemed ready to fall into place.

Ten

$\mathcal{F}$or the month prior to their planned visit to Virginia, the Waters household in Boston had been abuzz with excitement. No matter that there were but two of them to fill the huge house, most of which was vacant, Cherity's enthusiasm was as the enthusiasm of ten.

"Do you think I will be able to ride, Daddy?" she asked one morning.

"You did last time—why should it be any different now?"

"How many boots do you think I should pack?" Cherity went on without answering. "Maybe I should buy a new pair. What about clothes—I won't need a dress, will I?"

Again Waters laughed. "My dear," he said, "contrary to what you might think, you are a lady now, and about as beautiful a young lady as I have ever set eyes upon . . . since your mother, of course. Yes, I think you should take a dress, or two or three. Most young ladies of your age *do* wear dresses."

"But I had to wear dresses every day at school and I'm tired of them. Besides, I'm not like most young ladies, am I, Daddy?"

"You certainly are not! But you won't be riding horses *every* minute."

"All right . . . maybe I'll take two."

Cherity rose from the table and started toward the stairs. "Well," she said, "I think I will start packing."

"We're not leaving for a month!"

"It doesn't hurt to be ready early. By the way, Daddy," she added, "I thought you might like to know, I'm not going to go to that church again. In fact, I'm not going to go to any church again."

"Is your brief search to find the meaning of life at an end?" asked her father.

"I didn't expect to find the meaning of life, I only wondered what Mother found about it that was so interesting. In the meantime, I've decided that I am an atheist."

"What!" He laughed. Even in James Waters' own loss of belief, the word *atheist* from the lips of his own daughter shocked him.

"That's right. I've come to the conclusion that there is no God."

"How did you arrive at such a notion?"

"I've been thinking about it ever since that Sunday. I finally decided that if people who believe in God are like those three women, then God couldn't possibly exist."

"What about your mother?"

"I don't know, Daddy. That still confuses me. The only conclusion I can come to is that she must have been mistaken. I hate to say it, but I don't see how it could be any other way."

The visit had been arranged to begin during the third week of the month of August. Under any other circumstances, Richmond would have ridden to the station himself for their guests. But the weather being such as it was, with rain to all appearances on the way and the wheat harvest begun, an urgency existed to make what progress was possible as quickly as they could. He felt his presence, with Seth and Thomas, was imperative in the fields every minute that could be spared.

Thus it was that Carolyn and Moses stood on the landing at the Dove's Landing station to meet their new arrivals as the train pulled in, white steam screaming in great bursts from its iron wheels, and slowed to a stop.

Almost the moment the door opened and the conductor stepped onto the platform, a young lady of nearly eighteen, clad in men's trousers and boots, bounded off and came hurrying toward them almost at a run, her auburn-blonde hair bouncing as it reflected the sun, her face radiant and alive with joyful expectation. She was several inches shorter than Carolyn, perhaps five feet or five-two by now. At the moment she was not wearing a hat.

"Hello, Mrs. Davidson!" she said exuberantly, her boots echoing across the platform boards as she came forward. "I am so happy to see you again!"

She slowed and extended her hand, gazing deeply into Carolyn's eyes with all the eagerness of mother-hungry daughterhood.

"I am happy to see you again too, Cherity," said Carolyn, smiling and shaking hands but, as the first time they had met, with a peculiar sensation in her throat.

"I can't believe we're finally here!" said Cherity. "I am so excited!"

Carolyn now saw Cherity's father step, a little gingerly she thought, from the train. As he walked toward them smiling, she could not help noticing how much his appearance was altered in the years since she had seen him. His hair had noticeably grayed and thinned, and his cheeks, in spite of a general dark complexion, were pale and drawn. He was carrying a white cowboy hat, which appeared in distinct contrast to the brown business suit.

"Hello, Mrs. Davidson—," he began.

"Please . . . *Carolyn.*"

"Thank you. It is so good to see you again," he said as they shook hands. "My dear," he added to Cherity, "in your haste, you left this on the seat." He handed her the hat.

"We are happier than we can tell you that you have come," said Carolyn. "My husband and the boys are in the fields. You remember Moses, who works for us."

"Yes, of course . . . hello, Moses," said Waters.

The New Englander and free Southern black man shook hands.

"I'll go fetch yo' bags, Mister Waters," said Moses, ambling toward

the train where a porter was unloading their luggage onto the platform.

"I think we were the only passengers to get off here," said Waters,
following him. "It should be those two right there . . . here—let me
help you."

Two or three minutes later they were leaving the station together
and walking toward the carriage. The men loaded the bags in back,
then Moses stepped up and took the reins. Waters climbed up beside
him, while Cherity and Carolyn seated themselves in the leather-
padded seat behind them. Moses called to the horses and the carriage
bounced into motion.

As they made their way through Dove's Landing, Cherity looked
this way and that with wide-eyed pleasure, every sight a renewed
adventure.

As she chanced to glance in Carolyn's direction, she saw tears in her
eyes. Not one to keep her thoughts inside, she spoke up.

"What is it, Mrs. Davidson?" she asked. "Are you ill?"

Surprised in the midst of her reverie by the object of it, Carolyn
glanced over and smiled.

"Oh, no . . . Cherity, dear," she said, taking out a handkerchief and
wiping at her eyes. "I was just thinking about your name."

"My name?"

"It is one of the most beautiful names I've ever heard. The moment
I saw your face again, I thought how perfectly your countenance and
the meaning of your name were one. Whoever named you did so
perfectly and must have loved you a great deal."

"Why were you crying then?" asked Cherity.

"I was thinking how much God must love you too, and how very
special you are to him. It made me so happy that it brought tears to
my eyes."

Cherity remained silent. She recalled her father making occasional
remarks about Mr. Davidson's odd religious views and how he
brought God into everything. Apparently it ran in the family. Her
father smiled as he overheard Carolyn's explanation.

Still, as they went, she found herself warmed by Mrs. Davidson's words, and strangely moved that a woman could shed tears on her own behalf. What could account for such a thing?

 ⌒

They reached Greenwood twenty-five or thirty minutes later.

Once Carolyn got over her tears and Cherity the unaccountable feelings from being in Carolyn's presence again, the two women began to chat freely. Within minutes they were laughing and talking and sharing like Cherity had never done with an older woman in her life. They were true friends before reaching Greenwood.

In the front seat, an exchange almost as vigorous but far more humorous was taking place. Having never had the captive audience of a former Negro slave to himself, the reporter in him had filled James Waters with curiosity brimming over so full that he could hardly contain himself. His interest in the man was prompted, too, by the pride Waters took in considering himself a progressive and free-thinking liberal. He was anxious to canvass the old black man's views, in particular concerning his former master and boss, who at once so confused and also intrigued the former Christian and present agnostic Bostonian.

But the two men could scarcely understand a word the other spoke. Moses' broken and slurred Negro tongue was as great a mystery to Waters' ear as was the moderate New England to the black man's. Half their time was spent in repeating and interpreting what had already been said.

"Moses," Carolyn said from the backseat, "please take us by the field where everyone is working."

"Yes'm, Miz Dav'son," said Moses, turning aside on a narrow dirt road instead of continuing on up the driveway.

Glancing through the trees, Cherity was just able to catch sight of a few portions of the red brick and tile roof.

"There's your house?" she said, still peering through the trunks of oak and beech.

"Yes," replied Carolyn. "We'll be there shortly."

"I don't remember it being so huge!"

Carolyn laughed. "There is a lot of work that gets done here," she said. "There are several barns, some for animals, others for equipment, others for storage of grain or drying tobacco. And at one time the house was used to house field hands and white laborers, then with the increase of slaves, houses were built for them. See over there. That's what we call the Negro or colored village. The big house is not used so much for workers now but only family. There are many rooms that are scarcely used. There are just the four of us, now that our older daughter Cynthia is married and gone, along with Moses and Maribel who live in the house and help us there. The others, our black workers, mostly work in the fields and with the animals, and of course the mothers raise their children and that keeps them busy."

"It is a different world than Boston. There are certainly no slaves there."

"And you will see none at Greenwood either," said Carolyn. "We set our slaves free three years ago. They now work for us and receive wages like other hired workers."

"I remember, and I think your setting your slaves free was simply a wonderful thing to do."

"Thank you. We have never regretted it for a second," nodded Carolyn.

"Where is your daughter?" asked Cherity. "I was so sorry she was away visiting her future in-laws when I was here last. I have always wanted to meet her."

"She and her husband are in Maryland right now, but their future is uncertain. Robert just graduated from Annapolis and has yet to be assigned."

A few minutes later they came to a field of wheat, about a third cut, where to one side Richmond and Seth and Malachi, in that order— the latter two following as Richmond led, all bare-chested and the two Davidsons, father and son, brown from the summer sun and with blisters and callouses on their hands to match—were moving through the standing grain wielding razor-sharp scythes with which they made great swinging semicircular arcs that laid the ripened grain down with such skill and precision that the stalks simply fell softly to sleep on the ground. The three reapers were followed by Thomas and ten or twelve black gatherers, who picked up the sleeping stalks, tied them in bundles, and stood them as tents, each bunch leaning together toward a common center. Behind them eight black women carted the bundles to two wagons sitting at opposite sides of the field for transport to the threshing barn where the grain would later be separated from the stalks and chaff.

Moses led the carriage along one side of the field until they had drawn even to the lead reaper. Richmond glanced up, then set down his scythe and with a great smile walked toward them.

"James!" he exclaimed with outstretched hand. "You made it at last! I am so glad!"

Behind him, Seth walked toward the wagon, chest and shoulders and face dripping with sweat, for the day was hot.

"Seth, my boy!" said Richmond. "You remember James Waters—"

"Yes . . . hello again, Mr. Waters," said Seth as they shook hands.

"—and you remember his daughter Cherity."

"Hello, Miss Waters," said Seth, extending his hand. For one of the few times in her life, Cherity was speechless. The scene before her—grain being harvested before her very eyes, a field full of Negro men and women just like she had read about, spread out in front of her against a golden backdrop of wheat, green trees behind them, and haze covered hills in the distance stretching to the horizon where they met the dark gray of a sky that looked menacing somewhere far to the north—it might as well have been out of a picture book. In combination with the approach of this smiling, handsome, shirtless boy . . . it took her breath away.

"Oh, I'm sorry!" said Seth, removing his hand almost the instant Cherity touched it. "I'm all wet and dirty."

"Honest labor, Seth," said Waters. "Never apologize for the sweat and grime of honest toil."

"The journalist discovers inspiration already!" laughed Richmond. "You have an eloquent way with words, James . . . 'the sweat and grime of honest toil.' I like that. We've seen plenty of it today, haven't we, Seth."

"And *every* day," laughed Seth, "until the crops are in."

"Perhaps I am indeed inspired," said Waters, breathing in deeply of the warm air. "It is a spectacular sight—whites and blacks all out working in the fields together."

"Thomas!" called Richmond to Seth's brother on the other side of the field. "Come here, son. I want you to greet our guests. Malachi, you and the others take a break for water or tea."

He turned back to the carriage.

"I am sorry we are so involved right at the time of your arrival," Richmond said. "I would have preferred to welcome you back to Greenwood with tea on the veranda. Unfortunately, rain is on the horizon, and we must get as much of this grain into the barn as possible before it comes."

"Please, no apologies!" rejoined Waters. "If there is one thing I do not want to do it is interrupt your routine and necessary work. To tell you the truth, this sight is far more what I came here for than tea on the veranda! Although I am sorry that my health prevents me from being any help."

"Point well taken, my friend! I agree with you."

"Not that I won't enjoy a cup of tea with you as well, but I could not have hoped for anything better than this wonderful sight. In fact, after we get settled in, I would sincerely like to come back and watch."

"Hatching a little story about Dove's Landing already, James?" asked Carolyn with a smile.

"I'm on holiday, remember. Doctor's orders. Since joining the *Herald*'s staff two years ago on a part-time basis, my editor is very flexible. Unfortunately, I cannot say the same for Dr. Elliott."

"I would like to come back out too," said Cherity, at last finding her voice. "But I don't want to watch . . . I want to help! May I please?"

Richmond laughed.

"You and I shall join the women, Cherity!" said Carolyn.

"Do you really work with them, Carolyn?" asked Cherity's father.

"Absolutely. We all work together. Every extra set of hands is that much sooner the grain gets under the roof."

Thomas wandered up.

"Thomas, say hello to the Waters," said Richmond. "You remember Mr. Waters . . . and his daughter Cherity."

"Hi," said Thomas, then turned back to the field.

"I must say, young lady," Richmond added to Cherity, "you have indeed grown since you were last here. How old are you now?"

"Eighteen, Mr. Davidson," she replied.

"Well, we should get on to the house," said Carolyn, "and let our weary travelers settle in."

"I'm not a bit tired!" said Cherity. "I can't wait to see everything!"

"We will be in soon," said Richmond, taking hold of his scythe where he had leaned it against the side of the carriage. "What time is it?"

"About 11:30," replied Carolyn. "The train was scheduled for 10:40."

"We'll finish another pass east to west, then get these two wagons loaded and into the barn, then break for lunch."

Three hours later, James Waters sat under the shade of the roof of one of the Davidson's buggies to the side of the same field watching his daughter at Carolyn Davidson's side.

For one of the first times in his life, he thought with a smile, she was wearing exactly the right clothes!

It was true that Carolyn and all the black women were wearing dresses. But Cherity's trousers and boots fit in wonderfully with everything he saw around him, just as she already seemed to be doing herself. They had come here for him. But perhaps she was the one who would discover a way of life that suited her better than the city ever could. The smile on her face and the laughter he occasionally heard from her mouth where she and Carolyn and several of the black women were talking as they worked certainly did his heart good.

If the three ladies from Kathleen's church who had made an atheist of her could see his daughter now!

Well, let them eat cake, he thought. He would take his daughter any day, as she was at this moment, over their dark and dreary religion. And he would trust Cherity's soul to whatever God there might or might not be, rather than to the theology of those who would prefer to make judgmental saints, after their own likeness, of them all.

He leaned back against the leather back of the seat, closed his eyes, and breathed in deeply. He was beginning to feel better already.

Eleven

Whatever plans either the Waterses or the Davidsons may have made with regard to the visit of the former to the home of the latter, they were thrown out the window by the urgency created by the weather, and the eagerness of Cherity Waters to get the wheat in before the rain. She was downstairs almost the moment the sun was up the following morning. She found Richmond in the kitchen.

"Good morning, Mr. Davidson," she said cheerily.

"Good morning, Cherity," he said turning toward her. "I didn't expect to see you so early after your long journey of the last two days."

"Our journey was nothing compared with what you've been doing," rejoined Cherity. "That's hard work."

"And you were working fast!" Richmond laughed. "I kept an eye on you—you were outdoing some of the women."

"It feels good to work hard and sweat and get dirty. I don't get much chance living in Boston."

"Are you still planning to work on a ranch out west?" he asked.

"I don't know," laughed Cherity. "Sure, I dream about it. There's nothing I love as much as horses. But as you grow up, practicality creeps in. So I don't know—I will have to take my life as it comes and see what happens. But it never hurts to dream, does it?"

"No, Cherity, it certainly does not," replied Richmond. "Dreams often get us started on the road to where we eventually wind up."

"Where is everybody?" Cherity asked.

"Still asleep," laughed Richmond.

"I thought you would all be up at the crack of dawn and back out in the fields," said Cherity in surprise. "We've got to get that wheat in before it rains. It didn't rain yet, did it, Mr. Davidson?"

"No, it kept away for the night. Let's go see what it looks like."

He led her from the kitchen and outside, past the barns, then paused and looked about. The morning was still with but a hint of a breeze. The sun had just begun to creep out over the eastern horizon where, except for a few stray rays shooting through, the oaks and beeches blocked the view.

"Can you smell it?" Richmond asked.

"What?"

"The rain in the air?"

"I think so," said Cherity. "It smells good, a little like the ocean when it blows in toward Boston."

"That's it, the smell of moisture. And the little breeze, when it comes from that direction, usually means rain."

"You have to know a lot about the weather to be a farmer, don't you, Mr. Davidson?"

"I suppose so," he said. "More than anything, you have to understand land and growth and the kind of life God put into things that make them grow in different ways."

"Isn't that just what people call Mother Nature?"

"I suppose. But what is Mother Nature but how God works in his world? It is a colorful expression people use to say how God works."

"Isn't it just how the world works by itself?"

"Ah, Cherity . . . nothing works by itself. Nothing in the whole world works without God breathing life into it."

"What's that down there?" she asked.

"That's what we call our arbor. It is a special garden that Carolyn and I have been developing for many years to remind us how good God is."

"May I go in it?"

"Of course. Anytime you like. I'll give you the five-minute tour right now."

He led her down a gentle incline and soon they were hidden from view of the house in the midst of the garden.

"It's lovely!" Cherity exclaimed. "You could get lost in all these little pathways."

"Probably not for long. Eventually you would come out and look up and see the house or the oaks and beeches of the wood, and get your bearings again."

"I can't wait to explore it!" exclaimed Cherity.

"You are welcome to do so anytime."

They left the garden and walked back up the hill. This time Richmond took a different route. Suddenly Cherity found herself standing alongside a rail fence looking into a pasture where twelve or fifteen horses wandered about grazing leisurely on the grass at their feet.

"Oh!" she exclaimed. "Oh . . . they're beautiful!"

Richmond gave a whistle, and as if on command about half of them turned toward the sound. Some ran, some walked, some whinnied, and others came silently. Within a minute or two, eight long noses were snorting and sniffling about them, with Cherity in an ecstasy of delight.

"You should see Alexander call them, or Seth," said Richmond. "They are able to speak the horse-tongue far better than I!"

When they walked back inside the kitchen fifteen minutes later, Carolyn and Maribel were bustling about and the smell of coffee was in the air.

"Cherity is anxious to get back out to the wheat field, Carolyn," said Richmond. "She is worried about the rain."

"Is that true, Cherity?" smiled Carolyn. "Richmond is always pulling someone's leg."

"No, Mrs. Davidson," she said, "he's right—we have to hurry. Rain is coming. You can smell it in the air."

"She is right, Carolyn," said Richmond more seriously. "I'm going to go down to the village and tell Malachi to rouse the men as soon as he can. We might only have a few hours."

He turned toward the door.

"May I go with you, Mr. Davidson? I would like to see where the Negroes live."

"Sure, Cherity . . . let's go!"

They returned twenty minutes later. By then Seth and Thomas had been roused, rubbing their eyes a little sleepily, and had begun fortifying themselves for the day's work with Maribel's breakfast.

Within an hour, a little before eight, workers from both big house and Negro village were filing into the field of wheat, now about three-fourths cut, two-thirds bundled, and one-half safely inside and under the roof.

For the first few hours, Richmond, Seth, and Malachi bundled with the rest of the men, who also helped carry the bundles to the wagon so that the cut stalks would get inside should the rain come upon them suddenly. When the field was bare of stalks on the ground, once again everyone resumed their former positions and the rhythmic whooshing of scythe strokes got under way. Soon Negro voices began to rise in song—high strains from the women and deep voices of the men coming from opposite sides of the field, mingling harmoniously in the center—that must surely bring tears to the eyes of the angels in heaven to hear such beautiful melodies from such an oppressed race. As Cherity worked, she could hardly contain her joy to be surrounded by such music.

"I know we are in a hurry, Mr. Davidson," said Cherity during a break from the work about midmorning, "but may I try the scythe just once? I want to learn how to do everything!"

"Of course. I'll show you how to hold it."

A brief lesson followed, after which Cherity tried it herself.

"It's so unwieldy!" she giggled as the others all watched, some of the black men with grins on their faces. Malachi was intent with his stone, seated on the ground sharpening the other two steel blades.

"The key is balance," said Richmond, standing behind her and reaching around her, placing his hands atop hers as she grasped the two handles. "The odd shape and position of the handles has all been designed perfectly to allow the sickle to do the work. The blade is razor-sharp and if you balance the scythe and swing it in a gentle arc like this—"

Still holding on to the instrument with her, and as Cherity relaxed to allow him to do the work, Richmond sent the blade in a slow moving arc through a stand of wheat with a gentle *swoosh*. The next moment the stalks fell gently and silently to the ground.

"How did you do that!" exclaimed Cherity in amazement.

"Years of practice!" laughed Richmond, stepping away from her. "Now you try it!"

Cherity did so, and continued stroke after stroke. By the time the break was over she had begun to get the hang of it, to the admiration of the black women who would never have dared even try. Though tiny in stature alongside the men, she obviously had enough upper-body strength to manage the difficult instrument. With practice, Richmond maintained while telling her father of it at lunch, she could be a skilled reaper within a single season. She also tried her hand at bundling, and caught on to that too. She was not able to attain nearly the speed, however, of the lightning-fast black hands that gathered up just the right quantity of stalks from the ground and twined them into a tight bundle almost with a single motion. But they too, as Richmond said, had had years of practice, for they had been working in fields just like this all their lives.

Late in the morning a caller appeared at Greenwood's door.

"I'm here to see Seth," she said as the door opened.

"He be in da fields wiff da wheat harvestin', Miz Bowmont," said Moses. "Dey's all in da field on account ob da weather."

What the weather could possibly have to do with it, Veronica had not an idea.

"Which field?" she asked.

"Da ten acres . . . down wes' ob da colored village," replied Moses.

As he spoke, Veronica glanced behind him into the house where a man she had never seen before had just walked by. She did not like the fact that there were visitors at Greenwood she did not recognize. She turned and walked back to her father's carriage. She would have to talk to Seth about keeping her better informed. After all, she would soon be mistress of this place. Then she would teach Moses some manners toward his betters, or send him back to the fields where he belonged.

With a vague idea of charming Seth away from his work—and doing so in full view of both his parents would be a sweet victory indeed!—she did her best to maneuver her horse and buggy—with which she had become slightly more adept under Seth's tutelage, though she still considered horses among the ugliest and stupidest creatures on the planet—in the direction Moses had indicated. At length she drew nigh the scene of the day's pleasant labors which she could see in the distance. She reined in, surveying her options and trying to decide which way to go across the harvested field so as not to upset the buggy. Gradually the sound of rich harmony reached her ears.

Were the Negroes actually singing as they worked! What did they think it was, a picnic! Her father would never stand for such nonsense in *his* fields! There were going to be more changes around this place than merely to Moses' uppity manner toward whites.

For a few seconds she continued to gaze with unseeing eyes upon the scene, then heard an even more unexpected sound. A great lusty laugh of pure delight rose above the music, followed by the tinkling sound of high-pitched woman's laughter. The first had been Seth's. She recognized it well enough even though she had never heard him laugh with quite such abandon. What was this—singing, laughter . . . were they all actually enjoying themselves!

An inner premonition told her that efforts to lure Seth away from his work would not be successful on this day. With some difficulty, therefore, Veronica negotiated the beast in front of her in a circle, bumping uncomfortably across the rutted and pitted edge of the field, back onto the wagon track, and made for home more annoyed than disappointed. She did not like the thought of Seth enjoying himself quite so much without her.

Meanwhile, at the far end of the field, the enthusiasm of Cherity Waters had invigorated the entire family of laborers, both white and black. Whether they beat the rain or not, the previous afternoon and this morning had certainly been one of the most enjoyable harvests any of them had participated in. The blacks had already taken Cherity to their hearts in the same way they had Carolyn herself. And Cherity, who had never been around Negroes or wheat or harvests or country labor of any kind, except in her fantasies of the West, in which cattle came in for a larger part than wheat or former slaves, found herself in such an ecstasy of human enjoyment that she could hardly contain it. Her father's own words about the toil of honest labor were now fulfilled in her, for hard work is truly one of the great stimulants of the spirit toward health and growth and vigor. And to have so many people suddenly around her—young, old, white, black, fathers, mothers, sons, brothers, sisters . . . all different but so wonderfully typical of the family of humanity—filled the girl who had grown up as a virtual only child with a tingling pleasure of relationship between races, and a joy of diverse human fellowship that must surely be a foretaste of the kingdom of heaven!

By midafternoon they had taken a sizeable swath off what had stood that morning, and only an acre or acre and a half yet remained on the stalk.

A sudden gust of wind blasted across the earth in their faces. Richmond paused, looked toward the northwest, then gazed up at the sky. Seth felt the drop in temperature too. He looked over at his father.

"What would Mr. Brown say, Dad?" he called into the wind.

"I think he would take a deep lungful from that last gust and say, 'It's coming!'"

"Exactly what I was thinking myself!" rejoined Seth.

"Who's Mr. Brown?" asked Cherity, walking up beside him, for she had been gathering behind Seth's scythe most of the day.

"An old Indian fellow who was a friend of my grandfather's," replied Seth. "He knew the weather and all these hills around here like the back of his hand. I'll tell you about him later. Right now we've got to get this wheat to the barn!"

"I remember!" exclaimed Cherity. "The man you told me about up in the hills . . . the man whose house is up there . . . the Indian cave and all that."

"That's him!" laughed Seth. "You have a good memory. Do you also remember how scared you were in that cave?"

"I was not!" Cherity shot back with a smile.

Their banter was soon cut short. Already Seth's father was running to the two wagons piled high with golden bundles of the staff of life, shouting orders as he went. Seth tore off across the field after him.

"Why?" called Cherity, sprinting to catch up.

"It's about to burst!" yelled Seth over his shoulder.

The three scythes were now set aside, and every available hand set to bundling and tying the cut grain and racing the bundles to the two wagons. Carolyn and Thomas leapt up onto the beds. Soon the bundles were flying through the air up to them—so skillfully tossed by the black laborers, heavy grain end first, that not a single head of the precious wheat was lost—there to be neatly stacked with the rest. Quickly the load grew high until the wagon could hold no more without danger of the carefully laid wheat toppling to the ground.

Seth jumped up and took the reins of the two faithful workhorses who had been waiting patiently for the moment when they must make their contribution.

"Up behind me, Cherity!" Seth called.

"Where?" she asked, seeing but the one bench seat and a bed behind it piled high with grain.

"Up on top!" he answered. "To hold the wheat down. We don't want to lose any in this wind!"

Seth's father came forward, took Cherity by the hand, then hoisted her to the top of one wagon wheel. From there, and following his further instructions, she scrambled to the peak of the heap, and there took a somewhat tenuous and wobbly seat.

"Hang on!" called Seth as the wagon lurched forward.

"Oh!" exclaimed Cherity, grabbing her hat and trying to steady herself.

"Yell at me if we start to lose the load!" Seth called behind him. "You're my lookout!"

Behind them, what bundles remained were already flying up onto the mounting heap atop the second wagon, which, in less than five minutes and with Thomas perched on the crow's nest behind his father, followed the first.

As the redbrick of the house and various barns came into view, and as she rode triumphantly high atop the fruits of their labors like a conquering heroine returning home victorious after battle, Cherity thought she had never been so happy in her life. This wasn't the wild west of Kansas, but maybe it was even better. She was not a mere observer . . . she was part of it!

Cherity saw her father standing ahead beside the barn watching the grand arrival.

"Hi, Daddy!" she called down, waving and beaming proudly.

He smiled and waved as they passed. Seth urged the horses on toward the open double doors of the huge storage barn and drove straight inside. He jumped down, first helping Cherity to the ground, then quickly unhitching the team to make room for the second shipment from field to storehouse.

His father's wagon was not far behind, and was shortly also safely in the dry of the great enclosure. Within minutes—even as the troop of black workers made their way from the fields back to their homes, singing a happy spiritual whose strains of high and low rich harmonies could be faintly heard half a mile away at the big house—great drops began to fall.

Mr. Brown had taught the clan Davidson to read the signs well.

Twelve

The storm was neither of the fiercest nor the most drenching. Despite the precursors of gusty winds and black clouds, the rain that accompanied it fell gently and steadily and only throughout the night and for about half the following day. It did not damage the crops. What remained of the ten acres, as well as another wheat field of fifteen, was left standing, as was the cotton in several larger fields spread about the Greenwood estate.

But there would be no more harvesting for a while, until the stalks and their golden heads were dry again in the hot summer sun. In the meantime, activity shifted to the threshing barn, where the bundles of harvested grain were processed—the heads cut from the stalks in precise whacks from the skillfully wielded blades of three black men, which were then tossed and beat and threshed to separate the grain heads from the chaff. Though it was dusty work and there was little for her to do but watch, Cherity enjoyed it immensely. Had it not been for the rain, the men would still be in the fields and their women whacking and threshing the grain indoors. As it was, however, they remained in their houses and the men came up to work in the large barn. The songs that now accompanied the work gave a deep rhyth-mic cadence that seemed to drive the work from the thuds of blades on chopping blocks to the swishing of grain tossed in the air. Cherity could scarcely understand a word of the slow-paced spirituals of melancholy and masculine voice. But their mysterious tones struck deep into her soul, quieting her spirit and bringing a gentle smile to her lips. They made her feel happy and sad at once, and very content.

Later that day, when the rain had gradually stopped, Cherity stood at the fence of the horse pasture and corral. She heard footsteps behind her. She turned and saw Seth approaching.

"Hi," he said. "What are you doing . . . as if I didn't know."

"What do you mean by that!" she laughed.

"Only that every minute you're not doing something else, you're watching the horses."

"Is it really that obvious?"

Now it was Seth's turn to laugh. "Actually . . . yes," he said, still chuckling. "Alexander has begun to notice the way you have with horses and is beginning to worry about his job."

"Now you're teasing me!"

"Maybe just a little."

"I love horses—there's nothing wrong with that, is there?"

"Nothing at all. I love them too. That's why I recognize that look in your eye."

"What look?'

"That you are itching for a ride."

"How did you know!"

"Because you're just like me," said Seth. He jumped onto the fence and perched himself on the top rail with legs drooping over the other side. "I've loved horses all my life."

"Me too!" exclaimed Cherity, climbing up beside him. "Well . . . not *all* my life. I think I was always drawn to them, but when my father took me to Kansas on one of his trips, that's when I really fell in love with riding and horses."

"What was Kansas like?" asked Seth.

"I suppose it was a little rough. Everything I read about it now makes it sound like a battleground back then—John Brown and all the killing and fighting about whether it should be a slave or a free state. I'm still not sure why my father took me with him, but I'm glad he did. I was so young then. Now I see what a dangerous time it was out west."

A silence fell as both young people stared at the twelve or fifteen horses out in the pasture in front of them.

"Well . . . ?" said Seth at length. "Which one do you fancy?"

"What do you mean?"

"Pick one. Do you like Silverfoot, Moonbeam, Apricot Rose, Golden Cloud, Grey Laird—"

"Wait a minute!" laughed Cherity. "I can't keep them all straight. I've forgotten half their names from three years ago. Although I do remember old Diamond!" she added laughing.

"Unfortunately he's even older and slower than before."

"It sounds like you have some new ones too."

"We do," replied Seth.

"And do you still try to name them according to their color and personality, like you told me before?"

"Of course. That one there, for instance, whom you haven't met yet, is called Proud Lord."

"Why that?"

"Because he always remains a little way from the others, carrying his head high and a little aloof. He was rebellious and violent at first, but once trained he became as docile as a child."

"It's a perfect name!"

"And a little beyond him, the jet-black mare is called the Gentle Demon."

"It sounds like a contradiction."

"No more than all of the feminine of the species," said Seth with a twinkle in his eye. "Yes . . . a contradiction!"

"But why?" laughed Cherity.

"My mother, who named her, explains it like this—that she is gentle with women, but has a nasty streak that rears its head whenever a man tries to ride her. Mother says she is just like some women she has met—fine around other women, but antagonistic toward the slightest interference of male authority! So the minute she senses a man approaching with a saddle, back go her ears in defiance!"

"That's funny!" laughed Cherity. "Tell me the names of the rest—I want to learn the name of every horse at Greenwood."

"All right then," replied Seth, pointing farther into the pasture, "there are Malcolm and Midnight, and over there we have Swift Fire, Paintbrush, Blue Flash, and Dusty."

When he had completed giving Cherity a brief description of each horse and its temperament, Seth turned to her where she sat atop the rail and asked again,

"So . . . now that you know them all, which one do you fancy?"

"I think I like the beautiful hue of Golden Cloud best," replied Cherity, "although I love what you said about Malcolm and how he has noble blood but is humble and unpretentious."

"Well, then, pick one and let's go for a ride."

"Do you mean it!" she said. "Right now?"

"Sure," laughed Seth. "Pick any of the horses in this pasture."

"Oh!" squealed Cherity in uncontained delight. "Oh . . . oh—" she went on, gazing almost frantically about. "All right," she said, "I think I would like to ride Golden Cloud."

"An excellent choice," said Seth, hopping down into the pasture. "Though you have to be a little careful—an Akhal-Teke gallops differently than most horses, almost sliding over the ground in a flowing movement. It will feel different at first, but I know you'll do fine. She is spirited but not skittish." He gave a sharp whistle, then called into the field, "Golden Cloud!" Almost immediately, the Russian Akhal-Teke perked up its head and began to walk toward him.

Cherity bounded down from the fence and followed eagerly. "She came the instant you called her name," she said as she hurried to his side and fell into step alongside him.

"They like to be called. Once a horse is broken and taught that its master loves him, there is nothing that gives him greater pleasure than to be with his master."

"Which one are you going to ride?" she asked.

"I think . . . Blue Flash," replied Seth.

"Why him . . . he is a stallion, isn't he?"

"Yes—you have a good memory. And because I haven't taken him out for a while and don't want him to think I've forgotten him."

Again he whistled and called. "Flash . . . come!"

When the two horses had joined them, Seth turned toward the pasture gate leading to the stables and barn. As they went, the two horses followed behind without need of rope or halter or enticement of feed bag. Seth unfastened the gate and went through. They were soon under cover of the roof.

"How do, massa Seth," said a wiry black man, ambling toward them.

"Hi, Alexander. Miss Waters and I are going out for a ride."

"You want me ter saddle dem up fo' y'all?"

"I think we'll saddle them ourselves, but thank you, Alexander."

"Do you have any choice of saddle?" asked Seth as they went inside the barn and stopped at the saddle rack.

"A saddle is such a personal thing," said Cherity. "I don't have a saddle of my own at home yet." She walked slowly about the rack, looking at the saddles and letting her hand run across them. "I haven't found the right one for me yet . . . but I think for today I like . . . this one right here," she said, returning to a particularly worn-looking saddle whose brown leather was nearly black from age.

Seth smiled. "This is a worthy saddle indeed," he said. "It has seen a lot of use and has always proven faithful. But it is a man's saddle."

Cherity looked over at him with a look of mingled disgust and astonishment.

"You don't think I ride with a woman's saddle, do you! Sidesaddle . . . ugh! Surely you remember from last time."

Seth laughed at the abhorrence in her tone. They picked out two blankets and set about preparing the two patiently waiting mounts to take them out for their day's adventure.

Ten minutes later they rode out of the grounds, heading west toward the ridge.

About the same time the two riders had disappeared among the trees in the distance, Richmond and Carolyn were taking advantage of the reemergence of the sun and were walking toward the arbor with their guest. Maribel followed ten minutes later with a tray of tea, crackers, and small cakes. She found them seated in the summerhouse.

"Your daughter is positively delightful, James," Carolyn said as Maribel left the garden and they began to sip at their tea, "beautiful, vibrant, personable, and with such a wide range of interests."

Waters nodded appreciatively. "I have a great deal to be thankful for," he said. "Raising her without a wife has been full of challenges. She has grown into a young woman, yet at the same time she still has all the enthusiasm for life of a girl."

"And Cherity's two older sisters?"

"Both married, as you remember, and I am now the proud grandfather of three little ones."

"Congratulations," said Richmond.

"It is bittersweet, of course, in that having little ones around—though I am not able to see them often—not to mention seeing my daughters grow into women, cannot help but remind me of my wife."

"What was your wife like?" asked Carolyn. "As I recall, did you say she was a practicing Christian when you met her?"

"She was active in church," replied Waters. "She was from a Puritan background and brought that same Northern tradition into our family, with the older girls especially. Church was very important in her life. She and the two older girls were at church, it seemed, more than they were at home. And for a time it was important to me too. But I had spent a great deal of my own youth alone, and . . . well I will just say that raising Cherity without a mother was very difficult for me."

Carolyn and Richmond listened pensively but did not respond.

"It was during that time of my life, when I was nineteen or twenty, when I was saved, as the expression is, during a revival service some of us attended from the college where I had been enrolled. I became quite caught up in the whole thing for ten years or more. With no family of my own, it fulfilled a need I suppose. That's how I met Kathleen, in church, though in retrospect I have come to see, as much as I loved her, that we probably were more dissimilar in our outlook on spiritual things than I recognized at the time.

"In any event, when Kathleen died, the older girls stopped being quite so regular in church, and I certainly saw no need to push it, especially as Cherity grew. What good had belief in God done our family for the mother of these three girls to devote her whole life to the church, only to be taken away from them when they needed her most? And when the pastor of our church called on me as we were making funeral plans, he had only the absurdist of platitudes to offer, telling me that God must have had a purpose in taking Kathleen. Kathleen was dead—nothing could change that. People die, tragedies are part of life. All right, I can accept that. It was hard and I wept, because I loved her. But to say that God *took* her, even *wanted* her to die for some grand purpose that fit into his cosmic scheme . . . that I could not accept. What kind of God would do such a thing? Even if his role in the thing were more passive than the ludicrous view presented by our pastor, if he might have prevented it, why would he *let* her die? What kind of God would—"

Suddenly he stopped. He glanced at Richmond and Carolyn. Both were staring intently into his face as they listened. Waters smiled and laughed uneasily.

"I'm sorry," he said. "I didn't mean to go into all that."

"We are very interested, James," said Carolyn. "Everyone has a story, and sometimes the painful portions of those stories are the most significant. Please, do not be apprehensive about anything you want to share."

"Well . . . I don't suppose there is much more than that," smiled Waters a little sadly. "The conclusion is that my wife's death caused me, as the saying goes, to lose my faith. I did not return to the church and I have not been since. It could no doubt be argued, if my faith was so tenuous that it could be lost so easily, that it was probably on shaky ground to begin with. That may be true. It probably is true. So

I had nothing to fall back on. Once I started really thinking about Christianity as a mature adult, I realized I had no solid intellectual reasons for believing all I had been taught. That I was active in church and played at being a Christian for so long, and *thought* I was sincere and devout, cannot change the fact that within a year of Kathleen's death I no longer believed a word of it. But I would be remiss if I did not add that Cherity and I have managed to get along quite well together after those difficult first years. She is a very special girl and has brought great joy to my life."

"She is very special indeed," smiled Carolyn. "That much is clear after five minutes with her."

A brief silence fell. "More tea, anyone?" asked Carolyn, picking up the pot.

"Yes, thank you very much," said Waters.

"I believe I will have some also, my dear," said Richmond.

Carolyn poured out three more cupfuls.

"We have faced some difficult things in our lives too, James," she said when she had resumed her seat. "Would you be interested in hearing how we have discovered meaning and purpose through our grief?"

"I would, indeed. Though I have been around you both enough to suspect what you will tell me."

"If you think I am going to say that we discovered that meaning in God, and found in him the *answers* to the puzzle not the *cause* of the grief . . . then you are right. The more we understood God and his ways, the more everything that had happened to us fit into a wonderful pattern of purpose. In him we found peace rather than the frustration I seem to detect in your voice."

"A fair enough observation," nodded Waters. "And probably an accurate one."

"My wife has hit upon the most crucial point of all," interjected Richmond, "in what she said a moment ago—*understanding* God."

"It was my husband," said Carolyn, still speaking to their guest, "who taught me the importance of such understanding. I was like your wife. I was raised in church, my father being a supply preacher.

But when tragedy hit my life, the church was not enough. It did not sustain me or comfort me, and in fact had little to offer. I understand completely some of what you must have felt. I experienced those same doubts and emotions when I lost my first husband."

Waters took in the words with surprise. "I . . . I had no idea," he said.

"Like you," Carolyn went on, "I lost my faith for a time. But then I met Richmond."

"You were a Christian, I take it?" said Waters, turning toward his host.

"Oh, no," answered Davidson, "I had just been through a terribly tragic divorce. To have associated me with the word *faith* could not have been more inaccurate. I was a mess in every way. I don't think I believed in anything."

"But even in his unbelief," Carolyn now went on, "he showed me the pathway back into faith."

"An intriguing thing," said their guest. "How did he do that?"

"It was Richmond's insatiable spiritual curiosity, and his curiosity about God himself, that were, in a sense, the sustaining force in his life . . . in both of our lives, I should say. It helped us come through our difficult times to the place where you see us today where we are at peace with who we are and with life as it has come to us."

"I am more curious than ever," said Waters. "Would you care to explain further?"

Carolyn thought a moment. "Ever since the day I met him," she began, "Richmond has been on a quest, a mission, to understand God. So many merely accept what they have been taught, never pausing to ask whether it makes sense or whether it rings true with the world around them, or, for that matter, with the world inside them. I suppose it was one of the things that so drew me to him—his spiritual *curiosity*."

"You were not that way yourself?"

"Not really. I had to *learn* how to ask questions, and how to ask the right questions. Most Christians like myself do not learn it. They are not taught the value, even the *necessity* of spiritual questions. As I said,

I had grown up as the daughter of a pastor. I had been taught much about God. But I had never been taught to be *curious* about God and his ways. A short time after losing my first husband, Richmond walked into our church full of questions about who God was and how he could be a good God who always sought our best. I can still remember the tone of his voice and that wide-eyed expression on his face—"

Richmond broke out in a roar of laughter.

"To listen to my wife, James," he said, "you might think me a lunatic! I was as despondent as she. In the process of the divorce I mentioned, certain very painful charges were leveled against me."

"But in your grief, Richmond," Carolyn persisted, now turning to her husband, "you wanted to understand . . . you were *driven* to understand. You didn't want merely to react, and vent your wrath on the gods, so to speak. You wanted to know what it all meant. That's what set you apart from anyone I had known in the church. You were hungry for truth. You weren't willing to simply wallow in your grief and rail against God or life or fate for making you its victim. You stood up and said, 'God, I want to understand you! How can you be my good Father who wants and does your best for me when suffering exists, and when I am suffering myself?'"

"I suppose that is true," nodded Richmond. "I wanted to understand. I still do."

"Maybe it is the lawyer in you," laughed Carolyn, "always trying to dissect truth into its smaller and smaller parts in order to arrive at big-picture truth in the end. Or . . . " she added, pausing reflectively, "perhaps it is like your profession, James. That is the calling, too, of a journalist, is it not, like the attorney . . . to find truth, to investigate, to probe, to question, so that in the end, truth emerges."

"Actually, Carolyn," said Waters, "that is not how I have been accustomed to viewing my profession. Just the opposite, in fact. But I had no idea you were an attorney, Richmond. I thought you were . . ."

"Just a farmer?" added Richmond.

"I'm sorry, I didn't mean it like that."

"Think nothing of it."

"But, James," said Carolyn, "I don't understand what you mean by what you just said about your profession."

"I view myself as a reporter, not an investigator," Waters answered. "My job is to report things as they are, not try to figure out what they *mean*. That is best left to the philosophers!"

"Ah . . . I see. Yes, that makes sense, in contrast to what I said about Richmond trying to find meaning."

"Right. Have you heard of photography?" he asked, looking back and forth between the two Davidsons.

"I have read an article or two about it," replied Richmond. "As I understand it, the process involves the reproduction of images using emulsified silver on paper, which, depending on the degree of light it is exposed to, will turn varying degrees of black—the more light the darker, the less the lighter."

"You are remarkably well informed!" laughed Waters. "That is it exactly. Well, perhaps in a similar vein, I see my job as that of a photographer—to record what *is*, not speculate on what might be, or what any given photograph *means*. Mine is not to find truth but to record facts."

"But facts have meaning, James," put in Carolyn.

"Of course. But as I say, that is a job for the philosophers . . . or perhaps, if one is so inclined, for the theologians."

"Let me pose you a riddle, then," said Richmond. "Say you take a photograph of a man standing beside a tree in a wood. Your job as a reporter, as you see it, is to record that fact, to write for your readers: *A man is standing in a forest beside a tree. This is what he looks like. This is what the tree looks like. This is the expression on the man's face.* Is that a fair representation of your role in the affair—presenting the facts as revealed by the photograph?"

"Exactly. You could not have stated it better."

"All right, then, let me pose a further conundrum. Suppose the photograph does not reveal the most important of all facts concerning the man? You say the facts as we see them are enough. But what if they are *not* enough? What if the most important fact of all is one the

photograph does not show, and that, therefore, by recounting only
what you see, you actually are unable to accurately represent the facts
at all, and your description is at best a misleading one, or at worst, a
false one?"

"Go on," said Waters, for the moment intrigued.

"What if, for example," Richmond continued, "just beyond the
range of the camera, an enormous grizzly had charged at the very
moment the picture was taken, accounting for the look on the man's
face, and that twenty seconds later the man lay dead on the ground
and the photographer was running for his life? My question is: How
accurate is the mere photograph of the man standing beside the tree
in conveying either truth or fact? To omit mention of the bear seems
less-than-adequate journalism?"

"I see your point. It would all depend on whether I, as a reporter,
knew about the bear or not. But in a way it is merely academic. The
facts of the photograph can never in and of themselves reveal the
bear."

"But perhaps further investigation can. What if the photographer
survived? What if there were other witnesses? What if a great deal of
additional evidence indeed exists that *would* enable the shrewd journalist or investigator to get to the bottom of the mystery of the photograph? Would it not be well to find out, to look into that evidence to
see what it had to say?"

Waters smiled. "You would indeed have made a cunning attorney,"
he said. "Your analysis is keen. You plug the holes of possible objection before your adversary has the chance to poke his finger through
them! But it all still sounds merely theoretical to me. What does any
of this really have to do with you and me and your wife as we sit here
in your garden right now?"

"Everything, James," rejoined Richmond. "It has everything to do
with us."

"In what way?"

"We have all been handed a photograph of ourselves standing in the
midst of the world. But we don't know very much about that world
just from looking at the photograph. It is sometimes a confusing

world, and we are sometimes part of that confusion. And stare at the photograph as we might, we just cannot make sense of it. We need to know more. Now there are rumors that the world we are standing in has no meaning or purpose and all came about by accident. Some say the world is an intrinsically cruel place. There are rumors, too, of goodness and happiness and eternal purpose. There are rumors of various gods who had some role in the creation of the world that may or may not have anything to do with us. There are other rumors of a God who *does* have to do with us and who will share his paradise with us if we are good and believe certain things about him, and will punish us forever if we don't. There are all kinds of such rumors. But they all exist beyond sight of the photograph. Some people don't care, and just put the photograph of themselves in a drawer and never bother to look at it or ask what it means or what might exist past the edges of it if only we could see a little further."

Richmond paused and looked intently at their guest.

"But I was not such a one, James," he said. "When I walked into that church and heard Carolyn's father say, 'God knows each one of us personally, really knows us, and wants the very best for us if we will just let him give it to us,' something within me was suddenly no longer satisfied to look at a photograph of myself standing in the midst of a life that was complex and confusing and, in my case at that particular moment, painful. I wanted to know things about the forest and the trees and the landscape around me that the photograph didn't reveal. I wanted to know if there were bears about, or perhaps if there was a good God about, unseen in the photograph, incapable of being caught as an image on the paper but *there* nonetheless. From whence comes the light surrounding the entire photograph? What else existed that the raw fact of the photograph could never in itself fully reveal? I wanted to know what that photograph of me standing in the forest *meant*. I wanted to know *why* I was standing in that wood, *who* had put me there, who had taken the photograph, and who was the one who had made such a thing as trees and men and bears and photographs capable of existence in the first place. Furthermore, having made them capable of existence, what might he be doing now, and how might he *still* be involved with them?"

"You were full of many questions."

"I suppose, though I didn't formulate them all at once. But that's how it began. And a lifelong quest that has consumed me ever since—to know and understand the source of the light which enables such things as photographs to be taken at all. It has been my experience since giving my life to God some months after Carolyn and I met, that most who give to themselves the name 'Christian' have never investigated the source of light either. They call themselves by that name only because they have been told a great many things about the photograph. But they have never researched the matter for themselves. But such a policy could never satisfy me. I had to know . . . I had to understand."

"And what has been the conclusion of your quest to understand these things?" asked Waters.

"That the light behind the photograph comes from the overarching goodness of a loving Fatherhood."

As Seth and Cherity set off together, neither was in a competitive mood and they rode side by side, talking casually.

"Can we ride up the same mountain we did last time?" asked Cherity. "What was it called . . . some Peak or another?"

"Harper's Peak."

"That's it!"

"Sure—are you thinking . . . " Seth added, glancing over with a twinkle in his eye.

"Of racing?" said Cherity. "No. I want to enjoy every inch of the way, and see everything. I can hardly believe I'm actually here again! I don't want to miss a thing!"

They entered the woody region above the pastures, whose trees were wet with the leftover sparkles of the day's rain. Neither said much as they made their way through pine and oak and fir, gently ascending the ridge. Forty minutes later they emerged into the meadow where the race had begun at Cherity's last visit.

"It's so beautiful," sighed Cherity. "I remember it like it was yesterday."

"Maybe not a race, but how about a little canter?" suggested Seth.

"Why not!"

They urged their horses on and broke into an easy gallop across the green sward. They reached the opposite side, slowed, and continued up again, more steeply now over uneven terrain, in the direction of Harper's Peak.

"Did you ever get a horse of your own?" asked Seth.

"I did," replied Cherity. "And a beauty!"

"A horse but no saddle?"

"The right horse came along, but the right saddle hasn't yet. Until it does, I am content to borrow one from the stables where we board him. It is a couple of miles from where we live so I'm not able to ride any time I happen to want to. I can't believe that you have such a stable full of so many beautiful horses right outside your door!"

"What's your horse's name?"

"Whiteface."

"I don't need to ask where that came from! What color is the rest of him?"

"He's a Spanish Andalusian, mostly gray with speckles of black, one black foot, a light mane and tail, almost white actually, and a pure white nose."

"He sounds stunning, just like Babieca."

"You know horses!"

"Doesn't everyone know of El Cid's famous Andalusian who lived to be forty?"

"No, not everyone does! I've never met *anyone* who did!"

"What's his temperament?"

"My Whiteface is both gentle and fast. My only regret is not being able to completely give him the rein and let him run until he can run no more."

"Do you find that riding clears your mind, helps you think straight?"

"Oh, yes—there's nothing like it. You're out in the fresh air with a companion who maybe doesn't understand things the way people do, but still who is regal and maybe a little understanding in his own way, at least I like to think so . . . there's nothing I love so much."

"I know the feeling exactly. You're alone, but not alone. A horse won't bother your thoughts or intrude, yet gives a feeling of friendship at the same time."

"It's not like having a human friend, but it's almost as good in a different kind of way. I don't think I could ever be bored or be altogether sad if I was with my horse."

"Do you remember the last time you were here," said Seth as they reached the plateau and continued toward the peak. "You said you thought that including God in your life would be stuffy and boring."

Cherity chuckled at the reminder.

"Have you had any new spiritual realizations since then," Seth added, "or do you still believe that?"

"I don't know if you'd call it a realization or not," said Cherity, "but I've decided that I'm an atheist."

Seth began to laugh. His tone was not a mocking one, but one rather of humorous incredulity.

"You're kidding, aren't you?"

"No, I really am . . . I mean it."

For a moment Seth could not stop chuckling. Gradually he realized she was serious. He slowly stopped and looked over as their horses walked slowly along beside one another.

"You think it's funny?" asked Cherity.

"I don't know—maybe not funny," replied Seth, "if that's really what you believe. I've just never before heard anyone make such a straightforward admission. Why do you say you're an atheist?"

"I don't know exactly. I tried going to church once. I suppose I was curious about my mother and her faith. There were some ladies, friends of my mother's . . . they were intent on getting me saved, I guess you would say. All they could talk about was sin and hell and nothing that sounded appealing to me. Actually, yes . . . they struck me as stuffy and boring, and what they said made little sense anyway. It was like they had their own little private language. I don't think they cared if it made sense to me, they just wanted me to admit that I was a sinner and then pray and turn my life over to God or something. I didn't like it. I didn't like *them*. If Christianity made people like those three ladies, then I wasn't interested. Sometime after that I decided I didn't believe in God at all."

"Because of those three ladies?"

"I suppose in a way."

"I'd like to meet them!" laughed Seth.

"Why!"

"Your description fascinates me . . . although they'd probably try to get me saved too. I'm not sure I'd like that any more than you did."

Seth thought a moment, then turned toward Cherity.

"So you think that if people who profess something don't live by it," he said, "it makes the thing itself untrue?"

"I hadn't thought of it quite like that," said Cherity. "Do you think that's what I did?"

"It sounded like it."

"Hmm . . . "

"What if the people *themselves* are untrue," asked Seth, "not the thing they say they believe in?"

"I hadn't thought about that either."

"Don't you think that whether a thing, like Christianity, is true or false is independent of the people who believe it?"

"I don't see how it could be *completely* independent of them. How else are you to judge something like Christianity than by the Christians who believe it?"

"Maybe the two aren't completely independent, I agree with you there," rejoined Seth. "But I would still say you have to judge it on its own merits. You have to find out whether it is true or not. There are people who live consistently by their beliefs, and people who don't. That doesn't change the inherent truth or falsehood of the thing itself. It seems to me that you have to evaluate anything on the basis of truth, while recognizing that some people live more consistently than others."

"Maybe you're right. But being an atheist makes life a lot less complicated. You can just live and be happy."

"Maybe I should ask, then—do you *want* it to be true?"

"You mean that there's no God . . . do I *want* there to be no God?" Seth nodded.

"I don't know," replied Cherity slowly. "I never thought about whether I *wanted* it to be true or not. That's a hard question. But I don't see what it has to do with anything? Wanting something to be true won't make it true. I may want the sun to shine, or want to be taller, or want to live in the country . . . but it still may rain, I will still live in Boston, and I will still be a little runt that people mistake for a kid."

Seth roared. "You are hardly a kid!" he laughed. "I have the feeling you can hold your own with just about anyone!"

"You know what I mean! I'm too short."

"You're just right . . . you look lovely and I wouldn't change a thing about you if I—"

Suddenly Seth stopped and glanced away.

Cherity saw his embarrassment and shared it, knowing that she had inadvertently caused it. To hide the red also rising in her own cheeks, she dug her heels into Golden Cloud's sides and cantered off toward the peak. Seth waited a moment, then followed. When he caught her, Cherity had dismounted and was gazing about her down at the valley below.

"Harper's Peak," she sighed. "I've dreamed about this view ever since last time. It makes me so happy to be here again."

They stood for a minute or two in silence.

"Do you still see a lot of—what was their name, your friends who live down there on the other side of the town . . . Beau—"

"Beaumont," said Seth.

"Oh, yes—Wyatt was the boy's name."

"He's hardly a boy now," said Seth with a tone in his voice that Cherity couldn't exactly identify. "He's twenty years old and big and strong and . . . well, let's just say that he reminds me more and more of his father all the time. To answer your question—no, I don't see much of him these days, or Cameron either."

"The younger boy?"

Seth nodded. "He's no boy either. He's developed a mean streak. I don't know, they just . . . "

His voice trailed away. "I don't know," he said with a sigh. "It's funny how people change, that's all."

Even as he said the words, Seth was wondering to himself how he could shift the conversation so that the third member of the Beaumont trio did not come up.

"And what about their sister?" said Cherity. "She's your age, isn't she?"

"Uh, yeah," said Seth with an inward groan.

"What's her name—I forgot."

"Veronica," said Seth, his neck brightening again.

"Are you and she still . . . uh, good friends?" asked Cherity. The question had just popped out, and it was not until the words had passed her lips that she remembered the brother Cameron's tease from three years earlier. But it was too late to take them back.

"Yeah . . . " replied Seth hesitantly. "I guess I see her more often than I do her brothers."

"Maybe I'll have the chance to meet her."

"Uh . . . yeah, maybe. But I doubt if the two of you would hit it off."

"Why not?" asked Cherity.

"I don't know—you're just . . . I don't know, different, I guess. She's not interested in horses."

"I'm interested in more than *just* horses."

"I know, that wasn't what I meant."

Seth began walking about, trying to clear his brain. A few minutes later they mounted again and began the ride back down the ridge following the same route they had taken three years earlier. It was quiet as they went, a more subdued mood settling upon them.

"Can we explore the caves again?" asked Cherity excitedly.

"You really want to? You were scared last time."

"I wasn't, I tell you!" laughed Cherity. "And even if I was—which I wasn't!—I wouldn't be now. I'm older. I was just a little girl then. I want to explore for the Indian treasure."

"Who told you there was Indian treasure?"

"You did—or I thought you did."

"I did not," laughed Seth.

"You said there were legends and burial sites. So there has to be treasure."

"You are making up all kinds of things about last time! All I said was that there were rumors."

"But I bet there really is a treasure," insisted Cherity. "That's how rumors begin . . . I'm sure of it."

"Why would you think that?"

"Rumors have to come from someplace. And your mysterious Mr. Brown was an Indian. He must have had something to do with it. Can we go look in that house of Mr. Brown's—it's nearby, isn't it?"

"Not far."

"I bet there are clues if we just know how to look for them."

Not sure what to make of Cherity's enthusiasm, but seeing no harm in it, Seth led the way to that portion of his father's property they still called the Brown tract.

As they entered the house, Cherity expected a ramshackle place so old and run-down and full of dirt and cobwebs and decay that it might fall down around them. From what Seth had told her, she assumed the place hadn't been used in twenty or thirty years. Instead, as she walked in, the house even almost smelled inhabited. A few chairs were about, a table sat in the center of what must have been the kitchen, and all the windows appeared to be intact.

"I thought you said Mr. Brown left years ago," she said glancing around. "Look, this table isn't even dusty. *Somebody's* been here more recently than that!"

Seth did not reply at first, not knowing whether to divulge the fact that Greenwood's blacks used the place for secret church meetings, and that sometimes his mother met the black ladies here out of sight of prying eyes.

"And look . . . " said Cherity as she wandered into the largest room, at the far end of which stood a great wide stone fireplace, "here are more chairs, and rugs where it looks like people have been sitting on the floor. There have been people here . . . and not that long ago!"

"Yeah," said Seth, "my mom sometimes comes here with the black women."

"You never told me that before!"

"You didn't ask," laughed Seth.

"Why do they come here?"

"To make sure they aren't seen. You've got to remember that white people don't like how my parents treat black people."

"What's this?" said Cherity, approaching the fireplace and gazing at a strange emblem or painting on the wall above it. They stood looking a few moments at the odd symbols painted on a thin-stretched skin of light-colored leather, almost white.

"It looks Indian," she added.

"It probably is," said Seth.

"I wish I knew what all those symbols and drawings meant."

Cherity turned and continued about the large room.

"How did Mr. Brown wind up here?" she asked.

"I don't know," answered Seth. "You should ask my dad. But I'm not sure how much he knows. Mr. Brown was my grandfather's friend. My father was away when all the trouble happened."

"What trouble?"

"My father's brother was found dead—somewhere out here on the Brown land. And then Mr. Brown disappeared. Later his animals were found roaming the hills."

"Do they think *he* did it, and that's why he ran away?"

"I don't think they think that. From all I've ever heard Mr. Brown was one of the gentlest men you could meet. I never knew him myself—I'm too young . . . but that's what they say."

"So there's not just a mystery about the treasure," said Cherity, revolving everything in her mind, "there's also the peculiar circumstances of your—let's see, he's your father's brother, so he would be your *uncle*—of your uncle's death, and of Mr. Brown's disappearance. There are *three* mysteries!"

Seth laughed. "You sound like a detective! You turn everything into a mystery!"

"Don't you find it fascinating—especially when his house is still in such good repair . . . that Indian thing above the hearth. I'm *sure* there are clues, if we just knew where to look."

Again Seth laughed. Curious about an odd-looking board that caught her eye, Cherity pulled back the edge of a portion of an old faded woven rug.

"And look," she said excitedly, "here's a door in the floor!"

Before Seth could object, she had the rug off and the door pulled open on its hinge. Quickly she began to scramble down the steep stairway.

"Every house has a cellar," said Seth as he knelt down and peered after her. "It doesn't mean there's something sinister going on!"

"But this isn't just *any* house," came Cherity's voice from below. "This house belonged to a mysterious Indian! Maybe the treasure's down here! Do you think you could find a cand—"

"Wait!" interrupted Seth. He paused, then stood to listen. "I thought I heard something."

Cherity stopped on the stairs. It was silent a few seconds. Slowly she began tiptoeing back up into the room, listening intently.

"You're right, I hear a horse," she said.

"Someone's coming. Come on—get out of sight!" said Seth. He hurried to the wall and knelt down below the nearest windowsill. Cherity ran up and followed. He pulled her down beside him, then inched his head up to peep around the edge of the glass.

"It's Mr. Beaumont!" he exclaimed in a loud whisper. "What's *he* doing here! I heard he was in Washington!"

Cherity half stood to see for herself.

"He's coming straight for the house!"

Seth sat back down on the floor, obviously thinking what to do.

"Don't you want him to see you?" asked Cherity.

"Uh, not really . . . but mostly I don't want him to see *you*."

"Why not?"

"I can't explain. Let's—"

Seth glanced around hurriedly.

"You hide in the cellar," he said, crawling back over the floor on his hands and knees. "Hurry!" he said. "We don't have time to find a candle. I'll see what he wants."

Cherity scurried back down the steep steps into the darkness. Seth shut the door over her, then stood, went to the door, took a deep breath or two to calm himself, then stepped out onto the porch as the father of his fiancée rode up. Obviously taken by surprise, Denton Beaumont reined in abruptly.

"Seth, my boy!" he exclaimed. "What are you doing here?"

"I was just about to ask you the same question, Mr. Beaumont," replied Seth.

"Just out for a ride."

"You're a long way from Oakbriar."

"I guess I wandered out of my way without realizing it," said Beaumont, forcing an unconvincing laugh. "You know how fond your father and I always were of the Brown tract."

"I thought that was when you were young."

"You know what they say—old habits die hard!" laughed Beaumont again, though humorlessly. "Yes . . . I still love the old place. Why don't you talk your father into selling it to me—I've been unable to."

"What would you do with it, Mr. Beaumont?" asked Seth.

"Oh, I don't know, I'm just a sentimentalist, I guess."

"I don't think my father wants to sell it."

"That is clear enough," rejoined Beaumont. "But *why* he does not is what puzzles me. I am prepared to offer far more than it is worth."

"I don't think he feels he has the right to sell it."

Whatever caustic rejoinder may have been on Denton Beaumont's lips, he fortunately kept to himself. "Well," he said glancing about, "now that I see where I've come, I had better be getting back. I've been away long enough already."

He wheeled his horse around and rode off. Seth watched him go, then turned and walked back inside to retrieve Cherity from the cellar.

"Why didn't you want him to see me?" asked Cherity as she climbed back into the large room.

"He just wouldn't have understood, that's all," replied Seth. "He's a suspicious man. I don't want him asking questions about the Brown place. I'm glad he didn't see our two horses on the other side of the house. If he were to find out about the blacks coming here, or my mother teaching their ladies, there is no telling how much trouble he could cause. I wouldn't put it past him to have her jailed."

"Your neighbor and friend would do that!"

"He and my father don't get along very well anymore. Once we freed our slaves, that was the end of the friendship. He bitterly resents the stand my parents took. As the local commissioner, he could cause them a lot of grief. I would put nothing past him. There's something going on. I'm certain he came here on purpose."

"You think he lied to you?"

"To be blunt, I suppose yes. I don't know what he was up to. But one thing I am sure of—he knows these hills like the back of his hand. He didn't just accidentally stray this far from Oakbriar without knowing very well what he was doing. I only hope he hasn't gotten word of what's going on here, though that seems the only reasonable explanation. I'll have to tell my dad."

"There is another possibility," said Cherity.

"What's that?"

"He knows about the treasure and was sneaking around looking for it."

"There you go about the Indian treasure again!" laughed Seth.

"It makes sense, doesn't it? You said he's always been interested in this land. I bet he knows something even your father doesn't know."

"That's quite a theory."

They left the house and returned to their horses.

"How did your father come to own the land if it was Mr. Brown's?" asked Cherity as they began the ride down the hill.

"I've never been altogether sure of that," replied Seth. "It is a little puzzling. Like I said, Mr. Brown disappeared and . . . well, actually I'm not sure how the land came into my father's possession."

"Can we ask him?" asked Cherity.

"Who?"

"Your father, silly! Can we ask him about it?"

"I guess so. You're really that interested?"

"Of course! It might help us find the treasure!"

Seth laughed. "You are a determined one!"

"I want to ask him about everything! You said I should. Do you think he'll mind?"

"He won't mind," answered Seth, still chuckling.

Thirteen

The moment they arrived back at Greenwood, Cherity went in search of Seth's father. She found him seated with her father on the veranda of the house. The men were enjoying mint juleps and laughing and chatting freely.

"Mr. Davidson," said Cherity as she and Seth approached from the barn, where they had left their horses with Alexander, "Seth says I ought to ask you about Mr. Brown and the mystery of his disappearance and the treasure."

"Treasure!" laughed Richmond. "Did Seth tell you there was a treasure?"

"Not exactly," she answered with a sheepish smile, glancing back toward Seth as he came up behind her.

"I didn't think so," said Richmond. "It's the first I've heard of it."

"But don't you think there must be!" said Cherity excitedly.

"This girl of yours has quite an imagination, James!" laughed Richmond to his guest.

"She always has."

"Then why did Mr. Brown disappear so mysteriously?" persisted Cherity. "And why else would your neighbor be snooping around and lie to Seth about it being an accident that he had ridden there?"

Richmond's forehead wrinkled in question. He glanced toward Seth.

"That's right, Dad," said Seth, "though Cherity may be making it sound a little more devious than it actually was. We went for a ride up on the ridge. On the way back down Cherity wanted to see the Brown place. We hadn't been there five minutes when Mr. Beaumont showed up."

"What did he do?" asked Richmond.

"Nothing, once he saw me. We spoke for a minute or two, then he left. He said he was out for a ride and had strayed farther from Oakbriar than he had intended and hadn't realized where he was."

Richmond took in the information without expression.

"I still want to know about Mr. Brown," said Cherity. She sat down on the steps and waited. It was clear she was not going to leave until she had an answer.

Richmond's face clouded momentarily.

"Mr. Brown and my father were great friends," he began after a minute's reflection. "I doubt Brown was his real name, though my father didn't know either. As my father explained it to me after I returned from England, the man he knew as Mr. Brown had come to Virginia fifteen or so years before in 1818 or 1820 or thereabouts. I was just a boy of eight or nine at the time and hardly remember it. Apparently there were mysteries associated with him right from the beginning. All we children were terrified of him. Stories immediately began to circulate about graves and bones and buried people and ghosts. Children will make up anything about someone who is a little different!"

"I've heard those stories too," said Seth, "especially about the caves being haunted."

Richmond nodded with a chuckle. "The caves were always involved in the spookiest of the rumors. How much of his own past Brown divulged at the time he came to Dove's Landing, I don't know, but I later came to be aware that he was a Cherokee who, for reasons my father never completely knew, saw danger approaching for his people and decided to leave North Carolina and relocate farther to the north. So he came here, bought land, built a house, and established himself, then began farming and became friends with his nearest neighbor, who was my father, Grantham Davidson. One curious thing, however—and this will interest you, James," he added, turning to Waters, "—my father had the feeling, when he arrived here for the first time, that Brown had actually come from the North rather than from North Carolina."

Richmond paused reflectively. Waters, too, had grown quiet, turning many things over in his mind.

"It turned out that Mr. Brown was right," Richmond went on after a moment. "Trouble did come to the Cherokee nation. He had possessed as much prophetic foresight about events that would befall his people as we always thought he had regarding the weather. Who knows but that his coming here may have saved his life, though, as it turned out, the trouble eventually followed him here."

"What kind of trouble?" asked Cherity.

"A man by the name of Andrew Jackson," replied Richmond.

"Andrew Jackson . . . the president!"

Richmond nodded.

"What did he do? Everyone calls him a great leader—at least that's what we were taught in school."

"That is the white man's version, as I imagine Mr. Brown would have said," replied Richmond. "But he was the Cherokee's worst enemy. He was elected in 1828, the same year gold was discovered on Cherokee land in North Carolina."

At the word *gold*, Cherity glanced toward Seth with wide eyes, as much as if she were silently saying, *I told you so!* Quickly she returned her gaze back to Seth's father.

"Why did that make Jackson their enemy?" she asked.

"Some say he wanted their gold, others their land, still others say he was simply determined to remove the Cherokee nation from the Eastern Seaboard, gold or no gold, and would have used any means necessary to achieve his purpose. And he was successful in the end."

"That's terrible. How could he do that—it was their land, wasn't it?"

"*All* this land once belonged to various Indian tribes. But the U.S.

government can do anything it wants, even change its mind—especially when a minority people is involved."

"Like Indians and Negroes," said Cherity with annoyance.

"I'm afraid so," nodded Richmond.

"So what happened, Dad?" asked Seth.

"Whites flocked to the region and the first gold rush of the United States was on. They treated the Cherokee land as if it were free for the taking and the government in Washington did nothing to stop the injustices toward the Indians that followed. Andrew Jackson decided that there was no longer room for the Indians in their ancient homelands. It was in 1830, if I recall correctly, when his Indian Removal Act was passed in congress."

"What did it say?" asked Cherity.

"That all Cherokees had to migrate to a reservation in the Oklahoma Territory. Any Cherokees who refused to leave were forcibly taken to Oklahoma by the army of the United States."

"Was that the Trail of Tears?" asked Cherity.

Richmond nodded.

"What does all this have to do with Mr. Brown?" she asked.

"My father thought that Brown probably saw the handwriting on the wall years earlier and suspected what would eventually come to his people. So he relocated here to Virginia before the worst came."

"Maybe he brought gold here so that Andrew Jackson wouldn't get his hands on it!" said Cherity.

"Mr. Brown moved here years before gold was discovered in North Carolina."

"Oh, yes . . . I forgot," said Cherity, obviously disappointed.

All throughout the discussion, James Waters had remained strangely silent. The others were so caught up in the events of the past that none noticed.

"My father did say that Mr. Brown was different after Jackson's election, that he was anxious about the future, even, my father thought, concerned for his own safety. Sometimes he would leave for long periods of time, and some said visitors came to see him, coming and going at night so as not to be seen."

Cherity's eyes were wide at the intrigue of what she was hearing. "And then came a time when he asked my father to his house."

"What happened?" asked Seth.

As Richmond began to recount what he knew of his father's meeting with Brown, his listeners became uncommonly quiet. Within minutes Cherity had crept up the stairs of the porch and was sitting nearly at Richmond's feet. Seth sat beside her on the veranda, legs crossed. Both listened as intently as if they were hearing a ghost story around a campfire at midnight. Carolyn, not hearing anything from the others in a long while and going to investigate, stood in the open doorway, as fascinated as the young people, the dish towel in her hand long forgotten.

"The deed to the land wasn't all Mr. Brown gave my father that night," Richmond went on. "He also gave him another piece of paper."

"What was it?" asked Seth.

"A hand-drawn map—," replied Richmond.

A whispered gasp escaped Cherity's lips.

"A *portion* of a map, I should say," added Richmond. "For my father's first words upon seeing it were, 'But it is torn in pieces.'

"Brown explained that there were two other segments to the sheet that he intended to entrust to others, and that all three had to be placed togther at the same time for the map to reveal its secret."

Again Richmond stopped, seemingly finished with the story.

"But what happened . . . what *happened*!" said Cherity excitedly. "You can't leave it like that, Mr. Davidson. What was it a map to?"

"I don't know," replied Richmond. "Neither did my father."

"Mr. Brown didn't tell him what the map was for?" said Seth.

Richmond shook his head. "And the very next day Mr. Brown disappeared, to all appearances taking his secrets with him."

"But where is the map now, Mr. Davidson?" asked Cherity. "If Mr. Brown gave it to your father, what did he do with it?"

"He said he put it in the safe with the deed, but that it later turned up missing and he never saw it again."

"Oh no!" exclaimed Cherity. "And it's still never been found?"

"I'm afraid not."

"That's terrible!"

"Then a month or so later my brother went out for a ride and didn't come home, and when the next morning his horse was found, still saddled, beside the corral, a search was begun. They found Clifford's body that afternoon at the bottom of a small precipice about a mile from Mr. Brown's house.

"Of course my father and mother were disconsolate," said Richmond. "They notified me, and I returned from England. My father never heard anything of Mr. Brown again. Nor have I. After Brown's disappearance, Denton's father sought to annex the Brown land to Oakbriar. My father was forced to step forward and produce the deed. He registered it and took official title to the land. The Beaumont camp squawked and forced a complex legal proceeding—during which the question was raised by Denton's father that, if my father possessed the deed to the Brown land did not that make him a prime suspect in Brown's disappearance?"

"Like father like son," muttered Carolyn.

"In any event," concluded Richmond, "the transaction between Brown and my father was upheld, though my father continued to consider the land Mr. Brown's, and instructed me to deed it back the moment any of Brown's relatives should appear to claim it."

Fourteen

The runaway man and wife, their four children, and the young man Silas spent three days and nights in safety at the farmhouse where Silas' directions had led them.

They occasionally heard the baying of hounds in the distance from the direction of the river. They suspected that the barge had probably been found and a shoreline search instituted along the riverbank. But no one traced their steps up the small stream by which they had moved inland from the river without leaving a scent, and they seemed safe enough for the present.

On the third day they heard a wagon rumble into the farmyard. Ten minutes later, the barn door opened and the farmer walked inside into the dim light.

"Those second-class tickets you wanted," he said. "They've come through—your train's here."

An hour later the runaways were jostling along a bumpy back road on a bed of straw in the back of a rickety farm wagon, eight or ten bales of hay and straw piled in such a way to create a sort of fort that they hoped was sufficient to conceal them.

Their guide deposited them around dusk in a clearing in the middle of a dense wood through which ran a small stream.

"You'll have to wait here until your conductor comes," he told them. "It may be tomorrow, it may not be for several days. So make these provisions last."

He tossed down a bag of fruit and dried venison.

"You will be safe here. There is plenty of water and we are miles from any farm or plantation."

"How will we know the conductor?"

"No one else ever comes to this place. When he says 'Follow me,' do what he says. You can trust him."

On the afternoon of their third day in the clearing in the wood, suddenly footsteps sounded and a man appeared. The black man rose to meet him.

As the stranger approached, a gasp escaped his wife's lips. He turned and saw an expression of shock and surprise on her face. Before he could utter a word, she ran forward and began speaking in her native tongue. In astonishment he listened as the man, as surprised as the woman had been a moment earlier, replied also in the old tongue of their common heritage. For the next several minutes they spoke feverishly with one another as if they were old friends.

Listening in bewilderment, Silas walked up from behind.

"What all dat talk?" he asked in a low voice. "I ain't neber heard nuthin' da likes er dat!"

"As far as I can tell, Silas," replied the woman's husband, "they are speaking in the old native dialect."

"You mean *Indian* talk! Why dat?"

"Because my wife is an Indian."

"I knowed she looked different, but I neber knowed she wuzn't no nigger like us!"

The woman now turned and walked toward them with a smile.

"He is from my tribe!" she said. "I recognized him from years ago. He didn't remember me . . . I was just a child. But he knew my mother before she died and my father and many of the others from the old days."

"What is he doing here?" asked her husband.

"He is a conductor on the Underground Railroad. He has been helping blacks and Indians ever since the removal displaced most of our people. He was sent to lead us to the next station."

For the rest of the day's journey, well into the night, and halfway through the next day, the woman and their Indian guide talked almost constantly. She learned much about the fate that had befallen her people since her own enslavement.

Wherever her husband had been expecting their curious Indian guide to lead them, he was further surprised to find themselves welcomed into what was obviously a home of substance and refinement, even a degree of wealth, and greeted by a white farmer and his wife who spoke old-fashioned English. He had heard of the Quakers, but this was his first exposure to them. From an *Indian* guide to another *white* safe house . . . why were these people helping escaping *black* slaves! As at war with one another, in a sense, as the three races occasionally were, here they were joining as one in a remarkable display of unity, making common cause together on behalf of freedom.

The Indian conductor, after a parting that brought tears to the woman's eyes, disappeared, leaving them in the care of the white couple. They never saw him again.

In the days and weeks that followed, they marveled time and again at the types of men and homes which linked the Underground Railroad in such powerful but invisible bonds of sacrifice and service. Taken by a full-blooded native to the home of a wealthy white Quaker couple, they were led from there two nights later by a black man still a slave himself who was obviously taking great risks, though of a different kind, by having to return to his own plantation every night and work fourteen or more hours the following day.

"Why are you doing this?" the runaway asked their new conductor as he led them from the Quaker home to their next destination. "Does your master know?"

"He don't know nuthin'," replied the slave.

"Then why don't *you* escape too?"

"I don't got no complaints. I gots a good master—he trusts me. I ain't got a bad life."

"But you help others escape."

"Dey gots it worse'n me."

"Have you taken any of your own master's slaves north?"

"I wudn't do dat to him. We all love our master. But I know dere ain't many dat are kind to dere niggers. So I'll do what I can ter help who I can."

"But your master doesn't know?"

"Nope," said the man shaking his head.

"What would he do if he found out? Would he punish you? Would he make you stop?"

"I don't know. I doubt he'd du dat. He knows slavery ain't a good thing."

"But he keeps you as slaves?"

"He treats us kindly."

The man sent them on their way in the morning, leaving behind more questions than answers.

Two more black men followed, untalkative and from whom they learned nothing. Then appeared a black woman who could not have been more than twenty-eight or thirty, but with daring to make up for her years. She was leading out a man even younger whom they learned was her brother. She had already escaped to the North, but had returned at great danger to herself, all the way to Alabama, and was now leading him out the same way she had come.

They remained with her a week, moving nightly from one station or hiding place to the next with perfect safety. Gradually they learned the codes and passwords and secret signals and signs that passed along the railroad line. Then the woman and her brother were gone. The next night mysteriously appeared yet another to lead them.

Their trek continued. Slowly their steps drew ever nearer that promised land of Pennsylvania . . . north they went, ever north.

A great storm slowed progress to a halt. They were forced to remain in a barn in North Carolina more than two weeks. Other runaways and vagabonds came and went, and others, like them, remained to wait out the weather with the cows.

Silas continued as their constant companion. Questioned, he had no more specific destination than they—north to freedom.

They continued to be astonished at the variety of homes where, at great peril to themselves, they were hidden, fed, and sent on their way—from Quaker homes to poor farmhouses, from white to black, from homes of obvious wealth to the shacks of slave villages, from the basements of churches to the attic lofts of more barns than he could count. Always another came—men, women, old, young, rich, poor, slave, free . . . their only motivation to help the desperate travelers who dreamed of a better life a few miles farther along the route to liberty—*conductors*, as they were called, on this strange human railroad where freedom was the only destination.

Why did they do it? Why did they risk their lives for people they had never seen before and would never see again? What was it within them that inspired such heroism, such deeds of sacrifice to bring freedom to an enslaved people? How arose within them the courage and selflessness to change a country? It was clear that they were part of something wonderful, something huge, something historic.

As much evil as slavery produced, one could not escape the corresponding innate goodness of humanity that hard times and suffering produced. In the midst of terrible injustices and cruelty, brother yet sacrificed for brother.

What did it all mean? What did this enterprise of freedom say about humanity? How could such evil and such good coexist within the human heart?

It was a puzzle the leader of the small band could not entirely resolve. Even within himself he observed the dichotomy of both forces pulling him at once. He was, in a sense, giving—even, perhaps in a certain way, *sacrificing*—for Silas. The poor man was so inept and wool-brained that he probably could not have survived a week on his own. At the same time he was still haunted by the pleading words of the boy he had left behind: *"Take me wiff you."*

Yet he had refused.

What higher meaning existed in it all? And if so many strangers were willing to risk their own lives for him, for Silas, for his family . . . what obligation did that place on *him* toward others in need?

What did the fellow members of a common humanity owe one another? Was the precious thing called freedom to be found by individuals alone, or by the race of humanity as a growing interconnected whole?

Fifteen

The weather throughout Virginia warmed again. As soon as was possible, the wheat harvest at Greenwood resumed, and Cherity, now a full-fledged member of the women's crew, refused to be left out of a single minute of it.

When the work did not beckon or was finished for the day, during every free moment possible, sometimes early, sometimes as dusk was falling, and as the wheat fields gradually became bare and the harvest complete, she and Seth could be seen riding somewhere together—on the ridge, along the river, or on their way up toward the high pasture for a gallop.

Cherity's goal was to ride every one of the Davidson horses before she and her father returned home, and before the harvest was complete she was well on her way to accomplishing that goal. Seth had been concerned in two or three cases, for not all the animals were of gentle temperament. Two or three in particular had taxed all his and Alexander's combined patience and skill even to partially tame. But thus far there was not a creature in their stable that Cherity could not handle.

As Cherity and Seth rode along one hot afternoon after the day's work in the fields had been completed, they heard shouts coming from the direction of the river near the site of an abandoned mill.

"What's that?" said Cherity.

"It sounds like someone's in trouble," said Seth. "Come on!"

Within seconds both riders had accelerated to a full gallop toward the frantic sounds.

Seth emerged onto the riverbank and reined in, prepared to rush straight into the slow-moving current in answer to what he took for drowning cries for help. But an altogether unexpected sight met his eyes as he sprinted to the water's edge.

"Seth!" cried a gleeful voice from the middle of the river. "Look what I've got!"

A look of incredulity followed by a wide smile came over Seth's face. There was his brother, bare-chested and barefooted, trousers soaking wet, wobbling to keep his balance in the middle of the river on a makeshift raft of timbers and logs loosely held together with a few strands of decaying rope.

"Tom . . . what are you—," he began. But a shriek of pure boyish pleasure interrupted him as Thomas lost his balance and careened sideways into the water with a mighty splash.

"What's going on?" said Cherity as she rode up.

"Look—it's Tom!" laughed Seth. "He's got a dilapidated raft of some kind out there."

"Come in, Seth!" shouted Thomas as his head bobbed out of the water. Immediately he made for his craft with a great flurry of arms and legs. "I found an old raft!"

Already Seth was off his mount's back and his boots were on the ground. He tore his shirt off over his head, threw it up the bank, and dashed into the water with a great cry of delight.

Two minutes later he and Thomas were perched, struggling to keep their balance on the twisting, moving logs of the half-waterlogged contraption.

"Look out, Tom," yelled Seth. "The end of that log you're on is sinking!"

"Ow-eee!" shrieked Thomas and again flew into the water.

The motion upset Seth's precarious balance. The next instant he followed on the other side with a howl of ecstacy that ended abruptly with burbling suddenly submerged under the current.

Both rose above the surface like two corks. "What are you waiting for, Cherity!" cried Thomas making for the ship.

Cherity, who had not been seen in a dress since their arrival at Greenwood, did not have to be asked twice. She was already tugging at her boots. Seconds later, blouse and vest and dungarees soaked and threatening to weigh down her slight frame, she was making for the middle of the river with as much confidence in her stroke as she maintained on the back of a horse.

She reached the raft just as the two brothers were climbing aboard after another series of falls.

"Here . . . give me your hand!" said Seth.

He pulled her up, and with three of them now wobbling to maintain their balance, the craft was even more unsteady. It took two or three more tries, each ending with squeals and cries and splashing failures, before they gained a temporary equilibrium—Thomas straddling one log, Seth kneeling on the opposite side on a wide plank, and Cherity lying somewhere in the middle, legs dangling in the water, laughing with delight.

Slowly they recovered their breath.

"Where'd you find it, Tom?" asked Seth.

"Over there—in the mill."

"It's too waterlogged to keep steady."

"I know, but if we got dry wood and logs—there's a bunch of stuff over there. We could make it float high and level."

As Cherity lay wet in the hot sun, gazing straight up into the blue of the sky above and listening to the boys excitedly planning and scheming how to improve their raft-ship—for by now Seth had become a full partner in the vision—she thought she had never been so happy in her whole life. If only such moments might last forever.

On Seth's part, it was not until later that night—as he lay in bed reliving the day's adventure on the river and all the designs he and Thomas had hatched for the raft—that its deeper significance with respect to his own feelings began to dawn on him. It was a startling revelation.

He had never had so much fun with anyone in his life, male or female, as he had had during the past week with Cherity Waters!

Who was this girl, anyway, who loved horses and could ride as fast as he, who could talk about any subject not just dresses and hair and balls and beaux, who was not intimidated by anything, who would jump on the back of any horse whether broken or not, who would rush into the river with her clothes on just as eagerly as any schoolboy, who could laugh and joke and reflect on serious things and be equally natural with all three?

Was Veronica Beaumont even capable of the sheer pleasure of a swim in the river without some hidden girlish scheme in the back of her brain? And even if she claimed to be an atheist—the idea of it still brought a smile to his lips—at least Cherity gave thought to serious things. Had Veronica ever really *thought* deeply about anything?

Actually, there was one thing she thought about, Seth realized. How *deeply* she thought about it he wasn't sure. But she thought about it constantly.

Veronica Beaumont thought about herself.

But Cherity . . . she thought about life and nature and animals and the world and people and right and wrong. She had even thought about God too. Though temporarily she had arrived at some wrong conclusions, at least she was *thinking*. That was the important thing. Her mind was alive and eager to learn and know all it could. Veronica never expressed curiosity about anything.

As gradually Seth drifted from consciousness, with visions of boats and rafts, high seas and raging rivers spinning fancies in his youthful brain, throughout it all hovered the image of Cherity's face. By the time sleep overtook him, she had become the mistress of a mythical vessel of the clouds, an angel in white seated upon her ship's throne, billows of silky sail flapping high above them in the airy breezes of an eternal heavenly twilight, he and Tom her devoted skippers whose duty it was to sail her ship into the night . . . and sail it well.

Richmond Davidson was in his study when Carolyn walked in holding the large thick manila envelope. The look on her face told him he should probably open it sitting down. A glance at the return address told him why: *The Law Office of Harland Davidson, Richmond, Virginia.*

He drew in a breath, uttered a silent prayer, then took his letter opener, slit the fold, and removed the contents.

He looked them over, read a moment, then glanced up at Carolyn.

"Well," he said with a sigh, "it appears Harland and Stuart have changed their strategy to enveigle their way into Greenwood's assets."

"You mean the lawsuit against your mother's will?" said Carolyn. "*Changed* . . . how do you mean?"

"They are suggesting an out-of-court settlement."

A look of annoyance came over Carolyn's face. "I can tell that I am going to hate it already!" she shrugged.

Richmond smiled. "I cannot say I like it either," he said.

"All right—what is Harland's proposal?"

"He and Stuart have agreed to drop all further discussion of contesting mother's will in exchange for a monetary settlement."

"I should have suspected such a thing. For how much?"

"Twenty thousand dollars."

Carolyn gasped in amazement.

"That is for all four of them." Richmond held up four sheets of paper. "These are four promissory notes, executed in favor of Pamela, Margaret, Stuart, and Harland . . . in the amount of five thousand dollars each, at 3 percent interest, payments of seventy-five dollars per month, including interest on unpaid principal balance, to begin to each of them next month, and to continue monthly until paid in full."

"That is three hundred dollars a month!" exclaimed Carolyn. "That is a staggering sum. We will never be able to meet such an obligation."

Now *she* needed to sit down! Carolyn sought the couch opposite her husband's desk and collapsed into it, her face white.

"I almost expected it," sighed her husband at length. "Having heard nothing in three years, I had hoped perhaps they were reconsidering the veracity of Stuart's claim."

"Oh, but it is so wrong and unfair!" exploded Carolyn in a rare burst of antagonism. "I can't help it, Richmond—sometimes I wish you would fight back."

He smiled sadly.

"And sometimes I wish I were given leave to fight back," he said. "But I am an owned man, Carolyn. You are an owned woman. We do not dictate our own course."

Before they could discuss it further, a knock sounded from the door. They glanced toward it. There stood James Waters, newspaper in hand.

"Come in, James," said Richmond. "What's the news?"

"It seems it is your friend making it," replied Waters. "Apparently Senator Everett's health is declining and the party big wigs are using Beaumont as a substitute hard-liner. He just gave a speech in the capital a few days ago that has people talking. He—"

Now first he saw Carolyn, and suddenly realized from the look on Richmond's face that his host and hostess had been engaged in something of a serious nature.

"I apologize!" he said. "I did not know you were here, Carolyn. I did not mean to interrupt."

He turned to go.

"No, please, James," said Richmond, "join us. It is only a matter of something received in today's mail that has temporarily knocked us out of the saddle."

"Bad news?" said Waters, taking a seat in one of the overstuffed chairs.

"Let me just say that it is *difficult* news . . . though not entirely unexpected."

"Anything I might help with?"

"Not unless you happen to have twenty thousand dollars," snorted Carolyn, "which, I might add, contrary to the opinion of a certain attorney who shall remain nameless, we do not!"

"What my wife is so delicately trying to say," clarified Richmond, "is that we find ourselves behind a rather unpleasant and burdensome financial obligation owing to my late mother's will. A cousin has contested it on behalf of himself and his sister, as well as another two cousins, also on my father's side and likewise brother and sister. The four have agreed to settle and drop the suit . . . if I agree to a rather heavy settlement involving these—"

He held up the four documents still in his hand.

"—four promissory notes, one to each of them, for five thousand dollars each."

Waters whistled in astonishment. "No wonder Carolyn is upset," he said. "That is an enormous amount. They must have a strong case in the matter of the will."

"In truth, they have almost no case whatever. I more than half suspect the contestation of the will was but a ruse to see how far we might be prepared to go in effecting a settlement."

"What makes them think they can take advantage of you in this way?"

"Richmond always gives people what they want," said Carolyn, beginning to cool.

"Why not fight it?" asked Waters. "Ignore the notes. Let them pursue their case in court. If, as you say, their grounds for a claim are thin, they will not expend a great deal of expense on a court case before they will give up. If you need legal counsel, I know several attorneys in Boston who are highly respected in their fields and whom I am certain we—"

"Thank you for your offer," said Richmond. "But this is a battle I cannot fight in that way."

"I . . . don't understand—has the matter already gone to court?"

"No, nothing like that. I simply meant that I must fight the matter through in my heart, in prayer not in court."

"You will surely not agree to something like this if there are no compelling legal grounds binding you to the terms of those notes."

"I will have to see."

"But they could drain every dollar of income from this place for the rest of your lives. And what about your sons—it hardly seems fair to them to put the plantation in such financial jeopardy."

"God will see to our affairs, our finances, and our sons. I know there are times when you must not allow people to take advantage. If this proves to be such an occasion, I will fight. I am not afraid of a battle for right and truth, but I want to make sure the battles I fight are the Lord's, not my own. But if God speaks to me to relinquish my own rights in the matter, to trust our affairs and finances to him, to trust Greenwood to him, for it is his land not ours, then I will sign and abide by the terms of these notes."

Waters shook his head in disbelief, as if he were hearing a foreign language. "I simply cannot understand," he said. "What you are saying sounds absurd to my ear. You are a thinking, reasonable, intelligent man. I cannot grasp how you could possibly arrive at such a conclusion."

"I cannot explain it," said Richmond. "Sometimes the walk of faith means appearing the fool, though I doubt that many of God's people really look like fools when they attempt to walk in the integrity of Christlikeness."

"Are you actually saying that you attempt to model your life after the man Jesus Christ?"

"I do not do so very well," replied Richmond, "but yes, that is my attempt."

"And you, Carolyn," said Waters, turning toward the couch. "You go along with him in this?"

"Of course. It is my attempt too. Again, not as successfully as I might like, perhaps, but it is what our lives are all about."

Waters shook his head. "You two live in a different world than I've ever heard of, that's all I can say. Even my late wife did not carry her religion *that* far. In all my years in church, though I have heard hundreds of sermons on every theological point imaginable, I do not ever recall hearing the suggestion that we should pattern our lives in complete fashion after a man who lived 1900 years ago in a completely foreign culture. The thing is entirely unpractical, not to say impossible."

Richmond smiled. "Perhaps you are right," he said. "Completely unpractical."

He rose. "Well, I think I shall leave you two to carry on this discussion without me," said Richmond. "I need to seek consultation with my master." He left the room.

"What did he mean by that?" asked Waters when he was gone.

"It was his way of saying he needed to pray the matter through."

"It sounds like he has already decided?"

"Hearing from God is not an exact science, as they say. It is very subtle and emotive. In our humanity there are always uncertainties. And it has been three years since he went through this, at the time the lawsuit first reared its head."

"But why in heaven's name does he insist on moving ahead with such folly as to buckle to this pressure?"

"It may look like folly to you, James. To me it is a lovely and manly obedience."

"I hardly understand what you mean," rejoined Waters. "*Obedience* is never a word one hears associated with manliness. It sounds like servility."

"Not to one who recognizes the manhood of Jesus as the perfection of manhood," said Carolyn. "There is nothing so lovely in a man as the relinquishment of self-rule. What you are watching in my husband at this moment is the essence of what makes him who he is—a man who seeks not his own. In all that arises in his life, he seeks to lay down his *own* will that he might hear, and then obey, what is *God's* will. His is a hard life because of that commitment. It is the hardest thing a man can do. But then that also makes it the supreme act of which a man is capable. What you are witnessing explains why I love him, as much as I fight it within my own self upon occasion," Carolyn added, remembering her own annoyance of only a few minutes earlier, "and why I have cast my lot with him—because he is God's man."

"It sounds like you have seen this same mental process many times?"

"*Many* times. Though I would prefer to call it a solitary sojourn into the garden than a mental process."

"Your garden outside?"

Carolyn smiled. "No," she said, "a different garden. It is a battle, and not an easy one—the battle all God's men must wage—the battle against the *self* of the human nature. The battles against his manhood, against ambitions that are as strong and human as any man's, are difficult ones to wage. Richmond is a strong and determined man. These things are not easy for him. It truly is a battle. It is the most important battle, though an invisible one, in which humanity may engage."

"You say . . . *may* engage?"

Carolyn nodded. "To join in that invisible battle against self is always a choice," she replied, "not a matter of mere belief or point of view. It is not a matter of belief or creed. It is a matter of choosing to enjoin the garden battle, which is the laying down of self-will. I have seen Richmond in a near passion of frustration, even anger, at times, so desperate and strongly does his 'old man,' as Paul calls it in the New Testament, want to follow a certain course of action. But invariably a moment comes when he closes his eyes, draws in a breath, and becomes quiet. I know he has been to the garden, has once again followed the example of the higher manhood than the manhood of self, and has laid the thing down."

Carolyn paused, then looked seriously into the face of their guest. "Do you recall when I told you that Richmond's quest from the day he walked into my father's church was a quest to understand God?"

Waters nodded.

"What you are observing, right now, in the struggles he is going through, is the reason his quest has been successful and why he has come to a deeper understanding of God. Obedience to what God says to do is the door that opens the eyes of understanding."

"What do you mean, 'what he says to do'?"

"God's ways always follow the same pattern. When we pray for understanding, he will then give us something to *do*. When we obey by doing it, understanding will follow. When we pray to be made strong, he will give us something to lay down. When we pray to be made capable of forgiveness, he will bring someone to hurt us or speak untruths about us. When we pray for joy, he will bring something hard through which we have to discover that joy is not found in pleasurable circumstances but in a region of the heart where the ups and downs of fortune cannot reach. It is the formula for spiritual growth. There is always something to be *done* that brings spirituality to life. Richmond realizes what is at stake in this decision and does not want to make a mistake."

"If you ask me, to sign those papers would be the biggest mistake of his life."

"Not if it is what God wants," said Carolyn.

"How so?"

"In that case, *not* to sign would be an even bigger mistake."

Outside in the arbor, Richmond Davidson was engaged in one last brief skirmish with his old Adam. It did not last long. A few inward heart cries of resistance, a reminder of Christ's prayer in the garden, a sigh that was yet full of pain though he had uttered the prayer so many times before, the whispered 'Not my will' . . . and finally he turned back toward the house. He had no doubt that signing the notes would convince his cousins all the more that he was a fool. But doing so would only lower their opinion of *him*. To refuse would cause them to think of him as a hypocrite, and thereby lower their opinion of his God. And neither to save face, nor to protect his own financial standing, would he allow such a thing to happen.

He found Carolyn and James still in his small upstairs study. He smiled, walked straight to his desk, sat down, and took up his pen.

"They took the liberty to sneak in a clause," he said to his wife, "in the finest of print."

"What kind of clause?" asked Carolyn.

"A clause guaranteeing the notes with the land and the house."

"Surely you will not agree to that?"

"No. I will not place such a burden on Greenwood. We are told to be innocent as doves but also wise as serpents. I will obey, but not to the point of honoring outright deceit. Modeling one's life after Jesus, James," he added to their guest, "does not mean *being* a fool, it merely means not seeking one's own will. Although I do suppose," he added with a slight smile, almost as if speaking to himself, "as I said earlier, it sometimes means being willing to *appear* the fool. In any event, Carolyn, have no worry—I will strike through this clause and initial it before I sign."

"But you will sign?"

"I am afraid so."

"Oh, Richmond—," Carolyn began. Then she remembered her own words to James and paused, closed her eyes briefly, and nodded

Sixty seconds later the deed was done. Richmond rose again and joined his wife where she sat on the couch.

"Well, my dear," he said, taking her hand, "it would appear that another of those crossroads in our lives has come."

She nodded.

In one accord, they closed their eyes. "Our Father," sighed Richmond, "you know our frail hearts. You know our desire to obey you in all things. Yet surely you know how hard it is to hear your voice aright. We pray that we have done so now. Thus we come to you again, laying ourselves, our lives, and our future before you. We place ourselves again in your hands, Father. We know to do so is our only good, our only joy. We give Greenwood to you and ask you to accomplish your perfect will in everything that Greenwood stands for. We give our sons and Cynthia to you, our people, our finances. Accomplish your purpose in all, Lord, and let us not stand in your way by clinging to our own ambitions that do not see as deeply into your will as we might. We thank you that you are a good and loving Father whom we can trust to do your very best for us in all things. May all men and women come to see your goodness in the end."

When his voice grew silent, Richmond and Carolyn sat for several minutes in silence. Such prayers, and the circumstances leading to them, always exacted a toll.

James Waters, meanwhile, sat listening, quietly pondering what he had witnessed. But it brought him no joy. It stirred up too many feelings inside, too many memories . . . and, along with the discussion of Mr. Brown, too much uncertainty about much that he had not anticipated having to think about again.

Sixteen

For several days following Thomas' discovery of the ramshackle raft, he and Seth went to the river almost every moment they could spare. Often Cherity entered into the enthusiasm of their work, sometimes she remained onshore watching, at other times she quietly read a book in the branches of a great oak up the bank to the background music of endless talk and sawing and splashing and hauling and roping and nailing being carried out below her. But nonetheless did her presence preside over the construction of what turned out to be almost an entirely new craft as it had in Seth's airy dream fancy of the cloud vessel of the night.

And a worthy craft it was as it gradually took shape!

It was too heavy to dry-dock, but towing it back upstream they secured it to the decaying pier of the mill beneath which Thomas had discovered it. There they had set to work to make it seaworthy.

They managed, with Cherity's help, to tumble and roll two sizeable logs, each some eight feet in length, into the river. These, being dry and attached to opposite ends, raised the slimy watersoaked logs sufficiently to keep the whole thing floating on the surface. New ropes were brought from home to securely bind the logs of foundation, then great planks added and nailed across them laterally. Besides adding to her buoyancy, already envisioning adventures up and down the river for miles, these would make for a wide deck capable of supporting an entire ship's crew, even keeping them dry if need be during excursions when perhaps the sun was not so warm nor the river quite so inviting as in the midst of high summer.

A great launching was planned for the Saturday after the last of the stalks of wheat had fallen beneath the scythe. Word had already spread among the black children and youths of Greenwood, and Thomas, Seth, along with Isaiah and Aaron Shaw—the former, at eighteen, between Seth and Thomas in age, and the later, at fifteen, two years younger than Thomas—were excitedly planning an inaugural voyage that would take them some two and a half miles downstream, and to a calm pool where they could swim away the afternoon, braving a final stretch of white water before the raft would be loaded by a dozen of Malachi Shaw's men into the back of one of the Davidson wagons, and the wet and weary sailors in the back of another, to return to Greenwood via the land route.

One afternoon, seeing him nowhere about the house and barn, Cherity wandered off in search of Seth. She had a pretty good idea where she would find him.

She crept out of the wood on the bank above the old mill with a quiet step, then sat down to watch, full of many feelings she could not describe. The day before Seth had erected a tall mast beam vertically above the planks of the raft's deck. Upon this mast he intended to fly the flag they had obtained yesterday from Carolyn, an old white sheet torn in half to just the right proportions.

It was this flag, laying flat on the deck as he knelt before it, tin of red paint in one hand and small brush in the other, to which Seth had just added the final *N*. Almost the moment Cherity sat down to watch, Seth rocked back on his knees to inspect his work.

From above, Cherity felt a stab of something undefined pierce her heart as she saw the words of red on the white sheet: *T-H-E C-H-E-R-O-K-E-E M-A-I-D-E-N.*

Seeming to sense her eyes upon him, Seth turned.

"Cherity!" he exclaimed, rising to his feet. "How long have you been there!"

"I only just got here," she replied, struggling to get the words out from the choking in her throat.

"What do you think!" Seth asked with the exuberance of a thirteen-year-old. "How do you like her name?"

"The whole thing is beautiful," said Cherity, almost too pleased to be capable of a reply. "Do you think it will hold everyone!"

"We could pile two dozen on here and it won't sink."

"What is the chair for . . . tied to the base of the mast?" she asked.

"That's for you! I brought it from home . . . my mom said we could use it."

The spirit of excitement in anticipation of the voyage down the river, in the main house at Greenwood as well as the colored village, had mounted to a near frenzy of eagerness. Breakfast was scarcely over before Isaiah and Aaron appeared at the door. The four boys were at the river ten minutes later making final preparations.

Seth's first duty of the day was, its paint now dry, to hoist the white flag up the mast. That accomplished, the four boys—two white, two black—stood a moment at attention, then all saluted solemnly.

What boys can find to occupy themselves at a river, or at the site of an old mill, may be a mystery to mothers and sisters, but to the boys themselves the opportunities for activity and fun are endless indeed. Though the minutes waiting for the hour of launch went by slowly, there was little chance of boredom.

At last, sometime around eleven, the sounds of running, yelling, excited youngsters and teens began to filter toward the river. At last the entire Greenwood family of whites and blacks, owners and former slaves, field hands and house servants and even old Moses, Maribel, Alexander, Carolyn, James, and Cherity in a carriage with Richmond at the reins, began to appear through the trees.

No one wanted to miss this!

Onboard as they came stood the four proud skippers, flag above them beginning to wave a little in the breeze. Some of the children dashed for the raft. Others ran straight out to the end of the pier and into the river with shrieks of delight, then swam to the raft and climbed aboard.

Cherity walked down the pier. Seth turned toward her as she came, then extended his hand. She took it gently, then stepped down onto the deck and took her place in the chair of honor.

Onshore the chaos of a dozen men's and women's voices shouted final instructions to their youngsters, while husbands helped their wives down the bank to the water's edge.

As the excited mass of black boys and girls scampered and climbed aboard, slowly the raft began to feel their weight and pitched slightly.

"Aaron," cried Seth, pointing to the light side, "move some of the smaller ones over there! Isaiah, you get to that corner, I'll take this. . . . Tom, you stand there on the fourth corner."

Gradually they corrected the lopsidedness. The raft settled again level on the water. The babbling and chatter quieted. Soon all eyes rested on Seth.

"Stay seated carefully, you younger children," he said, glancing around at his wide-eyed passengers. "You mind anything Thomas or Isaiah or Aaron or I tell you. And Cherity too, for the raft's named after her in a way, though not exactly after her. We'll float down the river a while, then have a swim and then everyone under twelve will have to get off before the rapids."

"But massa Seff, I kin—" one eleven-year-old began to protest. He was immediately drowned out by a chorus of high-pitched black voices all proclaiming their swimming prowess.

"That is the agreement made by your parents," said Seth above the ruckus. "Anyone who does not agree may go ashore now."

A few groans and moans sounded. But they soon gave way to renewed shouts and cries of childish excitement and pleasure as Seth gave a shove against the shore with his pole.

"Cast off the rope, Tom!" he cried. "Aaron . . . Isaiah—man your poles. Steady now . . . here we go!"

Thomas flung away the rope attached to the pier, and with a few more shoves from the sturdy poles of the four skippers, *The Cherokee*

Maiden slowly drifted out into the water and then began to glide away as the current took them down the river. Hardly able to make himself heard above the din around him, Seth called to his father where he stood with Carolyn and James Waters, all three smiling and laughing at the joy of the great launching.

"Dad, we'll meet you and Malachi at Baker's Hollow to pick up the young ones!" he shouted.

Still laughing, Richmond waved in acknowledgment. Whether it was the sight of seeing white and black young people so happy together and so oblivious to their difference of race and background, or the quiet contentedness of mothers and fathers to see the joy on their own children's faces amid realities of life's toil of which their innocence was not yet aware, gradually a solemn calm settled upon the onlookers spread across the shore and bank. As the shouts and cries receded from across the water, softly now came the rich bass voice of Josaiah Black.

"*De—ee—ee-eep river, Lord,*" he sang, drawing the words out with slow, melancholy pathos. Immediately he was joined by Nancy and the rest of the women, rising high with the crystalline clarity of their soprano tones.

"*My home is over Jordan.*"

Now came in Malachi and the rest of the black men, until men and women together drifted into three, perhaps as many as five different harmonies and variations of the simple well-known black melody.

"*I want to cross over into campground.*"

While *The Cherokee Maiden* drifted from sight, she continued on her way by the multitude of fifteen or twenty black voices spontaneously intermingling with a complexity and richness scarcely achieved by the most renowned cathedral choir, reaching the depths and scaling the heights of what God made the human voice capable.

"*O, don't you want to go to that gospel feast,*
That promised land where all is peace?"

Carolyn Davidson stood listening in awe. She had heard their blacks sing many times, indeed, heard the harmonies of their voices drifting up to the house from their village on most evenings. But never, she thought, had she heard anything that gave such a foretaste of heaven itself. And surely this intermingling of white and black foretold that kingdom where the equality of all humanity in God's sight will be a reality rather than a dream.

"*Deep river, Lord,*
  I want to cross over into campground."

As the strains of the old spiritual died away over the river, calm now in front of them, though in the distance the shouts and chatter accompanying the vessel could be heard, the onlookers remained quiet a moment more, then slowly began to turn away from the river and climb back up the bank.

Only one there was among them whose heart was not filled with the joy of the occasion. Phoebe Shaw, holding the hand of her three-year-old son, realized that she had given up what remained of her childhood in a momentary season of foolishness. She was herself the same age as Seth. But she would never know the joy of youth again.

"Come, Malachi," said Richmond as they crested the embankment. "You and I had best be getting the teams hitched and on our way to Baker's Hollow."

Meanwhile, onboard the craft which thus far had proved seaworthy for its twelve to fifteen passengers, several of the teenage black girls, rather than entering into the raft revels of the younger ones, sat demurely at Cherity's feet. They had already grown in awe of Cherity from watching her in the fields and on horseback with Seth, amazed that any girl could be so skilled, so bold, so outspoken, so brave and confident around boys and men. To have called her a white goddess in their eyes would perhaps be an exaggeration, yet at the same time would not have been altogether off the mark. They sat at her feet as devotedly as if she were their mistress for life. On her part, however, Cherity was not content to sit silently while they stole shy glances at her. She engaged the three in such animated conversation that they were soon laughing and talking along with the rest. By the time they came round the bend and the raft slowed in the favorite swimming site known as Baker's Hollow, Cherity was one of the first off the raft into the water. Amazed at her freedom and abandon, and after no little coaxing, Darya, Kanika, and Recene all followed. Their initial reservation soon gave way to laughter and splashing and diving and jumping along with Cherity and the rest, while the younger boys all swam to the shore, scampered up the bank, and were soon flying into the water with the aid of a great rope swing tied over an overhanging bough of oak.

By the time Richmond and Malachi appeared an hour later with the wagon, though exhaustion had already begun to set in among some, groans and renewed protestations followed. It took the better part of yet another hour before *The Cherokee Maiden* could again be on its way for the second half of its voyage.

Wyatt Beaumont rode toward the river with three or four of his friends. Scully Riggs, who always seemed to turn up and was not so easy to refuse, was tagging along with them.

They were coming to fish, for Baker's Hollow, because the water ran deep in two or three pools where the river slowed, offered not only the best swimming hole for miles, but also the best fishing, and the trout were said to be biting.

The shrieks of laughter that drifted toward them while they were yet a long way off sounded strangely foreign in their ears. Had a troop of black urchins invaded their favorite fishing hole! Unconsciously the small posse increased its pace, some of its number already itching for a fight.

Before the river came into view, however, other voices could be heard among the rest—white voices. It was the sound of black and white laughing and making sport . . . *together*!

Wyatt slowed as the hollow came into view from the trail fifty yards away on the bank above. He took in the scene below with disgust. The others rode up and gathered around him.

"It's the two Davidsons," said Brad McClellan. "What are they doing with all those niggers!"

"Let's run 'em out, Wyatt!" said Scully. "We can run 'em out and teach that nigger-loving Davidson trash a lesson!"

The young Beaumont heir sat silently taking in the scene, running the options through his mind.

"Never mind," he said at length. "They've scared the fish off by now anyway."

"But that don't mean he got the right—"

"Forget it, I said."

"Come on, Wyatt. Why don't we have us a little fun?"

"Shut up, Scully," said Wyatt. "I'll deal with Seth Davidson in my own way. Come on, let's go."

He turned his horse around and led the small group of riders upriver to another hole, thinking to himself of some other means to exact vengeance on the Davidsons for their betrayal of Southern tradition than merely running them out of a swimming hole.

⟨~⟩

When Richmond and Malachi were on their way back to Greenwood with the youngest of the swimmers, *The Cherokee Maiden* continued its course downriver, now with only nine aboard: the two Shaw boys, the two Davidsons, thirteen-year-old Adam Lucas, and Cherity and her three young black maids in waiting, Darya Birch, sixteen, Kanika Black, fourteen, and thirteen-year-old Recene Patton.

Five minutes after leaving Baker's Hollow they began to feel the pull of the current, more swiftly now. Soon they heard the sound of white water ahead. The pulses of all nine quickened—the girls and Adam with fear, the Shaws and Davidsons in anticipation.

They rounded a bend, the raft tilted once or twice, a few screams of thrill escaped the lips of two of the girls, and quickly the raft picked up speed.

"Hang on!" shouted Seth. "Here we go!" Already the rush of water nearly drowned out his voice. "Steady on your poles, men . . . keep us off the rocks!"

Cherity had long since abandoned the chair and now knelt on the deck with the others, crying out in gleeful terror as the raft tipped and rocked and swerved dangerously from one side to the other. Yelling and shouting, the four older boys frantically wielded their poles, but could not prevent the unwieldy craft from crashing into boulders along the river's edge or submerged rocks beneath them. Whatever control they had had in calm water was gone, and they now spun and careened wildly out of control.

A great trough in midriver tipped them precariously upright. Screams sounded from all nine simultaneously. The deck splashed with white spray. Adam lost his grip and slid along the slippery boards. Isaiah grabbed his hand and pulled him back into the center of the deck. The next instant the leading edge of the raft crashed with a mighty thud into a rock rising out of the rapids in the center of the flow. The rear tipped up nearly twenty degrees before the rush of current swept it to the right and around the rock, then fell suddenly again to horizontal. The jerking up and down and sideways motion threw several off their feet and knees. Suddenly Recene slipped off the edge into the churning water.

"Seth!" cried Cherity.

But Seth had seen her and instantly fell to his stomach and reached over the side for her hand. "Grab hold, Recene!" he cried.

In spite of the rush and twisting of the raft, he managed to haul her back on deck. No sooner was she safe than another great *whack!* came from a boulder on the opposite bank. Adam, who had been trying to climb to his feet like the older boys, slipped and toppled into the current. Within seconds he was pulled into the center of the river and out of reach. Seth tossed down his pole, sprang to the near side of the raft, and dove in after him.

Thomas now climbed from his knees and stood with his pole, desperately trying to keep them from colliding with any more obstacles. But rocks and boulders were coming at him so fast and with such fury he could hardly keep them away. Suddenly his pole caught at the base of a huge rock as they sped past. It bent, then snapped like a twig. Losing his balance from the twisting and sudden shattering in his hands, Thomas fell sideways. His head crashed against the wooden deck, and he rolled off into the turbulent flow. It was obvious as his form floated lifelessly away that he had been knocked senseless by the blow.

Aaron and Isaiah glanced at each other, terrified by the sudden loss of their captain and his brother and paralyzed into inaction. Cherity saw their hesitation. The next instant, to the wide-eyed horror of the three black girls, she followed Seth into the river. Abandoned to themselves, the remaining black youths aboard were now more frightened than ever.

Luckily the worst of the rapids were behind them. By the time *The Cherokee Maiden* floated leisurely and none the worse for wear out of the last of the white water and into the first of a series of gentle bends that would take it to the pool at the end of her voyage, Seth and Adam were already sitting onshore catching their breath, and Cherity was lugging Thomas toward them. He had still only begun to come to himself, and it was with great effort that Cherity managed to keep his head above the surface of the water once she finally found her feet under her on solid ground.

"Guide her over here, Isaiah!" called Seth, standing to hail his first mate as he went to help Cherity with Thomas. "We'll take a breather and load everyone back onboard."

By the time Malachi and eight or ten of his strongest men, along with the four teenage boys, had lifted the raft out of the water and hoisted it onto the back of a flatbed wagon an hour later, the adventure had so grown in the imagination of the witnesses, that Seth and Cherity were heroes for saving Thomas', Adam's, and Recene's lives.

But Seth, Thomas, Isaiah, and Aaron paid little attention to the talk. Thoroughly enchanted with the success of the first, they were already planning their next adventure!

Later in the day Thomas found Cherity alone at the railing of the corral.

He walked up with a sheepish look on his face. "Uh . . . thanks, Cherity," he said. "I guess you saved my life."

"I don't think it was all that heroic!" laughed Cherity. "I'm sure the cold water would have brought you around sooner or later."

"Yeah . . . but what if it had been *later* and I'd have found myself standing at the gates trying to talk somebody into letting me in."

"What . . . you mean into heaven?"

"Yeah."

"You believe in heaven?"

"Sure, I guess. Doesn't everyone?"

"Not me. I'm an atheist."

"Really—I didn't think anyone was really an atheist. You mean you don't believe in God? How come?"

"I don't know . . . I suppose because when I went to church what I heard didn't make sense."

"Hmm. . . . Maybe I could agree with that. But . . . I don't know. I don't suppose I like all my dad's talk about God all the time, but that doesn't mean that God doesn't exist out there somewhere. I just don't like thinking he's got his eye on me all the time. My dad thinks he can't do anything without talking to God about it."

"I think your dad's great," said Cherity. "I just don't believe in God, that's all."

"You wouldn't think he was so great if he'd been preaching at you all your life," said Thomas, a little cynicism creeping into his tone.

Cherity glanced toward Thomas in surprise. Thomas almost sounded angry toward his father, something she had never detected from either him or Seth before. But she let it pass.

"Maybe . . . I don't know," she said. "My father never talks about God."

"Then you are lucky. That's all my dad ever talks about. I get sick of it. Everyone around here thinks our family is strange."

Seventeen

*E*arly one afternoon after Seth, Richmond, and Thomas had completed a job in the barn and the black workers were just finishing the last threshing of the wheat, Seth walked out and saw Cherity in her boots, trousers, and hat sitting on the top fence rail of the horse pasture adjacent to the stables.

Seth walked up behind her as if there was nowhere else in all the world she would rather be. He leaned against the fence. Cherity glanced down at him with a smile.

"You look at peace with the world," said Seth, "like you would be happy to sit here with the horses forever."

"Maybe I would be," sighed Cherity. "For all these years, I have dreamed of going to Kansas again. And yet now . . . "

Her voice trailed away.

"I thought you wanted to be a cowgirl out in the Wild West," said Seth.

"I did. But I don't suppose it was really *cows* that held such a great attraction for me, but horses. So what do I need to go to Kansas for—there are all the horses one could ever hope for right here!"

Seth continued to lean against the fence rails and Cherity sat for a minute in silence.

"So . . . you've ridden most of these," said Seth at length. "Which is your favorite mount?"

"For what purpose?" said Cherity. "They're all so different."

"All right, then . . . let's say for a cross-country race of, say, four or five miles?"

Cherity pondered the question a few seconds as she gazed intently into the pasture. "I think I would have to say Midnight."

"That would be my choice too," rejoined Seth. "Although I would put the Grey Laird as almost her equal."

"In a sprint, perhaps," said Cherity. "But over four miles, the Grey Laird would tire and Midnight would have more staying power."

"Would you like to put your money where your mouth is?" asked Seth.

Eyes alighting at the sound of it, though she had no idea what he meant, Cherity glanced over at him.

"What do you mean!" she said excitedly.

"Not only do you know the horses, you know the hills and trails around Greenwood pretty well by now too, wouldn't you say?"

"I think so, though not so well as you."

"We shall see," said Seth, looking up where she sat with a grin. "Here is my proposition: Let us each saddle a horse of our choice, and let us see who can reach Harper's Peak first—by different routes."

Cherity's face beamed in delight.

"You're on!" she said, turning around, bounding off the fence, and sprinting for the barn.

"Wait!" said Seth, dashing after her. "We have to start together!"

Cherity did not slow until she was inside. She ran straight for the saddle rack and removed the saddle that had come to be hers during her visit. It was old and almost black from years of use, fraying in a few spots but the most comfortable saddle she had ever used. In the meantime Seth called for Midnight and the Grey Laird and walked into the pasture to meet them as they came.

Ten minutes later, both horses saddled, they were ready.

"All right, we need some rules for this race," said Seth. "I know the terrain better—"

"But I have the best horse for the distance!" interjected Cherity with a grin.

"That, young lady, you shall have to prove! As yet I concede noth-ing!"

Cherity giggled with anticipation.

"But neither of us will take the direct trail straight up to the pasture and to the peak from there. That would be too easy. We will each have to find a different route. I will ride east, you will ride west from here. Then we will each find our own fastest way to the peak."

"When do we leave?"

"As soon as you're ready."

"Then I shall wait for you at the peak!" cried Cherity. She wheeled Midnight's head around to the west, dug her heels into her side, and with a great cry of "Go . . . go!" galloped away, leaving Seth standing at the Grey Laird's side, still tightening the cinches.

"I will get you for that" he yelled. Ten seconds later he was in the saddle and galloping in the opposite direction.

Seth knew that Cherity's assessment of the two horses' relative strengths was exactly on the mark. She was not just skilled in the saddle, but she possessed a keen knowledge of the equine temperament as well. She had chosen her mount well. He knew that if he pushed the Laird too hard too early, he would indeed tire long before they reached the peak. This was a race of strategy not mere speed.

Seth therefore did not urge the Grey Laird to a full gallop just yet. He would conserve his stamina as much as possible for a final sprint at the top of the ridge.

His way took him through a dense thicket of fir and pine. He did not have a well-marked trail to follow but this route would bring him out at the eastern end of the high pasture. From there his way would be rocky and steep and possibly shorter than Cherity's. If she chose her route well, however, she should reach the pasture first. In the direction she had taken a well-marked trail led from the western side of the pasture up to the high meadow. They had only been on it once together, and he wasn't sure whether she remembered. If she did, he would have a difficult time overtaking her.

Once they both emerged into the clearing of the high meadow, he would know how well she had chosen her route and how well she had ridden over the challenging terrain.

Cantering at about three-quarter pace, Seth reached the end of the low road and leaned the Laird's head toward the wood. The slope grew steep and soon he was fighting his way through the close-growing wood. He could not hope to gallop here but just keep the Laird going at a good gait until the trees thinned.

A mile farther on the trees grew less dense. Gently Seth now picked up the Laird's pace. Half mile more and he emerged onto the east-west path running halfway up the ridge. He wheeled the Grey Laird onto it and gave him rein. Still well within himself, Grey Laird broke into a gallop. A quarter mile farther on and the west extremity of the high pasture came into Seth's view ahead.

If he could just reach it and bear right across the grass to the slope before—

Suddenly in the distance a rider broke into view, its majestic black flying across the meadow with gigantic strides. Even from this distance he could see great clumps of sod flying up behind the powerful hooves.

"No!" Seth cried. "How could she—"

There was no use wondering now. Cherity was much farther ahead of him than he had imagined possible!

With his cry Seth saw her head turn toward him. On the wind he heard a laugh of mingled terror and delight to see her opponent across the way. She could have no way of knowing how they stood relative to one another. But Seth knew, unless the Laird was capable of a great sprint when he reached the high plateau, that she already had the race won.

Both sprinted across their respective ends of the meadow, then began the final ascent, according to the rules of the game, neither making use of the more direct trail that stood halfway between them. Cherity reached the slope a good minute ahead of him and disappeared into the trees.

Ten minutes of hard riding followed for both, having not merely to cover the rugged terrain but to pick the best footing while working their way toward the summit.

Both reached the plateau at about the same time. A little over a mile separated them, but Harper's Peak rose above the plateau closer to Cherity's position than Seth's. She slowed, glanced hurriedly to the right and left to make sure of her bearings, then kicked at Midnight's sides. With yells and exhortations to summon all the speed she had left, she galloped east toward the peak. At about the same time, as Seth emerged onto the plateau, he did not slow for he was aware of his danger and knew the way well enough. He wheeled the Laird westward with a great shout.

A minute or two later they each came into the other's vision, sprinting straight for one another at full gallop. By now the Grey Laird, the swifter of the two, was moving at enormous speed. But Cherity reached the slope of Harper's Peak first, turned toward it, casting a glance toward Seth about two hundred yards behind her, and made for the summit.

"Now, Laird . . . give it all you've got!" yelled Seth. But he could tell that the Laird was tiring. The gap closed to a hundred and fifty yards, then a hundred. Every five seconds he saw Cherity's auburn head turn back with a wild expression of unbounded pleasure and terror. But there was not enough ground left. Seth had closed to about seventy-five yards when he saw Cherity rein in ahead of him. He slowed, gave up the chase, and cantered in to join her at the peak.

Cherity was laughing with such abandon as he reached her that she could hardly stop. Seth laughed too, for who cannot share in a companion's joy.

The sides of both horses surged in and out as they gasped for air. Breathing heavily himself, Seth leaned over the thin mane of his valiant steed for a moment to gain his breath, then dismounted. Recovering her own wind, Cherity fell to the ground, still laughing.

"I have never had so much fun in my life!" she said. "Both times I saw you, it sent such a charge of fear through me . . . like one of those dreams you have as a child when you are being chased! And then when we were riding straight toward each other back there, it was so wonderfully terrifying! I was sure you would catch me!"

"I had no chance!" laughed Seth. "When I saw you so far ahead of me in the meadow, I knew I would never catch you."

"You almost did!"

"The Grey Laird had enough left for a final sprint, but not quite enough to overtake you. He ran out of energy up the final hill."

Seth walked to where Cherity lay and offered his hand.

"You indeed chose your steed well, my lady," he said affecting the voice of a medieval knight. "I congratulate you on a victory nobly won. I shall think of some suitable prize to bestow for your triumph."

She half sat and reached up. Their hands met. She nodded in receipt of his acknowledgment of her victory and shook his hand. Seth pulled her to her feet. Gradually their hands relaxed and they pulled apart. Still breathing heavily, they walked silently away from the horses, down upon the landscape below.

"You're right," said Seth at length. "That was just about one of the grandest rides I've ever had. No one around here can keep up with me. I don't say that boastfully, only that it's hard to find a challenging race. Not that I always want to be racing, but it's fun every once in a while."

"We'll have to do it again, taking different routes and different horses!" said Cherity.

"I don't know if I am a match for you!" laughed Seth.

As he glanced around, Seth spotted something. He ran a little way off, stooped down to the ground, then ran back and handed it to her.

"What is it?" she asked as she took it.

"It's called a Virginia bluebell. It will be your trophy—a memento of our ride."

Cherity took it with a gentle smile but said nothing.

⌣

Not only were both horses and riders fatigued, neither Seth nor Cherity was anxious for the ride to end. As they mounted, they therefore began their way back down from the peak slowly. Gradually their conversation drifted into more serious channels.

"Do you think it very bad of me not to believe in God?" Cherity asked as they went.

The question first struck Seth as humorous and a smile broke out on his face. Then he realized that Cherity was in earnest. He thought a moment.

"That all depends on the kind of God you say you don't believe in," he replied after a few seconds. "Or perhaps I should say the kind of God you think other people believe in."

"I mean the Christian God, then," added Cherity, "the God people talk about from the Bible."

"There are so many versions of the Christian God as to make some unrecognizable from others."

Cherity glanced over at him. "Is that really true?" she asked.

"It's something my mom says all the time," answered Seth. "And the more I have thought about it, the more I agree with her. Some of the images people have of God are so far from the reality of his true nature that it is better *not* to believe in them."

"It seems that must make belief a hard thing to find," said Cherity in an almost hopeless tone.

"I suppose that's true. In such a case, atheism is better than belief since the so-called belief is founded on a false idea of God in the first place. So to answer your question . . . no, I don't think it bad of you to say you don't believe. If the God in your imagination is not the true God, the best thing possible is *not* to believe in it."

"But you believe in God?"

"Of course. And so will you, I would say, when you come to see him as he really is. But why do you say you don't believe in him?"

Cherity told him about her conversation with her mother's three friends.

"Why did you go to that church?" asked Seth.

"I suppose I wanted to know more about my mother's faith."

"And because of those three women, you decided you were an atheist?"

"I guess."

"That doesn't seem very logical."

"Why not?"

"I mean, if you were trying to find truth, it must be higher than that."

"*Higher*," repeated Cherity. "In what way?"

"I mean that truth, if it can be found, must be loftier than what can be destroyed by a reaction to certain people who believe a certain way. Especially would that be true if the God they were presenting to you didn't represent God as he really is. It might be right to reject their image. Yet that might not in itself make you an atheist. It only means you haven't yet discovered God's *true* nature. I hope you won't misjudge truth because of *my* inconsistencies, any more than those of the three ladies. That's what I mean by higher—that truth has got to be higher than you and me, or anyone. We're only human and will all be inconsistent in how we live to some degree."

"Maybe you're right. It seems like that's what your brother might be doing. Still . . . what if I don't care anymore?"

"Fair enough," nodded Seth. "Then I'll turn the question back on you—what if you *ought* to care?"

"I hadn't thought of that before," said Cherity thoughtfully. "Do you think that's true, that I ought to?"

"Everyone ought to care what is true and what isn't."

"So what do you think I should do?" asked Cherity.

"It seems to me that you shouldn't give up so easily."

"What do you mean?"

"Try again. Try another church. Ask more questions. Talk to your father, talk to my parents . . . just don't base everything on the responses of those three women. You may one day discover that much of what they told you actually *is* true, but that the way they said it obscured that truth. You may find that God himself is true, while their representation of him is not."

"That is an interesting idea. I hadn't thought of that either—that maybe there was more truth in what they said than I was able to see because of the *way* they said it. I suppose it's sort of like those books

I read about the Wild West. Sometimes they make the Indians look like savages. But that can't be true about them all. You said your Mr. Brown wasn't like that at all."

"That's exactly it. I can't really say much about your discussion with those women because I didn't hear what they told you, but it might be something for you to consider. What I'd suggest more than going to another church is go to God himself and ask him your questions. Say, "God, there are some things I don't understand that I'd like to know about.'"

"It sounds funny to hear you say it like that!" laughed Cherity. Quickly she grew serious again. "But what if I still don't believe in him?" she asked.

"You can say the same thing. You can say, 'God, if you exist, show yourself to me somehow.' If you're sincere, I think he will."

"You think he actually does that?"

"Sure . . . if a person's sincere, and if a person looks for answers in the right way. I don't mean like asking God to show himself by some miracle or with a bolt of thunder or making you able to walk across water or something silly. God doesn't work that way. But I think he does always answer sincere and honest questions, though his voice might be very quiet when he does."

"How does he show himself?" asked Cherity. "What do you mean by saying that his voice is quiet?"

Seth thought a moment. "I don't know . . . that's a hard question," he said at length. "I suppose there can be a million ways—by things we feel inside, by the world around us . . . maybe like that little flower I gave you. Maybe he prompts us to ask, 'Who made you, little flower—and why do you bring joy to my heart?'"

"Just because we happen to like flowers doesn't mean there's a God."

"What if it *does* mean that? What if it is just that simple? I think that it is those kinds of questions that open up the human heart to be able to hear God's voice."

"You think flowers prove God's existence?"

"Not prove it. Nothing will ever *prove* God. Belief and proof are completely different things. We believe many things we can't prove. There may be a thousand signs all around us pointing to *belief* in God, yet not a single *proof* of his existence among them."

"How can you believe in something you cannot be sure about?"

"I didn't say we can't be sure, only that God can't be proven. But to answer your question, we must each discover belief in our own way."

"How did you discover it?"

"I was taught belief in God by my parents, of course. But then later I had to try to make sense of it for myself. I started thinking about some of these things we have been talking about . . . actually from horses not flowers. I guess I compare my belief in God with a horse's belief in me. One day the question dawned on me—Why are horses so regal, and why does it make me happy to watch them and be with them? I couldn't think of anything but that God must have established a connection in my heart with the rest of creation. Where else could it have come from? It isn't that I *heard* God telling me all that. God speaks quietly, even solemnly, like I said, through the things that are all around us."

"Like horses and flowers?"

"Yes. And we have to learn to see what they mean. Somehow the magnificence of the horse changed how I thought about God. Maybe it's not so much that God spoke to me but that I began to listen . . . and hear what he wanted horses and flowers to tell me about him. I felt God was speaking to me about the kind of God he is from my observation of horses, and what I felt inside when I was with them. At least that's how the process began, and I continued to think about many things. That's when I began to read the Gospels too, for myself . . . because I really wanted to know what they had to say to *me*."

"Will you answer me a question?" said Cherity.

"Sure."

"Do you think God—I mean . . . if there is a God—do you think he is angry with me for talking the way I do, and for saying I don't believe in him."

"Of course not."

"Aren't you worried about my salvation?"

"Not at all!" laughed Seth.

"Or that I might be on my way to hell?"

Again Seth laughed. "Not in the least. I would never think that."

"Those ladies were concerned about my soul."

"Well I'm not. I think God and you may be on closer terms than you realize."

"Why would you say that?"

"Because of the questions you ask?"

"What do they have to do with it?"

"They show that you *want* to know God in a true way. You may not yet be sure about him, and yet all the time, even in your unsureness, you may be drawing closer to him than you know. Your *brain* may not know him yet, but I have the feeling that your *heart* may actually have begun to know him. Besides, I don't believe in atheism."

Now it was Cherity's turn to laugh. "What do you mean by that?"

"No one is *really* an atheist," replied Seth.

"But I told you . . . I am."

"Do you mind if I ask you a question, then?" he said.

"Go ahead."

"If a mountain lion jumped out and attacked us right now—or even a huge African lion, though there aren't any here, but you know what I mean—and killed me and knocked you off your horse and then sprang at you . . . what would you do?"

"I don't know . . . try to get away."

"But if you couldn't get away and you knew you were about to die, you would yell, 'God, please help me!' just like anyone else."

"Maybe I wouldn't."

"But maybe you would."

"And if I did . . . so what would that mean? I wouldn't really mean it. It would just be a reaction to the danger. Everyone says things like that."

"You're right. Everyone calls out to God in times of trouble because down in their deepest hearts they know God is there and that he is the only one who can help them. People may *say* in their minds that they don't believe, but in their hearts they cannot help but know God exists."

Seth's argument was as profound as it was simple. For the moment Cherity had no answer to give it.

"Well, maybe you're right," she said at length. "But right now, I don't care. There are no mountain lions jumping out at us. But I will think about what you say. Maybe you are right: that it is my image of God that has been wrong . . . that it is not a question of atheism and belief, but more of what comes to my mind and what I mean by the word *God*. That is a new idea to me. So I will think about it."

By the time they reached Greenwood an hour later, both horses were spent. They took off their saddles and blankets, gave their regal mounts a thorough rubbing down, talking and chatting and laughing, the exuberance of their ride returning, then returned the horses to pasture with the bin next to the water tub filled with a fresh supply of oats.

"I'm going to check and see if there's anything my dad needs me to do," said Seth.

"I guess I'll go back inside," rejoined Cherity. "I'm tired!" She looked at Seth and smiled. "Thank you for the ride," she said. "That was really fun."

"Hey, you won the race! It's me who ought to thank you for letting me tag along!"

Eighteen

Cherity found Carolyn alone in the sitting room. She walked in, flush and exuberant in spite of what she had said about being tired.

Carolyn glanced up as she walked in. "You look radiant!" she said. "Where have you been?"

Cherity tossed her hat on the couch and sat down. "Seth and I had the most wonderful ride," she answered. "He challenged me to a race up to Harper's Peak!"

"That is a long way! Who won?"

"I did!" laughed Cherity. "Will you be honest with me, Carolyn?"

"Of course."

"Is Seth the kind of boy who would *let* me win? I don't think I could stand it if he did."

Carolyn laughed. "So you are as competitive as he in the saddle!"

"I just want to know if it was a fair race. Although he did give me my choice of mounts."

"Let me say this about my dear son," said Carolyn. "He loves for things to be *fair*. If I know him, he might have given you a slight advantage of some kind, I cannot say what, simply to add to the challenge to himself and make sure *he* received no advantage. Once that was done and he was convinced it was a fair race, he would fight tooth and nail to beat you. If you got there first, I am quite certain you earned it."

"Good. I do think he sent me a slightly shorter way, though I cannot be certain. Still, I am satisfied. Next time I shall send *him* the shortest way . . . and I shall win again!"

"Good girl! Would you like some tea, Cherity, dear? I am in the mood for tea and a nice long visit."

"Yes—that sounds wonderful . . . thank you."

The two went into the kitchen together to put the water on to boil, then sat down at the table.

As Cherity and Carolyn were seated comfortably waiting for their tea, Seth walked across the entryway from the barn toward the front door of the house. About halfway across it, he heard a clatter behind him. He stopped and turned. A buggy was coming up the drive.

Seth's heart went to his throat.

Veronica!

He stood frozen in his tracks. His first impulse was to flee. But that would be stupid. If she hadn't already seen him, she would before he could hide. If he ran, she would go straight to the house looking for him!

That was the one place she mustn't go!

He could just see it—his mother, the perfect hostess: *Come in, Veronica dear . . . have some nice tea with Cherity and me.*

Introductions would follow . . . questions . . . explanations. . . .

Seth spun around and ran to greet the approaching carriage.

"It is so peaceful here," sighed Cherity contentedly. Gradually the fatigue and exhilaration of the ride gave way to a dreamy happiness.

"I am glad," said Carolyn. "I hope your father is finding it so too, and is regaining his strength."

"I think he is," said Cherity, "though he does seem tired. Sometimes I worry for him."

"God will take care of him."

Cherity thought a moment about the words. No argument to counter them came to her lips because she knew how genuinely spoken they had been. She had learned to love Carolyn and knew that Carolyn loved her. Such was the most vital of all preparations for the receipt of the seed. Without love it is very difficult for germination of the word of truth to take place. A seed unfitly planted, as a word unfitly spoken, before love has ploughed and watered and made the soil soft, will wither and die and leave both unwise sower and unready hearer worse than before. Many who forcibly sow seeds of multitudinous words into unploughed ground that love has not softened accomplish far less for the kingdom of heaven than they imagine.

But Carolyn had loved. The soil was ready. Cherity's heart was fertile and had only been awaiting the occasion for it to be upturned and exposed to the light. After her time in this idyllic place, and her recent talks with Thomas and Seth, that upturning was well under way. New rays of light were shining in upon her from many directions.

"Veronica!" exclaimed Seth, running across the gravel entryway to intercept the carriage as it emerged from the shadow of the oaks. "How are you?" he added, taking hold of one of the reins and gently easing the horse to a stop. "What brings you here on such a fine day?"

Not pausing to inquire why Seth was so friendly all of a sudden, Veronica temporarily swallowed her intention for this visit. She had planned to be firm and tell Seth that she expected him to start calling more regularly at Oakbriar.

"Why to see you, what else?" she replied. A slight hint of snippiness intruded into her tone. "And to see if you wanted to go for a ride."

"Great!" said Seth, jumping up beside her and grabbing the reins. "Let's go."

He gave the horse a gentle whack, turned him around, and they flew back down the drive a little faster than Veronica was used to. As they entered the safety and cover of the giant oaks and beeches, Seth cast a quick nervous look back at the house.

"What are you looking at?" asked Veronica.

"Oh, nothing," laughed Seth uneasily.

"Then when are you going to notice my new dress?"

"Oh . . . oh, yeah—it's nice, Veronica."

"*Nice*—it cost over twenty dollars."

"Is that a lot for a dress?"

"Seth! It's a fortune!"

"Then why did you spend so much on a dress?"

"Because I have to look my best. What will people think if they see me wearing just an ordinary old dress?"

Seth secretly wondered what Veronica would look like in worn trousers and a cowboy hat.

"Do you really think God will take care of my father?" said Cherity. "He doesn't go to church. I don't even know if he believes in God anymore."

"God is still his Father," smiled Carolyn.

"Even if he isn't a Christian, or at least, doesn't believe like people say he should?"

"What people?"

"You know, church people who think you have to believe like they do."

Again Carolyn smiled. "Yes, I know the kind of people you mean," she said. "I am sorry to say that I used to be one of them when I was a young woman."

"You were!" said Cherity in disbelief.

"Christians have just as much to learn about God as do unbelievers," nodded Carolyn. "It is a difficult lesson, and one that many never do learn. It is something I believe saddens God terribly, for his own children to know him so little."

"That is like something Seth said when we were out riding."

"What did he say?"

"That we have to know what kind of God we say we believe in . . .

or *don't* believe in. He said that a lot of people don't really know what God is like at all . . . or something like that."

"I would completely agree. I used to say I believed, but now I realize how little I really knew who God was. *God* was the same—he is who he is. But I had never stopped to consider the implications of some of the things I said I believed about him. Many of those things I now see were false."

"You're not at all like that now."

"I thank God that he brought the pain into my life that forced me to learn who he really is. But to answer your first question—yes, of course God is your dear father's Father. Who else created him? God has created us all, and is our wonderful Father."

"Do you mean he is *everyone's* Father?" said Cherity. "Everyone's in the whole world?"

"Of course. Who else could be their Father? God is the creator of all the universe and everything in it. That makes him the Father of everyone and everything. When we speak of knowing who God really is, that is what we mean—who he really is, is our loving *Father*."

⌒

"As I started out an hour ago, before I stopped off in town for a while," said Veronica, "I thought I saw you riding up on the ridge."

"Oh . . . yeah, I guess you might have," replied Seth.

"Well, were you up there riding an hour ago or not?"

"Yeah."

"I thought I saw two riders. Were you with someone?"

"Uh . . . yeah. We went riding up there."

"Who were you with?"

"Oh, nobody . . . just some, uh . . . friend of my dad's."

"It looked like he was wearing a cowboy hat. Where is this friend of your father's from anyway," she laughed. "Texas! Ugh—the thought of the West gives me the shivers. I can't imagine anyplace so horrible!"

"It makes my heart so glad to hear you speak of God like that," said Cherity in reply to Carolyn's last statement. "If he exists, I mean . . . you make him sound so good! That is the kind of God one *could* believe in—and be glad about."

Carolyn laughed. "He *is* good, Cherity," she said. "He is so good and so loving and so generous and so forgiving and so patient that we cannot even think of words to describe how wonderful he is."

Cherity sat for a moment with a smile on her face, as if it were simply too good to drink in, yet as if she wanted to drink it all in . . . and more. Gradually, however, her face began to fall.

"But what about people like my father . . . or me," she said at length, "who say they don't believe in God, or at least don't believe in him in the same way—is God just as loving and kind, and all those other things, to them as he is to church people?"

"Does he love them just as much, do you mean?"

Cherity nodded.

"Of course he loves them just as much. He loves everyone as much as it is possible to love. But there are some people whom he can't get his love *inside* of."

"Why not?"

"They won't let him."

"But why?"

"They don't want it. He loves them, but they won't let that love in. Even though there is love in God's heart, it never gets inside the hearts of many men and women because they won't let it."

Carolyn rose to pour out two cups of tea.

"That seems a strange thing," said Cherity as she followed.

"It does, but many people don't know that God's goodness is waiting for them. The false images they have of God prevent it. Others don't let God's goodness in because they don't want it."

"Why would anyone not want it?"

"Because most people don't know how good God is. They have been told many things about him that sound unappealing."

"Again, it's kind of like what Seth said."

Carolyn nodded.

"But if they knew he is good," Cherity went on, "I mean *really* good, like you say . . . they would want it then, wouldn't they?"

"Not everyone, I'm afraid."

"I can't see why not."

"Because there is reciprocation involved. Love always flows two directions. When you let God's love inside, it changes you. Maybe there is a requirement involved too. Some people are afraid of that. They don't want to be changed. They especially don't want anything to be required or expected of them."

"So God feels the same way toward them, but everyone doesn't feel the same way toward him."

"That is something like it."

Cherity grew thoughtful for a minute.

"Something is bothering you?" smiled Carolyn.

"No . . . not bothering me," replied Cherity slowly. "I was just thinking about what you and Seth say about the importance of knowing God the right way, knowing who he really is instead of having some false image of him. How *are* we to know him as he really is? It seems impossible since we can't actually see him."

"That's why Jesus came—to show us and teach us what God is like. We can trust what he tells us because Jesus is God himself—God in human form."

"That is so hard to understand!"

"It is, I know . . . but it explains how Jesus was able to conquer death. And what Jesus told us is that God is a good and loving and forgiving Father."

⌒

"My mother and I have been looking at the calendar," Veronica said as she and Seth rode along. "We think a December wedding would be wonderful, with a grand Christmas ball to coincide with it. We have settled on December 11 as the date. So put it on your calendar, Seth, dear—you mustn't be late!"

Seth swallowed hard. He hadn't realized things had already progressed *this* far! He stared straight ahead at the horse's ears in a daze.

"And mother and I have already been shopping for material for the dresses," Veronica went on. "You must come by to see. It will be the most dazzling wedding in the whole county for the last ten years! I want it to be the wedding no one will stop talking about."

Seth struggled to bring his brain back to the present. He had to get out of here. He had to think of some excuse to bid Veronica a very pleasant good afternoon, while he went on his way . . . in the opposite direction!

As they took their cups, Carolyn sipped at her tea.

"I've noticed you sitting out on the rail gazing into the pasture," she said after a moment. "You love horses, don't you?"

"Oh, yes!"

"You love *all* horses?"

"Yes."

"But some of them won't come near you, will they? They don't know how much you love them."

"Oh, I know! If only they realized how full my heart is with love for them, and that I'm not mean but would be nice to them, I'm sure they would—"

Suddenly she stopped. A light dawned on her face.

"That's like God, isn't it?" she said.

Carolyn nodded. "What you described in your heart toward the horses is a tiny picture of what God feels toward mankind, and toward every man and woman and child in the world. God aches with love in his heart—oh, so much love!—and he wants to give that love to everyone even more than you want to be able to love those horses. But people are like horses—some of them won't come. Do you know the horse Moonbeam?"

"She is a proud one! Seth's told me how he and Alexander and

Mr. Davidson have been trying for months to break her, but she won't let them."

"Yet there are other horses who seem happy and content to be broken."

"They're happier and more content after they're broken too."

"Seth is a marvel with horses," nodded Carolyn. "Sometimes I am amazed at the way he has with them. They actually seem to understand when he speaks to them."

"I know!" exclaimed Cherity excitedly. "Seth is so—"

She stopped herself, her cheeks reddening.

"They know his voice, don't they? just like they do Alexander's" said Carolyn. "When either of them call, they come. They come because they want to. They have learned to love their masters just as Seth and Alexander love them. They have learned to return their love. They know they will always be good to them. They have learned to trust them and therefore they come when they call. But Moonbeam doesn't know it, so she *doesn't* come when they call. But it's only because she doesn't know Seth and Alexander like the other horses do.

"That's why a week or two ago they put her in with the riding horses, in hopes that by being around the others, she will see the love that flows between them. They hope in time that Moonbeam will also begin to recognize Seth's or Alexander's call as the voice of goodness and love."

It was silent a long while.

"Here, Veronica, take the reins a minute," said Seth. "I think I've got something in my boot." He handed her the reins and took off his boot. Gradually the buggy began to slow. By the time Seth had removed the offending twig, they had come to a complete stop.

"Get going, you!" cried Veronica. She yanked and whacked at the reins, but the horse had taken it into its head to stand right where he was and admire the scenery.

"You stupid horse!" yelled Veronica. "Move—get going!"

Seth was just pulling on his boot when suddenly Veronica grabbed the whip from its stand beside her and lashed violently four or five times at the horse's back. With the first stinging blow, the horse lurched forward at a run as she whipped its back.

"Veronica!" yelled Seth, grabbing both whip and reins from her hands in a single motion.

Her eyes flashed fire as he gently eased back on the reins until the horse was calm and had come again to a stop. Seth jumped down, ran forward, and began to stroke the horse's head.

"That was totally unnecessary," he said. Obvious anger sounded in his tone to meet the flames in her eyes. "There are reasons why horses behave the way they do."

But Veronica was no longer thinking about horses.

"Don't you *ever* speak to me like that again, Seth!" she said. "Don't you ever yell at me."

"Then don't take a whip to a horse," he said calmly. "I apologize for raising my voice. But an unnecessary whip is one thing I cannot tolerate."

He reached across and replaced the whip in its stand.

"I think it would be best if I walked back from here," he said. He handed Veronica the reins. "Good-bye, Veronica. Thank you for the ride," he said, then walked back along the road in the direction of the house.

Smoke coming out her ears, Veronica managed to get the horse to resume a slow walk toward town. She waited until she had gone far enough that Seth could not hear, then grabbed the whip again and beat the horse mercilessly. But it only took a few seconds of dramatically increased speed before she realized that if she wasn't careful she would upset the buggy and wind up in the ditch, possibly with the wretched thing on top of her. She stopped the chastisement, and somehow reached home safely. Her smoldering wrath toward both man and beast, however, was not abated.

"People aren't like horses, are they?" said Cherity at length.

"No," nodded Carolyn. "God put into people something different

than he did into any other creature. He made us able to *think* and to
choose. He doesn't force us to be broken. He calls our name and offers
his goodness, and then he gives us the freedom to come to him or not.
But even though animals do not have that same level of freedom to
determine what they want to become, in another way the choice is just
like the choice Moonbeam has to make—because when she finally
comes to Seth, it will be to let Seth become her master from that day
on. To answer Seth's voice means to let him put the bit in her mouth,
and then to let Seth ride her wherever he wants to go."

"Is it like that with God too?" asked Cherity.

Carolyn nodded. "God says, 'Do you want to be *my* horse, sugar
and bit and all? I offer you my love and all the goodness in my heart.
But it means more than just sugar chunks and apples—you also have
to let me put my bit in your mouth, and go where I want you to go.'"

They sat slowly sipping at their tea. Neither said anything further.
Carolyn did not push the discussion beyond its natural boundaries.
She knew that Cherity had enough to stir her heart and stimulate her
brain for one day. She was not one who viewed such eternally
momentous movements in the human heart with urgency. She knew
who was the Author of every man's and woman's story, and did not
intrude herself into his solemn and invisible work. That the still small
voice was calling to all the horses on the distant pastures of his kingdom was enough. Cherity had already heard the voice, and Carolyn
was not anxious to drown it out with her own. It was time to let
Cherity perceive the soft call of love on her own.

When Seth returned walking up the drive, he saw Cherity out in the
pasture.

She was walking slowly toward Moonbeam, gently inching closer
step by step, speaking quiet words of love which Seth could not make
out. Nor could he know that she was seeking thereby, observing the
horse's responses to her soft and gentle entreaties, as much to understand her own heart toward God as Moonbean's toward her. Cherity

was intelligent enough to have drawn the applicable parallel. With the horse's every move, every whinny, every bob of the head, every tentative step toward her and every reluctant jerk away, she intuitively recognized that she was watching an image and type of herself as she struggled to understand her own response to God.

Seth stepped back among the trees and watched a few moments more. But he recognized that the many-dimensioned exchange taking place in the pasture was a holy one that ought not be intruded upon.

He turned and stole quietly away through the trees.

At dinner that evening, both Seth and Cherity were unusually quiet. Both were thinking of the race to Harper's Peak and the very different interviews they had been involved in afterward.

"I saw you out with Moonbeam this afternoon," said Richmond, turning toward Cherity. "Or should I say, talking to her rather than *with* her?"

"Yes," smiled Cherity. "Carolyn and I had a long talk about horses . . . and other things. I wanted to see if I could understand what *she* was thinking and feeling."

"Any success?"

"I don't know," replied Cherity with a quiet smile. "I kept telling her that I mean only good for her. I don't think she understands yet . . . but she will. She just has to get used to my voice, that's all, and realize how much we all love her."

Nineteen

$\mathcal{B}$oth Waters lay awake in their rooms. Very different mental and emotional sensations stirred within each.

Cherity could not have identified what she was feeling. The human heart is like many ancient gardens, in which old and forgotten seeds, for eons buried under the mold of bygone years, when newly upturned toward invigorating rays and rain from above, will burst into new life. Who can tell, likewise, what diverse forms of divine life lie buried within each of us, planted by the hand of God when he created us, awaiting the moment when their blossoms are ready to flower.

Cherity did not know that a new place was dawning into wakefulness in her soul that had lain dormant in anticipation of the sun of a mother's smile. Most such beginnings—like the life that stirs in the heart of a seed as it begins the invisible breaking of the shell—are unlike their daily morning counterpart which we call *waking*. They occur slowly, sometimes over many weeks or months, even years.

The human plant called Cherity Waters had been planted eighteen years before in soil containing certain rocks and thorns, yet which was capable of producing physical growth. All the while other spirit seeds within the soil of the growing human tree had been awaiting their own moments of wakefulness. Like all such births of the implanted God nature within the human species, its first stirrings were silent, invisible, mysterious. Who can say whence begins the infinitesimal stirrings of that life, or in what form first beckons the faint call from the distant father tongue of our eternal Home.

As she heeded these stirrings, however, and flexed the limbs and muscles of that new consciousness and turned to the only place she knew to seek help, the churchy clichés of her mother's acquaintances had been unable to soften her heart in such a way as to allow the new life to burst forth. The whisperings had quieted. The new life had retreated back within its shell, disappointed, confused, but not extinguished. For that which had begun in the heart of Cherity Waters was the most vital of all eternal movements within the human soul—the mystery of being born again. Once begun, none can stop it but the man or woman himself. The Spirit of God is the Author and Originator and Divine Awakener of such rousings. He will not be thwarted by those who misrepresent him with contorted explanations of his ways. He will find whatever means are necessary to germinate the seed he himself planted. In his time, he will send the sun and rain and warmth of eternal Spring, ever hopeful for the moment when each is ready to break free of the husk and send roots down into the Soil of life, which is the *Spirit* himself, and then turn the face of its new-blossoming life flowers upward toward the sun of his being above, and say, "I will be my *Father's* child."

In truth, Cherity was much closer to such a blossoming than she realized. Her very nature had always turned itself toward the light because she was essentially *of* the truth. Her soul had been developing all its life toward more truth because, what truth she did see, that same truth she obeyed. That development had been protected and, to some degree even nurtured, by the lack of that very church education her mother's friends so condemned her father for not providing. Thus, her shoulders had not been heaped high from her very birth with degrading doctrines of a God whose justice would express itself to sinful man as the very opposite of love. She was not one who needed to be *convinced*—as useless a commodity for the growth of wisdom as could be imagined—she only needed her heart opened in the right directions. Nothing but opinion can result from argument where persuasion is the goal, and opinion, even right opinion, though better than wrong opinion, is of little lasting value in knowing God.

Like many who suppose themselves possessed of no belief, Cherity had never *really* been an atheist. What she called atheism was but the name she gave—knowing nothing else to call it—to her rejection of the dogma that had been presented to her as the gospel. In truth, she was no more an atheist than the horses she loved, who drew the breath for their great lungs from their Creator while knowing nothing of what to call him.

Cherity was, in fact, considerably less an atheist than the rebellious Moonbeam. Cherity had begun to look up and wonder who had given her life. She was but a thirsty young soul ready to look up to the fathering Sun of life.

Would that there were more such "atheists" in our churches, who, with courage and stout hearts, rose up to say, "I do not believe in your God. If God exists, he can be none other than the Father of Jesus Christ, and must be as Jesus describes him—the Father of lights, a Father of goodness, a Father of open arms and smiles and outflowing forgiveness, not an almighty autocrat wielding thunderbolts of retribution against all who dare tread on what some call his holiness."

Only out of such atheism can true faith emerge. He who worships a false god may in fact be worse than the honest atheist. At least the atheist acknowledges the perceived emptiness above him. The so-called "believer," whose belief is in a falsehood, is not nearly so close to the truth even as that.

As Cherity lay awake with a smile on her face, basking in the memory of the day, the shell surrounding her spiritual self was already splintering into a thousand pieces. In Seth Davidson she had experienced the camaraderie of human brotherhood. In Carolyn Davidson she had felt the warmth of human motherhood, which is no less a reflection of the divine character than human fatherhood. From the warmth of both loves, Cherity's fertile heart had been strangely stirred to look up with wonder at what, and Who, might be the source of Light above her. Like a thirsty plant, she had drunk, and had begun to be satisfied. In Seth she had met one worthy to be called a true *brother*. And in Carolyn she had met a woman worthy of becoming a home for a girl's heart.

⌒

In her father's room in another part of the house, a very different spiritual battle was under way.

James Waters was not at all pleased with what he was feeling. He was on edge, tense, irritable.

He could not blame his hosts for his condition. Richmond and Carolyn had shown him and Cherity every courtesy and kindness. Nor could he blame them for talking about spiritual things. He knew Richmond Davidson's predilections. If he didn't like it, in a sense he had no one to blame but himself. No one had forced him to come here. Yet he could not deny that their talk about God's goodness grated on him. If God was so good, what had he ever done for *him*?

His complaint was not with the Davidsons . . . his complaint was with God.

Unlike his daughter, James Waters was not feeling the warmth of the Father-Sun and gentle spring showers of his Spirit. Many of those, and in abundance, had already been sent to him through the years, not a few through his wife, whose sweetness of spirit far exceeded that of the five-pointed theology in which she had been steeped. That her intellect knew no better had not prevented God's true nature from elevating the character of her heart above that theology. Many there are like her who, though their doctrinal beliefs remain of the vilest, because their faces are turned toward the Light come to radiate Christlikeness in spite of the fact that they never grasp the reality of Christ's true work—to illuminate the character of a Father worthy of the name *Abba*, not an Almighty Holiness from whose wrath we are told Jesus died to protect us.

James Waters had been married to such a one. That it had not caused him to seek that divine character, but only to react against the lowness of that doctrine, is a sad but common result of unfortunate elder traditions that must, in a sense, be laid at the doorstep of both husband and wife. Now that she was dead, however, the responsibility to discover whatever truth toward which her life might have pointed shifted solely to him. And in that exercise he had thus far failed.

In his mind—and one fueled by analysis and intelligence, for his was an intellect both keen and shrewd—stood many imagined forms of God—some cruel, some weak, some malicious, some more interesting than others, yet all shrouded over with the uninspired and scripturally inconsistent conventionality of the religious training of his later youth and early adulthood. He had come to see their collective falsehood without feeling any corresponding compunction to discover what might be true. To refute and oppose is the easiest of all intellectual endeavors. But to *deny* is not to *know* truth.

James Waters had never sought the full truth of his Creator's nature and character because his deepest being recoiled from admitting to the possibility of a God to whom his obedience and submission might be due. The idea of a being with rights over him, or of obligations on his part toward such a one, was odious in his eyes. Thus, his self-reliance of heart hid behind his intellect, and what he considered the many unassailable arguments against God's intrusion into his life.

In his self-satisfaction James Waters had as a result steadfastly ignored many whisperings of his Maker. Like multitudes of believers and nonbelievers alike, the fact that he did not, as he supposed, *need* God, and was, as he further supposed, getting along fine without him, was to James Waters argument enough against attempted closer approach.

Scarce feebler argument exists for human relationship than "need." We do need him, of course, yet on a deeper level than most can apprehend. In the very act of creation, God placed within man a remarkable capacity to fend for himself and, in so doing, to sustain his own life. God gave man the capacity *not* to need him. Then he draws and woos and whispers, inviting us to need him anyway—to lay down our self-reliance and come to him with the empty hands of freely chosen childhood.

He invites us, in the absence of need, to *choose* to need him, to *choose* to rely on him, to *choose* to trust him, to *choose* to be a child though no one forces such spiritual childness upon us.

But when such wooings and whisperings against are not enough, when the warm sun and gentle rains of spring do not succeed in softening self-will, God may send harsh blasts of hail and freezing snows and bitter winds to see what they can do to crack open its stubborn outer shell, that the flames of hell will not be required in the end to melt and consume it.

James Waters had not felt many of life's severest pains. He had had it far easier than he realized. Yet his wife's sudden and unexpected death had blown a bitter gust of the Spirit's wintry winds against his face from which he had never fully recovered. Instead of softening him, however, it had hardened him yet further in his self-reliance. Rather than bow before it, he had silently cursed the bitter inevitability of what he called Fate. And thus, though he himself would have been the last to recognize it—indeed, all who knew James Waters considered him a genial, likeable, pleasant, and personable man—the embers of quiet anger festered and smoldered in his heart toward any God who would make *him* suffer.

As much as he spoke of Cherity's need of a mother—which need God was even now providing—in truth, his resentment stemmed from that all-too-common malady of thinking that he himself had been a victim of life's inequity. Most are not nearly so magnanimous as they think. As long as they are riding on the crest of good times, life seems to them a good thing. They are perfectly happy with the world until storm clouds blow over their own houses. They are not nearly so concerned about life's unfairness . . . until it bites into their *own* comfortable existence. Then suddenly are the accusations roused against God for masterminding such a tragic scheme, as the world and all human existence must surely be.

In spite of our accomplishments, such small-minded creatures we are!

Thus on this night, like his daughter, James Waters also lay awake. But whereas she lay smiling, he lay stewing. The openings of light in her heart were widening and she rejoiced to feel life flowing out from within her. He felt a crack in his comfortable level of self-reliance, and it brought only irritability and annoyance. And he fought tooth and nail inside himself to keep the precious shell of pride and independence intact.

How much his uneasiness may have originated from yet deeper places within him he had not yet considered. Cherity was not the only one who had had to endure youth without a mother. He had had to do so without mother *or* father. And certain conversations since arriving at Greenwood had forced a childhood he thought he had put to rest up out of the mists of memory to the surface of his consciousness. As the autumn of his life loomed closer and closer, suddenly he found himself unexpectedly pondering many questions anew.

Twenty

This time Cherity Waters rode toward Harper's Peak by herself. She had to be alone. She had to think. There was no place she would rather do it than on horseback, and no place she could think to do it other than this high outlook that had already grown special to her for many reasons.

But she was not thinking about horses or races or Seth on this day, but about her talk with Carolyn Davidson. She had not been able to forget it, nor forget what she had felt when trying to befriend Moonbeam. She had wanted the horse to see that she wanted only good for her . . . and not mere good, the very best!

Was that really how God felt about her?

It was too overwhelming a thought, that those same thoughts and feelings stirred in God's heart . . . toward *her*. That he knew her, loved her, and wanted to call her by name.

How long, she wondered, had he quietly been whispering to her? Was she now perhaps . . . at last ready to listen?

The thoughts that had been occupying the mind of Cherity's father for the past few days were much different than his daughter's. His agnosticism had resulted in a reaction against God for taking his wife.

In his grief, he had railed and complained against the Father-will of
the universe rather than asking what might be the higher purpose of
that Father-will to which he might bend his knee, sorrowfully
perhaps, yet in willing acknowledgment of the truth that his ways are
higher than our ways. By a series of self-centered responses rather than
truth-seeking responses, he had thus embittered himself against the
great truth that the Father-will of the universe has only the *best* for all
his creatures in its heart.

Cherity, on the other hand, had not reacted against God himself at
all but against an *image* of him which she could not in good conscience accept. Her announcement of atheism had, in reality, been a
step *toward* the reality of his being rather than *away* from it. By it she
had expressed her own heart's belief in the first of all spiritual truths,
the foundation stone of any quest to know God: the imperative necessity to know God *truly*. Many there are indeed whose belief is rather
in one of many false caricatures that are dreamed up by minds of men
who have never sought to know him by obeying him. They have never
paused to examine the vital question whether the god of their imagined belief is a God worthy to be believed in, and worthy to be called
the Father of Jesus Christ.

So while to appearances, upon their arrival at Greenwood, Cherity
and her father may have looked to be near the same point on a continuum of so-called belief, they were, in fact, miles apart. The *direction* of
spiritual progress or declension is of far more import than where one
happens to be on that continuum at any given moment. Two men or
women may intersect at an apparent common point of belief or unbelief, and yet the one may be on the road of *increase*, and thus gradually
becoming more God's child, while the other may be on the road of
decrease, and gradually becoming less his child. Belief is always growing or declining according to one's responses to life's circumstances.
Living things can never be stagnant. Belief is *alive*—it must either
grow or die.

James Waters had been for so long taking baby steps *away* from
God, allowing himself to become entrenched in his latent resentment,
that being at Greenwood was jarring to a heart that had become

comfortable in its unbelief. But he could not help being strangely warmed by the love and hospitality shown him. By the end of their time here, he would honestly have called Richmond and Carolyn *friends* of the deepest kind. If they just didn't have the annoying tendency to turn *everything* toward God.

That Cherity Waters, however, had been on the road of deepening spiritual hunger for longer than she herself realized had suddenly become clear from her recent conversation with Carolyn Davidson. Not only was she hungry after truth, she was hungry to be loved by a mother heart. The blossom of her spirit had therefore opened itself and drunk.

The next day Cherity came to Carolyn where she sat alone in the parlor.

"May I talk to you again?" asked Cherity.

"Of course, dear. Would you like to sit down?"

"I have one main question," said Cherity as she sat down. "Everything you say about God sounds good. But I have heard other things about him that are so different. I want to believe what you tell me, but how can I *know* it is true?"

"There is no way to prove it intellectually," replied Carolyn, "if that is what you mean. People have been trying to do so for centuries, but there is only one way—though it is not an intellectual one—for any man or woman to *know* God, and to *know* that he is."

"What is that way?" asked Cherity.

"By getting to know Jesus Christ himself more intimately and personally, and doing what he said."

Then followed a long talk with many questions, during which Carolyn told her anew the old tale of the man who was God, a story at once so familiar but to most so badly misunderstood, but such as few people, least of all Cherity, ever heard it—the story of the perfect man who told mankind how we could know God too, and said that he

could free us from sin and selfishness so that we could live as God's
sons and daughters.

The delight in Carolyn's eyes as she spoke was in itself enough to
draw Cherity all the way into the reality of the story. Carolyn spoke
now of this person to whom the Lord spoke and then of another,
removing this confusion, showing her the right reading of this or that
troublesome point. At last Cherity could not but believe that the
Savior Jesus had truly lived and walked the grassy hillsides and rocky
shores of Palestine, and said and done the glorious things of which
Carolyn spoke.

"And you see," Carolyn concluded, "by obeying his Word—which
until you are sure of him may be an obedience that takes the form of
personal duty and the following of your conscience—he will prove
himself to your intellect. Action always leads, understanding follows.
It is the way God established his world, and his human creatures, to
function. It is why he placed the conscience inside us, so that duty
would lead to light, and obedience would lead us to truth."

"You make it sound altogether wonderful to obey him."

"Of course—because through such obedience we will come to
know his Father. What could be more wonderful than that!"

"Then what do you think I should do right now," asked Cherity,
"today, this minute . . . even though I am still not *altogether* sure of
him?"

"If you have but the vaguest suspicion that what I have been telling
you is true, then it seems your first duty is to open your eyes and ears
and senses to the things he said and taught. Eventually you will not be
able merely to take my word for it, or anyone else's. The truths which
he spoke will have to get inside *you*. If you find within yourself that
they ring true to your conscience, ring true with the world around
you, and ring true to your experience . . . then what can that mean but
that the truth of the story, and the truth of Jesus himself and his
Father is *proving* itself to your whole being."

Cherity sat absorbing Carolyn's words.

"I would like to read some of it . . . for myself, I mean," she said at length. "Do you have a Bible? Can you show me where to begin. I want to read what Jesus said to do."

It did not take many minutes more before Cherity was walking outside, one of Carolyn's Bibles in her hands, with several slips of paper indicating places Carolyn had noted to read.

When Cherity returned three hours later and again sought Seth's mother, Carolyn knew immediately that there had been a change.

They sat down together and Carolyn waited. Cherity stared down at her lap for several long minutes before speaking.

"I realize now that I'm not as much of an atheist as I thought," she said at last. She looked up at Carolyn and smiled sheepishly. "Or else," she added, "if I was, I realize that I don't want to be anymore."

Carolyn nodded and returned her smile.

"I am ready to have him put the bit in my mouth," said Cherity. "I am ready to be broken and be God's horse. I want to know him as my master, Mrs. Davidson . . . just like you do, just like Jesus spoke about."

Tears filled Carolyn's eyes.

"Cherity, dear . . . " she began, then rose and rushed to where Cherity sat. The next moment they were in each other's arms on the couch.

"I am so happy for you," said Carolyn. "Once you know his voice and have begun to answer his call, life will never be the same again."

Gradually Carolyn pulled back and they sat together for a minute or two in contented silence.

"Will . . . will everything change for me now?" asked Cherity at length.

"Your outlook will change," replied Carolyn. "That is the main thing. Once we are aware that God is with us all the time—or I should say, that we are with him!—life takes on different meaning. We may talk to him about everything as a child talking to his father. We may ask him questions about what he wants us to do and how he wants us to think. Other than that, things don't change a great deal. You still have good days and bad days. Some things still go right and other things go wrong. You will not instantly become a different person. But you know all that already, don't you—once a horse is broken, he is still the same horse with the same personality, isn't he?"

"I see what you mean," smiled Cherity.

"One thing you musn't do is expect life as God's child always to be an easy life or a happy one. But it will always be a life full of meaning and purpose . . . because you have a new Father now, a heavenly Father who will be with you every moment."

"So . . . what do I *do*?" asked Cherity. "*How* do I take his bit? It's not like a horse, where there's a *real* bit. Everything takes place in your heart, doesn't it?"

"Have you talked to God about it?" asked Carolyn.

"A little, I guess. I don't really know what to say."

"Just tell him what you are thinking and feeling. Thank him for opening your eyes to him and for him revealing himself to you. Tell him you want his bit in your mouth. Tell him you want to be his daughter. Tell him you want him for your Master and Father. And then just place your heart into his care."

"But it's so . . . it's so new and different."

Carolyn smiled. "But it's wonderful too, isn't it, to realize, when you talk to him, that God has a smile of welcome on his face—like you did when you were speaking to Moonbeam—rather than a frown?"

Cherity nodded and smiled. It was such a happy thought to think of God as Carolyn described him—as a smiling Father!

"Then just think about him like you want Moonbeam to think about you. You don't need words for that, do you?"

"No," replied Cherity. "She couldn't speak to me in words anyway."

"But you would know the moment she was ready to come to you, wouldn't you?"

"Oh, yes. I would be able to tell immediately. I would know that there was a difference in how she was thinking about me."

"What would it be like? How would you know?"

"I've already pictured it in my mind. She would take a few steps toward me and give a low friendly neigh. It would have a different sound than the prideful whinny she makes when she tosses her head back and goes dashing off across the field. I would recognize the change as her quiet way of saying she was ready. She might bob her head up and down and neigh again, a little nervously because it was new to her. But then instead of backing away, she would come the rest of the way toward me, slowly, until she began to nuzzle her head against mine."

Carolyn thought she had never in her life heard so beautiful a description of what it meant to approach God with an open heart of childlike trust.

"What is to prevent you from approaching God just like that?" she asked. Her voice was soft and close to tears. "If you have words to say, speak them. If you don't, remember that Moonbeam has no words either. But you will know the change in her heart, won't you? The moment she decides to trust you. Do you think God knows your heart any less?"

"It doesn't seem possible, does it?" said Cherity.

"Of course not. He needs no words, only the bowing of your heart as you come to him. He understands the language of the heart. It is the language he invented to communicate with us. He knows the silent words of the heart better than any you could think to say with your mouth. So when you talk to your Father, let your *heart* speak."

Carolyn had participated in what is commonly called "the altar call" more times in her father's various churches than she could remember. But she had no desire now to urge upon Cherity any process of mind or decision other than what welled up from within Cherity's own heart. Many attempts at conversion are little more than inverted manifestations of spiritual pride and ambition within those of a prose-lytizing bent, who fancy themselves evangelists but who have never themselves been weaned from the milk of spiritual infancy.

Because Carolyn loved truly, and trusted God's Spirit completely, she knew as well when to be silent as when to speak.

Cherity nodded and smiled, then slowly rose. It was time for her to be alone again. She left the house and sought the arbor. There she walked about for twenty or thirty minutes, exchanging words with her new Father—who had in truth been her Father all along—in the silent, invisible, eternal language of the heart.

Eventually she came to the low stone wall over the brook and sat down. Slowly Cherity Waters began to cry, until great tears of quiet joy spilled down her cheeks.

"God . . . thank you so much!" she whispered. "Thank you for wanting me for your horse. But I'm not really your horse, am I? It's ever so much better than that. Because I'm actually your daughter. Thank you for wanting me to be your *daughter!* I can't believe I waited so long to realize how good you were. Help me to be just like you want me to be, and to give you pleasure whenever you think of me."

Twenty-One

*V*eronica Beaumont had been resolving a good many things in her mind since she had seen her fiancé.

The tone of Seth's voice and the look on his face during their last ride had startled her. She realized she had almost pushed him too far. He was sensitive about such things as horses. As ridiculous as it seemed to her, she had better watch her step, maybe even learn a few of the stupid beasts' names.

That would be sure to impress him, she thought, if she called them by name. She could hardly stand the thought of those huge ugly lips actually *touching* her, but maybe she even ought to go so far as to let him see her offering one of them a chunk of sugar from her hand.

It would be disgusting beyond words, but she could do it . . . if that's what it took to get back in control of Seth.

The thoughts of Cherity Waters had also to some degree revolved around Seth during that time. But very different were the nature of her reflections.

She had not spent a great deal of time wondering where she and Seth Davidson stood in relation to one another except for being new friends who, it seemed, found more every day that they had in common. If they both now, in a way, also shared the same mother—the one in a temporal, the other in a spiritual sense—that made them like brother and sister as well. In either case, whether friends or brother and sister, or both, they should have no secrets with each other.

Cherity knew she ought to tell Seth about what she and his mother had talked about, and of the changes that had been taking place inside her. She *wanted* to tell him. But something had grown suddenly shy within her ordinarily sanguine personality about this most personal and private exchange that had taken place deep within her. How would she tell one to whom she had made such a point of her atheism that suddenly she had been praying to God? She was not embarrassed to tell him. She wanted to tell him. But finding the right time to do so was not easy.

She and Seth were together every day. There had been a little additional harvest work, some fence mending, clean-up in the barn and stables. These they had all done side by side. With absolute fascination, she had watched Alexander teach Seth some of the finer points of horseshoeing, going back and forth between the patient Paintbrush and blacksmith's forge as he filed and ground and hammered and bent the shoe until it fit the waiting hoof better than any glove, all the while talking to them and telling them what he was doing and why. These and many other things they had done together. It had been a dream come true for the girl who had always loved horses. When there was nothing else to occupy them, they continued to ride together.

She and Seth had talked about a thousand things. But the perfect time to talk to him about her new relationship with God had eluded her.

Perhaps today, Cherity thought, when Seth invited her to accompany him into town with one of the small carriages to pick up some things for his mother. It would be quieter than being out on horseback.

She would tell him today.

⌒

When Veronica saw Seth in the distance in Dove's Landing, she could hardly believe her good fortune.

Her mother was still inside Baker's. Quickly Veronica stuffed her
hand inside her pocket where she had deposited two or three sugar
chunks just in case, then went to the front of the buggy and took a
deep breath.

"You had better not bite my fingers, you stupid horse!" she whispered. Then, waiting until she heard footsteps approaching behind
her, at last, trembling, she held her hand up. "Here you go,
Chasestop!" she said a little loudly. "Have some nice sugar like a good
little horse."

She heard a musical laugh, followed by a chuckle she recognized
behind her. In great relief, she withdrew her hand, still shivering from
the tickling of those horrid lips on her palm, and turned. The sight
that met her eyes drained the red from her cheeks. Who was that
incredibly attractive girl at Seth's side in a cowboy hat, boots, and
men's dungarees!

"Why . . . hello, Seth," she managed to blurt out.

"I am glad to see you getting better acquainted with the animal,"
said Seth, still smiling, "but his name is *Stopchase*."

"Well, I knew it was something like that . . . and I doubt he will
mind."

"What accounts for the change of heart?" asked Seth. "As I recall,
the last time I saw you exchanging words with the worthy Stopchase,
you were a little less understanding."

A far-from-gracious reply sprang to Veronica's lips. But she stifled it
and forced a penitent smile.

"I realized how right you were, Seth darling," she said demurely.
"I behaved like a perfect beast, and so I decided to make it up to poor,
uh . . . Stopchase."

"Well . . . that is good news," Seth mumbled, trying to recover
from his shock at the word he had just heard.

His apprehension of a week earlier for a face-to-face meeting
between the two girls had in no measure diminished. But as he and
Cherity had walked down the boardwalk, and as he had suddenly seen
Veronica seventy-five feet away, he realized there was nothing for it
but to keep going and put the best face on it he could. To spin around

and go walking off in the opposite direction, trying to think up some absurd excuse for doing so as he hustled Cherity away, would only make it worse.

So he had taken a deep breath and kept going, with Cherity at his side. But the sudden word *darling* from Veronica's lips sent his brain into a tailspin!

"Uh . . . " he struggled to add through a mouth all at once very dry, "Veronica . . . this is Cherity Waters, the daughter of my father's friend I was telling you about—Cherity . . . "

In the few seconds they had been chatting, Cherity had taken Veronica's place at the nose of the horse called Stopchase—sufficiently distracted not to have heard the fateful epithet or seen Seth's face go pale—and was gently stroking his nose and neck and whispering into his ear. At the sound of her name, she turned and smiled.

"—Cherity, this is Veronica Beaumont," said Seth. "Remember, I pointed out her father's plantation to you."

"Yes. Hello, Veronica," said Cherity with a pleasantness of voice that grated sharply against Veronica's ear. As Seth spoke, Veronica sent her eyes roving up and down Cherity's odd and unfeminine costume.

Cherity saw her doing so and laughed. "Before you ask if I am going to a costume party . . . " she said gaily, "I always dress like this!"

"How . . . fascinating," said Veronica, with the tone she might have used in speaking to a small child. "I take it you are not from around here?"

"Oh, no . . . can't you tell from my funny accent? I'm from Boston."

"I didn't think you could be from around here," smiled Veronica. "No young *lady* from Virginia would be caught dead looking like that."

Cherity again laughed good-naturedly.

"Neither would any young lady from Boston!" she rejoined. "I get strange looks all the time there too!"

"Then why do you do it?"

"Because it's comfortable and I like it. Who cares about looking like a lady anyway, I just want to be myself."

The depth of such a sentiment was entirely lost on Veronica. "Don't you care what people think of you?" she asked.

"Of course not. Who would care about something like that?"

Veronica bit her tongue. It was a relief to know that she had nothing to worry about from whoever this silly girl was. She couldn't be more than fifteen or sixteen and certainly knew *nothing* about boys!

Veronica turned to Seth, where he stood idly by trying to think of some way out of the strained meeting.

"Seth, dear," she purred, sliding her hand through his arm, "when are you coming over to look at the material for my wedding dress?"

"Oh, you are getting married?" said Cherity as again Seth gasped for air. "How wonderful for you."

"Yes, didn't Seth tell you?" said Veronica. "He and I are engaged. The wedding is set for December. You simply must come . . . that is, if you can make it all the way from Boston. It will be amusing to have someone there . . . in a cowboy hat."

Seth extracted himself from Veronica's grasp and stepped away.

"Well, we've . . . uh . . . we've got to be getting back to Greenwood," he said. "See you later, Veronica."

"Good-bye, Seth darling. Don't forget about the dress. It was a pleasure to meet you, Cherity, dear. You are just as cute as you can be in that outfit!"

Seth and Cherity walked toward Seth's buggy. The instant they were gone the smile faded from Veronica's face. *How dare he walk around town with another girl!* she fumed. Even if she was just a child who looked like something from out of a book, he should still know better. Gradually she was realizing just how many rough edges Seth had.

She had a lot of work to do before December!

⌒⌐

The drive back to Greenwood began in silence. Seth was mortified at what Cherity must be thinking. If only somehow he could keep the subject of his engagement from coming up again.

"That was a surprise," Cherity said at length. She tried to sound as cheerful as possible. "I had no idea you were engaged!"

One thing Seth was learning about Cherity Waters . . . if she had something to say, she came right out and said it!

"Yeah . . . it's just kind of one of those things," mumbled Seth feebly. "I was surprised too . . . you know, to see Veronica. It hasn't been exactly all that . . . official," he went on, groping to fill in the silent air space, but only making matters worse. "I mean . . . I didn't know a date had actually been . . . you know, set in stone like that. My folks don't even know!" he added with a nervous laugh.

"You must be very excited."

"Yeah . . . well, we've known each other a long time."

"December . . . wow—that's not too far away!"

"Oh, boy!" Seth laughed again, but without conviction.

Somehow they reached home, Seth encouraging Dusty along at a rapid clip. It was obvious something had changed between them. With excuses about needing to tend to the horse and buggy, Seth unloaded the supplies and made for the barn. Cherity was only too happy, for one of the first occasions since her arrival, to let him see to Dusty's welfare by himself. She instead sought her room.

Seth's secret was out. But what she had hoped to tell him yet lay stored away in her suddenly very confused heart.

Twenty-Two

A girl of approximately seven or eight, partially Negro though of tan complexion and the mixed blood of three American races, walked tentatively out of a cluster of trees, cast a nervous glance behind her, then continued toward the porch of a large brick plantation house.

That she had been asked to perform this same task a half dozen times in no way diminished the terror of it. She was chosen because she was the youngest, and for the innocence of her expression. But those hardly kept from her frightened imagination the many stories she had overheard as they traveled of cruel white people and the dreadful things they did to runaway blacks.

Just three nights ago she had lain awake at one of the countless stops of their endless journey, listening while a young man spoke in hushed tones to her parents.

"Dere's traitors everywhere on dis railroad," he had said. "Don't yer trus' nobody, spechully no w'ite man lessen he's one ob dose Quakers. Dere's a man called Murdoch—he's da wurst dere eber wuz, an' he's like er not already ter be on yer trail. He'll kill ye effen he fin' you—he'll du terrible things ter dose chilluns er yers. I seen him shoot a boy er ten—jes' shoot him dead as he wuz runnin' away. I wuz hidin' behin' a log an' I seen dat gleam in his eye like he took sum kind er evil pleasure in it. He rides a horse dat's da very devil hissel' an' he kin catch anything. Effen you hears horses, you git outer sight fast. He's a bad'n, he is. He knows every runaway from Alabama ter Maryland—dat's what dey seyz."

"How dat be?" she had heard another voice ask.

"Don' know dat, son—dat's jes' what dey say: dat he knows, dat he knows us all, dat he gots him a list ob every slave dat's missin'. I don' know how dat kin be, but dat's what dey seyz."

As the girl walked across the clearing toward the house, the words repeated themselves over and over in her excited imagination—*"He knows . . . he knows us all . . . he'll du terrible things ter dose chilluns er yers . . . he's a bad'n, he is . . . I seen him shoot a boy . . . shoot him dead."*

She knew her family was watching from the safety of the trees to see what manner of greeting she received, to see if this was the right house. But she could not help thinking that maybe this was the time some dreadful end awaited her behind the door, that her knock would be answered by a monster, a human fiend, a white man or woman with whip in hand who would kill her—maybe the man Murdoch himself! What if he took her away? What if she never saw her family again! What if she opened the door and saw his gun right in her face!

Slowly she continued on, trembling visibly now. She approached and hesitated at the porch. One at a time she climbed the stairs and crossed the veranda. She stopped again and raised her hand by now beside herself with terror—*"He'll du terrible things ter dose chilluns er yers . . . he's a bad'n, he is."* Finally, nearly paralyzed by fear, she knocked timidly on the door.

From the cover of a stand of oaks and beeches, the girl's family watched silently and with no little anxiety in their own beating hearts. The mother glanced at her husband with a look of wide-eyed silence as they saw their daughter's knock answered. The door opened but they could see nothing inside.

Usually the entreaties of a hungry-looking child were enough to elicit sympathy even from the sternest of plantation wives. Most were willing to part with a loaf or two of bread. Even when encountering runaways, though they might bluster a moment at the inconvenience of it, the compassion of a woman's heart usually rose to the surface, generally to leave the girl on the porch and return a few seconds later with something to give them. Such women usually said nothing if their husbands were not around. That's why they always waited until a time of day when they could be reasonably certain the woman of the place would be alone and the man out with his slaves.

Suddenly a gasp escaped the watching mother's lips. She glanced at her husband again. A white hand had reached out from inside and taken the girl's hand. Their daughter had disappeared inside the house. The door closed behind her!

The man gestured for continued silence. All they could do now was wait and keep watch.

Several long minutes passed where they knelt huddled together in the shade of the great stand of trees. They stretched to five . . . then ten. The father now grew anxious himself. This was far too long. Something must be wrong.

Slowly he rose. He would have to go himself to make sure she was safe.

He stood and walked into the light.

When men, like males of all species, first meet—the instinct of guardedness, skepticism, and latent suspicion usually rises to temper the encounter with wariness.

Women more readily approach one another on the common ground of shared humanity. Men, however, cannot so quickly ignore the face-off in which every other male is in a primal way his rival in an invisible contest for supremacy. The silently concealed inborn rooster of masculinity must subtly strut about to discover relative strengths, weaknesses, flaws, and insecurities to exploit, while hiding its own vulnerabilities behind a façade of self-assurance. Women interact, men spar.

Thus, *true* humility is more immediately apparent within the female of the species. Meekness is rarer within the masculine tempera-

ment than it ought to be, than it was intended to be—the humility of
seeking not one's own and counting others better than oneself. The
Man who was the supreme example of that manhood—God's design
when he infused his own Spirit into the Adam of the race—has sadly
been neither Master nor relational paradigm for the greater part of the
humanity he came to seek and to save.

There are, however, a few rare man souls who count the meekness
of Christlikeness the only worthwhile life-ambition. When such ones
meet on the foundation of manly humility, their shared masculinity
rises to the high realm of personhood, a realm where rivalry and ambition give way to love as it was meant to flow among strong men.

The black man and white man first saw one another some fifty feet
from the large redbrick plantation house. The one was approaching
from a wooded region of trees, the other had just rounded the wall of
the adjacent barn. Each paused momentarily in his step. Neither had
seen the other before that moment.

Their eyes met.

Though the color of their skin was noticeably distinct, each somehow recognized neither opposition nor enmity . . . but the universal
brotherhood of humanity.

The pause lasted but a second or two. A smile spread over the white
man's face and he continued toward the stranger.

"Hello," he said with outstretched hand. "I am Richmond
Davidson. I don't believe we've met."

Taken by surprise at the man's obvious cordiality and welcoming
countenance, the black man forgot the affected slave dialect with
which he spoke to whites, and unconsciously reverted to the more
polished tongue of his youth.

"I am . . . uh, Sydney LeFleure," he replied as Richmond walked
toward him. "My family and I are . . . traveling. We were hoping
perhaps to find food."

"You are a stranger here, I take it?" said Richmond as they shook
hands.

"Yes, suh, massa, suh," replied Sydney, recovering his surprise and
adopting the deferential speech of a slave. "We's on our way norf, an'

we wuz jes' hopin' ter git us sumfin ter eat. I gots me four chilluns an'
dey's parful hungry, massa. We'd be much obliged ter you, suh, effen
you cud see yo way ter help us wif sum food."

As Richmond listened, the smile returned to his lips.

"Do you think I am more likely to help you if you talk like a slave?"
he asked.

"No, suh, massa, I wuz jes' . . . dat is, I waz forgittin' my place
afore, dat's all."

Richmond laughed lightly. "Have no fear, Mr. LeFleure," he said.
"There is no place of station or race around here. We have no slaves
anyway."

"Dere ain't no colored folk here, suh?" said Sydney, in shock from
hearing the white man call him *Mister*. "Who be dose blacks we saw
workin' ober yonder?"

"I said we have no *slaves*," replied Richmond. "Those are our hired
workers. They are free blacks, and you may talk any way you like
around me, or say whatever you like without fear of reprisal. I suspect
that you are not a slave either."

"I was, Mr. Davidson," said Sydney, unable to keep from smiling
now himself at how easily this man had penetrated his deception.
"I have been a slave for sixteen years, since I was eighteen, though
I was not born into slavery."

"And you say your family is with you?"

"They are hiding in the woods," Sydney replied, nodding behind
him. It felt good to speak in the voice he had used but rarely since his
youth. Already he was feeling more relaxed. "We sent my daughter to
the door a few minutes ago. When she went inside and did not come
out, I became worried and was on my way to the house myself."

"Then let's you and I go inside and see where she disappeared to,"
said Richmond, leading the way toward the house. "You can bring the
rest of your family out of hiding—you will be safe here."

Sydney turned toward the trees and waved.

"Chigua . . . Silas . . . children," he called. "Come—this is the
place. We found it!"

When Richmond and Sydney walked into the kitchen, astonishment spread over Sydney's face. There sat his daughter at the table babbling away happily without a care in the world, a half-empty glass of milk in front of her and a large cookie with two bites removed in one hand.

"Daddy!" she exclaimed. "Dis lady gib me milk an' cookies, an' I wuz tellin' her 'bout dat barn we slept in wif dose goats an' cows an' horses all together. An' she says I kin help her feed da chickens later—kin I, Daddy . . . kin I please help her?"

Carolyn laughed and Richmond introduced her to the girl's father. A minute later they heard footsteps following through the open door behind them. They turned to greet the new arrivals. There stood Sydney's bewildered wife and three older youngsters, and their *very* bewildered traveling companion.

"Chigua, dear," said Sydney, "these are the Davidsons—Mr. and Mrs. Davidson, I would like you to meet my wife Chigua, and Azura, Darel, Milos, and you already know Laylie. And this is Silas," he added. "He and I escaped together down in Georgia and have been moving north together ever since."

"We are happy to know you all," said Richmond, thinking to himself what a stunning couple they were, though neither looked altogether like Negroes. Sydney's wife, in fact, more resembled an Indian, and he could not exactly place the ethnic appearance of Sydney's tan complexion.

"Sit down!" added Carolyn, pulling out a few chairs and nodding to the newcomers. "You look hungry! We'll get some food into you, and then you tell us how we can help you."

Within minutes nearly a gallon of milk had disappeared down the throats of the weary travelers, along with a dozen oatmeal cookies. Maribel, who had wandered into the kitchen at the first sounds of visitors, stood at the counter as she and Carolyn hurried a batch of biscuits into the cook oven to accompany a skillet of frying eggs and another of sizzling bacon.

Their other guests had also joined the kitchen melee, almost as perplexed as the strangers themselves, yet delighted by the unexpected developments. To see such a mix of skin colors and bloodlines all talking and laughing together could not but warm any but the coldest heart.

"James . . . Cherity," said Richmond as father and daughter walked in, "meet Sydney and Chigua LeFleure . . . their friend Silas . . . and their four children. These are—let me see if I can get them all!—Laylie and Azura . . . and Darel and Milos."

Waters hardly heard the children's names. At the sound of the woman's, almost more than from the distinctive features of her face, an expression of astonishment spread over his countenance. He shook first Sydney's hand, then hers, allowing it to linger a moment in his grasp.

"You are . . . *Cherokee?*" he said, more as a statement of fact than question.

"Yes—how could you tell?" said Chigua with a smile of curiosity.

"I, uh . . . recognize your name."

"It is not a common one, even in my tribe."

"I have . . . uh, I have known several Cherokees in my life," said James, his brain still spinning from the shock and implication of the uncommon name. "And I would . . . uh, like you to meet my daughter Cherity," he added, turning and indicating Cherity.

Cherity and Chigua shook hands, each probing the other's face for something neither could define. The two smiled, though neither spoke. It was a smile that went beyond words, different than when Cherity had first met Carolyn, yet touching places equally deep within her soul.

"I am still confused how you found us," said Richmond, bringing the conversation back to what Sydney had been about to explain before the interruption. "Perhaps I should explain, James," he added to the Bostonian. "Sydney and Chigua and Silas are runaway slaves. I hope you will not be too shocked. They came here seeking refuge."

"Why here?" asked James, who had taken a chair and was still struggling to regain his equilibrium.

"We been trablin' on dat Underground Railroad, suh!" said Silas excitedly. "Dis be our nex' stashun. We wuz sent here."

"Indeed, that is remarkable!" rejoined James. "I've heard of the Underground Railroad, of course. Probably most informed Northerners vaguely know of its existence. But I never dreamed I would actually see it for myself! This is fascinating. And you say *this* is one of the stations?"

"Dat it is, suh," answered Silas. "Dey gib us direckshuns an' den we cum here an' hid in dose trees out dere where we wuz hidin'."

As Carolyn continued to talk to the chattering children and keep food, which was disappearing as fast as she and Maribel could replenish it, on their plates, Waters turned to his host. "Richmond," he said, "you didn't tell me this! Greenwood—a safe house for the Underground Railroad!"

"How could I tell you, James?" laughed Richmond. "This is the first I've heard of it myself!"

"What!"

"Sydney," said Richmond to their new arrival, "what is this that Silas is saying?"

"He's right, Mr. Davidson," said Sydney. "We were given directions here. Our last conductor left us two nights ago and told us how to get here. We were told that there was a new house, a new station along the way where they knew about the wind in the horse's head. We looked and looked all around here, but we didn't see anything. But we were sure this was the right house. They said after we got here no more conductors would be sent to us because the people here would get us the rest of the way and over the border into the North."

Richmond listened with his mouth open in astonishment. By now Carolyn had overheard enough of the men's conversation that she had stopped what she was doing. She stood with a plate of steaming biscuits in her hand, as shocked as her husband at what Sydney had just said.

Husband and wife glanced at each other, both expressions silently saying, "*Do* you *have any idea what he is talking about!*"

"I . . . I don't know what to say," said Richmond at length. "We did have a young woman and her children here a few months back. We helped her get to Pennsylvania. But we've seen no one since. I've never heard about the wind in the horse's head." He glanced with a look of inquiry at Carolyn.

Suddenly she remembered.

"Of course—that was the sign Lucindy was looking for when we reached the town in Pennsylvania! I thought I told you about it, Richmond. It was a weathervane on top of the Quaker farmhouse where Caleb was. But what does that have to do with us?" she asked, looking again at Sydney.

He shook his head. "I don't know, Mrs. Davidson—only that it's the sign of a place where runaways can be safe. That was the sign we were told to look for here."

"Dat's why we wuz skeered!" said Silas. "We didn't see no win' in no horse's head."

None of them heard the horse as it rode up to the front of the house.

Moses, who had remained in the sitting room during the commotion, answered the knock and then walked into the kitchen. Richmond glanced up.

"Mr. Davidson, suh," he said, "Mister Beaumont's at da front door."

A gasp escaped Carolyn's lips. Every head turned toward her. The look on her face, suddenly pale, was enough to silence the entire room.

"Denton . . . *here?*" said Richmond.

"Yes, suh."

"He hasn't called on us in years!"

"He axed ter see you, Mr. Davidson."

Richmond thought a moment.

"Get them into the basement, Carolyn," he said. "Children, all of you—you must not say a word! Go with Mrs. Davidson. Maribel, you go down with them. Hurry . . . not a sound!"

When Richmond Davidson opened the front door about a minute later after taking a few deep breaths to calm himself, there stood his neighbor and boyhood friend on the porch, beginning to grow impatient.

"Denton . . . hello!" said Richmond, extending his hand.

"Hello, Richmond," said Beaumont, shaking his friend's hand. "I wanted to speak to you before leaving for Washington. I may be away a good deal in the coming months."

"Yes, I heard of your appointment as assistant undersecretary in the War Department—congratulations!"

"Thank you, Richmond—that is kind of you. The party leadership has requested an increase to my involvement in the nation's affairs. It is possible I may run for the Senate again when Everett steps down—we shall see."

"I wish you every success, Denton."

"There are reports coming to me," Beaumont went on, "of increased runaway traffic in the county. I have been instructed to be on high alert and to spare no efforts in apprehending them and making sure they are returned to their owners. Are you aware of these rumors? Have you heard anything in this regard from your own blacks?"

"I have heard nothing, Denton," Richmond answered, truthfully enough. "If our own people are party to anything of this nature, I am unaware of it."

Beaumont eyed him carefully. "Well," he said, "the reason for my call concerns the runaway problem. Because of my new duties in the capital, and in light of these reports of higher slave movement, we feel it imperative that I appoint a deputy commissioner to act in my stead during my absence. I felt perhaps, knowing of your background in law, that you might be interested. The remuneration, of course, is nominal, but there is the satisfaction of doing one's civic duty for the South."

Taken by surprise, Richmond hardly knew how to respond.

"I . . . appreciate your thinking of me, Denton," he said at length. "But I really do not see how I could devote myself to the runaway problem. It is no secret that you and I view slavery differently."

"No secret whatever," rejoined Beaumont a little testily. "Still, I felt it the neighborly thing to give you the first opportunity."

"I appreciate that. But I really must decline."

"Very well. On another matter—I would like to revisit our discussion of the Brown land one more time. If you would at least entertain it long enough to think the matter over, I would like to present you with a formal written offer. I have drawn up a document that I have here—"

He pulled a thick envelope from the pocket inside his jacket.

"—and which I feel is more than generous."

"Really, Denton, there is nothing that—"

"Please, Richmond," interrupted Beaumont, "just tell me you will consider it. You will see, in addition to an offer easily three times the value of the land, that I have enclosed a check in the amount of five thousand dollars. It is yours the moment you agree."

"That is a great deal of money, Denton . . . especially for a mere deposit."

"I wanted to get your attention and demonstrate once and for all how serious I am in this."

Richmond nodded. "All right, Denton," he said. "As you have taken so much trouble about it, I promise to read your offer through."

"Thank you, Richmond. Good day."

Beaumont turned, walked down the steps, mounted his horse, and rode away without once looking back, full of as many emotions, though of a vastly different nature, as the man he had just left standing on the porch watching him ride back down the entryway and disappear into the trees.

Twenty-Three

*D*enton Beaumont's strange visit, coming as it did almost exactly on the heels of Sydney's and Chigua's arrival, sobered the entire Greenwood household and reminded them how close danger was.

That the children were older than Lucindy's in some ways lessened the risk, though seven-year-old Laylie was talkative enough for all the rest.

But there were seven in all! What was to be done with them?

Where were they to sleep? How were they to be fed? When and how were they to be gotten to the Pennsylvania border?

The more pressing question that immediately occupied the minds of Carolyn and Richmond was how open should they be with the rest of their people about this sudden development? And what about Seth and Thomas?

"I don't know, Carolyn," said Richmond later that day when the two had a chance to be alone. "From what Sydney says we may have inadvertently become part of something we know almost nothing about. How word about us has spread, and why we are associated with this secret sign of a weathervane because of some farmer in Pennsylvania, may remain a mystery. But if that is being said and people are actually being *sent* here, we may not be able to stop this. We could have a stampede of runaways seeking refuge before it's over."

"How *do* they find us?" said Carolyn. "Over all those miles, through unfriendly country . . . it is a mystery."

"I have heard of a network of slave travel, hiding out, slaves helping slaves, moving at night from safe house to safe house. But I never expected Greenwood to become one of the regular stops!"

They sat some minutes in silence.

"What are we going to do, Richmond?" asked Carolyn at length. "We have Greenwood to think of, and the safety of our sons and our own blacks."

He nodded. "It is not as simple as being willing to help. Of course, we are willing to help any man or woman in need. But so much is at stake here. To help means continuing to break the law, and putting everything else here in jeopardy."

Richmond sighed and thought a moment.

"I see only three alternatives before us," he said. "Either we turn this family away to fend for themselves and probably get caught, or we report them ourselves and have them sent back where they came from. In either case, the rumors about us may eventually stop. Or, the third . . . we take them in, as we did Lucindy, in which case the rumors about Greenwood are bound to escalate all the more. These are our only choices."

"I could not live with myself, Richmond, if we knowingly sent them back into slavery . . . or perhaps, as a punishment for running away, a worse fate yet. Obviously we must help."

"Without a doubt," nodded her husband. "God's people do not turn away those in need. This family is in genuine danger. We must offer them refuge. I see no other way."

"Nor do I."

The silence that followed this time was longer. Both sensed that a turning point in their lives had come.

"How long do you think Sydney and Chigua will stay?" asked Carolyn.

"I don't know. I will talk to Sydney and see what their plans are."

"They are so delightful. It is hard to imagine a Cherokee girl

captured by fellow Indians and sold into slavery as if she were black.
Negro slavery is bad enough, but Indians enslaving one another!"

"Sydney is so refined and well educated. I cannot imagine him as a
slave."

"He could easily pass himself off as a free black. You and he could
ride into Oakbriar and Denton would never suspect a thing."

Richmond laughed at the suggestion. "I think it inadvisable to try
it!" he said. "As commissioner, Denton no doubt gets lists and updates
of runaways. Two such distinctive individuals as Sydney and Chigua
might actually be in *more* danger."

"Why *did* he offer you the job as his deputy?"

"That is a great puzzle to me—I am certain he had something in
mind. Meanwhile, what do you propose to do with our guests?"

"I thought we should put the LeFleure family in one of the second-
floor rooms, out of sight from the front of the house, and Silas in the
basement."

Richmond nodded. "I am thinking, too," he said, "that perhaps we
need to make provision for the horse and the wind. If people are
wandering about the countryside looking for us, I would rather they
know where to come rather than stumbling into Oakbriar or the
McClellan place asking for refuge."

"I hadn't thought of that! You are right. Their looking for us in the
very shadow of the home of a very unsympathetic commissioner adds
all the more to the danger."

Midway through the next afternoon, as the new guests had settled in,
Richmond went in search of Sydney, to find out more about their
plans, their destination, and to see what might be the most prudent
course to follow both in their protection and in getting them to the
North.

He found him alone in the library. Sydney was standing before a
tall shelf, a book in his hand, obviously engrossed in what he was reading.

He heard Richmond's step and glanced toward him.

"I hope you don't mind," said Sydney. "I couldn't help myself."

"Of course not," smiled Richmond. "Books are not relics to be admired on shelves, but tools to be used, mines of information and wisdom to be learned and gleaned from, treasures to be spent over and over not hidden away in vaults."

Sydney smiled as he spoke.

"I delight in few things more than seeing another with his mind buried in one of my books," added Richmond.

"You echo my sentiments exactly," rejoined Sydney. "Thank you so much. I have not seen such books since my father died. And to enjoy them after a bath and with clean clothes, and knowing my family safe and with friends . . . what can I say—I am more appreciative than words can express."

"We are happy to be in a position to help."

"When I walked in here an hour ago, I was assaulted by a thousand sensations of nostalgia—the sights, the smell of leather and paper and dust and the faint hint of mildew from some of the older volumes— there is nothing like the smell of a library!"

Richmond laughed. "You are a lover of books indeed! It is one thing all book lovers share in common—the pleasure aroused by the tactile, evocative sensations of books on the physical plane as well as the intellectual and spiritual."

"How right you are. And how I have missed them. Yet standing here like this, already my years as a slave . . . they already begin to fade as a dream."

"What is it that has taken your fancy today?" asked Richmond, nodding toward the open volume in Sydney's hands.

"The *Odes* of Horace," smiled Sydney.

"And in the original I see. You read Latin?"

"Only moderately. But this was a favorite of my mother's. The moment I saw it I was immediately reminded of her."

The two men found chairs in a nearby nook surrounded on three sides by books, one of several such alcoves through the room.

"How did you end up in slavery?" asked Richmond as they sat

down, "after what must have obviously been an upbringing of education. And your speech, when you are not pretending to be a lifelong slave," he added with a smile, "betrays, if my ears detect it correctly, a hint of the islands. Your name, too, I find intriguing."

"You are a perceptive man," said Sydney, returning his smile. "You have indeed deduced much about my past correctly. My mother was French, born in Europe. She spoke three languages, in addition to a working knowledge of Latin," he added, gesturing to the book in his hand. "Even in France as a free Negro, however, there were not so many opportunities as for whites. My mother worked as governess for a wealthy French couple. Monsieur LeFleure bought a sugar plantation on the island of Jamaica. My mother accompanied his family. Years later, upon the death of Madame LeFleure, Monsieur LeFleure gradually fell in love with their quiet black governess and they were married. I am their son—my father white, my mother Negro. Though I have never seen it for myself, I suppose one would say that I am entirely French, though as you noted, I still bear the noticeable accent of Jamaica."

"That is a remarkable story," said Richmond. "But it does not explain your slavery. Was the island raided by slave traders?"

Sydney shook his head. "I am afraid the treachery was closer at hand," he said. "When my father died, his two sons by his first marriage—though my father's will was explicit in leaving his affairs in my mother's hands—seized control of the plantation. They sold my mother and me to slave traders bound for the coast of the American south. I never saw my mother again."

"Sydney, I am so sorry!"

Sydney nodded appreciatively, though the memory saddened him.

They continued to chat. Gradually followed a lengthy discussion of many things touching on points spiritual, personal, and political, and in which both men shared more of their past lives than they would have anticipated doing with a relative stranger. Before another hour was out, both felt that they had been friends for years.

"What about you?" asked Sydney after some time. "From your remarks about spiritual things, and what you told me about freeing

your slaves, I cannot but presume you must have a story equally fascinating as mine, though obviously it has brought you along a different
path to this moment."

"I too have been on a pilgrimage," Richmond nodded, "though as
you say, a much different one than yours. We have both sought freedom, I suppose, but of different kinds."

"Are not all men and women on pilgrimages of some kind?" said
Sydney.

"Hmm . . . a fascinating observation. Or maybe it should be said that
all men *ought* to be. I cannot help but wonder if enough actually are."

"I see your point," rejoined Sydney. "You are right. But
continue—I did not mean to sidetrack you from telling me about
yours."

"In my own case," said Richmond, "mine has been what I would
call a *spiritual* pilgrimage. It was my father-in-law who in a sense set
the course of my search. Your quest has been to regain your freedom.
Mine has been for freedom of a different kind—freedom within
myself. But I don't want to bore you with—"

"Please . . . go on."

"You're sure?"

"Absolutely!"

"All right then . . . well, Carolyn's father was a minister. One night
I wandered into his church, as unbelieving a man as you could imagine. . . . "

James Waters had not seen his host for a good part of the afternoon.
He had been out walking, his mind full of more unexpected sensations
than he knew what to do with. Now he had returned to the house.
Hearing voices coming from the open door of the library as he made
his way along the second-floor corridor toward the room he had occupied during his visit, he paused briefly to listen. A vigorous discussion
was clearly in progress. Intrigued, he walked to the library door and
stood listening.

" . . . my unbelief was not out of hostility toward God," he heard Richmond saying, "but out of ignorance concerning who God actually was. Carolyn's father triggered something within me to remain in ignorance no longer."

"How so?" asked Sydney.

"When I walked into his church and heard him say that God knew us all personally and wanted to do his very *best* for us," Richmond went on, "I knew that I had to find out if it was true."

"Why?"

"I don't know. Something about the hugeness but simplicity of the claim struck me hard. No doubt my circumstances at the time contributed to my reaction. How can one separate the emotions and the intellect?"

Still James stood listening, filled with many mixed thoughts and emotions. Slowly he entered the library softly and continued to listen from the obscurity of a nook between two tall bookcases.

"I had to know if such an absolute goodness was indeed at the heart of the universe," Richmond continued. "The question was monumental in my mind. If God existed but was cruel, I had no interest in him. If God existed but was selectively loving and selectively cruel, then I had no interest in him. If God existed but his ways were ruled by rote formulas, I had no interest in him. If God existed but his means of conveying truth were dictated by the rituals and creeds of what went by the name 'church,' then I had no interest in him.

"But . . . if God was infinitely good, and infinitely forgiving, and infinitely trustworthy, and infinitely patient with saints and sinners alike—now there was a God I could believe in! And that, in brief, was the nature of my pilgrimage."

"So . . . where did you look for the answers?" Sydney asked.

"A shrewd and important question!" rejoined Richmond. As he spoke he glanced up and saw his other guest, where he had been inching closer as he listened, across the library.

"Ah, James!" exclaimed Richmond. "Come . . . join us. We have been trying to solve the riddle of the meaning of life!"

Sydney laughed as James approached and took a third chair. "Have you succeeded?" he asked.

"Speaking for myself," replied Sydney, "I am happy just to have found a place where my family can be safe. The greater meaning of life can wait!"

All three men laughed.

"But our host," Sydney added with a good-natured smile, "was about to tell me—at least I think he was—how *he* discovered the meaning of the universe."

"I don't know whether you've noticed," said James, "but he has a predilection to wax eloquent about spiritual things if given half the chance."

Richmond roared with delight. "James, my friend, you have come to know me well!"

"But I have not forgotten my previous question," persisted Sydney. "I remain curious *where* you sought answers to your quest about God . . . and what answers you discovered."

Richmond grew serious and thought a moment or two.

"In three places, I would say," he began slowly. "I call them three laboratories where the search for truth must be carried out."

"And they were?"

"The first and most obvious was in the Gospels themselves."

"But those are such ancient texts, written almost two thousand years ago," interposed James.

"And alive with power for any and all who would search for God and discover him in their words," rejoined Richmond. "But mind you, I say in the Gospels themselves," he added, "not in their *interpretation*. Many seek to interpret them whose minds are clouded by the fogs of doctrines passed down to them by generations of unbelief within the church, but not actually found within the Gospels at all."

"Unbelief . . . within the *church*?" said Waters, his voice betraying confusion.

Richmond nodded. "The church, or should I say, what is *called* the church, is the prime repository of unbelief in the world."

"How can you possibly say such a thing?" now asked Sydney.

"I have not been a churchgoer myself, though many of the slaves where we came from were highly religious. But I do not understand what you mean. How can the church, which supposedly exists to promote religion, be a storehouse of unbelief?"

"Because some churches, as I have subsequently found, attribute to God characteristics that are the most glaring of falsehoods."

"A strong statement."

"Worse still, they not merely encourage people to believe these falsehoods—a thing that ignorance alone might possibly account for—they go further and insist that their members believe them, and call those who question them unbelievers in danger of the fires of hell."

James nodded as he listened. He knew exactly the mentality his host was speaking of, though could not help being surprised at hearing him speak of it in such seemingly critical tones.

"The worst of it," Richmond went on, "is that these tenets of false belief are nowhere to be found from the mouth of Jesus in connection with his Father. Thus some in the church perpetuate from generation to generation what can only be called unbelief in the *true* Fatherhood of God."

"You astound me, Davidson," laughed James. "My, but you are plainspoken!"

Richmond nodded with a thoughtful expression. "Perhaps I am too much so. But I wander from Sydney's question. The other two places I sought to understand God were in the universe and within my own heart."

"Two very different places, it would seem," said Sydney, "for the prosecution of your inquiry."

"Not as different as you might think," rejoined Richmond. "And intriguingly, when the evidence from these two laboratories is analyzed, it yields a similar mystery that only the *gospel* explains."

"Linking the three laboratories of your search for truth."

"Precisely! In both the universe and within myself, I found the same puzzling dichotomy that has plagued man from the beginning of time—that which has been the mystery of the universe and has caused man to reject the idea of a good and loving Fatherhood—namely, the dichotomy between good and evil."

Now it was Sydney's turn to express astonishment. "That is remarkable," he said. "It is precisely that very question that has been gnawing at me for months as I have observed the diverse people we have encountered along the way of our journey. It is so clear that people are filled with *both* good and evil at the same time."

"It is a question that has puzzled philosophers, I presume, since people first began to look up and wonder where they came from. In the world there are beauty and ugliness, ecstasy and pain, happiness and sorrow, life and death, love and war, gorgeous sunsets and destructive hurricanes. And that same puzzling dichotomy, as you say, Sydney, exists in my own heart . . . in the heart of every man—a longing toward good, yet a propensity to do wrong . . . a reaching toward the right and noble and true, which is in constant conflict with a nature of selfishness. The problem of good and evil is foundational to much that man struggles to understand."

"You are so right," said Sydney. "Wherever one looks, one observes a fundamental war between opposites. What can account for it?"

"Indeed, what a puzzle it is. Yet in the gospel we find the answer to the riddle. *God* is the good, *sin* is the bad."

"Is that not too simplistic, Richmond," said James, "to explain all the cruelty and pain we see about us?"

"Perhaps in its very simplicity we discover the meaning we seek. Yes, it is a simple explanation, though also profound. Once I saw it in all its simplicity, the mystery of the universe for me was solved: everywhere and in everything, there is a live heart of goodness throbbing with love for all creation."

"A poetic and beautiful description," remarked Sydney.

"Yet," Richmond went on, "that creation, as typified in no other place so perfectly as in the heart of man, has gone bad—it has turned its own self-will in on itself."

"How so?" asked Sydney. He had never heard the ideas of Christianity explained with such clarity.

"We were created for a purpose we have failed to fulfill," answered

Richmond. "We are not at peace with the essential nature of our beings, with the essential nature of creation. We are out of step. Thus exists the divine and universal tension in all things."

"But *why* did the universe go bad?" asked Waters.

"Because God created it with the potential to do so built into it—the supreme expression of his love. It is called free will, the capacity to choose goodness, or reject it."

"Ah, now you're going theological on us!"

"I'm sorry. I did not mean to do that. All I meant by bringing free will into it was to say that every time any one of us makes a choice, from the simplest to the most profound, we become the living evidence, so to speak, both of God's existence and of his love."

"And that is at root of the distinction I have noticed—is that what you would say?" asked Sydney.

Richmond nodded. "Our power to choose between right and wrong," he said, "between good and evil, is the greatest evidence of the love at the heart of creation. And when beings with the power to choose exercise that power by choosing to relate themselves in obedience to their Father-Creator, then will all again be right with the universe. To the degree each of us begins to engage in that yielding in our present lives does that eternal coming right begin to take place."

"Perhaps your enthusiasm will get through to me yet," laughed Waters. "You continue to intrigue me. If more Christians in the world preached the Davidson gospel—"

"May I correct that, and say if more Christians in the world lived the gospel of the *Son of David,*" interposed Richmond. "In any event, this was the conclusion that I finally reached in my own personal quest. The universe is not really so hard to understand once one grasps that *we* are the reason for its wrongness, and that *God* is the reason for its rightness, and that the love of a perfect and infinitely redemptive Fatherhood will, and must be, victorious in the end."

"Perhaps you have just solved the riddle about human nature that I have been pondering," said Sydney thoughtfully. "I can see that I will have to reflect on this further. You indeed give a man much to think about."

They heard footsteps behind them.

"So this is where you men disappeared to!" said Carolyn. "We have all been looking for you. There is tea, coffee, bread, butter, and cake on the table in the dining room!"

Twenty-Four

Three days later, on the evening before Cherity and James Waters were scheduled to begin their return trip back to Boston, the mood around the dinner table was quiet and subdued. This had been a special time for them all. Each sensed that saying good-bye would not be easy. Sydney was also talking of moving on, though no firm plan had yet been devised for them to do so, and the next hundred miles could be the most perilous of their entire journey. Chigua would have remained indefinitely, but they knew they would never be safe as long as they were south of the Mason-Dixon Line. The mood of approaching separations had quieted the entire household.

Cherity was the first to leave the table. A few seconds later they heard the front door open and close. One by one the others rose also. Thomas disappeared upstairs. Chigua took the children to their room. Richmond and Carolyn, and James and Sydney made their way to the parlor where not long thereafter Maribel appeared with coffee, tea, and a few small cakes. Seth sought the out-of-doors, suspecting where he might find Cherity.

A few minutes later she heard his step behind her where she sat. She was wearing no hat. Her auburn hair fell down around her ears and neck past her shoulders. She did not turn around, but heard him climb up the rails, swing his feet over, and sit down on the topmost rail beside her. For some minutes they sat in silence gazing out across the pasture. A thin mist had begun to gather over the pasture and fields as the evening cooled.

"What do you think?" he asked at length. "How ought we to proceed with Moonbeam? sternly or gently?"

"Judging from my own personal experience," she replied, "—as one for whom the gentle approach of your mother helped me see things I had never been able to see before—I would recommend the soft word of encouragement rather than the whip."

"Spoken like one who knows horses!" rejoined Seth. "And loves them."

"I hope that I know them a little better than I knew them before . . . now that I know myself a little better. I hope I have learned to love and understand them a little better too."

It fell silent. The hearts of neither were thinking about horses.

"I hope—," began Cherity.

"I, uh—," said Seth at the same instant.

Both turned toward each other and laughed, but nervously. Their laughter on this evening was not like that after their race to Harper's Peak.

"You first," said Cherity.

"That wouldn't be right," said Seth. "Ladies first . . . I insist."

"All right," smiled Cherity. "I was just going to say . . . that I hope you and Veronica will be very happy together."

A stab of distress stung Seth's heart. He had *almost* succeeded in forgetting that anyone called Veronica Beaumont existed, even if just for one evening.

"Yeah . . . thanks," he mumbled.

Another long silence followed. Slowly the evening closed in around them. At this time of the year, it would not be dark for another hour or so. But the stillness of night had descended. The horses were thinking of sleep. The crickets were getting about their business in earnest.

"It's your turn now," said Cherity. "What were you going to say?"

"Oh, yeah . . . just that I, uh . . . that I've got something I want to give you," said Seth. "Kind of a going-away gift, I guess . . . though it's not much."

Cherity turned toward him expectantly.

"It's not here," said Seth, then turned. He swung his legs over the rail and jumped to the ground. "Come on."

Cherity leapt off the fence and followed. Seth led the way to the barn.

"Where are we going!" she asked excitedly.

"You'll see."

"But . . . what is it?"

"You'll see."

"Seth!"

"I can't tell you . . . I have to show you."

He opened the door and they went inside. A candle was burning in a rusty lantern, casting a yellow light about it.

"Remember our race to the top of the ridge?" Seth asked.

"Do I . . . what kind of question is that!"

"Do you remember what I said . . . that I'd give you your prize later, after I thought of one?"

Cherity nodded.

"Well I finally did."

He stopped at the saddle rail, hoisted down the saddle she had been using her entire time at Greenwood, then turned to face her.

"I never told you this," he said, "but this used to be my old saddle. It's the one I learned on, the very first saddle I ever called my own. It's a little small for me now . . . but it seems to fit you perfectly. I would like you to have it."

Tears of disbelief welled up in Cherity's eyes.

"That is," added Seth with a laugh, "if your dad will let you take it on the train!"

Still Cherity stood speechless.

"I don't know what . . . Seth, it's the most . . . I just—"

Suddenly she broke into tears and ran from the barn, leaving Seth still standing where he was holding the old worn saddle.

He left the barn carrying it, setting it upright on the bench on the veranda, then went inside. There was no sign of Cherity.

Cherity made sure Seth would not see her when he left the barn.

From her vantage point behind one of the nearby oaks, she watched him as he went inside. She couldn't bear to have him see her crying like a baby. He would probably ask her what was wrong! She didn't dare tell him.

Now she had two secrets. Perhaps she would have to carry both in her own heart for the rest of her life.

But she wouldn't trade her quiet new loves for anything. Even if the one came with a thorn that had pricked her heart with pain even as the other had flooded her with joy. She would bear the pain, and cherish the joy. For in the quiet place within her where such memories are kept, both loves, and all they made her feel, would always be as one.

Hearing the door of the house close in the distance, Cherity stepped out from behind the oak. She could not possibly go inside yet. She would walk about in the thickening darkness a while longer, visit the horses in the pasture one last time, maybe cry again, and, when she had closed the window to her heart a little more securely and could put on her smile again, then she would go inside.

Seth heard the door open half an hour later. He was in the parlor with his parents and Cherity's father, seated with his back to the door.

Footsteps came across the carpeted floor. He felt the gentle touch of a hand on his shoulder. He turned and looked up. Cherity smiled down at him.

"I'm sorry for running out like that," she said in a soft voice that bore trace remnants of the huskiness of tears. "I was just . . . too overwhelmed with happiness. I . . . I accept your gift. I cannot think of anything so special anyone has ever done for me. . . . I will treasure it."

She pulled her hand away and drew in a deep breath as she glanced around the room with a smile.

"I think I shall go upstairs to bed now," she said. "Good night, everyone."

After breakfast the following morning, with a few tears from Carolyn and Cherity as they embraced, but with silent stoicism from Seth as he shook the hands of father and daughter . . . they were gone.

Cherity did not once look into Seth's eyes. She hadn't dared.

Twenty-Five

The train ride north was somber and quiet. Neither Cherity, with the saddle sitting on the seat beside her, nor her father across from her, said a word for most of the morning.

Both Waters were changed. Their whole lives had been changed in the two short weeks since they had made this same train ride in the opposite direction.

James Waters did not thoroughly grasp the reason for his daughter's silence, nor appreciate the extent to which the spiritual foundations of her life had been forever altered. As she had not found a suitable opportunity to tell Seth about her conversation with Carolyn and subsequent ride and walk in the arbor, neither had she found opportunity to tell him. And now other things had pushed the urgency to do so from her heart.

James had plenty to think about for himself. Until this juncture of his life he had always been able to dismiss what he considered religiosity without much depth of thought regarding its deeper meaning. But now he had met a man and a woman who *lived* their Christian faith so practically and forcefully that it was impossible to ignore. Richmond and Carolyn Davidson could not be passed off as intellectual lightweights. Everything they believed they backed up with actions—from the way they opened their home to strangers of any background or color, to the freeing of their slaves, to their handling of financial obli-

gations, to the respect they showed one another and every other
person with whom they came into contact, as well as to the simple joy
and energy and optimism they brought into their lives. He had never
before connected living *character* with *faith*. Yet he could not deny
that the man and woman Carolyn and Richmond had become—both
apparently emerging out of hardships and suffering—were due in no
small measure to what they believed and how they had determined to
practice their Christianity. It was a remarkable thing. They were
people whose Christianity *mattered* with a consistency, even an appeal,
he had never encountered before.

He had met so many remarkable individuals here—from Malachi
Shaw and the other former slaves, simple but genuine humble blacks,
to Alexander the horse trainer . . . and the two remarkable LeFleures!
Into what an assortment of backgrounds and cultures he and his
daughter had been drawn during their visit!

But in a sense the mixing pot of people and cultures and personali-
ties all had Richmond and Carolyn Davidson at its foundation. Their
love and respect for everyone was the reason that Greenwood was such
an energetic center of *life* and activity and intellectual stimulation.

Like Sydney LeFleure, he found himself reflecting on this great mix
of humanity and thinking of the conversation in the library—how
every man and woman had within himself or herself roots of both
good and evil, the seeds of God's own goodness as well as the seeds of
sin. He had never thought about such things before in connection
with *himself*. Spiritual ideas had been for him distant and abstract.
Now the theological concept of free will took on a very practical reality. Suddenly the "Christianity" he once thought he knew had
changed. It was no longer a system of belief, but a daily opportunity
of choice between two opposing aspects of man's nature.

Within *his* nature.

Now he saw why Richmond Davidson insisted that faith was really
a very simple thing. It reduced to little more than *choosing* between the
good within him, or as Richmond would probably say, the *God* within
him, or the self-centered tendency toward sin which was also within
him.

He wasn't sure he liked the implications.

For years he had been satisfied with himself. He did not at all like the idea that something may be required of him—that Someone might have a claim upon him.

To what extent his unsettled mental condition might also have to do with the fact that neither could he dislodge from his memory the strange sensations that had risen within him whenever the conversation at Greenwood had turned to the enigmatic Cherokee called Mr. Brown, James Waters could not have said. And the startling appearance of Sydney's wife and what her name represented . . . suddenly so many things were staring him in the face!

Meanwhile Cherity continued to stare out the window, a book in her lap open to a page containing the small Virginia bluebell she had pressed between its pages.

Having somehow been apprised of the fact that the Davidsons' guests had departed on the morning train—though she had not been told details nor of the obvious emotional nature of the final good-byes on the station platform—Veronica made an appearance at Greenwood that same afternoon.

Borrowing one of Veronica's tricks, though the sighting had been purely coincidental, Seth saw her coming from an upstairs window.

Hating himself for it, Seth told his mother that by the time she heard the knocker sound on the door he would not be home and that she could truthfully answer to that effect. Then he dashed from the back door of the house to the cover of a empty chicken coop, and was disappearing into the woods behind the house about the same moment Veronica walked up the steps to the front door.

What kind of sneaking, waffling coward had she turned him into that he couldn't even face her!

He would have to think about his engagement to Veronica eventually. But right now his memories of the recent visit were too fresh to make that possible.

He circled around to the barn. There he hid out until he saw
Veronica ride away, well able to imagine her annoyance at having
come all this way for nothing. Then he went out the side door to the
corral, called for Malcolm, saddled him, and had a long, solitary ride
up to Harper's Peak, during which he thought about many things.

The next day, knowing their new black and Indian friends were planning to leave soon as well, Carolyn found Chigua LeFleure upstairs.

"Good morning, Chigua," she said. "I am on my way to meet with
some of the black women. We read the Bible together. I thought you
might like to join me."

"I would, thank you, Mrs. Davidson . . . what about the children?"

"I've already spoken with Richmond and Sydney. They said they
would keep close to the house until we return."

The two women left the house a short time later and walked to the
collection of homes where their black workers lived, formerly known
as the slave village. As stealth was required, some of the women had
already departed in ones, twos, and threes. Others would be taken in
the back of a wagon driven by Josaiah Black beneath a thin layer of
hay and straw for the animals.

Though Richmond had long used some of the higher pastureland
for horses and sheep, he had recently undertaken the cultivation of
several of the Brown fields, and also begun the establishment on the
Brown tract of a huge orchard of varied fruits, as well as grapes and
berries. These activities assured that there was always plenty of work
for their people, and also provided much-needed cover and protection
for the clandestine meetings that took place under the former Brown
roof.

Carolyn led the way to the Shaw house, then she and Nancy and
Chigua set out walking together the two miles through the gently
wooded hills.

"I am curious," said Carolyn as they went, "how you became a
slave, Chigua. Richmond told me briefly of Sydney's story. But other

than what you told us that first day, for a Cherokee to be a slave seems very unusual."

"Not as unusual as you might think, Mrs. Davidson . . . especially for one with skin as dark as mine. I am often mistaken for a Negro rather than an Indian. And I am sorry to say, but the Cherokees owned slaves too. They bought many black slaves to work their farms. But then we found ourselves enslaved as well. As slavery grew prevalent in the last century, I'm afraid it crossed ethnic and cultural lines without shame."

"It is such a travesty in our history."

"In the old times," Chigua went on, "many of our people lived in caves, but later the Cherokee had houses and owned farms and lived and dressed in most ways just like the whites, even to the point of operating sizeable plantations that used slaves."

"What was your background?"

Chigua nodded. "I lived a normal life," said Chigua. "My mother died when I was born and my father did not run a plantation with slaves. But I went to a Cherokee school. My father owned a reasonably large farm and we were considered moderately well-off. My father died when I was six and my sister and I went to live with my grandfather. But then came the removal to the West and I was captured by a Seminole raiding party. I never saw any of my family again."

"That must have been heartbreaking," said Carolyn. "I cannot even imagine it."

"I was nine when I was captured. I was frightened to death for what would happen to me."

"How did you meet Sydney?"

"He was captured by the same Seminole tribe several years later. He stayed close to me and told me he wouldn't let anyone hurt me. He was so gentle and kind, I knew immediately, even though he wasn't an Indian, that he would never hurt me. The Seminoles noticed his protectiveness of me. They knew Sydney was different from other Negroes. His whole bearing was regal. They thought we looked stately together. We were sold to the owner of a cotton plantation in Georgia. We were happy together and remained at the same plantation as slaves until just a few months ago. With our children growing older, Sydney feared that eventually they might be sold away from us. Once we began to hear about the Underground Railroad, he began looking for a chance to take us to the North."

"An amazing story," said Carolyn, "isn't it, Nancy?"

"Yes'm, Miz Dab'son. I ain't got nufin like dat. I wuz born a slave an' wuz always a slave. I lived my life right here on dis plantashun an' nowhere else."

"It is clear you value your Cherokee roots," said Carolyn.

"We are taught pride in our heritage," replied Chigua. "But it is hard to keep that heritage from the old days. Things have changed so much for our people. Our chief Moytoy was named Emperor of the Cherokee nation. One of our chiefs, Attacullaculla, my own ancestor, went to England and met the king. We have a wonderful legacy."

"It is so heartbreaking to see what the European influence has done to native tribes like yours. And yet . . . I am part of that—I am white myself. I am so sorry!"

"I do not know how we will keep our heritage and culture alive for our children," said Chigua, "and for their children. The old ways are disappearing. That is why I tell our four young ones about those who came before, about Chief Moytoy and Tame Doe and Attacullaculla and Nancy Ward, and all my ancestors. And I tell them about the five rivers—"

Suddenly Nancy's voice interrupted in astonishment.

"What dat you say! What five ribers?"

"It is a legend I heard as a child," replied Chigua. "I have always remembered it. I don't know where it came from. It is mixed in my mind with many legends from the past."

"What it say?"

"It tells of an ancient king from long ago, from a land across the sea. I don't know if I am descended from him, but I was told of the legend of the five rivers from before I can remember, and about an old king."

"But I been tol' dat same story!" said Nancy with wide-eyed excitement. "Malachi's mama tol' it jes' like you said! She made me promise ter tell our young'uns, an' we ain't no Indians, an' dat's da truf. She said he was an' ol' *black* king. You got nigger blood in you, Miz Leflur?"

"I don't know, Nancy," replied Chigua. "Perhaps I do. Look—" she said, holding out her arm next to Nancy's"—my skin is nearly as dark as yours. There are stories of an ancient one called Magoda just like the Cherokee chief Moytoy, who came from the king who knew the five rivers and whose son married one of my tribe and went to live with the Cherokee. Perhaps my dark skin comes from him. Do you know this name?"

Nancy shook her head. "I neber heard ob dat, Miz Leflur. My kind don' talk dat much 'bout da ol' days—we's always singin' 'bout da new times, 'bout freedom an' da promised lan' an' such like."

"And for you here, that freedom has come it seems."

"Dat it has, Miz Leflur, thanks ter Mister an' Miz Dab'son."

"My people are very particular to keep the legends of the old days alive," Chigua went on. "But over the years they cannot but fade from one generation to the next."

"What dat legen' ob dose five ribers mean, Miz Leflur?" asked Nancy.

"I don't know everything about it," replied Chigua. "I remember someone saying to look at our hands to remember, and to use the lines in our hands to think of the five rivers, to look to the land for strength and to take what strength it gives, and to remember the past for the wisdom of its heritage, and to remember that the blood of kings flows in our veins. But I don't remember who told me. It couldn't have been my own mother, and I remember nothing like that from my father."

She turned to Nancy and smiled. "I'm afraid that is all I know of it."

"But dat's right fine, ain't it, Miz Leflur. Hit makes my heart feel warm jes' hearin' you say it like dat."

"Just imagine—this must mean the two of you are related!" said Carolyn.

"Not me, Miz Dab'son," said Nancy. "I ain't come from dose ribers—dat's Malachi."

"Your children might still be distant cousins to Chigua's. How exciting!"

"If dat don' beat all!" said Nancy. "You reckon dat's really so, Miz Dab'son?"

"It seems like it could be—don't you think, Chigua?"

"I don't know, but why not, if we both are descended from the same ancient king."

"I am curious about what you said about the caves a while ago," said Carolyn. "There are local legends here associated with Indians and caves too—Cherokees, actually."

"There were Cherokees *here*!" exclaimed Chigua.

"We are going to the former home of a man named Mr. Brown who was Cherokee. I don't know if his *real* name was Brown, but that's what he was always called."

"What was he doing here?" asked Chigua.

"He came from the South. He was a friend of Richmond's father."

"Where is he now?"

"No one knows. He disappeared."

"This is the most amazing thing to hear!" said Chigua, now as surprised as Nancy had been before. "When I was young I heard about a man who left North Carolina years ago for the north. But his name wasn't Brown, it was Long Canoe, great-grandson of Attacullaculla, from another line than my descendants."

"What do you know of him?" asked Carolyn.

"Nothing really. He was a mysterious figure by the time I was born. I used to hear my father talk about him. Some say that when he left a boy accompanied him. It is said that he took the boy away to protect him. Did the Mr. Brown you speak of have a boy with him?"

"He was always alone as far as I know," replied Carolyn. "What do your legends say became of the boy?"

"Nothing at all. Nothing more was ever heard about him. No one knows what became of him, and I have heard nothing about my people since my capture."

"I wonder what became of him. Is it possible he could still be alive?"

"I don't know, Mrs. Davidson," replied Chigua. "That was many years ago and I was very young. So much time has passed. Even if there were such a one, and even if he did return, it is now too late. It seems likely that the secrets Long Canoe took with him may never be known."

꧂

They arrived at the Brown house. Chigua felt a wave of chill as she walked in even though it was a warm day. Most of the black women were already present, having arrived by different routes and at different times, and were waiting in relative silence inside. Though they had been meeting with Carolyn for several years, they were still aware enough of the danger, especially to their mistress, that they were watchful and wary whenever they ventured too far away from the precincts of the Greenwood plantation house.

"Hello, ladies," said Carolyn as she walked in. "You all, I think, have by now met our guest Chigua LeFleure. I asked her if she would like to join us today." Carolyn and Richmond had not specifically told their blacks what was the situation with Chigua and her family. From their speech and Chigua's distinctive features, most assumed them free guests of their master and mistress, as they still thought of them, and asked no questions. Judging it best for everyone concerned, thus it remained.

Gradually more women arrived. They sat down and Carolyn got out the supply of a dozen or so Bibles she had brought here and kept in a chest for just this purpose. She passed them around the group of women.

"I wuz in town, Miz Dab'son," one said as Carolyn came to her. "I wen' by Rev'run' Jones an' he said ter tell you he wuz ailin' sum an' ter pray fo him. He didn' seem too good, Miz Dab'son."

"Thank you, Wilma," nodded Carolyn. "I will pay him a visit this afternoon to see if he needs anything. . . . Now, shall we open to where we were before, to the sixth chapter of the book of Luke—do you remember where that is? If not, it is on page 937."

She waited while the women, sharing the Bibles as needed, found their place. Even so simple a task, for those who were still learning to feel comfortable with a book in their hands at all, took some time.

"I will begin by reading again what we talked about last time," said Carolyn at length. "Follow my words and see if you can see and hear them at the same time. I will start at verse twenty."

Again she waited a few seconds.

"And he lifted up his eyes on his disciples," Carolyn began, speaking slowly and enunciating each word with emphasized clarity, *"and said, 'Blessed be ye poor: for yours is the kingdom of God. Blessed are ye that hunger now: for ye shall be filled. Blessed are ye that weep now: for ye shall laugh. Blessed are ye, when men shall hate you, and when they shall separate you from their company, and shall reproach you, and cast out your name as evil, for the Son of man's sake. Rejoice ye in that day, and leap for joy: for, behold, your reward is great in heaven: for in the like manner did their fathers unto the prophets.'"*

Carolyn stopped and glanced around the room with a smile.

"For you who have been slaves and have been treated badly during your lives," she said, "what do you think when you hear that you should leap for joy because people hate you and do terrible things to you?"

"I ain't neber leaped fo joy at no whuppin, an' dat's a fact, Miz Dab'son!" said the outspoken Mary Sills.

"I can understand why!" laughed Carolyn. "How many of you have been whipped before you came here?"

About half the women nodded and mumbled and made comments in the affirmative.

"What do you think—can you forgive the men who whipped you?"

More comments followed, with several shaking heads.

"Yet just imagine—Jesus tells us that when we forgive, and when we are kind to those who treat us badly, that we will be rewarded in heaven. Listen to what he says: *'But I say unto you which hear, Love your enemies, do good to them which hate you, Bless them that curse you,*

and pray for them which despitefully use you.' That means that you are
to pray for your former masters that whipped you."

"What 'bout you, Miz Dab'son?" asked Mary. "You ain't neber
been whupped, has you?"

"No, Mary, I haven't."

"Den what you gots ter pray an' forgib like you say we has to?"

Carolyn smiled. "Right now, Mary, I am praying for some people
who are treating my husband badly."

"What kin' er people? Who wud do dat ter *him*?" she asked, incredulous that anything critical could ever be said of Mr. Davidson.

"Believe it or not, some of his own relatives," replied Carolyn.
"Sometimes those closest to us can be the most cruel of all. But you're
right, I don't have anything like whippings that I have to forgive. But
people can hurt us in many ways, with words and accusations as well
as whips. Those kinds of hurts have to be forgiven too. Some of you
might have those kinds of things to forgive too—hurt feelings and
cruel words and unkindnesses of many kinds. All hurts have to be
forgiven—so, Mary, why don't you begin our reading, there at verse
thirty-one."

Mary squinted down at the Bible in her lap, and then began to
read.

"An' as ye wud dat men," she said, each word coming out slowly,
one at a time, before she moved on to the next, *"shud do ter you—"*

She stopped and glanced up.

"Dis mean *women* too, Miz Dab'son?" she asked. "Or jes' men?"

"No . . . men *and* women, Mary."

"Why don' it say dat, den?"

"Because the word *man* in the Bible can mean men or it can mean
mankind, or both men and women together."

"Humph—seems a mite confusin' ter me." Mary bent down, found
her place again, and again, slowly and deliberately, continued: *"Do ye
also ter dem likewise."*

For the following forty minutes, with questions and interruptions
and many pauses and fresh starts, Carolyn guided and encouraged and
helped the ladies, reading in turn, through another seven verses.

"Very good, ladies!" Carolyn said enthusiastically when they had completed the section. "You are doing so well. I am very proud of you all. That portion Nancy read a moment ago is one of my favorite verses in the whole Bible. *'Give, and it shall be given unto you; good measure, pressed down, and shaken together, and running over, shall men give into your bosom.'*"

Carolyn paused and looked around the room at the gathering of simple and humble women whom she loved with all her heart.

"To give you an idea of what I mean," she went on, "imagine if you came and asked me for a container of flour to make bread. Now I could go to my bin and take out a meager scoopful and put it in your container and give it back to you. *Or* . . . I could fill it as full as I possibly could, then set it on the table and shake it about so that it would settle and make room for more. Then I could put *another* scoop in because of the settling."

Again she paused, allowing her image to settle into the women's imaginations just like the imaginary flour.

"But what if I still wasn't through. Because then I might set it on the table again and squash and press it down with my hands as tight as I could so that it would still hold even more. Then I could get my scoop and add *more* flour yet again. By now there would be so much more than the simple scoopful I had begun with. But I could even go further yet. I could scoop out more and put it on the top, and keep piling the flour so high that it was running over the edges as I handed your container back to you! Just imagine, that's how Jesus says God will bless *our* lives if we give to others so generously."

"Dat's how you an' Mister Dab'son is ter us," said one of the ladies. "You's always givin' ter us more'n we cud eber repay. Ef we ax you for sumthin', you always gib us more dan we ax for."

"That is very kind of you to say, Harriet. Maybe that is our way of repaying in some small measure how we feel God has blessed us," smiled Carolyn. "But more than that, we consider you part of our family."

"But we ain't *really*, Miz Dab'son," said Mary. "Look at us—we's black, you's white. Dat ain't sayin' we don' apresheate all you dun, cuz we do. But we's still black folks, an' you's still white."

"Of course," nodded Carolyn. "But we are all human beings together. That makes us brothers and sisters in an even *deeper* way than the color of our skin. In a wonderful way! Do you remember the verse Chigua read a few minutes ago, when she said, *'ye shall be the children of the Highest'*? We are all God's children together, and God doesn't see what color our skin is, only what is in our heart."

Carolyn paused thoughtfully a moment.

"That reminds me," she said after a moment, "of what Nancy and Chigua and I were talking about on our walk up here. They were talking about old legend of an ancient king and five rivers, and wondering if they were both descendants of that same king. But you ladies are descended from another king—Christ the king. And so am I. The Bible calls us heirs with him and children of the Father. Just imagine, we are children, not just of an earthly king, but of God himself who made the world and everything in it. He loves us as his children. I am a white lady. Most of you are black. Some of you probably have mixed blood. Chigua is a Cherokee Indian. She is married to a man who is half black and half white, so all three bloodlines run in her children. We in this room right now have within us the blood of all three races of America. Yet here we are *together*, true sisters because we are all children of the same Father. Isn't it wonderful! In God's eyes, I am not white and you are not black or brown or anything. We are simply children of God's heart."

"I have never heard anyone speak of God so personally as you do, Mrs. Davidson," now said Chigua, contributing for the first time to the discussion, "as if he were actually a Father who loves us and whom we could love back. Many Indians have converted to Christianity. Yet in our culture, God remains more like a spirit than a human being. He is nature, he is in the clouds and the sun and the water and the earth. He is over everything and in everything . . . but he is not the same as a *person*."

"He is God and Creator, but *impersonal* . . . is that something like it?" asked Carolyn.

Chigua nodded. "I would say so. Now you describe him as *personal*. This is new to me."

"I believe with all my heart that he is personal," said Carolyn. "Christianity says that God created the clouds and sun and earth and water and every plant and animal as well as mankind . . . but that he is distinct and separate from them. He created the sun, but he is not himself the sun."

Again Chigua nodded. "I think I see," she said slowly.

"But because we are unable to see God, even though he is personal, Jesus came to earth to tell us who God is . . . and to tell us that he is our Father—a *personal* Father."

Richmond had devised a plan to get Sydney's family the rest of the way to the North. It was not without risk—perhaps great risk. Yet it was so bold and daring that Richmond thought that it just might work.

Richmond had chanced to hear in town that Denton Beaumont would be traveling by train to the nation's capital in three days. The news set the wheels of his mind in motion. Manufacturing some business of his own in Philadelphia, which was in truth to visit an old friend whom he hoped might find a job and housing for Sydney's family, he told Carolyn, Sydney, and Chigua of his scheme. Carolyn was concerned for the danger. But as he listened, Sydney's glistening teeth gradually spread into a wide smile.

Richmond's plan, however, involved keeping Silas on at Greenwood temporarily, lodging with several other of the black workers. The possibility of his opening his mouth and saying more to their own blacks than they wanted was a risk they would have to take. But it would be far less than the risk of his blabbing something untoward in the presence of a federal commissioner sworn to enforce the Fugitive Slave Law by any means possible.

Then Richmond went to the young single man who still occupied the small room in their basement.

"Silas," he said, "I would like to talk to you a minute."

"Yes, suh, Mister Dab'son."

"I know you have been traveling north with Sydney's family—what is your goal when you get there?"

"Ter be free, Mister Dab'son . . . an' git me a job."

"How would you like to work for me—for wages?"

"But I's still a runaway as long as I's here, ain't I? I wants ter be a free man, dat's what I wants. Dis ain't da norf, is it, Mister Dabson?"

"No, Silas, this is Virginia. But there are no slaves at Greenwood, and you would be treated as if you were free. I think you will be safe here, as long as you say nothing to anyone. If you tell anyone that you are a runaway, I will have to send you away. You will simply be another black man I have hired to work for me."

"Dat soun's all right, I reckon," said Silas slowly, turning the thing over in his mind. "But I won't be no slave?"

"No, and you will be free to move on whenever you want to, as long as you never say a word about the Davidson plantation to another soul, even after you get to the North."

"I kin do dat, Mister Dab'son. Silas kin keep his mouf shut when he's got to."

And so it was arranged.

On the day of their scheduled departure, Sydney and Chigua and the children dressed in what clothes their hosts had been able to find for them to further the scheme, Sydney in one of Richmond's old business suits and Chigua in a dress of Carolyn's, neither the best-fitting but adequate.

Then they all loaded themselves into Greenwood's largest carriage, with appropriate luggage to complete the illusion, and set out for Dove's Landing and the station.

Richmond had timed their arrival to perfection. They had just finished purchasing three adult and four children's tickets to Philadelphia when Jarvis reined in at the platform and Denton Beaumont stepped down from his carriage. In obvious surprise, he looked over the family gathered with Richmond, a slender black man in a suit at

Richmond's side with briefcase in hand. Beaumont had never seen any of them before, and he did not like surprises of this kind.

"Denton, hello!" said Richmond expansively, walking toward him with outstretched hand. "You're not . . . taking the train today?"

"Actually, yes . . . yes I am. I am heading for Washington. Hello, Carolyn."

Carolyn smiled, though inside her heart was pounding for what the man was thinking.

"Why that's wonderful," said Richmond. "We will be traveling together. It will give us a chance to catch up."

Beaumont's eyes continued to scan the motley assortment of blacks with an inquisitive and not-altogether-happy expression.

"But you don't know my friends," Richmond went on. "Please meet Sydney LeFleure, his wife Chigua, and their four children. Sydney . . . Chigua . . . this is our friend and neighbor Denton Beaumont."

"I am pleased to meet you, Mr. Beaumont," said Sydney in his most flawless Jamaican English, extending his hand.

Reluctantly, Beaumont shook it. "Yes, I uh . . . had heard you had guests from the North," he said in Richmond's general direction. "What is it you do, Mr . . . .uh, LeFleure?"

"My background is in sugar exportation, mostly to Europe," replied Sydney. "More recently, however, most of my activities have been associated with the cotton trade."

"Sydney is French, Denton," said Richmond, "and his wife is a full-blood Cherokee."

"Ah, yes . . . I see."

"I am accompanying them as far as Philadelphia, where I have some business to attend to."

"And you, Carolyn?"

"No, I am staying here. I only brought Richmond and our friends to the station."

"Right . . . well, I need to see to my luggage," said Beaumont with uncharacteristic awkwardness. "It was, uh . . . a pleasure to, uh, make your acquaintance," he added with an unenthusiastic glance toward Sydney.

Beaumont continued inside the station. The slowing train was already visible coming toward them, and the six pilgrims and their surreptitious guide were already inside one of the coaches and comfortably seated before they saw Denton Beaumont again.

The Underground Railroad had temporarily hijacked the Baltimore and Ohio to transport its clandestine cargo on the final leg of its northern journey.

When Richmond returned five days later, Carolyn was as full of questions as he was of smiles and laughter.

"It all went without a hitch," he said. "Denton avoided us like the plague."

"And Chigua and the children?"

"They are situated in a small apartment in the outskirts of Philadelphia. I paid the landlord for two months' rent, and Travers assures me he will have work for Sydney within a week."

"Oh, that is wonderful . . . I am so relieved!"

"Sydney was beautiful! He played his role to perfection. After we had been on the train about an hour, he went over to Denton, who was seated alone, sat down with a great smile, and engaged him in conversation."

"I can hardly imagine it! Denton must have been beside himself."

"Let's just say that his discomfort was obvious. 'Richmond tells me you are an important man in Washington,' Sydney said. 'I am fascinated, Mr. Beaumont—I have been thinking of entering politics one day myself. . . .'"

Richmond laughed again. "I could hardly believe his audacity. And he sat there asking question after question, as Denton squirmed in his seat . . . it wouldn't have occurred to him in a million years that the articulate, well-informed, intelligent, good-looking man in front of him might be a runaway slave. There was even a man who boarded the trail for a short while called Murdoch—"

"Not the bounty hunter!" exclaimed Carolyn.

"I believe so. He and Denton exchanged words together. He was a man whose looks I did not like. But with Sydney sitting there across from Denton at the time, the man hardly took a second look at him."

"Oh, Richmond . . . that man is dangerous!"

"Well, nothing became of it, and now they are safely in Pennsylvania. Where are the boys?"

"Out in the shop. I think they are working on that project you gave them about the new weathervane."

Richmond found Seth and Thomas in the workshop as Carolyn had said.

"Hey, Tom . . . Seth!" he greeted them. "How are you two doing?"

"Good, Dad," replied Seth, setting down the saw in his hand. "When did you get back?"

"Just a few minutes ago."

"You have a good trip?"

"Great. Sydney and his family are safely in the North."

"But, Dad," said Thomas as if continuing with some previous conversation that had been gnawing at him, "what you are doing is breaking the law. I still don't see how you can justify it."

"A law that deprives freedom from any human being, especially one that perpetuates cruelty between men, is an evil law, Thomas," replied his father. "I take the command to obey the law of the land with utmost seriousness. But the Fugitive Slave Law and other laws upholding slavery in the South are wrong. Good men must stand against such evil. Too many in this country have been quiet for too long in the face of it."

"And why do we have to make this stupid weathervane?" said Thomas. "Why should we be in danger because of runaways? I don't want to go to jail."

"There is very little danger of that, Thomas. And if God has called us to help—"

"He hasn't called *me* to help them," interrupted Thomas irritably. "Who cares about blacks and slaves anyway?"

He turned and walked out, leaving Richmond dumbfounded. He sighed and it was silent a moment. Seth bent down and continued carefully sawing out the shape of the horse's head he had drawn on a slab of lumber.

"How is Silas doing?" asked Richmond.

"Seems okay," Seth replied. "Malachi is keeping a close eye on him."

Twenty-Six

Life at Greenwood gradually resumed its former routine. Yet how quiet the house seemed . . . dreary, empty, uninteresting. Carolyn noticed it as much as Seth. Since Cynthia's marriage, she had forgotten how much she missed having a daughter around the place. If Cherity had discovered a home of mother love in Carolyn's heart, Carolyn found her own soul enlarged as it made room for the motherless girl in that boundless region of being where mothers are capable of loving all young women as their own.

The following days were dull, drab, and silent. There was no doubt about it, Cherity made the house cheery, fun, and full of laughter. She seemed to *belong* there.

The "engagement," meanwhile, proceeded. All initiation came from Oakbriar, chiefly from Veronica and her mother. Seth remained almost bewildered by the vortex of events encircling him, accepting it with fateful inevitability as the way things were done. With every week that passed, he grew more and more uncomfortable being with Veronica.

Inwardly, Richmond and Carolyn had hoped the engagement would blow over before now. They were more aware of the nature of their son's struggle than he had any idea, but for now they gave him room to work it out on his own. They had learned most of what was being said through the normal channels of community gossip. It seemed clear that his naivety had landed him in over his head. But after two weeks with Cherity Waters, neither of his parents could bear the thought of Veronica as their daughter-in-law.

They hoped and prayed that Seth would come to his senses. All the while, however, they said to themselves that if it went on too long they would have to speak up. At the same time, however, they knew that ultimately Seth himself had to chart the course for his own future.

Meanwhile, weeks went by, then a month, then two . . . September . . . October . . . the colors of fall came and the air took on an occasional chill . . . and all the while the fateful day of December 11 drew inexorably nearer.

Denton Beaumont remained in Washington, D.C., for a month, came back to Oakbriar for a week, then returned again to the capital. None of the Davidsons saw him during that time. But, already beginning to cause a stir around Washington for an occasional rousing pro-Southern speech, the local favorite son was a star in Dove's Landing. There was already talk of Lady Daphne following him after the wedding. Such conversations inevitably also turned to Seth and Veronica, with speculations whether they might also follow Veronica's parents to begin their new life together in the capital. Invitations to the wedding had not yet gone out, but the celebration and Christmas ball to follow were being anticipated as the social events of the year for miles around.

In a self-serving press release for newspapers of central and northern Virginia, Denton Beaumont spoke of his new responsibilities in Washington on behalf of the state. It concluded, in response to the increasing problem of runaway slaves passing through Spotsylvania County on their way to the North, with the announcement of his having appointed his son Wyatt Beaumont to act as deputy federal commissioner in his absence. To the potential charge of patronage in regard to the move, Beaumont was ready with an explanation. "I had offered the post to one of our county's leading citizens, my friend Richmond Davidson," he was quoted. "But when Mr. Davidson declined I was unable to find another qualified individual. In the end I asked my son if he would be willing to assume the duties of the position."

As Richmond read the account, a smile crossed his face. Now Denton's offer made sense. He had planned to appoint Wyatt all along and needed an excuse to do so. Reading the piece reminded him that he had delayed too long in returning Denton's check for $5,000 along with a formal declining of his offer on the Brown land. He would do so today.

Thought of the runaway problem and Denton's comments, however, soon replaced the smile with a cloud upon Richmond's countenance. These were times of danger and he knew it. It appeared they were destined to be increasingly drawn into it. Nor could they continue to respond to requests for sanctuary haphazardly when runaways appeared at their doorstep. They had to make plans, for surely more would come. Neither could they keep hiding them all in their home indefinitely. Some other provision had to be made. It seemed clear, too, that some of their own people needed to be brought in on what was going on.

Already an idea was forming in his mind about who to share it with. He would talk to Carolyn and see what she thought.

Richmond and Carolyn Davidson were beloved by all their black workers. But everyone within the Greenwood community recognized that Malachi and Nancy Shaw enjoyed an especially close friendship with their master and mistress.

It was not, therefore, considered out of the ordinary when the two were to be invited to the big house one Sunday afternoon in mid-October. All assumed the master wanted to talk to Malachi about the upcoming week's work. As it turned out, it was Malachi and Nancy who were most surprised of all when they were shown into the formal sitting room to a spread of coffee, tea, bread, assorted cheeses, and a variety of cakes, and the doors closed behind them. They were accustomed to being treated with respect, but not as honored guests.

Malachi had not failed to note the new weathervane atop the barn over the course of the last three weeks where it bent a new and unfamiliar head to the wind. He had kept his curiosity to himself. As he had glanced up while walking to the house a few minutes earlier, he would not have guessed that today's invitation had been prompted for the same reason the horse's head had been erected in such plain view.

They sat down, Nancy's eyes betraying a little anxiety at the formality of the setting, and wondering if they were about to be released from service to Greenwood and sent away.

"Thank you both for coming," began Richmond as Carolyn poured coffee and tea and they sat down around the table. "We have asked you here because we need to discuss something serious and of great importance with you. We want to share with you confidentially, and ask your help in deciding what is to be done in this matter."

He paused a moment and took a sip from his cup.

"You both remember Lucindy Eaton and her children—"

Nancy and Malachi nodded.

"She was a runaway, as you know," Richmond continued, "and we helped her get safely into Pennsylvania. In doing so, we broke the law. Technically we could be jailed for what we did. What you don't know is that Lucindy was not the first to have come to us for help. There was one before her . . . and now more recently the LeFleure family, as well as Silas, were all runaways. We did not divulge it because we thought it best word of it did not spread. We are more concerned for your danger, and everyone's at Greenwood, than for our own. If word of this activity got out, technically you could all be reenslaved again too. We are *all* in grave danger."

Again Richmond paused, considering how best to say what he had to say.

"From Sydney we learned something that may change all of our lives forever," he began again. "Word has apparently been spreading through a secret organization called the Underground Railroad that

Greenwood is a safe house for runaway slaves. We do not know how. The result is that more and more runaways are sure to come. We cannot, nor would we, turn them away, therefore we must find ways to offer them protection and safety while preserving our own. Whatever we do must be kept absolutely secret. Not even the slaves from Oakbriar or the McClellan plantation can suspect a thing. If the tiniest rumor were to leak out, it could mean tragedy for us all."

Carolyn glanced toward Malachi, but remained silent as Richmond continued.

"You may have noticed a new weathervane with a horse's head on top of our barn. There is apparently a secret sign known to those traveling north on this secret human railroad. They are told to look for the wind in the horse's head, and when they find it they have come to a place of safety. We put the weathervane up so that runaways in the area who may have heard of it would not accidentally stumble into Oakbriar and ask if they were at the safe house."

Richmond drew in a breath, then went on.

"So now we come to the question of what to do. That's why we need your help. If we have become a part of this secret network, probably because of having set you and the others free three years ago, then it seems we must make preparations for whoever else may come. Should we tell the others?—we don't know. Not to do so would complicate things, but doing so would increase the risk of word leaking out. Malachi, I thought that perhaps we should make provision for more people in one of your smaller cabins . . . or perhaps build another home or two for the purpose. Nancy, we will need your help in determining best how to care for women and children who come. Up till now, we have kept all three groups of travelers in the big house with us. But we cannot do so forever, and there is the added problem of—"

Almost from the moment Richmond had begun, Carolyn had detected the hint of a smile on Malachi's lips, and steadily widening. She grew more and more curious at its cause, and now at last Malachi could contain himself no longer and began to chuckle aloud.

Richmond stopped what he had been about to say, smiling himself in curiosity at what Malachi found so humorous. "What is it, Malachi?" he asked.

"I's sorry, Mister Dab'son," replied Malachi. "I wuz jes' thinkin' dat it's a mite mo' complicated dan you gots any idea."

"What do you mean?"

"Jes' dat dat Lucindy girl weren't da first by *no* means—why dere's been black folks comin' through here lookin' fo da win' in da horse's head fo' da bes' part er two years now."

"What!" said Carolyn. "Do you mean . . . *you've* been helping runaways too?"

"Dat I hab, Miz Dab'son. I ain't exactly been a conductor or a stashunmaster . . . I reckon I been a little er both, jes' doin' what I kin ter help poor folks on da run from da commishiners an' bounty hunters."

"But how?" said Richmond. "Where have you put them?"

"Here an' dere . . . in da woods mostly. Dey don' stay long, not like dose dat you took ter da big house. I jes' sen' dem on ter da nex' conductor on da way."

"I am speechless!" laughed Richmond in incredulity.

"Usually I meet him up by da ridge on da Brown lan' in an out er da way spot. Effen dat Lucindy hadn't come right in ter Nancy an' effen I'd foun' her first, you'd likely neber hab seen her at all an' she'd been on her way by da nex' night."

"I am amazed!" said Richmond. "To think this was all going on under our noses . . . and we never saw nor suspected a thing!"

Nancy did not find her husband's revelation humorous.

"How cud you do all dis wiffout tellin' me?" she said with a hint of Mary's characteristic *humph* in her tone.

"I din't want no danger ter cum ter you or nobody," replied Malachi. "Hit wuz bes' I jes' dun it myself."

"But I neber seen nuthin' . . . I never seen you wiff nobody."

"Mostly dey came an' went at night. I'd git up an' sneak out an' git my railroadin' biz'ness done afore mornin'."

"An' all dat time, when I heard you creepin' out, I thought you wuz jes' takin' care ob your necessaries!"

"How did you feed them? . . . did they never have to stay for more than a short time? . . . what if the weather was bad or the next conductor was late?" asked Richmond.

"I had ter use a little imaginashun at times, dat's true enuf," chuckled Malachi. "I'd hide dem in one ob dem ol' Indian caves, or up in the high pasture in da shed dere."

"I can hardly believe you were able to find places to keep them without detection!" said Richmond, still shaking his head in disbelief.

"I eben took dem into da Brown house a time er two—I hope you don' mind, Mister Dab'son. Dere wuz a fearsome storm las' winter an' I had five at once, wiff two real youn'uns an' I didn't know what ter du wiff dem. Dat's when I foun' da big room underneath, in da cellar, an' I kept dem dere till da storm passed, an' dat's how I foun' da tunnel leadin' ter one ob da caves too. An' dat's where I been hidin' dem eber since—I hope you don't mind too much, Mister Dab'son."

"No . . . no, of course not, Malachi," replied Richmond. "There is a tunnel from the cellar under the Brown house leading to a cave?"

"Yes, suh. It's dry an' out ob da way an' it's 'bout as good er place ter hide runaways as you cud ax fer."

"Well, Malachi . . . it would seem that many of the questions I had you have already had to deal with. How many people normally come to you asking for help?"

"Can't say, Mister Dab'son—sumtimes nobody fo' a mumf or two. But den I led sum folks up ober da ridge jes' three nights ago when you an' da missus an' Nancy wuz all sleepin' like babies. But more's comin', dat's what everybody seyz. Dey say hit's a flood dat's comin' norf, an' gittin' ter be a bigger flood all da time."

Twenty-Seven

$\mathcal{T}$he night was late. A low fire burned before a small circle of six youths who sat around it. All were white and scions of well-known Virginia families. That they had been drinking no doubt heightened the sense of drama associated with the secret meeting called by the one all acknowledged as their leader. Their brains were yet clear enough to know what they did and recognize to some degree its import, though none could have foreseen where it would lead.

At last twenty-year-old Wyatt Beaumont spoke.

"My father has named me as his deputy commissioner while he is in Washington," he said. "As much as I respect my father in many ways, his inaction on the runaway problem is not one I can condone. This is the opportunity we have been waiting for to do something about it ourselves—to break the back of the Negro network once and for all."

"What can we do, Wyatt?" asked Brad McClellan. "We're just . . . well, not exactly kids, but you know what I mean."

"We have the law on our side, that's what," replied Wyatt. "We have been dealing with niggers all our lives. It's no different now, except now we're going to do it with guns and ropes and by putting them in jail or sending them back to their owners where they belong."

"Why us, Wyatt?" asked another.

"Because I can trust you, and I know you share my feelings about the problem. Just as my dad chose me, I have chosen you to be *my* deputies," said young Beaumont. "But no one must know. What we do here, and what I may call upon you to do in the future, must forever remain unknown. Breaking the vow of silence will be punishable by blood. If any one of you is are not prepared this night to swear absolute loyalty to our cause, you can get on your horse and leave us now."

He paused and looked around at the other five. The light from the flames flickered from their faces.

"Are we all agreed, then?"

Each of the five nodded.

"Then here is the vow of the Brigade of the White League. I want you to each say it after me: Long may the South endure . . ."

"Long may the South endure," they repeated slowly in unison.

"Death or prison to all runaways . . . "

"Death or prison to all runaways."

"May ruin come to all who harbor and give them aid or comfort . . ."

"May ruin come to all who harbor and give them aid or comfort."

"And we dedicate our lives to the rights of freedom for white men everywhere."

"We dedicate our lives to the rights of freedom for white men everywhere."

"Where did you learn all that?" asked one of the boys when they were done.

"I overheard my father talking to a man from Alabama. They were talking about a secret society of Southerners dedicated to the cause of slavery. That's when I decided to start our own brigade right here. And now that we have taken the vow together, you are bound to come when I call for you."

"How will we know?"

"I will arrange a series of signals and a place to meet."

"What about others . . . our brothers . . . guys like Scully and others around town? They'll want to join too."

"We will use them when we need to, but they must not know of tonight's vow. Too many loose tongues could bring us down too.

Whatever you do, say nothing to Scully. He's white trash and doesn't know when to keep his mouth shut. If anyone else proves worthy to be added to our number, I will decide that myself."

Even as he said the words, a cunning idea entered Wyatt Beaumont's brain that was so unexpected he hardly knew what to think of it.

A light carriage made its way along a lonely stretch of road deep in the Maryland hills. The young man at the reins knew how to handle himself well enough in a saddle. But the poverty of his boyhood on the streets of New York had taught him to appreciate life's finer things. The carriage notwithstanding, however, he had foregone his usual expensively tailored attire and was clad in the humble garb of a farmer. If he was seen by the wrong people, he did not want his appearance in so out-of-the-way a place to invite curiosity and comment.

Suddenly three horsemen galloped out of the woods and onto the road. Immediately he reined in. One of the riders signaled him to follow, then spun his horse around and led the way along the road in the same direction he had been going. He urged his single horse forward and the two other riders followed behind.

A quarter of a mile farther, they turned onto a narrow track, barely wide enough for the two carriage wheels, that led, by many turnings and up a steep incline, to an abandoned barn and corral.

Here they stopped again. He was blindfolded. One of the men jumped up beside him and took the reins. Again they bounded into motion. The route this time was similar. They climbed steadily, bouncing over rocks and potholes, until, after another twenty or thirty minutes, they reined in. His blindfold was removed. He found himself facing an imposing man of slender build but great height, whose pale eyes and fierce countenance stared straight through him.

He motioned him down and led him inside a small log cabin. They sat down across from one another at a rickety wood table.

"Are you the one they call The Owl?"

"I am."

"My name is Brown—John Brown. I understand you can get me guns."

"It is possible. Can you pay?"

"I can. What kinds do you have available?"

"Whatever you need—carbines, Winchesters, 45s, a range of pistols of various calibers."

"Where do you get them?"

"I have various sources—Lexington, Boston, Cincinnatti . . . I have contacts everywhere."

"You don't buy them through normal channels?"

"No," smiled The Owl. "That is why the prices of the people I represent tend to be somewhat higher than what is advertised in the catalogs. But no questions are asked."

"That should suit my purposes," said Brown.

"Then tell me what you need and I will speak to my contacts. As soon as they are paid we will arrange for delivery wherever you like."

"I will draw up a list."

The tall man paused, then lowered his voice, as if even here in his mountain hideout, prying unfriendly ears might be listening.

"There is one other thing," he said.

"I am listening," nodded The Owl.

"I need whatever information I can get on the disposition of troops at Harpers Ferry and the guard at the federal armory."

"When?"

"Next month."

"I will see what I can learn."

⟨‿⟩

Some troubles come upon us like sudden thunderbolts from a clear sky, after which life is never the same again. Other difficulties gather like slow-brewing storms whose clouds approach by infinitesimally closer degrees, until a day comes when finally, however long antici-pated, the rain of their difficulties at last breaks upon us.

Seth had seen a speck of darkness on his horizon the night he had ridden away from Oakbriar the previous May after being unknowingly backed into what gradually became an engagement to Veronica Beaumont. He had tried to ignore it. But it had grown steadily in size, inching closer day by day, until now his mental and emotional skies were filled with threatening dark clouds. Not a patch of light was visible anywhere.

By early November Seth realized the clouds would not go away of themselves. He and he alone could extricate himself from the quagmire in which he found himself.

Seth left the house and wandered toward the stables. Whenever he thought about trying to clear his head, the first place that came to his mind was Harper's Peak. He had to get as high as he could, into the fresh quiet air where he could look down on the world of his difficulties with detachment and perspective. How much his rides to that high vantage point with a certain girl from Boston in August contributed to the continual drawing of his soul in that direction in the months since was not a question he wanted to ask right now.

He stood at the fence and gazed into the pasture. He already knew that for this occasion, only the stallion Malcolm would do. He needed Malcolm's strength, humility, and clarity of vision. He would saddle him and ride to the peak.

He whistled and called his name. Twenty minutes later he was on his way.

He supposed he had been searching his soul ever since the Waterses' visit. Who could deny that alongside that certain other young lady, Veronica was unbelievably shallow. How could he have allowed himself to get swept into all this without seeing how things really were? Did he want to marry someone he couldn't talk to about serious things?

He reached the top of the ridge, his mind going in many directions. It was quiet and peaceful, just what he needed.

He climbed down from Malcolm's back and walked about. The words burst forth from him as if they had been building up for weeks:

"Lord," he prayed aloud, "what am I going to do! What *should* I do? What do *you* want me to do?"

The simplicity of the appeal in no way diminished its power. His unassuming prayer may indeed have contained the most powerful appeal possible to the human species.

Seth had grown up under the umbrella of his parents' faith. It was a faith his father and mother had wrestled through to make their own. But Seth had not yet encountered the birth struggle into his own sonship. He believed. His belief, as he had truthfully communicated it to Cherity Waters, had grown toward depths of personal authenticity. But he had not yet had to fight to transform that *belief* into trusting *faith*. Belief is the first step on the stairway of trust that leads to faith. It is a necessary beginning, but only a beginning. The season when Seth Davidson would have to climb that stairway was at hand. And in that upward journey would his own trusting sonship be born.

In truth, no better environment exists for the nurturing of the tender shoots of faith than under the loving and secure umbrella roof of a father and mother of truth. The so-called testimony that the angels in heaven rejoice at even more than to hear that one lost sheep has been found to rejoin the ninety-nine, is the simple witness: "I came from a home where God was honored as Father and Jesus was trusted as Lord." It is the finest testimonial possible to the method by which God ordained for his life to be transmitted throughout the generations.

Yet the umbrella of such an upbringing also casts a shadow out of which those fortunate young men and women must one day emerge in order that the sunlight from that Fatherhood and the obedience of that lordship might shine on their *own* faces and begin to guide their *own* life's footsteps.

This transition into that high obedient childship is often accompanied by temporary bouts of rough spiritual weather within the human soul. Yet only so do they begin to look up and depend personally for themselves upon their heavenly Father. They emerge from such storms on new and more intimate terms with both heavenly *and* earthly fathers. For with increasing trust in the former comes increasing respect for the latter. Mothers, too, come in for their share of this heightened awareness of life's roots and wings produced by such healthy steps toward spiritual independence.

In praying the few simple words that had proceeded from his mouth, Seth Davidson had taken huge new strides toward his own spiritual manhood. For he had taken the first step toward self-chosen childship. He had placed his affairs, his future, his fate, into the hands of Another.

No more would he try to "work things out," as is the common way, on his own. He needed help, and he knew it. He was not afraid to admit it. He was ready to be a child. And as a child, he would emerge a man. He would become a man because he would be a son.

Almost immediately after his prayer the words from the Lord's parable came to him:

I will arise and go to my father.

He stopped and stood a moment.

"Was that the answer you would give me, Lord?" he said quietly. "Did you just answer my prayer?"

Of course, he thought. It was so simple, why hadn't he seen it all along! God would speak to him through his father!

Thirty seconds later Seth was again on Malcolm's back and making for Greenwood as fast as he dared.

Seth found his father with the men where he had left them earlier, plowing the wheat field harvested two months before in preparation for its winter dormancy.

Richmond had known for days that Seth was in the midst of a struggle of some kind. He had sensed an hour or two before, when Seth had asked to be excused from the plowing, that it was coming to a head. He turned the plow he had been wielding over to one of the other men, and walked to meet Seth as he approached over the upturned furrows. The expression on Seth's face was serious.

"Dad," he said, "we've got to talk."

Half an hour later the two men, father and son, were mounted and riding into the hills on the back of two of their favorite horses. As soon as they were out of sight of the fields and buildings, Seth began to unfold his trouble to his father.

"I'm in a fix, Dad," he said, "and I don't know what to do. I'm talking about Veronica—you probably figured that, right? I'm just not sure I really want to marry her. The main reason I am in this pickle is because I didn't talk to you and Mom at the very beginning. It all just sort of happened. I was stupid, Dad. I guess I thought the situation would blow over, though that's pretty dumb—engagements don't just blow over. Or else I guess I thought that I could work it out on my own."

He laughed morosely.

"But obviously I haven't, have I," Seth went on. "Maybe I needed your help all along more than I realized. It wasn't that I didn't want your help. I just got into the whole thing . . . sort of by accident. I should have asked for help right at the beginning. I'm sorry, Dad."

"You're asking for it now," said his father. "Better late than never, as they say."

"Yeah, maybe . . . but I still wish I had been thinking clearly enough to come to you immediately. You would have helped me sort it out on the spot and we could have avoided all this."

"Why don't you tell me how it came about," suggested Richmond. "Sometimes the best way forward out of a problem is to go back to its origins and see where you went wrong in the first place. The quickest way forward is finding the place where you took the wrong fork in the road so you can go back and take the other one."

Seth nodded, then recounted the conversation that had taken place between he and Veronica's father the night he had gone to Oakbriar for dinner. His father nodded as he listened.

"So you see, Dad, it was all so vague," he said. "I had no idea he was actually talking about engagement. One minute Veronica and I were just neighbors and friends, the next minute we were engaged. Then she started telling people and word got around . . . then she told me she and her mother had set a date."

Seth shook his head as if unable to believe that any of it had really happened.

"I almost knocked on your door that night," he said, "when I came back from dinner to tell you about my talk with Mr. Beaumont. I knew I should have. I guess I was embarrassed, and I just didn't. I had misgivings even then. I knew *something* was wrong. But like I say, I was embarrassed . . . and maybe a little too proud to admit that I'd been a dope."

"You never need to be embarrassed with your mother and me."

"I know, Dad . . . but I felt stupid. I should have come to you right then and asked you what to do. And then as time went on, there just never seemed a good time. Sometimes, you know, it's hard to bring things like that up."

"I had the feeling something happened that night," said Richmond. "You were different after that, weighed down. You haven't been your-self since then. Well . . . except when the Waters were here. But after they left, you sunk back into whatever it was."

"That noticeable, huh?"

"To one who knows you as well as I do."

"Why didn't you say something, Dad? Why didn't you step in and clunk me over the head, and knock some sense into me? Why didn't you call it off?"

"Would you have listened?"

"I hope so."

"It's not always easy to listen to a parent's advice after you think you've done most of the growing up you need to do."

"Yeah, maybe. But I was being stupid, Dad—you should have told me."

"I couldn't tell you that, Seth, my boy, without you asking for my input and counsel."

"Didn't I ask what you thought of Veronica?"

"No, you didn't."

"I'm sorry, Dad. I thought I had. I wanted to know what you thought."

"Until you asked, I had to wait. I was pretty sure you had been

pulled in without realizing it. But don't worry—your mother and
I wouldn't have let you drown in a hopeless marriage. If it had gone
on long enough, eventually we would have spoken words of caution.
But we felt like you needed to see it for yourself."

"Well from now on, Dad, however old I am, if you see me about to
make such a colossal blunder again like this, you tell me! I don't care if
I am fifty years old and you are—"

He paused momentarily.

"How old would you be, Dad?" he asked

"Seventy-eight. I was twenty-eight when you were born."

"All right, then . . . I don't care if I am fifty and you are
seventy-eight, if you see me being stupid, box my ears and tell me! It
won't matter how old I am, you will always be my father, and will
always be older and wiser than me."

"I'll try, Seth, my boy!" laughed his father. "It might be hard, but
I shall try."

It grew silent and again Seth was serious.

"What we were talking about before," he said, "I guess maybe that
is the place to set it right, like you said, isn't it—where it went wrong
in the first place . . . in the parlor at Oakbriar."

"I think that may be a wise observation, Seth, my boy."

"I have to talk to them, don't I?"

"I think so."

"First I've got to decide what to say," said Seth with a long sigh.

As they rode back into the stables an hour after setting out, Seth
Davidson knew what he had to do. He would get his thoughts settled
and his mind calm. Then he would make a call at Oakbriar . . .
tomorrow. The day after at the latest. Word had it that Veronica's
father was back in Dove's Landing for two or three weeks in advance
of the upcoming congressional Thanksgiving recess.

He would use the opportunity to speak with him.

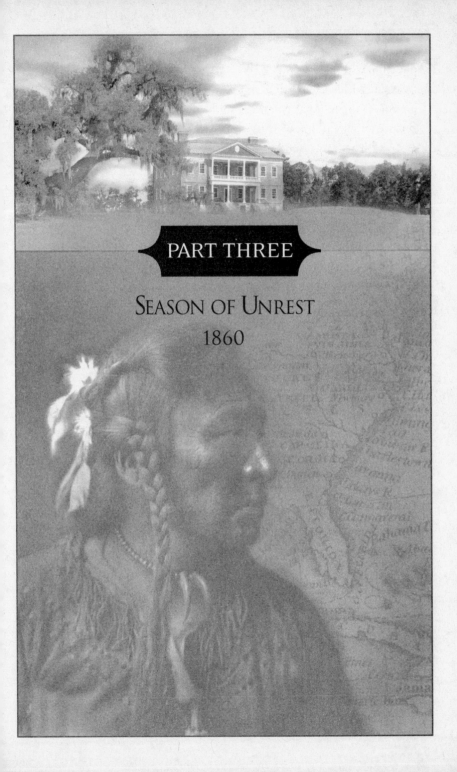

PART THREE

SEASON OF UNREST
1860

Twenty-Eight

$\mathcal{A}$ telegram arrived at Oakbriar before Seth Davidson made his planned visit to Veronica's father, carrying tidings that would, in the end, influence the lives of the Beaumont family far more than what Seth had to tell them.

In his study, Denton Beaumont heard the rider approach but had no idea what could be the man's business. Jarvis knocked on the open door a minute or two later.

"Dere be a telegram jes' come fo' you, massa Bowmont," he said.

"Come in, Jarvis," said Beaumont. "What are you standing there for like an idiot? Let me see it."

The black man handed his master the envelope, and retreated in silence. Beaumont slit open the envelope, removed and unfolded the single sheet inside, and sat back in his chair to read it. The message was concise and simple:

> SENATOR EVERETT DEAD OF HEART FAILURE.
> REQUEST PRIVATE MEETING SOONEST
> POSSIBLE. SAY NOTHING, COME TO RICHMOND
> IMMEDIATELY.
> —HENRY WISE, GOVERNOR,
> COMMONWEALTH OF VIRGINIA.

Beaumont exhaled a long sigh, his brain spinning. This was stunning news. What could the request possibly mean?

He was on the train for the state capital that same afternoon.

The following morning, Seth finally summoned the courage he sorely wished he had demonstrated earlier. He arrived at Oakbriar, walked up the steps, took a deep breath, and sounded the knocker.

From her room Veronica had seen him come. If the truth were known, she was more than a little put out with her fiancé, as she supposed him, for his gross inattentiveness of late. He never called on her, only she on him. Whenever they were together he was quiet and distracted. She had heard that men changed once becoming engaged. But she had never expected it of Seth.

When she saw him riding toward the house, therefore, after dashing halfway across the room, she stopped herself and thought a moment.

She would wait a few minutes in her room. She wouldn't run down eagerly as if she was actually *glad* to see him. Let him stand and stew a while on the porch. She might even tell Jarvis to send him away, and tell him that she was not receiving visitors today. Let him think about *that* if he thought he could get away with this silent treatment.

She sat down in her chair, looked at herself in the mirror, then played with her hair and fussed a little with her new necklace. But when she again heard the sound of horse's hooves outside, she jumped up and dashed to the window.

There was Seth's buggy . . . riding away!

She turned and flew to the door and down the stairs.

"Jarvis . . . Jarvis!" she cried out. "Was that Seth who called?"

"Yes'm, Miz Bowmont," replied the butler as his mistress reached the ground.

"Why in heaven's name didn't you come get me!" she said.

"He din't ax fo' you', Miz Bowmont, leastways not by yo'self."

"What do you mean by that!"

"He ax'ed fo' Mister Bowmont *an'* yo'self, Miz Bowmont. W'en

I tol' him dat Mister Bowmont wuz away, he thanked me den turned an' lef'."

"Without asking to see me!" cried Veronica in a passion of angry disappointment. She ran to the door and swung it open, intending to call after Seth and demand that he turn around.

But the back of his horse was already disappearing from sight. For half an instant she considered chasing after him, but just as quickly realized it would do no good. By the time she got someone to hitch a horse to a buggy, Seth would be halfway to Dove's Landing. She didn't much like the idea of trying to overtake him behind a horse at full gallop and turning the buggy over on herself.

Seething inside, she turned and went back up to her room. Stronger measures were apparently going to be called for.

Meanwhile in the office of the governor in Richmond, Denton Beaumont had just been shown a seat and offered a cigar.

"Beaumont," said the governor, "We are a year away from what may be the most historic presidential election in this nation's history. With Lincoln and Seward vying for the Republican nomination and some trying to persuade John Fremont to try again, with Jefferson Davis making noises about running, as well as the Democrats Douglas and Breckinridge trying to unseat their own president for the nomination, not to mention Bell for the Whigs likely to throw his hat in the ring, and with the guns of Harper's Ferry still sounding in our ears and John Brown likely to be hung within a matter of weeks . . . these are critically important times. And now with Minnesota and Oregon in the Union as free states, the South will never again gain parity in the Senate. We are already looking at an eighteen-to-fifteen advantage of free over slave states and that gap is sure to widen. The abolitionists are becoming more and more outspoken. John Brown was a lunatic, yet his cause has much sympathy in the North. Buchanan will no doubt be the last pro-Southern president this country will elect. Things are not moving our way and could get out of control. And here is Virginia right in the middle of it. If there is ever an armed conflict, I shudder to think of the implications for the citizenry of our state."

The governor paused momentarily.

"Now I am aware of your discussions with some in the party" he went on, "and of your recent appointment in Washington, and your plan to run again for the Senate in '62. But it would seem that events have stolen a march on us. Suddenly Everett is dead and I have a problem—I have to appoint someone to fulfill the remaining three years of the senator's term. I see no reason, as you are being groomed for it anyway, to select anyone else. You are the obvious choice. The long and the short of it is that I brought you here to ask if you want the job."

Beaumont sat stunned. It would not do in these august surroundings to fall all over himself with too much eagerness. But his heart was pounding so loud he could hear it. The governor just offered him a senatorial seat on a silver platter . . . without all the expense and bother—not to mention potential humiliation—of a second campaign!

He took a breath to still his trembling nerves, then tried to speak in a measured tone without betraying the quiver in his voice.

"Well, Governor," he began, "I am, of course, flattered. The death of Senator Everett has come as a great shock to us all. I am saddened, as I know you are, by the passing of a distinguished Virginian. As to your offer, I can only say that, for the good of our state, I am willing to serve, and am honored by the confidence you place in me."

"Come, come, Denton," chuckled the governor, "we have known one another long enough to dispense with all that. Save it for the press. A simple yes or no will suffice. I know how you had been longing to get to Washington. And had it not been for some last-minute pranks by our good friend Senator Hoyt, you would have been in Washington much sooner. But the fact is, there are any number of other men I might have invited here today who would be furious to know of this meeting. But . . . I want a man on the Senate floor who will be loyal to me when the time comes. And I will expect unswerving, and unquestioning loyalty."

"You shall have it, Governor."

"Then I suggest you get home, make whatever arrangements you must, then get back to Washington at your soonest opportunity and announce your resignation from that post in the War Department they arranged for you. As soon as you are situated and can send for your family, you will be expected on the Senate floor and sworn in."

"I will see to it, Governor."

"Good, then I will make the announcement to the paper, including heartfelt condolences from us both to Senator Everett's widow. I will send my official notification to the vice president in a couple days. Let me know by telegraph when you are in Washington."

Denton Beaumont left the governor's office twenty minutes later and nearly skipped down the stairs two at a time, a beaming grin spreading across his lips that he could not suppress if he tried. As he emerged from the capitol into the crisp November sunshine, he came very close to shouting *Hallalujah!* at the top of his lungs.

Frederick Trowbridge and Jeeves Hargrove and Upton Byford and even former President Tyler and all the rest of Virginia's power brokers who had chosen the fool Davidson over him to run in last year's election, and then come back to him last summer when their fortunes had changed and they needed *him* . . . let them all choke on it. *He* would soon be seated in the Senate, and without their help! He would remember who his friends were . . . and weren't.

By the time the train pulled into Dove's Landing the next day, Denton Beaumont was himself again—calm and sedate, yet still glowing inside from the developments.

"Hello, Mr. Beaumont," he heard his name called almost the moment he stepped out of the train.

"Oh, it's you," he said, turning. "Hello, Scully."

"Been out of town, Mr. Beaumont?"

"There's one thing you ought to learn, Scully," said the senate-appointee without slowing, "and that is to mind your own business. Your kind will never get far in life, but you'll get farther if you learn that one lesson."

"Yes, sir. You'll give my regards to Miss Veronica, won't you, Mr. Beaumont?"

"Scully, I don't know if you've heard, but my daughter is engaged."

"I heard, Mr. Beaumont."

"Then you know it wouldn't be proper for me to pass along to her the regards of another young man."

"Yes, sir. I only thought—"

"I know what you thought, Scully," interrupted Beaumont. "You're sweet on her, and you don't understand that girls like my daughter can never have anything to do with boys like you, whether they're engaged or not. Stay away from my daughter, Scully. I don't even want you thinking about her, do you understand?"

Beaumont did not wait for an answer but walked on, leaving Scully sulking where he stood leaning against the station wall.

The brief unpleasant exchange, as low on the human food chain as he considered a boy like Scully Riggs, did serve the purpose of reminding Denton Beaumont that there were matters that would require attending to, here as well as in Washington. He had affairs to place in order. One of the most pressing was this business of Veronica's marriage to the Davidson boy. If he knew Veronica, she would be as anxious to go to Washington as he was. He could hardly imagine her being happy at Greenwood alone.

His other pressing concern was Oakbriar itself. During his recent absences he had allowed things to continue without making too much of it. But the Senate would require far more of his attention. He could be gone for years. National office might not be out of the question if he played his cards right. He would have to make some definite changes.

Who would be in charge of operations at Oakbriar during his absence? Most of the white men were afraid of Slade. He had given the big black man far too much power. He was himself the only man who could keep him in line. Who would run the place? He wasn't about to let that fool of a Davidson boy settle himself at Oakbriar after December, even, as seemed inevitable, as his son-in-law. Before he knew it, the imbecile would be treating the slaves like whites and putting ideas into their heads. He and Wyatt would clash immediately.

Who could handle the whites, the slaves, and knew everything there was to know about Oakbriar?

Wyatt?

Possibly, but a plantation the size of Oakbriar required more experience and judgment than the bone he had tossed him regarding the deputyship. Wyatt would be able to do what was required, but he was still too young to command the respect needed from so many.

There was only one person. Beaumont hated to admit it, but he needed Leon Riggs back. He and Wyatt together—Wyatt as his eyes and ears, Riggs as his overseer—could keep the plantation profitable and orderly. Whether Riggs could handle Slade was another matter. But other than that, he was capable of running Oakbriar. And to ease his worries and allow him a seat in the Senate, he didn't mind dishing out a little humility in the man's direction.

As to Veronica, maybe he could get her to call off the whole thing and go to Washington with them. He knew it would never happen, but it was a pleasant thought. On the other hand, perhaps the wedding should proceed as planned, and then the two young people accompany them to Washington. Away from the influence of his fool of a father, who could tell, maybe something tolerable could be made of the boy.

He had to figure some way to make the best of it, Denton Beaumont thought to himself. Apparently they were going to be stuck with Seth Davidson as their son-in-law.

Lady Daphne went into a rapture of delight at the news her husband brought from his meeting with the governor. Veronica took the news more sedately. Immediately she began revolving within her own mind what effect the change would have on her.

"Will I have to go with you, Daddy?" she asked. "What about Seth and me and the wedding?"

"You do not have to come, Veronica," replied her father. "I merely assumed you would *want* to. What attractive young lady would not want to live and swirl about in the center of the nation's social vortex, with young men and dances and balls—"

"But, Daddy . . . what about Seth and the wedding?"

"Your mother and I will not be moving until after the first of the year. It will take me that long to find a larger house and see to moving what things we will need. Congress will be in recess for the holidays anyway. So by all means, my dear, go ahead with your plans, and bring Seth along. Perhaps the change will be good for him. One never knows," he added with a smile of intended humor, "he might become a diplomat or something."

Her father's words sent Veronica's brain spinning in heretofore unconsidered directions. To get Seth sufficiently out from under the wings of his parents such that she could mold him free from their daily influence had been one of her highest objectives for years. Her father's appointment would provide her just the right opportunity. Who could tell, with her father's connections and prominence, Seth might well become an important man too. He was just the kind of young man who could take the world by storm if put in the right places—good-looking, of good family and stock, well-spoken and educated. If he could be shed of the influence of his father's religious and social idiosyncrasies, there was no reason he couldn't run for office himself one day. Her father would appoint him as an aide or assistant of some kind. From there he would work his way up. When her father was ready to retire after two or three terms in the Senate, Seth, then in his thirties, would be in a perfect position to continue the family legacy.

Before the day was out, Veronica's castle building about the bright future she and Seth would have in the nation's capital had succeeded in making her as excited about the move as her mother. Immediately they began to revamp the wedding guest list, adding many new names from Washington whose friendships it would be well to begin cultivating as soon as possible.

Denton Beaumont was not one to let the grass grow under his feet. With the governor's public announcement due any day, sure to be the biggest news to hit Dove's Landing in years, he did not want to negotiate with a man like Leon Riggs from a position of weakness. It wouldn't do for Riggs to get the idea he *needed* him. The only way relationships worked in the calculus of Denton Beaumont's considerations was for people to need, and therefore fear, *him.*

Accordingly, the following morning he hitched up a buggy and headed for town, ostensibly on other business that would give cover to his true intent.

Arranging it so that he accidentally ran into Leon Riggs at the station, he greeted him with what he considered just the right touch of friendliness and aloofness.

"Hello, Riggs," he said, offering his hand.

"Mister Beaumont," nodded Riggs.

"How are things going for you here?"

"Can't complain, I guess. Pay ain't too good, but the work ain't bad."

"Well, if you ever decide to get back into plantation work, come see me. I can always use a good man."

Beaumont nodded and walked away. He knew the likely effect his words were having inside the brain of Leon Riggs behind him. Nor was he disappointed.

"Mister Beaumont . . . " he heard behind him after he had gone about twenty paces.

He slowed, then turned, casting on Riggs a look of interrogation.

"You mean what you said . . . ," said Riggs, "you know—about coming to work again at Oakbriar?"

"I don't know, maybe. Why . . . I thought you said it was going well for you here?"

"It's going all right, I guess. But I'd sure be obliged to be back out at your place."

"Hmm . . . " mused Beaumont. "Well . . . yeah, Riggs, I might take you back on. I'm a man of my word, and I said to come see me, so . . . tell you what—let me think on it a day. You come out and see me tomorrow."

"I'll do that all right . . . thanks, Mister Beaumont."

Leon Riggs was not the only one to see Denton Beaumont in town that day. Seth Davidson saw the Beaumont buggy on the street not far from the station and knew it could mean only that Veronica or her father were nearby. He waited until he saw Veronica's father walking toward it after concluding the Riggs gambit.

That's when Seth knew that today was the day.

⌒

Denton Beaumont's brief speech to Veronica the day before had almost succeeded in convincing himself as well as his daughter that, in Washington, the prospect of Seth Davidson as a son-in-law might not actually be so bad after all.

When Seth called at Oakbriar that same afternoon, therefore, he found Veronica's father downright pleasant, effervescent with friendliness heretofore unaccorded him.

"Come in . . . come in, my boy!" he said, shaking Seth's hand as he walked in from the sitting room. "Jarvis tells me you want to have a chat with Veronica and me."

"That's right, sir," said Seth stiffly. He was more nervous than he had been on the night of the candlelit dinner!

"Jarvis, go upstairs and tell Veronica her young man is here."

"Yes, Mister Bowmont."

This time Veronica was playing no games. The potential move to Washington had changed her outlook about everything. The moment she saw Seth riding up, she had rushed to the mirror, applied a few last-minute touches, and then flew down the stairs.

"Seth, Seth . . . you'll never guess what's happened!" she bubbled over as she ran into the room. "We're going to Washington!"

Seth stood unmoving, looking at her radiant face that was more excited than he had seen it in a long time, but having not an idea what she was talking about. Then he glanced back at her father.

"Veronica's right, my boy!" said Beaumont. "At least she means that I am going to Washington."

"I . . . thought you had already been spending most of your time there, sir," said Seth slowly.

"Oh that—no, this is far larger news. We are *all* going . . . Lady Daphne and myself, I should say. The rest of you will have to decide for yourselves—you and Veronica, I mean."

"I . . . I still don't understand," said Seth, now glancing back at Veronica in confusion.

"Daddy's been appointed to the Senate!" exclaimed Veronica excitedly.

"But . . . but how—"

"Senator Everett died four days ago," said Beaumont. "The governor has appointed me to serve out the remainder of his term."

Seth nodded. At last things were starting to come clear.

"Well, then . . . congratulations, sir," he said, shaking Beaumont's hand a second time. "I wish you the very best."

"Thank you, my boy . . . thank you very much. And now perhaps you see what Veronica and I have been talking about—that this affects your future as well as mine . . . the two of you. If you should choose to come to Washington with us, I am certain a position on my staff could be arranged. I don't know what interest you have in politics, but your future in such a case would be a bright one."

"Oh, Seth, isn't it exciting! It's like a dream come true," bubbled Veronica. "We will be married, and then the very next month be living in Washington itself! I can hardly believe it!"

Seth glanced down at the floor. This was going to be more difficult than he anticipated!

"So, my boy," Veronica's father was saying with a laugh, "how about that cigar now that I offered you last May!"

Seth's lack of corresponding gusto over the prospects had at last begun to dawn on Veronica. She had come to know this gloomy side of him sufficiently in the past few months to recognize something brewing that gave her an uncomfortable feeling in the pit of her stomach.

"What is it Seth?" she said. "You *do* think going to Washington will be exciting, don't you?"

The room fell silent. Veronica's father was beginning to get the same queasy feeling. A few days ago he would have rejoiced to hear what was on Seth's mind. Now that his pride, if that were possible, had reached to yet loftier heights, anyone who thought of raining on his parade at this moment of triumph did so at his or her peril.

"So, Seth," said Beaumont, "sit down and tell us what you came to talk to us about."

"I think I would prefer to stand, sir," said Seth. "I can think more clearly on my feet."

"Suit yourself . . . but I am going to sit down."

"Me too," said Veronica, her angst mounting. She did not care for Seth's tone.

Seth drew in a deep breath and unconsciously began to wander a bit from where he stood. He could not look either of them in the eye.

"I need to talk to you about the wedding," he began.

Veronica swallowed hard.

"Do you remember that evening I came over for dinner?" he said. "With the candles . . . when you and I spoke with each other, sir?"

They both remembered.

"It seems to me that is when the trouble began," Seth went on. "You asked me, Mr. Beaumont, about my intentions toward Veronica, whether they were honorable and everything, and of course I said they were. Then you asked me if we understood each other and if I was satisfied, as nearly as I can recall it, which I guess I answered a little too vaguely and said that we generally did and that I was. After that, everyone thought we were engaged. At first I thought it must be a mistake. But then I realized you were acting like we were engaged too, Veronica. And then gradually there was more and more talk about the wedding and then a date was set. And—"

He stopped and looked down at the floor. Finally he looked up and found Beaumont's eyes.

"What I'm getting at, Mr. Beaumont," said Seth, "is that I completely misunderstood you that night. I had no idea the questions you were asking implied *marriage*. I see now that my answers to you conveyed something entirely different than I intended. I apologize, sir. I truly mean that. It was entirely my mistake, and I should have come to speak to you about it long before now."

"Then why didn't you?" snapped Beaumont. This news he would have greeted with joy a week ago had begun to anger him.

"Because I didn't have the courage to, sir," replied Seth. "For that I also apologize. I was embarrassed. I knew I had made a mistake. I just didn't have the guts to admit it. It was wrong of me. Somehow I hoped I would get used to the thought of marriage, and realize that it was indeed what I wanted. So I let things go, thinking that the reservations I felt were common to young men anticipating such a change in their lives. But the fact is, sir—"

Seth stopped and took a deep steadying breath. He turned to Veronica where she sat staring straight at him. He mistook her pale face and trembling lips for impending tears, which made continuing with what he must say all the more agonizing.

"Mostly I must apologize to you, Veronica," he said. "I am so sorry to have let this go on so long, but as I started to say . . . the fact is . . . I am not ready for marriage."

The words, though by now well enough expected, landed like a bombshell.

"I wasn't when I came over for dinner and your father and I talked, and realize that I am not ready now. You *are* ready. You have, perhaps, matured more quickly than I. But for whatever reason, the fact is, you are ready to be married . . . but I am not."

Again Seth tried to take in more air. The strain of the interview was enormous.

"And that's why," he said, laboring to get the words out, "that I think it best for us to—"

"Stop!" suddenly cried Veronica. "I refuse to listen to another word. This is all about that horse-riding tramp from the North, I know it!"

"It has nothing to do with her," said Seth softly. "It's just that I realize I made a mistake and feel it best for—"

"Do you think I would actually marry you after this!" Veronica shrieked in a white fury. She jumped to her feet, trembling uncontrollably. "Get out of here, Seth Davidson! Get out and don't come back. I never want to see you again!"

She turned and walked from the room with haughty dignity, her head high. She refused to give Seth so much as a final passing glance at the face he had spurned.

Still standing in the middle of the room, still expecting perhaps some modicum of understanding from Veronica's father, he turned toward him. But on Beaumont's face, too, he saw only anger. Already Veronica's father had renewed his vow to get even with this idiotic clan of his neighbors one way or another. He still more than half suspected Seth's father of having a hand in the newspaper articles that had cost him last year's election. And now his son seemed determined to make a laughingstock of both him and his daughter on the very eve of his Senate appointment.

"I am sorry, sir—," began Seth.

A preemptory wave from Beaumont's hand silenced him.

"Save your words, young Davidson," he spat. "I want no more of your duplicitous apologies. They mean nothing to me. Now I suggest you do as my daughter said, and leave this house immediately. You are no longer welcome here."

Stunned at the hostility of their reactions, Seth turned and left the house. He mounted and rode off sad and mortified, and not once looked back.

Twenty-Nine

*I*f the news of Veronica's engagement to Seth had been gradual to spread, the shocking news of its cancellation was instantaneously the chief subject of conversation among the gossips of Dove's Landing and for miles around. How this came about was a mystery since none of the Davidsons nor the Beaumonts cast so much as a shadow of presence in town for a week, and none told a soul. Juicy news, however, will out. The juicier and higher up the social ladder those involved, the faster the word will spread.

Veronica pouted for a week. Lady Daphne cried for a week. Denton Beaumont fumed for a week.

In the end, none were the better off. For their pouting, crying, and fuming had a common source—they all felt sorry for themselves. Not once in said week did a fleeting thought cross any of their three minds concerning *right*, *truth*, or anyone *else* in the matter. Only themselves. What *they* had wanted, the plans *they* had made, and what others would think of *them* to have the self-righteous and priggish Davidsons spurn a match with one of Virginia's most distinguished and prominent families.

Therefore at week's end Veronica and her father remained incensed. Lady Daphne remained self-absorbed and sad—not on any of their parts for loss of Seth, but for the perceived reflection in the minds of others of his slap in the face of their dignity.

In truth, Veronica had never loved Seth at all. In actual fact, unknown to Veronica, he had done her one of the greatest services one human can do for another by heeding his conscience—he had saved her from a marriage founded in superficialities. She had never loved him, she only wanted to *possess* him—they two people not quite so far removed from one another as black from white, but nevertheless strangers in the matter of love between a man and a woman. The desire to possess, though it leads to probably half the marriages of the civilized world, can never provide a foundation for the true self-denying love upon which great marriages are built.

As for the principle mover in the drama, during the week when the three Beaumonts were sinking yet further into the despond of their self-preoccupation, Seth had taken several strides toward manhood. This same choice between opposites is before us all daily—between striding forward into maturity, or sinking backward into self-preoccupation. Seth had faced his own immaturity, stupidity, and lack of courage—as he saw them, though in truth they were not entirely so serious as he at this moment perceived them. He had faced them like a man, taken responsibility, offered apologies where they were needed, and sought to shift blame to no shoulders but his own. Finally he had taken action on the basis of duty, conscience, obedience, and right— a fourfold foundation that will never misguide the honest soul facing doubt or difficult circumstances. He would ever after use this foundation for evaluating decisions in his life.

To so act was one of the most difficult things he had ever done— as it usually is to follow duty, conscience, obedience, and right. But he had done it. He had been courageous in the end, however wavering he may have been in the beginning.

Thus, light slowly began to dawn in his heart. He began to breathe again. A smile returned to his lips. The weight had been lifted.

The brightening of Seth's emotional horizon was short-lived.

As the town and neighborhood reacted to the news, there were those who resented Seth Davidson bitterly for the pain he had caused poor Veronica Beaumont. Why that was so remained as great a mystery as how rapidly the word spread. Any of Veronica's friends might now go after Seth themselves. And while of course they felt bad for dear Veronica, it was doubtful that any of them would have spread evil reports about Seth. Already two or three were eyeing him, including Brigitte McClellan and Sally O'Flarity, and thinking what a victory it would be to corral the man who had rejected Veronica Beaumont!

How much Scully Riggs may have been a mover in the changed attitude toward Seth was also curious in that the moment he heard the news his heart leapt with new hope on his own behalf. Immediately he began planning a visit to Oakbriar in his best clothes. But he had not forgotten that he hated Seth Davidson and had made a vow against him. And now his hatred was increased tenfold for his having hurt Veronica and shamed her publicly. Even though Seth's breaking of the engagement gave Scully the perceived opportunity to pursue his own suit for Veronica's heart, he yet vowed that he would punish Seth for what he had done. The two opposites, in a brain like Scully's, did not work in natural opposition. What he should have thanked Seth for, in fact made him despise him all the more.

Thus, for whatever combination of reasons, the glances and looks that began to be cast in Seth Davidson's direction whenever he ventured from the serene surroundings of Greenwood were ones of silent accusation. He had cruelly abused the fair and lovely daughter of their favorite son and soon to be junior senator from Virginia, and talk throughout the community turned steadily more bitter. It soon became clear that this heightened animosity represented but the latent flowering of a widespread repressed resentment toward Richmond and Carolyn as well. No doubt contributing to it the more was a perceived need to shun the Davidsons in order to demonstrate loyalty to their suddenly famous United States senator.

Christmas came and went.

The season was festive at Greenwood, for they little suspected the growing ugly reports concerning Seth. The entire Greenwood family, black and white alike, gathered at the big house for a sumptuous feast and singing and laughter and entertainment lasting well into the evening. If the Christmas season was a little less celebratory at Oakbriar, it was certainly busy, for preparations were under way for the move to Washington. By the second week of January of the new year 1860, all the Beaumonts but Wyatt were settled into their new house at the capital.

If she were honest with herself, Veronica would have had to admit that she hardly thought of Seth once in the whole month prior to the move.

The encounter was unexpected.

Congress was back in session and the returnees had begun to make the most of the endless round of invitations by attending every social gathering possible.

The moment Veronica saw the face she knew she recognized it. But from where? Whoever it was and wherever she had seen him before, the man was much improved. In her mind's eye as she tried to recall their previous meeting was the vision of a somewhat lanky youth. But the man before her was mature, well-formed, impeccably dressed in a three-piece suit with expensive tie clasp and matching cuff links. His black hair, combed straight back, accented a more than commonly handsome face, she had to admit, and his gait with head high and mysterious smile gave him an air of bold confidence.

The surroundings in the consulate where they stood were indeed glamorous. It was everything any of the three Beaumonts could have hoped for. Background music came from a small string ensemble. The clink of glasses and waiters refilling drinks and the trickle of laughter and animated discussion from two dozen conversations around them in no fewer than four different languages, not to mention the formal attire of every man and woman present . . . everything about this evening reeked with the heady atmosphere of power and influence.

Veronica studied the face she had seen a moment before. Suddenly she realized that the young man was returning her gaze.

He smiled. Veronica returned it in kind. But he was a shrewder judge of people than she. He saw her uncertainty, then slowly approached.

"Cecil Hirsch," he said. "We met at your eighteenth birthday party."

"Oh, yes . . . ," said Veronica, still trying to place him.

"And you are now here as the daughter of Virginia's newest senator." He thought it prudent not to mention that she would have been here a year sooner had it not been for his efforts on behalf of Virginia's *senior* senator. She had grown, Hirsch thought, or at least matured in the ways of the world. If he had seen "like calling to like" in the girl before, that sense was even more pronounced in the *woman* he saw before him now. "How do you find the capital so far?" he asked.

"Wonderful . . . thrilling . . . exhilarating," replied Veronica. "We've been here less than a month. We hardly know anyone yet."

"Perhaps I can remedy that . . . because I know everyone," he added with a smile.

"Do you really!" Veronica did not even try to hide her excitement.

"Almost. I doubt I can get you into the White House to see President Buchanan. You might have to wait for your father to secure an invitation for that. But I think you would find yourself otherwise pleased with the results should you place yourself in my capable hands."

He smiled. She smiled. Both understood.

What Seth Davidson had never grasped about Veronica Beaumont, though having spent most of his life in proximity to her, Cecil Hirsch had understood almost the moment he laid eyes on her. Seth was not enough like Veronica to understand her. For both to its credit and its peril, innocence is always slow to recognize opportunism as the potent and subtle force it is. Cecil Hirsch and Veronica Beaumont were both users. As long as they both knew it, neither minded the trait in the other. In its own way it sweetened the attraction by adding to the risk.

Still smiling, Hirsch offered his arm. Veronica took it, and he led her to the refreshement table, and then, as the evening advanced, about the floor. At his lead, they dabbled here into one conversation, there into another, as Hirsch played the role for which he had already begun to be known in Washington. On this evening, however, he was playing it with just a bit of added flair and panache to an audience of one.

It suit Hirsch's purposes, also, to be seen with such a stunning young woman on his arm. New faces, especially beautiful ones, always roused comment and curiosity in Washington. The Senate was one of the world's most exclusive clubs. To have a new arrival join its ranks in an off year was in itself enough to make the name Beaumont one that everyone recognized. The fact that he was a controversial figure, and an outspoken pro-slavery advocate from the very state where the Harpers Ferry ruckus had taken place, increased interest in him all the more. And when word began to leak out that there was *another* Beaumont, a daughter, unmarried, reportedly beautiful, inquisitiveness concerning the name increased many times.

Hirsch had already caught wind of such whisperings. Thus he now made the most of this opportunity that had fallen in his lap to increase the cachet of his own standing in the eyes of Washington's elite.

"Why, Mr. Hirsch!" exclaimed Lady Daphne as the two approached Veronica's mother. "You do move in high circles!"

"I am only trying to keep pace with you, Lady Daphne!" taking the woman's hand and kissing it. "How nice to see you again. You are looking wonderful. I hope you haven't forgotten your promise about an invitation to one of your parties!"

"I haven't indeed, Mr. Hirsch," replied Mrs. Beaumont. "Veronica and I are already planning it." The truth was, however, Lady Daphne *was* willing to forget her suspicions with regard to this man's possible involvement in the news articles that seemed to have originated out of their private conversations. One flash of his smile and she was ready to let bygones be bygones. They were here now, that was all that mattered. The young man seemed nice enough. Perhaps she had been mistaken.

As they chatted, the new senator himself walked up, followed by three people none of the rest had ever seen.

"Hello, my dear," he said to Lady Daphne. "I see you have found plenty to keep you occupied. Veronica," he added, smiling to his daughter.

He glanced toward Hirsch. "I'm sorry," he said, "I seem to know your face, but . . . "

"That is a common malady this evening!" laughed Hirsch. "I am not quite sure how to take it! Cecil Hirsch, sir," he said extending his hand. "I was fortunate enough to attend your daughter's birthday celebration at your estate in Virginia a year and a half ago."

"Ah yes, of course," said Beaumont. "I remember you now. A newsman, wasn't it . . . you and I chatted informally for a few minutes. I see you have also renewed your acquaintance with my wife and daughter."

"Yes, sir, and found them as charming as ever. Let me take the opportunity to congratulate you, Mr. Beaumont, on your appointment. I am certain the Senate will be considerably livelier for your presence."

Beaumont laughed. "Thank you, Hirsch," he said. "I shall certainly try to do my part to keep things interesting."

He paused and glanced to his side.

"But I am being remiss!" he said. "I came over, my dear," he said to his wife, "to introduce you to Ambassador Fitzpatrick. Ambassador, may I present my wife, Lady Daphne Beaumont, and my daughter Veronica, and Mr. Hirsch. My dear, Mr. Fitzpatrick is the U.S. Ambassador to the Grand Duchy of Luxembourg, and this is his wife, Eloise, and son Richard."

Handshakes and greetings went round the small group. Even as she clung to the arm of Cecil Hirsch, Veronica could not help stealing a second glance at young Richard Fitzpatrick . . . and then a third. Already Washington seemed a veritable breeding ground of handsome young men! She would *never* condescend to thank Seth for it, of course, but she was thinking how glad she was not to be married!

"And where is Luxembourg?" asked Lady Daphne, to her husband's silent chagrin.

"A good question, Lady Daphne!" laughed the ambassador. "And a fair one. Most people have never heard of it, much less know where it is. Luxembourg is a tiny kingdom in northwestern Europe bordered by France, Belgium, Alsace-Lorraine, and Westphalia. The Luxembourgers like to think of themselves as at the heart of the European Empire."

"And what are you doing here?"

"We come back once or twice a year to consult with my colleagues in Washington about various European affairs. And to visit family and friends. New York is our home when I am not on assignment elsewhere."

"I see. Well . . . that is very interesting."

"It was very nice to meet you, Lady Beaumont," said Fitzpatrick. The two wives exchanged a few more words, and gradually the coterie broke up. The new senator and the ambassadorial trio wandered off. With an involuntary glance behind her at Richard Fitzpatrick, Veronica and Hirsch sauntered away in the opposite direction.

Lady Daphne was left alone.

As the gathering continued, groups forming, breaking up, and reforming in constant superficial social ebb and flow, Veronica remained at the side of Cecil Hirsch, as he purposed she should. Before the evening was out, she had been introduced to thirty or more people whose names she would never remember. Hirsch was well satisfied with the results. Within an hour or two of their meeting a tacit intimacy had been established between them that would give him leave to call anytime at the modest Beaumont dwelling in Georgetown. A few clandestine dealings with certain European governments and business interests of influence were in the offing. This fortuitous approach to the Beaumont family would give him expanded opportunity to move yet higher among Washington's elite in the sorts of negotiations by which he was able to afford just about anything he wanted.

From his very boyhood, Hirsch had learned to play any side of any situation to whatever advantage it could provide him. He could affect a half dozen regional tongues and pass himself off as from any class, culture, or occupation. He had been working on several Eastern European accents and could already add a cunningly persuasive Italian or German cadence to his native street English.

Long ago he had learned that people would pay for information. Information and what one did with it was the commodity of power. Information created deals, relationships, progress, opportunity. People would pay for information about socialites, about candidates running for office, about runaway slaves, about potential votes in Congress, about military plans and promotions . . . and about where to find things people wanted. He had cultivated friendships of supposed intimacy with no fewer than thirty prominent Washington insider wives. They little knew how many secrets they had inadvertently divulged during the last year or two which he had catalogued away for future use. Their slips of the tongue never failed to amuse, and meanwhile his file of useful information on the powerbrokers of the nation steadily grew, and he put his discoveries to use, matching people with needs on the one side with people who could supply those needs on the other, while he, the middleman, reserved the greatest profits for himself.

Meanwhile, Ambassador Fitzpatrick and his family had bid Senator Beaumont and several others of their acquaintance good evening, and Beaumont was now engaged in discussion with half a dozen men in a small parlor off the main ballroom. The room hung thick with the smoke of expensive Havana cigars, and eighteen-year-old Napoleon brandy flowed freely.

"What are your plans, Beaumont," the new senator from Virginia had just been asked. "Any . . . *national* ambitions?"

"Certainly not this year, Senator Douglas," laughed Beaumont. "I only just arrived. As I hear it, the field is already crowded with those who would like to oust our current president. Will *you* be the Democratic nominee?"

"You believe in speaking your mind!" rejoined the senator from Illinois, chuckling lightly. "I have heard that about you, Beaumont. But it is early yet. You Southern Democrats and our colleague John Breckinridge may have something to say in the matter."

"And the Republicans," asked Beaumont, "will they nominate your old nemesis Lincoln?"

"Not a chance," replied Douglas. "The party has any number of more well-known names than his—Seward, Cameron, even Governor Chase. Lincoln is too moderate to appeal to the Republicans as a whole. Seward will be the Republican nominee."

"Perhaps, Stephen," now put in another member of the discussion, one Alfred Whyte, a grey-haired diplomat from the old school of Whigs. "But for a new party like the Republicans to have a chance of winning, they might consider Illinois a must. Nominating Lincoln could give them Illinois and much of the North."

"Are you saying I would not carry my own home state?"

"I meant to imply nothing, only that your advantage in the North would also be Lincoln's. It would make for an interesting election— two candidates from the same state. If you and the vice president cannot come to terms about your differences and you Democrats split, it could give him the election."

Douglas nodded with serious expression. "You make a good point," he said. "Which is why you Whigs need to throw your support *our* way rather than nominating a candidate of your own."

"We are the nation's oldest party," rejoined Whyte. "Surely you do not expect us to lie down without a fight when the Republican party is less than a decade old."

"I only say that you could give Lincoln and the republicans the election."

"As could you Democrats if you split. Our fielding a candidate poses far less a challenge to you Democrats maintaining your hold on the White House than a split within your own party. Tell me—how serious is the Breckinridge challenge?"

"The Southern caucus does not confide in me."

"You are of the same party."

"Perhaps," nodded Douglas, "but with distinctly different views on the future of the South, the nation, and the question of slavery. Perhaps our friend Senator Beaumont here could enlighten us."

"I am sorry, but I must confess ignorance as well," replied Beaumont. "I have not yet met to discuss the election with my Southern democratic colleagues, and I have only met Vice President Breckinridge once. The subject of his presidential aspirations did not come up."

"Well if he does go through with it and split the party," persisted Douglas, "catastrophe could result. Lincoln may be a moderate, but his abolitionist views are well-known."

"As I understand it," said Beaumont, "he is not a strict abolitionist."

"Take it from me," rejoined Douglas, "he is more abolitionist than he lets on publicly. Perhaps not to the extent of a John Brown, but an abolitionist nevertheless."

"Do you consider him dangerous?" asked Whyte.

Douglas thought seriously a moment. Slowly he nodded. "If Lincoln wins their nomination," he said, "and should, against all odds, succeed in getting himself elected, I do not see how the Union can survive. The South would, perhaps literally, be up in arms at his election. But still," he added, "I cannot imagine it. If he could not defeat me two years ago for the Senate, how can he possibly hope to gain the presidency?"

The group became silent. A few took sips from their glasses or puffs from their cigars.

Thirty

*I*t did not come as a surprise this time when Nancy Shaw walked up the hill to the big house just as the first hints of dawn were breaking over the hills in the east, six coloreds in tow whose faces had never been seen in these parts before.

Richmond, as was his custom, had been up long before daybreak and had wandered outside onto the veranda a few moments before, cup of coffee in hand, to see what kind of morning beckoned. He had just drawn in a deep breath of the chilly January air when he saw movement in the distance from the direction of the workers' quarters. He squinted into the semidarkness. Gradually Nancy and her following band of blacks came into view.

He descended the veranda steps and went to meet them.

"Hit's happened agin, Mister Dab'son," said Nancy in a tone of some irritation. "Look at dis. What dey think, Mister Dab'son, dat you kin take in eb'ry stray dat takes it inter dere blame heads ter cum wanderin' in here? Lan' sakes—I don' know what dey's thinkin'! Don' dey know da danger dey's puttin' you an' da missus in?"

As Nancy vented her minor frustrations, Richmond quickly looked over the ragamuffin family of seven—father, mother, a girl of about eleven, a boy a couple years younger, and two more girls about seven, of which he couldn't tell which was the older, and another boy of about five.

"Well, I imagine the danger to themselves is considerably greater than the danger to us, Nancy," he said. "When did they come?"

"Just now, Mister Dab'son. Dey jes' walked in from outta da woods. Dey said they been hidin' out up on da ridge yesterday an' all night tryin' ter figger out which coloreds wuz da free ones an' which wuz da slaves, us or dem dey seen down where da Bowmont's coloreds wuz workin' yonder."

"Well, at least they came to the right place. I shudder what to think of the reception they would have received on the other side of the ridge. Where's Malachi?"

"He dun disappeart las' night. He ain't back yet."

"Hmm . . . " nodded Richmond. "Were you supposed to meet someone?" he asked, turning toward the man.

"Yes, suh," the father replied. "We wuz ter meet a black man sumwheres up dere near's I kin figger, but he din't cum an' we figgered maybe we dun got los'. We din't know what ter do effen no conductor come, so my boy here he sneaked down here an' he seen da horse's head yonder on da barn dere, an' dat's when we come an' looked our fer where da black folks stayed, an' den we met dis lady here—," he said, nodding toward Nancy.

"Humph," said Nancy. "I ain't no lady. I's a nigger jes' like you."

"Nancy," said Richmond in a tone of admonishment. "You *are* a lady. Now we have talked about all this, haven't we?"

"Yes, suh, Mister Dab'son."

"We told you that we would help people who come to us, didn't we?"

"Yes, suh."

"So I would like you to go back and wait for Malachi. Tell him what has happened and send him up to the big house."

"Yes, suh."

"All right, Nancy, thank you for seeing them safely to me . . . you may go home. I'll take care of it now."

Nancy turned to go, somewhat chastened but mumbling to herself as she returned down the hill. She was still annoyed at Malachi about this whole thing. When they were alone, Richmond turned to the head of the family where he stood waiting, all his family staring nervously at him waiting to see what he was going to do.

"Welcome to Greenwood," he said, offering his hand. "I am Richmond Davidson. You will be safe here."

Several hours later, in midmorning, Richmond and Carolyn walked away from the house in the direction of the arbor.

"Did you succeed in getting any more out of the woman?" Richmond asked.

"Only that she is Lucindy's cousin and was aware of the same reports, that if they could reach a certain plantation in Virginia, they would be safe and could find their way over the border from there."

"They heard about it from Lucindy herself?"

"No. When she never returned and apparently wasn't captured, after several months went by, they assumed she had made it to safety. So they set out to follow her. Like so many others, they found their way into the railroad network, then before long they heard about the wind in the horse's head."

"That explains most of it, I suppose," said Richmond. "For all our talk with Malachi about making preparations, we now find ourselves again unprepared. We should have started immediately but . . . here we are."

"Nancy still doesn't seem to like it much."

"That is clear enough," laughed Richmond. "She will get used to it. Some people have a more difficult time than others opening their hearts to those less fortunate."

"I will talk to her. We need her with us in this."

"And Malachi said several groups are expected in the next week or two. I am concerned about the future. What if it becomes like Malachi said earlier with a flood of refugees?"

"You always say we must just take one step at a time and wait to see what God does next. Now is apparently such a time in our lives. We took a new family in today. Now we have to see what God will do next."

"Right, as always, dear wife! We shall see what develops . . . and trust God that his hand is in the developments."

"We have a great deal of room in the house," said Carolyn, "upstairs, the second floor, the attic, the lofts above the barns. We could house fifty people."

"With a few modifications!" laughed Richmond.

He quickly grew serious again. "You are right," he said. "But all those places are so visible. How would we hide them during the day? How would we keep the children quiet? How would we feed them? How would we see to their basic physical needs? We do not have many visitors to Greenwood, but all it would take would be one unfriendly set of eyes and a few difficult questions. A delivery . . . a chance glance into an upstairs window, and all could be undone."

"The cellar?" suggested Carolyn.

"A possibility. But there are the problems of water, the outhouse, and other practicalities. This thing has many factors to consider."

"In the meantime," asked Carolyn, "what should we do with Lucindy's cousin's family?"

"Until we arrive on a strategy, our house will be the simplest solution," replied Richmond. "You said it—we have plenty of room. We must simply stress the importance of staying out of sight, and that, as hard as it is, the children mustn't run around outside. We cannot take any chances. Our goal must be to move them on as soon as possible. I am very concerned about detection. Malachi may have been lucky so far. But all it takes is *one* slipup, *one* misspoken word, and terrible things could result. We mustn't become cavalier, but must be extremely watchful and wary."

The result of this talk between husband and wife, and a ride later in the day during which Richmond and Seth spoke of many things, and yet another discussion with Malachi, was a sizeable order placed in town for lumber of varying dimensions which was delivered two days after that by Scully Riggs.

"Hello, Scully!" said Richmond as the wagon rumbled to a stop in front of the barn.

"What you building, Mr. Davidson?" asked Scully as he got down and helped Richmond untie the ropes around the load. "There's enough lumber here to build a whole house."

"Not quite that!" laughed Richmond. "We are making some major repairs and additions at our Negro workers' quarters, as well as some work in the barns."

The reminder that the Davidson Negroes were no longer slaves turned Scully's mood sour.

They had just begun unloading the first of the planks when Seth approached from the house.

"Hello, Scully," he said as he walked over to join them. "I haven't seen you in a while. How have you been?"

"All right, I reckon," replied Scully in a sullen tone.

"They keeping you busy at the station?"

"Yeah."

"Didn't I hear that your father is back at Oakbriar?" asked Richmond.

"Yeah. Mr. Beaumont put him back on when they went to Washington."

"I'm glad to hear it. Give your father my regards, and if there is any way I can be of assistance while Mr. Beaumont is at the capital, tell him to be sure and call on me."

Scully said nothing. To his list of grievances about these people, he now also had the fact that Veronica had left before he had the chance to pay her the visit he had planned.

Thomas and Carolyn now came out of the house. With another set of hands, the wood came off the wagon quickly. Carolyn added her own greetings to the son of Leon Riggs.

"When you are finished, come into the house with the others, Scully," she said, "and have something to eat. We've just taken some fresh bread out of the bake oven."

Scully nodded without a smile, and went on silently unloading the wagon with the three Davidson men. When the wagon was empty he climbed back up on the seat, whacked the reins, and rumbled off without another word and without taking advantage of Carolyn's invitation. Richmond stared after him, puzzled at his change in demeanor, then followed his sons inside.

Within the week, construction was under way on a new outhouse—closer to the main house and in proximity to a side door that was more easily accessible to the basement inside—as well as one entire new three-room cabin to be added to the Negro village. These new quarters would ostensibly house several single men who had been crowded more close than was comfortable into one of the other cabins. But it would have another distinction over the other buildings of the former slave quarters—a full cellar was already being excavated by hand, over which the cabin would be built, a basement which would have no visible communication or vents to the outside, and which, therefore, once the cabin was completed and the floor in place, would to all appearances not exist at all.

Such were their initial plans.

Seth's brain was already revolving more possibilities should they become necessary, involving the loft above the threshing barn, a disused stairway at the back of the main house that connected all four levels virtually without detection, as well as plans involving one or two tunnels from the basement to the outside. More far-reaching yet were his thoughts regarding one of the caves for which the ridge below Harper's Peak was known, a cave whose mouth opened onto the former land of Mr. Brown and was therefore said to be filled with the spirits of the Indian dead. A ride about the place with Malachi and Seth's amazement at learning about the tunnel already being used filled his imagination with many more possibilities.

What to *do* with the runaways, not merely where to hide them, was Richmond's chief quandary. As close to the border as they were, northern Virginia was crawling with bounty hunters. It wouldn't be as easy as simply sending them on. How many could Malachi's contact take? Perhaps, knowing that to many whites, especially in a crowd or from a distance, one black looked just about like any other, they could put a few to work temporarily, taking care that their work crews did not give the appearance of multiplying. That, however, could at best be a temporary measure.

In the present case, within a week their seven visitors were gone and safely in the hands of the conductor who usually met Malachi on the ridge. Where he led them they had no idea. Malachi thought it was to a Quaker home in the adjoining county. But Richmond knew that alternate travel arrangements would eventually have to be made.

In the meantime, as Greenwood again returned to normal and as they were beginning to wonder if they had overdramatized the potential influx of refugees that would land at their door, in the space of a week, three new arrivals appeared, independent of one another— a young single man of about thirty from Georgia, and a father and daughter who had fled from South Carolina upon overhearing that the girl was about to be sold off as a mate to a black man she had never seen. None of the three had ever heard of Nate Gibbons, Lucindy Eaton, Sydney LeFleure, or Lucindy's cousin. The single man met Malachi in the woods. The father and daughter saw the weather-vane and approached the house in broad daylight. All repeated the same report with astonishing similarity—that there was talk among runaways that there existed a certain plantation in Spotsylvania County, Virginia, above which the wind blew in the horse's head and where former slaves now worked as freedmen, where blacks in trouble or on the run could find refuge.

Thirty-One

*W*hy Wyatt Beaumont and Brad McClellan came to him in the first place was a mystery to Seth Davidson.

Did they really think he was one of them? Or were they testing him to see how far he would go? He even wondered if the whole thing was a ploy to draw in his father and thus justify reprisals on a much larger scale against Greenwood and all its free blacks? But he had no proof of that.

When they first came looking for him, he suspected nothing of where it would lead.

"We're looking for Seth," said Wyatt to Maribel where she was sweeping the front porch. They were still sitting on their horses in front of the house when Carolyn appeared a few seconds later.

"Why . . . hello, Wyatt," she said with a smile. "How are you!"

"Just fine, Mrs. Davidson," replied Wyatt, without returning the smile.

"And you, Brad—goodness, I haven't see you for such a long time!"

"Mrs. Davidson," nodded the elder McClellan with similar expression.

"How are your two families? How are Veronica, Cameron, and your mother doing in Washington, Wyatt?"

"Just fine—though Cam's back with me at Oakbriar. He hated it up there. But like I was saying to your darkie here, we're looking for Seth, Mrs. Davidson."

"As far as I know, he and Richmond and Thomas are with the men out on the west thirty acres of the Brown tract. They are putting in some new fruit trees."

"We'll find them," said Wyatt. He and young McClellan spun their horses around and galloped off.

"Tell your mothers both hello!" Carolyn called after them. No acknowledgment of her words came from the two retreating forms.

"Dey's a couple a angry-lookin' w'ite boys," muttered Maribel as Carolyn turned back inside. "Dey ain't up ter no good no how."

Carolyn had to admit that both had changed since she had last seen them. Now in their early twenties, they were men now. Neither did she care for the looks in their eyes.

The two young men found Seth where Carolyn said they would. They approached the work crew across empty fields from behind. At last they reached Seth and his father and Thomas and some of the black men, all with shovels in their hands.

They reined in, surveying the scene in which they found themselves. Whatever their feelings might once have been toward this family of their neighbors, it was clear that enmity had taken much deeper root in the rising new generation of young Southern gentlemen even than the animosity of their fathers toward their old friend. One glance in their eyes revealed clearly enough that they hated every black he had freed with venom, and, if it were possible, hated Richmond Davidson himself even more.

"Hello, Wyatt . . . Brad," said Richmond in the same friendly tone as his wife.

"Our business is with Seth," said Wyatt without smiling. "We need to talk to you," he said, turning toward Seth.

"We're a little involved right now," said Seth.

"That's all right. Come to my place tonight . . . after supper."

Without waiting for a reply, both young men turned their horses around and galloped off.

"What's that all about?" asked Richmond.

"I have no idea," answered Seth. "I haven't seen either Brad or Wyatt for six months, and then I only ran into them briefly in town."

That evening about 7:15 Seth Davidson rode up the entryway into Oakbriar in the gathering darkness with a strange mingling of sensations. He had not been here since breaking off the engagement, and he had to admit it was a relief knowing he would encounter neither Veronica nor her father.

What had brought him here in response to Wyatt's abrupt invitation, he couldn't have said—probably curiosity. What good could possibly come of it? The expressions on Brad's and Wyatt's faces earlier in the day didn't look like they wanted his help planning a church social. The ten or twelve horses tied up in front of the house told him he wasn't the only one to have been summoned to whatever this was all about. Immediately he recognized Dusty, Thomas' favorite mount. No wonder his brother had disappeared right after supper. He tied up Malcolm. Jarvis did not answer the door to his knock, nor were any other blacks anywhere to be seen. After waiting a minute, and hearing voices, he opened the door and went inside.

"Come in, Seth," said Wyatt as his neighbor and lifelong acquaintance entered. His tone was considerably more friendly than earlier in the day. Much of his jubilant spirit could be attributed to the fact that beer for the occasion was in no short supply. Most of the twelve or fifteen young men milling about the room had a tall frothy glass in their hand. For several it was their second or third.

"Have a beer," said Wyatt. "We are just waiting for one or two others, then we'll get down to business."

"No, thanks," replied Seth. He glanced about the room, thankful at least that Thomas, where he stood with Cameron Beaumont, was not drinking along with everyone else. The change on the sixteen-year-old Cameron's face since Seth last saw him was remarkable. He had grown six inches and looked mean and angry. That he and Thomas were to all appearances closer than ever sent a shudder through him. As he made his way about, greeting young men he had not seen in some cases for years, Seth knew almost everyone present, with the exception of one or two new arrivals to the area, each of whom seemed to subtly

react the moment the word *Davidson* was spoken in the various introductions that followed. The scions of every notable landowning family
for twenty miles had been invited. The beer continued to flow freely
until, some ten minutes later, Wyatt took the floor.

"All right, everybody," he called loudly, "I know you'd all rather get
drunk than listen to me, but I didn't provide all this free beer for that.
So find a seat or stand if you want. But let's get this thing going so
you can all stagger home before midnight!"

Seth stood to one side of the room. Most of the others took seats,
while a few, like him, leaned against one or another of the walls.

"Brad and I got you all together to talk about a problem we have
around here that is getting worse and worse," Wyatt began. "That's
runaway slaves—"

Seth's hands went clammy. He stole a glance at Thomas, but his
brother displayed no reaction to Wyatt's words.

"Runaways have always been a problem as long as there's been slavery," Wyatt went on. "But with all this abolitionist talk in the North,
it's getting worse all the time. I know we're not going to solve the
problem ourselves—that's for men like my dad in Washington," he
added with a laugh. "But we can do our part here. And word has it
that there are a lot of runaways coming through here. As you know,
my dad's now a senator and he appointed me deputy commissioner in
his place. So I have power to do something about the runaways. A
fellow from down South called Murdoch who patrols for runaways
says there are so many coming through Spotsylvania County that the
bounties on them alone could make us all rich. But it's more important even than that just to stop them. So I need your help, to be my
eyes and ears, and to report anything suspicious to me immediately."

"Are you talking about organizing a vigilante group, Wyatt?" asked
Seth.

All heads turned toward him, almost as if they had been expecting
him to voice some objection.

"I don't much care what you call it, Davidson," said Wyatt, his
friendly tone gone. "All I am saying is that we're going to put a stop to

it. We don't want renegade, runaway, or *free* blacks thinking they can use Spotsylvania County as some kind of second home."

Neither his emphasis of the word *free,* nor its implications, went unnoticed.

"And when they try to do so," he added, "we will make them wish they had never tried to get to the North this way!"

A few low rumbles of laughter circulated through the room. They were accompanied by evil grins of anticipated delight at what their host might mean.

"Where does this Murdoch fellow think they're coming from?" asked Miles Stretton, son of the owner of a plantation about ten miles south.

"He doesn't know," replied Wyatt. "He just says they've caught several trying to get north. They've all been coming through here. Word is that there's some kind of safe house somewhere in Spotsylvania County—probably close by."

At his words the room went quiet.

"Where could *that* be?" asked Stretton.

"Nobody knows. It might not be true," said Wyatt. "But my dad says there is a network of religious fanatics called Quakers all the way from Florida to Pennsylvania that help them. So we've got to find if there's a place like that around here. Because for whatever reason, runaways are getting through. If there is such a place, we've got to find it and bust it up."

"How do we find these runaways?" asked Jared Miller.

"That's why I invited you all here," replied Wyatt. "We have to work together."

"We'll all have to watch and listen to our own slaves," replied Brad McClellan. "They always get wind of these things. That's how we find out. Slaves will help other slaves if they get the chance. Whatever's happening, you can be sure the coloreds around know about it. But they can't know we're watching and listening."

"What are we supposed to do if we catch them?" asked Noel Perkins, son of Dove's Landing's banker, the only nonplantation

young man among them, whose father's wealth more than made up
for that fact.

"Murdoch says that is up to us," smiled Wyatt. "Most of them have
rewards on their heads."

He paused and glanced around the room.

"So . . . are you all with us? We'll have to arrange for communication between us so that at a moment's notice we can mount a search.
Every one of us will have to keep a horse saddled and ready to ride.
And of course, no one else must know—this whole thing must be kept
in the strictest secrecy."

"Why, Wyatt?" asked Brad's younger brother Jeremy.

"Because even in the South . . . there are traitors to our cause—"

A few heads turned in Seth's direction.

As much as he wanted to know where the rest of this discussion
would lead, his conscience was by now shouting too loudly to be
ignored.

"Come on, you guys," he said, glancing at all the faces staring at
him, "do we really need to take the law into our own hands? Nothing
good results from that."

Fifteen or sixteen faces all stared back at him in silence.

"Do you all think this is the best way?" he said.

The room remained silent. Wyatt Beaumont could hardly prevent
the hint of a smirk coming over his face. He had been hoping for Seth
to speak up, for just this reason.

"I think you might find more support for your pro-darkie sentiments in the North, Seth," he said.

"I'm no abolitionist," said Seth.

"Your dad's one."

"Not politically, just personally. He's a loyal Virginian. So am I.
I just believe in staying within the law, that's all."

"Stupid Yankee," muttered one of the boys across the room.

"Nigger lover!" added Jeremy.

Again it fell silent. Wyatt Beaumont eyed Seth with a smirk of
victory.

"Well count me out, Wyatt," said Seth. "I'm not afraid to say no to this little vigilante scheme, even if all the rest of you are."

He took two strides toward the door, then stopped and turned toward Thomas.

"Come on, Thomas," he said. "Let's go."

"I'm staying," said his brother.

"No you're not—you're coming home with me."

A tense moment followed as both brothers stared at each other.

"Thomas," said Seth in a voice of command. "Come with me."

Thomas hesitated only a moment more, then shuffled toward the door, seething with silent fury, and followed Seth outside. They galloped away separately. Seth did not see his brother again that evening.

Seth went straight to his father's study after arriving home. He found Richmond just preparing to retire. He recounted every word spoken at the gathering as nearly as he could recall. Richmond's expression as he listened, especially knowing that Thomas had also been included, was grave. He was reasonably certain Thomas would not betray them. But they would have to be even more careful from now on.

The delivery he had made to Greenwood last week had rekindled the flame of resentment in Scully Riggs's brain toward Seth Davidson. How could he act carefree and content, like nothing had happened, not even caring how deeply he had hurt poor Veronica?

And all of them pretending to be so friendly toward him!

But he knew their kind . . . thinking they were better than everyone else, looking down their noses at people like him.

He had heard about Wyatt Beaumont's meeting at Oakbriar, overheard two of them talking about it. Those high-and-mighties were all the same, the Beaumonts, the McClellans—they would never invite him. But he would show them that he knew how to take care of nigger lovers too.

Almost as if in response to his own thoughts, he looked up to see Wyatt Beaumont across the street. He ran over to meet him.

"Hi, Wyatt," he said. "How's Veronica?"

Wyatt glanced up but kept walking.

"She's all right," he said with obvious disgust.

"It's terrible what Seth Davidson did to her. I'd bust his face if I got the chance."

"Keep out of it, Riggs. Veronica doesn't want you doing anything for her. It's none of your concern."

"But we still want to teach Seth Davidson that he can't go around—"

Wyatt stopped and turned.

"*We?*" he said. "*Who's* going to teach what to Seth Davidson?"

"You and me, Wyatt . . . you and me and Brad and Miles—you know, the guys who were at your place last week."

Beaumont's eyes narrowed. He looked Scully hard in the eye. "What do you know about that?" he said.

"Nothing, Wyatt."

"Then why'd you bring it up?"

"Just because . . . I thought if you needed some help taking care of Seth Davidson—"

"Look, Scully," interrupted Wyatt. "It's none of your affair, just stay out of it. It had nothing to do with Veronica or Seth Davidson . . . and it's got nothing to do with you. Got that?"

"But, Wyatt—"

"Go crawl in some hole, Riggs. We don't need your help. And you keep your mouth shut or it'll go worse for you than it does for Seth."

Scully slunk back across the street.

Well, he didn't need Wyatt Beaumont, he thought to himself. He'd get his own revenge. He'd show them all!

As much as Scully Riggs hated being looked down on by other whites, he hated people like Seth Davidson all the more. The only thing that gave Scully Riggs what little status he could scrape together in the world was the knowledge that he was better than any colored man. The notion that the Davidson slaves had been made his equal, and now had the same rights as he did, filled him with silent rage. The desire for revenge that burned in his soul was not primarily about Veronica Beaumont, it was about his own warped and injured dignity. The fact that people like Veronica and Wyatt Beaumont looked down on him made him all the more determined to look good in their eyes. To earn Wyatt's favor, and thus, by his twisted logic, Veronica's, he would kill Seth Davidson if he had the courage. He little suspected how low on the scale of humanity Wyatt considered him, and that all his bravado only made Wyatt despise him the more.

There were other people in town, thought Scully as he returned to work, who might find it interesting to know that the Davidsons were improving their colored quarters. There were others, like him, that Wyatt Beaumont didn't consider good enough to ride with and hunt with, who never got invited to their parties and socials and whom their sisters never looked twice at. Maybe guys like Scully and his friends could take care of a few things too!

Over the next few days, with every errand and delivery he made, Scully dropped little hints about things he had seen and heard "out at that Davidson place."

His dropped comments circulated from mouth to mouth and store to store and house to house, not only about new quarters for the blacks, but coloreds walking about giving white men orders. What Scully had actually observed during the unloading of the wood, at a moment when Richmond Davidson had gone inside briefly with his wife, was Malachi Shaw asking Thomas to send his father to him when he had the chance for a question about one of the fences. Scully did not go into such details when recounting the incident. He also spoke freely about black women walking in and out of the big house like they owned it, again omitting the fact that he had seen nothing more than Maribel—whom everyone for miles knew had lived in the big house for twenty years—carrying a laundry basket inside.

Through innuendo and exaggeration, by week's end, Scully succeeded in stirring up old resentments sufficiently that when added to his stories and personal observation that the Davidson blacks got better treatment than many whites, the disgruntled gossip about the

Davidsons and the goings-on at Greenwood began to take on a life of its own.

Not that anyone had ever paid much attention to Scully Riggs or would give two cents for anything he said. But rumors care little for where they originate. Once implanted in the public ear, they take on a momentum that cannot be stopped. Scully's words produced exactly such effect. Before long most of the town's youths from lower station than those on Wyatt Beaumont's vigilante guest list were ready to run the nigger-loving Davidsons out of town by any means possible. In spite of how low he may have looked in the eyes of Veronica's brother, to the seventeen- and eighteen-year-olds in town who came from the same side of the tracks as he, twenty-two-year-old Scully Riggs soon took on the luster of spokesman and hero. More and more of the town's teenagers and troublemakers could be seen clustered about him as they walked the streets in the evening or on a Sunday afternoon, the unspoken general of a growing band of young hotheads.

The opportunity Scully was waiting for came a couple weeks later. He saw Seth Davidson in town, and from that moment did his best to keep an eye on his movements. The moment he left town for home, Scully dropped what he was doing and ran to the livery stable.

"Come on, Digger!" he said. "We're going to teach that nigger-loving Davidson a thing or two! Grab some burlap feed bags to put over our heads, then go tell the others. I'll meet you at the fork just out of town on the road west!"

Five minutes later the small mob had grown to eight strong as it galloped away from Dove's Landing in the direction of Greenwood.

Seth had taken one of the larger carriages into town to pick up supplies. On his way home he was not moving rapidly. The eight riders quickly overtook him.

He heard them coming behind him. Before he could look around to see who it was, eight horses surrounded the wagon and forced it to a stop.

Seth had no chance to utter a word. One of the hooded riders was quickly off his horse and onto the wagon. He yanked Seth from his seat, and threw him to the ground. Within seconds six bodies were on top of him, kicking and beating and pounding at his face and body.

"Nigger lover!" they yelled, and worse. "Maybe this will teach you the difference between black and white!"

The damage was quickly done. Leaving Seth moaning beside the road, the carriage overturned, its leather roof and seats slashed, all the supplies spilled and strewn on the ground, Scully and his fellow thugs fled.

And so it was that Richmond Davidson found his son just coming to himself an hour later, after the two horses, broken loose from their harnesses, had slowly made their way home, and sent their owner to learn the cause.

Word of the incident reached Elias Slade at the Beaumont Plantation. He had been awaiting his own opportunity for revenge against Seth Davidson for the blows he had received in the Oakbriar barn a year earlier. Slade's plans, however, involved more than a mere beating.

He intended to kill him.

Thirty-Two

*T*he hour was late. Fog hung thick and wet in Charleston Harbor. A man of age and race difficult to determine from a distance, with wide-brimmed hat pulled almost over his eyebrows, made his way slowly across the Ashley River.

From the opposite side another stealthy figure stepped out from the blackness next to an empty brick warehouse and began walking in the opposite direction over the bridge to meet him.

They stopped in the middle above the slow black current and stood face-to-face, or rather, silhouette-to-silhouette.

"Are you the one they call the Sleuth?" asked the one in broken English and an accent not native to these shores.

"I am called by many names," answered the other in a noticeable southern drawl.

"Do not play game with me. Have I or not found the one I was told about?"

"I deal in information and resources that are difficult to come by. Does that answer your question?"

"For now. My client is European."

"I have no qualms as to nationality. As long as he can pay, I care nothing for his home or his tongue."

"He can pay. He is wealthy man. He concerned about supply of bulk cotton to factories should hostilities break out between states. He hear rumors of possible blockades against South and trade with foreign markets. His business need raw material. Are rumors true?"

"It may come to that. My sources in the North intimate such a possibility."

"Then my client's fears are well-founded, no?

"Possibly so. But you need have no worries. I represent a consortium of plantation owners. We have high-placed contacts who are dedicated to keeping supply lines open."

"How will you do this?"

"We are working to establish trade connections in Latin America, and with Northern shipping interests. We will make certain that commerce with European markets is not jeopardized."

"My client will pay handsomely for such guarantee. How will I contact you?"

"You won't. I will contact you. Tell me where you can be reached. When the time comes, your client will be instructed how to proceed."

The foreign accent nodded.

"When I make contact next time, you must do what I say without hesitation. You may not recognize me."

"How will I know?"

"You will be told, the Sleuth is ready. You must be too."

As the two men parted, the younger tipped his hat back slightly on his forehead and watched the European disappear into the mist. Though he was but twenty-six he had risen rapidly in a game that had already taken him high into the centers of finance, influence, and power. At last his years of preparation in an endless string of two-bit street hustles was paying off.

This trouble between the states could make him a rich man before it was done!

In Denton Beaumont's absence, Leon Riggs had not been able to stop Elias Slade from sneaking out at night.

Wyatt was certainly no help. He was gone half the time. Riggs was more than half certain that Slade was sneaking over to the Davidson plantation.

That was all he needed!

Beaumont would fire him again if Slade proved unruly or troublesome.

Meanwhile, in the aftermath of Seth's beating, things calmed down around Greenwood. Scully and his hotheads had tasted victory sufficient to satisfy themselves for the present. Wyatt Beaumont was biding his time. Even Thomas had been helpful and cooperative in the aftermath of the incident.

No bones were broken and Seth was himself again in a week. But the attack turned him thoughtful. The resentment against him brought unnecessary danger to Greenwood. He still could not understand the reason for the animosity. But it could not be ignored.

Seth found his father on the floor of the new house at the Negro village. The cellar was complete, and Richmond was on his knees pounding nails through the last of the new floorboards.

"Hey, Seth, my boy!" he said. "How goes the work at the house?"

"Good, Dad," he replied. "There are a few things I need to ask you about."

Richmond stood, set down the hammer, and the two walked away together.

"This looks like it's going well too," said Seth, glancing over his father's work. "It was a great idea to use weathered lumber for the siding. It looks like it's been here a hundred years. You can hardly tell it from the other cabins. There's no hint of a cellar beneath the floor."

"We have you to thank for that. The cellar was your idea . . . actually, the new staircase up at the house was too. How does your devious brain think of these things!" Richmond added with a laugh. "How is it progressing?"

"It's coming along. Thomas and I have just about got the false wall in front of the old door on the second floor finished," Seth answered. "Once we plaster over and paint it, we'll have a completely invisible second staircase all the way from the attic to the basement."

As they went, Richmond sensed from Seth's countenance that

something other than the new staircase was on his mind. Slowly they continued away from the collection of small black houses. It remained silent for several minutes.

"How are you feeling?" asked Richmond at length.

"I'm okay . . . well, physically at least," replied Seth. "But I'm really confused about all this."

"It's more than just the beating on the way home from town?"

"Yeah . . . there have been a few other things too."

His father turned toward him with obvious concern.

"Nothing serious," said Seth. "No physical violence . . . just looks and comments and stares . . . a few threats."

"Do you think they're serious?"

"After what happened with Scully and the looks I got that night at Oakbriar, I suppose, yeah—they seem serious."

"Are you scared?" asked Richmond.

"I'm not thinking about it every minute . . . but sure, the threats worry me," replied Seth. "I can't help it. I'm confused as well as a little scared. And still feeling stupid besides. If I'm going to town alone now I take either the Grey Laird or Malcolm because I know they can outrun any horse in the county. I don't like having to look over my shoulder whenever I'm alone."

"I'm sorry, son . . . I didn't realize it had gone so far. What are they saying?"

"Oh, the usual . . . you know, about our slaves."

His father nodded. He knew that criticism well enough.

"And there's resentment about what I did to Veronica. I can't tell whether that's just Scully Riggs or whether the others genuinely think I besmirched her dignity or something by breaking off the engagement. Wyatt too—is he angry with me for what I did or is it because of freeing our blacks? Why do any of them care? What business is it of theirs? Veronica is long gone. I'm sure she has forgotten me by now. But along with the fact that our Negroes are free, they seem to think it necessary to teach me a lesson in what happens to young men who embarrass the pride of a woman whose good name they think it their duty to protect. As if Wyatt cares about Veronica's dignity," he added in a tone bordering on sarcasm.

"I'm sure it will all blow over."

"I don't know, Dad. Sometimes the threats are pretty ugly."

As Richmond listened, he grew more and more concerned.

"It's reached the point where there is no logic in it," Seth continued. "It's got nothing to do with Veronica or our slaves—it's just . . . *me*, Dad. They've got it out for me, that's all. You know how Scully Riggs and his kind are. They *want* to fight. They are itching to fight. Sometimes I think they are trying to goad me into doing something stupid. And now it's Wyatt and Brad too. I have tried to be nice to all of them, to befriend Scully. I have been trying for years to get past that chip on his shoulder. But nothing I do changes it. And Wyatt's really changed. What is it with guys like that, Dad?"

Again it was quiet. They were about halfway to the house by now. Richmond turned aside and sat down on one of the large stones that bordered this portion of the dirt road between the house and the Negro village. Seth took another.

"To answer your last question, I don't know, son," said his father. "I have encountered people like that in my life too. Whether it's boys settling things with their fists, grown men settling things with guns, or businessmen trying to get the upper hand through finances or politics, there is something in the flesh of man that wants to exercise power over others. It is exactly the opposite of how Jesus told us to live."

"So what do you do, Dad? Surely it's not smart to put yourself in danger. I mean, I know there are times you have to stand up and fight for some principle. But for me to take on Wyatt and his ruffian friends, or Scully and his thugs so they can pulverize me . . . I'm not sure *that* would serve any purpose."

"Of course not," said his father. "That is the kind of useless fight that is best avoided at almost any cost except cowardice, and we both know you are no coward."

"What do you do, Dad, when you know that people hate you for the stands you have made?"

"You have seen what I have done," replied his father. "I try as much as I can to ignore it."

"But how *can* I ignore it when they come after me?"

"I don't have an answer for you, son. This dilemma of yours requires some concentrated thought and prayer."

Unfortunately, before either Seth or his father had arrived at an idea of what they should do, circumstances took an even more malicious turn.

Thirty-Three

*W*hen the visitor called at the door of the Beaumont home, neither Veronica nor her mother had any idea that their chaperone for the evening had recently returned from playing a role as intricate as any they would see on the stage of Ford's Theater this evening. Indeed, his acting resume could have stood up favorably against any in the city.

"Are you ready, my lady?" said Cecil Hirsch with a smile and a slightly affected bow as Veronica opened the door.

"Oh yes, I am so excited . . . I can hardly wait. Mother is upstairs, she will be down in a minute. Come in."

"Thank you," nodded Hirsch, following Veronica inside. "Is your father at home?"

"No, he's at some Congress thing."

"You couldn't persuade him to join us?"

"He thinks Shakespeare is stuffy."

"We shall have to interest him in a good British comedy the next time one is playing."

"He says the theater is for the intelligentsia, whatever that is."

"The president is often seen at Ford's. And the man Lincoln, who may be our next president, they say, is a great enthusiast of the theater."

"My father hates him. He says it will ruin the country if he is elected."

"The country may ruin itself, with or without his help," commented Hirsch wryly.

They were interrupted by the appearance of Lady Daphne descending the stairs.

"Ah, Lady Daphne, you are radiant this evening!" said Hirsch expansively, walking toward her. "It is a pity the lights will be low in the theater. Otherwise all eyes would be on you."

"You are a charmer, Mr. Hirsch. But I fear a lying one!"

"Never!" he laughed. "Shall we go? Our carriage awaits on the street."

Forty minutes later, the three were shown to their seats in Ford's Theater by a uniformed usher. Still chatting amiably and spreading blandishments on unsuspecting Lady Daphne thicker than the fog in Charleston Harbor, Cecil Hirsch took his place between the two Beaumont women. The curtain rose fifteen minutes later. Fifteen minutes after that, concealed in the darkness, Hirsch had located Veronica's palm and was gently massaging both hand and heart with the same subtle cunning that he brought to all his affairs, foreign and domestic. The fact that she was in one of Washington's most famous theaters, surrounded by diplomats and dignitaries and congressmen, and being wooed by a man she took to be far more important than he was, caused Veronica's pulse to pound rather more rapidly than she could control, and it was with great difficulty that she tried to follow the somewhat confusing dialogue of *King Lear*. She was flushed with more emotions than she knew what to do with as they emerged into the cool night air some two hours later. She edged closer to Cecil Hirsch's side on the way home than she had on the ride into the city, telling herself that it was merely to stave off the chill. But deep down she knew the real cause. Being near Seth Davidson had never made her feel like *this*!

As the carriage slowed in front of their house, the intoxication of her fanciful passions had nearly reached a climax. This had been absolutely too lovely an evening to end now! Cecil felt the heat from her body next to his as they bounded gently to a stop, and shared her sentiments exactly.

"Lady Daphne," he said, stepping down, hurrying around the carriage, and helping her to the ground with his hand, "I cannot thank you enough for accompanying me."

"Oh, Mr. Hirsch, this was everything I had hoped for in coming to Washington. It is I who am indebted to *you*!"

He offered his arm to lead her to the house. In the corner of his eye he saw Veronica scoot toward the edge of the carriage seat to step down. With the slightest motion of his head, he turned to catch her eye, then checked her motion with an imperceptible shake of his head. She saw and divined his meaning. Heart pounding anew, she sat still . . . and waited.

"Lady Daphne," said Hirsch as they reached the porch, "you know, I've promised to show Veronica the lights of the moon and street lanterns reflecting off the water of the Potomic. It just occurred to me, as there is nearly a full moon tonight and the air is mild, that this would be a perfect—"

"Say no more, Mr. Hirsch," said Lady Daphne. "I am tired and not so young as you and Veronica. Denton is probably home by now and I would be happy for you young people to see the city together. Go on, and think nothing of me. I had a most lovely time. Thank you so much!"

"The pleasure was all mine, Lady Daphne," replied Hirsch. He took her hand, raised it to his lips, kissed it lightly, then tipped his head in a slight bow as she opened the door. He waited until she was inside, then returned to the carriage, where Veronica sat waiting with apparent patience but with face and neck warm with anticipation.

"Well, my lady," said Hirsch, bounding up again beside her. "What would you say to a midnight tour of some of the lesser-known sights of our magnificent capital!"

Veronica said nothing, only edged yet closer to his side, slipped her hand through his arm, and gently laid her head against the side of his shoulder. Hirsch urged the horse into motion. He was in no hurry as they went. He had no real destination anyway other than a ride along the shoreline. After that it would depend on Veronica.

They returned sometime after three in the morning. If the lovely face of Veronica Beaumont he had seen at the ball several weeks earlier had developed into that of a woman rather than a girl, that womanhood had now given the ultimate of itself to a man she scarcely knew.

But she was a mere trophy to him, one that lost its luster almost immediately in that it had been so easy a prize to win.

Thirty-Four

The new cabin at the worker's village had progressed rapidly. Its joists and roof rafters were now in place and ready for cross boards. Shingles would follow.

With nail pouch and hammer strapped to his waist, Malachi, bare-chested and perspiring freely, climbed the ladder, worked his way precariously across the joists then onto the rafters up to the crown of the small building. Once in place, he called down to Josaiah Black and the other men to begin handing him the twelve-foot cross boards to nail in place.

All went smoothly enough until Malachi was forced to shift his position. Suddenly his left foot gave way from the rafter supporting it. He slipped with a loud cry. Unable to catch himself, he toppled down, bounced dangerously off one of the joists and fell through down onto the floor, completed the day before. A roar of pain sounded that could have come from none but Malachi's throat, bringing everyone running in alarm.

"Somebody go git da master!" shouted Josaiah.

Richmond came running minutes later from the big house. He sent Carolyn and some of the men for ice from the ice house. He and two of the men lifted the groaning gentle giant and carried him home. In ten minutes Malachi lay, more angry with himself for his carelessness than concerned for his obvious pain, on his pad in his own house, surrounded by fussing black women adjusting and readjusting the compress of ice that had been crushed and bagged around his ankle. Already it was swollen to twice its ordinary size, which was saying something, for he was a large and muscular man.

Richmond confessed himself unable to determine for certain whether leg or ankle were broken. At the very least Malachi had suffered a major sprain and would not walk for days, if not a week. That same afternoon, Carolyn and Nancy set about devising a splint and tearing lengths of strong cloth to hold it in place. Richmond went in search of a pair of old crutches that had been in the family for years but had not been used for as long as he could remember and had been lost track of in some storage room or another.

By evening, aided by the ice, the pain had subsided. Malachi, however, was obviously agitated. When their supper was over he asked Phoebe to take her little boy outside for a while, then told Isaac and Aaron that he wanted to talk to their mother alone. When they were gone, having no idea what it was about, Nancy sat down in some trepidation and waited. Malachi still lay on his pad, his left leg, ice bag surrounding the ankle, elevated on two pillows.

"Wha'chu need ter talk ter me 'bout?" said Nancy, never one to beat around the bush.

"Jes' dis," said Malachi. "Dere's a family er railroad passengers dat's gotter be met—dey's gotter be met tonight, up dere on da ridge, an' I can't go no how. So I wants you ter go an' git dem safe ter da conductor what's planning ter take dem ter da nex' stop."

"*Me* . . . why me?" said Nancy. "I ain't goin' nowhere."

"You's got ter go. Dere ain't nobody else."

"I ain't goin', I tell you," she shot back irritably. "I din't approve ob what you been doin' before, an' I don't approve ob it now. An' it's God's truf dat I ain't gwine git involved in all dat mysel'. It's yor doin' not mine. We gots enuf ter do keepin' our own moufs fed an' our own chilluns cared fo' ter be goin' 'bout doin' what nobody oughter have ter do fer nobody else."

She crossed her arms with a gesture of finality and an unspoken *humph*, indicating clearly enough that in her opinion there was noth-

ing more to be said on the matter. The expression on Malachi's face as
he heard the tone of her voice was one of mingled shock and dismay.

"Wha'chu sayin', Nancy?" he said. "Why you talkin' like dat?
Mistress Dab'son'd neber say such a thing."

"What's dat ter me! Maybe I jes' want ter min' my own biz'nes an'
let other folks min' dere's, dat's all."

"But you help folks all da time. Why you don't want ter help now?"

"Dat's different. Dat's wiff folks I know."

"But you *gots* ter help!" Malachi persisted almost in a pleading
voice. "I's got no one else ter ax."

"Why? Why shud I do your work fo' you? You gots yo'sel' inter dis.
Den you kep' it from me an' din't trust me enuf ter tell me, so I don'
figger I owes you nuthin now."

To Malachi the words felt like a slap in the face.

"Nancy, wha'chu talkin' 'bout," he said. "Hit ain't dat I din't trust
you, I wuz tryin' ter proteck you an' da others, so dat ef sumthin
happened ter me, hit wudn't cum close ter none er you. Dat's why
I din't say nuthin. Hit ain't got nuthin' ter do wiff not trustin' you.
You's got ter know dat."

Nancy was silent. Already she was feeling foolish for her outburst.
In her heart she knew that Malachi was right. But knowing oneself in
the wrong, and having the courage to admit it, are two different
things.

It was silent several minutes. Malachi was not a man given to many
words, still less to preaching, still less to instructing his wife. But the
last three years had changed him. They had changed how he thought
about life. Most importantly, they had changed how he thought about
himself.

Learning to think about oneself correctly is one of the most fundamental processes of growth in which humanity can engage. Coming to
grips with who we are as beings created in the image of God provides
the fundamental truth root of all human experience. That so few
discover the reality of that truth stems from shadowy images of God
that humanity has devised out of the mists of prehistoric superstitions.

How can we rise into the dignity of what it means to be made in God's image if we do not know who he really is?

But Malachi Shaw had begun to discover the worth and value of his own personhood because he had an image—an incomplete one, it is true, but nevertheless a *real* one, pointing toward the *full* truth with *partial* yet growing reality—of God's nature in the person of his former master.

Richmond Davidson had helped Malachi embark on this inward journey. From the moment it had begun on the day his master and mistress had called their slaves to the big house and announced that they were giving them their freedom, Malachi had no way of realizing the full implications of the change. Nor even today was he aware of all the changes taking place within him. He still looked the same. He still spoke the same. But in the depths of his heart Malachi Shaw was no longer the same man he had been as a slave. He had become a man of worth in his own eyes, not for the strength of his muscular frame, but for the character of his heart. That worth was now measured by what he thought of himself, and by what Richmond, and thus, by extension, what God thought of him.

He was a man of value. His soul was of eternal significance. For the first time in his life he knew it. Richmond Davidson valued him. And if Richmond Davidson valued him, and told him that God valued him too, then Malachi could value himself as well.

It was a stupendous transformation—to be valued for who he was . . . as a person . . . as a human being.

At last he spoke, and Nancy had never heard the like from the mouth of her husband before.

"Eber since we's been free," he said, "I can't help but watch Mister Dab'son, an' dat's taught me sum mighty big things. He an' da mistress, dey treats us wiff respeck. Dey treats us like we's folks dat matter. Dey gib us our freedom as a gift. Dey din't hab ter free us. Nobody made dem do it, dey jes' done it. An' it's likely da bes' gift dat one man cud gib anuder. We din't earn it, dey jes' gab us da gift ob freedom. So I figger we's got ter pass on dat gift ter whoeber we can, in any way we can. Dat's what makes da gift so par'ful—'cause we kin pass it right on ter other folks. An' dat's what I'm doin'. I'm tryin' ter help folks dat ain't been so lucky as ter hab a master like Mister an' Mistress Dab'son. Desperate folk on dat railroad, dey be needin' our help, Nancy, an' since we's free, we *gotter* help dem."

Nancy had no reply to make. Malachi's words had already pierced her heart.

"My daddy an' mama used ter tell me dat we'd cum from kings," he went on, "an' dey tol' me neber ter forgit da five ribers an' dat da blood ob kings ran in my veins. It neber meant nuthin' ter me. We wuz all slaves, so what could we hab ter do wiff kings. But now I'm learnin' ter see dat maybe we did cum from dat ol' king, cuz nobody dat's got freedom in dere heart can eber be a slave through an' through. If you's free inside, den you kin walk tall cuz you knows what freedom really is. An' I'm thinkin' 'bout dat blood er kings more dese days cuz er Mister Dab'son, an' dat he treats me wiff respeck almost like I *wuz* a king. I ain't one, but he treats everybody like dey's as worthy er respeck as a king."

As she listened, Carolyn's words from the meeting at the Brown house returned to Nancy's mind:

"You ladies are descended from another king—Christ the king. . . . The Bible calls us heirs with him and children of the Father. Just imagine, we are children, not just of an earthly king, but of God himself."

"An' bein' free, an' bein' treated wiff kindness an' respeck," Malachi continued, "hit's changed me deep down like. Cuz hit ain't enuf ter jes' be free on da outside. We's got ter be free on da inside too. We's got ter learn not ter be low down niggers wiff stooped backs an' shufflin' feet who ain't got no self-respeck. We got ter stan' up tall an' be *free* black folks dat's got worth an' value. We's Americans too. But we can't stan' tall like dat effen we don' know inside dat we's got value an' worth cuz we's people dat God's made. He's made us like we is cuz he figgered we wuz worth makin'. All dat's what Mister Dab'son helped me see sum ob, an' I figger I can gib sum ob dat feelin' ob self-respeck ter others."

Realizing how long he had been talking, surprised to hear what was coming out of his mouth, suddenly Malachi stopped.

He glanced over at his wife where she sat. She was staring down at the table with a solemn expression.

"I'll go," she said softly. "Jes' tell me where you want me ter go an' what ter do."

⟞⟶

Nancy found the refugees waiting, huddled beside a small pool of mountain run-off beneath the overhang of a gigantic boulder that jutted out from a steep slope down which the stream trickled before finding its way into the pool and, two or three miles lower down, into the river. It was a remote place, far from any farm, plantation, or habitation. Though miles from anywhere, Nancy knew it immediately from Malachi's description.

The travelers perceived movement and heard her approach. As Nancy came into view, though they had been expecting her, the terror in their eyes was plain to see. Two young mothers, huddled with their three children. An older brother of one of the women stared up at her with question.

"I's here fo' you," said Nancy.

Sighs of relief sounded.

"I brung sum food," said Nancy. She set the bag she had been carrying on the ground and opened it. The six famished travelers tore into the cold provisions of bread, cheese, and hard-cooked eggs as if they hadn't eaten for a month.

"Thank you, missus," said one of the women. "Dis tastes like jes' 'bout da bes' meal I eber had in my life. We ain't had much fer most er a week. We got off da tracks we wuz supposed ter be on an' we wuz skeered real bad. Den anuder conductor, he foun' us an' brung us here ter dis big rock. But we wuz skeered nobody wuz gwine cum."

Except for the one talkative mother, the others ate in silence, stealing an occasional glance in Nancy's direction, looking at her with something like awe.

"Is you a *free* black, missus?" asked the other woman.

"Dat I is," Nancy answered.

"What it like?"

"Jes' like anythin' else . . . I reckon it's sumthin' a body gits used to."

"I hope we's be free sum day."

"You ain't got too far ter go," said Nancy, "effen what dey say is true, an' dat's dat the Norf's only 'bout a hundert miles from here."

"Don't you know?"

"I ain't neber been in da Norf. I ain't no regular conductor. But dey say hit's not much farther from here."

As Nancy watched them gobble down everything in the bag down to the last crumb, she could hardly imagine what it must have been like to travel whatever long distance they had come. Their clothes were shabby and torn. Though the night was cold, they had no jackets or overcoats, only a few dirty ragged blankets to protect them from the elements. Their faces were drawn and lean, their expressions filled with fear, doubt, and defeat. Not a trace of what Malachi had spoken of was visible upon them—self-respect. Suddenly in Nancy's mind's eye, she beheld something she had never herself known even as a slave on the Davidson plantation—the terrible worth-killing scourge of slavery. In that moment she saw how fortunate she had been. Yet in how many ways had she taken it for granted.

These poor, poor people! thought Nancy. And she had resisted coming to help them! What had she been thinking! The memory of her argument with Malachi made her so ashamed of herself, she suddenly felt a choking of remorse in her throat.

And as she sat in the night with six strangers whose lives were now in her hands, new wells of compassion opened deep in the heart of Nancy Shaw.

"All right, den," she said, her voice soft and just a little shaky. "Hit's time ter go . . . so foller me."

An hour later, aided by the light of the glowing gray moon, Nancy still led the ragtag group of weary runaways from Tennessee, through a densely wooded region of hills that ran nearly parallel with the ridge crowned by Harper's Peak. Their course was almost due west. As Malachi had explained where the rendezvous with their next conductor would take place, she had known the place almost instantly. Having grown up under lenient conditions at Greenwood under the old master, and being unusually adventuresome for a youngster, there were few places for miles she had not explored or hiked with the other slave and occasionally white children. Sometimes young Richmond himself led the romp of youngsters for an all-day adventure of many miles. She had not been in these woods and on these hills for years. But she remembered them fondly, and well.

As they went, Nancy now carried a sleeping child of two in her arms. The moment she had laid eyes on the mother, even in the moonlight she had perceived sheer exhaustion. How the poor thing could continue walking herself, much less manage her baby, Nancy could not imagine. The dream of freedom indeed inspired strength beyond the impossible. As they had risen from their meal, Nancy had taken the child, to a weary smile of gratitude, and led the way toward their next destination.

After a walk of five or six hours, daylight began spreading across the Virginia countryside, they reached their destination.

"I's leave you here now," said Nancy. "Anuder conductor's gwine cum fer you here."

"Please, missus," said one of the women, "don't leab us alone. What ef one er dem bounty hunters fin's us here?"

"Dey won't. My husband, he say dis place be good an' safe. But I reckon I kin stay a spell."

"Thank you, missus. You's been mighty good ter us."

Nancy smiled and sat down. The woman's words strangely warmed her heart.

Forty minutes later a white man appeared. Even Nancy started visibly at sight of him. Though Malachi had said nothing, she had assumed every conductor on this peculiar railroad was black.

"Ease thyself of concern," said the man in odd tones. "I am thy guide. You will be asleep in my barn and safe before noontide. Follow me."

Nancy rose from the ground where she had been sitting.

The travelers also stood. One by one they embraced her warmly.

"We can't thank you enuf," said one of the women. "You saved our lives. We wuz jes' 'bout ready ter gib up an' let dem catch us. We wuz so tired er runnin'. But you wuz so nice, so lovin', you gib us food, you risked yo own life jes' fo us—"

The woman began to cry. Nancy took her in her arms again and held her for several seconds. The other mother now spoke.

"Thank you, missus," she said. "What she said is right. We wuz plumb outer strenf an' hope. You's gib us hope agin. I hope dat sumday I kin help people like you's doin'. You's been so kind ter us. You's so wonderful. I dreamed ob bein' free all my life. An' now you is free, yet you's doin' dis fo' us, fo' people you don't eben know. You's jes' an angel, missus."

The words smote Nancy's heart. She stepped back and glanced away. Another brief silence followed. The women hugged again. Nancy stooped down, kissed each of the children, and then they were gone with the white conductor, whose Quaker network would see them across the border. Nancy's eyes flooded with tears as she watched them disappear in the distance.

As she made her way home, weeping for the first hour of the way, like her husband, Nancy Shaw knew a change had come. It was the flowering of compassion in a human heart, shedding its fragrance of tenderness slowly and invisibly into many hidden corners of character. For the first time in her life she began to think about herself not as a black and a former slave, but as a true woman, and as a child of God.

Thirty-Five

The sounds of horses outside stirred Seth from sleep. Seconds later he heard his name called from outside the window of his bedroom.

He struggled out of bed, turned up his lantern, then opened his window.

"Seth . . . come on, get down here!" It was Brad McClellan sitting on his horse looking up at the house. "Be quick about it . . . we've got to go!"

Sleepy and bewildered, Seth dressed hurriedly and stumbled his way out of his room. He met his father in the corridor, lantern in hand.

"What's going on, Seth?" he said.

"I don't know, Dad. It's Brad McClellan. I have no idea what it's all about. I'll find out."

He returned to his room, pulled on his boots, and rejoined his father in the hallway.

"Whatever you do, Dad," he said, "don't let Thomas leave Greenwood. I do not want him involved until I find out what's going on."

"Do you think he's mixed up in something?"

"I don't know, Dad," said Seth heading for the stairs. "I'm thinking of that gathering at Oakbriar."

A minute later he walked out the front door into the darkness. Brad sat holding the reins of *two* horses—his own, and Seth's Malcolm, saddled and ready.

352 *Dream of Life*

"Let's go!" said Brad.

"What's going on?"

"You'll see—come on."

"Look, Brad, I'm not going anywhere until I know what it's about."

Brad looked down at him with a piercing gaze. "You *have* to come, Seth," he said. "Wyatt told me that if you objected to tell you that there could be repercussions."

"What do you mean by that?"

"Just that what happened to you the other day could happen to others around here—your father, maybe your mother or brother . . . some of the darkies you are all so fond of."

The two young men stared at each other in the chill night air.

"Now, like I said," repeated Brad, "let's go."

He threw Seth the rein, spun around and galloped away down the drive. With reluctant forebodings, Seth climbed onto Malcolm's back and followed.

There was enough of a moon to ride by once they cleared the wood. It was some minutes, however, before Seth caught up and could move alongside his companion.

"What's going on, Brad!" he called out.

"A runaway! Spotted on the Beaumont place!"

"But I told you—"

Brad lashed his mount and again sped ahead. Before long Seth became aware that they were not alone. Three or four horses had joined them, when or where he didn't know. His misgivings mounting, Seth continued on. Whatever was going on, he told himself, he needed to know of it not only because of Brad's threats but to protect their own secrets.

They reached Dove's Landing and thundered through the deserted streets. A few more riders joined them. By now there were six or eight in all. Windows and street lanterns gave Seth enough light to recognize most of his companions. All had been at Oakbriar the night of the fateful meeting. No one spoke. The only sound was the pounding of a steadily growing number of hooves on the hard-packed dirt of the streets and the road out of town.

Ten minutes later Seth was certain they were somewhere on the Beaumont plantation. In the darkness he couldn't tell where. Four or five lanterns gave off flickering light ahead. Hounds were baying at the moon.

They began to slow. In front of him Brad reined in. Seth found himself suddenly surrounded by ten horses pawing, prancing, and snorting in the night. Four or five burning torches, flames dancing into the night sky, flickered toward them. In the lead walked Wyatt Beaumont.

"All right . . . everyone here?" he said. "Good. Okay, the dogs chased him into this wood here," said Wyatt nodding behind him. "Now that there are enough of us, we want to surround it then close in so he can't slip through. We don't want him getting across the river where the dogs won't be able to track him. So fan out around the edge of the wood. Leave your horses here, we'll go on foot—Brad, you go east. Cam, you west, till you meet at the river, then spread word back that the circle's been closed. Stay seventy-five to a hundred yards apart. If he breaks between two of you, give a holler. Between us and the dogs, we'll run that nigger down and teach him that this is the wrong place to come looking for freedom. All right . . . you all know what to do—"

Wyatt glanced up at Seth where he sat on Malcolm's back. In the light from his torch, their eyes met. A wily smile parted Wyatt's lips. Suddenly the truth dawned in Seth's brain—he'd been set up!

His only hope was to find the runaway before anyone else did. If he could slip him into the river, he would be able to come back for him later somewhere downstream and get him safely to Greenwood.

The poor black man was so anxious to get North that he had fled without getting full instructions. He knew only the name of the town nearest his destination. That partial information had been his undoing. For he had been seen snooping too close to Oakbriar. He was not to be so fortunate as to run into a friend among so many enemies. As Seth searched frantically and whispered in hopes that the man would hear him, ten minutes later he heard the shouts he had feared.

"We've got him. . . . Wyatt, over here—we've got him!"

A sinking feeling of dismay sickened Seth's heart. He turned and rushed toward the voices. By the time he reached the others, lanterns and dogs and ten boys he had grown up with, half younger than himself but old enough for evil to have turned into men before their time, were taunting and beating and kicking and cursing at a helpless black figure on the ground.

"Stop . . . what are you doing!" cried Seth, running into the middle of the fray. "You've found him, isn't that what you wanted? You don't need to beat him to death!"

"You got a problem with what we're doing, Davidson?" said a voice behind them. The small crowd of well-bred thugs parted to make room for their leader. Wyatt walked forward and looked with apparent satisfaction at their quarry where he lay half unconscious.

"Look, Wyatt," said Seth, "you caught the man. If he's a runaway, then send him back to his owner. Collect the reward—fair enough. I've got no problem with that. But you don't need to bash his face in."

Again Beaumont looked at his boyhood friend.

"So . . . you think we're being a little rough on him?"

"It's not necessary. If you're trying to stop runaways, send him back."

"Oh, we're going to stop them all right," said Wyatt, "by teaching their kind a lesson!" He broke out in an evil laugh. "That's right—a lesson. Maybe it'll teach you a lesson too, Davidson! Who's got the rope?"

Four or five voices answered at once. There seemed to be no shortage.

"Somebody find us a tree."

"No . . . you can't—Wyatt!" cried Seth. "There's no need for anything like—"

"Would somebody shut him up!" yelled Wyatt.

Several blows at Seth's face and stomach sent him to the ground beside the black man.

"While you're at it," said Wyatt. "Tie him up too. I don't want him running off. And put a gag in his mouth."

Dazed from the blows, Seth hardly realized what was happening.

A few minutes later, he gradually came to himself sitting against the trunk of a tree, feet bound, hands stretched behind the tree. A piece of his shirt had been ripped from his chest and stuffed into his mouth. He could barely move and couldn't utter a sound. The scene in front of him would haunt him as long as he lived.

The runaway slave, weak but conscious, sat on Seth's own Malcolm, whimpering and pleading for his life. In a circle around him, Wyatt Beaumont's accomplices laughed and shouted taunts and accusations, ridiculing the condemned man with the crude humor of their kind. A rope was stretched tight around his neck and up over an overhanging branch of the same tree at whose base Seth sat helpless.

"Please, massa," whimpered the man, "I's serb you all ma born days effen you jes' gimme er chance. I's be a gud slave, yessuh—"

Wyatt could contain himself no longer.

"You'll be a good slave, all right," he said, bursting into a great laugh. "Because you'll be a dead slave!"

With superhuman effort, Seth tried to cry out. But he succeeded only in producing a faint gurgle. Wyatt sensed that an objection had been voiced. He turned, walked toward Seth, and knelt down.

"Did you have something to say, *Davidson*?" he said, spitting out the name with revulsion. He yanked the cloth from Seth's mouth. "I'm waiting!"

"Wyatt . . . ," said Seth, his voice now pleading just like the black man's, "don't do it! It will be on your conscience forever. There's no reason—"

A blow from the back of Wyatt's hand filled Seth's mouth with blood.

"Save it, Davidson!" he retorted. "It's you and your kind who caused all this. People like you and your father are making these niggers so uppity they think they deserve to be free. Just remember— *you* caused this! And when you're lying in bed at night you can remember that this fool of a nigger was sitting on *your* horse when he died!"

Wyatt jumped to his feet and spun around. A great whack from his hand on Malcolm's rump sent the startled horse bolting into the night.

"No!" wailed Seth. His cry gradually faded into the blackness. No more sounds could be heard but the quiet flicker of flames from torches held by the surrounding circles of witnesses. A few momentary gurgles and gasps sounded from the black man's throat, and then gave way to silence.

Now that it had been done, the gruesome sight silenced all but the most hardened of the young men. They had been caught up in Wyatt Beaumont's vendetta for so long that they had not anticipated what it would *feel* like to watch a man die. Not until this moment had the reality sunk in that with their own hands they had actually *killed* a man.

The sobering thought sent more than a few chills around them as they gazed up at the figure swinging from the end of the rope. Each in his own way slowly realized that blood was on his hands. They were murderers.

Wyatt returned to the base of the tree. Again he knelt down and stared into Seth's face. "Hey, what do you know—poor Davidson's got tears in his eyes! Crying, little Sethy . . . what's the matter, Sethy! Ha, ha, ha!"

But none of his cohorts were laughing now. Even Brad McClellan was desperately fighting a rising lump in his throat.

Wyatt turned serious again.

"This is why I brought you along tonight, Seth," he said, looking hard into Seth's face. "I wanted you to see what freeing your slaves has done . . . and what will happen if more runaways come through here. And one more thing, none of the rest of us are going to squawk. So if word of this leaks out, about who was here and what happened . . . we'll know it was you that talked. You see, Seth—you're part of it now. You're one of us. You can't escape. You were here tonight. If you talk . . . we'll kill you next, or maybe one of your niggers. So you see, Seth—you're either with us . . . or you're dead."

He took a knife from his belt and cut the rope at Seth's feet, then freed his hands. The instant he was free, Seth struggled to his feet. He staggered forward, blindly thinking to get the man down.

"Somebody . . . help me!" he cried in desperation. "Help me . . . we've got to get him down before it's too late!"

They were still more afraid of Wyatt Beaumont than their own consciences. No one moved a muscle.

Suddenly a great explosion shattered the stillness of the night. Blood squirted from the side of the black man's head. What little struggle remained instantly ceased. His body shuddered briefly, then went limp at the end of the rope.

Seth turned to see Cameron Beaumont, at sixteen the youngest of the mob, pistol in hand, smoke yellowed from the light of the torches drifting lazily out of the barrel.

Hot tears blurred Seth's vision and he felt himself beginning to collapse. Hands grabbed him and he felt himself thrown over a horse's back and tied across the saddle like a sack of potatoes. The horse began to move, then the other horses also set out, until the scene of death was deserted. One by one the other riders moved away through the night. At length he realized he was alone with one other who continued to lead the mount on which he lay.

Drifting in and out of consciousness, Seth had no idea how long the journey lasted or its direction. At last he felt himself cut free and dropped to the ground. His captor rode off. Seth was left alone. A few minutes later he felt the warm breath and soft neigh of a friend near his face. Mercifully, they had brought him here on Malcolm, who would never leave him.

Again he fell unconscious.

When he woke, the dawn of morning was on its way into the sky. Hands and feet still bound, Seth struggled to sit up. He was somewhere halfway up the ridge on the Brown tract. Malcolm stood a few feet away nibbling on green patch of grass.

Struggling to loosen his bonds, and aching nearly everywhere, Seth finally managed to get free and climbed onto the faithful stallion's back.

"Home, Malcolm," he whispered in his ear. "Take me home."

Thirty-Six

*I*n the aftermath of the hanging, Seth was despondent. His father and mother were beside themselves with worry when he did not come home all night after his departure with Brad McClellan. One look when he rode into Greenwood the following morning told them that something terrible had happened. With difficulty he told them of the incident, breaking into tears more than once. By that same afternoon, after the stiff body had been found dangling from the tree by Leon Riggs, news of the hanging was spreading through the community like a brush fire.

Seth was sick with grief for days. The stakes of what the weather-vane on the barn signified had suddenly increased many times.

They could no longer conceal the constant stream of visitors that was discovering the wind in the horse's head at Greenwood on the route North. Over the following week, Richmond and Carolyn confided in the rest of their workers and brought them in on the scheme along with Nancy and Malachi. Nancy was so thoroughly changed from having taken Malachi's place as conductor that she was among the most eager of all to help.

There were, however, a handful whose loyalty they did not know if they could entirely count on. The danger of exposure stemmed mostly from undisciplined tongues rather than deception in the ranks of their workers. Accordingly, Silas and a few others were sent North with two or three groups of refugees. Their longtime workers among those were given enough cash to make certain they were provided for until jobs and lodgings could be found and they were comfortably situated north of the Pennsylvania border.

With danger increasing, the refugee stream indeed threatened to become a flood. When the family of eight appeared, two men with their wives, one sister, and three children, and one of the women in the late stages of pregnancy, they knew they would have to keep her in the big house until the baby came. None of the rest of the family would think of moving on without her. The sudden presence of so many extra blacks, and for what might be an extended time, posed difficulties they had not encountered before.

Only a week later, five children appeared. Carolyn's heart immediately went out to them. Questioned, the oldest, a competent and resourceful girl of fourteen called Ella Mae, told of their escape from a plantation in Alabama, of their mother's capture and their father's eventual death at the hands of a bounty hunter who had followed them. How the children had evaded him and how the girl had managed to lead her two brothers and two sisters to Greenwood without detection was nothing short of a miracle.

But . . . what to do with them!

The children too, it seemed, along with Eliza, should be kept in the big house, for the youngest was only four. Where else! Carolyn could not think of sending them on alone, with no family waiting for them in the North. What was to be done but *keep* them at Greenwood, and care for them? Perhaps indefinitely. After the recent hanging, the danger was too great to do otherwise.

It was Nancy who proposed a temporary solution.

She found Carolyn with Maribel in the kitchen. "Miz Dab'son," she said, "cud I talk ter you 'bout dem five young'uns dat come yesterday?"

"Certainly, Nancy," replied Carolyn.

"I been thinkin' dat maybe I cud help sum wiff dem. I wuz thinkin', since we gots ter keep dem from bein' seen, dat ef you'd want I cud cum an' sleep sumwheres in da big house wiff dem an'

watch ober dem, spechully dose two young'uns, Lilliana an' LeRoy.
Dat way you wudn't hab ter worry none 'bout dem wiff all da others
we got right now, an' you an' Maribel an' Mary cud keep watch on
Eliza down yonder below who's fixin' ter hab her a baby. An' maybe
sum er Eliza's folks' kids cud stay up wiff da others too, ef dat's what
you wanted."

"I think that sounds like a splendid idea, Nancy," said Carolyn.
"Are you willing to take on such a responsibility? What does Malachi
think?"

"We talked 'bout it, an' he seyz hit be a good idea. We's gotter help
dese poor folks what don' have no place ter go. Right now dey ain't
got no family but us, so we gots ter be dere family 'cause I reckon we
are."

And so it was that the first lodgers in the new hidden attic room
were Nancy Shaw as adoptive mother to Ella Mae and her four younger brothers and sisters.

On the third afternoon since their arrival, Carolyn walked up the
new hidden stairway with milk and a plate of fresh cookies. She had
seen none of the five children for several hours, or Eliza's daughter
and the other two little boys either for that matter. It was so quiet as
she reached the attic room door that she began to think no one was
inside. She walked in to see seven children sitting on the floor in a
circle surrounding Nancy—Ella Mae and her two brothers and older
sister, along with Eliza's daughter, Enisha, and the two little boys—
every one of them spellbound as Nancy spoke in such a thick Negro
dialect that Carolyn could scarcely make out a word. Four-year-old
Lilliana lay sound asleep in Nancy's arms.

"I wuz telling dem 'bout da ol' king from da ol' times," said Nancy,
glancing up.

"Well I won't disturb you," said Carolyn, setting down the tray. "It
appears they are enjoying it. I will just leave this with you."

Eight-year-old Hannah jumped up and ran toward her. Carolyn
stooped down to meet her.

"Look, missus," she exclaimed, holding out her palm to Carolyn's
face. "Dese are da lines ob da king!"

Now eleven-year-old Rufus ran to join her, sticking his hand almost into Carolyn's face. "An' dere's ribers too right here in my hand—dat's what Aunt Nancy seyz!"

Carolyn laughed and gave both a hug and sent them back to Nancy. "You all have quite a heritage, don't you!" she said as she stood. "It is something to be very proud of."

Carolyn returned downstairs with a wonderful feeling of contentment in her heart. *Aunt Nancy,* she thought, chuckling to herself. And the crowd was about to grow even larger.

The next day three black men, traveling alone and without families appeared!

"Dis be da place wiff da win' in da horse's head?" asked a bedraggled slave—he had been whipped so many times the scars on his back and shoulders were visible through his tattered shirt—speaking to the first person he saw, which happened to be Thomas.

"Yeah, that's what they say," Thomas replied. "Go up there and ask for my dad," he added, nodding toward the big house. He continued on with obvious disinterest.

Not sure what to make of the interview, the black man continued tentatively toward the large brick plantation house. Fortunately his next contact was black Mary, returning home from the pregnancy chamber. He asked her the same question, and two minutes later he was standing in front of Richmond Davidson.

"What is your name, son?" Richmond asked.

"Jackson, massa," the fugitive answered, "Jackson Riles. I be on da run from a turruble bounty huntin' man what's tryin' ter string me up. I be parful obliged effen you'd see fit ter let me hide out a day er two. I won't cause no trubble, suh, only thing is, dere's two other runaways wiff me. Dey's out yonder in da woods, an' dey's parful hungry too, massa."

So now the five children were in the new attic room, pregnant Eliza was in the basement along with those of her group the enlarged cellar could accommodate. Carolyn and Mary came and went from the cellar regularly, Mary caring for Eliza with the devotion of a mother, and, like Nancy in the attic far above her, sleeping on a pad most nights to be ready in case the baby came. A few of Eliza's group had been put in the cellar of the new house in the worker's village. And the three grown men were staying in a cabin of single men with the intent of moving on as soon as word could be got to Malachi's Quaker contact in neighboring Orange County and arrangements made for a meeting.

And all the while Wyatt Beaumont and his cohorts were prowling the neighborhood with heightened vigilance.

Thirty-Seven

*S*everal riders rode into the precincts of Oakbriar. Leon Riggs was the first to spot them. He walked toward the man in the lead and asked his business.

"The name's Murdoch," said the man. "I've got business with young Beaumont."

Riggs went in search in his boss's son. Twenty minutes later, Wyatt Beaumont was mounted and galloping away with them.

Father and son were seated on a bench a few yards into the shade of the woods bordering the drive. A deep change had come over Seth. He had been thrust headlong into the seriousness of life, and he would never afterward be the same.

"What do you think, Dad?" Seth had just asked. "Did I do the right thing with Veronica . . . calling it off, I mean?"

"You're not having doubts about that, are you?" asked his father.

"I don't know," shrugged Seth. "It almost seems like that's when these troubles began. They've all got something to do with Veronica."

"If you're going to trace your difficulties to Veronica," suggested his father, "I would think that many problems began by getting involved too deeply with her in the first place."

"Yeah . . . I see what you mean."

"It could never have worked. Calling it off took guts, and I am proud of you for it."

"But like you say, it might have been avoided if I had shown a little more backbone and sense earlier!" laughed Seth mordantly.

"The point is—it happened. You got yourself into a tough situation, then you had the courage to face it. There is no humiliation in admitting you made a mistake. It is only a fool who worsens his plight by going blindly forward without being able to admit his error."

"Is that what happened with your first wife, Dad?" asked Seth.

A hint of pain crossed Richmond's face. Sometimes he wondered where she was now, or if she was even still alive. He had tried to find out several years ago and had written a number of letters. But no replies ever came.

"No, son," he said with a sad smile at length. "An unfortunate marriage is not a mistake that can be undone like an engagement. Once the vow is made, very little can break it. Had you married Veronica, as great a mistake as it would have been in my view, I would never have counseled you other than to be the most devoted, sacrificial, and loving husband you could be. Even if she made your life miserable, as she might have done, she would nevertheless been your wife for life."

"Then what happened, Dad?" asked Seth. "Believing as you do, how did you come to be divorced and then marry Mom?"

A faraway look came to Richmond's eye.

"When I went to England," Richmond began after a few minutes, "it was with every intention of studying law. I was the younger of two sons and assumed I would not be part of Greenwood's future. I was alone and lonely. I met a young woman who was more than a little strange, I realized later. Yet somehow, her very peculiarities I found fascinating, almost captivating. She was beautiful in her own way, I suppose, though she had a distant, almost otherworldly air about

her. Whether I actually fell in love is doubtful, but she apparently fell
in love with me and her family was anxious for us to marry. Whenever
there is pressure to rush or accelerate marriage, my boy—take it as a
warning sign. Any woman who truly loves—I do not say who is *in*
love, but who truly *loves*—can afford to be patient. Many women are
not in love with their men so much as they are in love with an ideal of
love they have in their minds."

"I guess I have had some experience along those lines," said Seth.

"Right you are," rejoined Richmond. "You have indeed. And you
heeded the signs more astutely than I did. Sad to say, I did *not* heed
them. Her entire family conspired to make sure I was rarely alone with
her and I never learned how emotionally unstable she was. The father
presented himself as an erudite man who could teach me many things
and who knew many secrets of the universe hidden to most men. He
encouraged me to think of him as my father away from home. Yet as a
father, he proved anything but trustworthy. He kept from me much
in the family history that would have prevented the heartache and
grief that came later. I learned nothing of the fact that this man, the
girl's own father, had raised two entire families, completely abandoning the first which included three sons who were at the time older
than I. I learned nothing of insanity and suicides that had plagued the
family for generations. I was swept into depths of human misery without the least idea what I had gotten into.

"None of this lessens my own accountability. But I was very vulner-
able. Young men often do not recognize their own weakness, and
when someone comes along to feed their ego, they too eagerly allow it
to cloud their judgment. It simply shows that there are people in the
world who are less than honest, and who will deceive to achieve their
ends. While we are called to love those around us with the innocence
of doves, there come times in life when we must likewise be as shrewd
as serpents in judging the character of those with whom we have dealings.

"The long and the short of it is that we were married. I planned to
stay in England and make a new life for myself there. I entered Oxford
the next fall and began my studies toward a degree in law.

"Soon after the marriage, however, I began to realize that my wife had severe problems. Removed from the protective shield of her father and mother, her instability did not take long to manifest itself. At first I assumed the sudden change was due to the changes of marriage and leaving home. I tried to put the best light on it possible. I tried, and I honestly hope to God I did my best to love her in hopes that she would grow out of it. But in my heart I feared something was seriously wrong.

"She became pregnant. Instead of making her happy, the news turned her moody and withdrawn. Whenever we were with others in the family, I could not fail to pick up fragments of hushed comments and sighs from certain relatives indicating that they had seen such signs before. There was old uncle so-and-so . . . and a grandmother who died young . . . and who could forget the cousin who ran off, and so on. With every look and glance my forebodings grew.

"A son was born to us. The year was 1833. I was but twenty-three, far too young to be a father. Afterward, my wife was weak, delirious, ranting. The child was apparently healthy. The doctor was far more concerned for the mother, though he could ascertain no immediate physical cause for her condition.

"Several nights later she became raving and feverish. I didn't know what to do. The doctor had already been at the house to see us three times that day. At last, himself as exhausted as I, he went home saying he thought she would be safe till morning and urging me to get some sleep.

"But the night brought a worsening of her condition. She drifted in and out of consciousness, calling for the baby, then yelling at me and a servant girl to take the child away. She was incoherent and ranting. During one of these episodes, I sat on the bed, soothing and trying to talk to her. Gradually she calmed and eventually drifted into what appeared a peaceful sleep. Exhausted, and leaving the baby beside her I went to bed.

"She awakened several hours later, with images still in her brain, distorted by fatigue and her mental condition. She came a little more to herself and suddenly felt the child in the bed beneath her. Her hands went to it and discovered the body cold. She let out a hideous shrieking wail.

"The terrible sounds brought me to myself where I slept. I leapt from bed and rushed to the room where she was delirious and out of control. I bent down to investigate. She attacked me furiously, pummeling my face with her fists with a strength I could not imagine she could possess. All the while she was screaming that I had killed her baby. Finally I was able to scoop up the baby—"

His voice choked. Swallowing hard, he continued. "I rushed from the room calling for the servant girl to run for the doctor. In the meantime, I did my best to revive the child, but could not."

He looked away, and took several more deep breaths.

When Scully Riggs looked up from where he was loading an order his father had placed for Oakbriar, he saw six horses galloping by the supply yard at the station. He knew something out of the ordinary was going on.

Wyatt Beaumont rode in the lead. He recognized none of the others. They all wore serious expressions. Every saddle had a rifle sticking out from behind it.

Scully dumped the bag of grain from his back onto the wagon bed and dashed for his horse. He was sure to lose his job one of these days for running off. But this was a chance he wasn't about to miss.

In less than two minutes he was galloping west as fast as his horse would take him. He was not surprised when in the distance ahead he saw the dust from the six riders turn off the main road toward the Davidson place.

Father and son continued to talk, unaware off the danger approaching them.

"What had happened, Dad?" asked Seth.

"In her sleep, and unaware of herself, the poor delirious woman had rolled over on top of the child and suffocated him."

"Gosh . . . Dad—I never knew. I'm sorry! That means I had a half brother in England."

"It is the kind of thing I didn't want to tell you until the right time," sighed Richmond, tears standing in his eyes. "It was not something I wanted to tell anyone."

"I was disconsolate," nodded Richmond. "My wife never recovered emotionally. As she grew stronger in the coming weeks, she remained convinced that I had come in while she slept and murdered the child. And as she spread the tale, there were many who believed it. Strange to say, knowing as they did her unbalanced condition, her family also turned against me. I found myself isolated and alone, completely unable to concentrate on my studies. My life crumbled around me. Not only was my marriage in ruins, there was a possibility of my being brought up on charges of murder."

"Surely, Dad, it couldn't have gone *that* far."

Richmond smiled. "Don't be so sure, son," he said. "It is one of life's profound mysteries that lies are more readily believed than truth. Let people report that a man is kind, good, unselfish, and fair, and that he will seek the good of his neighbor above his own, and they will either register disinterest, or else laugh in your face and say that such men do not exist. Men do not want to believe such of others. To do so only indicts them in their own self-centeredness. But let people report that a man is a liar, is unfaithful to his wife and beats his children, and that he will cheat in the name of profit, and everyone *will* believe it, and will believe it without undertaking the slightest investitgation to discover whether the reports are reliable. Human nature delights in believing the worst. Such it was in my case. I honestly expected the authorities to set in motion an investigation on the basis of my wife's charges."

"What happened?"

"We buried our son and somehow managed through the next few weeks. My wife spent most of that time in bed and not once spoke to me. Gradually she regained her physical strength. She was so changed as to be unrecognizable—hard, cold, uncommunicative.

"After some time she began leaving for long periods. I had no idea where she went. Whenever we saw one another she gazed at me with both hatred and fear. I think she had come to believe her own lies and had talked herself into being afraid of me. Whether this was conscious, or a subconscious response to the guilt of knowing she had smothered her own child, I never knew. To this day I do not know whether she ever fully knew the truth of what transpired that night.

"Then I began to hear rumors that she had been seen out walking the streets alone at night, and worse, that she was taking up with men throughout the city willing to take advantage of her mental weakness. I did not see her for weeks at a time. Every time I did, her condition had deteriorated yet more.

"A day came when a man called at the door. I thought I was about to be arrested. But he was a solicitor, not an agent of the police. He handed me a set of papers that had been filed against me for divorce. I cannot say I was completely surprised.

"I went through an intense period of soul searching. I had always hated the idea of divorce. Yet I found myself in an impossible situation. At first I said to myself that I would not sign the papers. The idea of being divorced was repugnant to me. I tried to find my father-in-law in hopes of talking to him to see what I could learn about his daughter. He refused to see me. Through the solicitor, I managed to learn enough to convince me that the reports I had heard about her were true, that there were other men involved. Eventually I realized that if my wife had any chance of finding mental and psychological freedom, she would have to put this part of her life behind her. Whether that was possible, I did not know. But for me to refuse to sign and contest the divorce, and drag the matter into court, might destroy her. Was this a time to stand and fight, to defend myself, to answer the charges against me? Or was it a time to lay down my arms and put the conflict to rest? And all the while I was grieving the loss of our son. Can I say that it did not hurt to have such said against me? Surely not—every word of accusation was a slice of the knife into my very heart, for I had tried to love her. I don't know, Seth, my boy, I don't know if—"

His voice caught and he looked away. Tears flooded his eyes at the agony of uncertainty that had accompanied his decision. He wiped at his eyes.

"I will never be 100 percent certain that I did the right thing, Seth," Richmond struggled to go on. "I was convinced at the time that it was best for her. In any event, in the end, reluctantly, I signed the papers of divorce. I never saw the solicitor, any of her family, or my wife again. It was as if from that moment, once they had me out of their life, they pretended I had never existed at all."

"Dad, I'm . . . I'm really sorry," said Seth. "I can't imagine what it must have been like. My problems with Veronica were nothing alongside what you had to go through."

"We each are given trials to bear, Seth. They cannot be compared in difficulty. Life is difficult for *everyone*. We must face with fortitude, courage, faith, patience, and hope—let us not forget hope!—those unique trials that come to us. Mine came to me and I had to face them. Yours came to you. More will come to us both, and we will have to face them. Through our response to them is character built."

"What was her name, Dad . . . the lady—your first wife."

"Naomi," he replied in a melancholy voice, again dabbing at his eyes, "a beautiful name for a troubled soul."

Wyatt Beaumont reined in at the base of the Greenwood drive. The other five riders clustered around him.

Their leader had just begun to lay out his plan of action, when he was interrupted by another horse suddenly galloping into their midst and pulling up abruptly, choking them with dust.

Wyatt looked toward the newcomer with an expression of condescending irritation.

"Scully, what are you doing here?" he said.

"I figured there was some kind of trouble, Wyatt . . . I figured I could help."

"Well you figured wrong."

"Come on, Wyatt—I won't be no trouble."

"We don't need your help, Scully. Get back to town where you belong."

"Just hold on, Beaumont," said the man in charge. "Another look-out might come in handy."

He turned toward Scully. "Can you do what you're told?" he asked.

"Yes, sir."

"All right, you can stay. My name's Murdoch, and you do every-thing I say."

"Yes, sir, Mr. Murdoch."

"What's your name?"

"Riggs . . . Scully Riggs. What's it all about, Mr. Murdoch?"

"Runaways, Riggs."

"I knowed it! I figured they had some no-account coloreds here that didn't belong! I knowed them Davidsons—"

"Shut up, Scully!" barked Wyatt. "Let Mr. Murdoch do the talk-ing."

"All right, here's what we're going to do," said Murdoch. "We'll ride straight in and hope to catch them by surprise. Likely as not, they're hiding in their colored village with their own coloreds. Either of you two locals know where it is?"

Wyatt nodded.

"I do, Mr. Murdoch," said Scully eagerly. "I sure do. I know right where it is!"

"Good . . . then you two take Pete here and get to where you can keep an eye on the whole place. I want to know if there's sudden activity there or if they try to get somebody out and into the woods. They'll likely have signals arranged and things'll happen fast. They make a run for it, you grab 'em or shoot 'em. You got a gun, Riggs?"

"Yes, sir, but not with me."

"Pete, give him your pistol when you get in place."

"You want us to shoot, Mr. Murdoch?"

"'Course I want you to shoot. The price on this one's head's not worth the food it'd take to keep him alive."

"What about the local coloreds—the ones of this man Davidson?" asked the fellow called Pete.

"A darkie's a darkie," replied Murdoch. "If a few of them get shot by accident . . . who can tell the difference? That's the price they pay for trying to help runaways."

⟨────⟩

"Is that when you decided to come back to America?" Seth asked his father.

"Not immediately," replied Richmond. "I didn't know what to do. I still hoped to complete my law degree at Oxford. Yet everything had changed. My life was in chaos."

"I've felt that way lately too," sighed Seth.

"Shortly after the divorce was final," Richmond went on, "I received yet another blow, the news that my older brother, Clifford, was dead. With the same letter from my father—your grandfather Grantham—came the urgent request that, as I was now divorced, I return home to help with the plantation. My parents were growing older and there was no one else to run Greenwood when they were gone. My professional career ended at that moment. Despondent and utterly broken, I sailed for New York."

"Is that when you met Mom?"

"Shortly thereafter," nodded Richmond. "I happened to be in Richmond and was walking along a sidewalk next to a small church where her father was preaching. I had never been interested in spiritual things but I might certainly be said at the time to have been searching for *some* meaning in life. I wasn't thinking about God. But neither was I opposed to thinking about him. If God had anything to offer a despondent young man like me, I was willing to listen. For some reason the open door of the church drew me, and I walked inside. I sat down in the last row, and as the service progressed, there were no great voices of angels. But I heard things that made me think seriously

about just who God might really be. The service ended and I kept
sitting there thinking about what I had heard. When next I looked up,
the church was empty except for one young lady with a sad expression
picking up the hymnals.

"Mom?"

Richmond nodded. "Somehow we began to talk," he said. "Our
conversations continued the following week, and the week after that.
I asked her many questions. At first she said she had no answers. But
gradually she explained many things to me, even though she did not
hide the fact that she had doubts of her own. It was obvious to me
that there was concealed pain in her life too that made her doubt the
very truths she was telling me. You've heard the old saying, that sharing the gospel is nothing more than one thirsty sinner telling another
thirsty sinner where to find water. Well your mother and I were two
lonely thirsty downcast souls, and *neither* of us knew where to find
water. Yet gently and tenderly God took us by our hands and led us to
himself."

The silence this time was lengthy.

"What did happen to Uncle Clifford?" asked Seth at length.

"He was out riding and apparently fell from his horse," replied his
father. "His head struck a rock. He was dead when my father found
him the next day. My father saw prints from another horse. But if
Clifford was with anyone else at the time, it was never discovered who
it might have been."

"And what about old Mr. Brown?" asked Seth. "It happened up by
his place, didn't it?"

Richmond nodded. "That's the strange thing . . . there is no way he
could have been involved in anything nefarious. But the fact is, he was
never seen again. My father always said—"

The sound of horses galloping up the driveway put a stop to their
conversation. Richmond rose and walked out of the shade of the trees.

Some inner caution prompted Seth to remain where he was.

Thirty-Eight

The name's Murdoch," said the lead rider without prolonged introduction. "I'm looking for a man by the name of Davidson."

"I am Richmond Davidson," said Richmond, glancing over the group of men. He had never seen most of them before, though he observed Wyatt and Scully among them. "What can I do for you?"

"I track runaways, that's what," replied Murdoch. "We got a report that there might be some from the Carolinas that came through here. I've been tracking an ugly cuss for about a week that goes by the name of Jackson Riles."

From where he and his father had been seated, Seth was not able to make out the conversation in progress. But he knew he had seen the man before. It only took a few seconds to place him as the bounty hunter who had questioned his mother about runaways when they'd taken Lucindy north to Pennsylvania. Quickly he rose, ducked behind a few trees, made for the arbor, and, still keeping out of sight, ran for the side of the house.

Seth burst into the back door, and ran through the kitchen in search of his mother.

"Mom," he said when he found her upstairs, "we've got to get everyone hidden . . . hurry!"

"Who, Seth . . . what's—"

"Get them into the cellar and the kids up into the attic and out of sight—is Nancy here with them? And keep them away from the windows. There's a man outside who's looking for runaways!"

Carolyn dashed up one more flight to the rooms where they had put their recent arrivals.

"Hurry, all of you!" she said. "Don't make a sound . . . follow me. Bring all your clothes, bring everything . . . not a word—hurry! Nancy, take the children upstairs . . . keep away from the windows!"

A great scurrying of bodies, children, babies, men, and women suddenly turned the house into a beehive, with enough questions from the youngsters to prompt at least a half dozen more *Shhh!* warnings from Carolyn and the other adults.

Mary and Maribel, meanwhile, were in the basement room with Eliza when Carolyn appeared.

Mary looked up. "Miz Liza's baby's comin', Miz Dabson!"

"Oh no . . . not now!"

"I's jes' 'bout ter sen' fo' you. She started 'bout ten minutes ago."

Seth was flying down the stairs, doing his best not to pound so loudly he would be heard outside. He ran through the basement hardly aware of the drama of life taking place, and into the tunnel they had built to the outside. Moments later he was making for the colored village.

Carolyn turned back toward the terrified troop of runaways who had followed her downstairs. Three of the children were staring at her. Ella Mae and her four had returned to the attic room. "Elijah . . . the rest of you," said Carolyn, "you've got to keep the little ones quiet until we find out what is going on. The basement will be safe. Go into the little room there and close the door.

"But, Miz Davidson, what 'bout Eliza?" asked Eliza's sister.

"We will take good care of her. If Mary and Maribel need your help, they will—"

Carolyn paused. "On second thought, Janna, you take Maribel's place right now. I think I had better take Maribel upstairs so that everything will look normal."

Outside, Richmond's interview with the bounty hunter Murdoch continued.

"I don't know how you got the idea there are runaways here, Mr. Murdoch," Richmond was saying, "unless it is the fact that our colored folk are free. They work for us now as hired employees. It is true that some of them have gone North, but with our full knowledge and permission."

"Yeah, I heard of you, Davidson," rejoined Murdoch with a sneer. "We all heard of you and despise what you done. You're a traitor to the South."

"I don't happen to see it that way, Mr. Murdoch. I like to think that perhaps what we have done here is ahead of its time. Freedom will come to Negroes throughout the South eventually. We see no reason not to embrace the future peaceably."

"Well, it don't matter. It's not your own darkies I'm looking for," said Murdoch, boring his eyes into Richmond's, probing for any hint that would tell him that the man was lying. "Once you give them their papers, there's not much I can do about it. No, Davidson, I'm looking for runaways that've got nothing to do with you, unless you're hiding them. Then they'll have everything to do with you—'cause you'll go to jail and they'll hang. So you had better tell me the truth."

"You are certainly welcome to have a look around, Mr. Murdoch," said Richmond.

"We intend to, Davidson . . . with or without your permission. Boys," he said, turning to the men with him. "Search the place. If you see anything that looks suspicious, come get me."

As they spoke, Richmond noted both rifles and ropes with which their horses were equipped. With Seth's experience with Wyatt's gang of hoodlums so fresh, it was clear that the stakes in this dispute were increasing daily. The freedom of blacks was no mere political issue—life and death were involved.

Lord, he prayed silently, *keep bloodshed and death from Greenwood.*

Blind the eyes of these men, Lord. Do not let them find what they are looking for.

From the corner of his eye he glanced toward the house.

"Would you and your men perhaps care for a julep?" he said. "I'll just go in and tell my wife—"

"We're not looking for your hospitality, Davidson," growled Murdoch. "But maybe we will just go see your wife." He urged his horse on toward the house as his three men dismounted and ran off in the direction of the barn and other buildings. Richmond hurried after him.

He caught Murdoch as he was walking up the steps onto the veranda. He led him inside. Carolyn and Maribel stood in the entry-way as if expecting them. Murdoch looked them over, gazing up and down over Maribel's form with angry contempt.

"What are you staring at?" he said.

"Nufin', suh," replied Maribel in a trembling voice, though in truth her eyes had drifted down to the gunbelt strapped to the man's waist.

"Then why are you standing there looking like you've got some-thing to hide?"

"I don' know, suh . . . I's jes' standin' here wif da missus."

"You live here?"

"Yes, suh."

"You seen any strange coloreds around?"

"No, suh."

"And you'd tell me the truth whatever I asked?"

"Don't know, suh. A body can't likely say what she'd do effen she ain't gotter do it, can she?"

"I thought as much. You're a liar like all the rest."

Without further question he turned, spotted the staircase and quickly strode up the stairs two at a time. Richmond sent Carolyn a quick glance. Her eyes were wide with fear. With her head she gestured imperceptibly toward the cellar door, hidden by a tapestry hurriedly hung on the wall in front of it. He nodded, then followed Murdoch. By the time he reached the second floor, Murdoch had already kicked two of the doors wide with his foot and was searching roughly inside them. He continued from room to room, rudely knocking open closet doors, looking under beds, and tossing chairs and blankets about.

"You got a lot of furniture and wardrobes and linens for just one family," he said.

"There are several servants who live with us in the house," replied Richmond. "We have our two sons, and our daughter has not been gone long . . . and we occasionally have guests."

Murdoch continued through every room, did the same on the third floor until he was satisfied, then descended the stairway back to the ground floor.

"You don't mind if I have a look around down here, do you, ma'am?" he said to Carolyn where she stood waiting at the bottom of the stairs.

"No, sir."

He paused and eyed her carefully. "Do I know you?" he said.

"I don't think so," replied Carolyn.

"I could swear I've seen you someplace before. Well, no matter— it'll come to me. That's why I'm good at what I do, I remember faces. I can even tell one darkie from another, which most white folks can't."

He proceeded to search the ground floor in the same manner as he had those above it. Three or four minutes later he walked toward the door. "Sorry to inconvenience you, ma'am," he said to Carolyn, "but I've got a job to do."

He left the house to rejoin his men.

"Show me your darkie quarters," he said to Richmond, still following.

When they were gone, Carolyn removed the tapestry, opened the door a crack. "Just a little longer," she whispered down the cellar steps, then again closed in their fugitives and rehung the tapestry over the door.

Almost the instant she did so, a scream sounded from below.

"Hit's comin', Miz Dab'son!" Mary's voice called out. "Dere's no stoppin' dat baby now!"

Carolyn flew down into the cellar and ran to the bedside.

"Eliza, dear," she said, "I know how badly it hurts, but there is a bad man outside who is looking for you. You must try to keep quiet."

Carolyn motioned to Mary and Eliza's sister, and they came to her with obvious fear in their faces. "If she starts to cry out again," said Carolyn, "clamp a cloth or towel over her mouth. It is the only way. That man *must* not hear her!"

They nodded.

"I am going to join them outside," she added. "Richmond might need help."

She turned to go. Again Eliza started to cry out. Mary was beside her in a moment and stuffed a towel onto her mouth to muffle the sound.

"I's sorry, 'Liza dear, but dere ain't no other way."

As Richmond and Murdoch walked away from the house, Murdoch hesitated at the faint sound of a cry. He turned back briefly, a look of question on his face, then continued on. He called out to his men to join them from where they were ransacking the barn, workshop, ice house, and other outbuildings.

Richmond led the way to the black village.

As they reached the workers' quarters, immediately all activity about the place—talking and singing and laughter and sounds of playing children—ceased. Every set of black eyes turned to face their master and his unfriendly looking visitors.

One of Murdoch's men emerged from out of the woods, rifle in hand. Wyatt Beaumont and Scully Riggs followed. As they walked forward, neither acknowledged the presence of their father's friend.

"Scully . . . Wyatt . . . what's this all about?" said Richmond. "You know our people are free, not runaways. What have you been telling this man?"

"I told you, Davidson," snapped Murdoch, "this isn't about your people. You just keep quiet. Pete . . . Harv, Jesse, Beaumont, you see anything peculiar going on here?"

"Nothing, Murdoch," replied Pete. "Just lazy darkies and all these women and their brats."

Murdoch nodded as he looked around. Slowly a cluster of curious black children began to draw near, followed more slowly by the men who happened to be about. "Boys," said Murdoch, taking no notice of them, "search every inch of this place. If anybody's hiding, I want them found. Any of these coloreds get in your way, you know how to deal with their kind—Beaumont, Riggs, you two go along. If you see anybody that don't belong, I want to know it."

Carolyn now approached from the direction of the house. She gasped in astonishment to see their two neighbors carrying out Murdoch's orders along with his men.

"Wyatt, how can you do this!" she said, walking toward them. "You've known us all your life. And what about you, Scully? I used to take care of you when you where a child after your mother passed away. How can you—"

"We're men now, Mrs. Davidson," interrupted Wyatt rudely. "We're not little boys. We got things we need to do, a way of life we've got to protect even if some people are bent on destroying it."

Carolyn was shocked at his cold and impersonal tone. "What are you talking about, Wyatt?" she said "We're not bent on destroying anything. Surely, Wyatt, you don't think your father and mother—"

"Look, Mrs. Davidson," said Murdoch, taking two strides toward her, "like I told you, we have a job to do. If you get in our way, I'm going to have to ask you to go back to your house."

He laid a rude hand on her shoulder to pull her away.

"Mr. Murdoch," said Richmond in a tone of quiet authority. He walked forward and took firm hold of Murdoch's forearm. "I am going to have to ask you to keep your hand off my wife." With a determined grip he removed Murdoch's hand from Carolyn's shoulder. "If you have a request to make, either to my wife or myself, you may make it in a gentlemanly fashion."

Murdoch spun around and yanked himself free from Richmond's grasp. Almost the same instant the gun from his holster was in his hand. Terrified, Carolyn jumped behind her husband.

"Don't you ever touch me, Davidson!" he spat in obvious threat, pointing the gun straight into Richmond's chest from less than two feet away. "And don't you try to stop me from doing *anything* I want to do. One word from me and every one of these shacks goes up in flames, and your own house with them. You watch your step, Davidson! I am a man you do *not* want to get in the way of."

Murdoch's men took threatening steps toward them, their rifles inching higher in their grasps. They were ready to defend their leader at the slightest provocation. At the same time, all the Davidsons' blacks tensed and also crept forward. Only shovels and hoes and rakes were in their hands. But every man among them would have not hesitated to use them to the death in defense of their master. From the gleaming looks in the eyes of Murdoch's small outnumbered band, it was clear they hoped the coloreds would start something, so that *they* could finish it.

The two men stood eyeball-to-eyeball without flinching.

From the corner of his vision, Richmond saw Wyatt Beaumont staring straight at him. In his face he saw his father at a younger age. He wore an expression that said he would feel no compunction to kill.

The standoff lasted but a few seconds.

Richmond backed away, keeping a steady eye alternately on Murdoch and Denton Beaumont's son. If they tried to hurt one of his blacks, he *would* interfere.

"Carolyn," he said, "you can go back to the house. These men are nearly done here."

Afraid to leave him alone, but knowing she must obey, Carolyn slowly backed away up the hill toward the plantation house.

"Malachi . . . all the rest of you," Richmond continued, glancing at the circle of tense black faces surrounding them, "get back to work . . . you women can go back to your homes and return to what you were doing. If these men want to search anywhere inside or outside your houses, you may let them."

Slowly his eyes drifted again toward Murdoch's. "They will not hurt you," he went on slowly, as if disguising a subtle command as he reassured his people. "As soon as they find that you have nothing to hide, they will leave in peace."

Slowly the circle of Negroes widened then backed away. Not a sound could be heard.

Straining to hear in the dark underground room of the new cabin where he sat with Jackson Riles and his two companions and a half dozen other runaways he had hurried below, Seth could make out very little. He had no idea how near the incident had come to breaking into a major incident.

"Now, Mr. Murdoch," said Richmond. "Get on with your search. Wyatt and Scully will tell you these are all blacks they have both known for years. Then take your men off my property."

Murdoch lowered his gun and replaced it in the leather at his side. Again their eyes locked momentarily.

Both men knew it would not be the last time they saw one another.

Carolyn dashed for the house. The moment they were gone ten minutes later, she burst through the door, hurried across the floor, flung back the tapestry, then flew down the cellar stairs, expecting any moment to hear Eliza scream out again from her bed.

Instead the cry of an infant met her ears.

Thirty-Nine

*W*ith a newborn now at Greenwood, additional complications had to be considered. If Eliza could not move on while pregnant, neither would either she or her new little girl be in any condition to travel for a good while, perhaps months. The three single men were taken west by Malachi to continue their journey. Others came to replace them, and also moved on.

The Underground Railroad in central Virginia was doing a brisk business.

After two months, with Eliza well enough to travel and her little girl gaining strength rapidly, and having received word that Wyatt Beaumont would be gone for two weeks, Richmond decided once again to make use of the delivery wagon with the deep bed and hidden compartment that had taken Lucindy and her family north. Their route on this occasion, however, would be almost directly west, where Richmond wanted personally to meet the Quaker man and woman who had already taken so many travelers from them as Malachi's contact.

He therefore drove the wagon himself with the youngsters and one adult, and was accompanied by Malachi leading a smaller wagon with the others.

They were gone four days, made the transfer of cargo without incident, and Richmond returned excitedly to tell Carolyn that the man was none other than the cousin of Frederich Mueller of Hanover, Pennsylvania, at whose farm Lucindy had found her Caleb. The underground network, it seemed, was all around them, yet they had never suspected it.

Spring advanced and the summer of 1860 approached. Though slavery had come up in 1852 and 1856, the election to be held in November of 1860 would be the first presidential election dominated by slavery and states rights. The nation watched with interest to see what stances the old Democratic and the young upstart Republican party would take.

The first of three Democratic conventions was held in April. At that time the Northern Democrats nominated Illinois Senator Stephen Douglas as their presidential candidate. Neither Democratic President Buchanan nor his vice president could support Douglas, a longtime Buchanan foe over slavery. Southern Democrats demanded that the party adopt a platform in strong defense of slavery. Douglas could not agree. Some Southern delegates walked out. After fifty-four ballots, Douglas had still not received the two-thirds majority required for nomination. The convention adjourned, with plans to reconvene in Baltimore in June.

The Republican national convention was scheduled for mid-May as another major barometer of the nation's feelings on the issue of slavery.

Richmond opened the morning newspaper of Saturday, May 19.

"Look, dear," he said as he perused the front page. "The dark horse Abraham Lincoln won the Republican nomination for the presidency last week. That's astonishing—he was way down the list of favorites."

"I thought Senator Seward was the favorite," said Carolyn.

"He was. Apparently he won the first ballot, but didn't get a majority—let me see . . ."

Richmond continued to read the account. "Ah," he said after a few minutes, "this explains it—it took three ballots before Lincoln gained a majority. After an unexpectedly strong showing on the first ballot, some backroom wheeling and dealing took place by Lincoln's supporters. The Pennsylvania delegation switched its vote and Lincoln led on the second ballot. By the third vote the momentum was moving entirely his way. Suddenly a man whose only national experience was a single two-year term in the House of Representatives more than a decade ago has come from out of nowhere and is now the Republican candidate for the presidency."

"That's remarkable. Who is his vice presidential candidate?"

"Senator Hamlin from Maine."

"Who do you think they will run against for the Democrats?" asked Carolyn.

"Either Vice President Breckinridge or Senator Douglas," replied Richmond. "I see no other possibilities. Although after Douglas's failure to win the nomination outright last month, I'm not sure what will happen. Maybe when the Democrats meet again, they will come up with a completely different candidate."

"Might the president himself run again?"

"I doubt it," replied Richmond. "President Buchanan has lost so much support, even among his own party, I don't think he is even seeking the nomination. So though he tried to curry favor of the Southern party leadership, he didn't satisfy them, and in the process lost favor with Northern Democrats as well."

"Who do you think will win in November?"

"A good question. If Douglas is nominated, he has already beaten Lincoln once so I would say he would have to be considered the favorite."

"That was only for a state election. The national electorate might see things differently."

"True. And against Breckinridge, I would guess that the electorate would go along North-South lines, pro-slavery versus antislavery. In that case I would put my money on Lincoln."

Richmond chuckled as he continued to read. "Listen to this," he said. "Here is a photograph of Lincoln . . . but the description is even better."

By now Carolyn had walked over and was looking over his shoulder at the paper as he read.

"'In personal appearance,'" Richmond read, "'Mr. Lincoln, or, as he is more familiarly termed among those who know him best, Old Uncle Abe, is long, lean, and wiry. In motion he has a great deal of the elasticity and awkwardness which indicate the rough training of his early life, and his conversation savors strongly of Western idioms and pronounciation. His height is six feet three inches. His complexion is about that of an octoroon[2] ; his face, without being by any means beautiful, is genial looking, and good humor seems to lurk in every corner of its innumerable angles. He has dark hair tinged with gray, a good forehead, small eyes, a long penetrating nose, with nostrils such as Napoleon always liked to find in his best generals, because they indicated a long head and clear thoughts; and a mouth which aside from being of magnificent proportions, is probably the most expressive feature of his face.

"'As a speaker he is ready, precise, and fluent. His manner before a popular assembly is as he pleases to make it, being either superlatively ludicrous or very impressive. He employs but little gesticulation, but when he desires to make a point produces a shrug of his shoulders, an elevation of his eyebrows, a depression of his mouth, and a general malformation of countenance so comically awkward that it never fails to "bring down the house." His enunciation is slow and emphatic, and his voice, though sharp and powerful, at times has a frequent tendency to dwindle into a shrill and unpleasant sound; but as before stated, the peculiar characteristic of his delivery is the remarkable mobility of his features, the frequent contortions of which excite a merriment his words could not produce.'"[3]

"It seems that it would be marvelous to see him speak in person," said Carolyn. "He sounds fascinating."

"He claims not to be an abolitionist," said Richmond, "but in trying to explain his position, Lincoln is quoted as saying from two

---

[2]Octoroon—a person of one-eighth Negro blood.
[3]Quote from *Harper's Weekly*, Vol. IV, No. 178, New York, May 26, 1860.

earlier speeches: 'I have always hated slavery, I think, as much as any Abolitionist. I have been an Old Line Whig. I believe I have always hated it, and always believed it in course of ultimate extinction. If I were in Congress, and a vote should come up on a question whether slavery should be prohibited in a new Territory, in spite of the Dred Scott decision I would vote that it should. I nevertheless did not mean to go on the banks of the Ohio and throw missiles into Kentucky, to disturb them in their domestic institutions.'"[4]

"That sounds almost like the abolitionist position," said Carolyn as Richmond set down the paper and she returned to her chair.

"Similar to it," nodded Richmond, taking a sip of his coffee. "He is clearly against slavery, and would fight tooth and nail against its expansion into new states and territories. But I think he still hopes to find a peaceful, negotiated solution in the areas where slavery presently exists."

Carolyn thought a moment. "Perhaps his position is a little like ours," she said. "We have freed our own slaves because, like Lincoln, we have come to hate slavery, but we have not embarked on an effort to force Denton Beaumont or William McClellan do the same. It is a personal conviction that we are trying to live out in our lives without insisting that everyone share the same conviction."

"Well put, wife! I have the feeling such may exactly reflect something like the man's views. However, if he becomes president he will not have the luxury we do of being able merely to live out his personal convictions. He will then speak for the nation, and I fear it will be a seriously divided one if he is elected. But he sounds like a fascinating man. I wish I could sit down with him for an hour or two!"

Carolyn, Nancy, and Mary went into Dove's Landing to call on Reverend Jones, as was their custom. He lived in a run-down shack behind Baker's store and, though she did not much care for Negroes, his usefulness with odd maintenance jobs to a widow like Mrs. Baker

---

[4]Lincoln quote from *Harper's Weekly*, Vol. IV, No. 178, New York, May 26, 1860.

was more than sufficient to offset her discomfort with the arrangement. She did not exactly give him the place without charge, but he had been more than able to offset the rent she required with the work he did for her, supplemented by similar light jobs for others about town.

During the last several months, as he had been ailing, Carolyn tried to see him weekly if not more often, and had been bringing him cold meals to sustain him from visit to visit.

When they appeared in town on this day, Mrs. Baker spotted Carolyn and her two black friends the moment the carriage drew up in front of her store. She hurried outside to intercept them as they walked around the side of her shop to the little house in back.

"Mrs. Davidson," she said, "could I have a word with you?"

Carolyn stopped and turned with a smile. "Hello, Mrs. Baker," she said.

The shopkeeper's quick perusal of Mary and Nancy at Carolyn's side revealed a condescension that she made no effort to conceal.

"I feel I should tell you, Mrs. Davidson," she began, glancing toward the basket of food in Carolyn's hand, "since you obviously consider his care your affair, that Mr. Jones has not been able to do any work for me in more than a month."

"He has not been feeling well, Mrs. Baker," replied Carolyn.

"That is obvious. He does nothing but lie in bed all day."

"He is not a young man, Mrs. Baker. Last winter was a difficult one for him."

"Be that as it may, he is now a month behind on his rent."

"Please, Mrs. Baker, have no concern. If he is unable to make up his work for you, my husband and I will gladly ensure that his obligations are met."

"As I said, Mrs. Davidson, he is *already* a month behind."

"I see . . . well, then—Nancy, will you please take the basket?" she added, turning momentarily to Nancy. Nancy took the basket of food and Carolyn opened her handbag. " How much is his rent per month?"

"Well, as I say . . . he takes it out in work . . . but, it comes to the equivalent of six dollars, Mrs. Davidson."

A few inaudible words escaped Mary's mouth which it was just as well Mrs. Baker, who could not decipher more than fifteen or twenty percent of what any Negro said, did not understand.

"Well then," said Carolyn, pulling out two bills and two coins, "here is twelve dollars. I hope this will cover last month he has been unable to work, as well as one more."

Surprised but clearly pleased, Mrs. Baker took the money from Carolyn's hand. "Uh, yes . . . thank you, that will be just fine."

"If there are similar difficulties in the future, Mrs. Baker, will you please come see me rather than worrying Mr. Jones about it."

Mrs. Baker nodded, attempted a smile, then returned to her shop.

"Effen dat woman thinks dat shack where dat poor man lives be worf six dollars a munf," huffed Mary, "she's nufin' but a thief! Why hit ain't a sight as good as ours, no how! An' you an' Mister Dab'son only hab us pay two dollars a munf."

"But she also gives him work to do, Mary," smiled Carolyn. "And Mrs. Baker is a widow. She has herself to think of too."

A few more mumbled comments and *humphs* accompanied them the rest of the way to Rev. Jones' door. Several knocks went unanswered. They heard nothing from within. Carolyn tried the latch. The door swung open and they entered.

From the moment Carolyn walked inside, she perceived that a change had taken place since her last visit. Rev. Jones lay on his bed at the far side of the room beneath a single blanket. They hurried toward him. His eyes were barely open. He smiled feebly at the sight of his visitors. Though his eyelids hung heavy, what portion of his eyes were visible below them brightened noticeably.

"Ah . . . ladies, you's good to come see me," he said in a voice barely above a whisper.

"Rev. Jones," said Carolyn, disturbed by the sight. She knelt at the bedside and placed a hand on his shoulder. She trembled inside as her hand touched him. His body was on fire. "What is it?" she said. "Have you been taken more ill since I saw you last?"

"Da cough's got worse an' worse," he said, his voice weak and rough. "Den I got so weak I jes' couldn't git up. But I'm happy an' da

Lord is good to me an' I've got dear friends to love an' dat's good ter me. What more does a body need dan dat?"

Carolyn felt a tug at her arm. She turned. Nancy motioned her away from the bed.

"Dis was lying on da floor at da foot ob da bed, Miz Dab'son," she said, showing Carolyn a towel covered with stains that could be nothing else than blood.

"Oh, Lord!" Carolyn breathed, closing her her eyes briefly. She took a deep breath, then opened her eyes and looked at Nancy again. "He's been coughing up blood. How long has he had this cough, do you remember?"

"He got sick fo dat spell last winter, den he's been coughin' eber since, close as I kin recall."

"Oh, Lord . . . Lord, bless the dear man!" she whispered. "How could he have failed so quickly! We were just here five or six days ago. Listen, Nancy," she said, "I am going to run for the doctor. You and Mary do everything you can to get him to drink some water. And see if you can manage to get a little of the soup we brought inside him."

Carolyn turned and hurried out through the door. By the time she reached the street and passed the entrance to Mrs. Baker's Mercantile a few seconds later, she had lifted the edges of her dress and was running as fast as she could along the boardwalk.

Carolyn found Dr. Meade in his office. She knocked but did not wait for a reply, and rushed straight through the door.

"Doctor . . . please!" she said out of breath, "you've got to come. It's Mr. Jones. I'm more than certain he has pneumonia—I fear it is advanced."

Dr. Meade sat behind his desk, gazing over the top of his spectacles at this sudden intrusion into the quiet of an uneventful afternoon. He rose heavily, and glanced about for his coat and bag.

"What are the symptoms?" he asked.

"He's had a prolonged cough," answered Carolyn, catching her breath but obviously still frantic, "and now has a fever. And recently he's been coughing blood."

"I see," nodded the doctor gravely. "That sounds bad all right," he added, putting on his jacket. He picked up his black bag and led the way to the door. "Where is he?"

"At his house . . . behind Baker's Mercantile."

Dr. Meade stopped in his tracks halfway through the open door. He turned to face Carolyn. "You don't mean that old man, the darkie that does odd jobs . . . not *that* Jones?"

"Yes, Doctor . . . old Mr. Jones. Please—we've got to hurry!"

The doctor shook his head, turned and took a few steps back inside his office, and set his bag on his desk.

"I can't treat *him*, Mrs. Davidson," he said. "You ought to know that."

"He may be dying, Dr. Meade!"

"Be that as it may, he's colored. After the hanging and everything else, I just can't risk it. I'm sorry."

"Dr. Meade—he is a human being! And a dear one! I thought the physician's oath was color-blind."

"I'm sorry, Mrs. Davidson. I can't help you."

He sat down in his chair. It was clear he did not intend to budge.

"Dr. Meade—this is the most disgraceful thing I have ever heard!" said Carolyn, her anxiety for Rev. Jones boiling over. "I might expect something like this from . . . from . . . Denton Beaumont . . . but from *you*, Dr. Meade! I cannot believe my ears! A doctor's vow is to preserve life. Do you intend to just let a poor man die . . . and do nothing to stop it!"

The room went deathly silent. Dr. Meade sat and returned her stare but said nothing. He was angry, too, at being accused of playing false to his oath by a ranting abolitionist like this Davidson woman. The fact, also, that Denton Beaumont was one of his closest friends did not prejudice him in Carolyn's favor. But he was one of those who kept his anger to himself, and chose other and more subtle means to express it than unleashing a verbal torrent of attack. She would pay for her outburst, but at a time and by a method of *his* choosing.

Only a second more Carolyn stared back at his expressionless face, then turned and ran from the office. Before she had passed the threshold, her anger gave way to an uncontrollable flood of tears. Even if Dr. Meade had come, she knew the symptoms well enough to realize he may not have been able to stem the tide of the infection. But that he refused to come at all dashed what little hope she had carried to his office into heartbreaking despair.

Without a doctor's assistance, there was nothing any of them could do to help. Their friend Rev. Jones was in God's hands now.

For the rest of the afternoon and throughout the night, one of the women remained beside the sickbed. They could only make him comfortable, try to get him to eat and drink, and apply cool compresses to ward off the fever.

But the disease had progressed much too far before they had realized its severity. Neither did Rev. Jones himself recognize the full state of his body's collapse. Now in its final stages, there was no hope of reversal.

Four days later, the dear man slipped away to be with his Father in a home prepared for him of considerable more luxury than Mrs. Baker's shack where he had lived happily and died in great peace surrounded by three or four of his dearest earthly friends.

The Davidsons held a service in the colored portion of Dove's Landing's cemetery. All the black workers from Greenwood, and a number of slaves from Oakbriar and the McClellan plantation attended. The Davidsons were the only whites among them.

The following Sunday came. No black services were held. There had been none for several weeks as their humble leader's health had deteriorated. With Rev. Jones now gone, some of the blacks from the various plantations for the first time began to think of the future.

Who would take his place? Even though they had to meet in secret, and even if their so-called church was the abandoned home of a Cherokee farmer, they had to have a pastor. And black ministers in and around Dove's Landing were in short supply.

For years Virginia law had prohibited blacks from meeting, assembling, or conducting their own church services at all. It also threatened imprisonment for whites who undertook to teach blacks or slaves to read, to better themselves, or about spiritual principles. The secret church meetings Rev. Jones had conducted for several years remained undetected by virtue of an ingenious plan among the religious blacks of rotating between the clandestine black services and the authorized services held every Sunday morning at the Dove's Landing church, where several pews at the rear were sectioned off for the sole use of coloreds.

Though most of the blacks of the area thought highly of the Davidsons for what they had done and envied their blacks their freedom, there were nonetheless a few who resented them their good fortune. But the loyalties even of these to fellow blacks was the strongest bond of all. None would have thought of betraying either Rev. Jones, the Greenwood blacks, or Richmond and Carolyn Davidson as the obvious unspoken "sponsors" of the black worship services, in spite of their personal feelings in the matter.

Thus, on most Sundays, a few token blacks from every plantation including Greenwood—the individuals comprising this small black congregation shifting membership from week to week—walked silently into Dove's Landing to attend the white services, sitting in the black section in unexpressive silence, while other of their fellows, by means secretive, circuitous, and constantly changing, made their way over hill and valley and through woodland and pasture, to the services held on the Brown tract by Rev. Jones.

Thus the assortment of blacks at each service was always different, though always representing a mix from all the surrounding plantations. Over the course of time, every black was seen at some time or another in the Dove's Landing church. And as all blacks looked similar to most whites, this constantly shifting diversity of worshipers never aroused the slightest suspicion in the community that there was another invisible congregation existing simultaneously but unseen.

Carolyn's teaching of Greenwood's own women, however, was never discussed.[5]

Spearheaded by Nancy and some of the women, who then spoke with their men, a plan gradually began to be discussed among the Davidson workers. They contrived to visit two or three of the other plantations, ostensibly on other business, and speak in secret with the leading slaves in a matter that did not divulge the women's meetings. While the full reasons for their suggestion of a pastoral replacement, therefore, were not made clear to the slaves of other plantations, they were persuaded to go along. The reactions to their proposal were mixed, but in the end, in that no better solution presented itself, a general consensus among the community of blacks in the region was reached.

Accordingly, a deputation of four women and three men of Greenwood's blacks, scrubbed clean with faces shining and wearing their best Sunday clothes, appeared one Sunday afternoon at the front door of the Davidson home. Answering their knock, Moses opened the door. His jaw dropped in astonishment. He found Richmond and Carolyn in the parlor a minute later.

"Mister . . . Miz Dab'son," he said in a more formal expression than usual, "da two ob you's got a group ob *visitors*."

---

[5]By the eve of the Civil War, Christianity had pervaded the slave community. Not all slaves were Christians . . . but the doctrines, symbols, and vision of life preached by Christianity were familiar to most.

The religion of the slaves was both visible and invisible, formally organized and spontaneously adapted. Regular Sunday worship in the local church was paralleled by illicit, or at least informal, prayer meetings. . . . Slaves forbidden by masters to attend church, or, in some cases, even to pray, risked floggings to attend secret gatherings to worship God.

His own experience of the 'invisible institution' was recalled by former slave Wash Wilson:

"When de niggers go round singin' 'Steal Away to Jesus,' dat mean dere gwine be a 'ligious meetin' dat night. De masters . . . didn't like dem 'ligious meetin's so us natcherly slips off at night, down in de bottoms or somewhere. Sometimes us sing and pray all night."

Slaves frequently were moved to hold their own religious meetings out of disgust for the vitiated gospel preached by their masters' preachers. Lucretia Alexander explained what slaves did when they grew tired of the white folks' preacher: "The preacher came . . . and he'd just say, 'Serve your masters. Don't steal your master's turkey. Don't steal your master's chickens. Don't steal your master's hawgs. Don't steal your master's meat. Do whatsomever your master tells you to do.' Same old thing all the time. . . . Sometimes they would . . . want a real meetin' with some real preachin'. . . . They used to sing their songs in a whisper and pray in a whisper."

Slaves faced severe punishment if caught attending secret prayer meetings. Moses Grady reported that his brother-in-law Isaac, a slave preacher, "was flogged, and his back pickled" for preaching at a clandestine service in the woods. His listeners were flogged and "forced to tell who else was there."

Slaves devised several techniques to avoid detection of their meetings. One practice was to meet in secluded places—woods, gullies, ravines, and thickets (aptly called 'hush harbors'). Kalvin Woods remembered preaching to other slaves and singing and praying while huddled behind quilts and rags, which had been thoroughly wetted "to keep the sound of their voices from penetrating the air" and then hung up "in the form of a little room," or tabernacle. (From *Christian History* magazine, Issue 33, p 42.)

Having no idea what his emphasis of the word could signify, but assuming possibly that a new troop of runaways had arrived, Richmond rose and followed Moses to the veranda. The sight that met his eyes brought a smile, then a chuckle of good humor to his lips.

"We's wantin' ter talk ter *Missus* Dab'son," said Josiah Black, whom the others had designated spokesman.

"I see," nodded Richmond, still smiling though now more bewildered than ever. "Then come in—she is in the parlor."

They followed him stoicaly inside.

"Carolyn, my dear," he said as they entered the parlor, "you have guests."

"Me?" said Carolyn, glancing up in surprise.

"It seems they are here to see *you*," replied Richmond.

"Dat don't mean you can't stay, Mister Dab'son," said Nancy. "It's jes' dat our biz'ness is wiff da mistress."

"If you don't mind," said Carolyn, "I *would* like him to stay so that we can both hear why you have come. But sit down, please . . . make yourselves comfortable."

They did so. An awkward silence followed. Richmond and Carolyn glanced at each other with expressions of humorous curiosity. Neither had so much as a clue what it was all about. The eyes of their black visitors all rested on Josiah. Finally, with obvious nervousness and a bit of stammering, he managed to begin.

"We's been talkin'," he said, "us an' others down yonder, 'bout what ter do 'bout the Sunday services wiff Rev. Jones now passed away like he dun, God rest his sowl. We needs us a pastor, 'cause dat church's 'bout da only time we see da blacks at da other places roun' 'bout, an' Rev. Jones he taught us good outta da good Book an' helped us ter know 'bout God an' Jesus, an' dat white preacher in town, he's nuthin' but a white man's preacher dat tells coloreds dat dey ain't as good as whites an' ter obey der masters an' such like. An' dere ain't no other colored preachers dat we know ob. An' our ladies, dey been tellin' us 'bout dere meetin's wiff you, Miz Dab'son, an' 'bout all you dun taught dem. An' we figger you likely knows as much 'bout God an' da good Book as Rev. Jones. So we's here axin' effen you'd be paster ter us coloreds out yonder at da Brown house."

Richmond and Carolyn sat in surprised silence. Whatever they had expected, it was surely not this!

"But why me . . . I'm a woman," said Carolyn at length. "I'm no preacher. What about Richmond?"

"I'm no preacher either!" laughed her husband.

"But you boff know a heap mo' 'bout God den we do," now said Nancy. "An' I's sure you knows jes' as much as yor missus, Mister Dab'son . . . but you's been teaching us ladies 'bout God all dis time, Miz Dab'son. You's already been like a pastor to us."

"But what about the slaves from Oakbriar and the other plantations," asked Carolyn. "What would they think of such a suggestion?"

"We already dun ax'd dem, Miz Dab'son," replied Josiah. "We din't tell dem nuthin' 'bout da meetin's wiff our ladies. We only said dat you wuz a fine lady dat knows 'bout God an' da Book an' how ter live like Christians is supposed ter do. Dey's willin' ter go along."

"Well," said Carolyn, glancing with question at Richmond again, "you've quite taken me by surprise. I suppose all I can say is that I will pray earnestly about it and that Richmond and I will talk the matter over further. I will take your request seriously, and then see what God would have us do."

When Carolyn and Richmond were alone a few minutes later, they continued to discuss the unexpected request.

"They're not looking for a *preacher*," Richmond commented after some time, "so much as a minister, a teacher. And you are both, Carolyn. You are a natural teacher—you've been teaching our ladies for years. And your compassionate nature has a heart for ministry. They trust you, and that is probably the most important qualification of all."

"The slaves from the other plantations don't really know me."

"True, you will have to earn their trust. But that will come in time."

"It sounds like you think I should do it."

"I do."

"But . . . I'm a *woman!*" laughed Carolyn again. "You know what the Bible says about women teaching and preaching."

"Of course. But you have to read the Bible for its larger themes. When Paul says, 'I suffer not a woman to teach,' I presume he had some specific reason for doing so. But that certainly cannot be taken as a large general truth of Scripture. Goodness, I would be lost without your wisdom and counsel and balancing influence in my life."

"Do you think Paul was wrong to say it?"

"I wouldn't go so far as to call it *wrong*. But it may be that he overstepped himself in that case. He is not above error, and his attitude toward women, especially in that as far as we know, he was not married himself, may have been one of his blind spots."

"So do you think women *should* occupy leadership roles?" asked Carolyn.

"Perhaps under certain circumstances, yes. We always have to look to the larger truths. Look at how Christians are so divided on slavery, each side pointing to specifics from the Bible to justify its view, but not seeking the overarching themes of compassion, justice, freedom, equality, and the liberty of life in God. In the same way, many of Paul's instructions to the early church cannot be turned into ironclad rules that can be applied in all situations. Error always results from trying to turn a single scriptural instruction into a larger general truth."

Carolyn nodded, taking in her husband's words thoughtfully and seriously.

"These are new times, Carolyn," Richmond went on. "We have to ask what is best for our people, and perhaps for all the blacks of the community. I feel strongly that God's call is on you to do this. You have unique gifts. You have a special way of communicating with the women especially. They love you with all their hearts. How wonderful it would be if that could be extended to the slaves of the other plantations."

"I suppose you are right, but wouldn't that increase the danger of detection?"

"Sure, there would be risk involved. Not all the community's blacks are as loyal to you as our own. But risk also means the opportunity for growth. I see that great good could be done."

Carolyn sighed and shook her head. "I must say, I am a little surprised at all you say."

"I believe in you, my dear. I think God is in this."

"I will need to pray about it," said Carolyn. "*We* need to pray about it. In one way it goes against what I've always thought. Seeing women temperance leaders has always made me uncomfortable."

Richmond took her hand. "It is *you* they have asked for, Carolyn, not a fiery woman out championing some cause. I honestly do think you should seriously consider it."

〜

The second Democratic convention convened in Baltimore a month after Lincoln's nomination, hoping to break their deadlock. But the fight between Northern and Southern interests continued, neither side willing to budge. More ballots were taken. As he had been in April, Douglas was again the clear winner, but without receiving the two-thirds majority required. Again the Buchanan Democrats representing the Southern states walked out.

In their absence, eventually the convention voted to make Stephen A. Douglas the Democratic nominee for president in that he had now received more than two-thirds of the votes of the remaining delegates who were present.

Outraged at having their votes ignored, Southern Democrats met a week later in Richmond, Virginia, and convened a Democratic convention of their own.

President Buchanan's attempted policy of compromise had not proved effective. The Southern delegation put forward in his place Buchanan's vice president John Breckinridge. With two antislavery candidates from Illinois on the ballot, they hoped a split in the Northern vote would propel pro-South Breckinridge into the White House. But their strategy obviously involved risk, for in putting forward two Democratic candidates, the vote of the Democratic party would likewise be split.

A month later, complicating the upcoming election all the more, the old Whig Party nominated John Bell as yet a fourth national candidate.

Only time would tell whether Breckinridge would defeat the split vote of two Northerners, or whether Lincoln, the Republican, would defeat the split vote of two Democrats.

Forty

Seth left the house in a thoughtful mood and walked slowly toward the arbor. It was a quiet Virginia evening in early September . . . warm, peaceful, humid, with whispers and fragrances in the air of the coming night.

He had been deeply shaken by the attack by Scully Riggs and his cohorts, by the cold-blooded hanging of the black man he had been forced to witness, and by the tense visit to Greenwood by Wyatt and the small posse of bounty hunters led by Malone Murdoch.

In his more rational moments when reason ruled his thoughts, he could intellectually convince himself that the heightened atmosphere of danger was not actually his *fault*, but simply evidenced the growing danger of the times. In his more morose moments, however, he could not but feel a heavy weight of personal responsibility for the sudden increase in violence that seemed to be taking place with Greenwood at its center and focus.

He had been thinking about the things his father had shared with him before Murdoch and his men had ridden into Greenwood. The incident confirmed all the more the danger they were in. One more attack like Scully's, or close call with a man like Murdoch, and he or his father could wind up dead! Or one more midnight hanging by Wyatt's vigilante mob and one of their *own* blacks might be the victim. What if Wyatt captured Malachi cutting across some distant corner of the Oakbriar property on his way back from a railroad rendezvous? Then it would be Malachi at the end of Wyatt's rope!

Even though his father's situation as a young man had been so different, thought Seth, he too had been faced with a crisis. Yet rather than meet it head-on and contest the charges against him, he left England and returned to Virginia. His father had met his crisis by avoiding a confrontation. He had not done so to run away, but because it was the most prudent course of action.

How might he learn from his father's example? Seth wondered. Maybe this was no time to hang around and endanger himself and his family further. Perhaps the time had come when it would be wisest to diffuse his own personal crisis—and lessen the danger to everyone else at the same time—by leaving the area so that the flames of anger against him could simply burn themselves out.

Was he facing a time to meet conflict head-on and fight it . . . or to avoid a confrontation altogether?

How many times through the years had Seth seen his parents disappear into the arbor together. It was only recently as he began exercising a faith of his own that he realized that they went there to pray, to seek God's guidance. He knew the decision to free Greenwood's slaves had originated there. He suspected they had prayed for him and Cynthia and Thomas many times in the depths of their garden sanctuary. And how many other decisions and quandaries had been resolved within its sheltered paths and hidden places of personal retreat?

Now he was facing a critical decision that would represent a major turning point in his life. He had watched his mother and father live out the practicality of their beliefs. As his teen years had advanced, he had grown more and more capable of seeing how deep those wellsprings of faith went within them. Through the years he had gradually made their faith his own. There had been no single moment of conversionary fire, no event to which he could point like the evening his father had walked through the open door of that church.

For Seth Davidson, the realization that he *wanted* to live as God's man had been a slow-growing one—a commitment and dedication that had deepened steadily within his heart as he had matured from fifteen to eighteen and now as he approached twenty-one.

And now a moment had come to put that commitment to the test more than he had ever had to before.

It was different than his entanglement with Veronica. Once his way had been made clear in that situation, he had known what to do. All it had taken to navigate that dilemma had been common sense. True, it had taken him some time to see it. But the decision itself to end the engagement was not in itself a difficult one. It had been hard to carry out. But once he came to his senses and knew what he needed to do, his course was obvious and he had done it.

But he was now facing something entirely different. He *didn't* know what to do. His parents couldn't tell him. There was no commonsense decision to make. He honestly didn't know what was best.

Only *God* could tell him what to do. He needed help. He needed guidance to make the *right* decision. For one of the few times in his life, Seth Davidson knew that he needed to hear from God.

As the trees and shrubbery of the arbor closed around him, a sense of calm and quietness of spirit descended upon him. He had been here dozens of times, probably hundreds. But for the first time a sense of what this place *meant* stole over him. This was his parents' closet of prayer. What a wonderful thing, what a precious opportunity, to be able to touch the generational flow of prayer like this. It was the generational flow out of which he had been born—both physically and spiritually! Out of his parents' prayers had their love for one another emerged. And out of their prayers his own faith in God emerged.

They had prayed for him!

The simplicity yet magnitude of that simple fact suddenly overwhelmed him in gratitude. In a sense, this place represented his own spiritual birthplace, the spiritual soil in which his roots of personhood had been nourished, and given the strength for potential growth when the time came for him to make those roots his own.

As he walked, Seth's gratefulness deepened to have been given

Carolyn Davidson as a mother and Richmond Davidson as a father. What son could be more blessed!

Thank you, God and Father, as my own mother and father have taught me to call you, prayed Seth silently in his heart. *I thank you, as I grew to become the person I am, that you drew me to seek you, that you placed within me the desire to know you and serve you and obey you. Thank you for my dear mother and father whom I love, and for their devotion to you, and their courage to obey you, which has been such an example to me. Help me to follow their example, and to continue to be a faithful son. Let me never think I have outgrown my need for their wisdom.*

Prayer for his parents reminded him of the very practical perplexity of his current dilemma.

Lord, he began to pray in a more serious vein, *I pray for the safety of my family and Greenwood and all the people who call this place home. Let no danger or harm come to them. Protect them like the caring Father you are.*

As for me, Lord, you know my perplexity well enough. I hardly need recite it to you. You know my heart, you know my thoughts, you know my fears. And you know that I don't know what is best to do. I ask you to show me, Lord. Guide me into your perfect will. Please, God, show me what you want me to do. And give me the fortitude, courage, faith, patience, and hope to obey you when you make your will clear.

Seth prayed for another ten or fifteen minutes, sometimes in words, occasionally in silences, then rose and continued to walk about the garden until dusk gradually settled over Greenwood. Even before he began making his way back toward the house, he sensed that God may have begun to provide fragmentary answers to the questions plaguing him about his future.

A sense had been growing upon him for several weeks that a change was coming. Almost the moment he said the words an hour earlier, *Please, God, show me what you want me to do,* that sense grew strong. Almost the same moment he had been reminded of his older sister.

The idea of actually leaving Greenwood, perhaps even leaving Virginia, was one he had never before considered. This was his home. It had always been his home. He had assumed it would remain his home indefinitely. The idea of leaving did not fill him with a sense of adventure but of sadness. He had no desire to leave. He loved Greenwood. He could never feel at home anywhere else.

And yet . . . what if the threats and the danger might be lessened by his absence? Might his not being here lessen the animosity of his one-time friends like Wyatt and Scully and cause them to lose interest in Greenwood as their perceived enemy?

Denton Beaumont was gone. The local people of Dove's Landing had grown accustomed to the freedom of Greenwood's slaves. Wyatt's resentment wasn't really with the senior Davidson, Seth realized. The competitive animosity of youth was between the oldest sons of the two families—him and Wyatt. If he was gone, Wyatt might lose interest in Greenwood as an object of his hatred. Maybe the broken engagement with Veronica was part of it, maybe it wasn't. He really had no way to know. But the fact was—he was at the center of the resentment, whatever its cause.

He was himself the lightning rod for their anger. Not only was he himself in danger, he increased the danger to everyone around him. If he were gone, Wyatt's and Brad's and Scully's eyes would turn elsewhere. Perhaps, thought Seth, if he were gone, Thomas might even grow closer to their parents. Who could tell but what some of Thomas' animosity stemmed from living all his life in the shadow of an older brother.

Again his thoughts returned to Cynthia. Perhaps she was the answer to the dilemma of where he ought to go for a while.

Forty-One

$\mathcal{A}$ tall wagon rumbled into Dove's Landing, clattering and banging
with pans and pots and brooms and mops and paraphernalia of every
diverse kind, its side panels painted in bold letters and announcing to
curious passersby: *Professor Weldon Southcote, A Woman's Best Friend:
Housewares, Utensils, Tools, and Supplies.* The man seated gaily atop
the bench seat guiding his two sturdy draught horses through the
town's main street was himself as colorful as the lettering on the sides
of his traveling emporium.

The women who happened to be out glanced curiously at the
wagon and the assortment of goods hanging and dangling from hooks
and pegs. The good professor's *Ho* of welcome was slower today than
usual as he looked about. Eventually he took note of his potential
customers, tipped his hat and greeted them warmly, pulled his emporium beside the boardwalk of what appeared the main street, and
thence proceeded to do a brisk business for the rest of the afternoon.
Mrs. Baker in her store two doors away was anything but pleased as
she stared out her window, for every dollar spent with Professor
Southcote was a dollar not spent with her. But there was little she
could do about it but fuss under her breath.

Professor Southcote was full of more questions for his local clientele
than usual. His queries in particular concerned nearby plantations
whose good women he might visit with his merchandise. Thus it was

that, as the day advanced toward evening, the wagon of Professor Southcote, A Woman's Best Friend, was heard slowly clattering and jingling up the winding incline over the gravel drive toward the large redbrick plantation house of Greenwood.

Upon his arrival, Maribel did her best for five minutes to send him away on behalf of her mistress, over the man's most energetic requests to speak with the woman of the house. At length Carolyn herself approached, on her way back from the worker village.

"Would this be Mistress Davidson now?" said Professor Southcote, his face brightening as he stood beside his wagon.

"Dat's da mistress all right," said Maribel, 'but she ain't gwine want none er yo' junk no how. I tol' him, Miz Dab'son," she said, as Carolyn came closer, "but dis be one stubborn an ornery man what won' take no—"

"Hello, good lady," said Southcote, smiling and tipping his hat. "If I might just have a minute of your time?"

"It will be all right, Maribel, thank you," said Carolyn with a smile. "Who knows but what this gentleman might have something we could use."

Mumbling to herself, Maribel shuffled her way back into the house.

The moment they were alone, the demeanor of Southcote's salesman's persona vanished. His expression immediately grew serious. "Is your husband at home, Mrs. Davidson?" he asked.

"Yes . . . yes he is," she answered, puzzled by the sudden shift in tone.

"I need to speak with him."

"I doubt if he will be as interested in your wares as I am?" laughed Carolyn.

"No doubt. But I seriously need to speak with him, ma'am. While I am doing so, I will be happy for you to look over my goods . . . happier still if you should find something which might be useful to you. But that is not primarily why I have come."

Carolyn eyed the man. He was obviously in earnest. She nodded slowly, then turned and left him where he stood. She returned from the direction of the stables a few minutes later with her husband at her side.

"I am Richmond Davidson," he said, extending his hand. "My wife tells me you want to see to me."

"Yes, sir," said their strange visitor. "I am Weldon Southcote. If you don't mind, Mrs. Davidson, if you could look at my merchandise as we speak . . . if might keep us from being noticed should anyone be watching."

"What is this all about, Mr. Southcote?" asked Richmond.

Southcote slowly led Richmond around the wagon, pretending to show him one tool or another as he lowered his voice.

"It is about slaves, Mr. Davidson," he said in confidential tones scarcely above a whisper, "runaway slaves."

Richmond's eyes flinched imperceptibly, but he held the man's gaze.

"What about them?" he said.

"Where they come from . . . where they go . . . where they hide."

"What does this have to do with me, Mr. Southcote? Why do you want to talk to me about runaway slaves? Perhaps you heard that we freed our own slaves a few years ago. While it is true that some of them left and went North, they all had papers and I assure you, none of them—"

"Mr. Davidson," Southcote interrupted, his voice still soft, but urgent, "I *know*."

A pregnant silence followed.

"Know what?" said Richmond after two or three seconds.

"I know about the wind in the horse's head. I know everything— what is going on here, what you have been doing, and about your safe house for runaway slaves."

The words stunned Richmond into another brief silence.

"I see," he nodded, visibly shaken.

"But I am not here to expose you, Mr. Davidson, or put you in more danger than you are in. I am here to warn you . . . and help you."

"All right, you have succeeded in getting my attention," sighed Richmond.

"You are not alone, Mr. Davidson," Southcote went on. "There are others who can help. But the dangers are increasing on every front. Search parties are on the increase, especially here in northern Virginia. The times are as perilous for those who help as for the runaways themselves. You must watch your every move. You have been seen."

"What do you mean?"

"Your occasional midnight flights to the border, one of your black men's regular overland sojourns to Orange County . . . they are on the lookout for you, though they do not know who you are yet. That is why I am here, to caution you to lay low. Take no more trips to the border yourself. It is too far from here. You will be discovered eventually."

"My wife and son have only been once, and myself—let me see, three times. Mostly we move people by other means."

"I understand, but you are too important a link to be jeopardized. The Quaker network is being closely watched, and all who are connected with it. You can be a great asset in our cause. You can save many lives. But you must be more cautious. More eyes are upon you than you know."

Richmond took in his words soberly. He could hardly believe what he was hearing. "How do we know we can trust *you*?" he asked.

"You have no choice, Mr. Davidson. I know about the secret cellar under the new house in your slave village. I know of the hidden staircase at the back of your house. I know of the tunnel connecting your cellar with the oak wood. I know that there are caves and tunnels to some house in the hills that you occasionally use. I know too much for you not to trust me. You simply *must* trust me. I don't know how to put it more simply than that."

Richmond's eyes widened in dismayed amazement. How could the man possibly know so much!

"What is your role in all this?" he asked slowly, visibly shaken by the strange man's revelation. "Why are you telling me? How can you help?"

"I am an eccentric who knows every main road and back road between Pennsylvania and Georgia," replied the strange salesman. "I have been traveling these roads for thirty years. No one suspects me because my wagon is a familiar sight and I make no attempt to hide. Neither do they suspect my loyalties. I come and go as I please. I have become a traveling conduit of information. I know who is friend and who is foe. I am often able to put people in touch with others, that they might help one another."

"What should we do, then?" asked Richmond. "We have a family now with relatives waiting in Pennsylvania. If we cannot transport them . . . will you take them in your wagon?"

"No, I move too slowly. I am merely a vehicle of information. As to what you should do . . . for now simply wait. All I can say is that they will continue to come, and I will work with my contacts in the network to find safer means to move them on from here. You and your own blacks are too valuable to conduct them yourselves. The way will become clear. In the meantime, I want you to give me a word, a phrase, some secret expression of your own choosing."

"For what purpose?"

"As a password or sign between you and me."

"Till now we have relied on the wind in the horse's head to let us know that refugees are seeking asylum. That is why we put up the weathervane."

"That has come to be a widely recognized phrase," said Southcote. "Unfortunately, too many ears have heard it. The network is even now being infiltrated by those who would destroy it. I need something that only you will recognize, as a means for you and me to communicate with one another and no one else."

"I see," said Richmond. He thought a moment.

"Then if one comes from you," he said, "Tell them to say, *We come as children of our Father.*"

Southcote nodded his head. "So it shall be," he said. He then walked around to the other side of his wagon. "Ho, good lady!" he said, assuming again the mantle of seller of wares, "have you found anything to interest you!"

The expression on Carolyn's face replied well enough that she had not been examining brushes, brooms, and cutlery, but had been listening around the corner of the wagon. She had heard every word that passed between her husband and the good professor.

"Come, Mrs. Davidson," said Southcote, "select two or three items to account for our being here so long. Not even your house lady must know about me. No one must know but the two of you."

⌒

As they had concluded their clandestine talk, a lone black man, raggedly dressed, walked up the drive toward the house. He appeared seemingly out of nowhere like so many others who had come. Richmond looked up, saw him walking toward them, and assumed him yet one more runaway seeking refuge.

Observing the strange wagon and three white people standing beside it, the black newcomer walked in their direction.

"Dis be da Davidson place?" he asked.

"Yes it is, young man," replied Richmond, "I am Richmond Davidson. I am the owner of the plantation."

"Thank the Lord I found you, Mister Davidson," said the black man. "I been searchin' high an' low fo' days ter git here . . . "

Professor Southcote's eyes narrowed slightly as he listened. He scrutinized the newcomer carefully, then, as the man spoke to Richmond, slowly and with steps so tiny that neither man noticed, began inching his way around to the one side and then behind the black man.

"I cum from da Souf lookin' fer freedom," the man was saying, "an' dey tell me dat you help black folks in need. . . . "

Gradually Richmond saw Southcote come into his line of vision behind their strange visitor. He became aware that Southcote was subtly attempting to get his attention.

"—an' hide out runaways dat are in trouble." The man went on. "I's hoping you can hide me wiff da others, so I don't git caught."

Richmond let his eyes drift over the black man's shoulders. He saw the professor slowly begin to move his head back and forth. The expression on his face, along with the gesture, said clearly, *Do not believe this man!*

Richmond brought his attention back to the man in front of him.

"I, uh . . . " he began a little hesitantly, "I don't exactly know what you mean," he said. "We do have free blacks here, but that is because we set our own slaves free several years ago. If you are looking for work, perhaps I might see if we might have something for you. But otherwise . . . "

He let his voice trail off, glancing at Southcote. Again the professor shook his head with an expression of warning.

"I don't want no work, Mister Davidson," replied the would-be traveler, sounding almost angry with Richmond's reply. "I's a runaway. I need fo' you to hide me out." He spoke in a tone of demand. The humility, fear, and gratitude that were uniformly present with every other refugee that came asking for help were completely missing from the countenance of this man.

"I'm sorry," said Richmond. "But I just cannot help you."

The man stood a moment more, seemingly confused as well as angry, then slowly turned and retreated back along the drive until he was out of sight.

As Southcote came toward him, Richmond's face wore a look of perplexity. "You were warning me against him, I take it?" he said.

Southcote nodded. "And fortunate for us all that you were able to discern my meaning."

"Do you know him? Have you seen him before?"

"No, I have never laid eyes on him in my life. But I sensed immediately that he was lying. He was a spy, I am convinced of it. From where I have no idea. Do you have someone you could trust to follow him? We might learn something."

"I'll get Seth," said Carolyn who had heard everything.

Ten minutes later Seth was on his way toward Dove's Landing, following a route through pasture and woodland paralleling the road where he would be able to keep his eye on the man for most of the way.

He returned an hour later. The traveling emporium of Professor Southcote was nowhere to be seen.

"You were right, Dad," said Seth. "Halfway to town, who should step out of the trees and onto the road with two horses to meet the guy—Wyatt Beaumont. They mounted and I followed them just long enough to see that Wyatt was taking him back to Oakbriar."

Richmond shook his head and let out a long sigh.

"That was close," he said. "If I hadn't been warned and we had taken the fellow in, it would have been as good as telling Wyatt everything that is going on here."

"Wyatt sending spies," sighed Carolyn in disbelief. "I just cannot believe it."

"It appears we are going to have to be more careful than ever."

Forty-Two

*H*eeding the warnings of the strange purveyor of tools, instruments, pots, pans, cleaning supplies, detergents, and cure-all remedies for every ailment known to man, Richmond began to consider alternate routes in and out of the plantation besides those that Malachi had been using that were apparently now in jeopardy. The region to the north and west of Dove's Landing became increasingly mountainous in the direction of the Alleghenies, of which Harper's Peak and the ridge it overlooked were a distant eastern outcropping. Malachi contrived a meeting between Richmond and the Quaker Brannon, the cousin of Mueller, and the two men set in motion a new series of rendezvous points and routes, as well as methods of contact by which to get runaways safely to the hills about fifteen miles west, and from there to move them northwest toward that part of the state where abolitionist sentiment ran strong, and where Brannon had many more contacts in Ohio and Pennsylvania. They hoped these new measures would prove a less perilous conduit to freedom than more direct routes.

In accordance with this new strategy, Seth and Malachi Shaw sat wearily one morning in mid-October on the seat of a wagon returning along the little-used western road, the bed behind them piled with an assortment of hay bales, boxes, and various pieces of equipment made to look like a usual load that might be seen around any plantation.

A few hours earlier, however, they had let out six single young men in the middle of the night, who were, they hoped, by now safely inside the abandoned barn in the Allegheny foothills to which they had been given directions by Brannon and where the runaways would sleep the day away until Brannon's conductors should come for them.

It was about daybreak. They had just turned onto a path, barely wide enough for a wagon to pass, on their way back to Greenwood by backroads and through isolated woodland.

Seth, at the reins, was suddenly awakened from his sleepy reverie by a large dark figure darting across the road a hundred yards ahead.

He glanced over at Malachi.

"Did you see that!" he said.

"Dat I did," he replied, "but what wuz hit?"

"I don't know . . . could it have been a bear?"

"Don' think so, massa Seth. Dat be a black man fo' sho'."

This close to Greenwood, near the border between the Beaumont and Davidson properties, Seth's first thought was that another runaway was hiding out and perhaps in search of the wind in the horse's head. Leon Riggs had clamped down so tight at Oakbriar in his boss's absence that none of their blacks could move ten yards on their own without reprisals from the whip. The Sunday services at the Brown house which his mother was now conducting had been very sparsely attended by the Oakbriar slaves as a result. Certainly none of their own people would be out this early and so far from home.

"Must be a runaway trying to find us," said Seth.

Malachi wasn't so sure. A suspicion had entered his brain as he turned the shape of the bearlike figure over in his mind. But he kept it to himself.

Seth continued on, then gradually slowed as they approached the spot where the figure had run into the trees. He glanced into the wood. Slowly he reined the two horses to a stop. But Malachi was anxious and unsettled.

The morning grew still and quiet. The horses snorted and moved restlessly. A few birds had begun to herald the arrival of the sun from the trees.

Seth handed Malachi the reins and slowly got down off the wagon, scanning the woods. Gradually he began walking into the trees.

"I wudn't go no further, massa Seth," said Malachi. "Dey ain' no way you's gwine fin' no black man in dere what don' want ter be foun'."

"What if he is looking for us? What if he needs help?"

"Don' matter now, massa Seth." came Malachi's voice behind him. "Hit's too late. I's reckon we orter jes' keep goin'. We ain't gwine fin' nobody in dere no how. He be long gone whoeber he wuz."

"Whoever you are," said Seth aloud, "we're friends. You have nothing to fear from us."

No response came from the early morning forest.

Two eyes were gleaming at him from behind a tree, watching his every move. But their owner did not move a muscle.

Seth continued, occasionally breaking a twig beneath his feet.

"If you need help," said Seth, "my name is Seth Davidson . . . "

He waited, hoping that the mention of his name would bring the runaway out of hiding.

"Seth *Davidson*," he repeated. "It may be that I can be of assistance if you—"

Suddenly from behind a tree, powerful arms seized him and yanked him back against a massive bulk of chest. The same instant he felt cold steel against his neck.

"I know who you is well enuf," growled a deep voice. "I been waitin' fo' dis chance to put it right atween us, an' it looks like you dun gib it to me!" He laughed a low wicked laugh. Seth could smell his foul breath.

"What do you want, Slade?" said Seth. "You've got me where you want me."

"I gots what I want, w'ite boy. I want *you*. I wants ter see yo' blood on the ground, dat's what I want."

"You'll never get away with it, Slade. You'll hang."

"Mister Beaumont won't let me hang. He knows his slaves'd run wild effen it weren't fo' me, speshully wiff him gone. Riggs ain't nuthin'. It's me what keeps dem all in line. An' after I'm dun wiff you, maybe I'll jes' take care ob dat father er yers da same way."

"What did he ever do to you, Slade?" said Seth. "I can understand your being angry with me, but why my father. He gave you your freedom. You owe him more than you owe any man alive, certainly more than you owe Mr. Beaumont. You ought to thank him for what he did."

"He's w'ite. Dat's enuf."

"He gave you your freedom, Slade. Does that mean nothing to you?"

"Effen da man's a fool, dat ain't nun er my concern. Ef he wants ter let me go, dat's his affair. But he's still a w'ite man, and you's his son, an' I's gwine kill you."

Slade's arms stiffened and Seth felt the knife blade against his skin. But a voice from behind him postponed the murder.

"What's takin' you so long, massa Seth?" it called out. "You be all right in dere? Who dat you's talkin' wiff?"

Seth did not reply.

Malachi slowly crept forward into the wood.

"Massa Seth," he repeated. "What's you—"

"Git outta here, Shaw!" spat Slade, inching out from behind the tree. He still clutched Seth in a vise-grip. "Me an' dis w'ite boy's got biz'nes dat don' concern you. Now you jes' go git on dat wagon dere an' you go back ter yo' massa like da good ol' nigger you is, an' you tell him where he kin fin' what's left ob his son—dat is effen he's got da stomach fo' it, an' den you tell him he's nex'."

"I won't let you hurt 'im, Elias," said Malachi as he came forward through the trees.

"You fool nigger—he's a w'ite boy! Wha'chu care?"

"He's ma boss's son—dat's why I care. He's da son ob da man dat freed me, an' you too. An' he's a good boy too, dat treats da black man an' da white man da same."

"What dat to me!"

"It orter be plenty ter you, Elias Slade, dat's what. An' it means a heap ter me, an' dat's why I ain' gwine let you hurt 'im."

"Who's gwine stop me?"

"I will, Elias."

"Den maybe I's jes' have ter kill you bof. Den I's take Phoebe wif me nex' time she an' me's—"

"You been seein' my Phoebe agin!" cried Malachi.

"Where you think I jes' been?" laughed Slade cruelly. "I come ober 'cross da ridge mos' eber week, an' she an' me—"

The words and tone of scorn was unwisely chosen.

The righteous indignation of the father, and the loyalty of the free man to his liberator, rose up in the heart of Malachi Shaw. With a great cry he rushed forward.

Momentarily taken by surprise, for no one willingly attacked *him*—What was it with the absurd courage of these Davidson people? Were they all determined to get themselves killed!—Elias Slade hesitated for the merest instant.

Seth felt the change. If he were unable to break loose from Slade's grip it would surely cost him his life. But he had no choice. With all the force he could summon, he sent his booted foot down on Slade's foot and his elbow into the big man's ribs.

It was enough to get his neck away from the knife. The same instant the avenging angel flew with vengeance against Seth's accuser.

Slade released his grip to ward off the attack. Seth fell to the ground as the two titans collided in a fury of wrath and hatred. But in the dawn darkness of the wood, Malachi had not seen the glint of the blade in Slade's hand. The skirmish was thus brief. Nor in the commotion of shouted curses and threats had any of the three heard the clatter and clanking of a wagon on the seldom-used road.

Suddenly a shot exploded behind them. As its echo died away, Elias Slade groaned in pain. A bullet to his shoulder had thrown the red-stained knife from his hand. At his feet, Malachi Shaw lay with a gaping gash in his chest pouring blood onto the forest floor.

The small stout white man wearing a peculiar top hat and holding a rifle did not look imposing. But the expression on his face said clearly enough that he knew how to use the weapon in his hand, and would not think twice about sending a second bullet after the first.

Slade saw the look and did not hesitate. He turned and fled through the trees. A second shot chased after him as he disappeared, though in the dim light did not find its mark. The same instant Seth rushed forward and knelt at Malachi's side. A moment later Weldon Southcote was beside him.

"Quick . . . help me get him back to the wagon!" cried Seth.

But the man merely stared down at the face of the man on the ground.

"Hurry," implored Seth, leaning down and slipping his arms under Malachi's shoulders and knees and somehow lifting the great bulk off the ground.

"Son . . . " said the top-hatted man quietly.

"Please!" said Seth, struggling with his heavy burden, "there are some blankets in my wagon. Get them for me . . . we've got to stop the bleeding!"

"Son!" repeated Southcote with more force.

At last the urgency in his voice arrested Seth's attention. He stopped, holding Malachi's limp form, blood staining his shirt down the front of his own chest. He looked into the man's face with an expression of helpless confusion and horrified disbelief.

"Son . . . he's dead."

At the words, Seth's eyes filled with tears. He looked at Malachi's face as he held his body in his arms. One look told him it was true.

Slowly he stumbled forward to the road with a strength he did not even know he had, and carefully set Malachi's broken form on the straw in back. Only then did he collapse on the ground and weep.

He heard footsteps behind him.

"It we're going to catch the man that did this," said Southcote, "we had better hurry."

"I know who he is," said Seth, staring down at the ground.

"You know him?"

Seth nodded.

"What was this all about?"

"He was after me. He was about to kill me. Malachi saved my life."

"Is he free or slave?"

"Free," said Seth softly. "Both of them are free."

"Well, then, the law will do nothing, one free black killing another. This was one of your freedmen?"

Again Seth nodded.

"Only thing we can do, then, is go after him and kill him ourselves."

"You'd never catch him," said Seth, "even with that bullet of yours in his arm. The man possesses superhuman strength. We'd never catch him now. And we can't just ride into Oakbriar, ask to see him, and then shoot him. That would be murder."

"I don't know about that. But if he's going to be executed for this, it will have to be you that does it."

"I'll ask my father what to do," said Seth. "But he will never go along with murder, justified or not."

"Well, whatever you do, my involvement in the affair cannot be known of. No one must know that I came along this road. The proximity is too close to your father's plantation. You talk it over with your father and mother, but no one else. Make up whatever story you want about how you got away from that big darkie's knife . . . but I was never here."

"What about Slade's gunshot wound?"

"He won't talk. His kind never do. He doesn't know who I am anyway and didn't get any better look at me than I did him. If we're lucky, maybe he'll die from it, though from what you say, I doubt it. All right, I've got to get out of here."

Seth glanced up with a forlorn expression. But consolation in time of grief was not Weldon Southcote's forte.

"What you do about that man I shot is your own affair," he said, climbing back up onto his wagon. "I should have aimed a little lower and to the left. But it's done now and he's gone, and I've got to be well away from around here before the day advances and I'm seen. You get yourself home, son . . . and quickly."

A minute or two later, Seth heard the clattering and clanking of Southcote's wares as he eased his rolling merchandise emporium around the Greenwood wagon, used to take six persons to freedom the night before, that had now become a hearse.

Slowly he rumbled away, and Seth was left in silence.

Weeping on and off the whole way, Seth reached the outskirts of Greenwood then went the long way around, so as to avoid the black houses, and straight to his home. He would have his mother and father know first so that they could be with him when Nancy Shaw was told. He dreaded to think what the reaction among their blacks toward Phoebe would be to learn that her continued and secret relations with Elias Slade had cost her father his life.

He walked to the door, his eyes filling with tears again. Carolyn let out a scream when she saw his shirt. Seth continued past her and collapsed in his father's arms.

"Oh, Dad . . . !" was all he could utter before bursting into sobs.

Forty-Three

The murder of Malachi Shaw rocked the entire black community for miles around Dove's Landing. Even whites were more concerned than they might otherwise have been. Everyone knew the name Elias Slade, and now they had more reason to fear him than ever.

Malachi's funeral, to the loud weeping of nearly every one of Greenwood's blacks, was attended by every slave from every plantation for miles, and even a few whites. Richmond delivered a powerful eulogy in which he spoke out more vocally than he ever had in public against injustice and violence of all kinds, breaking into tears as he described with great emotion the friendship and deep affection that freedom had allowed to develop between himself and his former slave. Poor Nancy was devastated by grief but tried to put on a brave face for the husband who had gone to join the old king of the five rivers and his other ancestors of a proud heritage. The mourning would have been far greater had the dozens, perhaps a hundred, been present who were now living in freedom because of the simple, humble man's courage.

As the only eyewitness of the affair, Seth's account was understandably sketchy from having to be vague about what he and Malachi had been doing at the remote place east of Dove's Landing at such an hour, as well as having to omit all word of Southcote's involvement. Slade's wound from Southcote's gun did not become widely publi-

cized anyway. But the fact that Slade had attacked Seth and had killed
Malachi when he had come to Seth's rescue were straightforward
enough.

Charges might have been brought, not for black killing black for no
court would care, but for Slade's attack against Seth. But as no injury
had resulted to stand in proof of it, and as Denton Beaumont, Slade's
boss, or his son Wyatt, would have been the local authorities in the
case to bring such charges, both of whom would probably have taken
Slade's side in a legal contest, a successful prosecution seemed
unlikely. A legal battle involving the Beaumonts was the last thing
anyone at Greenwood wanted, and nothing more was ever done.

It did not take long after the incident for Seth Davidson to reach
the decision he had been wrestling with for a month.

His despondency over the killing was deepened by a tremendous
burden of guilt. Had he left Greenwood when the thought first came
to him, perhaps Malachi would still be alive. It was Slade's hatred of
him that had precipitated the incident. Nor had he forgotten Slade's
threats against his father. But even that had spilled over as a result of
Slade's hatred of him. It all went back to the day he had taken on
Slade with his fists to keep the big man from raping Veronica. He
doubted Slade would do anything if *he* weren't around.

He *had* to leave.

Now more than ever. He was in danger. And as long as he
remained at Greenwood, so were his parents. So was everyone.

He had no alternative. He had to get away from Dove's Landing
long enough to let the hatred cool down.

Two days after the funeral, Seth found his parents alone and told
them of his decision.

Carolyn cried. Surprising to Seth, however, after listening atten-
tively to his reasoning, Richmond did not argue against it.

"There is more to it, though, isn't there, Seth," he asked, "than
Veronica and reaction against you by the town bullies?"

"That's a lot of it, Dad," replied Seth. "But there's so much involved—Slade, Wyatt, Scully, the hanging . . . everything somehow stems from the fact that those guys have it out for *me*. It seems like everyone else is in danger as a result."

"Are you afraid?" asked Richmond.

"I suppose . . . sure. After what happened with Slade, how could I not be? I have the feeling Wyatt's going to keep trying to draw me into his vigilante activities. I see no solution to all this but my absence. Yeah, I guess I'm afraid, but more than that—I see no other way. Everybody's in danger, not just me. Do you think I'm a coward, Dad?"

"There's nothing wrong with fear," replied Richmond. "I don't see your wanting to leave as cowardice. You are trying to be prudent enough to recognize how to avoid an unnecessary confrontation, and protect other people in the process."

"You're not just trying to make me feel better by saying that?" smiled Seth mordantly.

"Maybe I am," smiled Richmond. "But it is the truth. If your life *is* in danger, which we now know it is, there is no sense, like they say, in being a dead hero. Why not remove the source of Slade's resentment, and maybe Wyatt's and Scully's also. Let their hot heads cool down a while. I think you are trying to look realistically at the big picture, and have come up with a well-thought-out solution. Of course we will miss you. But it will only be for a short time and I will sleep better at night knowing you are somewhere safe."

Seth wandered into the kitchen midway through the afternoon two weeks later. The house was mostly quiet. His father and Thomas were out. Maribel and Moses were resting. Carolyn's back was turned as he entered.

"Hi, Mom," he said, sitting down at the table.

For a moment she did not reply, then turned and smiled. Her face and eyes were red.

"What is it, Mom?" said Seth in concern. "What's wrong?"

"I am just going to miss you, that's all," she said. "I wasn't ready to lose a son just yet."

"You're not losing me!" laughed Seth. "I'm just going away for a little while. I'll be back."

"I know . . . I keep trying to tell myself that. But it doesn't help. You are leaving home and moving north, and at a younger age than I planned on having to say good-bye. Who knows when I'll see you again? You must just be patient with this mother's heart and let me cry."

"All right, Mom. How can I complain that you love me too much! But really, I will be fine. It will be an adventure. At least I am trying to convince myself of that. And you know it's for the best."

"I suppose I do," she sighed. "I am afraid for you here. How can I not be? I just don't know why all this has happened. But it has. I would rather have you safe and with Cynthia than in danger here."

Seth rose, walked to his mother, and embraced her.

"Oh, Seth, I love you," she said, breaking into tears again. "I am going to miss you so much! You're not just a son. You are my friend. I'm going to miss our talks . . . I'm going to miss *you*!"

"I'll miss you too, Mom . . . but we can write. I promise, I will be back after things cool off around here. You don't think I'm going to become a Northerner for good do you? Somebody's got to take over Greenwood, and take care of you and Dad when you get old, right!"

Carolyn stepped back, wiped at her eyes, and forced a smile.

"Seth," she said, placing her hands on his two shoulders and looking him straight in the eyes, "you have a great time in the North! My tears will dry, and I want you to remember me with a smile on my face."

"Okay, Mom," he smiled. "I will. That won't be hard. For what crying you sometimes do, you have a smile on your face *most* of the time. How else would I remember you! You're just about the best mom anyone could have."

"What a nice thing for you to say! You had better be careful, or you'll have me crying again!"

"Then maybe I should finish my packing!"

Carolyn watched him go, then drew in a deep breath. She would be all right now. She'd had a cry and had held him in her arms one last time.

She was ready to be strong again.

⟨⟩

Seth left Dove's Landing on the 2:15 train the following afternoon. It was Thursday, November first. The year was 1860. His parents and Thomas saw him off.

From a street away, so too did Scully Riggs. As he watched him board the train, however, Scully did not feel the elation of victory. Instead, he had a hollow feeling inside. He may have succeeded in running Seth Davidson out of town—at least, so Scully interpreted the string of events. But for what? Veronica was gone. Now Seth was leaving. Rich people like them could come and go as they pleased. But he was stuck here. He'd be stuck here the rest of his life. What good had it done him to get even with Seth Davidson? He had done him a favor. Now he was getting out of this place.

A few final waves as the train pulled out of the station, then the three Davidsons turned, Carolyn wiping at her eyes again, and returned to their carriage. The ride back to Greenwood was quiet. Thomas was silently envious, wishing it were him on the train instead of Seth.

In the meantime, Seth sat back as the train picked up steam. He was already feeling pangs of loneliness. For all his bravado, he would miss his father and mother more than they realized, maybe even more than he realized. They were his two best friends in the world. He depended on them in so many ways.

But, he said to himself, it was a relief knowing they would be safer with him gone. And it was a relief knowing that with every minute that passed the distance between himself and Elias Slade and Wyatt Beaumont was widening!

He settled into his seat and picked up the day's newspaper he had brought along.

"Election Nears," read the headlines, "Dems Split North/South Vote. Lincoln Appears Unbeatable."

"The strategy of Southern Democratic leaders in placing their own candidate, Vice President John Breckinridge, on the presidential ballot," Seth read, "in opposition to the candidacy of Senator Stephen A. Douglas of Illinois, now seems likely to have been a serious miscalculation. In splitting the Northern vote in next Tuesday's election, as they supposed, between two antislavery sons of Illinois, Breckinridge would carry the South, and with it the election. But with the wild-card Whig candidacy of John Bell showing surprising strength in border states, and with Old Uncle Abe demonstrating more force against Douglas in the North than anticipated, it may be that the worst fears of Southerners—Republicans, Democrats, and Whigs alike—are about to be realized.

"If Douglas does not bring home at least 73 electoral votes in the North, or if Bell should manage a stronger election-day showing than anticipated by stealing two or three states away from the Breckinridge camp, it will likely be the log-cabin-born son of Quakers Abraham Lincoln who is the next occupant of the White House."

Seth finished the article, then his eyes scanned farther down the page until they came upon the caption: "Tension Mounts in South Carolina, Secession Talks Intensify."

"It is no secret," the article began, "that the states of the deep South are up in arms at the possibility of a Lincoln presidency. None has been so strident in its opposition to the Lincoln agenda. For months, that state's legislature and nearly all its newspapers have promised the rest of the nation that it would withdraw from the Union if Lincoln is elected.

"Though widely reviled throughout the South, Lincoln is not a strict abolitionist. In all likelihood, if elected, he would do nothing to upset that age-old institution as it presently exists in the Southern states. He is a politician not a firebrand like John Brown. But he has pledged absolutely to halt the farther *spread* of slavery in new states and territories. 'On this point,' he has said publicly, 'we must hold firm, as with a chain of steel. The tug has to come, and better now than at any time hereafter.' South Carolina's obstinancy has caused Lincoln to add a second inviolate conviction to the spread of slavery, that is that no state has a right to leave the Union. On those points, he has declared, he will not budge.

"Is the talk of South Carolina's leaders a bluff intended to bolster support for Vice President Breckinridge? Or is it a threat backed up by a promise of future action?

"No one can know at this time. Only the election and its aftermath will tell the story. A showdown seems inevitable.

"The larger question concerns not South Carolina, but all the South. If Lincoln is elected, and should South Carolina prove good on its threat, what will be the response of other Southern states? Will they side with Lincoln and the North and remain true to the nation as it exists? Or will they follow South Carolina's lead and also secede?

"And what will be Washington's response? If secession comes prior to Lincoln's inauguration on March 4, what will President Buchanan do about it during the final four lame-duck months of his presidency?

"These are momentous questions upon which the future of the nation may turn. All eyes will be on the voting booths next Tuesday, November 6, just as all eyes will be on South Carolina in the weeks that follow."

Gradually continuing through the paper, Seth's eyes were arrested by a small item under the heading "Capital Social Column."

"Virginia senator Denton Beaumont and his wife, Lady Daphne MacFadden Beaumont," Seth read, "have announced the engagement of their daughter, Veronica, one of last year's bright new faces on the capital social scene, to Richard Fitzpatrick, son of Michael Fitzpatrick, U.S. ambassador to Luxembourg. No more details are known other than that a Christmas celebration is in the planning stages in the couple's honor. A wedding date has not been set, although rumor has it that the nuptials will take place in the first month or two of the new year, after which the couple plans to honeymoon on the French Riviera before returning to Luxembourg where the ambassador's son and his bride will accept a post in the consulate."

Seth smiled at the announcement. *Well, Veronica,* he said to himself, *it looks like you finally got what you wanted!*

PART FOUR

THE NATION EXPLODES
1861

Forty-Four

Seth traveled by train to Fredericksburg, then through Baltimore, Philadelphia, New York, finally arriving on Sunday afternoon at Cynthia and Jeffrey's small naval home in New Haven, Connecticut, where Cynthia's husband had been assigned upon graduation from Annapolis.

The much-anticipated election was only two days away. Seth had only been able to settle in to Cynthia's extra bedroom and shake off the fatigue of travel and begin to familiarize himself with the city in hopes of finding a job when the election suddenly dominated the news, the city, and the entire nation.

The headlines shouted by paperboys throughout New Haven told the story: "Lincoln Wins. Crisis in South Looms."

"As most political experts had expected," read Jeffrey aloud as he and Cynthia and Seth sat at the breakfast table several days later, when the majority of votes had been counted, "pro-slavery advocates in the Southern states are in mourning this week, while rejoicing can be heard throughout the North at the election in last Tuesday's election of Abraham Lincoln as the next President of the United States.

"While official balloting will not take place until the electoral college of delegates from the states convenes, Lincoln's sweep of the North leaves no doubt as to the inevitable result. Though Southerners had hoped for a split decision in the North, Illinois senator Stephen

A. Douglas disappointed backers by carrying but the single state of Missouri. Pro-slavery prospects were further dashed by Whig John Bell's surprising victories in Virginia, Tennessee, and the vice president's home state of Kentucky. While Lincoln in the end is expected to garner some 40% of the nationwide popular vote, his electoral-college victory will be far more convincing, if not an actual landslide. At present, Lincoln stands with 173 likely electoral votes. Results have not yet come in from the two western states of California and Oregon, but their seven combined electoral votes will surely give him a total of 180. John Breckinridge, carrying Texas, Arkansas, and the seven states of the deep South, will gain 72 electoral votes, Bell with his three states 39, and Douglas 12.

"While Lincoln is an outspoken opponent of slavery, he has never indicated an inclination to abolish that institution, but only to prevent its spread to additional states and territories. Among Republicans, Lincoln is considered a moderate unlikely to make slavery a dominant issue. Even his moderation, however, is seen in the South as a threat to the Southern way of life. What kind of Union will it be that Abraham Lincoln takes charge of when he is sworn in as the sixteenth President of the United States on March 4 of 1861? The answer to that question may rest with a handful of men in the legislature of the state of South Carolina. Will pride and arrogance outweigh allegiance to the Constitution and the law of the land? We must only wait to see, and pray that it will not be so."

Jeffrey set down the paper. The three were silent a moment as they pondered the import of what he had just read.

"Will it come to war, Jeffrey?" asked Cynthia.

"I don't know," he replied with a sigh. "I do not have much faith in South Carolina's leaders to place the good of the nation above their own petty interests."

"What do Mother and Father think?" said Cynthia, turning toward Seth.

"They didn't really talk about the election much," replied Seth. "They were planning to vote for Lincoln because they felt his views were closest to their own. But I did not talk much to Dad about whether South Carolina would make good on its threats. I don't think he took it that seriously."

"I have a feeling they are deadly serious," said Jeffrey. "To secede from the Union would be suicidal. But I am afraid those men down there are so blinded that they might be stupid enough to do it."

"You are indeed a Northerner, Jeffrey!" laughed Cynthia.

"Perhaps . . . but stop and think about it—do *you* want me to go to war?"

"Goodness, Jeffrey, do you actually think it might come to that?"

"If South Carolina secedes . . . yes. It could come to war. If a handful of men can take a country into war by their own pride, then I call them stupid to do so. But I fear the worst. I do not think they will back down. Neither, I'm afraid, will Mr. Lincoln."

Again the breakfast table was silent.

Cynthia had never seen her husband of three years like this. His tone sent chills through her body. Attempting to change the subject, she turned again to Seth.

"What will you do today, Seth?" she asked, trying to sound cheerful.

"I'm going down to the docks," Seth replied. "I am going to talk to that man whose name Jeffrey gave me about work."

Walking through the city several hours later, Seth sensed everywhere a mood of buoyancy and happiness as a result of the election. He wondered if the reaction was quite so optimistic back home. He had only written once to his parents since his arrival and had not yet heard back. He was anxious to hear news of reaction to the election from south of the Mason-Dixon Line. He was especially anxious to hear his father's insights concerning what appeared an impending crisis in the matter of South Carolina's continued belligerence toward Washington.

Seth had been on his new job about a week when, in the third week of November, he received a letter in his father's familiar hand. It was thick and promised to be a good read!

He had just returned from work, Jeffrey was still at the base, and

supper was about an hour away. Seth boiled water, fixed himself a pot
of tea, then sat back to relish every word of his father's missive.

"*My dear Seth,*" he began to read,

"*The news here, as I am sure it is there, is all about the election.
Virginia, of course, is not nearly so up in arms over Lincoln's election as are the states of the deeper South. Virginia's vote went unexpectedly for Mr. Bell. Sentiment around here, however, especially in
Richmond and Fredericksburg, was decidedly pro-Breckinridge.*

"*Despite being held in general low esteem by many of my
colleagues, I was nevertheless invited to a gathering of state leaders to
discuss what should be Virginia's posture if and when events should
come to a head. There were probably thirty in attendance, from
both parties and a wide variety of interests. Both of our esteemed
senators, Hoyt and our friend Denton, as well as most of the state's
congressmen, and the governor, and many of the state's large plantation owners. Denton and I spoke but little. Frederick Trowbridge
and some of the others were likewise cool. But I was treated with
more cordiality by most than I might have expected.*

"*One might, of course, say that my inclusion was owing to the
openness of state leaders to moderate their views. I am sorry to say
that it was clear that I was but a token representative of what is a
one-man view. The glances and expressions and hushed conversations that ended abruptly as I approached all said clearly enough
that little has changed. I endured it, however, hoping that I might
demonstrate that I am a normal human being and neither madman
nor traitor.*

"*I am still not sure why I accepted the invitation—a whim of
civic duty must have struck me! Still . . . it was enlightening, though
not encouraging. I would have to say the outlook for the future
appears dark. How the issue of slavery will be resolved peacefully,
I cannot see. Though there are moderates in Virginia, even throughout the South, by far the prevailing consensus seems to be that South
Carolina will withdraw from the Union, and that Mississippi,
Alabama, Georgia, Louisiana, and North Carolina as well. That*

*will place Virginia in the precarious position of having to choose
whether to join the rebel states with all the risk that entails, or side
with the Constitution, the Union, and the North. The future of
Virginia, as well as other border states such as Tennessee and Maryland and Kentucky and Missouri, will hinge upon response to these
two options.*

*"With Mr. Lincoln on record as saying he will not attempt to
abolish slavery where it presently exists, I am mystified at the hostility of my Southern colleagues against accepting our position peacefully as a regional minority. It is obvious that slave states will never
again control the U.S. Senate. But why should that lead to secession
and war?*

*"Perhaps the separation of the North and South into two nations is
the best solution. But I cannot imagine it working. Neither would the
new President allow it. He is more strongly against breakup of the
Union than he is slavery. Slavery, I believe—though I am personally
against it—would be allowed to coexist with the rights of Negroes in
nonslave states to be free. That is how I read Mr. Lincoln's point of
view. But he will not allow the country to break apart. Upon that he
is firm. At what point, then, will one side or the other attempt to
enforce its position with military force and bloodshed?*

*"When is a principle worth the shedding of blood? And how
much bloodshed is any given principle worth? Is slavery such an
issue? Is the right of states to govern themselves, even to the point of
withdrawal from the Union, such an issue?*

*"I do not have the answers to such questions. But as a father with
two sons of potential fighting age, I came home from the gathering
deeply distressed. Loyal Virginian as I consider myself, the men of
the South are belligerent and arrogant to a degree I have never
before seen in politics. Our South Carolina brothers appear almost
eager to push the North toward a provocation of hostilities. Their
antagonistic rhetoric cannot but end in their own destruction. Yet
they are blinded by self-interests. It adds not so much as a straw to
the scale of the argument that the freedom of all men, black and
white, is right. They do not care. As it looks to me at this moment,*

they will die before they will back down. Nor do they care how
many others may die . . . they will never admit to being wrong.

"It is one of the curses of Adam that has fallen to our sex, Seth, my
boy—this absurd manly refusal to be able to admit oneself in error.
'I am sorry . . . I have been wrong,' must surely be among the most
difficult words in any language for the male of the species to utter. But
as long as such a mentality prevails among leaders and men of power,
and with it the stubborn refusal to acknowledge the march of civiliza-
tion and society toward an increasing of the freedoms and liberties to
which all humanity is entitled under God, and equally toward which
men of conscience and foresight ought to dedicate themselves because it
is right not because of any advantage to be gained by themselves, then
I see little hope for a peaceful settlement of the crisis to which the
outcome of the recent election is sure to lead to in the end."

The letter that arrived at Greenwood two weeks later, in the first week
of the last month of the year, was greeted at Greenwood with as much
rejoicing as had it been an invitation to his inauguration signed by the
new president-elect himself.

"It's a letter from massa Seff!" said Moses returning from the front
door with the morning's mail. A shriek sounded from the kitchen.
The envelope was snatched away from him by Carolyn's eager hands a
few seconds later. A moment or two after that, she was seated in the
parlor and had begun to read.

"*Dear Mother and Father,*" Seth wrote.

> "*Greetings from New Haven!*
>
> "*Your letter about the election and the meeting you attended,*
> *Dad, I devoured with great interest. It was so good to hear from you*
> *I read it over four times! Actually, I began this letter of reply that*
> *same evening. But I had only begun work at my new job a few days*
> *before and I have been so exhausted that several evenings I have*
> *fallen asleep after supper.*
>
> "*Jeffrey knew a man whom he sent me to see at the docks. I have*

been working ever since loading and unloading ships. It is tedious
work after living so long at Greenwood doing work that I love. And
strenuous—my arms and shoulders ached badly for a week and a
half! But I am used to it now and find it not so difficult as at first.
The men I work with are generally of a rougher sort than I might
choose, though there are one or two among them who seem made of
gentler stuff than the rest. But most treat me well enough now that
we are somewhat acquainted.

"At first I felt badly ill suited for city life and was downcast and
depressed, thinking I had made a terrible mistake coming here. It
has been good to see Cynthia again and she has done everything she
can to make me feel welcome. We are enjoying talking over our lives
as children, remembering things neither knew the other had remem-
bered, and laughing a good deal. The years have a strange bonding
effect as brothers and sisters become reacquainted on the level ground
of adulthood. Years that once seemed so significant—Cynthia always
seemed to be so much older to my boyish eyes—melt into nothing-
ness. It now seems we are the same age.

"As I said, to begin with I felt a great burden of melancholy. I tried
to find work but was not immediately successful, invariably sensing
strange looks and glances whenever I opened my mouth. My accent, it
seemed, prejudiced people against me at the outset. And when it was
learned that I came from a plantation in the South, a plantation that
grew crops and where black men and women carried out much of the
work, I rarely had a chance to explain that my father's blacks are free.
In these tense times, no one wanted to hire, as they thought, a slave
owner's son. I had always considered Virginia's the mildest of tongues,
and to my ear the New England twang sounded harsh and edgy.
What I sounded like to the natives of this region, I can not imagine.
I have even noticed that Cynthia has lost some of what I consider the
genteel sweetness of her native speech.

"But again, I digress from what I was saying! After a week,
Jeffrey's contact at the dock hired me. Now that they know that I am
not the son of slave owners, they accept me—accent and all—as one
of them. The work is hard, as I say, but I am used to it now

*and—almost!—find myself looking forward to it every day. If I am
not yet actually making friends, I am making acquaintances that
I hope may become friendships.*

*"The mood here after the election is much different than what
you described in your letter, Dad. No one seems concerned in the
least about war or any of the rest of it. They have no idea how strong
is sentiment in the South. Jeffrey, however, is sober in his assessment.
He recognizes the danger. I know Cynthia is worried too, though she
does her best not to show it.*

*"You only mentioned Mr. Beaumont briefly, Dad. What did you
and he talk of at that meeting, or have you seen him around Dove's
Landing? Is the situation there improved at all . . . Wyatt, and so
on? Of course I am very curious whether you have had any interesting guests or visitors, though I will understand if you are unable to
write about them.*

*"My greetings to all, especially Thomas and Nancy and Aaron
and Isaiah and Phoebe. I pray for them daily and hope they are
coping with the loss of Malachi with strength. I cannot imagine
what it must be like. He was a good man.*

*"My love to you both, and to Thomas. Cynthia and Jeffrey send
their greetings and love along with mine.*

"Your son,
"Seth Davidson"

Carolyn set the letter down, smiled peacefully, and let a few tears
fall down her cheeks unchecked. She did not like having two of her
children so far away. At least they were with each other.

In the middle of a dark night, over a thousand miles to the south,
farther south even than Seth's own Virginia, a slave man and his wife
carried two of their four children, still asleep, to the waiting arms of a
cousin hiding in the woods a few hundred yards from the slave shack
that was the only home they had ever known. Silently they hurried

back for the other two. When they reached the woods again with the two littlest ones, the rest of their small party was ready.

It was somewhere between midnight and two in the morning and deathly silent. Even the dogs at the big house had not heard their movements.

"You still want ter do dis?" whispered the father.

"Ain' no life ef we ain' t'gither, Macon," she said. "We got's ter try."

"Den let's go," he nodded. "An' may der Lawd hep us, cuz we' neber make it all dat way wifout it."

He glanced around at the few other eyes waiting in the darkness, then nodded.

"All right den," he whispered, "hit's time. Let's git as fer away from dis ol' place as we can afore dem dogs wake up."

Ten hours later the troop of nine runaway slaves slept soundly as far away from any other sign of life as they could get. They had one night's walk in the dark behind them, but already one or two of them were beginning to wonder if this had been a mistake.

How would they ever make it so far.

⌒

Once again Seth sat down wearily after a hard day's work and opened an envelope from home. There were two letters inside, one from his mother and one from his father.

After his mother's had caught him up on affairs at Greenwood, and his father's on the current political outlook in his home state, Seth continued to read with interest of his father's conversation with Veronica's father.

"*You asked about my conversation with my old friend Senator Denton Beaumont,*" Richmond wrote.

> "*Though the discussion accomplished little to mend the fences between us, at least we talked. Perhaps that is a good thing. But he wore the prestige of his new position with condescension. Seeing it on his face saddened me.*

"'It is good to see you again, old friend,' I said to him when we found ourselves alone. 'Your influence is being felt in Washington, from the reports.'

"He nodded in what seemed begrudging acknowledgment of my words.

"'Sometime when you are in recess, we must go for a ride together,' I suggested.

"'We were younger then, Richmond,' he said. 'Times were different.'

"'Do you remember the day I rode over excitedly to tell you of Cynthia's birth, and you three years later rode the same road to tell me of Wyatt's? Those were the days, eh, my friend! We used to keep nothing from one another. I regret that we have drifted apart.'

"'It can hardly be helped, Richmond. I, at least, am a loyal Virginian.'

"'I would say the same of myself,' I said. 'The following of my conscience hardly makes me a traitor to my state.'

"'Some would say allegiance to the South ought to supercede the voice of conscience.'

"'Only one whose conscience gave him no trouble would say such a thing.'

"'There you go with your preachments again. But times of change are coming, Richmond. It might be well for you to consider your position. Make no mistake, I will carry Virginia's future with me. When that day comes, it may be that you will need a friend. It may not go well for men of your political leanings.'

"'If that day comes, I hope I shall have one. You, at least, Denton, will always have a friend at Greenwood.'

"His expression made it clear that such a friendship, if he would even call it by that name, meant less than nothing to him.

"'I reiterate, Richmond,' he said, 'that you would do well to consider your position. It is still not too late for you to rekindle your passion for our shared Southern heritage.'

"'If you mean go back on the promises of freedom I gave to our *people, I could not legally do so even if I would. How can you even suggest such a thing?'*

"'*I am thinking of your future, Richmond. I simply do not want to see you dispossessed along with those who side with the North once the fighting begins.'*

"'*Are you actually suggesting that Greenwood could be taken from us?' I asked in astonishment.*

"'*I am saying nothing more, my old friend,' he added, speaking the words as if in derision, 'that in times of war, traitors often pay a heavy price. It is a time to choose one's loyalties with care.'*

"With the words he moved off, leaving me more depressed than ever. I spoke with him briefly one other time, though only to ask about his family. As you know, Veronica is to be married in a month or two. I conveyed our regards, told him that you were in New England and that I was sure you would want me to convey your best wishes to Veronica. He acted as though he didn't believe me.

"Things at Greenwood are much the same, though every day brings new challenges. If Denton only knew what comings and goings there are in cellars and up and down hidden staircases and through tunnels! We have new guests, as we call them, every week or two, though their appearance continues to be random and unexpected. With Malachi gone, we now realize how much he had done. But Nancy is doing the work of three in his stead. And to think that at first she resisted being part of it! She is now the most enthusiastic to help of all. Sometimes it is one, sometimes as many as six or eight traveling together. Slowly we are making more contacts who are willing to help, many whites, mostly Quakers, among them.

"Your mother is well, misses you terribly, but is of good cheer. I do not know if a letter from her own hand is capable of conveying the depth of her love, but it is there and I know you treasure it. We are too busy with the work of the place and the flow of 'guests,' to worry overmuch about our troubles, which, in truth, are very few.

"You are constantly in our thoughts and prayers. We love you."

Seth set down the letter and exhaled a long sigh that expressed many things. Hearing from home always made him thoughtful, a little melancholy, but also filled him with a quiet and peaceful joy mingled with sadness. And word of Veronica made him feel strangely sad in a way he could not explain.

Forty-Five

*O*n an isolated road in the hills of North Carolina, a strange-looking wagon rumbled along. Around a bend ahead of it, a troop of Negroes plodded in the same direction, looking like they had been walking all night, or perhaps for several nights. They were bedraggled, hungry, and exhausted.

As the wagon came into hearing of the pilgrims, a few glances behind were sufficient to scatter them into the trees beside the road. The driver of the strange vehicle continued on, then reined in his two sturdy equine manservants. He could hardly keep from smiling at the sounds of rustling in the undergrowth.

"You can all come out!" he called, then waited in silence.

"Better come out and greet a friend," he said, "than have the dogs set on you! You'll never make it another twenty miles without my help."

Again it was silent.

"There're search parties about looking for you. I ran into one of them about an hour ago. If you're from the Mulholland plantation, they will find you eventually."

He saw another rustling and movement of bushes and brush. Out from it a tall lanky black man emerged and climbed out onto the road. Professor Southcote stared down at the man a moment from his perch high atop the seat of his strange-looking wagon.

"A word of advice, friend," he said at length. "You'd best keep your people off the road, or else listen a little more carefully. This region is crawling with vigilantes looking for people like you."

"We's mighty tard, suh. We din't hear you comin'."

"Well you'd better listen, or next time you won't be lucky enough to find a friend in the road. Where are you bound?" Southcote asked as a few more timid black faces emerged from their hiding places.

"Anywhere we can git ter freedom, suh," the first man replied, apparently their leader.

"How long you been on the road?"

"A few weeks, suh. We had ter hide out a spell after gittin' away from da plantashun. Den we got an da road an' headed norf."

"At this rate, you'll never make it without getting caught, man. You've still got all of Virginia to cross, and winter's coming."

"We gots ter make it, suh. We gots ter make it fer da chilluns."

"What's your name?" asked Southcote.

"Diggs, suh . . . Macon Diggs."

By now Southcote realized that there were four young faces staring up at him with big round white eyes in the middle of frightened black faces, along with four more adults in addition to Diggs. He shook his head. There were too many . . . and they kept coming, more every month. They had no idea how far it was, no idea what it took to elude capture. They were so ignorant, yet so hopeful, so determined. The lure of freedom outweighed everything.

Suddenly Southcote's reflections of what seemed the hopelessness of his mission were interrupted by a sound in the distance—a sound he knew all too well. He cocked his ear to listen.

"Riders coming . . . and this way!" he shouted, jumping down off his perch with an agility marvelous for one of his build. Before his feet hit the ground every one of the runaways had scattered and were rapidly disappearing into the wooded undergrowth.

"Wait!" he called after them. "Diggs—get your people back here . . . hurry!"

With wonderful trust for one he hardly knew, and displaying great judge of character, the man called Macon Diggs gave a whistle and a shout, with the result that by the time Weldon Southcote had reached the back of his wagon and had removed an odd-shaped iron bar from somewhere and had inserted one of its ends into a hole at the base of the bed, nine black faces were clustered closely around him with wide, curious, but fearful eyes. The fact that they now heard the galloping horses too, and coming closer, was clear indication that, though they hadn't the slightest idea what he was doing, they were willing to place their lives in his hands.

"Turn this, Diggs," said Southcote, indicating the iron lever, "just like an auger. Be quick about it."

The black man took hold of the bar and began to turn, while Southcote stepped to one side and began to shove against one side of the wagon.

Gradually an awesome spectacle unfolded before their eyes . . . two halves of the tall, merchandise-laden wagon began to separate. The more Macon Diggs twisted his auger, and the more Walter Southcote pushed and shoved and coerced the gears of his cunning machinery, the wider yawned the door into the hidden interior of his traveling hideaway.

"That's enough—get in, everyone!" he yelled. "I think it will hold you all. If not, you'll have to crowd together."

The children needed no persuasion. Quickly they scrambled up and into the little cleverly constructed human cave. And now for the first time did the children, followed by Mr. Diggs and the others, see that there were already five or six blacks sitting inside wondering what was happening no less than themselves. Crowding together, and cramming into every available nook and cranny, children on laps and held tight to mothers' breasts, within seconds the strange contraption began to close as it had opened.

"Not a peep out of any of you!" said Southcote as he now cranked his iron bar in the opposite direction. "Squeeze in tight."

Slowly the light faded from their view. Again Southcote was left alone, thinking that it would be a miracle if he could secure the latch. The thing had been designed to hold six, and by his count—though he had lost track!—there were something on the order of fifteen inside his empty wagon shell at this moment.

He had just managed to clamp the sides together, run back around and climb onto his bench, and give his horses a whack with his reins, when eight riders came into view galloping toward him.

They stopped and he reined in as if he had been moving along at a constant pace for an hour or more.

"You seen any blacks along this road, old-timer?" asked the lead rider.

"Can't say I have, mister," replied Southcote. "But if you and your men have just a minute to spare, I have a product that I am more than certain would be of great benefit to you and add years to your lives besides."

He rose, turned around, and from somewhere in his assortment of goods produced a bottle, which, turning back to face them, he held aloft. "Now, gentlemen, if I could just have a moment of your valuable—," he began.

Already Malone Murdoch and his posse were disappearing in the distance.

Southcote watched them a moment, with a keen gaze from beneath the brim of his well-worn top hat, then muttered a few words, uncorked the bottle in his hand, took a long healthy swig, sat back down, and once again prodded his horses into action.

Forty-Six

*W*ord began to spread around the New Haven docks about midway through the day of December 20, just five days before Christmas. By quitting time everyone in the city knew. Seth bought an extra edition of the paper, rushed into print, on his way home. Its headlines emblazoned the news that would change the course of a nation's history:

"South Carolina Secedes From Union!"

Seth opened the paper where he stood beside the street as people bustled about him talking about the astonishing developments. The rest of the announcement continued in print so large as to cover most of the front page:

"Passed unanimously at 1:15 p.m., December 20th, 1860. An Ordinance to dissolve the Union between the State of South Carolina and other States united with her under the compact entitled The Constitution of the United States of America.

"We the People of the State of South Carolina, in Convention assembled, do declare and ordain, and it is hereby declared and ordained, that the Ordinance adopted by us in Convention, on the twenty-third day of May, in the year of our Lord one thousand seven hundred and eighty-eight, whereby the Constitution of the United States of America was ratified, and also, all Acts and parts of Acts of the General Assembly of this State, ratifying amendments of said Constitution, are hereby repealed; and that the Union now subsisting between South Carolina and other States, under the name of The United States of America, is hereby dissolved."

In disbelief, Seth folded the paper under his arm and hurried home. The look on Cynthia's face when he rushed in said well enough that she too had heard the news. She ran straight into his arms.

"Oh, Seth!" she exclaimed. "I'm so afraid!"

"Have you heard from Jeffrey?" he asked.

"He's not home yet. I only heard the news an hour ago."

Seth set down his things, then showed her the paper. Cynthia read it, slowly shaking her head in disbelief.

"I just don't see how they can do it," she said. "It's . . . it's so wrong!"

"Don't you wish we could talk to Mom and Dad right now."

"Oh, wouldn't that be wonderful!" sighed Cynthia. "I would *so* like to know what they think! And just to be with them."

She paused and drew in a deep breath. "That's one thing I miss," she said thoughtfully, a faraway look coming into her eyes, "one thing I don't like about growing up. Sometimes, I don't know . . . I just want to be a little girl again. As much as I love Jeffrey and wouldn't trade our life for anything . . . you know, there's part of you that misses childhood. It was so safe, so happy."

"We couldn't have had a better place to grow up," nodded Seth. "I feel that way too. And I *am* still just a kid compared to you, old sister!"

"You look like a man to me. You've grown up so much since I saw you last . . . and now doing a man's work on the docks!"

"I don't feel like a man," said Seth. "Sometimes I feel, just like you said, like a little boy and I want to go back to being ten or twelve. But . . . I don't suppose you can ever go back, can you?"

"I guess not. And now I wonder if the country will one day look back and wish it could go back to more peaceful times. Seth, what's going to happen!"

"I don't know, sis . . . I honestly don't know. But," he added, pointing to the paper on the table, "it can't be good if things continue like this."

Christmas five days later was bittersweet at both homes in New Haven and Greenwood. Though Cynthia and Carolyn did their best to make the day festive and gay, the miles of separation could not but cast a cloud of melancholy over the celebration of Christ's birth.

The packages so lovingly sent and so excitedly received at both ends, and the gifts they contained, while the cause of much mirth and happy laughter, could not replace the presence of loved ones so dearly missed at such a special family time.

Seth's presence buoyed Cynthia's spirit, yet the uncertainty of Jeffrey's future added an invisible weight she could not dismiss from her heart. And though preparation for the great annual celebration at the big house for the entire Greenwood family kept Carolyn busy in the kitchen with Nancy, Maribel, Mary, and several other of the black women, in the quietness of her heart she was missing her daughter and oldest son more sorely than ever.

Their traditional family time alone on Christmas Eve the night before, with only the three of them, had been painfully quiet. Thomas had seemed more gloomy than ever. Nothing they did, it seemed, could please him. Any gift they gave, whatever words they spoke, were met with a shrug of the shoulders. The evening ended, Richmond and Carolyn together on the couch in front of the fireplace, Carolyn leaning against Richmond's chest, his arm around her shoulders. Tears softly fell from her aching mother's eyes for the son and daughter who were together but so far away, and for the son so close, alone upstairs in his room, and yet also so far from their hearts.

Events did, true to Seth's words to his sister, continue to slide in a direction that in the end could only result in confrontation.

Seizing the four-month opportunity when the government in Washington floundered with a lame-duck president, and while President-Elect Lincoln watched powerless from his home in Illinois, the states of the South followed South Carolina's lead. On January 9,

Mississippi voted to secede from the Union. Florida did so on the tenth, and was quickly followed by Alabama, Louisiana, Georgia, and Texas.

Suddenly nearly a fourth of the country had broken away.

Wasting no time, and continuing to act before Lincoln or the congress in Washington could stop them, representatives from the seven breakaway states met on the fourth of February in Montgomery, Alabama, and formed a new nation called The Confederate States of America. Former senator and secretary of war Jefferson Davis of Mississippi, who was not even in attendance, was elected president of the new nation's provisional government.

Jefferson Davis left his home to take up his new duties in Montgomery on February 11. Abraham Lincoln left Springfield, Illinois, for his new duties in Washington, D.C., on February 12. They were two presidents bound for two very different destinies.

As Lincoln made his way to the capital for his inauguration, all eyes from both "nations" turned their eyes in his direction. How would the new president respond to the events that had taken place since the election?

He would not be an impotent observer much longer.

What would Lincoln do?

And how would the Southern states respond?

Forty-Seven

The first action of the seceding states was the attempted takeover of federal lands, buildings, forts, and other property within their borders. For the most part control of these installations was turned over peaceably. Where those in charge or command were loyal to the South, they remained. Otherwise officers loyal to the Union left their posts and returned North to await orders. In the few instances where federal installations were seized or captured by force, there were no injuries or exchanges of gunfire.

In South Carolina, however, the mood from the outset was tense. In order to avoid the unnecessary shedding of blood in an atmosphere where all South Carolina, it seemed, was ruled by hotheads eager to start a tragic and needless war, six days after South Carolina's secession the handful of federal troops stationed at Fort Moultrie in Charleston, removed themselves to unmanned and unfinished Fort Sumter, located in Charleston Harbor, where, they hoped, they would be left in peace until the crisis blew over.

As a symbol of their belligerence and resolve, six thousand South Carolina militiamen with artillery capable of bombarding the fort, took up positions on the land in a semicircle around Fort Sumter and demanded that Major Anderson surrender the fort. But the commanding officer, Major Robert Anderson, was loyal to the Union and would not give up his post without orders to do so. On January 9, a ship attempting to bring him supplies was fired upon and forced to turn back. From that moment, the sixty-six soldiers inside were separated from the outside world, and cut off from provisions and supplies.

Weeks passed, then a month, then two. The small Union garrison at Fort Sumter remained hunkered down and isolated, surrounded by cannons and guns and South Carolina hotheads eager to open fire. Throughout both the Union and the Confederacy, all eyes watched to see how the standoff would end. Tensions rose.

Lincoln reached Washington, D.C., under threat of assassination, and all the capital turned out on the fourth of March for the inauguration of the new president. After being sworn in, Lincoln spoke directly to the seceding states of the South in his inaugural address. He promised not to interfere with slavery where it already existed, but again he insisted that no state had the right to secede from the Union, vowing to hold, occupy, and possess all federal installations.

"In your hands, my dissatisfied countrymen," he went on, "and not in mine is the momentous issue of civil war. The government will not assail you. You can have no conflict, without being yourselves the aggressors. . . .We are not enemies but friends. We must not be enemies. Though passion may have strained, it must not break our bonds of affection. The mystic chords of memory, stretching from every battlefield and patriot grave, to every living heart and hearthstone, all over this broad land, will yet swell the chorus of the Union, when again touched, as surely they will be, by the better angels of our nature."

With President Lincoln and the new government at last installed in the capital, the anxious waiting seemed about to end. Major Anderson's troops at Fort Sumter were running low on provisions. The fort either had to be evacuated and turned over to the Confederacy, or else it had to be provisioned with new supplies.

Many of Lincoln's advisors and new cabinet officers argued in favor of abandoning the fort. Meanwhile, at the Confederate capital in Montgomery, the advisors of Jefferson Davis were clamoring for him to strike a blow for the Confederacy and order an attack on the fort.

Both sides continued to wait.

"*Dear Mother and Father,*" Carolyn read aloud as she and Richmond sat at the kitchen table, each with a cup of tea, midway through the morning of March 11, a week after Lincoln's inauguration.

"*The country, it seems, or what is left of it, has a new president at last. I am glad to know, for the present at least, that he is your president in Virginia too.*

"*How long do you think he will be Virginia's president? The news here is full of speculation about what states will join the Confederacy.*

"*I must admit, it is peculiar indeed to be a Sutherner, here in the North. Sentiment is so strong here against South Carolina as well as the other states of the so-called Confederacy. Fort Sumter's Major Anderson is almost a national hero. One cannot help being swayed by the talk and the pro-Northern sentiment. And yet, as I say, it is peculiar in that by heritage I am a son of Virginia and the South. If war comes it cannot be but tragic, and doubly tragic in that it is so unnecessary. We are a nation of law, of mutual commitment, of duty, a nation ruled by a Constitution which cannot be set aside.*

"*These things dominate discussion here, on every street corner and at home. Jeffrey and Cynthia and I talk of little else. How much would I give to be able to speak to the two of you face-to-face, my dearest friends and worthiest counselors in the world! Alas, I am here. But I am grateful to be with Cynthia during these troubled times.*

"*Jeffrey, of course, is full of the military perspective. The threat of potential hostilities worries Cynthia terribly. And this brings me to the real news of this letter, and the urgency with which I write and am desirous of a reply.*

"*New orders arrived yesterday for Jeffrey's crew to be dispatched. He has no definite destination as yet, but they have been put on alert to sail on twenty-four-hour notice. All expect hostilities. Wherever he goes, they will be leaving New Haven. Cynthia, though anxious, is expending her energy packing things away for a move. Whether it will be a few days, a week, two weeks, or a month, no one knows. Jeffrey says it could come at any time.*

"This places my life, too, suddenly up in the air. I have no particular allegiance to New Haven and cannot imagine staying once Cynthia and Jeffrey are gone. I would have to find new lodgings and that is not an appealing thought. Most of the young men my age are all talking about enlisting.

"Such talk turns my thoughts immediately inward in reflection upon my own loyalties. Am I or am I not obligated to fight for a cause I do not believe in? I cannot be said to be completely loyal to either side. My sentiments of right or wrong are clearly on the side of the North. But am I to take up arms against my countrymen, especially my own native Virginia should she side with the Confederacy? Perhaps the larger question is, could I take up arms at all . . . on either side . . . against anyone? I seriously doubt it. Whether I believe in war in a larger sense, I cannot now say. But I do not believe in this war, if it comes, for it is an unnecessary war, in which, as I see it, principle is not so much involved as people think, but stupidity. Lincoln would allow slavery to remain. Therefore, there is no reason for war.

"I am very much in a quandary about my own future. Thus, I covet not merely your prayers, which I know I have in abundance, but your advice and counsel.

"Perhaps I should return home. In light of these national matters of such import, those factors I felt driving me away four months ago—Wyatt, Scully, and all the rest—seem far away and unimportant. Only you can advise me on the current state of affairs there, and what you would wish me to do.

"Desirous of posting this as soon as possible, in haste, I am,

"Your loving son,
"Seth"

⌒

"22nd March, 1861
"Dear Seth,
"Be assured, of course, as you know, you have our constant

prayers. We appreciate the trust you show in still desiring our counsel and advice.

"The situation here is tense and uncertain. Virginia's newspapers are full of inflammatory talk, mostly pro-Confederacy here and in the east and south, and, from the reports, decidedly pro-Union in the northwest of the state. So heated has the debate become that there are some who call for Virginia to split into two states.

"I must say, as I read the situation, if hostilities break out, I see no other possibility than that Virginia will side with the Confederacy. Some of the South's loudest voices in favor of secession are coming from Virginians. With Richmond and Washington so close as two such important cities and centers of power, it is possible that Virginia itself will become the chief battleground. My heart breaks at the thought of it.

"To return here would put you in the middle of all that, and in the middle of strong pro-Confederacy sentiment. You must follow your convictions and your conscience. I would simply say that this may not be the best place for you to wrestle through the matter of loyalty, especially since, as I read your words, they are not of a secessionist, pro-slavery bent.

"Speaking as your father—and I admit a strong bias in favor of keeping you out of harm's way!—my recommendation is that you remain where you are at present. Being here, as you presently feel, would make your situation even more untenable than before. All the locals are talking of nothing but enlisting and killing as many Yankees as they can. It is distressing to see how quickly pride turns American against brother. Things are volatile. Nothing will be lost by your remaining in the North a little longer.

"If you should fight, my prayers will go with you. But my earnest prayer is that as God's man you will not. Christians in both North and South are invoking God as on their side. It both saddens me and angers me. Where is the unity of the brotherhood! Few wars have been fought where right and wrong did not exist on both sides. Perhaps there are just and necessary wars . . . but not nearly so many

as men suppose. If war between the North and South comes, it will certainly be neither a just war nor a necessary one.

"*As to your immediate plans, might I recommend you consider paying a visit to our friends the Waterses in Boston? I am sure they would take you in for a week or two if Cynthia should leave abruptly. It may be that James would have a recommendation, as Jeffrey did, for potential employment. Not knowing the economy or work situation there, I am at a loss myself to advise you. Of course, everything hinges on whether war breaks out. A visit to Boston would not solve your greater quandaries, but might give you some breathing room to see how circumstances develop.*

"*You of course know it—you are not only welcome here, this is your home. Our arms ache to hug you again, and I miss our talks about so many things. If the country were not teetoring on the brink of chaos, I would say, Come home! in an instant. But I question whether that is truly in your best interest at the present time.*

"*I hope you will not mind—I intend to send James a letter, which I will write upon completion of this, telling him what I have told you, assuring him that he is under no obligation on my behalf if this is not a convenient time for a visit. I hope by so doing to prevent any awkwardness for either of you.*

"*Our prayers, affection, and love are with you always. I will write again if I feel I have anything constructive to offer in your situation and the decisions facing you.*

"*Much love,*
"*Father*"

The prospect of a visit to Boston filled Seth with an immediate surge of optimism. While his second cup of tea still sat warm beside him, he set his father's letter aside and took up pen and paper to begin a letter at once to James Waters.

He had but begun, however, when a knock at the door interrupted him and preempted the completion of his efforts. He rose to answer it. There stood a uniformed messenger.

"Telegram for Mr. Davidson, sir," he said.

"I am Seth Davidson," said Seth, his heart quickening. What could a telegram mean but some ill tidings from home!

"That's fine, then . . . sign here please."

Seth anxiously walked inside a moment later and sat down again and opened the envelope, then removed the single sheet inside. It read:

> RECEIVED LETTER GREENWOOD RE: YOUR SITUATION.
> EXTEND WARM INVITATION BOSTON. LETTER WILL
> FOLLOW. DAUGHTER ALSO EAGER SEE YOU, ADDS
> GREETINGS.
> J. WATERS.

James Waters' letter arrived two days later, emphasizing his eagerness to extend to Seth their hospitality and to welcome him for as long as he chose to stay. He might, Waters said, be able to assist him in the matter of work, which he hoped he was not presuming to have gathered from his father's letter was a matter of some pressing concern. There were always opportunities of interest available for young men of aptitude who were willing to work hard and he looked forward to discussing one or another of these with him. He himself had not been at the paper every day during recent months, his health having again taken a minor turn for the worse several weeks before Christmas. But he had enough contacts throughout the city that he was reasonably certain of being able to turn something up for him. He concluded by saying that their guest room would be ready immediately and he was welcome at his earliest opportunity and convenience.

Seth put the letter aside with grateful heart that his father could open doors for him, as fathers have done for sons throughout the ages.

He would go to the station this very afternoon and investigate the schedule of trains to Boston.

Forty-Eight

*T*hat Cherity Waters had not heard from Seth Davidson in so long was easily enough explained in her mind by the simple fact that he had had other things on his mind. Namely, Veronica Beaumont.

Cherity had scarcely begun allowing herself to build fantasies in regard to Seth before Veronica's simple statement in town rendered such daydreams foolish and moot.

Then why, she had asked herself a hundred times since that day, had Veronica's simple, *"Yes, Seth and I are engaged, didn't he tell you?"* thrust such a knife into her heart? Seth owed her nothing but his friendship. And that he had freely given. They had been perfect strangers before. He owed her no explanations. Why should he have told her about Veronica? What business was it of hers?

She knew the answers to every such question that plagued her. Why then did every reminder of Seth Davidson twist her stomach in knots?

The letter from Mr. Davidson, though she had not actually read it, did not, from what her father told her, mention either the wedding or Veronica. But why else would Seth be in New England? Why would he be looking for work other than to start out a new life with his young bride?

Why would that make it hard to see him? She should be overjoyed at the prospect.

All Cherity could think of, however, though she kept such thoughts from her father, was that she wanted to run away and hide. She was not at all certain she could face Seth and Veronica together . . . and staying in their guest room just down the hall—she and Mrs. Porterfield waiting on them along with her father during his convalescence . . . the thought was too uncomfortable to imagine!

But her father had extended the invitation—what could she do about it?

⌒⌒

The orders Jeffrey had been expecting came on April 6.

Earlier that same day, President Lincoln made a momentous decision—he would provision Fort Sumter. This time no Northern vessel would be forced to turn back.

Dispatches went out from Washington in two directions:

To the South he notified the Governor of South Carolina that he would soon send food, but neither arms nor reinforcements, to the men barricaded at Fort Sumter, reiterating that if hostilities came, it would be by South Carolina's initiation. As president, he would not provoke an unnecessary war. But neither would he abandon the fort or its men.

Lincoln had drawn a line in the sand. He hoped for peace, and would do all he could to preserve peace. But he was willing to risk war.

At the same time, orders went out to federal troops in the North.

When Jeffrey burst through the door late on the afternoon of the sixth of April, one look at his face and Cynthia knew.

"I ship out in two days," he said.

"Where?" was all Cynthia could ask.

"Fort Sumter," Jeffrey replied. "The president has ordered us to sail on the eighth for Charleston to provision the fort."

Cynthia's face went ashen.

"And . . . and then?" she asked faintly, groping for a chair.

"I will be stationed either in Baltimore or Washington. Already there is talk of having to protect the capital against an invasion from the South."

"What shall I do, Jeffrey?" she asked. "I am mostly packed."

"I think it best that we put our things in storage here, and that you return to Greenwood. When I am stationed permanently you can join me and we will send for our things. But," he added, "if war breaks out, I may not be back for some time. My home may be aboard a ship for a few months until it is over."

Cynthia sighed. They had been expecting it. Yet now that the day had come, hearing the words from Jeffrey's mouth felt like an omen of doom.

"What about Seth?" Jeffrey asked.

"He has been planning to make sure I am situated elsewhere or on my way home, then go to Boston. He said he would travel with me wherever I go, if need be. But if I am going home, I hardly think that necessary."

Jeffrey nodded. "As long as he can help you pack our things and get on the train, that would be a great relief to me."

Seth returned home from work about an hour later and heard the news. He wrote to James Waters that same evening. Whether his letter would arrive ahead of him he couldn't know for certain. He assured them that he would manage to find their home by cab.

Jeffrey sailed from New Haven on April 8th.

The next day, after seeing to the last of their belongings, Cynthia and Seth set out together for the train station. After still more hugs and tears, Cynthia boarded a train for New York, the South, and home to Greenwood, Seth, an hour later, the northbound to Boston.

As Seth's train pulled into the station he saw James Waters standing on the platform waiting for him. He was disappointed to see him alone. But his disappointment was quickly overshadowed by shock. He hardly recognized the man where he stood leaning heavily against a cane. He looked so much older than Seth remembered him!

As soon as he stepped from the train, Waters approached slowly from across the platform, limping visibly.

"Seth," he said with outstretched hand, "welcome to Boston!"

"Hello, Mr. Waters," rejoined Seth. "It is good to be here, and to see you again. I didn't expect you to be here at the station to meet me."

"I wouldn't hear of you taking a cab. But let's get your bags! We can talk in the carriage once we get on our way."

Still unable to accustom himself to the dramatic change that had taken place in his father's friend, Seth took both bags from the porter himself as they were set on the platform.

"Did you hurt your leg?" he asked, nodding toward the cane as they made their way through the station.

"Oh . . . this—no, just a precaution. My doctor is forever fussing at me, talking about circulation and worrying about my heart. I feel fine, but I humor him with this cane. He would have me in bed all the time if I listened to him."

They continued to chat as they returned to James' carriage. Soon they were seated and bounded into motion.

"How is Cherity?" asked Seth.

"Just fine . . . very well in fact. I tried to talk her into coming with me to meet you. As you can see I was unsuccessful. But you shall see her soon!"

They reached the house. James led the way inside. Seth followed with his bag.

"Cherity!" called out her father. "Cherity, we're home . . . Seth is here."

No answer came to his call.

"This is odd," he said. "Where could she have gone? She knew you were coming. Well, the mystery will resolve itself in time . . . ah, Mrs. Porterfield," he added as an older woman appeared, "meet our guest, Seth Davidson. Seth, this is our housekeeper, Mrs. Porterfield."

The two exchanged handshakes and pleasantries.

"Where is Cherity?" asked James.

"She went out, Mr. Waters," answered Mrs. Porterfield. "I had presumed to meet you."

"No, I haven't seen her. This is very strange. Did she say nothing?"

"She and I were adding the last minute touches to Mr. Davidson's room—a vase of flowers it was. An odd expression came over her face. She said something about thinking they would be more comfortable in Anne's room, with the larger bed, and I said that you had told me to prepare the guest room. She said something softly I could not hear, then left the house."

"Why did she mean by *they?*"

"I couldn't say, Mr. Waters. She has been quiet and has kept to herself all day."

"Hmm, well . . . right now let me show you your room, Seth," said James. "It is the same one your father used when he was our guest."

He led the way upstairs. A minute later Seth was alone in his new quarters. He set his bags down on the bed and wandered about. He came to a stop in front of a large window opening upon a spacious garden below at the back of the house. He stood in front of it absently. Gradually he became aware that he was staring at the back of a person diminutive of stature walking slowly amongst the shrubbery and trees. The dress confused him at first . . . but he would know that light auburn hair anywhere!

The next second he was flying back down the stairs. When he hit the bottom, without pausing to look for his host, he searched hurriedly for the quickest way outside.

Seth walked across a short-clipped green lawn half a minute later toward the figure he had seen from the window. His steps were so soft on the grass that she did not hear his approach.

"Cherity?" he said slowly.

Startled, Cherity instantly knew the voice. Heart pounding, she hesitated a moment, then turned to face him.

"Hello, Seth," she said with a smile.

"I didn't recognize you at first," he said, "from the window, I mean. What's the occasion?"

"What do you mean?"

"The dress and everything—where are your hat and boots?"

"I thought your visit deserved something a little better."

"I'm honored—you look great!"

Cherity glanced behind him toward the house with a puzzled expression.

"Where is . . . you know?"

"Where's what?"

"You know . . . where is she?"

"*She* . . . she who?"

"You know . . . your wife."

"My *wife*!" exclaimed Seth in a bewildered tone, breaking into a half smile of utter confusion. "What are you talking about!"

"Veronica, I think her name was."

"*Veronica!*"

"Yes . . . the girl you introduced me to."

"Veronica and I aren't married!"

"But . . . I thought . . . didn't she say you would be married in December . . . and that was right after our visit?"

"Oh . . . you mean . . . that day we saw her in town!" said Seth. At last the light broke over his face. "Yeah, I could have killed her for that!" he added with a light laugh. "Gosh," he said, "I'm sorry for the confusion . . . no, it was nothing like that."

"But then, I don't understand . . . what—"

"You thought . . . I mean, when your father wrote to invite me . . . you actually thought *she* was with me!"

Cherity's head was spinning.

"I . . . I didn't know . . . what else to think," she said, struggling for words.

At last a serious expression came over Seth's face as he saw Cherity's confusion, though he still did not fully grasp what it signified.

"Veronica was right," he said. "She and I were sort of engaged."

"How can you be *sort of* engaged?" asked Charity, head still reeling.

"Well, it's a long story, and one I'm not particularly proud of," answered Seth. "It was all a mistake. I broke it off over a year ago. Veronica and I have not seen one another since."

Cherity's face was suddenly very hot.

"I am sorry for not writing," said Seth. "To tell you the truth, after the thing with Veronica, I didn't know what to say. I felt so stupid. I figured you probably thought I was an idiot for being engaged to a girl like that."

"I would never think that."

"Well if you had, you'd have been right. I *was* an idiot. But it's over and done with now. Veronica's father was appointed to the Senate. He and the family—well, except for Wyatt—all went to Washington where apparently Veronica got herself engaged to the son of an ambassador. Like I said, I haven't seen her since."

"Oh, I . . . uh . . . I see."

"I guess I'm not much of a letter writer, huh? I'm sorry . . . I never really thought of writing letters till I left home a few months ago. Then all at once I had to. I was so used to talking to my mom and dad about things. Suddenly they weren't there so I had to write them."

They walked about the garden in silence for a minute or two. It was not like Greenwood's arbor, with endless paths and walks. They quickly returned to the point where Seth had walked up behind Cherity on the lawn.

"Are you . . . uh, all settled in inside?" Cherity asked at length.

"I suppose. Well . . . actually all I did was toss my suitcase on the bed. Then I saw you and ran down and outside. I didn't even open it yet."

"Why did you leave Virginia? Was it to visit your sister?"

"Only partially. There were some unpleasant things going on at home. My dad and I thought it best for me to get away for a while."

Briefly he recounted the series of events, leaving out details of the hanging and Malachi's death.

"That's awful!" said Cherity. "Can nothing be done about such people?"

"Not really. Whatever anyone might do would only make them retaliate all the more. I was worried about my folks and Greenwood."

"What about yourself?" said Cherity with obvious concern. "I would be worried about *you*!"

"Well, that too!" Seth laughed. "I wasn't especially anxious to be a target either. But I especially didn't want to be a target that brought retaliation on anyone else. I thought it would be better for everyone if I was gone for a while. My sister's husband was stationed in New Haven, so I came up here."

By supper a few hours later that evening, Cherity had regained her composure and had hidden away the feelings that had threatened to betray her. She was again the spunky, lively young lady whom Seth remembered from her visit to Greenwood.

"There is so much I want to show you," she said enthusiastically. "And we can go riding . . . it won't be like where we went in the hills behind Greenwood, but I think you will like it. Can we go riding tomorrow, Daddy?"

"Give Seth a little time to get settled, Cherity!" her father laughed. "Not everybody was born with quite your energy!"

"What are you talking about!" said Seth. "I haven't been on a horse in months. I'm ready!"

"I was planning to go into the office."

"Do you feel well enough, Daddy? You remember what the doctor said."

"Oh, what does he know—I feel fine. I thought Seth might like to go with me. I was thinking of making a newspaper man of him."

Seth laughed at the prospect. "Me . . . a journalist!" he said.

"Actually I had something else in mind," rejoined Waters. "Or at least something other than journalism in the normal sense."

"Can't it wait a day, Daddy? I want to take Seth riding."

"I suppose it might. But I think I will go in anyway. I want to talk to a few people and see what might be available."

"Are you seriously thinking that there might be a job at your newspaper?" asked Seth.

"Why not? It would be better than dock work, I would think. Isn't that what you said you were doing in New Haven?"

"Yes, sir. I took the first thing that came along, and that was it."

"Well I think you would find newspaper work far more interesting and mentally stimulating. Tell me . . . what do you know about photography?"

"Nothing at all," added Seth with a laugh. "I've only just heard of it. What is it?"

"The reproduction of images, pictures, on paper."

"Do you mean art and drawing and that kind of thing?"

"No, actual photographic reproduction . . . the transmission of an image, exactly as it is, onto a special kind of paper. It's new. Your father and I discussed the developments. They are very exciting. It is in the earliest stages of development. Unless I am mistaken, it is a field that will ultimately change the news business, and perhaps much else in the world."

"It sounds fascinating. But what does it have to do with me?" asked Seth.

"Does it sound like something you would be interested in learning more about?"

"I don't know, possibly. Why?"

"My paper is just beginning to develop a photographic staff. We publish a weekly magazine and there are hopes that photographs will eventually be able to be reproduced in its pages. The editor happens to be looking for a field assistant he can train. I heard him talking about it just last week. I think a bright young man like you might be exactly what he wants."

"I would be willing to learn," said Seth. "Do you think I might actually have a chance of getting the job?"

"I don't see why you wouldn't have as good a chance as anyone. That's one of the things I want to talk to him about tomorrow when I tell him about you."

The following afternoon, while Cherity's father went into the city, Cherity took Seth by buggy to the stables where she kept her horse. Half an hour later they were far from the center of Boston in a wooded region of wide horse paths and roads. As they went, the year and a half since they had seen one another evaporated as if it had been a day. They were young again, happy, carefree, full of exuberance, relishing, though neither would have dared put it into words, the simple pleasure of being *together* again.

"We can't exactly race," said Cherity when they were away from the stables and, to all appearances, far also from any other human beings. "You never know when you might run into riders or a buggy, and there's no place like Harper's Peak to ride to. But shall we have a gallop?"

"Lead the way!" replied Seth. "I want to feel the wind in my hair!"

Cherity dug her heels into her horse's flanks. Seconds later they were flying along the wide hard-packed trail.

They rode and chatted freely for over an hour, catching up on the nineteen months since Cherity and her father had left Greenwood. Cherity was especially interested in their expanding involvement in the Underground Railroad.

As they made their way back, more slowly now, walking their horses side by side, Seth brought up what that had been on his mind since his arrival.

"Your father seems . . . uh, not particularly energetic."

Cherity smiled sadly. "He is very ill, Seth."

"What is it?"

"Doctors are vague, and Daddy's even worse. He's always trying to downplay it and pretend it's not really so bad."

"But the change in him is obvious. I hardly recognized him."

Cherity sighed. "He fell pretty badly before Christmas," she said. "He was in bed for two weeks."

"What happened?"

"I came on him standing a few steps up from the landing on the stairway, leaning over on the banister as if he could hardly stand."

"'Daddy, what is it!'" I cried as I ran to him. But he couldn't even answer me. His face was dreadfully pale and his left arm was hanging limp. He was gasping for air as if he could hardly breathe. I ran up the stairs for Mrs. Porterfield and I will never forgive myself for leaving him. For just as I reached the top I heard a thud from below. He had fallen down the two or three steps and was lying on his back on the landing. My scream as I ran back to him brought Mrs. Porterfield running. We let him lie there and gradually he began to come back to himself and breathe more easily and after twenty or thirty minutes we got him to his bed. By the next day he was fine, though of course we had sent for the doctor."

"What did he say?"

"Oh, he talked about excitement of the heart and how my father needed to be careful not to put undue strain on his nervous system and that agitation of all kinds should be avoided. But he's been telling Daddy all that for years. That was the reason he recommended an extended stay in the country, and why we went to visit your family."

"But what is the cause? Is there nothing that can be done?"

"A weak heart and poor circulation, I think is what it is. After Daddy's fall he said that there was no immediate danger of a recurrence of the attack. Yet neither could he guarantee that there wouldn't be. He said it was a disease whose outcome could not be predicted, that sometimes people lived for many years after such an incident, but that sometimes—"

Cherity glanced away.

"Sometimes . . . what?" persisted Seth.

"Sometimes, where circulation in the arteries and extremeties is poor, the heart can fail suddenly without warning."

"How has he been since then?"

"His spirits have been good," replied Cherity. "But even now I don't think he's fully recovered. The bruise on his hip isn't healing. It's swollen and discolored. I can't help but worry. But the doctor says nothing when he comes—just the same thing, keep him from too much excitement. I know Mrs. Porterfield is worried too. Daddy tries to put on a brave front. But I think he is afraid."

"Is it really that serious?" Seth asked.

"I . . . I don't know," replied Cherity, beginning to cry. "But I am afraid it might be. When the doctor spoke about the heart suddenly failing, though he didn't actually use the word *die*, I know that's what he was talking about."

Cherity drew in a deep breath and wiped at her eyes.

"I wrote to both my sisters, without him knowing about it. Their families both came to visit for Christmas and it was a very happy time. But they were shocked to see the change on him too. We are all worried."

Forty-Nine

A black form stole with stealthy step toward an abandoned house in the foothills of central Virginia.

He had been watching the place most of the day and, perceiving no activity, now dashed across the open field to the front door. He tried the doorknob. It turned. A moment later he was safely inside. He would sleep there for the night.

The following day, the watcher crept closer to the plantation of which the abandoned house was a part. He was looking for no weathervanes nor wind horses. He knew well enough what manner of people dwelt here. Nevertheless, he would keep watch from a distance, make sure it was safe and that he had not been seen or followed, before making closer approach.

He must do nothing to endanger the friends who had risked so much on his behalf.

When Wyatt Beaumont saw the little black figure scampering across the road a hundred yards in front of him, and into the undergrowth, he immediately knew something was wrong. None of their slaves could possibly be this far west, not with loose children running around. And the uppity Davidson blacks weren't taking to hiding out these days.

This smelled like runaways. And where there was a kid, there were bound to be more. Slowly Wyatt eased his horse forward until he came to the place where he had seen the bedraggled black urchin disappear.

He stopped and waited, but heard not a sound. His eyes scanned the brush and woods for any sign of life.

"All right . . . come on out of there!" he called after a minute. "I know you're in there. I saw the kid."

Again it was still and quiet.

"Maybe I can help you," he said loudly. "Otherwise, I'll have to bring the dogs back. So you might as well come out and let me help you now."

Still there was no answer.

"All right, if that's the way you want it," said Wyatt, beginning to turn his horse around. "I'll just have to go get the dogs."

Two or three clomps of his horse's hooves was enough. He heard a voice behind him.

"Hey, jes' you' hold on er minute," he said. "You say maybe you kin he'p us?"

Young Beaumont turned and saw a tall black man walking out from the trees.

"That's what I said, mister. If you and that kid I saw a minute ago just want to come with me, I'll see that you get all the help you need."

"Dat's fine, den, cuz we cum as chilluns ob da Father."

Wyatt eyed him with a puzzled look.

"What are you talking about?"

Behind him, Wyatt now saw the brush and woods filling up with blacks of all sizes and shapes coming out of hiding. There were nine of them! This would be his biggest haul yet.

"I wuz jes' axin' effen dis be da right place," said the man.

"This is the right place, all right," said Wyatt. Even as he spoke, his brain was calculating how to get this catch back to Oakbriar and whether to contact Murdoch. This could be a huge feather in his cap, and who could tell but there might be a sizeable reward. But he didn't have a gun with him, and two of the black men, not to mention that big burly teenager, looked tough. It might not be such a good idea to risk it on his own.

"Where you from?" asked Wyatt.

"Norf Carolina, suh."

"Well, that's just fine. I'll tell you what, so that you won't have to walk so far, because I'm sure you're all plenty tired, I'll just ride back and hitch up a wagon and come back for you. How does that sound? You all just wait right here for me. But get down out of sight like you were until you hear me again. You can't tell when someone might be coming along who's not as friendly to runaways as me."

"All right, suh . . . I reckon we kin do dat."

Wyatt spun around and galloped off as fast as he could make his horse move. He would be back within fifteen minutes . . . with help, and with guns.

"I don' like dat boy's looks, no how, Macon," said Mrs. Diggs at his side. "He don' look like no frien' ter me."

"But he said dis was da right place."

"Only cuz you put da words right in his mouf."

Diggs felt a tugging of his shirt at his side. He glanced down at his seven-year-old daughter.

"Daddy," she said, "you said it wrong. You wazn't supposed ter say nufin' till he ax'ed you who we wuz from."

"He did ax where we'd cum from," said Diggs.

"Da girl's right, Macon," now said his wife's cousin, the only other grown man of the group, who had come along with his sixteen-year-old son. "He din't ax dat till you'd already spilled it 'bout bein' chilluns ob da Father. You wuz su'pozed ter wait."

"An' he ax'd *where* we'd come from," now said the other woman of the group, Macon's widowed sister. "He neber ax'd *who* we wuz cum from."

"I din't like his look, no how," repeated Emily Diggs. "An' duz you recollect what he said w'en you said it, Macon? He said, 'Wha'chu talkin' 'bout?' Dat don't soun' right ter me."

Macon only had to run the conversation with Wyatt Beaumont through his brain one more time to realized he had blundered badly.

"We got's ter git outer here!" he said. He turned and fled into the woods, with eight others on his heels.

When Wyatt Beaumont returned to the spot with Brad McClellan and found the nine runaway slaves gone without a trace, he cursed himself for being such a fool to have forgotten the dogs. With two rifles between them and enough rope to tie them all up in the back of the wagon, the threat of using dogs had never crossed his mind again. He hadn't intended on having to go after them—he figured the simpleton had believed him.

He glanced around at the empty road and quiet forest.

"You sure this is the spot?" asked Brad.

"Of course I'm sure . . . what kind of a fool do you take me for! This is where they were, all nine of them."

He swore loudly again, then grabbed his rifle and emptied it into the surrounding woods. When his temper had cooled and the echoes of the useless shots died away, Brad spoke again.

"What do you want to do?" he said. "They can't have gotten far, especially if there were kids. We can't just let them go."

"I don't intend to let them go. If there's a reward, I intend to collect it. If not, I intend to see that lying nigger swinging from one of these trees. But we're not going to find them without the hounds."

He paused and thought a minute.

"You stay here," he said. "Keep out of sight, but just in case they are close by and come out when they think we're gone. I'll make a lot of clatter with the wagon so they'll think we're leaving. Keep both rifles and the rope. I'll go for the dogs and get back as soon as I can. I shouldn't be longer than three-quarters of an hour."

On a not-too-distant part of his estate, Richmond Davidson heard the shots. He had no idea of their cause, but shots fired from an unknown gun rarely signaled welcome news. Fortunately Dusty was saddled and nearby. He was in the saddle and galloping in the direction of the sound almost by the time echoes had ceased.

It was not a suspicion exactly, but from the sound of the shots in relation to his own position, the ridge, and the Brown tract, Richmond guessed where he might possibly gain a vantage point to tell him something. He gained the bare crest of the ridge a couple miles east of Harper's Peak about ten minutes later. He reined in and gazed into the valley below him. There was a wagon in the distance making for Oakbriar. Whoever was at the reins might have had nothing to do with the shots, but he was moving fast and that might tell something in itself.

He gazed about and thought for a minute. What the occupant of the wagon could possibly have been doing on the isolated and mostly abandoned road between Dove's Landing and the old Brown place, he hadn't an idea. But as the land was his, he ought to at least investigate.

He wheeled Dusty around, and made for the valley.

Brad McClellan was feeling very proud of himself. Not only had he single-handedly coerced all nine runaways out of the woods with a pretended slave dialect, he had managed, with threat of the rifle in his hand—a threat aided immeasurably by Wyatt's violent volley of shots a few minutes earlier—to tie up the three men. The women and children would be easy. Wyatt, of course, would never condescend to speak a word of praise, but he would be pleased with Brad's efforts. The only ones who wouldn't be pleased, he thought to himself as he tied up one of the women, were the dogs.

He had just secured the last of the men to a tree when Brad heard something behind him. He grabbed his rifle, spun around, but saw nothing.

As he resumed his task, several of the blacks saw a strange sight, a man without boots and wearing no shirt emerging from behind a tree with a finger to his lips indicating silence. What it could mean, they didn't know. But the boy with the gun and his friend certainly weren't about to help them. Whoever the man was, therefore, they had nothing to lose by doing as he said. And thus, though the eyes of the children widened, fortunately none of them made a peep as he approached, tiptoeing in stocking feet and with shirt in hand toward their captor.

For all his gentleness, Richmond Davidson was yet a large and powerful man, several inches taller and easily outweighing Brad McClellan by thirty or forty pounds. As the gun again lay on the ground at his side and he was occupied with the ropes with his back turned, in one swift movement, Brad found some soft object thrown round his head and eyes and his chest and arms suddenly clutched in a grip of great strength.

He shouted and swore but to little effect. It required but a few eye signals and nods of the head for Brad's silent assailant to bring the women and children quickly to his aid. Within seconds, Brad was facedown on the ground with Richmond's shirt so tightly bound around his eyes, and part of it stuffed in his mouth, that he would be able to see or say nothing however hard he struggled. Emily Diggs and her sister-in-law busied themselves with the ropes meant for them.

"Who is dat man?" finally said one of the children, breaking the strange silence of the rescue.

"Shush, chil'," she said.

The moment Brad was secure, though the women were taking no chances and continued to coil the rope around him, Richmond leapt to his feet, grabbed the gun and tossed it into the brush, made another deliberate and forceful gesture with finger to mouth, especially toward the children, to silence, then sprang at the ropes binding the three men who watched the marvel unfold with expressions of silent wonder.

Within three minutes, the troop of nine, led by their strange savior—who had retrieved his boots but left his shirt behind as the only evidence, he hoped not sufficient to identify him, that he had ever been here—were making as quickly as possible through the woods.

"But who dat man?" asked one of the children again.

"I said shush, chil'," snapped Emily. "He's a frien', dat's who he is, an' effen he wants ter tell mo', he'd do it w'en he's ready. Till den, you keep yo' mouf shut."

They continued for perhaps four minutes, until Richmond judged them out of immediate earshot, though he continued to listen for sound of the return of reinforcements, which he now had no doubt was the purpose of the wagon he had seen from the ridge.

He stopped, then gazed around at the five adults as they gathered close around him.

"The lady is right," he said, speaking softly. "I am a friend. Where are you from?"

"Norf Carolina, suh," answered Macon.

Judging him to be the leader of the group, Richmond looked into his eyes.

"Who do you come from?" he asked.

The man hesitated and glanced at his wife. She nodded.

"We come as chilluns ob da Father," replied Macon Diggs.

Richmond smiled. "I thought as much, but I needed to know. You are safe now. You are with others of his children. Now," he added, "I must retrieve my horse. If they find it, my identity will be discovered. You must never speak of what happened back there, or what you will see and hear later today. Many lives are at stake. And though we are children of the Father, we must be quiet and prudent children. Do you all understand?"

"Yes, suh," said Macon, as eight heads around him nodded vigorously. "But, suh," he added, "dat man, he say he wuz goin' fo' da dogs, an' I's feared dey'll come follerin' us."

Richmond stopped to think. "Yes, you're right," he said, "we had better go by a different route than I had planned."

He thought again. He would take them up toward the ridge, and, if need be, hide them in one of the caves. Though that would be risky too. How could he get the dogs off their scent? One thing he must *not* do was head straight for Greenwood!

"All right, then," he said at length, still pondering his options, "wait right here. Do not move. You will be safe until I return."

Fifty

~

Cherity's father returned from the offices of the *Herald* early in the afternoon, weary from exertion but obviously optimistic over what he had heard. "The magazine's editor would like to talk to you," he said to Seth. "I think the job is yours if you want it."

"Even though I know nothing about it?"

"Nobody knows anything about it," he laughed. "It's that new. He is looking for someone who can learn."

"I suppose I can do that."

"There is a photographer in the city who is familiar with all the latest developments and has equipment we can either rent or buy. He'll train you first, then you'll bring what you learn to the magazine."

"You make it sound like I've already got the job!" laughed Seth.

"Just come in with me tomorrow and meet my editor."

"Fair enough."

"I'll introduce you myself," said James. "We'll go in after breakfast. I think he may want you to begin immediately."

True to his prediction, by ten o'clock the following morning Seth had been hired at the *Herald* and was on his way to meet the man who would train him in photographic techniques. He spent several hours at Mr. Phillips' studio, then returned to the paper where he was introduced to the typesetting department. He returned to the Waterses' home late in the afternoon, hands smudged with black ink and enthusiastic with the prospects of his new job.

"Are you going to like it?" asked Cherity.

"It's remarkable!" answered Seth buoyantly. "You can reproduce anything you want on photographic plates, creating an image that's just like the thing looks in real life. I could hardly believe what I saw! Mr. McClarin, that's the paper's editor—"

"Yes—I know him. He's been over for dinner."

"Oh, right . . . of course. Anyway, he says eventually we will be able to run photographs in the paper right along with the news reports. That may be years away, no one knows yet. It's all new. For now they are concentrating on the magazine, possibly with woodcuts from the photographs."

"What will your job be?"

"I'll go out—once we get the equipment—and take photographs to go in the magazine. If President Lincoln, say, comes to Boston to give a speech, I might go and photograph the event. The next week when the people open their magazine they will see a picture of the president and the crowd and everything."

"That is amazing."

"Or I might take portraits of people—close up, just their face, I mean. Hey, I might take a picture of you!"

"Not for the magazine!" Cherity laughed.

"No, but for your father to hang on his wall. What a great job . . . yes, I am going to like it! Your father was right—it sure beats loading cargo onto ships at the docks. And I have him to thank for it. Which reminds me, I need to talk to him about paying for my room and board now that I am working again, until I find another place."

"What—you're not going to move? You just got here!"

"I know, but I can't presume on your father's hospitality."

"Why not?" laughed Cherity. "We have a house full of empty rooms. Your parents didn't make us pay when we came for a visit."

The thought of such a thing brought laughter to Seth's lips. "But this is different," he said. "I came to Boston to work."

"I don't think it's different at all. We are not a hotel! I won't hear of you paying for room and board."

"Well, I think it is only right that I talk to your father about it."

Meanwhile, events back at Seth's Virginia home were about to take a startling and unexpected turn.

Still not altogether sure how he was going to get the troop of runaways to the plantation, and at the same time throw off Wyatt's dogs—if he could smell them himself from twenty feet, thought Richmond, the dogs would easily track their every step!—Richmond led them by a circular route, away from Greenwood at first, then toward the ridge and in roundabout fashion across a distant corner of the Brown tract.

But he was not the only one who had heard the shots from Wyatt's rifle forty minutes earlier. Even now, unknown to him, Richmond was being watched and his movements monitored by someone other than either Wyatt Beaumont or Brad McClellan.

When the watcher judged that no harm would come to anyone by the revelation of his presence, at last he stepped out from the shadows where he had been moving in a line along with the little group. He now waited as they approached.

Richmond detected the movement, froze momentarily in panic, then, as the sunlight fell on the face in front of him, broke into a great smile.

"Sydney!" he exclaimed. "What . . . I cannot believe my eyes!"

He dropped the reins of his horse and ran forward, shook Sydney's hand vigorously, then embraced him warmly.

Macon Diggs and his group of fugitives stood watching the display with mouths hanging open. What kind of white man was this who not only risked his life for them, but actually embraced blacks!

"My friend . . . *what* are you doing here!" said Richmond.

"I came back," answered Sydney, obviously sharing Richmond's joy.

"I can see that! And your family?"

"They are well and safe. We are still near Philadelphia where I am working for your friend Travers. He has been very good to us. But I had to come back."

"But why? Haven't you heard—war is about to break out."

"I have to help," replied Sydney. "I have to help our people. I found myself unable to sleep at night, words haunting me from the day I escaped my old plantation. There was a boy sleeping beside me who heard me getting up. 'Take me with you,' he pleaded. But I refused, because of my family. Perhaps I had no choice, I will never know. But his words have haunted me ever since. I finally had no choice but to try to help him, and perhaps help others get North, just as you and so many helped us, just as you, I presume, are even now risking so much to help those standing behind you. Can I do less? Ought I do less? So I am going back."

"I applaud your courage, Sydney," said Richmond. "But it is becoming more perilous all the time. You will bring great danger upon yourself."

Sydney nodded. "Freedom comes with a price, my friend," he said. "But there are so many in bondage who dream of a new life, how can I not try to help them? And these?" he added, gesturing behind Richmond.

"A group of runaways I just snatched from capture a few minutes ago. There is much to tell you, Sydney! Many are now coming to us. But first we must get these people, and you, to safety. Will you help me?"

"That is why I returned. What can I do?"

Richmond thought a moment, then turned to the leader of the band of refugees.

"Diggs," he said, "this is Sydney LeFleure. He is a runaway slave like you, and a friend. He will take you to safety. Sydney, can you find our house from here?"

"I have been watching you and your house for a day," replied Sydney. "I needed to be certain I would bring no danger to you. Yes, I could find your home almost with my eyes closed."

"All right . . . good . . . but we have to throw the dogs off. Hmm . . . let me see . . . right, it could work—follow me, everyone."

Richmond took the reins of his horse from Diggs, who had picked them up when Richmond ran forward, and led out again, with Sydney at his side, as quickly as possible, until they came to a small stream that tumbled down the near side of the ridge not far from the Brown house and toward the river.

They arrived at the water's edge. Richmond stopped and turned to face the group.

"Now, we must be very, very careful," he said, untying a rope from his saddle. "We must fool the dogs, and they are not easily fooled. Diggs, take off your shirt. All the rest of you give me something you are wearing, scarf, shirt, cap . . . anything."

Confused but not inclined to argue, they proceded to do so.

"Sydney," said Richmond, "take them downstream a hundred or two hundred yards. They must stay in the middle of the water and not so much as touch a rock at the edge. By then you should be safe. Take them to the house. Carolyn will know what to do."

"What about you?"

"I will drop this lad's shirt," Richmond said as he began to collect the clothes, "on the other side, then tie the rest to the back of my horse and drag them from there on a wild-goose chase up the ridge. The dogs will follow the scent straight across the stream. At least that is what they will try first and I am confident they will pick it up and come after me. Then I will dispose of these things and make my own way back through town. Oh—Sydney—would you be willing to give me the shirt off your back?" grinned Richmond. The words had scarcely been asked before Sydney's shirt was over Richmond's head.

Two minutes later the scent decoy was tied in a bundle and attached to his saddle. Richmond crossed the stream, dragged the clothes about the ground, tossed the shirt a short distance away in the brush, then turned to watch the troop splashing their way carefully along the course of the streambed.

"See you at the house, Sydney!" he called.

He turned again and urged Dusty away, followed by the bundle of wet smelly clothes bounding on the ground behind him, and up the ridge. Already he could hear the baying of hounds behind him.

Thirty minutes later, having completed a complex and circuitous navigation of the ridge, and judging from the sound of it with the dogs having by now closed about half the distance, Richmond carefully made his way through thinning woods toward the plantation of Oakbriar. He was not afraid for his safety, for he knew well enough that Wyatt was not on the premises. But it would not do to be seen by Leon Riggs or any of the Beaumont slaves. Slowly he worked his way within two hundred yards of Denton's huge storage barn. Closer than that he probably ought not to press his luck.

He reined in, glanced about as he dismounted, then retrieved and untied the bundle of clothes. One by one he tossed the items into the brush and woods over as wide a distance as time permitted. Sneaking yet closer on foot, he threw two of the shirts almost to the barn. Then he crept back to Dusty, remounted, retraced his steps the way he had come until he crossed one of the well-worn wagon paths connecting various of the Beaumont fields, turned onto it, and galloped away.

Skirting the edge of Oakbriar so that he would not be seen, he made his way back to the main road, then galloped for Dove's Landing. He reached town, moving now at a leisurely pace, just about the time he judged Wyatt's hounds would be arriving in the precincts of their own home. What Wyatt would conclude to find himself staring at the back of his own barn when the trail finally went dead, he could only imagine. Stopping in at several shops to make certain he would be seen, Richmond then proceeded back to Greenwood.

Except for his recent accompaniment of Murdoch and his small mob, this was the first call Wyatt Beaumont had paid on Greenwood in three years. Back then he had been in a friendlier mood than he was today.

He rode up to the house with Brad McClellan at his side. Richmond had half expected to see one or another of them and thus had remained around the barns and stables all afternoon since his return. Sydney and their other guests were safely hidden away where no possible search would locate them. Seeing the sons of his two neighbors ride up, Richmond went out to meet them.

"Hello, boys," he said walking toward them as they dismounted. "I hope, Wyatt, that the circumstances of this visit are not so unpleasant as the last time you were here. I must say that I was disappointed to see you throwing in with a man like that Murdoch fellow against lifelong friends."

"Like I told your wife, Mr. Davidson," said Wyatt without a smile, "there are things that have to be done. We brought back your shirt," he added, tossing the shirt on the ground that he had untied from Brad's face.

"What do you mean, Wyatt," he said. "I am missing no shirt."

"You didn't lose that earlier today?" he said nodding toward the shirt on the ground.

"I did not lose a shirt."

"If I'm not mistaken, I believe I have seen you in that before."

"I don't know how you could have seen me in it."

"Have it your own way. You won't mind if we just have a look around, then?"

"Do you mean like your friend Murdoch did?" asked Richmond, "rummaging through our home, treating my wife rudely. . . . I am afraid if that is the sort of thing you have in mind, then I do mind, Wyatt."

"So you refuse to let us carry out a search?"

"For what purpose do you want to search Greenwood."

Wyatt, who had been absently glancing about, suddenly spun around and took a menacing step toward the man who had once been his father's friend.

"To look for runaway slaves, you old fool!" he shouted. "What do you think we would be looking for!"

"Wyatt," said Richmond, staring straight into his eyes, "if you were to ask with a gracious tone, and have good reason for doing so, and were respectful to my wife and workers, of course I would let you go

wherever you wish on Greenwood land. But if you cannot speak with
more respect than you just have, whatever our differences may be,
I am going to have to ask you to leave my property."

Wyatt uttered a vile imprecation, then walked to his horse.

"You cannot win, Davidson!" he yelled rudely. "You will be found
out!"

Fifty-One

*E*vents quickly overtook Seth's enthusiastic outlook about his future. President Lincoln would be delivering no speeches in Boston anytime soon. Whether he would be photographing portraits of Cherity only time would tell.

Midway through the morning, word suddenly clattered by telegraph into the offices of the Boston *Herald* that preempted all the other day's news. Everything planned for the front page was immediately scrubbed. Within the hour, new headlines read:

"War Breaks Out. Insurgents Fire On Ft. Sumter. Battle in Charleston Harbor Rages. Civilians gather on rooftops to cheer."

After returning to the *Herald* building from his morning at the Phillips' studio, Seth's first thought when he heard the news was for Jeffrey. Had his ship reached South Carolina and was *he* now involved in the fighting?

He searched the editorial offices for James Waters, but he was nowhere to be found. As he had the day before, what remained of Seth's afternoon was spent in typesetting, helping to prepare an extra edition that would broadcast to all Boston that war had begun.

Seth returned to the Waters home late in the afternoon as the edition he had been working on hit the streets. Cherity's father had been home for several hours. Seth found father and daughter in the kitchen. The serious expressions on their faces made it obvious that they had heard the news.

James was seated at the table, staring straight ahead. His face was pale.

"You heard?" said Seth, walking in and sitting down.

James nodded. "I came home as soon as word began to spread around the office," he said. "I suppose there are historic stories to be written, but I wanted to be with Cherity."

"What does it all mean, Daddy?" asked Cherity. "What will happen?"

"Do you remember when we were in Kansas?" James asked.

"Of course."

"You were reading dime novels then about make-believe stories. But now the country is facing a real-life tragedy. It means that our country may be falling apart . . . or else about to break into a terrible war no one can stop."

They sat for a while contemplating James' words.

"But . . . I still don't understand *why*," said Cherity. "I know what's happening. But I cannot see why—what good will it do either side?"

"Probably none," answered her father. "The conflict five years ago was about whether Kansas should be admitted to the Union as a slave or a free state. In a way, this war is still over the same question—but whether people should be slaves or free.

"They say it is about states' rights. But it's not really about that either. States' rights are perfectly secure. But leaders in the South see their power diminishing as free states more and more outnumber slave states. Yet for the life of me I cannot understand the mentality of those who want war. Pro-slavery forces still control the Senate. Lincoln says slavery will not be tampered with where it already exists. Perhaps our Virginian friend can enlighten us as to why the South seems bent on its own destruction," James added, glancing at Seth with expectant expression.

Seth shook his head and sighed. "I'm sorry, I can't. I think it's idiotic to send the country into a war when nothing is really at stake. It is like you said—slavery is secure in existing slave states. The Senate still supports slavery. So why do they want to form their own country? I think it's nonsense."

"You don't sound much like a Southerner," said James. "But then neither does your father."

"I am a Virginian," said Seth. "But I am also the son of Richmond Davidson."

"Then what *is* this war about?" asked Cherity again.

Both men glanced at each other and shook their heads.

James closed his eyes and began to breathe rapidly. His face grew yet more pale. Seth glanced at Cherity in concern. She had taken note of the change and recognized the look on his face from the previous episode.

"Daddy . . . what is it?" asked Cherity in alarm.

"What do you mean, dear . . . I'm . . . I'm fine. . . . " In spite of his words, James' voice was weak.

"You look . . . tired and pale."

She stood and walked over to his chair. "Seth and I are going to help you to bed."

James seemed to come to himself and glanced at his daughter with a thin smile. He struggled to draw in a deep breath and winced slightly as his hand went to his chest. Gradually his breathing eased. "This news has, I suppose, been a blow," he said. "Now that you mention it, I do feel rather tired. It has been a stressful day."

"Daddy . . . let me send for the doctor."

"Don't be silly . . . I'll be fine. It is just this terrible news. I'm worried for the country, my dear. I shall be fine. I would like a cup of tea, if you don't mind. Actually," he added, "I think I *will* let you help me up to my room, and I will take it there."

⟲

The next few days answered many uncertainties, even though Cherity's question, Why? remained a tragic conundrum. After a day and a half of ceaseless bombardment, Major Anderson ran the white flag of surrender up Fort Sumter's flagpole. He and his men were soon on their way North, with a Confederate flag flying over Ft. Sumter in place of the Stars and Stripes. The first battle had produced no casualties and had resulted in a resounding victory, as it was hailed in South Carolina, for the Confederacy. Optimism for a quick, painless, and easy victory swept through the South.

As the Union had a regular army of a mere 17,000 men, mostly on duty in the West, on the 15th of April President Lincoln called on the states for 75,000 volunteers to serve for three months. He was clearly expecting widespread fighting. Two days later, the president offered the field command of all Union forces to the most capable and experienced man in his army, General Robert E. Lee.

Lee hesitated, postponing a decision until he saw what his native state would do.

Virginia seceded from the Union on April 18 and the capital of the new Confederacy was moved from Montgomery to Richmond. Within the week, however reluctantly, Lee offered his services to the Confederacy and was given command of the Army of Virginia.[6]

Lincoln's call for troops was received in the South as a summons to war. Suddenly Confederate flags could be seen across the river from Washington, D.C., and Lincoln feared an invasion and takeover of the capital before Union troops could reach Washington to defend it.

Tennessee, Arkansas, and North Carolina followed Virginia's lead and seceded to join the Confederacy. In every city and community throughout both North and South, passions ran high. Young men flocked by the tens of thousands to join the fight. So many joined on both sides that thousands were sent home.

The news of Virginia's secession, and Lee's decision, were more bitter blows to Seth than had been the firing on Fort Sumter. He was now a young man torn between two countries. He hardly slept that

---

[6]Lee confided to a pharmacist that he "was one of those dull creatures that cannot see the good of secession." But in the end he went with his state, and on April 23 accepted command of the Army of Virginia. He wrote a farewell note to a Northern friend: "I cannot raise my hand against my birthplace, my home, my children. I should like, above all things, that our difficulties might be peaceably arranged. . . . Whatever may be the result of the contest I foresee that the country will have to pass through a terrible ordeal, a necessary expiation for our national sins. May God direct all for our good, and shield and preserve you and yours." (*The Civil War,* Geoffrey C. Ward, Alfred Knopf, NY, 1990, p. 52)

night, his mind tormented by uncertainties and anxieties, confused thoughts and indecision.

What he would have given for an hour with his father to put everything into perspective!

James Waters spent most of the next day in bed tended by Cherity while Seth went into the city to work.

The outbreak of war, however, changed everything. He found it difficult to concentrate. Everyone at the paper, as was the entire city, as was the entire country, was swept up in war fever. Seth could think only of Greenwood and Cherity and James and Cynthia and Robert and his parents.

It was with great relief that he returned to the Waters home that evening to find James up and about and fussing at Cherity for babying him. The color in his face had returned and he seemed back to normal. Everyone's spirits were buoyed as a result.

The next several days passed like a blur. Seth continued to go into the city to work. Gradually he settled into a routine, learning the ropes at the paper. His apprenticeship with Mr. Phillips the photographer progressed rapidly. He began taking photographs and learning to process the chemical baths to develop them. The doctor called at the Waters home, but offered no more information than Cherity had already confided to Seth. And every day brought fresh news of national import that seemed to heighten tensions and ensure all the more that terrible things were on the horizon. Both armies, reports said, were growing by the tens of thousands. The clash when it came was destined to be horrific.

Seth spent the evening after the announcement of Virginia's secession writing to his parents, trying to put his thoughts into words, once again asking what they thought he should do. He had begun to wonder, he shared with them, whether his presence in the Waters home for an indefinite time as a guest was entirely proper, though, with James' health as it was, could he be useful? He shared briefly about James' medical condition which he knew they would be concerned about. He had wanted to talk to James about room and board, but had not found a suitable opportunity to do so. Should he, he asked, seek lodgings elsewhere? He was also anxious to know the mood in Virginia now that, technically, Greenwood was no longer even part of the United States. Finally, he asked his father's opinion of recent events, inviting him to share whatever insights and thoughts he had. As for himself, he confessed himself troubled and confused by developments.

Fifty-Two

*O*n the second Saturday afternoon following the outbreak of hostilities at Fort Sumter, Seth and Cherity went riding again in the afternoon. The mood was different. Both sensed that a change had come, that the innocence of youth had suddenly vanished in a past they would never know again. The happy season of their visit during the harvest at Greenwood a year and a half earlier and even their happy ride of a week ago now seemed fading into a mist of pleasant memory, while ahead loomed a future of uncertainty and doubt. It was a time to reflect and assess where they stood in a suddenly dramatically changed world.

"What will you do?" asked Cherity as they went. "Will you enlist to fight too, like they say every young man in the country is doing?"

"For which side would I fight?" laughed Seth morosely. "My loyalties are so confused I don't know what to think. I am a Virginian in Boston, a Southerner in the North . . . what am I supposed to do? It's not as if I could fight anyway? Me . . . *kill* another man? I do not think I could—even if I believed in a cause with all my heart. But there is no cause here that I believe in at all, except that the states of the South are wrong. I could certainly never kill for the cause of slavery. I hate slavery and I could never fight to preserve it. I would sooner fight to abolish it. But even for that, I don't think I could kill. How can Americans fight against themselves?"

"Aren't wars part of history?"

"A tragic part. They only happen because men are stupid, greedy, and arrogant. I hate the very thought of it. This war especially is just so wrong!"

"Will you go home then?" asked Cherity.

Seth sighed. "Of course, there is nothing I want so much, in one way, as to be home and with my parents right now. But to go home, now that Virginia has seceded, would put me right in the middle of Southern sentiment where, if I *didn't* fight for the Confederacy, I would probably be more ostracized than before, and maybe cause danger for my family. At least this far north I can blend in. My accent betrays me, I suppose, but I'm in no danger of being beat up or hanged or shot. I don't know what to do. I ask myself that same question every day—what should I do? Until I hear back from my father, I will do as he taught me—just do the thing that is set before me. So every day I will go to work and try to do the best job I can, until the Lord indicates that I am supposed to do something else. Sure, I feel an obligation to the country. But like I said, on which side do my loyalties lie? If there was only some way to fulfill my duty as an *American* without taking sides with either the Union *or* the Confederacy. I am very torn."

"Who knows . . . maybe God *will* show you such a path to walk."

Seth glanced over in surprise, not knowing how to respond to Cherity's statement. She was looking in the opposite direction and did not see his questioning expression.

A brief silence followed. The next words changed the subject in an unexpected direction.

"Do you mind if I ask you a personal question?" asked Cherity. "You don't have to answer if you don't want to."

"Sure."

"Why did you break off your engagement?" she said. "No, I don't mean it like that—I'm sorry. That was too blunt. It's just that you and Veronica seem so very different. It has puzzled me all this time. That's probably not a fair question either, I just—"

Cherity glanced away, her face suddenly very red. Why hadn't she just kept her mouth shut!

"No, that's okay—I don't mind," said Seth. "I'll answer your questions—yes, we were different. That's why I broke it off, because I finally realized how little we had in common. There was no real *friendship* between us. She doesn't even like horses."

"How can *anyone* not like horses!" exclaimed Cherity.

"That was Veronica," laughed Seth. "And really . . . I have you to thank."

"For what?"

"For getting me out of the engagement."

"*Me* . . . what are you talking about?"

"It was your visit that made me see how little Veronica and I had ever really talked or shared about anything. After you and your dad left, I began to realize—"

Seth stopped himself. Now it was his face that began to grow warm.

"Let's just say that I never had so much fun with anyone in my life as with you during those two weeks," he added. "Veronica suddenly seemed very, very boring."

"I *think* I will take that as a compliment," said Cherity, a hint of playfulness in her tone. "But . . . how did it happen then? I cannot imagine you proposing to her."

"Actually . . . I didn't."

"Then how did you become engaged?"

"It kind of came about by accident."

"You said something like that the day you came. But how can something so important as an engagement happen by accident?"

"Do you really want to hear about it?"

"Only if you want to tell me."

"It's horribly embarrassing, but . . . well, maybe it's been long enough that I can finally see the humor in it."

"What happened?"

"Well, Veronica invited me to dinner with her family . . . "

Seth went on to recount the details of the fateful evening at Oakbriar and his unpleasant conversation with Denton Beaumont.

"That is hilarious!" laughed Cherity. "Now I see why you say it just sort of happened."

"By the time I realized the mess I was in," said Seth, "I was too embarrassed to own up to it and face the music. I didn't even tell my parents and that was something I had never done before. Well, eventually I did, but it took me long enough. I should never have let it go on so long."

"What happened when you did?"

"Veronica yelled at me and said she never wanted to see me again—which she hasn't—and her father said some insulting things, and I left with my tail between my legs . . . but *greatly* relieved to be out of the pickle I had gotten myself into!"

"That is really a funny story!"

"It wasn't funny at the time! And there have been dangerous consequences—the vendetta against me and Greenwood has been terrible."

Again it was silent for a minute or two. Then Seth spoke.

"All right, then," he said, "it's my turn to ask *you* a personal question."

"Uh . . . I suppose fair is fair," rejoined Cherity, having no idea what Seth might be thinking.

"Something has changed about you since I saw you last," said Seth. "I don't just mean that you're older . . . you seem, I don't know, more at peace with yourself and life and everything. There have been a couple times, if I didn't know better, when I've looked in on you sitting beside your father's bed . . . that it seemed like you were praying. And then that comment you made a minute ago, that God would show me what I'm supposed to do. I guess what I'm asking is . . . are you . . . I mean, do you still consider yourself an atheist?"

Cherity smiled. "No," she said. "I know now that everything you told me about God is true."

"Why the change?"

"Actually, it happened when we were in Virginia with your family. I wanted to tell you before we left, but I suppose I was a little embarrassed at first too. I just couldn't find a good time. It's hard to talk about such personal things. I mean . . . it's not that hard once you are talking, but it's hard to bring them up out of the blue. Do you know what I mean?"

"Sure."

"The time has to be right."

"Do you want to tell me about it now?"

"I've wanted to ever since. I should have written to you too, but . . . well, maybe I'm no better at letters than you. . . . Well," she added, looking up shyly, "I didn't know if it would be proper with . . . you know . . . with you being engaged and all."

Cherity paused and looked away, then drew in a deep breath.

"I had a long talk with your mother," she began. "I can't remember where you were right then, out somewhere. It was one of the most wonderful times I've ever had with anyone. I felt . . . I don't know, almost like I had a mother of my own for the first time in my life. It's different for a girl to feel loved by a woman, and I felt so loved by your mother. She was so warm to me. And when she told me about God being my Father and caring for me in a special way because I'd grown up without a mother . . . I don't know how to explain it, but something happened in my heart . . . her love got inside me and somehow God's love came along with it. After we'd talked I went out for a long ride—"

"Let me guess—Harper's Peak?"

Cherity smiled. "Where else? I had already grown so fond of it up there, I could think of nowhere else to go to be alone. Maybe that's where I began to learn how to pray, though it was in your parents' arbor the next day, on that little stone bridge, where I first told God that I wanted him for a Father, and that I wanted to be his daughter too."

"That's wonderful," said Seth. "I'm so happy for you."

"I wanted to tell your mother too. I must have started ten letters to her since. But somehow I could never say it exactly like I felt inside."

"She would love to hear from you. I know you were very special to her too . . . you *are* special to her, I should say."

"Maybe I'll try again."

"Does your father know?" asked Seth.

"I think he does . . . sort of," nodded Cherity. "I've tried to tell him. But I haven't told him directly. Knowing of his own struggles about God and church and everything, it's hard to know what to say. I love him so much, I don't want him to think it makes me respect him any less that I have found a fulfilling life with God that he was not able to experience himself."

"Give him time. Maybe he will eventually."

"I worry about how much time he has left."

"God gives every man as much time as he needs."

"Do you really think that is true?"

"I suppose I'm too young to have the lifetime experience to back up such a statement," replied Seth. "What do I know about time, right—I'm only twenty-one! But I've heard my dad say it many times. He wasn't even walking with God when he was my age and look at him now. He always says God takes as much time to accomplish whatever he purposes in the life of every man and woman."

Cherity sighed. "I hope you're right. But I can't help worrying."

The silence that followed this time was more lengthy as they made their way along a narrow path beside a small river.

"We probably ought to be heading back," said Cherity as they drew alongside. "I'll take you by another route than we came."

They began making their way, by many turnings and paths and trails Seth had not yet seen in several rides with Cherity, again in direction of the stables.

"Hey, by the way," said Seth as they came out of a small wood. The edges of the city were again visible in the distance. "I've meant to mention it and keep forgetting—nice saddle!"

"Thanks! A friend gave it to me."

"Some friend—giving you a beat-up old thing like that!" rejoined Seth, his eyes twinkling.

"I know it's old and worn, but I like it better that way. It makes it all the more special a gift. My friend used it himself for years and broke it in for me."

As she spoke Cherity turned and smiled radiantly.

All at once a revelation filled Seth's brain—this was no little girl riding beside him. This was a young *woman*! Suddenly it dawned on him—Cherity Waters was just about the most beautiful young woman he had ever seen!

He glanced away, unable for a moment to catch his breath, then back. She was still gazing straight into his eyes.

"What!" she said, smiling yet the more. "Why are you looking at me funny!

"Oh, I . . . I didn't mean . . . was I looking at you funny!" Seth stammered. He was unable to hold her eyes. "Sorry, I don't know what I was thinking."

He gave his horse a gentle whack of the reins and cantered ahead.

Wow! he thought, drawing in several deep breaths. Would he ever be able to look into her eyes again without being undone?

They were nearly back to the stables. Ahead they looked up to see a horse galloping toward them at great speed. As it neared they reined in.

"Miss Waters," said the rider, out of breath and pulling to a hasty stop.

"Yes, I am Cherity Waters," said Cherity.

"I was sent to find you," he said. "It's your father . . . he's had a bad fall and—"

Whatever else the messenger was about to say was lost in the hooves of Cherity's horse thundering away. Seth shouted to his mount and was soon flying across the heath toward the stables after her. By the time he pulled up and dismounted, she was already running for the carriage.

Fifty-Three

$\mathcal{A}$s they pulled up in front of the house, Cherity recognized Dr. Elliott's buggy on the street. She jumped down, ran through the gate and up the porch steps, burst through the door and rushed straight upstairs to her father's room.

The doctor was standing beside the bed. A figure lay upon it, thin, motionless, and white, covered by a single sheet whose color was nearly indistinguishable from the pallor of the face looking up from beneath it with eyes closed.

Slowly Cherity approached. The doctor heard her steps and turned.

"Is . . . is he . . . ?" Cherity began in a whisper.

"He is alive," replied the doctor, also in a soft voice as if in reverence for a nearby world of which he knew nothing and whose closer approach he could not control. "But I will not mislead you, Miss Waters, the attack your father has had is more serious than the others. I am not altogether hopeful."

"Can you do nothing?"

"All we can do is wait."

Cherity breathed in deeply, trying to calm herself.

"Every other time, Doctor," she said, "you have been vague. I want you to tell me exactly what it is and what to expect."

"I suppose you deserve that much," he replied. "Your father's condition, in its simplest terms, is a weakness of heart. There can be many causes, but generally it stems from what we call a fatty degeneration of the heart muscle."

"And what is the prognosis?"

"It is my duty to tell you that death from this ailment can be sudden. At the same time, such is not inevitable. Conditions such as your father's often persist for ten or fifteen years. The results are unpredictable. However, the fact that your father has had a series of minor episodes, leading now to this severe attack, no doubt brought on by the excitement of his nervous system caused by recent events and overexertion . . . we must be realistic. It may have proved too much for a system already weakened, as I say, by prior episodes."

"What are you saying, Doctor? Is . . . is he dying?" asked Cherity, her voice trembling slightly.

"His system is weak. He may be near the end, but I can say no more. There may be a full recovery, but it would be misleading to tell you to expect it."

Cherity's hand went to her mouth and she turned away. Seth was standing in the open doorway. He had heard everything.

Slowly she walked toward him as her eyes filled. She walked straight into his arms, where she stood for a few moments quietly sniffing in jerky breaths.

Gradually she came to herself, realized what she had done.

"I'm . . . I'm sorry," she said backing away, looking up with a forced smile. "I forgot myself."

She left the room and sought her own bed, where she lay down and wept.

Seth and the doctor were left alone. Seth approached with outstretched hand. "I am Seth Davidson," he said. "I am . . . a friend of the family, you might say. I've been staying here about a week."

"Dr. Elliott . . . Garth Elliott, Mr. Davidson," replied the doctor, shaking Seth's hand.

"Is there anything to be done, Doctor?"

"Only rest. We must wait to see how his system responds. I have done all I can do for him now. Mrs. Porterfield is downstairs. You will, I assume, be on hand?"

"Yes, of course."

"Then keep him comfortable and notify me if there is a change. If he comes to, try to get water into him, perhaps some soup. Do not let him get up even if he says he feels well, which I doubt after what has happened. But he is a determined man and one never knows . . . in any event, as I say, do not let him get out of bed or eat solid food. Even that could tax his system. But if he does wake up, send for me."

"We will. Thank you, Doctor."

With another shake of the hands, Dr. Elliott left the house. Seth pulled the straight-backed chair from in front of the desk across the room and took a seat beside the bed.

The rest of the day and evening passed quietly. Cherity, Mrs. Porterfield, and Seth sat alternately by James' bedside. He came to himself several times, took a few sips of water, tried to speak with Cherity, but was too weak to carry on a lengthy conversation.

He slept most of the night, and the next day the prayerful waiting continued. Cherity tended him faithfully, forcing smiles when she must but with a heavy heart.

Her father awoke midway through the morning, seemed more alert, drank some water and managed several spoonfuls of broth from Cherity's loving hand.

The house was preternaturally quiet the rest of the day, as if James' condition required soft steps and whispered voices, and as if noise itself would push him through the veil into the next world. Somehow the scarcity of words, perhaps augmented by the brief moments in her father's doorway when, as she said, Cherity had forgotten herself, heightened each of the young people's awareness of the other. Indeed, how could the presence of the other not loom larger than life in such an atmosphere where life itself hung in the balance, and where their ministering hands and loving hearts were working in such close proximity toward a common goal. All senses seemed suddenly attuned to greater pitch, especially the senses of the heart.

In pouring out her love upon her father, Cherity's heart thus opened likewise, though she had fought against it a year earlier, toward this uncommon young man—strong, handsome, giving, humble, and fun—who was suddenly, after a long absense, so close again. But how could her heart battle on two fronts at once? How could she protect herself from the pain of losing her father, without at the same time yielding in vulnerability to that other love from which she had already suffered once?

How could she fight it? Her heart was weakened by her father's condition. Perhaps the greater question had now become: Did she *want* to fight it?

She had been in grave danger before, but she was in love with Seth now . . . and she knew it.

Yet she *must* not betray her feelings. Not now. She could not give way to her emotions, or she would collapse entirely.

That Seth's thoughts were likewise gathering themselves about Cherity Waters in fuller fashion than previously was not a suspicion that once crossed Cherity's mind. He had never, not now, not in Virginia, not even in telling her about Veronica, given her the least reason to suspect that he regarded her as other than a good friend who shared a love for horses. True, he had said some nice things, but they were no more than *any* friend might say. Especially a friend like Seth. He was *nice*—a true Southern gentleman. He was gracious to everyone. He had been such a gentleman toward Veronica, whom apparently he did not love, that he had nearly married her to keep from hurting her feelings. She could not, Cherity told herself, allow her feelings to be betrayed by the kindness of his nature. Even a mere friend would offer the arms of consolation at a difficult time. She had wept momentarily on his chest, feeling the strength of his arms around her. It meant nothing. If Mrs. Porterfield's father were dying, he would probably embrace her too.

And Cherity's growing admiration for Seth—almost awe of him—as a spiritual being more like his parents than she had realized, only accentuated the gulf she supposed existed between them, and made all the more unlikely the possibility of intimate approach. He was so entirely *God's* young man, was there even room in his heart for one such as she? Did such devotion to God allow a sharing of the deepest regions of the soul? True, his parents had room for God and one another. But did Seth?

That Cherity Waters, in Seth's mind, was as far above Veronica as a young woman of developed character and maturity and spiritual hunger, as he seemed above her to hers, prompted corresponding thoughts to pass through the heart of the young squire so recently arrived in the North from Virginia.

Nor let it be supposed that for this young man and this young woman, at this crossroads moment of their lives, because their thoughts and feelings and heart pulsings mingled love of God with love of man toward woman and woman toward man, that such indicated less love on either side. The truest love of woman for man and man for woman will be that love which is lifted to the heights of its own fullness on the wings of love for God, in whose heart are born all loves human and all thoughts divine.

There is no separation, no dividing line, in *Love*. True love for God draws up into itself all other forms of the great *Agape*, including that holy *Eros* designed by him as no less a reflection of his own being than other loves—the wonderful mystery that draws a man and woman into oneness of heart.

Fifty-Four

The Sunday sun of late afternoon had begun to drift toward the western horizon beyond the city of Boston. Cherity's father had had fits of wakefulness on and off all day, though by the weakness of his body and the pallor of his countenance he appeared not appreciably better. He had managed to drink a little but had eaten nothing other than what broth Cherity could spoon into his mouth. He had exchanged tender words with Cherity, who had been at his bedside nearly the whole day. Though she had wept, she had done her best to hide her tears from him. He had been asleep again for several hours.

Suddenly he awoke, more alert and clearheaded than since the attack. Cherity, in the chair at his side, had dozed off. She was startled into wakefulness by his voice.

"Cherity, dear," she heard him say in a firm tone, "are you still there?"

"Yes . . . yes, Daddy, here I am," she replied. She came quickly to herself and leaned toward him.

He turned his head toward her and smiled feebly. She saw immediately that his eyes were wider and brighter than they had been all day. She bent down and kissed his forehead.

"How are you feeling, Daddy?"

"Better . . . but tired. So tired. But I shall be out of this bed in no time. Is Seth at home?"

"Yes, Daddy. I think he is writing a letter to his father."

"Ah, yes . . . a good man, a good friend. Ask Seth if he would come up for a moment or two."

Cherity nodded and left the room. Seth appeared a minute later at Cherity's side.

"Ah . . . Seth, my boy," said James from the bed, "do you have a minute to spare an old man?"

"I have all the time you would like, Mr. Waters. You sound much improved."

"Cherity, dear," said James, "do you mind . . . if we men . . . are alone a few minutes?"

"Of course not, Daddy."

Cherity left the room a bit curious, closing the door behind her. Seth sat down in the chair she had vacated, and waited.

"Seth, my boy," James began after a moment, his voice gradually gaining strength for what he knew he needed to do, "there is an errand I need you to run for me."

"Of course, sir."

"But first—what does the doctor say? I am . . . I am asking you because Cherity and Mrs. Porterfield would not be altogether honest with me. They would either cry . . . or keep the worst from me. It is time . . . for us to be men together. You must not pamper me with niceties. What did he say?"

"That you had a serious attack," replied Seth, "worse than the previous episodes, and that there was little he could do but wait and see how your system recovered."

"I see. Well, that is a more direct reply than the women would have given. Now for a more difficult question. I realize you are young . . . this may be awkward for you, but . . . your father is not here and I must depend on you instead. I think . . . I hope . . . I am a good judge of character and think . . . that you are able to the task."

"I will try to be, sir."

"Good. All right, Seth, my boy . . . does the doctor say I am dying?"

Seth gulped. James was right—this wasn't easy! "He, uh . . . did not say so," he tried to reply.

"Does he *think* I am dying?"

"I am not sure, sir. He was vague."

"Then tell me what he said."

"He said that people with your condition can die suddenly or live for years. He said that your system has been weakened. Though he could not make a definite prediction, he said . . . that is, he urged Cherity to be realistic, as he called it."

James took in the words thoughtfully, nodding slightly.

"All right . . . I see. It would seem that he *does* think I am dying, but could not bring himself to say it to Cherity in so many words. Is that how you would assess it, Seth?"

"I don't know, sir . . . possibly so. He did not seem to speak with a great deal of hope—I'm sorry."

"Don't apologize. I asked for candor and you have given it."

It was silent for several minutes. James was obviously thinking hard. The stark revelation of his condition, though not unexpected, was sobering.

"I hope what I said has not troubled you, Mr. Waters," said Seth at length, not sure what Cherity's father was thinking.

"What you said does not trouble me," rejoined James seriously. "But the reality does. I am not ready to die."

Seth did not know how to reply. "I'm . . . I am sorry, sir," he said. "I suppose no one is ever completely ready."

There was another pause.

"I loved her, Seth," said James a little sadly after a minute or two. "My wife, I mean . . . Cherity's mother."

"I know you did, sir."

Seth paused, wondering if he dared say what had just come into his mind.

"But . . . but did you love her enough," he added, "to trust God when he took her?"

"What are you talking about?" said James, startled at the bluntness of Seth's question.

"Forgive me for being bold, sir," said Seth. "But you said yourself that this was no time for niceties . . . and as I understand it, you turned your back on God because you were angry with him for your wife's death."

"Who told you that?"

"My father."

"What right had he to discuss my affairs—," James began irritably, then calmed again. "I'm sorry," he added. "Why shouldn't he have told you? Yes, it's true—but did I have no right to be angry? My wife was dead."

"I am not sure we ever have a right to be angry with God."

"Why not?"

"He gave us life."

"That gives him the right to take it away?"

"I don't know . . . but it seems likely."

"Will he send me to hell, then?"

"I doubt that. You have made your peace with him by now, I hope."

"I am trying. But it is hard, Seth, my boy. I am not sure he will listen to me."

"He listens to everyone."

"I have neglected him too long."

"Then don't continue to neglect him."

"It is too late to make right a wasted life."

"Not altogether wasted, sir. You have done much good by your writing. And you raised one of the loveliest of daughters. That is surely a wonderful legacy to leave the wife you loved."

At the word *legacy*, James seemed to start briefly where he lay. His brain spun off in an unexpected direction. But soon his thoughts returned to the more recent past.

"I should have given Kathleen more," he said.

"You gave her what you could, Mr. Waters."

"I'm sure Kathleen wished for better."

"She will forgive you—I am sure she already has."

"If only I could see her again face-to-face."

"You will, sir."

"Ah, but that implies I will go to heaven. To get there, God will have to forgive me too."

"Do you think his forgiveness, which created hers, will be less? He *will* forgive you, sir. All his forgiveness requires is a humble heart."

"A humble heart," James repeated with a long sigh, as if puzzling over the simplicity of it. "That is all, you say . . . " he added softly as if about to fall asleep again, "a humble heart."

He closed his eyes and continued to ponder Seth's words. For the moment death was easier to face than the condition of his heart.

He opened his eyes again.

"Are you there, Seth?" he asked.

"Yes, sir."

"I had nearly forgotten about the errand . . . go into the city. I want you to fetch my lawyer, a Mr. Glennie. He lives in Paul Revere Court, anyone can tell you the way. Tell him to come at once . . . I must dictate a will. I know it is Sunday . . . tell him he can bill me double if he likes, as if he is not already rich enough."

A brief spasm of chest pains followed, which rendered him too weak to speak further.

Seth left him. Cherity resumed her place by the bed and Seth left the house in search of Paul Revere Court.

Fifty-Five

Seth returned in the thin light of dusk an hour later with Mr. Glennie, who was shown immediately into the sick chamber. He was instructed to close the door behind him.

Seth went to his own room and fell dozing onto his bed. He was aroused by the sound of Cherity's voice. He turned on his bed and saw her standing in his doorway. The light of evening had fallen. It was a little after seven-thirty. He must have slept longer than he intended.

"My father wants you again," she said.

"How is he?"

"He is weak . . ."

"And his lawyer?"

"He left half an hour ago."

Seth rose and followed Cherity from the room. He found James much the same as before, though his skin, if anything, looked even paler, and his eyes stood out from a face grown gaunt.

"Ah, Seth . . . ," he whispered as Seth approached. "You do not mind leaving us again . . . do you, my dear?" he said to Cherity.

Cherity turned and walked from the room, handkerchief to her eyes, and once more closed the door behind her. Seth sat down at the bedside.

"I have . . . thought hard about . . . some of the things you said," began James. "You were right . . . I have much to answer for. I have tried to make a beginning . . . but they are difficult matters to face."

"Yes, sir."

"You have proved yourself worthy of my trust, Seth, my boy," James went on. "I asked you direct questions about my condition . . . you gave me direct answers. You had the courage even to tell me what I did not want to hear. I knew you were made of good stuff."

He drew in a deep breath, summoning the last strength his body possessed for what he must do.

"Now I am going to trust you even more, Seth, my boy," he said. "If I am dying, there are things I need to tell you, things I have never told another soul in my life."

"Wouldn't you . . . uh, I don't know, sir—rather speak with Cherity?" asked Seth.

"She is the last one who must know," rejoined James. "But someone must, in the event it becomes important for reasons I cannot now see. What I have to say is not in my will, or anywhere. But it must be known, and you are here with me. There is no one else. More importantly, I know I can trust you. I know you care for Cherity and will guard this information and do with it what is best."

"I will try to be worthy of your trust, Mr. Waters," said Seth solemnly, "if you truly think I am the one to tell."

"I do. Your being here is no accident. Perhaps you were sent to us for just this purpose. But first, bring me some water. I am very thirsty. Then I will tell you my story."

Seth left the bedroom, found an anxious Cherity waiting distractedly downstairs, told her that her father wanted to talk to him about something, he didn't know what, but had requested a drink first. Then he returned to James' room.

With effort he helped James prop his head on two pillows, then drink about half the glass of water. James lay back as Seth resumed his seat, closed his eyes for several long seconds, then drew in a deep breath and spoke.

"My name is not actually Waters," James began as Seth listened in amazement, "—that is, originally," he added. "It is Waters now, and is the legal name of my daughters, for I have been going by the name Waters for more than forty years. But I was born Swift Horse Brown. Neither am I a native New Englander. I was born in Georgia as a three-quarter-blood Cherokee."

As he listened, Seth's astonishment grew.

"I was orphaned at twelve," James continued. "My uncle brought me north to protect me from times of danger that had come upon our people. I was enrolled in a boarding school, my name was changed, and I was cut off from my roots. My father's name was Swift Water, and my uncle, in filling out the necessary forms, listed the name "Water" as my family name—which was somehow mistakenly copied later to *Waters*. He gave me the first name James, and that was that. Our family had descended from the great chiefs Moytoy and Attacullaculla. My grandmother, Nakey Canoe, daughter of the warrior Dragging Canoe, married an Englishman by the name of Alexander Brown. Their son, Swift Water Brown, was my father. In time I almost forgot that past altogether, aided by my surroundings and my uncommonly light complexion. Those were not good times to be an Indian in this country back in the teens, twenties, and thirties. A great rift threatened our tribe. My uncle made every effort to make sure my heritage would not be learned. My mother and father, you see, were killed by our own people when I was twelve. The danger to my life was also great.

"But I did not quite forget my roots, as you can see by Cherity's name," James went on, gathering strength as he spoke. "She does not know that her name is a reminder of the Cherokee blood that flows in her veins. The name on her birth certificate, though she has never seen the document, is Cherokee. Our visit to you brought to the surface many long-forgotten memories. Since then, especially as my health has failed, those memories have become important to me."

"But Cherity should know," said Seth.

"It is not yet time," replied James. "Dangers remain. This is still not a time when people of dark skin, whether colored or Indian, are looked upon with favor. Persecution is widespread. You will know when the time is right, but I do not think that time is yet."

Though his voice was soft, it seemed to summon one final surge of strength as he spoke. In some strange and mystic way, Seth felt that he was in the presence of an ancient heritage he scarcely understood but that called to deep places within him.

"I kept my Cherokee past from my daughters for the same reason that my uncle kept my identity from those at the boarding school to whom he entrusted me. When Andrew Jackson was president, Cherokees were treated as are Negro slaves today. I did not want such a fate to befall my daughters. I thought it in their best interest never to know. And I was the last descendant in my family line since my uncle never married."[7]

James paused and smiled. "I always wondered if Cherity's fascination with the West and Indians originated with her Cherokee blood."

Again he paused briefly, thinking.

"And yet . . . times are changing," he went on. "I want you to know. If the right time comes . . . you will know what to do with the information I will share with you."

"I know Cherity would treasure her heritage," said Seth.

"Perhaps that day will come. But there remain forces in this country determined to prevent our people laying full claim to their birthright. If her true identity were known, her life could be in danger. There is much at stake. The Cherokee future as Americans is in doubt, as is that of the Negro race. There are three races of Americans, but at present two of them do not share in the dream of life enjoyed by those of pure European ancestry. What I have done, for good or for ill, I did to protect my daughters from the hatred I have seen toward our kind. You must promise me, Seth, not to tell Cherity unless—"

A fit of mild coughing stopped him briefly.

"Unless what?" asked Seth.

"Unless . . . you are *sure* the time is right."

"I will do my best to be faithful to your request," nodded Seth.

James continued for another thirty minutes, telling Seth of a rich legacy of an ancient people, and his own part in it. By the end of that

---

[7]See Appendix Note 9—Hiding Cherokee Blood

time, his voice had again begun to weaken. The effort was taxing him. But he was determined to see it through.

"So you see, Seth," James concluded, "the visit to you and your parents rekindled much because of your strange Cherokee neighbor called Brown. Ever since I have wondered if he and my uncle could be the same man. Imagine it—my uncle your own grandfather's friend, and then your father and I meeting coincidentally after all that time! Of course there is no way now to know. But what your Brown told your grandfather, that Brown was not his real name, may tell us something, or it may not. Both my father and uncle were Browns by birth, though they were simply known as Long Canoe and Swift Water. After my uncle brought me to New England, he disappeared from my life for fourteen years. But the moment I heard about your enigmatic Mr. Brown, I had my suspicions."

"But you said nothing?"

"I remained concerned for Cherity's safety. It was only two years before her birth when three Cherokee leaders were assassinated in Oklahoma, two of them, John Ridge and Buck Watie, my own cousins and childhood friends. That is how close the treachery comes. It is not that long ago. There remain bitter rivalries. My other cousin, Stand Watie, has grown to be an important man. Yet why should Cherity know?"

"Did you ever see your uncle again?" asked Seth.

"Only once, long after I was out of school and married to Kathleen and both of Cherity's sisters already born. Out of nowhere he appeared one day. How he knew where to find me, I do not know. Tumultuous times were again on the horizon for our people, he told me. He counseled me to continue as I was, not to divulge my identity because of possible repercussions. My home, my possessions, could be taken from me. My identity must further be kept secret, he said, because he had things to give me that I must safeguard if something should happen to him."

"What kinds of things?" asked Seth.

"It is all safely hidden away . . . in a packet, in the bottom drawer of my desk over there. I want you to take it . . . make sure Cherity gets it all when the time is right. Go . . . get the packet."

Seth walked across to the desk. After a few more instructions from James, he located the packet and brought it to the bedside.

"Open it," said James.

Seth did so.

James took it with a feeble hand and turned the envelope upside down. Something heavy plopped into his hand. He held it out. There Seth saw a thick ring of pure gold.

"This will belong to Cherity one day," said James. "It is one of seven ancient rings that were once in the possession of Chief Attacullaculla. It is all explained in the letter my uncle left me when he brought me the ring. I am leaving all this with you. Give it to her when the time is right, when our people do not have to fear for their lives or that what they have may be taken from them."

He replaced the ring and handed Seth the packet.

"Keep it for her, Seth."

"I will, sir. But what happened after that?"

"I never saw my uncle again. Your Mr. Brown apparently disappeared about the same time. Perhaps they are indeed the same man. And there is the matter of your uncle's strange death, also about the same time. Is it possible that *your* uncle and *my* uncle were involved in something together that your grandfather knew nothing of that resulted in *both* their deaths? Is that why your Brown and my uncle were never heard from again? I have puzzled over it ever since I was with you and am no nearer a solution in my mind than your father. Yet I do not see how we will ever know the full story now, after all this time."

James closed his eyes, and laid back on the pillows. To all appearances he was soon asleep.

Fifty-Six

$\mathcal{S}$tuffing the packet into his shirt where Cherity would not see it, Seth rose and left the room. He nodded to Cherity, who came and took his place at her father's side.

He did not see her for thirty or forty minutes, when she again walked out and smiled sadly. Her eyes were red but she seemed at peace.

"We had a good talk," she sighed. "But I am tired and he is dozing."

"Why don't you have something to eat?" suggested Seth. "I'll sit with your father again."

Cherity went wearily downstairs and Seth reentered the bedroom. James glanced over from the bed.

"Oh . . . Seth," he said, "you're back . . . good. Sit down."

Seth did so, and after another minute James began to speak again.

"There are some things I want you to tell your father," he said. "He had a more profound impact on me than he probably knows."

"In what way?" asked Seth.

"He and your mother are the most thoroughly Christian man and woman I have ever known," rejoined James. "After Kathleen's death, the more I looked back on our church life together, the more I saw cliché and dogma rather than living reality. It wasn't really her death that made me lose my faith, it only brought to the surface the flaws in what I thought I had believed up till then. And as you said . . . yes, I became angry at God."

"Perhaps your wife's faith was more real than you knew," suggested Seth.

"You may be right. But after she was gone, I made the mistake— God forgive me—of discarding the reality because of my inability to see it in those I knew from the church. Your parents helped me realize, as you yourself have too, Seth, my boy, that the worst hypocrisy wasn't in others, it was in myself. Instead of seeking reality beyond the dogma, I discarded the whole thing. I hid my anger so deep under an affable exterior that even I didn't know I had anger toward God lurking in my heart.

"Your father had the courage to speak the truth to me, as you have. And I finally see myself for what I have been. I have much to apologize to God for, much to ask forgiveness for. And now," he added with a wan smile, "I feel a little like the thief on the cross. There is so much I want to make right. But it is too late."

"It is never too late, Mr. Waters."

"Please, Seth . . . we are going to be men together, remember. I am dying and we both know it. Don't begrudge a dying man the right to feel like a fool. That is the prerogative of the dying, to wish they had made more of the opportunities of life when they had them."

The words pierced Seth's heart.

"I hope I have made my peace with God about it by now," James continued, "or at least in the last hour I have tried to make a beginning. I look forward to being able to make my peace with Kathleen too, and tell her I was not the husband I wish I had been, or the father to her daughters I should have been after she was gone. I can only hope, like he did to the thief on the cross, that he will welcome me though repentance for my folly has come so late."

"He will," nodded Seth.

James smiled. "You are a good young man, Seth Davidson," he said, reaching his hand toward Seth. Seth took it and held it firmly in his own. "But even your kind words cannot keep me from feeling like a fool for waiting so long. Why does it take the deathbed to awaken the soul?"

"I cannot say," replied Seth. "Perhaps because eternity suddenly seems so close."

"No doubt. And perhaps God is watching out for my Cherity in spite of me. You are here, after all. So now promise me—"

He paused once more. His voice had grown weak again. He struggled for a breath and tried to continue.

"Don't you think you should tell Cherity, if not about her past—and I will honor what you said before—at least about making your peace with God," said Seth.

James forced a sad smile. "How to tell a daughter to whom you have presented yourself as an agnostic all her life . . . how to tell her such a thing . . . that is what I have struggled with. It is—"

Seth saw that there were tears in his eyes.

"You must, sir . . . you must tell her. Don't wait until it is too late."

"But I have wasted all these years with her . . . foolishly turning my back on the God I should have known all along . . . should have helped her to know . . . I have failed her so badly . . . don't know how . . . but now . . . it is too late." He had begun to cry.

"It is never too late," said Seth again.

James squeezed Seth's hand. "Seth," he said, "men—remember."

Seth nodded.

"About Cherity . . . promise me, Seth, that . . . that you will take care of her."

"I will, sir," replied Seth, his eyes beginning to fill.

"Be good to her."

"I will."

"Whatever she needs . . . she will be provided for . . . the house . . . see that she—"

"Have no worry," said Seth. "But . . . please talk to her, Mr. Waters. Tell her you have spoken with God about your life. She needs to hear it from your own lips. I think she has something she would like to tell you too."

Without awaiting an answer, Seth turned and left the room. He went in search of Cherity. He found her in her room. The door was open. He knocked softly. She turned. Her face searched his for any sign.

"You need to talk to your father," he said.

"Is he . . . "

"He is awake but very weak. He has something to tell you. And you need to tell him about your ride to Harper's Peak, and your time on the stone bench in the arbor."

Cherity hesitated, looking at him with question.

"Tell him, Cherity," repeated Seth. "*Tell* him."

She nodded and left the room. She spent the next half hour seated beside her father on his bed. They would be the most treasured thirty minutes of her life. When Cherity emerged from the room, her eyes were wet with tears. Seth was waiting on the landing outside the door.

"He is . . . I am afraid, Seth . . . I don't know what to do," she said softly. "He seems unable to speak."

Seth hurried in, Charity at his side.

James' eyes seemed to brighten as he saw them approaching together. "Seth . . . Seth," he whispered, his lips parting in a faint smile, "I . . . told her . . . like you said . . . and now—I'm going—I've got to—an apology to . . . make. Seth, take care—"

The sentence remained unfinished. The light began to fade from his eyes.

"Daddy!" cried Cherity, rushing forward and sitting on the bed beside him. She leaned down and gently scooped him off the pillows toward her.

With daughter's arms beneath his shoulders cradling his face to her cheek, he breathed a few last whispered words, so faint she could barely make out his final sigh of life, "I love you, my . . . my little Cherokee."

With them, the man with a mysterious past that now seemed from another era altogether, and who had become a child of the Father in the end, slipped across into that other world where Cherity's mother was waiting for him.

Cherity held him a few moments more, gently laid his head back on the pillow, then stood, turned toward Seth, and broke into sobs. She went straight into his arms and wept on his chest. He closed his arms around her and held her close. This time she did not pull away.

Fifty-Seven

On Monday morning, Dr. Elliott came to the house, along with Reverend Morrison, pastor of the Evangelical Presbyterian Church where Cherity occasionally attended, to speak with Cherity about funeral arrangements. The latter was an honest seeker after truth, whose sermons, it is true, relied a little too heavily on platitudes. But from them Cherity gleaned what meat she could and had grown spiritually thereby, and for the pastor, therefore, she held a fond regard. He had met her father, though briefly, and was particularly tender in his care for Cherity after learning of James' passing.

Seth took the opportunity to go into the city late Monday morning. He arrived at the *Herald* offices and went straight to Mr. McClarin's office to inform him about James. As well as apologizing for being late that morning, he said that he would not be to work for several days, until funeral arrangements were finalized and Miss Waters' situation settled. He could not promise, he added, that he would be able to continue at the magazine. As much as he appreciated the job and wanted to continue, other concerns had now become paramount.

"Will you return to Virginia?" asked McClarin.

"I don't know, sir," replied Seth. "I need to make certain that Miss Waters is provided for and in a comfortable and adequate situation."

"What will she do?" asked the editor.

"I don't know, sir."

"War is coming you know—do you intend to volunteer?"

"No," answered Seth. "Which side would I fight for?" Briefly Seth explained the quandary of his mixed loyalties.

"I see what you mean. When your father freed his slaves it made quite a stir—sold a lot of newspapers and magazines . . . well, take as much time as you need," said the editor. "Your job will be waiting for you. I will think about your dilemma. In the meantime, give my sympathies and kind regards to Miss Waters and tell her that if there is anything I can do, not to hesitate to call on me. Her father was a good man and gave this paper many good years. We owe him a great deal. And of course, please notify me about the funeral. Many of James' colleagues will want to attend."

"Thank you, sir," said Seth, rising and shaking the editor's hand.

The moment he was gone, McClarin put on his coat and hat and set out for the Phillips photographic studio. An idea had come to him that bore looking into.

⌒

They had notified Cherity's two sisters of James' death, as well as Seth's parents, by telegram late Sunday night. With Rev. Morrison's help, and two or three telegrams back and forth from Anne and Mary, the funeral was scheduled for Friday.

Condolences came by telegraph from Greenwood on Monday. Seth's parents said that one or the other of them would try to make it north if possible, but that there were visitors at Greenwood that might make such a trip impossible. Wyatt Beaumont had been extremely troublesome of late. They did not know whether they could risk being away.

Anne would arrive from Albany on Wednesday evening.

Mary and her family would arrive from Norfolk on Thursday.

On Wednesday morning a messenger came to the door. Expecting more condolences, Seth was surprised to see his own name on the envelope. He opened it and read the brief message:

Please come see me as soon as is possible. I know this is a difficult time.

However, I have a matter to discuss which could impact your job prospects and decisions with regard to the future.

It was signed, *M. McClarin, Boston Herald.*

Seth showed it to Cherity.

"What is it about?" she asked.

"I have no idea. Perhaps I ought to go in this morning and find out."

When Seth returned to Constitution Hill several hours later, his own horizons filled with sudden new opportunities, he found Cherity alone in the sitting room crying.

"Cherity, what is it?" he said as he entered.

"I'm just feeling sorry for myself," she replied, dabbing at her eyes with a handkerchief. "And missing Daddy. Oh, Seth . . . what am I going to do! Anne's going to be here tonight. Suddenly I realize how alone I am with Daddy gone. I know they will both treat me like the little sister I have always been. They'll feel sorry for me and want me to come live with them. But how can I? I would never feel at home with either Anne or Mary, and I dread the thought of being an imposition. What am I going to do? I can't stay here . . . alone."

Seth had already been thinking through just this dilemma on his return from the city, as well as praying determinedly about the decision McClarin had suddenly set before him. How to fulfill James' dying charge with regard to Cherity, and yet heed his own obligations to himself and his country—the perplexity had been gnawing at him incessantly for two days. Suddenly McClarin had shown him how he might accomplish the latter. And he could see but one way to carry out the former.

"There is another possibility," he said.

"What is that?" asked Cherity, looking at Seth questioningly.

"You *do* have a home now," he said, "only not here."

"Where, then?"

"Greenwood," he replied.

A gasp escaped Cherity's lips. Her heart leapt at the thought. She *would* feel at home there! But . . . so many questions flooded her brain.

"Would they . . . your parents, I mean . . . " Cherity floundered. Her mind was racing. "Would they . . . actually want me?"

"Are you kidding?" said Seth. "They would *love* having you!"

"How can you know that without asking them?"

"Because I know my father and mother. And it wouldn't all be just for your benefit. You could help them too. I know you would be a help and comfort to my mother."

"A comfort . . . what do you mean? How could I help them? Why would she need comforting?"

"Because . . . I won't be there," said Seth. "And I have the feeling neither will Thomas for much longer."

His words landed dissonantly against Cherity's ears. Her heart and brain were spinning in so many directions! What was Greenwood without Seth!

"Why . . . what do you mean?" asked Cherity. "Are you . . . I don't understand . . . do you mean you are going to stay *here* . . . in Boston?"

Seth shook his head. "No," he said. "Whatever you decide, I will be leaving both Boston *and* Greenwood."

"I . . . I don't under—but . . . where would you go?"

"Mr. McClarin has offered me a way out of my dilemma," said Seth, "about where my duty ought to lie. He says I can keep my job with the *Herald*, and be loyal to *both* sides at the same time. Apparently Mr. Phillips thinks I have an aptitude for this new photography. He seems to like what I have chosen for subjects so far and would like me to continue to work with him."

"How?"

"He wants to send me on assignment, traveling with a regiment but as a civilian, probably of Union soldiers to begin with. He wants me to photograph what I can of the war. He will pay for my travel as *Herald* staff. He would allow me the liberty to travel on my own, or, if need be, with soldiers of either side. I would be an entirely neutral observer."

"It sounds dangerous," said Cherity, her tears from earlier drying as thoughts of Seth's safety became uppermost in her mind.

"It may be," he replied. "But I cannot stand by as a spectator when our country is at such a critical time. I have to be loyal as an *American*, even if I cannot fight for the North *or* the South. I hope you can see why. It is important to me that you understand."

"I suppose I can," said Cherity. "Women don't feel those kinds of things. But I guess all men do. It's what makes women love them, but hate the causes they fight for."

Even as the fateful word escaped her lips, Cherity wondered if she had said too much. But Seth seemed to take no notice.

"I can do my duty without taking sides," he went on. "This is my way to be of service to the *whole* country."

Cherity stood and faced him.

"Oh, Seth," she said, "I can't help it—I am afraid."

Seth walked toward her, opened his arms, and enclosed her in his embrace.

"I know," he whispered. "These are frightening times. I suppose I am afraid too. We cannot see to the end of it. But . . . but we have each other now. We must let that help us get through it."

Cherity sighed. The contentment she felt was tinged with remnants of melancholy. Her grief was still fresh. Yet for the moment she was content, and her heart quietly glad. She would think about what Seth's words might mean later. For now she would just let them bathe her in peace.

"And you really think . . . ," she began.

"Yes," he whispered, in answer to the question she had been thinking, gently stroking her hair as he continued to hold her. "Greenwood is your home now. We will leave as soon after the funeral as you are ready."

Funeral services for James Waters were held on Friday at Boston's Evangelical Presbyterian Church, and was attended by more people than anyone expected, most of whom none of his three daughters recognized. Neither Richmond nor Carolyn was able to come.

The will was read by Mr. Glennie later in the afternoon. The house on Constitution Hill was left to Cherity. Approximately four thousand dollars in the bank and various investments were to be divided equally among the three daughters. James' personal possessions and the home furnishings, they could divide among themselves as they saw fit.

As Cherity had anticipated, both Anne and Mary urged her to come live with one or another of their families. She had decided instead, Cherity replied, to accept the offer of Seth's parents, received by telegram the day before, of an extended stay at Greenwood. She appreciated their kind invitations, she told her sisters, and the time might come when she would want to take advantage of one or both of the offers. For the immediate present, however, she felt Greenwood was the right place for her to get her feet on the ground, where she could work hard and feel useful, and could accustom herself to life without their father.

Anne and her family left Boston on Saturday.

On Sunday, Cherity, Seth, and Mary attended Rev. Morrison's church in the morning. Mary and her family left the city by train that afternoon.

On Monday Seth and Cherity packed what they each would need and made final arrangements with Mrs. Porterfield for the house during Cherity's absence. Seth paid one last visit to Mr. Glennie on his own.

On Tuesday morning, Seth finalized his plans with Mr. McClarin, promising that he would return within three weeks to complete his photographic training.

By that afternoon he and Charity were seated on a southbound train on their way to Virginia.

Fifty-Eight

The reunion on the platform of the Dove's Landing station on the following Thursday was tearful, joyous, and bittersweet.

The two men greeted one another with a vigorous shake of the hand, followed by a manly embrace between father and son. The two women dispensed with handshakes and smiles altogether, and ran tearfully and without preliminaries straight into one another's arms. The men were already talking about crops, weather, and luggage before spiritual mother and adoptive daughter began to release their hold sufficiently to stand back and gaze into the other's liquid eyes.

"Cherity . . . my dear," said Carolyn softly with an overflowing heart. "I am so sorry about your father. But I am also so happy to see you—welcome!"

"I feel like I have come home," whispered Cherity. Her voice, though soft, exuded utter peace.

"You *are* home!"

"Hi, Mom!" exclaimed Seth, interrupting the tender scene by scooping Carolyn into a great embrace.

"Seth!" she said, "you look . . . so grown up!"

"It's only been, what—five months," laughed Seth. "I can't have changed that much!"

"I suppose I had forgotten what a man you had become."

"What are you talking about—I'm still the same me."

"Hello, Cherity," said Richmond, now approaching with outstretched hand. "Welcome back to Dove's Landing."

"Thank you, Mr. Davidson," smiled Cherity. "I cannot tell you how happy it makes me feel just to be here again."

"We are so sorry about your father. He had become a good friend."

"Thank you. He died peacefully and I am thankful for that. He and I shared many things on that last day. I will treasure them as long as I live."

"Where's Tom?" asked Seth.

For the first time since their arrival, Carolyn's face fell. Seth saw it, then glanced toward his father with an expression of question.

"Cynthia is at the house, but I'm afraid Thomas is gone, Seth," said Richmond. "He left without warning last week, said he was going to enlist for the Confederacy, and we have not heard from him since."

The news hit Seth hard. He had expected it, yet suddenly the reality of impending war came very close.

"Most of the others are gone too," Richmond went on. "Wyatt, Brad, Scully Riggs, even Cameron and Jeremy . . . they've all joined up. Our only consolation is that Thomas will probably be in the Virginian army under the command of our friend Robert Lee. But I must confess that your mother and I have a difficult time finding much consolation even in that."

"But *you* two are here!" said Carolyn. "That's what matters now."

The next few days were like walking back into a dream for Cherity. No place could have assuaged her grieving heart like the hills and pastures, gardens and giant trees of Greenwood. And though having a mother to love could not make up for the loss of a father, it made it easier to bear. For Carolyn's heart opened wider now to receive the orphaned girl even than before. And with Cynthia for a friend, sharing with her, if not the loss of death, the anxiety of an uncertain future, Cherity soon felt almost more at home than she had anywhere in her life.

When Seth at last broke the news to his parents three days after their

arrival that he would be leaving soon too, they were both relieved to
know he would not join the fighting and yet anxious anew because
necessity would surely bring him close to it. They admired his stand,
however, and knew he had to follow his convictions wherever they led
him.

Richmond, Carolyn, Cynthia, and Cherity saw Seth's train off two
weeks later. The good-byes were sad. The women cried. Seth held
Cherity several long seconds, though neither found words suitable for
the occasion. They fell apart, located each the other's eyes, and tried in
one last fleeting second to say with them what neither had been able
to in words. Seth attempted a smile, such as it was, then turned one
last time to his father. Richmond's heart wept, though his eyes
remained dry.

The train pulled out. The watchers stood stoic and silent, crying
again. Seth, from an open window, waved and shouted a few last
words of farewell. He would save his own tears until he was alone.

The train picked up speed and disappeared from sight. The four
waited a minute longer, then slowly turned and made their way across
the platform to the waiting carriage.

"We are all together," said Carolyn, "the four of us . . . yet suddenly
it feels very, very lonely here."

⁓

The Virginia papers were full every day of news proclaiming the
buildup of the Confederate Army and predictions of a quick end to
the conflict. With the army under generals Lee and Beauregard growing rapidly and far readier for battle than Union forces, a march on
Washington and takeover of the capital seemed about to commence
any week. It was well-known that Lincoln's call for troops to reinforce
the capital had not yet materialized.

But no march on defenseless Washington was planned throughout
the month of May, nor even June. By then Lincoln's reinforcements
arrived. The Union Army began amassing for an attempted invasion of
northern Virginia and march toward the Confederate capital of Richmond.

Both sides were impatient to invade, yet neither was ready to make a move. The waiting continued.

The first indication that the war had begun in earnest, and was close by, came in early July. Hearing rumors that Beauregard's forces were on the march from the Carolinas, Richmond disappeared early one morning by horseback and took the road east. Within ten miles, from the vantage point of a low hill, he saw stretched out below him the vast throng of grey-clad soldiers heading north in endless columns. The sight took his breath away. All he could think was, *Might Thomas be among them!*

He watched until they were gone, saddened anew at what now seemed inevitable, then turned and made his way at a more leisurely pace home to Greenwood. Whatever the future held, there seemed little doubt that this region of Virginia, sitting almost directly between the two capitals of Washington and Richmond, would find itself in the very middle of it.

Carolyn and both girls heard the approach of hooves and hurried out to the porch.

"What did you see?" asked Carolyn.

"It is as reported," sighed Richmond, dismounting and walking toward them. "General Beauregard's troops moving north to head off an invasion from Washington."

"Was Thomas there . . . did you see him?" asked the anxious mother.

"Carolyn . . . there were thirty or forty thousand men. It was a vast throng."

"Forty . . . *thousand*!" exclaimed Carolyn, reaching for a chair and sitting down.

"There is no doubt now," said Richmond, "this is a war. Many will die. My heart breaks to imagine it."

The invasion of the Union army into northern Virginia came on the eighteenth of July. It met General Beauregard's forces at Manasses

Junction beside Bull Run Creek just a few miles into Virginia on the twenty-first. Over seventy thousand men, Americans all, finally clashed and their rifles and cannons echoed deadly volleys across the ground that separated the two armies.[8]

The fighting lasted most of the day. Finally Beauregard's forces sent the badly disorganized Union army fleeing back toward Washington in a panicky mob. By day's end, over forty-five hundred Americans were dead or wounded. A national tragedy had begun.

News of the resounding Confederate victory brought no joy to Greenwood. They mourned the dead on both sides, and wondered with fearful hearts if their Thomas was among them.

Even the unexpected joy that arrived two days later would prove painfully brief.

They heard the approach of a borrowed buggy early in the evening. The women were in the parlor sewing. Wondering who it might be, Moses went to the door. The visitor, however, did not knock, but walked straight in.

"Massa Seff . . . ," Moses began in surprise. Shrieks from the women in an adjacent room drowned out whatever he had been about to say. The three women dropped the things in their hands and were out of their seats in a second. Seth only managed to set down the camera and other equipment in his hands before he was mobbed by a

---

[8]On July 18, the volunteer Union army, 37,000 strong, marched south into Virginia. A reporter for the *Washington Star* described the spectacle:

"The scene from the hills was grand . . . regiment after regiment was seen coming along the road and across the Long Bridge, their arms gleaming in the sun. . . . Cheer after cheer was heard as regiment greeted regiment, and this with the martial music and sharp clear orders of commanding officers, made a combination of sounds very pleasant to the ear of a Union man.

"The Northern troops had a good time despite the fierce heat. They stopped every moment to pick blackberries or get water,' General McDowell remembered, 'they would not keep in the ranks, order as much as you pleased. . . . They were not used to denying themselves much; they were not used to journeys on foot.'

"Hundreds of Washington civilians rode out to join the advancing army, hoping to see a real battle. Some brought binoculars, picnic baskets, bottles of champagne.

"Some of the troops rather liked the notion of fighting their first battle in front of illustrious spectators. 'We saw carriages and brouches which contained civilians who had driven out from Washington to witness the operations,' a Massachusetts volunteer remembered. 'A Connecticut boy said, "There's our Senator!" and some of our men recognized . . . other members of Congress. . . . We thought it wasn't a bad idea to have the great men from Washington come out to see us thrash the Rebs.'

"Beauregard knew the Northerners were coming. Mrs. Rose O'Neal Greenhow, a prominent society leader in Washington and the aunt of Stephen A. Douglas, was one of those who had seen to that, sending him word of the advance, her coded note concealed in the hair of a sympathetic Southern girl. And he had ordered his men to form a meandering eight-mile line along one side of Bull Run Creek near a railroad center called Manassas Junction." (*The Civil War*, Geoffrey C. Ward, Alfred Knopf, NY, 1990, p. 62-65)

frenzy of hugs and questions. After her own share in the excitement, Cynthia ran out to the barn to tell her father that Seth was home, and soon the handshakes, backslaps, and hugs began all over again.

"I've been attached to the Sixth Massachusetts Regiment," Seth told them. "I was with the Union army at Bull Run two days ago. It was horrifying. The army fled back into Washington in such disarray that if Beauregard had pursued us, he could have walked into the capital and taken over the White House. For now Washington remains in Union hands. But the troops are badly shaken by the outcome, as is the president—at least that's what they say. I don't know what's going to happen. The Confederate army may overrun Washington and Philadelphia and New York by the end of the summer."

"But what are you doing here!" exclaimed Cherity, overjoyed to see Seth again.

"Mr. McClarin told me to get on a train back to Boston with my plates and photographs after the first battle. After that he would decide what to do with me. But I was so close to home! As long as the trains are still running and no battles imminent, it wouldn't have been right not to come down, even if only for half a day. I still have plenty of unexposed plates—I thought I would practice my photographic techniques on you tomorrow morning! I've even been trying to figure out a way to get a photograph of all of us at once . . . including me!"

"Do you . . . *have* to go back so soon?" asked Carolyn. She did not understand photographs, she only wanted her son!

"I'm sorry, Mom, I hate what I have seen. I despise the hatred both sides have for each other. But I will be faithful to this job. I love this country. So I must do my duty as I see it. So yes . . . I do."

Seth paused, and an expression came over his face that none, not even his father and mother, quite knew how to define. "Before I do anything," he said, "I need to go for a ride on Malcolm."

He turned and offered his hand to Cherity. "And what steed will you choose, my lady?" he asked.

Radiant, shyly embarrassed before the others, heart beating with more feelings than she could have described, and unable to find the voice to give him an answer, Cherity followed Seth from the room.

She was wearing a dress but did not change it, and stood in patient silence while Seth saddled two horses, then again offered his hand to help her up. There was no race on this day, not even a gallop, but a quiet walk up the high ridge even more memorable than any of their previous rides together. No one else ever knew the words that were spoken that day on Harper's Peak. But when the two returned to Greenwood several hours later, everyone knew that Cherity Waters and Seth Davidson had each claimed the heart of the other.

Seth left to return to Boston two mornings later. This time, as they again said tearful farewells on the station platform, all five knew they may not be together again for a very long time.

A hunter, a woman, a child

c. 30,000 BC–c. 10,000 BC

The land called the New World was ancient with civilization long before the first European set foot on its eastern shores. How and why the species *homo sapiens* first came there had more to do with weather than conquest.

In a time now lost in the mists of antiquity, a man, well bundled in skins and with feet wrapped in layers made from sea otter pelts, trudged forward, spear in one hand. With the other he pulled a small wooden sledge behind him along the surface of the frozen ground.

A bitter wind blew against his cheeks. His breath from nostrils and mouth sent white puffs of warmth into the chill air. He was used to the cold. He had spent his entire life in it. His father had taught him to hunt the big game at the edge of the ice. It was the only way he knew.

He glanced back at those who followed—his wife, with child though he did not yet know it, her father, and his younger brother and his wife. They were primitive Paleolithic hunters from the sparsely populated upper regions of Siberia. Their existence was nomadic. They followed game to survive. This was the farthest north they had ever ventured. Strapped to the sledge behind him—sliding on rails of ivory tusk connected by means of smaller bone with skins tightly stretched between them—were various stone tools and implements. These included additional skins for warmth and shelter, flints and

supplies to make fire and weapons and for skinning animals and tearing meat, as well as sharp-tipped spears, hammers, and crude stone
axes that gave them an advantage over four-legged beasts twice their
size and more.

That they were now crossing a narrow isthmus of frozen land no
human had trod before them was not planned. A chance sighting of
game had brought them this way in the ceaseless trek after food. Had
they taken a different route, another of their kind would have
wandered onto this new continental corridor soon enough. But fate
decreed these five as the first.

They would not be the last.

They struggled to survive during an age known as the Pleistocene
ice epoch when enormous glacial sheets up to half a mile thick covered
much of the world's northern landmass. The seawater here was frozen
in solid inland mountains of white. With much of the globe's water
mass locked away above land, its oceans were much lower than they
would later become, and many sea floors turned into dry land.

The planet's fortunes, however, were continually changing. When
atmospheric conditions brought a warming trend, slowly the ice began
to melt. As the Northern Hemisphere again turned its face toward the
sun, the boundaries of the glacial ice moved northward. Hearty
animals that could endure the cold and find food in the new forests
created by the northward spread of spruce and oak, migrated in the
direction of the melt. Hunter gatherers of men tracked these beasts as
they went. By slow degrees, over thousands of years, the regions
exposed by the retreating ice pack became thinly populated with life.

The retreating ice and low sea levels exposed temporary land
bridges connecting all the globe's continents. This first small band of
humanity to discover the northernmost such isthmus had been following a herd of caribou for a week. The animals did not travel with great
speed. The humans had been able to keep pace comfortably out of
sight, then approach to kill one from the herd every several days and
eat their fill.

Though grassy provision was sparse with half the ground still frozen, sensing they were being followed, the caribou moved eastward. The band of hunters continued in leisurely pursuit.

Others would follow over the next few thousand years. The opening of this climactic door provided the opportunity for increasing handfuls of Siberian, Mongolian, and northern Chinese hunters to lead the way into a previously uninhabited world. As long as they were able, creatures ventured across this Beringia land bridge, just as others were doing across similar land bridges around the world.

The five humans continued on. In reckonings of the future it was sometime late in the month of May. They camped that night, as they had for the last several days, on the low causeway. In a few more days the land under their feet began to rise in elevation. Gradually both four-footed and two-footed creatures left one continent behind and crossed over into a new history.

When another month had passed, they were moving across what would one day be called the Seward Penninsula. By now the human explorers had lost track of the caribou herd. But they had spotted other game—moose, elk, and a great white bear whose furry hide the man coveted to keep his wife warm.

The small party of five managed to get far enough through the vast Alaskan ranges to winter successfully in a cave near the valley of the Yukon River, overlooked by gigantic towering peaks the likes of which struck terror into their hearts.

They kept sufficient meat frozen in snowdrifts outside the cave's mouth to prevent starvation. Many nights they heard mournful howls from roaming packs of wolves. But fire not only kept them warm, it also kept the wolves away.

The man and woman's child was born—the first true native to this place that would one day be called the Americas.

The winter months were black and fearsome. During some weeks storms raged outside their cave-home for forty or fifty hours at a time. They had not known such deep blackness on the Kamchatka Penninsula they had left on the other side. In their voyage they had come five or six degrees farther north, and in those climes the loss of winter daylight was enormous. Fearing they had entered a land of perpetual darkness that the gods had cursed, it was with great rejoicing that at length they saw the sun creeping again into the sky.

When at last winter loosened its grip on the land, the band, now six, prepared to take up again its pilgrimage. They left their cave and set out again in search of new provision. This winter had been severe. All they could think now was to seek the sun. As it rose in the southern sky, imperceptibly higher each day, the great ball of yellow-orange fire in the heavens became their guiding source of strength. Gradually the land began to thaw as they moved south. They encountered creatures of increasing variety—bear and deer, huge birds, abundant fish in the rivers and streams, even some small animals they had never before seen. The earth seemed sprouting new life of itself. Life again took on hope.

They recognized enough of times and seasons to know that the white cold would come again. But never could they imagine enduring another such winter as that just past, especially with the fragile life of an infant now to protect. Following the sun thus became the sole guiding principle of their movement. When the sun rose high, their skin felt its warmth and made their hearts happy. They would follow the bright god of the sky wherever it led. They would follow it every day. Perhaps, before the freeze came again and the tiny flakes of frozen air began to drift from the sky and bring a chill to the earth, the sun would lead them to a place where ice and snow could not get its fingers of death so deep into their bones.

So they trekked south, in the shadows of the mighty peaks with perpetual crowns of white. When they killed more than required for food, they sacrificed the remainder on altars of stone to the god of the sun as they had been taught by their forefathers, though they knew not why, chanting before the blinding orb of the sky, exulting in the blessing of its warmth.

Southward they continued . . . toward the sun.

A year passed . . . another winter came, though less severe . . . then another thaw. The baby survived, bundled in its swaddling share of the white fur of the great northern bear, took strength from its mother's hearty constitution, and grew strong.

Others came after them in the years that followed. Those who ventured between the continents too late in the season were caught in the clutches of winter, their bones disappearing under vast drifts of snow and ice. But some made it, as had the first, and survived to move south.

The man and his woman had another child, then another, as did his brother and his wife. More years passed.

The old grandfather died . . . the young ones grew.

South their steps still pointed . . . ever in the direction of the sun.

Occasionally they met others of their kind. At first they were able to communicate with those they met, for all these first explorers had migrated from the same regions.

Again for a time the great ice returned to the earth. The isthmus they had crossed was covered once more in glacier, only to be flooded again by the sea several more times over the millennia in a climactic ebb and flow of thaw and freeze.

The last opening across the Beringia land bridge connecting Alaska with the outer reaches of Siberia was created approximately 10,000 BC. The two continental ice packs froze one final time to allow hunters of big game from the most distant outlying portions of Asia across this lowland strait, then south toward the rich plains of North America. In ever larger numbers than before, they poured into this new land by threes and fours, then by hundreds. While the door remained open, the new continent slowly became peopled with what would become a new American race. Its characteristics would retain traces of its Oriental, Siberian, and Mongolian ancestry, though love of the sun would brown and toughen its skin, forever distinguishing it from its Asian forebears.

The ice ultimately relinquished its hold on the north. When the final thaw was complete, the oceans of the Arctic and northern Pacific again washed over the land bridge. The passage of eastern migration was closed off—this time forever.

By then many thousands had come. They little thought of themselves as discoverers of a new land. Only as hungry men and women who must follow the source of food wherever it led. How could they foresee that their adventurous spirit would give a whole new side of the globe—unseen from the population centers of China, Europe, and the Near East—the opportunity to grow and expand with the life-giving seed of a new race of humankind.

Migrating still farther south, the human newcomers multiplied and spread in all directions across and down the two huge American continents. They found the land teeming with animal life—a few camel, mammoth, sloth, large cats, prehistoric species of horse, and casteroide, innumerable moose, deer, bear, antelope, and bison, as well as abundant smaller game.

While retaining vestiges of common roots, these who trekked from Siberia to Alaska diverged over millennia into separate peoples with their own individual cultures. Very different destinies would follow the various tribal groups of these first Americans. The most advanced and skilled continued to follow the sun southward, eventually migrating past the high mountains and expansive open plains of the north into the hot equatorial region near the Tropic of Cancer. Others spread out eastward toward the shores and island regions where Europeans would one day encounter them and mistakenly give them the name of another brown-skinned race half a globe away.

Their ethnic origins, however, remained forever linked throughout a history that would one day know them all—from the *Eskimo* of the Arctic, to the *Koyukon* and *Montagnais-Naskapi* of Alaska and Labrador, to the *Tehuelche* of Argentina, to the *Inca* of Peru, to the *Iroquois* of the northern forests, to the *Navaho* of arid rocky regions, to the *Aztec* of Mexico, to the *Apache* of the Great Plains, and to the *Cherokee* of the southeastern coastal plains—simply as *Indians*.

As the civilizations of Sumaria, Egypt, Assyria, Babylon, and Greece rose in other parts of the world, altogether lost from their sight, far to the south in the mountains of Peru and in the warm crescent of Oahuaca, these ancient ancestors of America peopled the mainland

and established two advanced civilizations that grew and prospered without influence from the rest the globe.

Meanwhile, though their Aztec and Inca cousins built cities, others of their kind, finding the nomadic life peaceful and the expansive plains and coastal regions north of Mesoamerica temperate and abundant with life, built no empires but continued to follow their food in perpetual migrations that became as predictable as the patterns of weather that drove the animals they stalked up and down throughout the great land.

On the plains, in the forests, in the fertile lands of the Ohio Valley, along the shores of the great river called Mississippi and the fertile expanse between the two coastlines, many native tribes formed out of the common root stalk of humanity, developing cultures and societies, living as their ancestors had for centuries, each gradually carving out its own sense of *place* within a continent too massive to be crowded by their sparse numbers. Some of these tribes continued as nomads, others gradually learned, like the Aztecs to the south, to grow things, to domesticate animals, and to construct semipermanent dwellings and shelters. Among these, the Iroquois in the north, the Hopewell in the Ohio Valley, and the Cherokee to the south, led the advance toward civilization, with laws and society, construction, trade, and culture.

Who could tell to what these remarkable tribes might have risen, and what their civilizations might have become. History will never know. For at the height of their march toward civilization—later than in many places on the globe, but moving steadily in that direction— a new race of men of fair skin, and with them a race of blacks, arrived from over the sea.

The destiny of what these newcomers called the *New World*, and the three races that would all call it their home, was suddenly altered forever.

Ani-Yunwiya—The People

1680–1725

*A*matoya Moytoy and his woman Quatsy stared into the water flowing past them. An infant son slept peacefully in his father's arms.

Seven hundred or more generations had passed since their intrepid forebears had crossed the land bridge from a continent now forgotten into this new home of their ancestors. That past had long faded from memory, though the strength of its heritage would never die. These were a rugged people for they had survived, and, if not tamed the land, learned to dwell in harmony with it. The land and its bounty was their mother, for it sustained and nurtured them. They took what they needed for life, but no more. They were a people whose diverse tongues contained no expression for *greed*. To hoard, to grasp, to possess more than one's fellow, were concepts unknown among them.

The land fed, the land provided, and to the land they would return in the end. They were one with the land, with the animals, with the sun, with the weather, and with the great river who spoke secrets for those who knew how to listen. They had learned the ways of rain and drought, the haunts of wild creatures, the secrets of the land. As they multiplied in numbers they occasionally made peace with neighboring tribes, and occasionally war. From earliest memory, their people, the *Ani-Yunwiya*, had dwelt here. Even in the 1500s when the Spainard DeSoto came up from the south he found the Cherokee a mighty people.

Moytoy was the greatest among the people called Cherokee in the region of Great Telliquo and even throughout the region of Tannassy. He had taken his newborn son to the river of the same name to learn what the Great Spirit would call him, and to hear, if he might amid the tumult of the waters, the voice that would speak to him of his son's destiny in this land growing gradually crowded with the fair-skinned strangers from across the sea.

Amatoya and Quatsy stood silent before the rushing headwaters of the Tannassy.

"Oh spirit of the waters, hear my request," said the chief at length. His voice was solemn and strong, melodic in unison with the rippling white water flowing past him. "I bring before you my son. Let his life be as your waters, flowing ever onward with power and strength. May he bring you honor, Great Spirit of the earth and water and sky. May his children forever love and respect this land. As your waters never end but flow on and on, may our people also flow on and on in this land of our fathers and their fathers before."

He turned. Quatsy removed the soft-skin blanket from the child, then his father knelt and gently lowered the frail form to its neck into the icy flow. Startled awake, the young one cried out. Three more times Moytoy dipped his son into the flow. He stood again, held the dripping boy a moment, then handed him to his mother who wrapped him in the garment of warmth.

A few minutes more they stood. Slowly Chief Moytoy began to nod. He had listened. The spirit of the river had spoken. The name had been given.

Once more he turned to the woman at his side.

"It is as you expected," he said. "The spirit of the river would make us one, though we are two. The name will continue. May I be worthy of it, and may he be worthy of it."

Amatoya and Quatsy turned away and left the river which would one day be called the Tennessee, and began the trek of half a day back to Telliquo with their son.

As they approached the village, warm greetings from the rest of their tribe met them. The cousin to the chief's wife led the procession out from the camp.

"We rejoice in the return of our chief and his family," said Kunnessaway. "What name has the great river brought forth for your son?"

"My son will also be known as Moytoy," replied Amatoya. "He will be called Okoukaula. He will follow in my path, wearing the white feather of peace."

The face of Kunnessaway clouded with doubt. "I fear our chief sees not the marks of the future. More of our future chiefs will wear the red feather of war."

Moytoy the elder, as he would henceforth be called, shook his head as he handed the infant into Quatsy's arms.

"We will live in peace with the newcomers from over the sea," he rejoined firmly. "There is land enough for all. They do not roam as we do. They stay near the great water and do not venture inland toward our villages. We will live in peace."

The boy Okoukaula grew to follow his father as peace chief of the Cherokees, and in time came to be called Moytoy the younger. Though a few of the village war chiefs may have disputed his claim as headman of all chiefs, none disputed that among their people he eventually rose in stature even above his father. By the time he had taken his own sons to the river in the early years of the eighteenth century, new times were advancing upon them rapidly.

Whether the chiefs of war or the chiefs of peace would rule the Cherokee, not even their wisest seers, priests, or conjurers could yet foresee.[1]

---

[1]See Note 1—The People of the Caves

Attacullaculla,
Chief of the White Feather

1730–1759

$\mathcal{F}$or centuries the Cherokee people lived in relative peace in the mountains and valleys between Carolina and Kentucky, Virginia and Georgia. It was their home. Yet from the moment the English colonists took root in the land called America, the Cherokee nation began to be pushed farther and farther into the mountains.

The new treaty with King George II of England in 1730 brought relative peace to the tribe for the next twenty years. But the seven Cherokee men who had visited the great palaces of England little anticipated how soon a series of colonial wars would ravage their region, and that within a generation the so-called treaty would be little more than a memory, trampled underfoot by the stresses of expanding American colonialism.[2]

Elected peace chief of the Cherokee while still a young man, Ukwaneequa was renamed Attacullaculla and for the rest of his life did his utmost to promote favorable relations with the English. In 1736 the French sent emissaries to the Cherokee to try to win back Cherokee loyalties from the English. But Attacullaculla convinced his people to remain loyal to the English. In spite of his efforts, however, clashes between the two cultures increased. Cherokee villages were often burned without question. Gradually many in the tribe, led by Oconostota, spoke out for war.

---

[2]Much detail is available on the Cherokee visit to England, including Cuming's journal, in *The Cherokee Crown of Tannassy* by William Steele, as well as *The Cherokees* by Grace Woodward. Also see Note 2—Seven Cherokee in England, and the Articles of Friendship and Commerce.

A new treaty was signed with the English in 1754. But it did not lead to peace. It gave up large amounts of Cherokee land as well as made provision to allow the British to build forts in Cherokee territory.[3]

⟨~~~⟩

Moytoy the younger died about 1753. Attacullaculla was peace chief and Oconostota was war chief, and there were many other prominent chiefs at the time. Moytoy's son Dreadful Water claimed the Emperor title, but the Cherokee national council made their own choice of headman, Standing Turkey of Echota, called Old Hop because he was old and lame. Despite this selection, Attacullaculla was considered the most influential chief in the nation, and Oconostota was known as the Great Warrior of Echota.

The encroaching English colonists were not the only concern of the Cherokee. Their perennial enemies the Creek and the Seminoles coveted the rich hills, valleys, streams, and rivers of the vast Cherokee territory. Cherokee towns were constantly threatened by war parties from both tribes. Though friendly relations between the Cherokee and English gradually resulted under Attacullaculla's leadership in Chero-kee land being used for English settlements and forts in exchange for trading privileges and goods, the Cherokee did not so easily desire to cede land to their Indian rivals. Thus centuries of old disputes and tribal border warfare with the Creeks and Seminoles continued.

The Muskogee tribe of the Creek mounted a major assault against the Cherokee in 1755. Hearing of the death of Moytoy, and attempt-ing to seize upon a moment of weakness in Cherokee leadership, four battles took place. Despite the efforts of Oconostota and the leader-ship of Attacullaculla, many warriors were lost and the Creeks seemed slowly eroding the strength and resolve of the Cherokee.

In grave danger, and with no help coming from their so-called allies the English, the Cherokee made plans for a final effort against the Creek, summoning even the aid of their women in battle. It was a daring and dangerous plan. If they were overrun, massive damage

[3]See Note 3—The Difficult Years of 1730-1755.

could be done to the entire fabric of Cherokee life. But the alternative was capture and annihilation.

"You must join me in battle, Nanye'hi," said the young warrior called Kingfisher as he came into the lodge that had been his home for three winters.

His young wife glanced up at him in anxious question.

"The Creeks again raid our villages," he went on. "The Great Warrior of Echota has spoken to the council. He says that to save our towns and villages, our women must take up arms with us."

The young wife looked down at the infant son in her arms, then over at her two-year-old daughter asleep on the furry skin of a bear across the lodge.

"What if I do not return?" she said. "Who will take care of them?"

"You will return to our children," replied her husband.

"But I am afraid."

"Fear is not an evil thing," said Kingfisher, placing a gentle hand on her shoulder. "One who meets what he fears with courage is known for his bravery. You and I will face our fears and be brave together."

Though the Creek force was huge, a thousand or more, the five hundred Cherokee dug in throughout a forested and hilly region and were prepared for them. With screams and bloodcurdling cries, the first wave of Creeks rushed toward the waiting Cherokee. The air erupted with explosions from the muskets with which both sides were well supplied. As the echoes from the initial volley died out for reloading, arrows whished through the trees in both directions. Soon muskets exploded again. Within minutes the air hung thick with dense blue-gray smoke. Screams and yells and war cries of battle and death sounded everywhere.

Most of the Cherokee women who had accompanied their warriors crouched low behind trees and small mounds of earth or logs, reloading rifles and handing bullets and arrows to their men as quickly as they could load rifles or string bows, take aim, and refire. All around was fear, blood, and death as the Creek horde gradually advanced upon them.

In the hollow behind a fallen log knelt the nineteen-year-old Cherokee maiden of the Wolf clan, her heart filled with terror for the two young children she had left back at the village. Her husband, Tsu-la, also known as Kingfisher, a few yards away was firing at the Creeks as rapidly as he could reload the musket in his hands. Young Nanye'hi, named for her grandmother, daughter of Tame Doe and Fivekiller, had only been married three years. She had born her husband two fine children, Catherine and Fivekiller, named for her mother and father. Beside her sat a small pile of musket balls. One by one she placed them in her mouth, chewing the soft lead to roughen its edges and make them more deadly. The explosions from her husband's gun were deafening, and the smoke so thick after twenty minutes that she could scarcely see any of the rest of their tribe scattered through the pine wood.

She crept toward Kingfisher with a fresh supply of musket balls. He turned, took them from her. She saw in his eyes what she herself felt—that the battle was not going well and that the Creeks were too numerous to hold off much longer. He turned to face the battle, and Nanye'hi returned to her place of safety.

Suddenly behind her she heard a great shriek. She glanced into the smoky wood to see a Creek warrior twenty feet from them. Kingfisher had just loaded and quickly raised rifle to shoulder.

But he was too late. A puff of white burst from the barrel of the enemy's gun, followed instantly by its explosion. Kingfisher's body jerked back. The gun fell from his hands, and he toppled down the ledge toward his young wife.

In panic she fell to her knees and crawled to him, then cradled his head in her hands. His chest was covered in blood.

"Nanye'hi," he whispered faintly. "I . . . Nanye'hi . . . "

He said no more. The rest remained unsaid as his lungs emptied in a dying sigh.

A forlorn cry of agony rent the forest. Its sound sent a chill through all the Cherokee who heard it above the gunfire, for they knew whose cry it was. Immediately rose within every Cherokee breast a flame of indignation at the enemy, and a surge of determination for the battle.

Nanye'hi had no time to grieve. In the ten seconds that had passed since the fatal shot, the Creek warrior rushed forward to see if his aim had been true. Nanye'hi saw the movement and glanced up.

Acting more from instinct than plan, in less than a second the great hunting blade from her husband's waist was in her hand. She leapt to her feet and rushed the foe, who, in the smoke and confusion did not recognize his danger. Before he could unsheath his own knife, Nanye'hi plunged the razor-sharp steel between his ribs with all the might she could summon. The warrior staggered back and fell. Seconds later she had avenged her husband's death. The Creek warrior lay dead at her feet, her hand and the blade dripping with his blood.

What happened next she could not remember. Turning to grab up her fallen husband's musket, and shouting war cries in the ancient Cherokee tongue, Nanye'hi flew toward the battle, heedless of safety, in a passionate madness of ferocity. Her tribesmen had heard her cry. A few had seen what had happened and witnessed her bravery. From thirty or forty feet away, Oconostota sounded a war cry of his own. It was echoed by renewed exortations from Attacullaculla on the other side of the wood. Within minutes every Cherokee knew what had happened and surged forward in mighty rage to follow Nanye'hi's example.

When the battle was over, what remained of the Creek force fleeing for their lives—leaving behind livestock, wounded, and the handful of black slaves whose job was to keep ammunition in the hands of the warriors—Nanye'hi was at the front of the victorious Cherokee force, five Creeks scattered about the battlefield slain at her own hand by her husband's musket and blade.

Nanye'hi stood in a daze. Silence slowly returned to the field of death. The rifle dropped from her hand to the ground. Still she stood, unable to comprehend the magnitude of what had taken place. Not twenty years of age, she was already a widow.

Soft footsteps sounded behind her. She turned a forlorn face. Her two uncles approached, the great chiefs of the red feather and the white feather who had come together in common cause against the Creek's threat.

She fell into the arms of Chief Attacullaculla. The sobbing wail that echoed through the forest was one that would be carried for the rest of their lives in the heart of every Cherokee warrior and woman who had witnessed her bravery that day. The defeat of the Creeks was so great that they were driven from upper Georgia and never returned. Having led the Cherokee in so great a victory, by which most of North Georgia was gained from the Creeks, Oconostota would be known for the rest of his life as the greatest of all Cherokee warriors.

As the sun slowly set, Nanye'hi followed on foot the horse that carried her husband's body back to Chota. Many women had lost their men that day in the battle to save their city, and all the nation stoicly grieved for the fallen.

Two weeks later, a solemn ceremony was held. The highest honor that was possible for a Cherokee woman to receive was about to be given. All the village turned out to see their much beloved Nanye'hi, widow of Kingfisher and slayer of five Creek warriors honored before the entire tribe. Henceforth she would be known as *Ghigua*, a Beloved Woman, and would sit on the tribal council in recognition for her brave and heroic action.

Nanye'hi stood in a robe of white deerskin with her two youngsters, one at her side the other in her arms, her beautiful tan face stoic. Even in her honor, her heart wept though no tears fell from her eyes. Her uncle, Chief Attacullaculla stepped forward, then spoke to the assembly, recounting as if they were already legendary, her deeds on the field of battle.

He then placed around her neck a necklace of shell-wampum of great value and named her a *ghigua* of the Cherokee nation. Then he motioned for one of the black slaves who had been captured in the battle to be brought forward. He was now presented to Nanye'hi as the most prized of the spoils of the battle.

But Nanye'hi cared little for the honors bestowed on her. She grieved for her young husband and fatherless children. She could not know the legacy and example of her heroism she would become for Cherokee women everywhere, and for all time.

⌒

Attacullaculla continued to be the primary voice among the Cherokee for peace on the council, as the "civil" or *white* chief. Oconostota, however, especially after his defeat of the Creeks, did not share Attacullaculla's wish for friendship with the English settlers, reminding the other chiefs at every opportunity that their ancient borders had been pushed back to half their original extent, that the wild game had diminished, that their children were forgetting the ways of the ancestors, and worst of all, that whole villages had been decimated by the smallpox from which he himself had suffered and was still scarred. The only hope for Cherokee survival was to drive the English and all white settlers from their lands.

Attacullaculla, however, had seen with his own eyes the advantages and strengths and appeal of a civilization far more advanced than his own. He continued to argue for adaptation, saying they should accept what they could of the white man's ways, and did all that lay in his power to promote good relations as beneficial for the Cherokee. To Attacullaculla's grief, his eldest son sided with the war party. Dragging Canoe had his father's gift of persuasive speech and the young men flocked around him. The outbreak of war between the French and the English over control of Indian lands, mostly in the North, in 1755 precipitated a new era of fighting and violence throughout the colonies, even among those tribes not directly involved. More than ever the English needed forts and allies in Cherokee territory.

⌒

Three new forts were built, one within five miles of the Cherokee capital town of Echota, and fighting and skirmishes continued— fueled by hostilities between the two European powers. Within a short time the tenuous alliance between the Cherokee and the English colonies was hanging by a thread. Time and again only the eloquence of Attacullaculla prevented it breaking apart altogether. His diplomacy and tact saved as many English lives as Cherokee. He pled the cause of his own people with the military leaders of the colonies, but just as often prevented his cousin and the war party from ruthless attacks against the whites. Attacullaculla helped persuade the Governor of South Carolina in 1757 to construct what would be Fort Loudon, both to strengthen English control in the area and also to encourage more trade between the Cherokee and the towns of the eastern coast. He invited colonial traders to establish headquarters in Chota, to promote yet more trade and commerce, and at the same time encouraged these white traders to take Cherokee wives.

But an incident in 1759, in which a militia of Virginians killed and scalped twenty Cherokee after a joint mission against the French and Shawnee, pushed the chief of the white feather too far. Even Attacullaculla vowed revenge.

The reaction within the tribe was outrage and horror. Attacullaculla's son Dragging Canoe and many other young warriors immediately clamored for retaliatory raids upon the English. The chiefs did their best to dissuade them, saying they would first attempt to negotiate restitution for the killings with the colonies of Virginia, North Carolina, and South Carolina. But their requests fell on deaf ears.

Within months, led by Attacullaculla's son, young warriors began raiding and burning colonial settlements. South Carolina declared war on the Cherokee and mobilized its militia.

Oconostota and a party of thirty prominent Cherokee chiefs rode to Charleston in an attempt to negotiate peace with the Governor before all out war erupted. The Governor perceived an opportunity that might not come again. Though the delegation had come in peace, he immediately arrested Oconostota and the Cherokee leaders. He gave orders for the thirty hostages to be marched under military guard back to Fort Prince George, where they were imprisoned.

Governor Lyttleton then sent for Attacullaculla, known friend of the British.

The hour was early. A stocky man, shorter than many of the women of the village but strong in mind and limb, wrapped an otter skin around his bare shoulders and walked quietly from the village.

Smoke rose from a dozen or more lodges as he went. The women had begun to stir. Within an hour the village would be alive with activity. The sky was clear and promised warmth, but the chill of night just past still held the gray dawn in its grip.

He walked to the creek, stepped across the log over it, and continued up the hill on the opposite side. After a few minutes he paused and glanced behind him. A figure followed. He waited.

"You are out on the hills early, White Owl," she said approaching.

"No earlier than you, my sister."

"I saw you leave the village. I knew you were burdened. Your face speaks of much thought."

"It is not only for the gentleness of your countenance that you are called Tame Doe," he said. "You have the keen eyes of one quiet of spirit who sees what many cannot."

"That is only because I know you so well, my brother. I have been watching your many moods since before I can remember. Tame Doe looked up to White Owl."

Again he smiled, the older brother recalling with fondness the years now long past when his sister was so young in his youthful eyes. Now she stood three inches taller than he, though he was ten years her elder.

"You are weighed down by what you must do. When do you leave to see Governor?"

"Soon . . . later today."

"What will be outcome?"

"I do not know, but I fear preventing war will be difficult. What else can I conclude with Oconostota and the others not returning but that he took them hostage? Perhaps he will imprison me as well."

"He would not dare. British respect you as most powerful Cherokee chief of peace among our people."

"I am not so certain, my sister. This governor is more American than English."

"And Oconostota?"

"If he has his way, I will have no opportunity to achieve peace. He is full of anger. He will not give my way a chance to succeed."

"He went to governor seeking peace."

"Only because he saw no other choice."

"He would say your way has been tried with settlers and has failed."

"Perhaps he is right. Every promise they make is broken. They take more and more of our land. They enslave our people. They kill without compunction."

"Would they not say the same of Oconostota and our young warriors who kill and burn their homes? I have heard them call us savages."

"It is true. In their eyes, such we must seem. But it is not we who have taken their land. Many of their traders cheat us. They lie. They drive us to retaliate. Truly this white race from the land called England can be a cruel and heartless people. I do not understand how they have so little honor, so little care for justice to fellow men. And yet—"

Attacullaculla drew in a deep sigh and shook his head slowly.

"And yet . . . you desire peace."

"I cannot give up the hope that it may be so, that men even of different colors can live together without bloodshed. Our father taught me to love peace. I have worn the white feather all my life."

"That is why you still wear ring of peace," said Tame Doe, nodding toward her brother's right hand, whose middle finger was encircled by a band of gold.

He glanced down at his hand and nodded.

"You are only one of seven who still wears ring of peace."

"It was agreed among us that the rings would honor the white feather of peace, and that they would not be worn in times of war. Before the delegation set out for Charleston with Oconostota, even though the mission was to negotiate peace, five of the seven removed their rings and gave them to me for safekeeping. We feared lest they be stolen or captured by our enemy."

"The fears were well founded. Now they are all captive."

"If the English knew that four of the chiefs they are holding were honored by their own king in his own court . . . perhaps it would mean nothing. They can be a ruthless people."

"But were not all rings given to you?"

"Ounakannowie has abandoned our cause. He has come to despise me. His ring is now in Oconostota's possession."

"Where are others?"

"They are safe, my sister," smiled Attacullaculla. "For your own safety it is best you do not know. There are some who consider the rings filled with magical powers. I fear the result if they were controlled by the chiefs of the red feather, though Oconostota now possesses one."

"Yet you still wear yours?"

"I must be a symbol of peace to our people as long as I wear the white feather."

"What will happen?"

"I will speak to the governor. Even now my son would mass our warriors to march on the fort to rescue the captives. But I will try again to make them see the folly of open war. Their numbers are too great. Peace is the only way our people will survive."

They glanced up to see a young woman of twenty-three approaching.

"Ah, young Nanye'hi," said the chief with a smile, "you are out with the beaver and rabbit."

"I was out for a walk before children awake," said the girl, walking toward Tame Doe. "I wish to speak with you, Uncle."

Attacullaculla stared at his niece for a moment, as if seeing her dawning maturity in the well-defined angular features of her face in a new way.

"I have noticed that trader Ward at the post has a fondness for you, Nanye'hi," he said.

The girl's cheeks flushed slightly.

"He is kind to me."

"Do you love him, Nanye'hi?"

"How is one ever sure? He is English, Uncle."

"That is why the young have elders, to keep them from foolishness. You have your mother who is a Tame Doe and has the wise and watchful eyes of a quiet heart. You have a father who is a brave warrior, who has killed to protect our people yet has the gentle touch of a kind father. By trusting their wisdom, you too will grow wise."

"And by trusting your uncle, our chief," added Tame Doe. "What is it you wish to say?"

"I do not find it pleasant to own my black man," said Nanye'hi. "Why should I among all the Cherokee have slave?"

"You are kind to him," said Attacullaculla. "As he came to you for your bravery, you honor our people by being kind to him. He reveres you almost as much as do our people. Slaves were treated cruelly by the Cheeks. In his eyes, you saved his life."

As Nanye'hi left them a few minutes later, uncle and mother watched in silence as she disappeared down the slope in the direction of the village.

"She is a remarkable young woman, Tame Doe," said the chief. "She too, I think, loves peace. But she is a feisty one who has courage and grit—she possesses her father's blood as well."

"She will be better equipped to make her peace with it than I. I do not like the scalps outside our lodge. I grieve at the thought of death. But my husband is Fivekiller."

"You are indeed a Tame Doe," smiled Attacullaculla. "Your Nanye'hi will rise high among our people. She is a daughter to make a mother proud. I perceive greatness in her eyes. She will encounter much that we cannot foresee. Times are changing. Our people must change with them. It will not be easy for some."

⌣⁀

Upon Attacullaculla's arrival at Fort Prince George, the South Carolina governor explained that his fellow chiefs had been imprisoned and were being held pending a solution to the recent massacres. Governor Lyttleton then demanded that Attacullaculla turn over twenty-four Cherokee warriors who were accused of killing whites in the recent raids. One of them was the peace chief's own son.

"I will do what I am able," replied Attacullaculla. "But you are asking a great deal."

"They are murderers," returned the Governor insolently.

"Are they any more so than the whites who scalped my own people."

"I am told that was done by the French."

"They were Virginian Englishmen," said Attacullaculla calmly. "If you are seeking causes to this recent violence between our peoples, it is to your own colonists you must look first."

"There were many charges of theft of horses and poultry in Virginia."

"Some of those charges were true," nodded Attacullaculla, "but only because our warriors were left starving after the Shawnee war, and were deserted and left helpless by the very colonists they were assisting. You know the truth of the incident as well as I, my lord Governor. For twenty years I have done everything in my power to preserve the peace between our two nations. I have saved more white lives than I can count. But even my patience has limits. I have not forgiven the Virginians for the heartless murders of my people, nor their Governor for paying his colonists bounty for Cherokee scalps. I do not forget treachery, my lord Governor. There are many of my people who clamor for war against you, even should our entire tribe die in the attempt to preserve our heritage. I hold them back as one man trying to stop a river that is swollen to a flood and is ready to burst. If war comes, many will die, and I will be unable to prevent it. We have given you everything. We have sold you the best of our lands. Our people are dead from your guns and your diseases. This is our land and you take it and treat us as vermin beneath your feet. Does your thirst to consume us have no end!"

Governor Lyttleton sat in silence, astonished and angered to hear the ordinarily calm Attacullaculla lecture him with such passion. But the man's noble bearing and command of the facts were irrefutable.

"I regret what happened in Virginia," began Lyttleton in reply. "What Governor Dinwiddie did in the matter of the scalps is without excuse, and I would never—"

"There are many who would say," interrupted Attacullaculla, "that your imprisoning my brothers, when they came to you on a mission of peace, is the act of a traitor and a coward."

"How dare you speak to me like that!"

"I speak the truth, my lord Governor. Do you deny that what you did was an act of treachery?"

"In times of war, extraordinary measures are called for. I did what was necessary."

"Your colonists broke the treaty your own king, and your own colony made with my people. Your colonies break *every* agreement we make with you."

"I thought you were a man of peace!"

"I hope I am. That is why I am here. I will do what I can to bring those responsible for the killings to justice. But on your part, you must release my kinsmen to show your good faith. They will help me among our people to convey your demands."

"I will do no such thing!" snapped the Governor.

"Then I fear there is little I can do," replied Attacullaculla. He rose to leave the room.

"Wait," said the Govenor behind him. "I will tell you what—I will release three of the prisoners."

"They are not *prisoners*, my lord Governor," said Attacullaculla, "but Cherokee chiefs whom you took hostage under false pretences."

"Bah—you are splitting hairs. I just offered to release three of them."

Attacullaculla thought a moment, then nodded in agreement.

Within an hour, he was on his way home with Oconostota and two others, discussing their options for freeing the rest of the hostages. Angered by the Governor's duplicitous tactics, Oconostota was no longer thinking of peaceful solutions.

When Attacullaculla next left for the British fort with two of the warriors that had been demanded, Oconostota took the opportunity of his absense to ride among the towns and villages raising a party of warriors to be ready in the event his cousin's negotiations failed. Attacullaculla's return a few days later, without the hostages, was all the answer Oconostota needed.

The war chief sent word to the commander of Fort Prince George requesting a conference. The meeting took place in the dead of winter in the early months of 1760. Oconostota rode with his party of warriors to the meeting on the Savannah River near Fort Prince George where their Cherokee brothers were still captive. But there would be no more talk of peace from his mouth. This time Attacullaculla remained behind.

As they drew near the site of the meeting, Oconostota instructed some of his warriors to move in a circular route through the wooded region in order to gain a closer vantage point to the white men. The main party came to the bank of the river. On the opposite side stood the captain and two officers from the fort and their interpreter. Suddenly Oconostota raised his arm. Gunshots from his warriors in hiding burst out. All four white men were wounded. Knowing they had been double-crossed, they fled and made for the fort.

Raising the war cry, Oconostota and his party forded the river, galloped after them, and stormed the fort. But their few numbers and guns were no match for the barricaded and well-armed English troops. The attack was repulsed and Oconostota and his party could do nothing but take their dead and wounded and retreat. Two days later Captain Cotymore died from his wounds. All the Cherokee hostages, most of them respected chiefs of the tribe, were murdered the same day.

The chief of the white feather had done all he could. But Attacullaculla could no longer hold back the violence. Within months, full scale war erupted between the Cherokee and the English colonies.[4]

---

[4] www.keetowah-society.org; *The Biography of Nancy Ward*, by David Hampton, The Association of the Descendents of Nancy Ward. See also Note 4—The Legacies of Attacullaculla, Oconostota, and Dragging Canoe.

Nanye'hi Ward, Beloved Woman of the Cherokee

1754–1802

*A*ttacullaculla's predictions about his niece Nanye'hi, daughter of Tame Doe and Fivekiller, proved true. As she grew from a young widow to a self-reliant mother at twenty to a beautiful woman at thirty, to a majestic matron at forty, to a queen of the Cherokee at fifty, her fame throughout the Cherokee nation grew into legend. Even white men throughout the colonies and then the states of the new nation heard rumors of the tall Wild Rose of stunning beauty and stately dignity of the Cherokee. It was said that her glistening long silky hair was blacker than a moonless night, and that her delicate tan skin was as soft and fair as rose petals. Her piercing black-green eyes were of deeper green than the emerald of any mountain stream and were capable of enchanting all who laid eyes on her. Whites did not know the strange word *Ghigua,* but they knew that the Beloved Woman of the Cherokee was held in higher honor than many of her chiefs.

A few years after her husband's death, the white trader Bryan Ward, a widower with his son John, had come to live among the Cherokee to operate a trading post at Chota, and gradually began to show an interest in the young widow. He had long been kind to her, but now seemed looking out for her with as much kindness as those of her own tribe. He was more attentive to her two youngsters, Catherine and Fivekiller, than could be accounted for by mere friendship. By now Nanye'hi was twenty-six-years of age, and her carriage had grown all the more lovely. Slowly the white trader and young Cherokee widow fell in love. They were married in Chota where they continued to live for many years. Though Nanye'hi took her new husband's English name for her own, she remained faithful all her life to her duties and loyalties to the Cherokee people. Forever after, among whites, the legendary Ghigua of the Cherokee was simply called Nancy Ward.

Like an increasing number of the Cherokee of her time, Nanye'hi did not find it distasteful to integrate into American life. Like her uncle she valued white life as much as Indian life, and saw in her third child, daughter Elizabeth—half white, half Cherokee—the future of her people. Many times Nanye'hi risked her own life to save another, the color of whose skin her eyes did not see. She had shed the blood of fellow humankind and the memory of it never left her. She devoted the rest of her life to prevent its being shed again whenever it lay in her power.

As Beloved Woman, it was Nanye'hi's role to lead the women's council of the tribe, and also to sit for life on the men's tribal council of chiefs to represent the women, where she had a full voice and vote. The Ghigua was also granted supreme pardoning power of the entire tribe, above even the prerogative of any of the chiefs. It was her duty to prepare the Black Drink for the Green Corn ceremony. Hers was expected to be a voice for peace. The Ghigua was one of the permanent negotiators in all treaty discussions. In a meeting with American John Sevier in 1781 at Little Pigeon River to discuss terms of peace, she was amazed and distressed that no women negotiators had accompanied him. He was equally incredulous to find that she, a woman, had been entrusted by her tribe with so important a task. When the negotiations were concluded, she told Sevier to go back to his people, and tell the women of the terms of their agreement. "Let your women hear our words," she said.

Because Nanye'hi was so respected, honored, and revered by her people, her word often swayed a council discussion and changed a course of violence that had been set in motion by Cherokee warriors. One of the most important powers of her position was the right to pardon condemned captives, a power she exercised many times through her life. The power of Oconostota was absolute during times of war, but at all times, in war *and* peace, inspired, as they saw her, by the Great Spirit, even the great chiefs of the nation gave way to the will of Nanye'hi Ward.

Jeremiah Jack and William Rankin, two white settlers, came by canoe downriver to Chota to purchase corn from the Cherokee. They encountered an angry young crowd of rowdy Indians who grabbed them, took them captive, and made plans to kill them. Hearing the commotion, Nanye'hi rushed to the scene and commanded the young men to release the whites instantly. The Ghigua had spoken and the young warriors obeyed. Two hours later the two white men were on their way home, their canoe loaded with corn.

The wife of a homesteading family was taken captive in 1776. William Bean had been one of the first settlers to the region years before. Some of the Cherokee had never forgotten the name Bean and his incursion into their lands, and they had vowed revenge. His wife, Lydia, was brought back to Cherokee land where Nanye'hi's cousin Dragging Canoe ordered her to be burned at the stake. Mrs. Bean was tied to a pole on a small hill and a great pile of kindling heaped about her feet. Hearing of it, Nanye'hi hurried to the scene. Outraged at the sight that met her eyes, she ran forward, cut the ropes at Mrs. Bean's feet, and commanded that she be set free.

"It revolts my soul," she shouted angrily, glaring around at her cousin and the others, "that Cherokee warriors would stoop so low as to torture a squaw. No woman shall be tortured or burned while I am Ghigua."

Even a determined warrior and the son of the chief like Dragging Canoe had to obey. Nanye'hi finished cutting Mrs. Bean down, then took the white lady to her own home. As soon as it was safe, Nanye'hi sent Mrs. Bean back to her husband with the escort of her own brother Tuskeegeeteehee and son Hiskyteehee. Thereafter a long friendship existed between the two women. Like her uncle, Nanye'hi sought to learn from the whites. Mrs. Bean taught Nanye'hi the art of weaving, how to make butter and cheese, and other aspects of dairy farming, which were all then introduced into Cherokee life.

To the end of his life, Attacullaculla clung to his hope for friendship and brotherhood between the great king across the water and his own people. As his eyesight failed and his strength grew feeble he realized that he must entrust that hope to the next generation. But the American colonists seemed bent on destroying the once-proud Cherokee nation, which made his vision of friendship all the more difficult to achieve.

Who would be capable of carrying his posterity into the next generation, and, after that, into the next century?

His headstrong son Dragging Canoe was out of the question. He had become too much like his warrior uncle—restless, eager for bloodshed, too quickly angered. Though Oconostota had come to see much through the eyes of realism as his years had advanced, Attacullaculla wondered if such would ever be true in the case of his own son.

Dragging Canoe's speech at Sycamore Shoals on the eve of the American war with the British made his position clear enough. He was reportedly still leading raids of the Chickamaugua. Dragging Canoe would certainly make no ambassador for peace.

What about Dragging Canoe's son and daughter, his own grandson Young Dragging Canoe or his granddaughter Nakey Canoe? Nakey had married a white trader and now had three very young sons, his own precious great-grandsons—Alexander Saunie, named for her husband, Long, and Swift, who had both been given Cherokee names.

No, Attacullaculla thought. They were too young. It was impossible to tell to what extent they would follow his own dream, or that of Dragging Canoe.

The thoughts of the aging chief turned to other of his children.

Little Owl . . . he lacked resolve. It was as easy to persuade him as it was for the wind to bend a tree. He could change his mind ten times in a day.

Turtle-At-Home . . . he was well respected among the people but due to a defect at birth could not speak clearly.

His daughter Ollie wished for peace but had no voice among the people.

The Badger . . . Tah-Chee . . . his cousins Tassel and Doublehead, one of whom would likely be head chief before many more years. . . . With none could he feel sure that the legacy from the English king would be preserved.

Slowly Attacullaculla's thoughts turned toward his niece Nanye'hi. She had grown to be the most respected and loved woman of the Cherokee, surpassing even the men of the nation in honor. *She* would realize the importance of friendship *and* hold the ear of the council.

Yes. Nanye'hi would carry the legacy of peace to the generations of the future.

When the aging chief of the Cherokee rode toward the house with the attached trading post, the dwelling could have been any white man's house, for the spacious log house was the largest dwelling in the Cherokee capital.

Nanye'hi's two older children, both in their twenties, were already married and gone, but fourteen-year-old Elizabeth ran out to greet him. She was followed by one of several black slaves, who met the chief, helped him down, and took the reins of his horse. Attacullaculla was dressed in his finest chieftain's robes, skins, and adorning finery of beads, silver, feathers, and gold. Upon his graying head sat the symbolic leather band of the white feather.

Nanye'hi walked out of the house and greeted him with an affectionate embrace. "Uncle," she said, looking him over with some puzzlement. "What is the occasion that you have come in your regal attire? Has the council been summoned?"

The aging chief nodded. "Yes, Nanye'hi, but only a council of two."

"I do not understand, Uncle."

"It is a council of two, and I have summoned it," he replied. "It is a solemn council regarding the future. You and I will be the only members present. There is much we must discuss . . . alone. Come, Nanye'hi—you and I must ride up the mountain to the sacred site where the Great Spirit spoke to our ancestors."

Nanye'hi sensed from her uncle's voice that something momentous was at hand. She nodded and left him. When she returned some minutes later, she too wore her council robe of white deerskin. Her flowing black hair was adorned with a band of colorful feathers she placed upon her head only for the most solemn of occasions. At nearly forty, she was stunning and commanding. No queen of any empire bore herself with more regal dignity.

A few words to her husband were enough. He understood her role in the tribe. She leapt on the bare back of the pony that stood waiting beside her uncle's mount. Bryan Ward and young Elizabeth watched them ride out of town, the aging chief and the Beloved Woman of the Cherokee. As they rode away, already eyes from half the town followed the two legendary figures as they disappeared from sight toward the hills.

They rode to the top of Ooneekawy Mountain whose peak looked down on the most ancient of Cherokee villages. When they had reached the top, they dismounted and gazed about in silence.

"All that our eyes can now see was once the land of the Ani-Yunwiya," said Attacullaculla in a voice whose very sound filled his niece with memories of her childhood. "Now the white settlers claim much of it for their own for their towns and forts and farms. Our people are dwindling, our land is shrinking. Yet we are also learning to adapt and change and grow. We have learned much from the white man. It is his land now too, no longer only the land of the Indian. We must live *with* the white man, not against him."

Attacullaculla paused as he continued to gaze down upon the beloved land of his people.

"But I am old, Nanye'hi," he said. "I have not many seasons of the sun left."

"You will be honored among our people for many years, Uncle—"

"Nanye'hi," interrupted Attacullaculla, "you must look to the future, not the past. You must be brave, as I know you will be, for you have shown your bravery on countless occasions. You are honored among our people. It is time for you to be strong. My time has passed. The future will go with you. That is why I have brought you up the sacred mountain. Like old Wasi[5] of the ancient people, I will not see the future. I can but gaze from the mountain, but you must go down and lead our people into their future."

He paused and held up his hand. Nanye'hi's glance immediately went to his middle finger, where, for as long as she could remember, since her very childhood, she had seen the gold ring and been told by her mother that it had come from the king in England.

He now pulled off the ring and took Nanye'hi's right hand. Gently he slipped the ring of royalty onto her thumb.

"I have worn this ring since it was given me by the king over the water," he said. "Now I pass on my ring of peace to you."

Too awestruck to speak, Nanye'hi watched as her uncle now pulled out a soft leather pouch of coveted white deerskin that matched his council robe. Slowly he opened it, then poured five rings of pure gold into his palm.

Nancy's eyes widened at the sight.

"And now, Nanye'hi," he said, "I give you these other five too. They were entrusted to me by my comrades during the settlement wars twenty years ago, to keep and preserve for the time when permanent peace would come to our people. They were all massacred when

---

[5]When the early missionaries came among the Cherokees, they were astonished at the similarity of the religious tradition of the Cherokees to the biblical accounts. . . . They claimed that Yehowa was the name of a great king. He was a man and yet a spirit. . . . His name was never to be spoken in common talk. This great king commanded them to rest every seventh day. Yehowa created the world in seven days . . . made the first man of red clay and he was an Indian, and made woman of one of his ribs. All people were Indians or red people before the flood. They had preachers and prophets who . . . warned the people of the approaching flood. . . . A little before the flood men grew worse and worse. At length God . . . told a man to make a house that would swim, take his family and some of the different kinds of animals into it. The rain commenced and continued for forty days and forty nights.

The Cherokees detailed to the missionaries parallels to practically every one of the stories of the Bible. They called Abraham Aquahimi; Moses was called Wasi. These accounts were so circumstantial that many investigators were led to believe that the Cherokees were of Semitic origin. (*History of the Cherokee Indians*, Emmet Starr, pp. 23-24)

my cousin attacked Fort Prince George. Only I of the original seven am left. Now you must keep them safe for our people as I have done."

"But where, Uncle?"

"Wherever they will be safe. In time you too must pass them on as I am passing them on to you. You must give them to one or more who will preserve the legacy of peace. The whole country is full of war as the Americans and British fight to control this land. We cannot see to the end of it. It may be the British, it may be the Americans with whom we will have to live. But we must live *with* them. Such is my pledge, and such legacy I now pass on to you."

"Were there not seven rings, Uncle?" asked Nanye'hi.

"Oconostota now wears the last of the seven. I fear it is for him a symbol of power and war. That is why we must preserve the legacy of peace. I will go to our fathers longing for the day when all seven rings may be joined again, when our people will be united as one, again to rise to greatness—not by conquest but by the character that makes them the real people, the *Ani-Yunwiya* of a new time, *The People of Peace.* When you are old, like me, you must pass them on to one who will preserve the legacy of the rings, and who will preserve the heritage of our people. Perhaps such a one will be your Cata'quin who has married the Harlan. Perhaps it will come from my seed, one of the sons of my granddaughter Nakey, if one should inherit her gentle nature rather than that of her father. In tiny Long, as she gave him into my arms, my aging heart leapt to see what appears in his eyes. If he is not a chief among our people, surely he will be a wise man. When the time comes, Nanye'hi, you will know, whether him or another. The future of our secret is now yours."

Within two years Attacullaculla had departed to return to the spirit of his fathers. His memory was revered and his passing mourned by the entire Cherokee nation, and equally by the many white Americans who had known him as a man of dignity and honor.

The once great warrior Oconostota, however, had by now became a relic of the past, drinking and wandering and lamenting his past glory as chief of a warrior race, eventually even selling the gold ring on his finger to a trader who never knew where it had come from, in exchange for five dollars of whisky.

With the death of Attacullaculla in 1778, and Oconostota in 1782, Old Tassel became the chief of the Cherokee. But it was a new era. And though Old Tassel strove to prevent yet more incursions into Cherokee land, the new American nation, flush with its success against the British, was determined to take anything it wanted. It was quickly clear that the new government felt entitled to *all* the land on the continent.

Nanye'hi was a major negotiating force during peace and treaty talks of the 1780s, urging both sides to exist together peacefully. Like Attacullaculla, there were those Cherokee who thought she placated the settlers too readily. But though Nanye'hi Ward did not like the encroachment of whites any more than the rest of her tribe, she would not stand by to see whites murdered in cold blood. "The white men are our brothers," she said. "The same house holds us, the same sky covers us all." Upon numerous occasions, hearing of planned attacks against colonial "overmountain" settlements, she secretly informed one or another of the Indian traders who lived among the Cherokee to get word to those in danger. In time, as a result of such warnings, she became as greatly honored by white settlers as by her own people. In spite of such seeming betrayals, her esteem among her own people grew yet more. Many did not agree with her, but all respected her.

Over the years Bryan and Nanye'hi Ward enjoyed a certain degree of wealth. Their home was furnished with primitive splendor and style. In addition to Ward's trading post, they became successful raising cattle. They purchased a home on the Womankiller Ford of the Ocowee River which they converted into an inn which Nanye'hi operated successfully for many years.

After the conclusion of the War of Independence with England, the new government of the United States agreed to yet another treaty in 1785 at Hopewell in South Carolina. Its final clause read: "Any settler who fails to remove within six months from the land guaranteed to the Indians shall forfeit any protection of the United States, and the Cherokee may punish him or not as they please."

Nanye'hi Ward spoke on behalf of the Cherokee at the treaty signing.

"I am glad," she said, "that at last there is peace. I take you by the hand of friendship. I have a pipe and tobacco to give the commissioners to smoke in friendship. I look upon you and those of my tribe as my children. Your decision for peace is pleasant to me, for I have witnessed much trouble during the wars between our nations. I am growing old, but I hope yet to see children who will grow up and people our nation, as we are now under the protection of the Congress and shall have no more war between us. The talk I have given you is from the young warriors I have raised in my town, as well as from myself. They rejoice that we have peace, and hope that the chain of friendship will never more be broken."

She gave two strings of wampum, a pipe, and some tobacco to the representatives from the government.

But in matters of greed and power, the waters of peace do not run deep. In 1802, as a chilling portent of things to come, the third president of the new nation, Thomas Jefferson, struck an agreement with the state of Georgia. The Georgia Compact stated that, the conflicts and disputes being what they were, with the white populations exploding, with towns and cities springing up all around them, it would doubtless be best for the Cherokees to be removed from Tennessee, the Carolinas, and Georgia altogether, and relocated in one of the less-populated western territories. Toward this end, Jefferson made a pact with the state of Georgia to purchase for $1,250,000 all its western lands, which would become U.S. government property, along with the guarantee that the federal government would extinguish at its own expense "as early as the same can be peaceably obtained upon reasonable terms, the Indian title to the lands lying within the limits of that state."

It was several years before the terms of this policy began to be known among the Cherokee. But as Jefferson's plan was seen for what it was, it gradually split the Cherokee nation apart. Some welcomed the offer of new lands as a new chance to return to the old ways and not worry about encroaching settlement. Others resented it as the final insult of a government determined to be rid of them forever.

Changing times, as it always does, brought new figures of leadership to the fore, rising out of the same lineages of chiefs that had gone to their fathers. As Cherokee politics had essentially been dominated for most of the eighteenth century by the Moytoy, Attacullaculla, and Oconostota dynasty, now began to rise a powerful new family out of the old that would itself grow into a new dynasty symbolizing the new times of the American nation. It descended from Attacullaculla through his son Tah-Chee.

In 1771 was born to the son of Attacullaculla's grandson Oganosta and his wife, Sehoya, a child called Nung-noh-nut-tar-hee, or the Pathkiller, who later changed his name to Kah-nung-da-tla-geh, the Man Who Walks the Mountain. Another boy was born called Oowatie, the Ancient One. By the time they were young men, the former was simply known as The Ridge. The brother patriarchs of a powerful Cherokee family were in the making. Though in his early years, The Ridge was a violent traditionalist opposed to accommodation with the ways of the white man or relinquishment of tribal lands, his son and two nephews would come to symbolize the transition of the Cherokee into American culture. Oowatie and his wife were converted to Christianity, adopted many ways of the whites, and took the Christian names Christian David and Susanna Charity with Watie as surname. The lineage of those two brothers would remain at the center of a half century of strife for the Cherokee.

Eventually the conflict over whether to continue to sell their land to the government, or whether to fight to the death to preserve what was theirs, erupted into armed conflict within the Cherokee nation itself. Brother took up weapon against brother in the dispute. Whatever their differences in policy, Attacullaculla and Oconostota had managed to keep their people as one. But now murder and treachery

spread through the nation, Cherokee against Cherokee, as a proud
people fought to retain their heritage and their land before all was lost.

Attacullaculla's vision of peace and unity among his people seemed
like a dream that would never again be realized.[6]

[6]www.pinn.net; "Sunshine for Women," Cynthia Kasee, and *Native American Women: A Biographical Dictionary*, by Gretchen Bataille (ed.), London, Garland Publishing, 199e, pp. 272-74; *The Cerokees*, Grace Steel Woorward, p. 130

Long Canoe and
the Secret of the Cave

1786–1816

*N*anye'hi Ward never forgot her pledge to Chief Attacullaculla. She kept the secret of his legacy in her heart, and the secret of the rings in an ancient hiding place of the Cherokee, high on the sacred mountain where she was certain they would not be found.

Nor had she forgotten the aging chief's words about the grandson of her cousin Dragging Canoe. The words the great Attacullaculla had spoken on the mountain, and the sacred trust he had placed in her hands, had been with her ever since: "*You must pass on the legacy as I am passing it on to you . . . to one who will preserve the heritage and will treasure the unity of our people.*"

Many of their people said that the Great Spirit spoke through her. It was true that voices, feelings, and thoughts came to her that she could not account for by ordinary means. She first noticed it on the stormy day of the birth of her cousin Nakey's second son. That was many years ago, only two years before Attacullaculla's death. She had accompanied Nakey to the river where the naked infant had been baptized in hardiness. The moment the boy had cried out from the cold, a chill swept through Nanye'hi's body. Almost the same instant, a distant rumble of thunder sounded. Even as Nakey lifted the dripping boy from the river, Nanye'hi glanced up to the peak of

Oononhway shrouded in clouds and mist. Less than a year later, the great chief told her he felt the boy was destined to wisdom. Had the Great Spirit, even before, been telling her the same thing?

Nanye'hi stared up at the mountain, now grown eerily silent. As they made their way back to the Cherokee town where Nakey lived with her husband, Alexander, Nanye'hi continued to ponder the strange events of the child's water birth. Ever since that day, whenever she saw Nakey's growing boy, the thumb on which she still wore the great chief's ring tingled momentarily, and the far-off gaze of Long's eyes reminded her of the rumble from Oononhway after his birth.

She listened to the young boy's every word as he grew. She observed him with piercing eyes. Many children of the Cherokee could claim closer relation to the great Ghigua. But never was one more devoted to the grandson of a cousin than was Nanye'hi Ward to young Long, son of Nakey Canoe, grandson of Dragging Canoe, as he grew into boyhood, then youth. He was a quiet boy, attentive to nature, to weather, to the ways of the animals. By the time he was twelve, he was considered a master cultivator of the earth, knew exactly when and where to plant maize and squash and many other crops, whose ways he had learned from his elders and the white man to get the best yield. It was obvious he would be a man of the earth, not a warrior like his fiery grandfather Dragging Canoe. But when at fifteen, he announced, though he loved and respected his white father, he had chosen to take to himself the name of his mother's family rather than his father's, out of respect for the heritage of his Cherokee roots and blood, Nanye'hi knew that the spirit of Attacullaculla had indeed chosen wisely. From that moment, she knew that the day would come when she would take the young man now known as Long Canoe to the top of the mountain as her uncle had taken her.

Long Canoe grew and matured alongside his cousins Ridge and Oowatie and his more distant cousins Doublehead and Old Tassel. As one of these promising young leaders of the nation, the grandson of Dragging Canoe was selected along with a few other Cherokee young men to attend the white man's college at Dartmouth with one of the scholarships given to a select group of Cherokee for educational advancement. During his time in the North, Long spent many hours studying the ways of his fellow men, both those with dark skin and those with light. By the time he reached manhood he had seen many changes come to his people and to the land they called home.

Once the sovereignty of the new nation calling itself the United States of America was established by treaty with Great Britain in 1783, the most far reaching of the Cherokee knew that their hope for national sovereignty was dead. The thirteen colonies, now thirteen states of a new nation, were too powerful. Their expansion could not be stopped. They had defeated the most powerful nation on earth. They would not be stopped from taking anything they wanted.

The first two decades of the nineteenth century were troublesome for the Cherokee nation. The Cherokee gradually split into two factions, both convinced that they represented the best for the future of their people. When Thomas Jefferson began to encourage a westward migration of Cherokee, the debate grew fierce about whether to relocate and leave lands their people had occupied for centuries, or whether to fight to preserve them.

The divisive split came to a head in 1808 when Chief Doublehead signed an agreement to move west. When the hard-liners learned of the agreement, Doublehead was brutally murdered by his own kinsmen, the death blow being struck by none other than The Ridge. A break in the Cherokee nation had begun that would not be fully healed for many generations.

In spite of the danger from his fellow tribesmen, another chief, Tahlonteskee, took a band of 1,100 Chickamauga Cherokees west to the land provided them in the Arkansas Territory. The peoples of this first migration of Cherokee would later be known as the Old Settlers, and, though danger from their own people remained high, many would join them. A western migration of families and small groups continued. The hostility between the two factions of Cherokee intensified. Those who sold their lands continued to be in danger of assassination by their own people.

The dispute grieved the heart of aging Nanye'hi Ward, now a stately woman of seventy-six, whose life spanned an era of much change in the fortunes of her people. She knew the time was approaching when she must do her duty to posterity.[7]

⟨~~~⟩

Long Canoe returned from Dartmouth, his view of the world broader, his toleration for peoples of diverse backgrounds widened, and his love of his own Cherokee roots deeper. In his absense, the dispute between those advocating removal to the West and those vowing to remain in the East and fight to the death to retain their lands had grown more bitter than ever.

A major campaign against the Creeks was waged in 1813–14 in which commander Andrew Jackson conscripted seven hundred Cherokee to fight with U.S. forces. Jackson's life was saved during the conflict by a young chief called Junaluska. But it was well-known that Jackson hated native peoples and was using the Cherokee only for the purposes of expediency in ridding the South of Creeks. Once that was accomplished, none doubted that he would use equally ruthless tactics to rid the mountain regions of the Cherokee. It was during the Creek War that the elder Ridge was promoted by Jackson to the rank of major and his brother Oowatie to captain. The Ridge was thereafter known as Major Ridge. Promotions notwithstanding, however, when it came to native peoples, it was clear that Andrew Jackson represented a new breed of American leader who cared nothing for native rights.

In spite of threats from their cousin, now called Major Ridge, Long's younger brother, Swift, became one of the loudest voices urging their kinsmen to sell their land while there was still time to profit by it and move West to join their Cherokee cousins. Although his stand was unpopular, his words carried weight in light of the recent plight of the Creeks. The United States government had declared the Creek enemies

[7]See Note 5—The Old Settlers vs. the Eastern Cherokee

of the American people and had confiscated their property. How long could the Cherokee hope to retain *their* rights before the same fate befell them? They must sell their lands and move beyond the government's reach. So at least argued those, like Long Canoe's brother, Swift, who advocated joining the Old Settlers in the Arkansas Territory.

To demonstrate his loyalty to their Cherokee heritage, however, Swift followed his brother's example and took a Cherokee name rather than their white father's, calling himself Swift Water. His son he called Swift Horse.

Long Canoe found himself in the position of peacemaker between his older brother Alexander Saunie and his little brother Swift Water. But speaking out in favor of the Old Settlers had placed Swift Water in great danger with those in the tribe intent on putting a stop to westward migration. Doublehead had already been murdered for his sentiments. Those intent upon stopping migration would not be afraid to kill again.

Long Canoe matured as one of the Cherokee nation's new leaders, recognized for his wisdom, intelligence, and cunning. Half white and half Cherokee, his features were light and his hair a dark brown rather than the pure black of his race, and his eyes blue as the sky. Some complained that his years away had turned him into a white man. But never lived a more dedicated Cherokee than Long Canoe, son of Nakey Canoe, grandson of Dragging Canoe, great-grandson of Chief Attacullaculla.

A new wave of immigration West followed the Creek War of 1813–14. Secretly Swift confided to Long his intention to take his wife and son, Swift Horse, to Arkansas when the time was right. He was already speaking privately with a certain South Carolinian inter-ested in purchasing their land and house.

Long Canoe worried for the safety of his brother. "What if you are discovered by the elders?" he asked.

"They will not find out," replied Swift. "I make sure I am not followed when I go to the city. Nothing is imminent. I am waiting for the right time. Many of our people are changing their views."

In actual fact, a few hard-liners like Major Ridge were slowly seeing the necessity to modernize and educate. Perhaps fighting alongside Andrew Jackson and witnessing the fate of the Creeks had changed him. Slowly he grew more moderate.

David Waite, brother of Major Ridge, and his wife, Susanna, had several children, including Kilakeena, or Buck, and Degadoga, meaning "he stands on two feet." Buck later changed his name to Elias. After his conversion, David Watie changed his second son's name from Degadoga to Isaac. For a time he was called Isaac S. (for "Stand"), but later dropped the Isaac and became known as Stand Watie.

More and more young Cherokee men were sent to white schools. Major Ridge and and his brother David Watie were determined to send all three of their sons, the cousins John Ridge, Buck Watie, and Stand Watie—boys about the same age as Long Canoe's nephew Swift Horse—north to New England to be educated when they reached fifteen or sixteen. Whatever the future held, it seemed clear that the education and Americanization of the rising new generation of Cherokees would play a role in the destiny of their people.

At last, thought Nanye'hi, the time had come when she must do as she had long anticipated. Dangerous times were coming to their tribe. There was continual talk of migration West. Strife was everywhere within the nation. How much longer she herself would live was even doubtful.

It was time to secure Long's pledge on behalf of his great-grandfather.

When the cousin of his grandfather, the Beloved Ghigua of the Cherokee, came to him, Long Canoe assumed at first that the visit concerned his brother Swift Water. He and Old Granny, as she was known, had always enjoyed a special bond. When she looked at him she pierced his very soul with her deep green-black eyes. Had she received wind of his plan to migrate West?

Aging Nanye'hi appeared at his home in her finest deerskin robe with all the finery of her position in the tribe, including the same feathers in her hair she had worn on the similar sacred occasion so many years ago. By now Long himself was a respected man in the Cherokee community.

As the two left the town together on horseback, most of the eyes of their friends and neighbors followed them with curiosity. Nanye'hi led the way up the familiar trail to the top of Ooneekawy Mountain. Not a word was spoken until they reached the same site where Attaculla-culla had given his sacred charge when Nanye'hi was still a young woman.

They paused at the summit of the sacred mountain, and stepped off their horses.

"I am not as young as I was years ago," she said, breathing heavily, "when I rode up this mountain with the great chief. At that time the land in every direction belonged to the Cherokee. Now that river marks the eastern boundary." She shaded her eyes with her hand and stared at the glittering line of silver that wound through the valley.

Now it was Nanye'hi whose eyes probed what could not be seen. Her ancient visage beheld the legacy of the ancients. Now it was the pulsings of her own heart that she had to pass on to another, as the great chief had passed them on to her. When at last she spoke, her voice, like his in her memory, bore the weight of the centuries.

"I have a story to tell you, Long Canoe," she began. "It is the story of our people, what they were, and what they can become again."

He listened with reverence, sensing the import of her words.

"I too was brought to this place, though I was older than you are now," Nanye'hi continued. "I was brought here by the great chief Attacullaculla, your own great-grandfather. He was dressed in his chieftain's robe and told many things about the heritage of our people. He chose me to carry a sacred mission of trust, and I have carried it all these years. He commanded me to choose another when my time was done. That is why I have brought you here, because I have chosen you to pass on what was given to me. I have chosen you, Long Canoe, to preserve a sacred and secret legacy of our people."

"What legacy, Nanye'hi?"

"This legacy," she replied, holding up her thumb.

"Your ring?"

"It is not merely a ring—it is one of the sacred council rings that came from the king across the water, a lasting symbol of peace and the unity of our people. Now come, there is more I have to show you."

She led the way to a great oak about three hundred yards from the summit.

"You see this mark where the bark has swollen around the cut of the knife. I enscribed my own sign here thirty-eight years ago as a marker. You know the secret of the triangles. This oak is the first of the three corners. To find the location of the secret, you must find the other two corners, then, with the midpoints of each line joining them, locate the center. That is where I will take you now."

She led the way a little farther pausing often to glance at the tree trunks around them. The young man followed, noting carefully the signs carved on the trees. They came to another tree bearing a triangle with a dot in the middle, noted it, then continued the search. When they reached the last corner of the triangle, marked with an identical sign, they had the perimeter of the triangle set.

Within minutes they closed in on the center. The roar of a waterfall became audible. Soon they could see the falls. The cascade poured over the lip of the rock and fell twenty feet in a graceful arc before continuing its descent to the valley. Nanye'hi led toward it. A cave was hidden in the rock behind the falls. Presently the two entered its mouth hidden behind a pile of boulders which would have been next to impossible to see without knowing the precise center of the triangle. Nanye'hi lit a torch, then led the way inside. Deep into the cave they crept, crouching low. Finally Nanye'hi stopped. She handed the torch to Long Canoe, then fumbled with several stones in the wall of the cave. At last she removed one large rock, and thrust her hand into a cavity in the wall. When she removed her hand she held a small deerskin pouch.

She turned to Long Canoe, took one of his hands, then opened the pouch and into it poured five rings of pure gold.

"The council rings!" he exclaimed. "I thought they were a legend."

Nanye'hi's eyes grew deadly serious. "They are legend," she said. "But they are none the less real and true that they are legend. I have worn the ring of Chief Attacullaculla all this time, and now I pass on the sacred charge of these five to you. The times are more dangerous than ever. You must learn to understand what the rings mean, Long Canoe. You must protect what they symbolize, and, as I have done, when your own time comes, pass them on so that the legacy will be preserved."

"What should I do with them? Where should I keep them?"

"Where they will be safe. Perhaps they are best left here for now. No one knows of this place but we two. When time comes for a change, you will know it. The sacred trust is now in your hands. In time you too must pass them on as I am passing them on to you. We must preserve the legacy of peace."

"But, Nanye'hi," he said, "there are six here—I thought there were seven, the sacred number of our lodges and clans."

"Yes, the remaining one has been lost through one of our war chiefs. But," she added, her voice becoming distant, "the great chief told me that he would go to his fathers longing for the day when all seven rings would be united again, when our people would be united as one, again to rise to greatness—not by conquest but by the character that makes them who they are, the real people, the *Ani-Yunwiya* of a new time, *The People of Peace*. When you are old, it will be you who who will preserve the legacy of the rings, and who will preserve the heritage of our people."

They returned from the mountain several hours later. Long Canoe was somber, with many things to think about.

"What of your brother Swift Water?" asked Nanye'hi. "Is it true what is being said, that he may join those in the West?"

"I do not know," replied Long. "He has spoken of it. He too wants to preserve the old ways and thinks that may be the best way to do so."

"It is dangerous to talk of it openly," said Nanye'hi. "My hearts grieves for the division that has come to the Ani-Yunwiya."

Secret Mission

1819

*H*olding the secret of his sojourn up the mountain with the aging Ghigua in his heart, a year later, along with Major Ridge and David Watie, Long Canoe was added to the tribal council as a sign of the growing esteem in which he was held. That he had no wife or family meant that he had time to devote to matters of the troubled nation. Nanye'hi was not able to attend all meetings of the council because of her age. But whenever she was present and their eyes met, the powerful secret that bound them together sent chills through Long Canoe's spine.

Still hopeful that the Cherokee would be able to maintain their national sovereignty within the greater U.S., as had been promised many times by American leaders, plans were made for a new Cherokee constitution, modeled after that of the United States. Long Canoe helped draft the document.

By the end of her life, seeing that whites were continuing to pour into their land and showing the Cherokee little respect, Nanye'hi moderated her views on friendship with the whites and advised against giving up any more land. Nanye'hi's daughter Cata'quin, or Catherine and known as Katy, took up her mother's crusade on behalf of their people. With her mother and several other Cherokee women, they presented a memorial to Cherokee delegates in 1817, urging that no more land be ceded to the United States.

When it came time for the ratification of the constitution by the full council in 1819, the eighty-one-year-old Ghigua was unable to

attend. Her daughter Katy Harlan appeared in her stead, wearing
Nanye'hi's gold ring as a symbol of her proxy, and voting in favor of
ratification, as she had done at times in the past, by means of
Nanye'hi's fabled walking stick.

Long noted the ring on Katy's finger. Did Katy, he wondered,
know of the other five rings? And where was the ring of Oconostota at
this moment? Had it passed out of Cherokee hands altogether?[8]

⟍⟋

Only two weeks after ratification of the new Cherokee constitution,
Swift Water came to Long Canoe late one night in secret.

"It is done," he told his brother.

"What is done?" asked Long.

"The constitution decided it for me," said Swift Water. "It is a
white man's document. It is a betrayal of our people. We will never
live as Cherokees again."

"It is for the best, Swift," said Long Canoe.

"That I do not believe, my brother. That is why I am taking my
family West. We will follow Tahlonteskee and Oolootskee and the
other brave settlers. It is the only way to preserve what is being lost.
The deal I told you about before has at last been made."

"But, Swift—"

"Do not try to dissuade me, Long. I believe the council has
betrayed our heritage."

"They say the same of those who sell their land to whites to go West."

"I see that as the best way to preserve our heritage. I know you are
following the path you think best. But I must follow what I think
best. Perhaps you, and even Nanye'hi, would feel differently if you
had the charge of the next generation. I must look after my family."

"You heard the Ghigua and Cata'quin and the other women pleading that we give up no more land."

---

[8]In the Cherokee nation, women and men are considered equal contributors to the culture. It is ironic that
American women struggled for hundreds of years to achieve the kind of equality that Cherokee women had
enjoyed for more than 1,000 years and how Europeans tried to reverse that. (*Cherokee Women in Crisis*,
Carolyn Johnson, Univ. of Alabama Press, 2005, from review by Eddie Chuculate)

"Yes, but the whites will take *all* the land eventually. Do you not see it? Even Major Ridge is softening his view. I think even he will come around to seeing things my way eventually. The next generation of leaders, like John Ridge and the two Watie brothers, surely will. I hope for my own son, Swift Horse, to be one of them. I want to start him toward leadership among our people where he can do the most good—in the West."

"You may be right," replied Long Canoe. "I have myself heard the Major say that he may have been wrong in killing Doublehead. But there are still many who believe in the old blood law that tribal lands cannot be sold under penalty of death."

"Nevertheless, I must cast my lot with the future," said Swift. "The American Jackson will see that all the tribes are brought to ruin, not merely the Creek and Seminole. You and the others who believe in the promises and treaties will see their deception in time. All Cherokees will have to go West eventually. The intermarriage here is rampant. Before long no one will know a Cherokee from a white. To move West is the only way to preserve the purity of our race."

"I fear for your safety, my brother," said Long Canoe. "But I wish you the best. May the Great Spirit protect you wherever you go. When will you leave?"

"Soon. As soon as my business is concluded."

"And Swift Horse and Rose Blossom?"

"They know nothing yet. Swift Horse is young. Rose Blossom is afraid. It is best that they not know until we are away."

The two brothers embraced with deep affection, then parted.

Long Canoe lay awake long into the night pondering his brother's words. How to know which side was right in this difficult dispute? One thing was certain: passions ran high on both sides. He prayed his brother knew what he was doing.

Three nights later, Long Canoe awoke suddenly. A sound had disturbed his sleep. He lay and listened intently. Gradually he became aware of light outside . . . an unnatural, orange, flickering light. Panic seized his heart. He jumped from bed and grabbed shirt and trousers and boots.

He rushed into the night. In the distance flames leapt high into the blackness. He knew it was his brother's home. He ran toward it. Halfway there, he suddenly stopped abruptly. A voice called his name. He glanced about.

Again came the frightened cry. "Uncle . . . Uncle, is that you?"

He ran to the edge of the wood. There stood twelve-year-old Swift Horse, trembling in terror. He questioned the boy briefly but could get nothing out of him other than that his father had thrown him out of a low window and told him to run as fast as he could.

He asked a few more questions. The boy opened his mouth, but no words would come. He could only tremble in terror.

"You know my house, Swift Horse," said Long. "Run to it . . . run now. The door is open. You will be safe there until I return. Go . . . go now. I will see to your father and mother."

The boy dashed off through the night. Long Canoe continued toward the blaze, fearing the worst.

By the time he reached it, the house was engulfed in flame, surrounded by a band of six young warriors.

"Is this your idea of justice!" cried Long Canoe angrily.

"He sold the house to the white man," replied the leader of the group. "He was a traitor. This is the penalty as demanded by ancient law."

"You are murderers. I will bring you all before the council!"

"You may do what you like, Long Canoe. You would not be wise to raise objection. Your home could be next."

Tears rising in his eyes at this horror that had infected the Cherokee nation, Long Canoe stared another few minutes at the house. It was long past the time when escape was possible. It was clear his brother and Rose Blossom were dead.

He turned and walked away into the night, leaving his murderous kinsmen to ponder their hideous deed. As he walked, he had much else to ponder. Suddenly his own fortunes had changed. He had no time to waste. It was possible they had seen young Swift Horse escape and may come for him next. His first thought was not for his own safety, though that too had to be considered, for he had made a sacred vow to the Ghigua and could not carry it out if he was dead. Treachery had come to the tribe. He must protect its heritage, and protect his suddenly orphaned nephew. Swift Horse was great-grandson to Chief Attacullaculla. Who could tell what might be his destiny one day, or that of one of his offspring. He must be protected from those who would kill him as Swift Water's son. Now at last he understood why his brother had been compelled to leave. The words were seared into Long's brain with the flames of the burning house: "*If you had charge of the next generation . . .*"

Before he reached his home again, Long Canoe had reached the decision that would change his life forever. None doubted that he was one destined to rise among the new generation of leaders alongside Major Ridge and Stand Watie and John Ross, even perhaps one destined to be chief of all the Cherokee one day. But that would never happen. It was time for him to leave his homeland . . . for the good of his Cherokee posterity . . . to protect and preserve a heritage that would always be in danger as long as he remained in this place.

But he would not sell his land. He would do all he could to maintain unity and peace with all his people.

Two hours later, Long Canoe and Swift Horse made their clandestine flight through the night. Though there were rumors of the boy's escape, most assumed he had died in the blaze that had taken his parents.

Nanye'hi Ward died in her home at Womankiller Ford in 1824. Those at her bedside vowed that they had seen a light rise up from her body, take the faint form of a dove, and disappear through the window and fly toward the sacred town, Nanye-hi's birthplace of Chota.[9]

⟶

Two aging Cherokee chiefs, Pathkiller and Charles Hicks, died in 1827 within two weeks of each other, prompting the new government of the Cherokee nation to hold its first formal election for chief. Major Ridge by this time held such prestige as elder statesman of the Cherokee that he was appointed acting chief until the election could be held. But Ridge saw the need for change among the Cherokee. He felt a chief was needed with more formal education and familiarity with the white man's world than he possessed. Though his son John was rising rapidly in influence, he was yet a young man, as were John's two cousins. Thus Ridge supported the predominantly white John Ross for the position of chief, a well-educated son of a Scottish planter and part Cherokee mother. Though Ross was but one-eighth Cherokee, he was wholeheartedly committed to the Cherokee cause and seemed to be a man representative of the changing times who would be respected and would be able to deal effectively with Washington.

Ross was elected chief in 1828. In that same year, the Cherokee's old adversary Andrew Jackson was elected President of the United States. The fate of the Cherokee nation was sealed the moment the results were announced.

A major discovery of gold at Dahlonega on Cherokee land in North Carolina the same year as the two elections set in motion a course of events that would doom any hope that the Cherokee nation could remain an autonomous entity. The first gold rush of the new country was on.

---

[9]Katy Ward, like her mother, married an American trader to the Cherokee, Ellis Harlan. The Harlan line remained among the Cherokee and continued to marry within the Cherokee nation. Their son George Harlan married Cherokee Nannie Sanders. Their son Ellis Harlan married Nannie Barnett, whose son Oce Harlan married Mary Ann McGhee, the great-great-granddaughter on her mother's side of Chief Doublehead, and whose parents had been removed to the Oklahoma Terrotory on the Trail of Tears. Their daughter Mary Ann Harlin, fifth generation descendent of both Nancy Ward and Doublehead through father and mother, known as Mayme, married John Seiler. Their daughter Cherokee Seiler married John Robert Carter, whose daughter Judy Carter married Michael Phillips.

Meanwhile, Long Canoe continued to support his nephew's education in the North. A few of his tribesmen, trusted friends, came to know his whereabouts. Through the years, by means of secretive travel and midnight meetings, he managed to keep contact with a handful of close friends and, aware of the changes taking place among his people, seeking joint counsel with them what course they should all pursue in the white man's world.[10]

---

[10]See Note 7—Gold, the Ridge/Ross split, and Cherokee Removal From the East.

Trail of Tears

1846

*B*y the mid 1830s it was clear that Andrew Jackson's Indian Removal Act would eventually be carried out. The New Echota Treaty of 1835 gave the government the legal cover to do so. A deadline was set for the last voluntary Cherokee migration as May 23rd, 1838. All Cherokee who did not comply would be rounded up by force and sent to camps where they would await their time to be herded west.

The Ridges and Waties were not the only Cherokee to attempt to preserve the heritage and wealth the land had given from its rivers and streams and caves. Almost from the moment the New Echota Treaty was signed, plans were made, led by Chief Rising Fawn, to hide as much treasured wealth from each clan as possible. A sympathetic white man, Jacob Scudder agreed to act as caretaker and guardian of the treasure after the Indians were gone, in hopes that one day they would return to recover what was hidden.

Over the following two years, clans and families hid gold and other valuables, in clay pots and leather bags and beneath rocks in numerous caves spread over 250,000 acres of forested mountain terrain. Additionally, a great tunnel was begun deep into the earth from one of the largest of the caves. Work on the tunnel continued for two years, mostly at night, in preparation to become the most massive secret depositories of wealth in American history. But no gold was placed inside the tunnel until it was certain that Andrew Jackson's order would be carried out.

Meanwhile, hundreds of Cherokee families set about marking oak and birch trees and boulders with ancient mystic symbols, creating sign trails to the caves where their gold had already begun to accumulate, as well as marking directions to the great tunnel under construction. Many paper and leather maps were drawn with further directions. All over the area the traditional signs of the triangles were notched into trees and hammered into stones—a carved triangle with a dot in the center—each showing a third of the clue, one corner, needed to locate the entrance to the hidden center of the triangle.

When the grim inevitability of the removal bore down upon Cherokee leaders with a crushing weight of despair, their people began bringing their treasures into a multitude of hiding places. All through the Cherokee nation, gold was secretly transported to the caves and the great tunnel. During the week before the final deadline of May 23rd, tremendous activity took place every night, hundreds of bags carried by foot and on horseback, packs loaded on sledges and sleighs pulled by oxen or horse, and small boats and barges gliding silently down the Etowar River. On the last night, a huge stone was placed over the tunnel entrance, sealing away the Cherokee gold in its permanent vault of hiding, never to be opened again.[11]

Thousands of Cherokee left on their own. But those who refused, or who vainly hoped that a negotiated settlement would be reached, finally faced the reality that had long been feared. To the very end Ross tried to forestall a forced removal. And as he was trusted by so many thousands who remained where they were, the majority of the Cherokee tribe ultimately lost their chance to move West on their own.

Finally Andrew Jackson's ruthless victory over the once-proud Cherokee nation was complete. Having allowed its gold to be plun-

---

[11]www.ngeorgia.com and www.thelegendsestates.com. Tales of discovery of bits of this Cherokee gold throughout northern Georgia have been told for more than a century. But despite 150 years of searching the area, and thousands of rumors of small stashes being found, the great tunnel and huge quantities of gold remains one of the tantalizing mysteries surrounding the Cherokee removal.

dered, its lands to be stolen, the final legacy of Jackson's political life
was about to be realized in one of the most heartless, humiliating,
degrading episodes in the young nation's history.

In May of 1838, suddenly the army troops arrived. Any hope for
voluntary migration was gone. They did not even allow the Cherokee
to pack or gather clothes or blankets, but broke into homes to drive
men, women, and children like cattle to Fort Campbell. There they
were kept for months in the outdoor stockades, enduring dreadful
conditions until all had been gathered. Almost as if intending to make
the journey as cruel as possible, the army kept the captives in the
stockades through the warm and stifling summer months and did not
begin the march until the month of October, when weather and traveling conditions were far worse.

As they finally set out, many of the 16,000 who began the journey
were already sick and dying from exposure, disease, and malnutrition
from the dreadful conditions in the stockades.

A twenty-eight-year-old army private, who had spent years in Cherokee lands as a trapper and counted many Cherokee among his dear
friends, was among the company to arrive at Fort Campbell that fateful day in May of 1838. He had played with Cherokee friends as a
boy, and as a young man had saved a wounded Cherokee man from a
band of hunters.

What young John Burnett was forced to do, the humiliating duty
of driving men, women, and children from their homes, and the sights
he witnessed, seared his conscience for the rest of his life. Never again
would he consider the white man "civilized" and the red man a
"savage." During those dreadful months he saw true dignity and true
cruelty at work, and they were not as many supposed.

They reached Tahlequah in the Oklahoma Territory at the end of
March in 1839, four thousand of the Cherokee dead from unspeak-
ably cruel conditions and buried on the side of the trail. Whatever
most of the soldiers felt at what they had been ordered to do, Private

John Burnett quietly wept inside as his detachment finally turned away and began to retrace its steps home. For the next several weeks he worked alone at night beside the light of his campfire on a long letter to his father and mother, attempting to explain the terrible things he had seen. He knew that if his commander learned of it, or if his letter was discovered, it could be used to bring charges of treason against him. But his conscience was too troubled, and his anger had been too stirred, not to tell what he had seen.

"*Dear Mother and Father,*" Burnett wrote,

> "*At last it is over and I am bound for home. But I must write of what I have seen, or go mad.*
>
> "*In the year of 1828, a little Indian boy living on Ward Creek had sold a gold nugget to a white trader, and that nugget sealed the doom of the Cherokees. In a short time the country was overrun with armed brigands claiming to be government agents, who paid no attention to the rights of the Indians who were the legal possessors of the country. Crimes were committed that were a disgrace to civilization. Men were shot in cold blood, lands were confiscated. Homes were burned and the inhabitants driven out by those gold-hungry brigands.*
>
> "*Chief Junaluska was personally acquainted with President Andrew Jackson. Junaluska had taken five hundred of the flower of his Cherokee scouts and helped Jackson to win the Battle of the Horse Shoe, leaving thirty-three of them dead on the field. And in that battle Junaluska drove his tomahawk through the skull of a Creek warrior, when the Creek had Jackson at mercy.*
>
> "*Chief John Ross sent Junaluska as an envoy to plead with President Jackson for protection for his people, but Jackson's manner was cold and indifferent toward the rugged son of the forest who had saved his life. He met Junaluska, heard his plea, but curtly said, 'Sir your audience is ended, there is nothing I can do for you.' The doom of the Cherokee was sealed. Washington, D.C., had decreed that they must be driven West, and their lands given to the white man, and in May 1838 an army of four thousand regulars, and three*

thousand volunteer soldiers under command of General Winfield Scott, marched into the Indian country and wrote the blackest chapter on the pages of American history.

"Men working in the fields were arrested and driven to the stockades. Women were dragged from their homes by soldiers whose language they could not understand. Children were often separated from their parents and driven into the stockades with the sky for a blanket and the earth for a pillow. And often the old and infirm were prodded with bayonets to hasten them to the stockades.

"In one home death had come during the night, a little sad-faced child had died and was lying on a bear skin couch and some women were preparing the little body for burial. All were arrested and driven out leaving the child in the cabin. I don't know who buried the body.

"In another home was a frail mother, apparently a widow with three small children, one just a baby. When told that she must go, the mother gathered the children at her feet, prayed a humble prayer in her native tongue, patted the old family dog on the head, told the faithful creature good-bye, with a baby strapped on her back and leading a child with each hand started on her exile. But the task was too great for that frail mother. A stroke of heart failure relieved her sufferings. She sank and died with her baby on her back, and her other two children clinging to her hands.

"Chief Junaluska who had saved President Jackson's life at the Battle of Horse Shoe witnessed this scene, the tears gushing down his cheeks and lifting his cap he turned his face toward the Heavens and said 'O my God, if I had known at the Battle of the Horse Shoe what I know now, American History would have been differently written.'

"Being acquainted with many of the Indians and able to fluently speak their language, I was sent as an interpreter into the Smoky Mountain country in May 1838, and witnessed the execution of the most brutal order in the history of American warfare. I saw the helpless Cherokees arrested and dragged from their homes, and driven at the bayonet point into the stockades. And in the chill of a drizzling rain on an October morning I saw them loaded like cattle or sheep into six hundred and forty-five wagons and started toward the West.

"One can never forget the sadness and solemnity of that morning. Chief John Ross led in prayer and when the bugle sounded and the wagons started rolling many of the children rose to their feet and waved their little hands good-bey to their mountain homes, knowing they were leaving them forever. Many of these helpless people did not have blankets and many of them had been driven from home bare-footed.

"On the morning of November 17th we encountered a terrific sleet-and-snow storm with freezing temperatures and from that day until we reached the end of the fateful journey on March 26th, 1839, the sufferings of the Cherokees were awful. The trail of the exiles was a trail of death. They had to sleep in the wagons and on the ground without fire. And I have known as many as twenty-two of them to die in one night of pneumonia due to ill treatment, cold, and exposure. Among this number was the beautiful Christian wife of Chief John Ross. This noble-hearted woman died a martyr to childhood, giving her only blanket for the protection of a sick child. She rode thinly clad through a blinding sleet-and-snow storm, devel-oped pneumonia and died in the still hours of a bleak winter night, with her head resting on Lieutenant Gregg's saddle blanket.

"I made the long journey West with the Cherokees and did all that a private soldier could do to alleviate their sufferings. When on guard duty at night I have many times walked my beat in my blouse in order that some sick child might have the warmth of my overcoat.

"I was on guard duty the night Mrs. Ross died. When relieved at midnight I did not retire, but remained around the wagon out of sympathy for Chief Ross, and at daylight was detailed by Captain McClellan to assist in the burial like the other unfortunates who died on the way. Her uncoffined body was buried in a shallow grave by the roadside far from her native mountain home, and the sorrow-ing cavalcade moved on. The Anglo-Saxon race would build a towering monument to perpetuate her noble act in giving her only *blanket for comfort of a sick child. Incidentally the child recovered, but Mrs. Ross is sleeping in an unmarked grave far from her native Smoky Mountain home.*

"Being a young man, I mingled freely with the young women and girls. I have spent many pleasant hours with them when I was supposed to be under my blanket, and they have many times sung their mountain songs for me, this being all that they could do to repay my kindness. And with all my association with Indian girls from October 1838 to March 26th, 1839, I did not meet one who was a moral prostitute. They are kind and tender-hearted and many of them are beautiful.

"The only trouble that I had with anybody on the entire journey to the West was with a brutal teamster by the name of Ben McDonal, who was using his whip on an old feeble Cherokee to hasten him into the wagon. The sight of that old and nearly blind creature quivering under the lashes of a bull whip was too much for me. I attempted to stop McDonal and it ended in a personal encounter. He lashed me across the face, the wire tip on his whip cutting a bad gash in my cheek. The little hatchet that I had carried in my hunting days was in my belt, and McDonal was carried unconscious from the scene.

"I was placed under guard, but Ensign Henry Bullock and Private Elkanah Millard had both witnessed the encounter. They gave Captain McClellan the facts and I was never brought to trial.

"When Scott invaded the Indian country, some of the Cherokee fled to caves and dens in the mountains and were never captured. At this time we are too near the removal of the Cherokees for people to fully understand the enormity of the crime that was committed against a helpless race, truth of the facts are being concealed. We are living on lands that were taken from a helpless race at the bayonet point to satisfy the white man's greed for gold.

"Future generations will read and condemn the act. I can truthfully say that I did my best for them when they certainly needed a friend. However murder is murder whether committed by the

villain skulking in the dark or by uniformed men stepping to the strains of martial music.

"Murder is murder and somebody must answer, somebody must explain the streams of blood that flowed in the Indian country in the summer of 1838. Somebody must explain the four thousand silent graves that mark the trail of the Cherokees to their exile. I wish I could forget it all, but the picture of six hundred and forty-five wagons lumbering over the frozen ground with their cargo of suffering humanity still lingers in my memory.

"Let the historian of a future day tell the sad story with its sighs, its tears and dying groans. Let the great Judge of all the earth weigh our actions and reward us according to our work."[12]

---

[12] The foregoing was actually not written in a letter home, but was in fact composed in 1890, on the occasion of John Burnett's 80th birthday to his children. It is one of the most well-documented accounts by a white man of the Trail of Tears. After the first two fictionalized sentences of the letter, the above is taken word for word from Burnett's account as a private in Captain McClellan's Company of the United States Army, 2nd Regiment, 2nd Brigade, Mounted Infantry. Ironically, the land "given" to the Cherokee in the Arkansas Territory actually belonged to the Osage tribe and was not the U.S. government's to give at all. But by now the commitment to the Cherokee nation was viewed as the higher priority in white eyes, and thus, to accommodate the massive influx of Cherokee from the East, the Osage were now driven from *their* land. Also see Note 8—Vengeance and the Cherokee Blood Law.

Notes from the Old Books

Note 1—The People of the Caves

The Cherokee represented but one tribe of many between the great Mississippi River and the Atlantic coast, all outgrowths and related offshoots of the once mighty Hopewell and Mississippi mound-building native societies of ancient times. The Cherokee, or *Tsaragi*, were originally also known as the Ani-Kituhwagi, people of Kituhwa, the largest ancient city of the early nucleus of their nation. The actual origin of the name Cherokee is uncertain, and has been conjectured to mean Ancient Tobacco People, Red Fire Men, Children of the Sun, Brave Men, or People of the Caves. Many of the tribes of the two American continents called themselves, not by the names given them by later European explorers, but simply *The People*. It is no doubt revealing of the Iriquois' perception of themselves, and indicative of the status to which they would later rise among many indigineous tribes in European eyes, that they called themselves Ani-Yunwiya, *The Principle People.*

Cherokee culture and survival depended on hunting and fishing, but they were not as nomadic as their cousins of the northern plains. They had learned to grow a number of crops and made widespread use of maize as did the Sun People Cortez had encountered far to the south in Mexico. Water, fire, and the earth were the source of life and sustenance. From the great Mississippi, tribes spread in all directions up the rivers that fed it, and up the streams that fed them. Water gave the earth life, and from it they took abundant fish and hunted the animals that depended upon the waters for survival. Clans formed from family groups, then tribes formed from clan groups, and gradually villages sprouted up and down the river valleys. Along the banks of what they called the Tannassey, the land was rich and the Cherokee thrived.

Numerous Cherokee villages were separated by a day's walk from one another. Some became cities and centers of trade and activity. Homes and lodges were made of wood, woven cane, and stone, and usually covered by bark, mud, or animal skins. Outside the villages grew fields of maize, tobacco, beans, and many varieties of squash. Smokehouses cured meat. Ovens and open fireplaces made baked goods from ground maize, and cured clay pottery. As villages and towns and cities grew, the greatest of the native tribes enlarged into nations with customs and laws and networks of travel, trade, and commerces. Some among them were fishers, others hunters, others warriors, others farmers. Women gathered nuts, wild roots, and berries, made pottery and baskets, cured skins, tended crops and fires, and even occasionally took up the bow or spear against the enemy. Each village had numerous chiefs, and the most important of these sat on the national tribal council. Some chiefs were leaders of war, others of peace. Women were as vital to the survival and provision of the tribe as were the men and had their own women's council.

When Spanish explorer Hernando DeSoto landed on the coast of Florida in 1540, quickly conquering and enslaving native peoples both to guide him and carry his supplies, and then began his trek inland in quest of New World gold, hundreds of thousands of native peoples inhabited the southeastern portion of the continent north of the Mexican gulf. As the first white man to lay eyes on the Cherokee, DeSoto found a populous people throughout the river valleys of the southern Appalachians. Though there had already been much native blood shed by the Spaniards, DeSoto's encounters with the Cherokee were peaceful and the Cherokee hospitable. Rumors of Cherokee gold led DeSoto into the inland regions inhabited by the Ani-Yunwiya. But though his men found evidence of copper mining, the gold buried beneath the ground eluded them and they did not remain long.

As the societies of Native American nations became more sophisticated over the centuries, it was not a sophitication of technology, invention, construction, knowledge, or wealth as was growing up in other parts of the world. It was rather a sophistication in knowledge of the earth and its ways. When DeSoto and his men appeared among them, wearing strange suits of metal, and carrying knives and chains and guns and swords, and confronting a people bare-skinned or clad in the skins of animals slain for food, and adorned by the simple feathers of the eagle or with necklaces of shells traded from the sea tribes, it was a clash of cultures from which there could be no turning back. These were peoples who had learned to live upon the earth while preserving its natural beauty, provision, and balance. They took no more from it than they needed, and it gave all they required. Theirs was a life based on natural balance and order and unity with creation.

It was a life not Spaniard, Englishman, nor Frenchman could grasp. To the European mind they were backward savages, to be exploited. They could not apprehend that perhaps these bare-skinned people were not so simple as they appeared, but had developed a way of life upon the earth that possessed as many benefits to humankind as ancient Athens or Rome, or modern Paris, Madrid, or London.

As a settled, agricultural people, the Cherokee lived in approximately two hundred villages, some of good size, usually consisting of thirty to sixty houses or lodges, and a large council house. These villages were spread out in three geographic regions: the Lower settlements along the headwaters of the Tugaloo River in the Blue Ridge Mountains, Middle settlements in the Joree and Unicoi Mountains between the Little Tennessee and Hiwasse rivers, and Overhill settlements between the Tennessee River and Smokey Mountains. Each had many villages and towns, numbering some thirty or forty in all.

The Cherokee Nation was comprised of seven clans: the Aniwayah or *Wolf* clan (the largest and most prominent of the clans), the *Blue* (or panther or wildcat) clan, the *Long Hair* (or wind) clan, the *Deer* clan, the *Bird* clan, the *Paint* clan, and the *Wild Potato* (or Kituwah, bear, or raccoon) clan. Most war chief's came of the Wolf clan, peace chief's came from the Long Hair clan. From the Bird clan came the keepers of the birds, those skilled in hunting and trapping birds. From the Paint clan came sorcerers and medicine men who made the red paint used in battle. From the Deer clan came the keepers of the deer, fast runners and messengers. Those of the Wild Potato clan gathered food in the wilds for their people, at first near the ancient capital town of Kituwah.

Cherokee society was matrilinear, like that of the ancient Picts of Scotland. Women were held in higher esteem in Cherokee culture and carried more responsibility than in white societies of the same era. Descent and clan designation progressed through the mother's side of the family. Every newborn became a member of its mother's clan. Houses were owned by the women. Men and other kinsmen resided in their women's homes at the discretion and pleasure of wives, mothers, aunts, and sisters.

Occasional Beloved Women, or *Ghigua*, were chosen for bravery in battle or outstanding personal qualities. The Ghigua headed the Council of Women and held a voting seat in the Council of Chiefs. The Ghigua was given the responsibility for prisoners, was considered a sage and spiritual guide, and acted as ambassador and peace negotiator. After Nancy Ward, the most famous of all the Cherokee Ghigua, her name became almost synomous with the term itself.

A river, or Long Man—any stream, creek, or body of moving water—was considered sacred, and its water used for purification and other ceremonies. A day or two after the birth of a child, a priest waved the infant four times over a fire while he addressed a prayer to the fire for special blessings. On the fourth or seventh day, the same priest took the child to a river and commended it to its Creator, praying that it might enjoy a long and happy life. While holding his hand over the infant's mouth and nostrils, he immersed it seven times in the water, then returned the child to its parents. Then a naming ceremony was held. Most names were bestowed by a prominent elderly woman of the community or one of the Beloved Women, and were based on the infant's fancied resemblance to some object, on upon something said or done at the moment of birth, or perhaps upon a physical or behavioral trait observed in the child. Later in life, depending on personality or achievement, a new name might be earned or given.

To some extent the tribal priesthood was hereditary. Yet some children were also chosen for the honor. A child born in unusual conditions, or during strange circumstances (an earthquake, storm, eclipse, draught, etc.) might be groomed as a visionary or prophet. Such a career was particularly marked out for twins. Such selected children were kept secluded during the first twenty-four days of their lives. They were not allowed to taste their mother's milk, but instead were given water soaked in corn hominy. While such youngsters were growing up, they were encouraged to go out from the village alone in order to find comfort in solitude. Sons promised to the priesthood were called "devoted sons," and their training was more demanding even than for young warriors.

Cherokee homes were circular with an interwoven framework of logs and branches plastered over with mud and occasionally bark and animal hides. In later periods log cabins came into use much like those observed in white settlements. Each village also had a much larger council house, up to fifty feet in diameter and located on a mound in the center of the village. They were used for meetings of the chiefs, general meetings, religious ceremonies, and to preserve the sacred fire, a vital ingredient of Cherokee culture and religion. These council houses were true "town houses" or community centers used by the whole town. Village inhabitants came and went freely, gathered together for meeting, discussion, or celebration, or merely came to sit alone and smoke a pipe of the tobacco plant whose properties they had discovered and would one day give as a dubious gift to the white man.

On a high mound in the national capital sat a large heptagon or seven-sided national council house of which each village council house was a smaller replica, its seven sides representing the clans of the nation. From this council house national festivals were celebrated and the nation was ruled by its leading chiefs.

As the ancient Cherokee lived in an alternating state of war and peace, their way of life called for a dual organization of tribal government ruled by the white, or peace, council, and the red, or war, council. Each had interdependent chiefs and functions.

White chiefs were often but not exclusively hereditary, subject also to appointment by the Great High Priest or tribal council. Each town was governed by its two chiefs, the white chief in peacetime and the red chief during war. An assembly of women, the "War Women," was present at every war council to serve as counselors to the chiefs, and to regulate the treatment of prisoners.

The white council was made up of men fifty years and older. Most were chiefs and they performed both secular and religious functions. The highest authority in the nation was the Great High Priest, whose Cherokee name was Uku. The Great High Priest had a principal assistant, a speaker, and seven counselors representing the seven clans, whom he consulted on all matters of importance.

On the red council sat military officials who had been elected or acquired their rank from bravery in battle. They were honored with victory and scalp dances and sat in places of honor in the town council houses. The national white and red chief had up to a dozen officers, the two highest were the *right-hand man* and the *speaker*.

Upon any threat of war or attack, messengers were dispatched to the Uku and the national tribal council summoned. If it was determined that war was required, the war chief summoned his advisors to make plans for the battle strategy.

Each warrior carried his own provisions into battle, as well as his own weapons and armor—a shield and club for defense, an ax, knife, lance, bow, and quiver of arrows. Helmets were worn for head protection—three-inch-wide headbands of thick buffalo hide, whose upper edge held a tightly packed circle of upright feathers painted red. Twenty-four-inch-wide shields were also made of thick buffalo skin, boiled and hardened in the sun. When starvation threatened from long engagements away from home, some warriors roasted and ate their shields, and were afterward called "shield eaters."

The Cherokee crafted precision war bows of oak, ash, and hickory, and arrows of deadly accuracy. For maximum flexibility, the bows were coated with bear oil, then warmed by fire so that the oil would penetrate the wood. War bows were up to five feet in length and could support more than a fifty pound draw. Strings of great strength and durability were fashioned from twisted bear gut. Stone-headed cane arrows averaged thirty inches in length and were fletched with split turkey feathers.

When warriors from each town and village were assembled, armed, and ready, their war chief and their war officers led them in rapid procession for the long march to the place of meeting at the national capital. The Great War Priest wrapped his divining crystal in seven sacred deerskins from the treasure house and gave the bundle to his assistant. The priest then took up a pottery ark filled with live coals from the sacred fire. With his assistant and the war chiefs behind him, he marched through the town to bestow his blessing upon the upcoming battle.

Once the entire army was assembled in the capital, a twenty-four-hour fast was celebrated, and then the war chief led his warriors away to battle.

On their return to their own village after battle, the warriors stayed at their town council houses for twenty-four days before returning to their wives and families. This was a time for extensive purification rituals to rid themselves of uncleanness contacted during fighting, and also for the treatment of wounds and injuries. Warriors who distinguished themselves in battle were honored by a new name that was publicly bestowed by a general council of town leaders. Killer was the highest name that could be given, and the names Raven, Owl, Wolf, and Fox were also common.

Though DeSoto himself died in the New World without finding the gold he sought, a century later, the Spanish were smelting gold, silver, and copper on Cherokee lands. The invasion had begun. Gradually the French claimed more and more of the land drained by rivers flowing into the Mississippi. As the European population in the Americas grew and the more adventuresome of its number spread west, competition for control of vast tracts of verdant and forested land, as well as economic rivalry for the Indian fur trade became fierce between the rival European powers. The French enjoyed friendly relations with the Indian tribes in the Mississippi and Tennesse regions, who found them polite and gracious, even-tempered, and understanding toward native ways. As French influence among native tribes expanded north and east, control of the Indian trade on the headwaters of the upper Tennessee River valley took on heightened importance to the British colonial economy of the Carolinas.

In the early 18th century, both English and French in America edged their colonial claims closer and closer to one another. The nation of the great Cherokee tribe was caught in the middle of inevitable conflict between them.[13]

Note 2—Seven Cherokee in England, and the Articles of Friendship and Commerce

Sir Alexander Cuming took his charges once again from the Mermaid Tavern up the rise to the summit of the hill where Windsor Castle looked out over the surrounding countryside. The Baronet led the way . . . behind him in single file came the Indians, and trader Wiggan brought up the rear.

Seayagusta was second in line. He wore a scarlet jacket and breechclout, but the rest were dressed only in breechclouts, which were called aprons in the newspaper.

The Cherokee had spent much time on their face and body decorations. Each had his own distinctive style, streaks and whirls and spots of reds and blues and greens.

The warriors had gathered their long black hair into strands tied with ribbons so that these queues of hair arched from the back of each head like a horse's tail. Several had turkey feathers thrust into their hair. Collannah wore the gaudy feathers of the Carolina parakeet, and the young Ukwaneequa was decked with the iridescent feathers of a wood duck.

The people of Windsor had become accustomed to seeing the Indians about their town, but they had never seen them painted and

---

[13]*Fire in the Mountains* by D. Sheppard and J. Wolfe, *Seven Clans of the Cherokee Society,* Marcelina Reed, Cherokee Publications, Cherokee, NC, 1993, www.cherokeehistory.com., www.cherokeebyblood.com.

adorned as they were this day. Men and women cheered as they passed, and merchants ran out of their shops to view the parade (*The Cherokee Crown of Tannassy*, William O. Steele, pp. 109-10).

London newspapers of the day reported that the Cherokees' audience with His Majesty went off splendidly, the seven so-called savages from North America kneeling, as did Sir Alexander, at the proper time. As related by Sir Alexander in his journal, he (Sir Alexander) "laid the Crown of the Cherokee Nation at His Majesty's Feet, with the five Eagle Tails, as an Emblem of His Majesty's Sovereignty, and four Scalps of Indian Enemies; all of which His Majesty was pleased to accept of."

When afterward the group was conducted to the gallery over the terrace, one Cherokee carrying a bow caught sight of an elk in the park below and had to be restrained from demonstrating his marksmanship to his royal host. Later, at the command of His Majesty, Cuming's wards were provided a banquet of leg of mutton and saddle and loin of mutton at The Mermaid. This repast was unquestionably devoured without the aid of cutlery.

After their reception at Windsor Castle, the Cherokees became the rage of London. Wined, feted, and followed by great crowds, they visited the Tower, attended theatrical performances, fairs, and were entertained sumptuously by a group of London merchants interested in South Carolina trade at the Carolina Coffee House in Birchin Lane. Habited in rich garments laced in gold presented to them by His Majesty, they strolled through St. James's Park, visited Westminster Abby and the Houses of Parliament, and sat for a group portrait and single portraits for His Grace the Duke of Montague. And, in early September, they were grandly driven in two coaches to Whitehall, escorted "by a sergeant of the Foot Guards and file and a half of grenadiers," to meet the Lords Commisioners, who acquainted them with the Articles of Agreement drawn up to regulate trade in their country—articles of agreement that would bind the Cherokee Nation to England for the next fifty years (*The Cherokees*, Grace Steele Woodward, pp. 64-66).

After the seven Cherokee who had accompanied Sir Alexander

Cuming had been in England for three months, a document was drawn up and, in September of 1730, the Articles of Friendship and Commerce were presented to the seven Cherokees for approval. They were signed in Sir Alexander Cuming's home in London, and included the following provisions: The Cherokee committed to trade exclusively with England, whites commiting crimes in Cherokee lands were guaranteed trial in English colonial courts, and the Cherokee pledged to English military service should England go to war with France or any foreign power.

A last minute misunderstanding, however, nearly turned the signing into disaster.

After meeting with the king's representatives, the seven returned to their quarters. There they demanded an exact translation of all that had just occurred in the meeting, and what exactly the Articles of Friendship said. When Wiggan translated, and they learned that Oukah-Ulah had recognized "The Great King's right to the Country of Carolina," several of the seven were furious and immediately went into formal counsel. The majority voted to repudiate the claim by killing both Wiggan and their chief Oukah-Ulah. Eventually calm returned to the discussion. They agreed to submit the treaty to their priest and let him decide the outcome.

A great ceremony was held to formalize the agreement. Ukwaneequa, now speaking for the group, addressed the King's Commissioners in English, impressing the British with his dignity and stature that was in inverse proportion to his slight frame.

"We look upon the Great King George," said Ukwaneequa in English, "as the Sun, and as our father, and upon ourselves as his children. For though we are red, and you are white yet our hands and hearts are joined together. What we have seen, our children from generation to generation will always remember. In war we shall always be with you."

With a dramatic flourish, Ukwaneequa laid the white eagle feathers brought by the seven on the table along with the document. "This is our way of talking," he said, "which is the same thing to us as your letters in the book are to you, and to your beloved men we deliver these feathers in confirmation of all we have said."

The seven Cherokee men returned home after five months with many tales to tell of the strange land across the sea called England. They were not accompanied home by Sir Alexander Cuming, who was detained in England on charges brought against him by the colonists of Charlestown for embezzlement and fraud. He remained beloved by the Cherokee, however, with many of whom he had become close friends. Ever after, he was honored as "a man whose talk is upright and who came to the Cherokee like a warrior from His Majesty."

It was upon his return that the stature of Ukwaneequa, though both the youngest and smallest of the group, began to grow. Though Oukah-Ulah had been appointed leader of the group at the outset, Ukwaneequa's knowledge of English and skillful persuasive and oratory powers was thereafter looked to by his comrades to tell of the visit to their people.

When the Articles of Friendship were explained to the tribal counsel of the Cherokee nation, the older chiefs questioned the seven intently about what promises they had made to "the Man who lives across the Great Water," and whether they had, as some rumors were reporting, given away ancient Cherokee lands. But they were assured both by Ukwaneequa and Eleazar Wiggan, their faithful friend and translator, that the seven had been loyal and had represented the tribe faithfully.

Ever after his trip Ukwaneequa lost no opportunity to recount in great detail, to young and old alike, their adventures in England, and what amazing and spectacular things he and his comrades had seen. Ukwaneequa gave this personal account of the events twenty-five years later: *"He said . . . that it would have much better effect if some of us would go along with him. But after some questions were asked about England and how far it might be to it not one of our people would consent to go. . . . At night Mr. Wiggins the Interpreter came to the house where I was, and told me that the Warrior (Cuming) had a particular favor for me, and that if I would consent to go he would be indifferent whether any other went; and Mr. Wiggan pressed me very much to accept of his Invita-*

tion. I was then a young man but I thought it would be right to Consider before I spoke, I told him I understood England was a great Way off. That I should be long in going there, I should be detained there a Considerable time, and would be long in returning and I did not know how I should get back. But he assured me the distance was very much magnified and that I might be back at the end of the Summer or at least some time in the fall.

"Upon which assurances I agreed to go. Early next morning One of our people came to me. . . . He then told me that neither he nor any other had intended to have gone but since I was to go That I should not go alone, for that he would accompany me and that he knew of Two or three more that he could persuade to go accordingly they were spoke to and agreed making it all Six and we Immediately got ready and soon set off."[14]

Note 3—The Difficult Years of 1730–1755

It was not only war that brought change to the Cherokee. The effects of the white man's encroachment were felt in many ways. DeSoto and those who followed him to the New World brought both conquest and strange diseases that the natives were unable to withstand, diseases capable of wiping out entire villages. Most southeastern tribes suffered a 75 percent decimation from European epidemics after 1540. No one knows how many were lost in the first epidemics, but by 1674 the combined native population of the southeast U.S. was estimated at about 50,000. Their once great cities of commerce were gone, their numbers reduced to a fraction their former levels. Gradually the population of native peoples increased. But another series of smallpox epidemics in the 1730s and 1740s cut the number of Cherokee remaining in half again. Carried by slave ship to the Carolina coast in 1738, the disease spread inland and resulted in the death of more than half of many villages. The natives had no medicines or methods to deal with the unknown killer. Their common practice of plunging not only infants into cold rivers and streams for consecration, but also the sick for healing, could not have been a worse remedy. The disease was

---

[14]www.freepages.genealogy.rootsweb.com—"Attacullaculla."; www.freepages.genealogy.rootsweb.com— "Ancestors of Attacullaculla"

not only horrifying in its result, the proud Cherokee were so humiliated by the disfiguring effects of the pox that some of their warriors killed themselves because of it. Priests and medicine men, unable to control the disease, fell out of favor and the influence of Cherokee religion began to decline in the eyes of the people.

During these years, too, neighboring tribes, such as their centuries-long adversaries the Creek and the Seminole to the south, continued to raid the new colonial settlements. The retaliation of the English did not honor their treaty with the Cherokee nor differentiate between one indigenous tribe and another.

The French and the English continued to dispute their right to various territories, pursuing each other back and forth across Cherokee land. Their agreement with the English king did not prevent American colonists, assuming the land was free for the taking, from seizing Cherokee land as more and more of their number trekked westward.

By the time twenty years had passed since the visit of the Cherokee to England in 1730 and the treaty with representatives of the English king, division was rampant within the Cherokee council. Once again the old war and peace factions were divided on what course the Cherokee should pursue in response to the white man's greed for land.

Note 4—The Legacies of Attacullaculla, Oconostota, and Dragging Canoe

When Daniel Boone sent his adventurous eyes westward and began to explore the region of the Alleghenies in the 1760s, he encountered a very different Cherokee nation than that of the wild and untamed land braved by traders and trappers two generations earlier.

All the eastern seaboard of the growing nation, and inland no mere dozens but hundreds of miles, had become increasingly civilized. Settlements were becoming towns, towns were becoming cities. Trade with Europe was mounting, and immigration from many countries exploding. The African slave trade was mounting steadily as great plantations spread throughout the South. The economy of the colonies was no longer that of a mere frontier outpost but was becoming a force to be reckoned with throughout western Europe. The American colonies were maturing toward nationhood, and the nation of the Cherokee was being changed along with it toward modernity. Whether that trend was good or bad for the Cherokee people would be for posterity to determine. Inevitability perhaps propels as much history forward as do discoveries, decisions, and the destinies of peoples. Whereas the history of black America in the eighteenth century was largely determined by the cruelty, greed, and inhumanity of its oppressors, and though many chapters of the history of native America would likewise be written in that same language of oppression, at the same time the sheer *inexorability* of time's march forward was a yet deeper source of the momentum that gradually pulled the Cherokee, along with native peoples the world over, out of antiquity into the modern age.

It would thus also be for his posterity to determine whether the great chief Attacullaculla would be viewed as one with prophetic eyes of foresight for seeing the necessity of embracing new times with dignity and realism, or as a traitor to his people for too easily allowing the ways of European colonialism to infiltrate Cherokee lands, customs, and loyalties. For whatever reasons, his voyage to England as a young man in 1730 forever changed the youthful Ukwaneequa, later to become the powerful peace chief Attacullaculla, and as a result changed the future destiny of his people. He saw the English colonists not merely as an "enemy" to be repulsed. Attracullaculla viewed them, rather, as *people*—from a different race and culture, to be sure, but yet as fellow citizens of a common humanity. They were people to *learn from*, people to *cooperate with*, people with whom *mutual respect* was possible as the inevitability of time's march brought them ever into closer contact.

The thirteen years following 1763 were ones of rapid change and mounting conflict in America. The colonies themselves were changing, not merely toward the Cherokee but toward their motherland. An infant nation was flexing its muscle and growing feisty and independent. The colonists no longer saw themselves as British but as *Americans*. In the years following the end of the French and Indian War in

1763, that independent spirit grew into a conflict that began to surge toward the boiling point.

Colonists flooded west across the mountains in increasing numbers. The attempt to fix a permanent boundary of Cherokee land resulted in more treaties with the colonies. But each treaty was ignored. Settlers simply came, found land they wanted, and built homes and refused to leave. For years Indians had been striking blows against frontier settlements to preserve their land. But it became more difficult with every passing year. Homes of settlers on their lands had once numbered in the dozens. Now they numbered in the many thousands. It was now *American* colonists who were taking Indian land, and a treaty of long ago with the king of England meant nothing to them.

With this expansionary invasion came an inevitable intermingling of white and Indian cultures. Cherokee homes and towns gradually came to resemble those of the colonies. More and more Cherokee spoke the English tongue. The lifestyle, habits, clothing, and economy of the Cherokee gradually took on more characteristics common to their white neighbors. Colonial men took Cherokee wives, gave their children English names, and a robust, talented, new generation of mixed English and Cherokee began to emerge that would take the proud tribe of the ancients known as the *Ani-Yunwiya* into the future.

All these changes came slowly, one adaptation leading to another, and that leading to yet another. Much stemmed directly from the leadership and convincing oratory of Attacullaculla, and his determined loyalty to the British. To the end of his life he remained convinced that such progress was in the Cherokee's best long term interest. The great chief invited Moravian missionaries to live among the Cherokee on the condition that they would build schools and teach Cherokee youth in the language and ways of the English. Many of these changes were forced upon him by circumstance, and by the knowledge that resisting change would result in the needless slaughter of his people. At the same time, Attacullaculla saw th benefits of such adaptation and change. He was a realist who would rather cede portions of ancient Cherokee land than see the blood of both Indians and colonists spilled upon it. It was a realism that found advantage for his people where it could. But these changes toward cultural integration did not come without growing pains, conflict, and bloodshed.

Everywhere the same story was being told in a thousand distinct but similar ways. The world and its populations were exploding—in knowledge, in economics, in culture, in art, in technology, in the understanding of freedom. Former barriers were being pushed aside. And at the edge of all change existed the conflict between the old and the new. Thus, as the colonies expanded westward, absorbing and assimilating native populations in a massive intermingling of peoples, there was conflict. The entire New World was a microcosm of newness, change, and conflict. The great melting pot of "American" peoples and races was forging a *new* identity whose meaning each racial group—white, black, native—would discover for itself.

For whatever reason the Cherokee in time became one of the most widespread and mightiest of native tribes, not because of its ability to make war like the Sioux or Apache, but because of its ability to adapt and grow from change. Even in the seeming defeat of the Cherokee, by adapting to new ways and by using their gifts and intelligence to move their people forward, they became a modern people rather than an anachronistic historic footnote that posterity would forget. Instead of a forgotten race, the Cherokee became a race of energetic people like the Scots, assimilated but never eradicated, a people with a language, a culture, a heritage, a written history, books, and a Bible in its own native tongue, yet at the same time less *pure* Cherokee and gradually more *American*.

The Cherokee came to represent *all* the peoples of native America who had sprung from common roots. They were one people, *The People*, and in truth none was more principal than any other. They were *The People of America*.

In many ways, the examples of cruelty upon Indian peoples, though numerous, tell but one portion of the story. Many white settlers were good and hard-working men and women who did not realize the implications of their westward expansion. They saw the Indian natives as their neighbors. Many desired friendship, and were kind and devoted husbands to Cherokee wives. In 1772 a group of settlers met with Attacullaculla to forge a lease and friendship pact in which all sides could maintain peace and positive relations. It resulted in a ten year lease of Cherokee land for which the Cherokee were to receive some £400 in trading goods, along with the promise not to advance farther into the Cherokee Overmountain territory. As always, some were sincere and abided by the agreement, others did not.

In the 1760s and 1770s, some fifty Cherokee towns and villages were burned, all crops and livestock destroyed or taken, and hundreds of men and women killed, scalped, or sold into slavery. By 1775, the nation of the Cherokee was desperate and nearly facing extinction if something was not done. By then Attacullaculla and Oconostota were aging. The war party, ironically, was now led by Attacullaculla's son, himself a chief, Dragging Canoe. His daughter Nakey Canoe was one of many of her generation to marry a white man, and Dragging Canoe was increasingly isolated as a voice from the past, even within his own family.

A major treaty was concluded, more sweeping than any that had come before, with the Henderson Purchase of 1775, which sold all lands north of the Cumberland River which included most of what eventually became the state of Kentucky and mid-Tennessee. In exchange, the Transylvania Company gave the Cherokee £10,000 in trade for goods, including guns and ammunition, on display in a log cabin next to the Cherokee Council ground beside the Watauga River at what was called Sycamore Shoals. Neither Attacullaculla nor Oconocstota were able to resist the huge payment and the enormous quantity of goods to be gained in exchange for the land. Both of the great chiefs sanctioned the purchase.

Dragging Canoe did everything in his power to prevent his father and uncle from signing the the gigantic Henderson Purchase. His eloquent speech at Sycamore Shoals after the fateful deed was done poignantly symbolized the dying gasp of the old times.

"Whole Indian nations have melted away like snowballs in the sun before the white man's advance," said the proud son of Attacullaculla. *"We had hoped that the white men would not be willing to travel beyond the mountains. Now that hope is gone. They have passed the mountains,*

*and have settled upon Cherokee land. They wish to have that usurpation
sanctioned by treaty. When that is gained, the same encroaching spirit will
lead them upon other land . . . finally the whole country, which the Cherokees and their fathers have so long occupied, will be demanded, and the
remnant of the Ani-Yunwiya, the Real People, once so great and formida-
ble, will be compelled to seek refuge in some distant wilderness. There they
will be permitted to stay only a short while, until they again behold the
advancing banners of the same greedy host. Not being able to point out
any further retreat for the miserable Cherokees, the extinction of the whole
race will be proclaimed. . . . Should we not therefore run all risks and
incur all consequences, rather than submit to further loss of our country?
Such treaties may be right for men who are too old to hunt or fight. As for
me, I have my young warriors about me. We will have our lands. I have
spoken."*

War broke out the next year between England and the new nation
that would call itself the United States of America. It was hardly to be
wondered at that the Cherokee, frustrated and angered by twenty
years of greed, duplicity, lies, and cruelty on the part of the colonies,
sided with the British and did everything in their power to assist them.

Despite the treaty and Henderson Purchase, one faction of Cherokee, the Chickamaugas, led by Dragging Canoe, refused to honor it
and continued to raid settlements of the region for another quarter
century. Dragging Canoe stole from and killed and scalped whites
throughout Tennessee. He murdered one David Crockett and his wife
(whose grandson of the same name would become famous in the next
century), killed some of his children, and took two as prisoners and
kept them for seventeen years.

As America gained its independence from the British in 1783, it
assumed a right to all lands belonging to native tribes. Tennessee
became a state. A young congressman who had fought the Cherokee
in the wilds years before, made his voice heard in the new nation's
capital in favor of brooking no compromise whatever with the Indians. The young congressman's name was Andrew Jackson. His prejudice against and hatred of Indians would doom the Cherokee fate
forty years later.

As the old century gave way to the nineteenth, many Cherokee joined the life of the new nation. The Cherokee became known (with the Chickasaw, Seminole, Choktaw, and Creek) as one of the five "civilized" tribes—with houses and businesses and plantations and farms and slaves. Henceforth neither Indian nor British would determine the course of events in this land. Now known as the United States of America, its people would forever after be called *Americans*. Diverse ethnic backgrounds and races had to look *forward* to changing times with realism, rather than trying to preserve that which no people can ever preserve—the *past*. They must now somehow forge a future . . . together.

Some Cherokee began to acquire wealth in plantation life as the economy of tobacco and cotton took over more and more of the South. Yet they also worked diligently to preserve their traditional native heritage, and continued to fight to keep what remained of their native land. But with statehood now surrounding them, it was a losing battle. There continued to be treaties and token payments. But the result in every case was a continual shrinking of the lands that had once been theirs.[15]

The land cessions which the Cherokee Nation was pressed into making with the federal government in the latter part of the eighteenth and the first quarter of the nineteenth centuries did not please the Cherokees. The methods used by the various administrations between 1798–1819 were disillusioning to a people who had written laws and were seeking to pattern their government after that of the United States.

President Adams' administration sought to gain land cessions from the Cherokees by settling their overdue debts with trading companies or with the government-operated store or factory at Tellico. The Cherokees had bought more goods and supplies than they could pay

---

[15]cherokeehistory.com by Ken Martin

President George Washington made a speech in 1796, saying that the Cherokee would be an educational "experiment" in how the federal government dealt with all Indian tribes. Accordingly, three years later Dartmouth college set up a program to include Cherokees at the school and established a loan program. Other forms of aid were extended to the Cherokee involving education in the use of tools, carpentry, agriculture, animal husbandry, and weaving. Even with such programs, however, whites continued to take Cherokee land whenever it suited them.

for. Adams' commissioners artfully arranged with the council to
revoke Cherokee debts in exchange for cessions of land. Pressed in this
way, the Indians had no alternative but to cede their land from time
to time to the federal government. Thus, between 1791–1819 the
Cherokees negotiated twenty-five land cessions with the federal
government.

Since the government goods sold to them at the factory were
frequently things that had been damaged in their conveyance from the
east, the Cherokees asked Presidents Adams and Jefferson to discon-
tinue the factory and permit them to buy their supplies from traders as
in the early days. But both Adams and Jefferson refused.

Instead (during Jefferson's administration particularly), manufac-
tured goods were forced on the Cherokees by the factor (storekeeper),
who had instructions from Jefferson to keep the Cherokees in debt so
that their lands could more easily be obtained by the government (*The
Cherokees,* Grace Steele Woodward, pp. 127-8).

Note 5—The Old Settlers vs. the Eastern Cherokee

Many of the Cherokee who migrated early on from Georgia and
North Carolina owned houses and lands and even plantations, which
they sold to whites before leaving. They were later called the Old
Settlers. Whites were capable of paying more than their fellow tribesmen. Better to receive something for the lands than be driven off later
and receive nothing. But their exodus was bitterly resented by those in
the east who hated to see their holdings of land shrinking all the more.
In spite of persecution against them, small bands continued to trickle
West.

The Old Settlers considered themselves the true lineage from the
past, and saw their move westward as the only means of preserving the
purity of the proud and ancient race. They saw the impossibility of
preserving the Cherokee nation through treaties and laws and accom-
modations. The Creek and Seminole wars of recent years demonstrated clearly enough the fate of native tribes who tried to resist the
growing might of the white man's government. The same fate was
sure to come to the Cherokee eventually. They hoped that in the West

where land was plentiful, in a place that seemed remote from the white man's thirst for settlement and conquest, they would be free to live in freedom as in former times.

Those who sold their land and migrated West, however, were seen as traitors by hard-line eastern Cherokees, who vowed, under penalty of assassination, that no more would sell their homes and lands and move West to join the traitors.

Note 6—Progressive Change in the Cherokee Nation

The years of the 1820s brought great change to the Cherokee and the others of the five civilized tribes of the southeast United States. While the Old Settlers in the West attempted to live by the old ways as much as possible, the Cherokees of Georgia and Tennessee continued moving their people forward into new times. The Cherokee language was codified into a written script by Doublehead's nephew George Gist, known as Sequoyah.

Gradually more and more Cherokee integrated into the life of the growing and expanding nation. Their people traveled and intermarried, took European names, built homes, established farms and successful plantations. Wealthy Cherokees owned slaves and sent their sons to the North to be educated. Ever since Attacullaculla had invited Moravian missionaries into Cherokee towns, the Cherokee people had discovered much in Christianity to confirm their own myths, religious tradition, and reverence for nature, the land, the animal kingdom, and the unifying spirit connecting them all. And now the Christianity of America with its pilgrim roots found a receptive home in the hearts of an increasing number of Cherokee. Cherokee David Brown translated the Greek New Testament into Sequoyah's new Cherokee language. Progressive Cherokee leaders adopted aggressive educational, religious, and political programs to bring the Cherokee population, especially its youth, into the new age of mainstream America. The new constitution and capital of the reorganized nation at New Echota replaced the old tribal system of war and peace chiefs with a republic of laws modeled after those of the United States. If they could gain respect as a modern

"American" people, Cherokee leaders hoped to preserve both what remained of their lands and some measure of national autonomy.

Measured by the white man's "land stealer" or compass, the Cherokee nation measured now but 200 miles east to west and 120 miles north to south, its greater portion lying in the Georgia area wherein were concentrated approximately two-thirds of the nation's population. On the white man's map the Cherokees' holdings of approximately ten million acres resembled a small, wind-blown leaf bleakly clinging to a wet stone.

Acutely aware of the impending disastrous enforcement of Georgia's Compact of 1802, the Cherokee nation, between 1819–27, firmly adopted as its main objective the preservation and protection of its remaining lands.

In a supreme effort to forestall the removal of their people from ancestral homelands promised to the state of Georgia by the Compact of 1802, progressive Cherokee leaders, many of whom were mixed bloods, undertook an ambitious and aggressive program that would further Cherokee education and religion; replace ancient Cherokee culture with that of the educated and Christianized white man; and—of utmost importance—convert the Cherokees' tribal government (already altered by the written laws of 1808) into a republic substantially patterned after that of the United States. By adherence to this program, the Cherokees hoped to convince the United States government that the Cherokee nation merited respect. So convinced, that government would then, they hoped, bring its compact with Georgia to a close by compromise or by some method other than that of extinguishing the Cherokees' title to their lands.

But, ironically, the Cherokees' phenomenal advancement—unparalleld between 1819–27 by any of the other American aborigines—hastened, instead of deterred, enforcement of the Compact. For, upon perceiving the Cherokees' advancement, which, in some respects, outpaced her own, Georgia abandoned both dignity and ethics and through her government, press, and courts, began, in 1820, a vicious attack upon the Cherokees that was to continue for eighteen years (*The Cherokees*, Grace Steele Woorward, pp. 138-140).

John Ridge, Buck Watie, and Stand Watie grew to lead a new movement of young intellectuals within the Cherokee nation, convinced that education and literacy were the paths for the survival of its people. Both John Ridge and Buck Watie married young women from white New England. After his conversion to Christianity, Buck changed his name to Elias Boudinot after his adoptive father in the North, and returned to Georgia. In 1828, he started the first Cherokee newspaper, written in Sequoyah's native alphabet, called the *Cherokee Phoenix*. Major Ridge, John's father, became a significant force in the Cherokee nation, often traveling to Washington as a diplomat, working on behalf of all Indian tribes. In the mid-1820s he helped the Creeks forge a treaty with the government that returned much land to them that had been taken away, for which the Creeks gave Ridge $10,000 in expression of gratitude, making Ridge a wealthy man. He became a considerable land owner and cattle rancher and owned many black slaves.

Note 7—Gold, the Ridge/Ross Split, and Cherokee Removal from the East

With the discovery of gold on Cherokee land in 1828, whites—the "twenty-niners"—poured into Cherokee lands, more greedy now for gold than their ancestors had been for land. If the Cherokee harbored lingering doubts, it was clear now that in the eyes of the governments of Georgia and Washington they possessed no rights to the ownership of their lands. Soon after the discovery, the state of Georgia nullified all Cherokee laws and claimed the land for itself.

Strife on all fronts escalated. Georgia appealed to Washington on the basis of Jefferson's 1802 Compact to force the removal of all Cherokees from their state once and for all. No more pretence of fairness was left. The government of Georgia wanted *all* remaining Cherokee land. At last a century of appeasements, broken treaties, and ceding of vast territory seemed about to climax in the loss of what small quantity of Cherokee land remained. And the state of Georgia, lusting for Cherokee gold, could not have had a more agreeable ally in the White House. Andrew Jackson rushed the Indian Removal Act through

Congress in 1830, finally placing into the law of the nation what many Cherokee had long feared—the final removal of *every* Cherokee man, woman, and child from Georgia, Tennessee, and North Carolina.

Chief John Ross appealed to the U.S. Supreme Court and received a favorable ruling in support of the Cherokee maintaining their lands. But Jackson's response was defiant. "John Marshall has rendered his decision," said the president. "Now let him enforce it."

By now some of the Cherokee old guard was rethinking its position. If the president of the United States and the state of Georgia could defy the Supreme Court and get away with it, it seemed that hope was lost. Elias Boudinot had long been a staunch advocate of the Cherokee right to their native lands. He had written of this right repeatedly in the *Phoenix*. But now he began to favor negotiation, with removal to the West as an ultimate goal. It was the only possible means to keep the Cherokee nation intact. Gradually his cousin John Ridge joined him in this dramatically changed view. Finally even John's father, Major Ridge himself, in a complete reversal, came to the same conclusion—that the Cherokee cause in the east was lost. If the nation was to survive, it *must* move West. Right or wrong, the three became convinced that their lands *would* be taken. The only solution was to join the Old Settlers in the Arkansas and Oklahoma territories.

As Major and John Ridge and Elias Boudinot, and to a lesser degree the fourth of the Ridge-Watie spokesmen Stand Watie, spoke out in favor of this radical new view, a major split with Chief Ross developed. The members of the Ridge-Watie-Boudinot family were viewed as traitors by Ross and many eastern Cherokees. The tables had completely turned. The old full-blood Ridge-Watie family became advocates for moving the nation West, while a predominently white man, John Ross, now stood as the voice fighting to hold traditional Cherokee lands in the east.

In 1834, the Cherokee Treaty Party was officially organized by Major Ridge. For the next two years, he and John Ross represented the two opposing factions of the Cherokees, factions that had been disputing ever since the first of the Old Settlers had left in 1808. Now, however, Ridge was the leading spokesman for the side he had once so violently opposed. Though the majority of Cherokees considered Ridge's call for a new and final negotiation with the U.S. government as betrayal, Ridge and his followers traveled to Washington in 1835 to conclude what was called the New Echota Treaty. At last Andrew Jackson had what he wanted, a timetable signed by prominent Cherokee leaders for complete removal of the Cherokee nation to the West. And, though reluctantly, the Treaty Party had what it wanted, the promise of five million dollars payment for the final remaining Cherokee lands. Such payment, they were confident, would be succifient to establish their people comfortably in a new western homeland.

A deadline was set for the last Cherokee migration of May 23rd, 1838. All Cherokee who did not comply and leave voluntarily would be rounded up by force and sent to camps from which they would be herded West.

Though the New Echota Treaty was seen as betrayal by many eastern Cherokee, some began to leave Georgia and North Carolina for the West, including the Ridge, Watie, and Boudinot families. Over three hundred left in the fall of 1837. John Ridge and Elias Boudinot led almost four hundred West shortly thereafter. And two hundred fifty more left in early 1838. In thirty years of a slow-trickling exodus, about five thousand, or a fourth of what remained of the once mighty Cherokee nation, had now migrated West. But the majority of Cherokees numbering some 15,000, continued to believe that Chief Ross would negotiate some eleventh-hour solution that would allow them to keep their lands. And thus they remained where they were as the deadline drew closer and closer.

Note 8—Vengeance and the Cherokee Blood Law

Once the great majority of the Cherokee were settled in the Arkansas and Oklahoma territories, whatever had been the conflict between the Old Settlers and the new arrivals, the fact was they were all Cherokees together and most desired to heal the wounds of division from the past. Passions ran high, however, among a few of the "Ross faction" as it was called, who had held out to the end and never betrayed the sacred ancient law by selling Cherokee land. Their hatred still seethed toward those responsible for the travesty of the removal, and they vowed revenge. Their hatred was no doubt fueled at seeing the Ridges and Waties, who had preceded them West, living in relative ease and prosperity, with slaves and cattle and building large new homes on the choicest sites in the new territory, after they themselves had so recently endured the horrors of the removal.

In June of 1839, three months after the arrival of the weary wagon train from the east, a general council of leaders met at Takotoka to attempt a formal union of the two groups of Cherokee, the Old Settlers and the New Immigrants. Though reviled by many of the recent arrivals, Major and John Ridge, and both Watie brothers attended, hoping to heal the wounds of recent years. Their presence so angered a splinter group of Ross loyalists that the latter began speaking privately in the days to follow about taking action against them. This small group convened a secret council of its own in the evening a week later after the general council had adjourned.

The Cherokee blood law, they agreed, from times ancient and immemorial was plain: the penalty for selling tribal lands was death. The new constitution may have said differently, but this was a time to appeal to the way of the ancients, not a law modeled on that of the white man. The gathering of radicals unanimously condemned Major Ridge, John Ridge, Elias Boudinot, and Stand Watie to death. They would carry out the sentence themselves.

Early the next morning the executions began.

While still in bed at Honey Creek, John Ridge's home was burst into by three masked men. John was dragged from bed and outside where the rest of the assassins waited. With his wife, Sarah—a New Englander who had married John during his days in the North and lived among the Cherokee ever since—and his children watching, John Ridge was stabbed twenty-five times, and his throat cut. His murderers stamped on his body as ritual demanded, then fled. In shock at the horror they had witnessed, Sarah and her sons managed

in their agony to get their husband and father back inside. He died
on his bed, bleeding so profusely that the blood drained through the
bed onto the floor.

Major Ridge, John's father, had arisen early that morning to travel
to Van Buren in western Arkansas. A messenger was sent immediately from Honey Creek to overtake him and tell him of his son's
assassination and warn him. When he arrived, the courier found The
Ridge lying on the road with five bullets in his head. He returned to
tell Sarah of yet another murder, this time of her father-in-law.

At Park Hill Elias Boudinot was building a new home. He was
busy with his carpenters when four men he did not know
approached, saying that Dr. Worcester had sent them for medical
supplies. Boudinot turned to glance toward the doctor's home a
short distance away. As he did one of the strangers quickly pulled a
knife and plunged it deep into his back. Before he hit the ground,
another had his tomahawk in hand, which now split the dying man's
skull.

In a matter of a few hours, three of the Cherokee nation's brightest,
most gifted, intelligent, and educated leaders, who might have led
their people through the tumultuous times they were sure to face in
the coming years, all lay brutally murdered at the hands of their own
brothers of veangeance.

Also condemned to execution, Elias's brother and John's cousin,
Stand Watie, got wind of the assassinations in time to flee the area and
escape the vendetta.

The entire Cherokee nation was stunned by news of the brutal
assassinations. Word of them eventually reached the caves of North
Carolina and Tennessee, where yet a few hundred brave and determined Cherokee were hiding out, scraping out an existence as best
they could, refusing to be herded West but now with nothing whatever to call their own, except the vague hope of one day rebuilding
Cherokee pride in the East.

More assassinations followed among the Cherokee, leading to what
amounted to a civil war in the tribe between 1839 and 1846. Hostilities rose to such heights that federal officials were forced to intervene

in 1846 and impose a treaty upon the tribe officially reuniting the two factions of the Cherokee nation. Bitterness and hatred, however, smouldered between the two groups for years. Ever after, whether or not he was directly involved, Watie blamed John Ross for the killings of his brother, cousin, and uncle. Gradually Stand Watie became the leader and primary spokesman for the treaty party—a divisive split and rivalry between the two men for leadership within the Cherokee nation lasting for the next twenty years.

While John Ross remained principal chief of the Cherokee, Stand Watie continued as the leader of the opposing faction. The rivalry remained contentious as Watie became more active in politics, eventually becoming speaker of the Cherokee National Council.

When the states of the South seceded from the union in 1861, Watie sided with the South and was commissioned a colonel in the Confederate army. He raised a following of many Cherokee, called the Cherokee Regiment of Mounted Rifles, hoping not only to fight for the Confederacy but to seize complete leadership of the Cherokee nation from Ross, who supported the Union. Watie went to Ross and gave him two options: sign an alliance with the Confederacy or face a coup for the chieftainship of the entire Cherokee tribe. Reluctantly Ross agreed and sided with the South. In 1862 he fled Oklahoma Territory for Philadelphia where he later died. In August of 1862, Stand Watie was elected principal chief of the Confederate Cherokee nation.

Watie saw action throughout the Civil War, was promoted to brigadier general in 1864, and, at the end of the war, was the last Confederate general to surrender.

Of the five million dollars promised to the Cherokee by the New Echota Treaty, the Cherokee tribe ultimately received from Georgia and the U.S. government a mere ten thousand dollars.[16]

Note 9—Hiding Cherokee Blood
These precautions of James Waters accurately reflect an entirely different cultural outlook than most of us have today. In the current

---

[16]Encyclopedia of North American Indians, Houghton Mifflin, "Pitter's Cherokee Trails."

climate when pride in one's roots is high and prejudice against those of dark skin or different ethnicity is on the decrease, it may be difficult to understand to what extent being of Indian blood was *not* something to be proud of—even something to keep secret—not so very many years ago. Many Cherokee people of mixed blood had light skin and had adopted many so-called white ways and customs. When American governmental and colonial attitudes became so harsh, even dangerous, toward Native Americans, it seemed better to some to assimilate than to be treated as "Indians." When the U.S. government began creating Indian registration rolls for the purpose of documenting payment for Indian lands for those who had moved West, many Cherokee who had resisted giving up their lands refused to register. Others registered themselves as white to avoid the stigma of being known as *Indian*.

"In my own family, my great-great-grandfather—Katy Harlan's half-Cherokee son George—registered himself as entirely white on the roll. My grandmother told of many family members, like him, who tried to hide the true extent of their heritage because of how badly Indians were treated long into the twentieth century. The result is that all the rest of us who followed this particular one of our ancestors through Nancy Ward's line, though increasingly proud of our heritage as the years have gone by, are registered with less Cherokee blood than is actually the case. This is true of many Cherokee on the rolls. For some reason my grandmother, even two generations ago and despite having grown up during difficult years in Indian territory in Oklahoma, was proud of her Cherokee heritage. She taught her children—my aunts and uncle—to honor the past, and named my own mother *Cherokee*." —Judy Phillips

Note 10—Bucks for Buttons
"List of the Price of Goods", 1751

During the mid-eighteenth century, trade between the British and Cherokees was at its peak. The British commissioned several traders in the Creek and Cherokee nations to trade rifles, woolens, tools, and other European goods for skins.

A Blanket	3 Bucks or 6 Does
2 Yards Wool Cloth	3 Bucks or 6 Does
Paint, 1 Ounce	1 Doe Skin
A Knife	1 Doe Skin
Pea Buttons, per Dozen	1 Doe Skin
Fine Rufel Shirts	4 Bucks or 8 Does
A Large Knife, Cuckhandled	1 Buck
60 Bullets	1 Doe
Silver Earbobs	1 Buck the Pair
Swan Shott (large lead pellets)	200 per a Buck Skin
Handkerchiefs of India	2 Bucks
1 Riding Sadle	18 Bucks or 16 Does
Women's Side Sadle	20 Bucks or 40 Does
2 Yards Stript Flannel	2 Bucks or 4 Does
Men's Shoes	2 Bucks or 4 Does
Callicoes	2 Bucks or 4 Does
1 Gun	7 Bucks or 14 Does

(*Cherokee Voices,* Vicky Rozema, pp. 15-19)

Note 11—Cherokee Names

Cherokee names are both fascinating and confusing. Every well-known Cherokee chief is known by multiple names and nicknames, in both Cherokee and English. This difficulty is added to by the fact that the ancient Cherokee tongue was a spoken not written language. After the European conquest, when Cherokee names were attempted rendered into English, diverse spellings could not help but result. When nicknames and honorary names were added, a given chief or warrior might be known by many names, complicating the study and interpretation of Cherokee history. Chief Pathkiller's death in 1828, precipitating the election from which John Ross emerged as chief, is complicated by the fact that Major Ridge, Nungnohnutarhee, was also known as Pathkiller.

The honorary titles Raven, Owl, Wolf, and Turkey were so common that Old Hop, Oconostota, and Old Hop's nephew were all known at one time or another as Standing Turkey. There are likewise numerous Ravens, Owls, and Wolfs among the chiefs.

The great peace chief of the Cherokee was known as Ukwaneequa, Oukandekah, Chuconnuta, Onacona, White Owl, Attakullkulla, Leaning Wood, Little Carpenter, as well as Attacullaculla. Whether some of these are mere spelling variations or perhaps mistakes that have crept into the historical record it is impossible to determine.

More than anything, Cherokee names and nicknames are melodic, lyrical, poetically musical, and uniquely descriptive, as the following examples illustrate: Groundhog Sausage (Oconostota), Tuskeegeeteehee (Nancy Ward's brother), Hiskyteehee (Fivekiller, Nancy Ward's son), Kahnungdatlageh (Man Who Walks the Mountains, one of Major Ridge's names), Kooweeskoowee (John Ross), Omitositah (Old Tassel), Kunnessee (Green Corn Top, or Young Tassel), Going Snake, Turtle at Home, Dreadful Waters, Soft-shelled Turtle, Running Waters, Rising Fawn, Rolling Thunder, Pumpkin Boy, Crying Bear, Lying Fawn, Bone Polisher, Beanstalk, Buffalo Horn, Corn Blossom, Lightening Bug, Mad Wolf, Morning Blossom, Nanye'hi (One Who Goes About), Moytoy (Water Conjurer, Rainmaker), Oowatie (the Ancient One), Sequoyah (Pig's Foot), Untsiteehee (Mankiller), Tsi'yugunsini (Dragging Canoe), Degataga (He Who Stands on Two Feet), Cunne Shote (Standing or Stalking Turkey), Cheratahegi (Possessor of the Secret Fire), Uskwalena (Bull Head).

Bibliography and Source Materials

The Cherokee Crown of Tannassy, William O. Steele: John Blair Pub, Winston-Salem, NC, 1977.

Seven Clans of the Cherokee, Marcelina Reed: Cherokee Publications, Cherokee, NC, 1993.

Cherokee Legends and the Trail of Tears, Amanda Crowe: Cherokee Publications, Cherokee, NC, 1956.

Trail of Tears, John Ehle: Random House, NY, 1988.

Cherokee Tragedy, Thurman Wilkens: Macmillan, NY, 1970.

The Cherokees Past and Present, J.E. Sharpe: Cherokee Publications, Cherokee, NC, 1970.

The Story of the Cherokee People, Tom Underwood: Cherokee Publications, Cherokee, NC, 1961.

Cherokee Voices, Vicki Rozema: John Blair Pub, Winston-Salem, NC, 2002.

The Cherokees, Grace Steele Woodward: Univ of Oklahoma, Norman, OK, 1963.

History of the Cherokee Indians, Emmet Starr: Warden Co, Oklahoma City, OK, 1921.

Families in *Dream of Life*

Davidson

Albert Davidson (1757–1821)
m. Zena Ann Baker (1759–1811)

- Grantham Davidson (1781–1841)
  m. Ruth (1779–1853)
  - Clifford (1809–1834)
  - Richmond Scott (1810–)
    m. Carolyn Hope Peters
    - Cynthia Jane (1836–)
      m. Jeffrey Verdon
    - Seth Robert (1840–)
    - Thomas Edward (1842–)
- Sarah (1783–1851)
  m. William
  - Stuart
  - Margaret
- Mary (1785–1785)
- Oscar (1786–1844)
  m. Polly
  - Harland
  - Pamela

Beaumont

Sir Richard MacFadden
- William MacFadden
  - Denton Graves Beaumont (1809–)
    m. Lady Daphne Downes MacFadden (1814–)
    - Wyatt Andrew (1839–)
    - Veronica Lucille (1840–)
    - Cameron Metcalf (1843–)

Waters

James Waters (1807–)
m. Kathleen McSweeney (1808–1841)
- Anne (1828–)
- Mary (1830–)
- Wade (1832–1832)
- Cherity Michel (1841–)

About the Author

Californian Michael Phillips began his distinguished writing career in the 1970s. He came to widespread public attention in the early 1980s for his efforts to reacquaint the public with Victorian novelist George MacDonald. Phillips is recognized as the man most responsible for the current worldwide renaissance of interest in the once-forgotten Scotsman and one of the world's foremost experts on MacDonald. After beginning his work redacting and republishing the works of MacDonald, Phillips embarked on his own career writing fiction. Since that time he has written and cowritten 48 novels and it is primarily as a novelist that he is now known. His critically acclaimed books have been translated into eight foreign languages, have appeared on numerous best-seller lists, and have sold more than six million copies. Phillips is today considered by many as the heir apparent to the very MacDonald legacy he has worked so hard to promote in our time. Phillips is also the publisher of the magazine *Leben*, a periodical dedicated to bold-thinking Christianity and the legacy of George MacDonald. Combining all categories that have made up his extremely diverse writing career, *Dream of Freedom* was Phillips' 100th published work. Phillips and his wife, Judy, make their home in Eureka, California. They also spend a great deal of time in Scotland where they are attempting to increase awareness of MacDonald's work.

The American Dreams Series

*Best-selling author Michael Phillips brings
readers an epic series of love and sacrifice leading
up to the turbulent Civil War.*

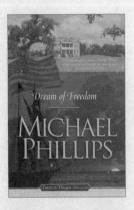

Dream of Freedom

In the midst of a nation's
turmoil, a few will stand. A few
will fight. And one man will
make a decision that has the
power to change his family and
the South forever.

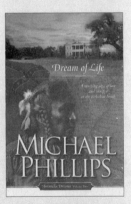

Dream of Life

Secession has begun. Loyalties
and families are divided. And
every man must decide for
himself the true cost of freedom.

BOOK 3 COMING SUMMER 2007!

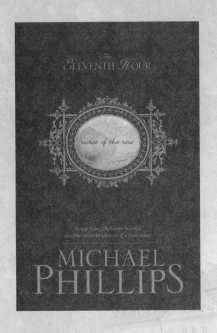

have you visited
tyndalefiction.com
lately?

Only there can you find:

→ books hot off the press

→ first chapter excerpts

→ inside scoops on your
favorite authors

→ author interviews

→ contests

→ fun facts

→ and much more!

Sign up
for your **free**
newsletter!

Visit us today at: **tyndalefiction.com**